THE
ANTHONY
BOUCHER
CHRONICLES

THE
ANTHONY
BOUCHER
CHRONICLES

REVIEWS AND COMMENTARY
1942-1947

THE
ANTHONY
BOUCHER
CHRONICLES

REVIEWS AND COMMENTARY
1942-1947

Edited by

Francis M. Nevins

RAMBLE HOUSE

ISBN 978-1-60543-002-7

ISBN 1-60543-002-1

Published: 2001, 2005, 2009 by Ramble House
Artwork: Gavin L. O'Keefe
Preparation: Fender Tucker

INTRODUCTION:
THE WORLD OF ANTHONY BOUCHER

Francis M. Nevins

An Anthony Boucher walks the earth but once. He treated every day of his adult life as the bountiful universe's invitation to create, to enjoy and help others enjoy creations, to care. Whatever he touched he made come alive with his informed love. He excelled at all he did, and what he did best no one will ever do better.

He was a native Californian, born in Oakland on August 21, 1911 with the rather ordinary name of William Anthony Parker White. Both his parents were doctors but his father died seven months after the boy was born and his grandfather, a lawyer and Civil War veteran, helped William's mother raise him. "His grandfather... meant a lot to him," Boucher's widow said a few years before her own death. "He had come to America from Scotland, where he had been an iron worker in Glasgow. I think there was an arrangement for men to get free passage if they would fight in the Civil War. I doubt he could have afforded it otherwise. I gathered he was something of a rake. Quite an old rogue. My husband enjoyed that in people."

Asthma and other ills kept William bedridden for half his childhood and made him a voracious reader and writer even in youth. Despite missing school so often, he was a bright and precocious boy—so gifted in fact that Stanford University researchers included him in a special group of California children whose future careers were to be studied for clues to the origins of genius.

Early vocational aptitude testing indicated that he should become an architect, and his first intellectual interests were scientific in nature, but in his mid-teens he turned decisively to language and literature. At age 15 he made his first fiction sale, a short spoof he called "Ye Goode Olde Ghoste Storie" (*Weird Tales*, January 1927) and later described as "so abominably written...that the editor who bought it must have had a sadistic grudge against his readers." His health improved in high school and college so that he was able not only to keep up with his studies but to immerse himself in dramatics and journalism, to go regularly to plays and concerts and movies, to start collecting stamps, coins and phonograph records, and to write—stories, plays, book reviews, translations, poetry in Spanish and German. He graduated from Pasadena High in 1928 and from the University of Southern California in 1932, taking with him from USC a Bachelor of Arts degree, a Phi Beta Kappa key and a fellowship to the University of California at Berkeley. While studying there for his M.A. he met Phyllis

Mary Price (1915-2000), who was in her first year of college and a few years later was to become his wife.

"I met my husband at a student party at my parents' house," Phyllis White recalled. "My father was Lawrence Marsden Price, of the University of California German Department, and my parents often entertained students. I remember the first time he came to our house he addressed just one remark to me. He asked whether I knew what became of the cookies. After he had been to a couple of parties at my parents' house, he invited us all to dinner at an apartment he had near the campus with his mother. At the end of the dinner he made a date with me to go to the theater with him.

"His mother was an unusual woman because in her time there weren't so many woman doctors. And what was also pretty unusual for her time, she smoked and drank too. She was about average height with white hair and blue eyes. She was very intelligent and very opinionated. We used to have lively discussions. She was a Republican and we were Democrats. The fact that we were to her left made us personally responsible for everything the Communists did.

"My first date with my future husband was the first date I ever had. I never dated in high school. One of the things we talked about was how much we liked the old theater stock companies. That was a great institution but it had died by the time we met. There was at that time an attempt to revive it in Oakland and we went to check it out." The play they saw, at the old Fulton Theater, was called *Gambling, Gambling!* "It was a bit disappointing. It wasn't like the real old-time stock companies at all."

William Anthony Parker White was one of those brilliant students who never needed to study. Despite a courseload in German, Spanish, Portuguese, Russian and Sanskrit, he spent most of his time writing, acting and directing in the little theater movement, and continued to attend as many plays, movies, concerts and football games as he could squeeze in. He had concentrated heavily on language courses with the original aim of becoming a teacher but decided early in his two-year stint at graduate school that academia was not for him. "One reason," said Phyllis White, "was that he felt he didn't have the patience to make it as a teacher. Another thing that bothered him was that he was surrounded by people who took no interest in contemporary popular literature but at the same time were trying to research the popular literature of a few centuries back." Rejecting the professorial life, he resolved instead to become a writer. In 1934, after completing his Master of Arts thesis ("The Duality of Impressionism in the Recent German Drama") and receiving his graduate degree, he returned to Los Angeles in the hope of launching a literary career. Discovering that the Library of Congress catalogues already listed 75 authors named William White, he adopted the byline of Anthony Boucher (his own second name plus the maiden name of his maternal grandmother, which rhymes with voucher) and wrote stories and poems and plays and translations with concentrated fury. And sold not a word.

His only published work during this period was the theater and music criticism he wrote for a political weekly, the Los Angeles *United Progressive News,* beginning in 1935. He was paid in the form of free tickets to plays and concerts, no cash. As for the quality of his unpublished stories and dramas of those years, he said in 1952, "when in morbid moments I now go back and reread them, I'm ashamed of my exceedingly slow development as a writer....I, a dull and muddy-mettled rascal, went on well into my middle twenties producing stuff for which unprofessional is the kindest epithet."

In 1936 he tried his hand at a classical detective novel, because of the discipline a strict form would impose on him and out of admiration for puzzlemasters like John Dickson Carr, Agatha Christie and Ellery Queen. The manuscript was sent out to eight publishers and rejected by each. Then one day early in 1937 Lee Wright, mystery editor at Simon & Schuster, picked that submission at random out of the slush pile and took it home to read. At two the next morning she woke up her husband with the excited cry that she'd just found the first unsolicited manuscript she ever wanted to publish.

THE CASE OF THE SEVEN OF CALVARY (1937) is set on the Berkeley campus and features as amateur detectives the erudite professor of Sanskrit Dr. Ashwin and his eager young graduate student Martin Lamb, who's a transparent stand-in for Boucher himself. The model for Ashwin was Professor Arthur William Ryder (1877-1938), who had taught Boucher Sanskrit at Berkeley. "I never met Dr. Ryder," Phyllis White recalled, "but I used to hear a lot about him. Tony was studying with him when we met. A pleasant habit of Dr. Ryder was to invite my husband over for an evening of talk occasionally, and he would have on hand a bottle of Scotch. At the end of the evening he would present him with what was left to take away with him." No wonder Boucher felt inclined to say thanks by making his mentor the model for the detective character in his first novel. *Ashwin* is a Sanskrit word meaning a rider. The plot of THE CASE OF THE SEVEN OF CALVARY hinges on a fairly obvious alibi gimmick but Lee Wright's excitement over the manuscript was well justified. No other mystery so lovingly evokes the academic atmosphere and the joys of learning and thinking as this whodunit debut.

In May of 1938 and on the strength of first success Boucher married Phyllis Price, who meanwhile had graduated from the University of California's Library School. "He was a Catholic so the wedding was at Newman Hall. That was the old Newman Hall, which has been torn down for parking." The newlyweds moved to Los Angeles, where Phyllis worked as a librarian until the birth of their first child. While hoping for a screenwriter's contract at a movie studio, Boucher wrote and sold six more detective novels. Four of these deal with amateur of crime Fergus O'Breen, a sort of Southern California Ellery Queen with brogue, and/or his LAPD counterpart, Lieutenant Jackson. The other pair, published under the byline of H.H. Holmes (the real-life pseudonym of 19th-century mass murderer Herman W. Mudgett), star Sister Ursula of the Order of Martha of Bethany, a nun variant on G.K. Chesterton's immortal Father Brown. All of Boucher's seven novels hold up well today as specimens of the grand deductive tradition, full of locked-room puzzles and bizarre clues and intellectual fireworks, enlivened by the author's love of language and literature and theater and opera and Sherlock Holmes and science fiction and bawdy humor and the tolerant, socially concerned wing of the Catholic Church. Like his idols Doyle and Chesterton and Carr and Queen, Boucher infused the classical detective form with his own multifarious enthusiasms, and enriched the genre in the process.

His career as a novelist ended when he found work at which he was even better, writing about the novels of others. In early 1942 the family moved back to Berkeley, which was to be Boucher's home base for the rest of his life. "Larry, our first son, was with us," Phyllis White said, "and we were soon joined by his brother James [Marsden White]. For the first five years we lived in a rented house on Ellsworth Street. Then we moved to our own house on Dana Street and we never moved again. Berkeley suited my husband just fine as a place to live. He liked being near the University, where he could use the library and attend the sporting events and the concerts. He particularly liked being near San Francisco."

Between October 1942 and the summer of 1947 Boucher spent much of his time writing the material collected here: articles and reviews covering mysteries, fantasies, science fiction and other books for the San Francisco *Chronicle*. As a result he had to cut back his own imaginative output to an average of four or five magazine stories a year, either mysteries or fantasy-science fiction or, like most of the short exploits of Fergus O'Breen, both at once. Perhaps his most fondly remembered "pure" detective stories of the period are the cases of alcoholic ex-cop Nick Noble which appeared in *Ellery Queen's Mystery Magazine (EQMM)*, but there were others as well—Sister Ursula stories, O'Breen exploits and non-series tales—and all are represented in EXEUNT MURDERERS (1983), a collection I was privileged to edit.

Boucher's short mystery stories, like his mystery novels and science fiction, reflect all the interests and enthusiasms that filled his life, with religion, opera, football, politics, movies, true crime, record collecting and an abundance of good food and wine alongside the clues and puzzles and deductions. His stories are further enhanced by a dimension whose value has increased with the passing years. "He used to say," Phyllis White remarked, "that the heresy of our age is the perceived dichotomy between art and entertainment: if something is one, it cannot be the other. Things that are now being studied in school were in their own time great popular successes. The public avidly awaited the next installment of a current Dickens novel. There was a popular following of the Elizabethan theater and of the Greek theater. He used to say you could get a better idea of just what it was like to be alive in that time from reading the fiction of an earlier period than you could from reading a factual history." In his critical writing Boucher stressed again and again the function of mysteries as (in Hamlet's words to Polonius about the players) the abstracts and brief chronicles of the time. The whodunits of any period bear witness to later generations about the way we lived then, and Boucher's tales of the early and middle 1940s, with their ambience of rationed consumer goods and gung-ho patriotism and defense plants and rumor mills and returning combat heroes, capture the sensibility of the American home front during World War II like nothing else in the genre.

In those years the tradition of the amateur mastersleuth whose brilliance solves crimes where police work failed was still vital and flourishing, and to devotees of that tradition the roots of Boucher's protagonists will be evident. In Nick Noble for instance there is quite clearly a bit of the historic Poe and even more of Baroness Orczy's Old Man in the Corner. Boucher created the character in 1942 for the then infant *Ellery Queen's Mystery Magazine,* which is still happily with us (if only Boucher were himself!) almost sixty years later. The Screwball Division was a translation into colloquial American of THE DEPARTMENT OF QUEER COM-PLAINTS in Carter Dickson/John Dickson Carr's 1940 collection of that title. The Chula Negra was based on a little Mexican cafe on Second Street in Los Angeles where in the mid-1930s Boucher and other *United Progressive News* journalists "used to gather to talk about the stories we were going to write and eat the best *lengua en mole* I've ever tasted and drink sherry...at ten cents per water-glassful." Sister Ursula, as we've seen, derives from Father Brown and Fergus O'Breen, as the cadence of his name suggests, from Ellery Queen.

During the years he wrote most of his short detective stories he also edited his first two anthologies, THE POCKET BOOK OF TRUE CRIME STORIES (1943) and GREAT AMERICAN DETECTIVE STORIES (1945), both of them prized collector's items today. In addition he translated several Georges Simenon stories for publication in *EQMM* and did other translations from the Spanish and Portuguese. On one of his regular business trips to New York he became a charter member of the Mystery Writers of America organization (MWA). "He was always proud of carrying card number five," Phyllis said. Along with fellow *Chronicle* reviewer Joseph Henry Jackson, he took the lead in forming a San Francisco scion society of the Baker Street Irregulars, giving himself the designation Brother Scanlon of the Scowrers. "My husband was rather ahead of his time in his views as to the equality of women. The Baker Street Irregulars was a stag organization. He insisted that there must be not only Scowrers but also Mollies." (For the benefit of tyros in the literature of Sherlock Holmes I should mention that both the Scowrers and the Molly Maguires figure prominently in the 1915 novel THE VALLEY OF FEAR, fourth and last of Sir Arthur Conan Doyle's book-length Holmes tales.)

In collaboration respectively with Denis Green and Manfred B. Lee, Boucher wrote scripts for the *Sherlock Holmes* and *Ellery Queen* radio programs. *The Case Book of Gregory Hood,* a detective series heard irregularly on the Mutual radio network between 1946 and 1950, was created and scripted by Boucher and Green and at various times starred Gale Gordon, Elliot Lewis and Martin Gabel as the San Francisco importer-sleuth. "Even during the period when his main occupation was writing radio plays," said Phyllis White, "shows that emanated from Los Angeles and New York, he stayed in Berkeley and commuted. He was on a schedule of Hollywood roughly every six weeks and New York every six months." While juggling all these activities, Boucher also found time to teach a writing class once a week in his home. Among his students who went on to professional careers were the science-fiction writers Ron Goulart and Philip K. Dick and the novelists David Duncan and Jean Backus. "For a while," Phyllis added, "he was in the Berkeley Lawn Bowling Club. And for a while there was a group of serious students and collectors of the limerick....Then there was a group of people who got together once a month to drink wine, and I am sure there are many other things that I am not thinking of."

What was it like to live with Boucher while he was working and playing so intensely? The most vivid account we are ever likely to have is that of his older son, Lawrence White. "As I remember, a typical work day for my father would begin with the sound of the alarm clock somewhere around eight o'clock in the morning. The purpose of the alarm clock was to notify anyone else who was awake, usually my brother or myself, to start giving wake-up calls every few minutes. If that didn't work, we had to escalate the wake-up shakes and deliveries of hot coffee passed under the nose until he could finally get himself out of bed. After he got up it was quite a while before he could work himself into a normal breathing pattern. He was a lifelong asthmatic. He never had what most of us consider a healthy day in his life. The period right after waking up was the worst for him. After a considerable breathing stabilization period and some coffee, he would be ready to repair to his study for his first workshift of the day, usually around nine or ten o'clock.

"His study was on the top floor of our large split-level house, on the side where he got the sun in the morning. This was nice because our cat gravitated toward the sun, and so he would have his muse there in the corner by the window, lying there saying, 'Yes, it is time to get to work.' So the door was shut, and he was doing whatever he did. He might emerge around midday to come down to the kitchen, fix himself a nice tartare steak, and return to his study until about four o'clock in the afternoon. At this point he would try to nap for a couple of hours until dinner time. Then we went through the whole waking up ritual again between six and seven o'clock; usually he'd go through a review copy while he was waking up.

"We always had dinner together in the evenings, which I remember as a very pleasant time. We were all on our own for the other meals. Dinner was the one time of the day when everyone was together, but after dinner he was back to his study for another four or five hours of work. After my brother and I were in bed, at eleven or twelve o'clock, we could often hear my father and mother playing records from their large opera collection and talking animatedly. They both liked to stay up until two or three o'clock in the morning. But generally my father's schedule was to put in two shifts on a normal, full workday. We had to go through this terrible waking up period twice a day.

"The actual process of his work was not really visible to me. I saw a lot of reading. He seldom went anywhere without a review copy under his arm or in front of his face. I could hear a lot of one finger typing and the occasional slap of cards from some solitaire breaks. I couldn't hear him working the cyphers or cryptograms and double-crostics and other forms of what he called relaxation that he would sometimes do for breaks. Occasionally large envelopes would be passed out of the study to be taken to the nearest mailbox. His level of concentration I am sure was quite high when he was in there. He didn't care too much to be disturbed....

"The study was a large room, I guess about twelve by twenty feet, maybe even larger because it was lined with books all the way around. The windows were not covered but every other part of the wall was. The main type of bookcase was an orange crate, which was nice because it is modular and you could stack books two deep. In his study he had his mystery collection, his science fiction collection, his Sherlock Holmes collection, his true crime collection, his limerick collection, his pornography collection (very small—it mostly overlapped the limerick collection), and a lot of reference books. They were mostly books on words and dictionaries in many languages. There wasn't much of what you would call office equipment—a typewriter, a few rubber stamps.

"It seemed to us as children that our father was kind of a rationed commodity because he was around so much, but yet he was off limits so much of the time. From my perspective now I see we probably had more time with him than most kids do with fathers who go to work and have golf and a bunch of other things; they're not home very much. There was a lot of play time, which kind of had its own schedule, but competed very strongly with the work schedule and the deadlines. No matter how bad the pressures, among the entertainments were: going to plays (musical comedies were big on the agenda); opera (they didn't drag us kids along to that); a lot of fine dining; a lot of sports spectating, which my mother didn't participate in; and lots of home table games. There were lots of parties involving the local writing crowd, and we went at least once per year to Playland at the Beach.

"My father got involved in so many things. He went to all the football games, the Cal basketball games, track meets, rugby games, gymnastics. He was doing all this just on the side."

Perhaps Boucher's most lasting contribution to world literature came in the months after he'd left the *Chronicle* and was supporting himself and his family with periodical and radio work. Scholar of Latin American mystery fiction that he was, Boucher translated from Spanish, and persuaded his colleague in crime Frederic Dannay (Ellery Queen) to publish, the first story by Jorge Luis Borges to appear in the English language ("The Garden of Forking Paths," *EQMM,* August 1948). But his most important editorial and critical accomplishments still lay ahead of him.

During the late 1940s, while his science-fiction reviews were appearing in the Chicago *Sun-Times,* Boucher's reviews of current mystery fiction were being published in occasional *EQMM* columns and in odd corners of the Sunday *New York Times Book Review.* Beginning July 1, 1951, he took over as the *Times'* regular mystery critic, and his "Criminals at Large" column graced every issue of the *Book Review* for just short of the next seventeen years. Although his primary allegiance was to the fair-play detective novels of the sort he used to write himself, he was so eclectic in taste as to appreciate all kinds of crime fiction—suspense, Gothic, espionage, psychological, farce, private eye, police procedural, high adventure—and he insisted in his first *Times* column that "the important distinction is not between the schools of the whodunit but between the good and bad books whatever the school."

By practicing that credo Boucher brought mystery criticism to a perfection it will never see again. Six or eight times a week for almost seventeen years, he would tell us whether a book was good of its kind, whether the author succeeded within the chosen framework or formula. When a whodunit was truly excellent his praise would ring to the sky, as when he reviewed 23-year-old Ira Levin's first novel, A KISS BEFORE DYING *(NYTBR,* October 25, 1953): ".... superlatively enviable sheer professionalism....Levin combines great talent for pure novel writing—full-bodied characterization, subtle psychological exploration, vivid evocation of locale—with strict technical whodunit tricks as dazzling as anything ever brought off by Carr, Rawson, Queen or Christie." If the book was a weak effort with some saving grace, he'd pinpoint the flaws precisely and take pains to note the good side: "....a slow-moving routine plot, weakly detected, but partially redeemed by a convincing first-hand picture of northernmost Alaska." To the hopelessly shoddy or inept work he'd give short shrift but usually with a dash of wit, as when he called a particularly boring John Rhode novel "the dreariest Rhode I have yet traversed." He never wrote maliciously.

Did I say never? Well, *hardly* ever! On the occasions when he encountered a book so atrocious it should never have been published at all, he didn't hesitate to say so bluntly. And during the early 1950s, the evil days of McCarthyism and HUAC, his single *bete noire* was Mickey Spillane, whose best-selling thrillers Boucher despised for their neo-fascist political slant, joy in sadism, sniggering approach to sex and slapdash prose and plots, all the antitheses to Boucher's own values which were rooted in Christian intellectualism and the liberal humanist tradition. In the 1960s when Spillane's influence had faded, Boucher mellowed toward the creator of Mike Hammer and began to see in him the last of the old pulp storytellers. His take on Spillane's first novel, I, THE JURY (1947), is included in this collection.

Boucher was an awesomely rapid reader, capable of finishing and fully comprehending a novel in two to three hours. After the reading he'd arrange all the relevant information about the book, from bibliographic details to a plot summary to any factual errors he'd caught, on one or both sides of a 3x5 card.

The space limitation led him to employ his own system of abbreviations on these cards: OH, for instance, stood for Our Hero, and IH for Idiot Heroine, a creature he must have encountered hundreds of times in so-called novels of romantic suspense. On completing the file card he'd write his review of the book, a process that generally took him thirty minutes or less. Even though most of the titles Boucher reviewed are long forgotten, his thousands of *Chronicle* and *Times* critiques are so full of wit and insight and infectious readability as to defy being laid down. Any publisher with the sense and tenacity to assemble all of them in book form will have given us the definitive critical history of the genre during one of its richest quarter centuries. For now the present collection from the *Chronicle* must suffice.

```
     Apr 4 66              (NOVELETS)
2/1 McBain, Ed
80 Million eyes: An 87th Precinct mystery novel
NY: Delacorte (c66)  $3.50  20 cm  192p  64,000
Ad fr 80 Million eyes Arg Feb 63 22,000 EQMM:May 66
The dear hunter   c65    Pyramid (what mag?)
Loc:  the city & env
Time:  Oct 13/19 1965
Tecs:  the 87th, esp Carella & Meyer in 1st, Det 3/g
       Bertram (Bert) Kling in 2d

V satisf blend of 2 nts into n by counterpointing them in action & theme (misuse
of love), 1st top TV comic strophanthine-poisoned on camera; 2d, violent psy-
chotic who (echo of Tobit) will allow no o men in life of girl he hasn't yet met.
As always, superbly readable, & this time unusually solid plots (though I do
think somebody shd've thought of enteric coating before p176). Gd plodding, gd
labwork (esp in 2d).  Best 87th since Ax 64.
```

Boucher lived and worked at 78 rpm while the rest of the world revolved lazily at 33. His speed-reading gift left him many hours for a legion of other activities during his years with the *Times*. Through most of the 1950s Boucher and his colleague J. Francis McComas co-edited the monthly *Magazine of Fantasy and Science Fiction* and the annual BEST OF FANTASY AND SCIENCE FICTION anthologies culled from the magazine. One of Boucher's duties was to check the scientific accuracy of submitted manuscripts, and thanks to his boyhood interest in science, he said, a bell would ring in his head whenever he read a questionable statement of technical fact. Boucher, McComas wrote years later, "combined an unerring sense of what was 'commercial' with excellent literary taste....He was essentially a *kind* editor... especially gentle with beginning writers....If a submission showed any merit at all, he was ever ready to take the time for written encouragement, with detailed suggestions for plot revision, or character strengthening, or style polishing....His proudest boast was the number of first stories he had bought."

And somehow he *still* found time for other work. He and McComas co-edited the excellent but commercially unsuccessful magazine *True Crime Detective* during the last year (Fall 1952-Fall 1953) of its brief life. He wrote a monthly review column in *EQMM* for much of his tenure with the *Times*. He and several other members of the Northern California chapter of MWA turned out a collaborative suspense novel, THE MARBLE FOREST (1951), which was adapted into director William Castle's 1958 movie chiller MACABRE. His science-fiction reviews as H.H. Holmes migrated east from the Chicago *Sun-Times* to the New York *Herald-Tribune*. He wrote entries on Dashiell Hammett and Erle Stanley Gardner for a new edition of the *Encyclopaedia Britannica*. From 1962 through 1967 he edited the annual BEST DETECTIVE STORIES OF THE YEAR anthologies, supplying not only warm and thoughtful introductions to each tale he selected but also an invaluable "Yearbook of the Detective Story" appendix listing the year's short story collections, anthologies, prize-winning crime novels, and sad but necessary notes on the mystery writers who had died during the year. For Pacifica's public radio station KPFA he conducted a regular mystery-review program. He served as regional vice-president and eventually as national president of MWA and won three richly deserved Edgar awards from the organization for his criticism. He selected and wrote introductions for the novels in several series of quality paperback mystery reprints. And to every piece of work he brought such enthusiasm and knowledge and love that he seemed not to be working at all but just having fun.

Superficially he might have resembled the hopeless workaholic but Boucher's lives as writer, editor and critic were never the alpha and omega of his existence. He had enough hobbies for a small army—gourmet cooking, wine culture, football and basketball, Gilbert & Sullivan, theology, limericks, multilingual Scrabble, poker—and gave time and attention to each. Indeed his kitchen skills were such that for a period during World War II when his wife had her hands full with two small children, Boucher took over as the family cook, and despite wartime rationing and food shortages did better than satisfactorily.

"Another development," Phyllis White said, "was his turning pro with what had been a lifelong hobby. He had always been an opera buff and a collector of records. As a boy he laid the foundation for his record collection back in the Twenties when the new orthophonic records were introduced and the old acoustic records were sold off for a dime. He acquired quantities of records of the great singers of the so-called golden age of opera. In later years he kept haunting thrift shops and got on the mailing lists of specialist dealers....After his death, his record collection was acquired by the University of California for their music library at the Santa Barbara campus." Around that collection of more than nine thousand old operatic discs he built his public radio series *Golden Voices*, which ran on KPFA every Sunday evening from 1949 until his death. "Each week he would take up a different singer, talk about the career, and play illustrations from his collection. This led to television work at KQED—programs about the San Francisco Opera and interviews of singers." An opera buff *par excellence*, he loved to put on top hat and white tie and tails once a year for the San Francisco Opera's gala first nights. He wrote countless notes for the company's printed programs and, from 1961 until his death, served as local correspondent for the Metropolitan Opera's magazine *Opera News*, arguing for increased attention to the form's dramatic aspects. "He served one term as president of the Berkeley Democratic Club," said Phyllis, "and two terms on the State Central Committee." After giving up political activity on doctors' orders he remained in constant demand as a speaker on campuses, at liberal and labor fund-raisers, at conventions of science-fiction fans. And overarching all his work and all his play (the two for him being indistinguishable) were family and faith. He was committed to Catholicism with all his fervor and learning and love, donating time to the weekends of spiritual renewal sponsored by his parish church, volunteering as a lay reader at Sunday Mass in the mid-1960s following the liturgical reforms of Vatican Council II, helping to translate some of the liturgy from Latin into contemporary English.

What makes Boucher's many-lives-in-one even more astounding is that he so rarely enjoyed a day of truly robust health. Although he compared himself to the sundial with the motto "I count only the sunny hours" in his ability to blot out weakness and pain, he and Fred Dannay often said to each other only half in jest "that if both of us had been blessed with good health, how much more we could have accomplished!" Bouts of illness often forced Boucher to scrap or postpone projects to which he'd made commitments. But his spirit outfought his body and he kept working with courage, gusto and relentless intelligence. Until the spring of 1968.

That was when he was admitted to Kaiser Foundation Hospital and diagnosed as suffering from advanced lung cancer—too late for surgery to do any good. "He never knew about the cancer," Phyllis White said, "because it was very hard to diagnose him and by the time that they figured it out, he was out of it and couldn't be told anything." On April 29, at the unbearably early age of 56, he died. What he did with his life would have been staggering if he'd lived ten times as long.

The eulogy at his funeral was read by Father Brian Joyce, his closest friend among the clergy. "He had that quality so characteristic of the truly Christian and of the fully human life," the priest said, "the quality of joy." Like the two other deeply religious major figures in crime fiction, G.K. Chesterton and Dorothy L. Sayers, Boucher taught with his life a lesson of inspiration to people of his own faith and of another and of none: that living creatively is itself a sacrament, ennobling and liberating those who live that way, so that they relate to their lives as God is said to relate to the universe. He was one of those who make us proud we are of his species, who give us ideals for our own lives. We'll never see his like again. An Anthony Boucher walks the earth but once.

This book is organized in a simple and straightforward way which I trust Boucher would have approved. Part I brings together the articles on mystery fiction that he wrote for the *Chronicle* once a month; Part II collects his weekly columns reviewing the current mystery crop; Part III contains the generally longer reviews in which he covered other kinds of books ranging from fantasy and horror to a new translation of the Bible. All material in parentheses is Boucher's. Material in brackets is my own, added where I felt it necessary to explain something relevant to Boucher's remarks that he took for granted or that happened after his comments were published. I've taken the liberty of mitigating Boucher's tendency to use semicolons, commas and capitalized words where they struck me as distracting, and of correcting his rare factual slips and the much more common typographic errors in the published versions of his material.

This book is a reality only because fellow Boucherolater Karen Duncan located, reproduced and sent me copies of the hundreds of *Chronicle* pages on which Boucher material appeared. Ecstatic hours of poring over those photocopied pages convinced me that these treasures had to be shared with the world no matter what it took. My secretaries Pam Boyer and Mary Dougherty deserve thanks for their help in putting the material on disk, and Saundra Taylor, curator of manuscripts at Indiana University's Lilly Library, for giving me access to the carbons of Boucher's essay and review typescripts. This project has brought me many pleasures but also one great sadness: that Phyllis White did not live to see this tribute to her husband published.

THE
ANTHONY
BOUCHER
CHRONICLES

REVIEWS AND COMMENTARY
1942-1947

VOLUME ONE:

AS CRIME GOES BY

Monthly Articles

To get any use out of a reviewer, you've got to be able to tell (a) what he means and (b) whether his tastes are apt to agree with yours. So this first long column will be mostly an explanation of how the Boucher system works.

Telling what I mean will be easy. If the wording is at all ambiguous, just look at the face. There are four of these faces.

The first, the man whose hair has risen right off his head, will be used sparingly—only for the absolute masterpiece that some Howard Haycraft to come will positively have to include in his book on whodunits.

The second, whose hair still clings to the scalp but points straight up, means a sweet job that belongs on your reading list.

The third, the dubious and not quite happy one, means a fair enough mystery that'll do if there's nothing else in the library.

The very unhappy fourth face will, I hope, be even more scarce than the first: it will mark incompetent work that should never have been published. [For technical reasons the faces have been eliminated from the reviews as printed in Part II of this book.]

(Note: Last week something went wrong between my typewriter and the printed page, and the faces got shifted down one step. My apologies to Helen McCloy, Jerome Barry and A.R. Hilliard, whose admirable books I intended to urge you to read, and to George Harmon Coxe and Richard Hull, who may have deserved the third face but certainly not the fourth.)

As to whether your tastes and mine are apt to jibe, you'll have to find that out largely by experience. But my tastes in the mystery are fairly catholic, and as a reviewer I'll try to make them ever more so. Anything that is a good job of what it means to be will get a good notice.

But two warnings. The one form of whodunit that I do not like is the school of gallant characters, glamorous adjectives and heroines with male names—what Ogden Nash calls the H.I.B.K. school, from their favorite phrase, Had I But Known.... I'll try to play fair with these, but if you're a fan of theirs you'd better mark the faces up one notch.

Contrariwise, I am, like Mr. Doyle before me [Edward Dermot Doyle, the *Chronicle's* previous mystery reviewer, who had just left to join the military], more of a sucker for meticulous slow-paced British novels than is the average American mystery-renter. I'm quite apt to give the first face to a Freeman Wills Crofts or an R. Austin Freeman. Again you are fore-warned, and in these cases mark them down a notch.

The weekly box will usually give you, for each of the crop, a sentence of synopsis, a sentence of judgment and a face. This monthly column will take up at greater length the opuses that deserve it. As for instance, this month we have a couple of phenomena to consider.

One is Mr. Frank Gruber. Writers used to stand in awe of the incredible fertility of Lope de Vega or of [Alexandre] Dumas *pere*. Then came Edgar Wallace and later Erle Stanley Gardner, and Lope and Dumas began to look like amateurs. Now there's Mr. Gruber; and even Wallace and Gardner commence to pale. The only possible rival to compare with Gruber is an oyster in a month without an R.

And, as with the well-bred oyster, the quality of his output is astonishingly high. For smooth speed only Gardner can touch him, and for ingenuity and detail of dividend he has few competitors. (A dividend, Constance, is what a mystery is about besides murder—like the bell-ringing in [Dorothy L.] Sayers' THE NINE TAILORS or the nursery rhymes and mathematics in [S.S. Van Dine's] THE BISHOP MURDER CASE.)

No arrangement of one or two names could do for the Gruber output, and he's used an assortment. (For my money, the best book he ever wrote was THE LAST DOORBELL by John K. Vedder.) And what all this leads up to is a spot of reputation-staking: I hereby state the Boucher hypothesis that the newest Gruber guise is Stephen Acre, "a new writer" (according to the jacket) who has just published THE YELLOW OVERCOAT (Dodd Mead, $2). [Boucher's theory proved to be correct.]

It's chiefly worth mentioning so that loyal Gruber fans can keep up with the master's output. It isn't major Gruber. Joe Devlin, who inherited a detective correspondence school and several pecks of trouble, isn't going to steal your affections from book salesman Johnny Fletcher, and for once there's no dividend worth speaking of. But it's fast enough, and the solution is certainly an astonishing one, if a little hard to follow.

The other phenomenon of this month is that Anna Katharine Green of the grinds, Gypsy Rose Lee, who may work for [the famous showman] Michael Todd, but would understand the murderous soul of the great Sweeney Todd, the Demon Barber of Fleet Street.

There've been celebrities' mysteries long before Miss Lee's THE G-STRING MURDERS. I can recall one by a great tennis player, two by a Metropolitan [Opera] soprano, one by a British archaeologist, one by a translator of the Bible—even one in which the President of the United States took a hand. But they've been freaks, curiosa—sometimes good, sometimes bad, but never part of the regular mystery trade.

But when Miss Lee makes with the book words she becomes a complete professional. [Boucher didn't know it at the time but both of the Gypsy Rose Lee whodunits had in fact been ghost-written by one of his favorite mystery writers, Craig Rice.] No need to emphasize the publicity value of her other activities, to be kind, or to make allowances. She belongs not with the "celebrities" but with men like the poet Nicholas Blake or the psychologist C. Daly King, who have other careers, yes, but who are important to readers of this column purely because they write first-rate mysteries.

The new Lee, MOTHER FINDS A BODY (Simon & Schuster, $2), I come out flatfooted and say is better even than THE G-STRING. The plot is tighter knit, there is even more fine rowdy shoptalk, the characters are sharper (especially Biff Brannigan, now Gypsy's husband, who emerges as a keen and challenging new detective). And then there is Mother, who buries bodies, seduces sheriffs, confesses killings and never stops worrying about her daughter's disreputable profession.

The setting is no longer strictly burlesque, but don't let that worry you. A Texas border honkytonk is even riper Lee material. So run, do not walk, to your nearest bookstore and—but you were probably there last week, only to learn that they were sold out and had reordered.

This monthly column, to get back to our explanations, will also include random "bests." As for instance:

Neatest Clue of the Month: the curious behavior of the housefly in Helen McCloy's CUE FOR MURDER.

Best Dividend O.T.M.: the entrancing lore of string tricks in Jerome Barry's LEOPARD CAT'S CRADLE, which will keep you up the rest of the night practicing them. (You should see me now at parties.)

Trickiest Plot O.T.M.: the intricate involutions of Judson Philips' THE FOURTEENTH TRUMP. (Equally insoluble for me is the meaning of that title.)

Most Exciting News O.T.M.: the rumored discovery of a never-printed Sherlock Holmes story.

Now you have an idea of what to expect, and I leave you with the official fifth toast of the Baker Street Irregulars:

The game is afoot!

November 29, 1942

This is Mass Murder Month, when the publishers bountifully bestow whole massacres upon us for the usual price of a single corpse, an agreeable practice that should tempt mystery fans to the bookstore for a change instead of to the circulating library.

CRIME CLUB ENCORE (Doubleday Crime Club, $2) is a book that certainly belongs on your shelves. Howard Haycraft, the admirable author of MURDER FOR PLEASURE and editor of several whodunit anthologies for boys, regrets, as any lover of the field must, the short life of the average mystery story. Unless it attains high sales in its first trade edition, it vanishes out of print and is sold off by the libraries, and word of mouth praise and critical plaudits can do nothing to revive it.

Here Mr. Haycraft has tried to give new life and possibly even a permanent status to four of the finest crime novels of recent years: Raymond Postgate's VERDICT OF TWELVE, Selwyn Jepson's KEEP MURDER QUIET, Philip MacDonald's WARRANT FOR X, and Margery Allingham's THE CASE OF THE LATE PIG.

If you know even one of those opuses, you will realize the high caliber of the selection. The omnibus title is perhaps unfortunate, since these are not typical Crime Club novels. Only the last is strictly a detective story; the others belong to the admirable British school of the literate and chilling murder novel.

Sally Benson called the turn when she labeled this Haycraft collection (complete with an interesting preface by the editor) "the best detective omnibus to date." I can only cast my vote with hers.

A different sort of omnibus is THE FOURTH MYSTERY BOOK (Farrar & Rinehart, $2.50). The stories here are not revivals, but mark the first appearance in book form of material from such magazines as *The American.*

The jacket promise of "six full-length mystery novels" is a bare-faced lie. In fact there are five novelets and a short story, by Mary Roberts Rinehart, Mignon G. Eberhart, Philip Wylie, Hugh Pentecost, Q. Patrick, and the promising newcomer Dana Lyon.

Quality is uneven, ranging from the superlative Eberhart to a disappointing Rinehart. The collection is possibly not up to the earlier F&R MYSTERY BOOKs (no [Rex] Stout this time, no David Frome), but it's a lot of mystery reading for the money.

The month's third omnibus, a unique classic, is SPORTING BLOOD: THE GREAT SPORTS DETECTIVE STORIES, edited by Ellery Queen [Frederic Dannay] (Little Brown, $2.50). Those who read the previous Queen anthologies, CHALLENGE TO THE READER and 101 YEARS' ENTERTAINMENT, realize the Messrs. Queen [referring to Dannay and his cousin and collaborator Manfred B. Lee, who in fact did not work with Dannay on the Queen mystery anthologies] know more about the detective short story than you'd think possible, and those who have followed Ellery's own adventures know what they can do with the combination of detection and sports.

But you may not have realized—certainly I hadn't—how many excellent sporting detective stories there are. In this volume you'll find Sherlock Holmes involved (rather reprehensibly, as R.K. Leavitt has pointed out in 221B) in horse racing, [Stuart Palmer's schoolteacher-sleuth] Hildegarde Withers solving a polo murder, [Leslie Charteris' rogue known as] the Saint engaged in a novel poker game, [Dorothy L. Sayers'] Lord Peter Wimsey and [Ernest Bramah's] Max Carrados appositely engrossed in crimes involving rare books and coins (for hobbies are included as sports), and Ellery Queen himself, modestly and for lack of any competition, investigating the criminous aspects of baseball, football and philately.

For fans of either sports or murder, here is a 360-page treat. My only objection is to the omission of Percival Wilde's card-sharping detective Bill Parmelee, but that slight dissent is swallowed up in gratitude to the editor for unearthing a whole new field of detectival delight.

While on this Queenly subject I direct your attention to *Ellery Queen's Mystery Magazine,* the only successful magazine ever aimed specifically at the reader of mystery novels. Dedicated to the revival of obscure masterpieces and the discovery of new ones, it's a sort of periodical anthology of the best in short detective fiction, and a cover-to-cover must for all true aficionados. The just-out January [1943] issue contains stories, among others, by Dorothy [L.] Sayers, E.C. Bentley (a [Lord Peter] Wimsey parody), [BEAU GESTE author] P.C. Wren (of all people), H.G. Wells, and your reviewer.

OBITUARY DEPARTMENT. No obit that I have seen on that fine character actress Edna May Oliver so much as mentioned what must be to mystery followers one of the outstanding facts of her career, her creation [more precisely her portrayal in a series of RKO movies] of Stuart Palmer's schoolmarm detective, Hildegarde Withers.

Occasionally an actor becomes completely identified with a detective, so completely as even to influence the later writing of that character. Warner Oland as Charlie Chan, William Powell as Philo Vance and Nick Charles, William Gillette as Sherlock Holmes—these are the great examples, and Miss Oliver as Miss Withers ranks with them.

So a moment's reverent silence for the death of Hildegarde in the flesh, and a further moment of prayer for her prompt reappearance on the printed page.

PSEUDONYM DEPARTMENT. Dutton, publishers of the brilliantly hard-boiled DIG ME A GRAVE, invite the public to guess at the author hidden behind the pseudonym John Spain. The only clues of internal evidence are that he knows Los Angeles (as distinguished from Hollywood) very well indeed, L.A. politics somewhat but from the outside, and Dashiell Hammett by heart.

One sound guess might be Raymond Chandler, best until Mr. Spain of the Hammett followers. Another (a least-suspected-person solution) might be Hammett himself. I've heard rumors that he's been afraid to put out another mystery since his reputation became so overwhelming; a pseudonym would give protection.

But my own guess is James M. Cain. It's hard to justify objectively. There's a certain amount of interest in music and in Mexicans that fits in. There's the fact that Cain's non-mysteries stem so directly from the Hammett mysteries. There's the rhyming resemblance of the names. But I confess that what really gave me the theory, which I am hereby stuck with, was a Mexican girl mentioning an iguana. [The senorita and the iguana figure prominently in Cain's 1937 novel SERENADE. But this time Boucher guessed wrong. John Spain turned out to be hardboiled mystery writer Cleve F. Adams.]

Odd confusion of pseudonyms: the Q. Patrick novelet mentioned above has as its leads Peter and Iris Duluth, heretofore star performers for Patrick Quentin.

Apropos of all which: there are reasons, as my predecessor Mr. [Edward Dermot] Doyle acutely surmised, why I may neither discuss the identity nor review the novels of H.H. Holmes [which was a pseudonym of Boucher himself]. So for Mr. Holmes' latest I present to you a guest reviewer: Alfred Meyers, whose novel MURDER ENDS THE SONG last year proved equally satisfactory to connoisseurs of music and of murder. [Meyers' rave review of the "Holmes" novel ROCKET TO THE MORGUE is omitted from this collection.]

November 29, 1942

The saying that you can have too much of a good thing is manifestly false when applied to so infinitely good a thing as the adventures of Sherlock Holmes.

Sixty of those adventures have been transcribed for our reverent delight, 56 of them by the faithful John H. Watson, two by the master himself, and two by an unknown third hand, perhaps that of Sir Arthur Conan Doyle.

(This count does not include the two anonymous records of the master's failures recently discovered by Christopher Morley among the miscellaneous works of the aforesaid Sir Arthur.)

But 60 adventures have nowise sated our appetites, and we have continued devoutly to hope for more. For "somewhere in the vaults of the bank of Cox & Co., at Charing Cross," Watson wrote in the twenties, "there is a travel-worn and battered tin dispatch box...crammed with papers, nearly all of which are records of cases to illustrate the curious problems which Mr. Sherlock Holmes had at various times examined."

All loyal aficionados of Holmes, and particularly the Baker Street Irregulars, those hierophants of the sacred writings who number among their members Christopher Morley, Vincent Starrett and Elmer Davis, have prayed for the day when that dispatch-box might be opened and a new adventure of Sherlock Holmes be revealed to his palpitant admirers.

And now comes news from London that a sixty-first adventure has indeed been discovered but that (and I shudder to speak of it) it is deemed unworthy of the master and may never be published.

The following are the facts as ascertained by the industry of those indefatigable Irregulars, Edgar W. Smith and Charles Honce.

The noted biographer Hesketh Pearson is now preparing a life of Sir Arthur and has been probing through long-neglected Doyle family papers. Among these he and Doyle's son Adrian found a manuscript presumably extracted from the dispatch-box and turned over to Doyle, who acted as Watson's agent in his dealings with publishers.

The case is entitled "The Man Who Was Wanted," is treated in some 7000 words, and concerns the problem of finding a business executive who has disappeared because of financial difficulties. Holmes solves the matter by showing the man's photograph to all concerned and making his deductions from their reactions.

The opening scene in Baker Street, Pearson declares, is "quite as good as anything that Conan Doyle (sic) did, but the plot is weak." Adrian Conan Doyle agrees that "it is not up to scratch," and the manuscript is accompanied by a note from Doyle's wife stating that he did not intend to publish it because it was not up to standard.

The outcry of protest from Irregulars and even from more normal devotees has, of course, been terrific. That the case was one of Holmes' poorer ones from a plot standpoint seems to us irrelevant; we would tolerate any plot for the sake of a great opening scene in Baker Street. (And fine opening scene plus weak plot describes so many of the already published adventures.)

The announcement of the suppression has naturally failed to dampen the enthusiasm of publishers. At least two American firms are already in the field with ardent bids. But the Doyle estate is making no definite decisions pending the return from America of the elder son, Denis Conan Doyle, who is rumored (bless him!) to favor publication.

There the matter rests. For the nonce we can only hold our breaths and pray that Adrian Conan Doyle will see the light.

And we can speculate on the nature of the case.

For Watson left many hints as to the contents of that dispatch-box, and several of them might apply to this adventure. Unfortunately the name of the man who was wanted has not been revealed.

Was it Crosby? In 1894 Holmes was involved in the repulsive story of the red leech and the terrible death of Crosby the banker.

Was it Harden? On April 23, 1885 Holmes was immersed in a very abstruse and complicated problem concerning the peculiar persecution to which John Vincent Harden, the well known tobacco millionaire, had been subjected.

We cannot hope that it was Mr. James Phillimore who, stepping back into his own house to get his umbrella, was never more seen in this world; for that case, we know, was one of Holmes' rare failures, and one gathers that he was successful in finding the man who was wanted.

My own conjecture is that the name is Maupertuis. "The whole question," Watson wrote, "of the Netherlands-Sumatra Company and of the colossal scheme of Baron Maupertuis are (sic) too recent in the minds of the public, and are too intimately connected with politics and finance to be fitting subjects for this series of sketches."

The doctor wrote this in 1893, referring to events of the spring of '87. His reluctance at that time is understandable, but it is at least likely that some time in the twenties he decided that the time was ripe to remove the Maupertuis papers from Cox & Co. and entrust them to Sir Arthur.

But Holmes himself would be the first to reprove me for drawing conclusions before I am in possession of all the facts. We can but wait breathlessly for "The Man Who Was Wanted," secure in the knowledge that the sixty-first adventure of the master, no matter how inferior to the others, can hardly fail to be the highpoint of any publishing year. [The story was in fact published after the war but turned out not to be by Conan Doyle at all.]

December 6, 1942

MURDER FOR CHRISTMAS, title of one of [Agatha] Christie's most debated novels, is likewise an excellent motto if you're wondering what to send to your man in the Army.

The men in service read and like mysteries. You may have been hearing how much more serious-minded our soldiers are in this war, and pictured them devoting their reading time exclusively to texts on higher mathematics. But the army is buying unprecedented quantities of mysteries for its libraries and still failing to keep up with the demand.

Whodunits make ideal presents because they can be enjoyed and passed on. No soldier wants to be cluttered up with gifts that he has to tote around. When your present is a mystery, it's a gift not only to him but to all his friends and eventually to the USO or the camp library.

If the ideal book present is a mystery, the ideal form for a mystery is a Pocket Book, attractive, inexpensive, and equally easy to carry about and to part with. And the ideal PBs are the mystery anthologies edited by Lee Wright.

Miss Wright is the admirable and astute individual who edits Simon & Schuster's Inner Sanctum Mysteries, writes the delightful *Gory Gazette,* advises PB on its mystery reprints, was Gypsy Rose Lee's bridesmaid, and knows more about the mystery, whether esthetically or commercially, than S&S knows about book promotion.

These anthologies are three: THE POCKET BOOK OF GREAT DETECTIVES, THE POCKET BOOK OF MYSTERY STORIES, and THE POCKET MYSTERY READER. It isn't possible to pick and choose among the riches offered by these three; they're the best mystery anthologies ever offered anywhere near their price and among the best mystery anthologies period.

If you want novels rather than anthologies, PB offers a notable choice, including the following which I nominate for any list of the best mysteries ever written (and if you've unfortunately missed any of these, get an extra copy for yourself):

IT WALKS BY NIGHT, by John Dickson Carr; THE A.B.C. MURDERS, by Agatha Christie; THE RED WIDOW MURDERS, by Carter Dickson [John Dickson Carr]; THE CASE OF THE COUNTERFEIT

EYE, by Erle Stanley Gardner; DEATH IN A WHITE TIE, by Ngaio Marsh; THE RED HOUSE MYSTERY, by A.A. Milne; THE SIAMESE TWIN MYSTERY, by Ellery Queen [Frederic Dannay & Manfred B. Lee]; STRONG POISON, by Dorothy [L.] Sayers; and THE SAINT-FIACRE AFFAIR, by Georges Simenon.

You'll find others almost equally good by each of these save Simenon and Milne, to say nothing of lesser masterpieces by [Earl Derr] Biggers, [Dorothy Cameron] Disney, [Leslie] Ford, [David] Frome [a pseudonym of Leslie Ford], [Frances & Richard] Lockridge, [Van Wyck] Mason, [Elliot] Paul, [Patrick] Quentin, [Mary Roberts] Rinehart, [Rex] Stout, and [Phoebe Atwood] Taylor.

An impressive list? Well, I have yet to see a less than first rate whodunit picked by Pocket Books. And, to top it off, there's a Sherlock Holmes PB [THE POCKET BOOK OF SHERLOCK HOLMES] with two complete Holmes novels and three short stories.

Avon Books, through less pleasingly made and creatively edited than PB, offer a few excellent mysteries, notably Freeman Wills Crofts' WILLFUL AND PREMEDITATED, as fine a job as I know of the detective story from the murderer's point of view, and Simenon's MAIGRET TRAVELS SOUTH, which includes the French [actually Belgian] novelist's atmospheric masterpiece, LIBERTY BAR.

Best buy in Avon is THE AVON BOOK OF MODERN CRIME STORIES, not, as the title suggests, an original anthology, but a reprint of LINE-UP, the splendid collection published in 1940 by members of the Detection Club of England, distinguished not only by tales from all the masters but by invaluable discussions of the detective story by [A.A.] Milne, [G.K.] Chesterton, [J.J.] Connington and [R. Austin] Freeman.

All the above-mentioned books are paper-bound and cost a quarter apiece. If you want more substantial gifts, you'll do better with anthologies and omnibuses than with the individual novels which afford only one night's entertainment. Here follows a list of the best collections currently available.

THE OMNIBUS OF CRIME. Edited by Dorothy [L.] Sayers (Harcourt Brace, $2.95). The classic among anthologies.

101 YEARS' ENTERTAINMENT. Edited by Ellery Queen [Frederic Dannay] (Little Brown, $3). The challenge to Sayers' championship.

CHALLENGE TO THE READER. Edited by Ellery Queen (Blue Ribbon, $1). An ingenious fusion of anthology and guessing game.

SPORTING BLOOD. Edited by Ellery Queen (Little Brown, $3). A perfect gift for the sports fan too.

FOURTEEN GREAT DETECTIVE STORIES. Edited by Vincent Starrett (Modern Library, 95 cents). Sound selection of standards and novelties.

CRIME CLUB ENCORE. Edited by Howard Haycraft (Doubleday

Crime Club, $2). Novels by [Raymond] Postgate, [Selwyn] Jepson, [Philip] MacDonald and [Margery] Allingham.

THREE FAMOUS MURDER NOVELS. Edited by Bennett Cerf (Random House, $1.98). Novels by [Francis] Iles, [E.C.] Bentley and A.E.W. Mason.

THREE FAMOUS SPY NOVELS. Edited by Bennett Cerf (Random House, $1.98). Novels by [E. Phillips] Oppenheim, [Eric] Ambler and [Graham] Greene.

THREE STAR MYSTERY NOVELS (Harper, $2.50). Novels by [J.B.] Priestley, [James] Hilton and [Ethel Lina] White.

THE COMPLETE SHERLOCK HOLMES. By A. Conan Doyle (Garden City, $1.69). The canon of the Sacred Writings.

The following are recommended if your man's tastes go beyond the whodunit to fantasy and horror (you'll find some of them in the Sayers and Wright collections too):

THEY WALK AGAIN. Edited by Colin de la Mare (Dutton, $2.50). The standard supernatural anthology.

GREAT GHOST STORIES OF THE WORLD. (Originally published as THE HAUNTED OMNIBUS.) Edited by Alexander Laing, illustrated by Lynd Ward (Blue Ribbon, $1). The most imaginative ditto.

THE MIDNIGHT READER. Edited by Philip Van Doren Stern (Henry Holt, $2.75). The definitive ditto.

January 31, 1943

I talked last month about the best mystery novels of 1942, but possibly the most important book in the field last year was not a novel. For the rare critical and scholarly works on whodunits have a permanent value that only the very cream of the novels can hope for, and by their diligence and skill the criminous scholars are at once raising the standards of mysteries and raising the mystery field as a whole in general critical esteem.

As 1941 was marked by Howard Haycraft's MURDER FOR PLEASURE, 1942 was distinguished by Ellery Queen's [Frederic Dannay's] THE DETECTIVE SHORT STORY: A BIBLIOGRAPHY (Little Brown, $4). A work of prodigious scholarship, this bibliography lists every volume of short detective stories in English known to the editors, which is equivalent to saying every volume known period.

I don't need to stress the book's value as a reference work, but it has an additional and unsuspected merit: it makes first-rate reading. For the strictly factual data (in themselves fascinating enough) are enlivened by Mr. Queen's own acute comments on the nature and importance of many of the books.

The fan more interested in reading the stories rather than acquiring the first editions would welcome more information on U.S. publication of British books, and fan and bibliophile alike may regret the omission of figures on number of pages. On the question of inclusion or omission of given works you can't argue with an editor; the border line of the detective story is an impossible one to draw.

But you'll be amazed to see how much falls within that borderline. And the next time one of your loftier friends scoffs at people who read detective stories, you can find consolation in Mr. Queen's collection. It's hard to be ashamed of a field which boasts among its early writers [Charles] Dickens and [Thomas] Hardy and [Nathaniel] Hawthorne and among its living practitioners [Aldous] Huxley, [T.S.] Stribling and [W. Somerset] Maugham.

RUEFUL APOLOGY DEPARTMENT. Books published early in January are apt to be overlooked in annual surveys; you read them so long ago. That's my only excuse for omitting in my "bests of 1942" the finest new detective character of that or any of the past several years—Admiral Wetherbee. The cantankerous and magnificent retired officer made his debut in FULL CRASH DIVE by then Lieutenant (now Lieutenant Commander) Allan R. Bosworth. It is doubtful if he will appear again for the duration, but if you missed him, you'd better discover him now and then sit around, like me, drooling for another Admiral Wetherbee mystery.

CINEMA DEPARTMENT. Among current films, EYES IN THE NIGHT is [based on] Baynard Kendrick's THE ODOR OF VIOLETS, with Edward Arnold as blind Captain Duncan Maclain; A NIGHT TO REMEMBER is [based on] Kelley Roos' THE FRIGHTENED STIFF, with Brian Aherne and Loretta Young as blithe detectives Jeff and Haila Troy; and STREET OF CHANCE is [based on] Cornell Woolrich's THE BLACK CURTAIN, with Burgess Meredith as amnesiac Frank Townsend.

These were all much better than average mystery novels, and have therefore been probably altered as much in plot as in title.

Cleverest Window Dressing O.T.M.: the quotations from the writings of one of her own characters, an odd neurotic pleasingly influenced by T.L. Beddoes, which head each of the chapters in Melba Marlett's ANOTHER DAY TOWARD DYING.

REPRINT DEPARTMENT. The novels of Dorothy B. Hughes, like olives and the Marx Brothers, are never simply tolerated. Their admirers see in them brilliantly poetic fantasies of terror. Their detractors call them unbelievable nonsense (though even the staunchest detractors should be won over by her latest, THE FALLEN SPARROW).

The first three of these extraordinary books, THE SO BLUE MARBLE, THE CROSS-EYED BEAR and THE BAMBOO BLONDE, are now gathered into one volume succinctly entitled TERROR (Duell, Sloan & Pearce, $1.98), an unusually distinguished omnibus for which Hughes fans will be loudly grateful.

There's almost as much divergence of opinion on the later works of Dorothy L. Sayers, but there is little argument about the excellence of her THE NINE TAILORS, now reprinted (Pocket Books, 25 cents). Myself, I can only say that I don't know a better mystery novel. (Argumentative counter-nominations gladly received.)

Most Ingenious Murderer of the Month: The absentee killer in Baynard Kendrick's BLIND MAN'S BLUFF.

Best New Detective O.T.M. (or in fact since Admiral Wetherbee): Inspector Napoleon Bonaparte in Arthur W. Upfield's MURDER DOWN UNDER. This Australian half-caste, with his curiously formal speech, his parabolic passion for termites, his sentimentality, his patience passing even that of [Georges Simenon's Inspector] Maigret, his stubborn pride (a compensation mechanism), and the startling versatility with which he functions equally well as bush tracker or as armchair detective, belongs undeniably in the gallery of the great.

February 28, 1943

John L. Nanovic, the able editor of Street & Smith's detective magazines, has had the ingenious notion of sending book reviewers a copy of the latest *Detective Story Annual* with a letter saying: "We feel that this collection of action detective stories ranks right along with the best in mystery books, and would like to offer it for review or comment in your columns... pointing out that the fiction magazines generally known as 'pulps' really produce excellent stories for all."

I'm all for Mr. Nanovic's campaign. The pulps are the backbone of the American mystery novel. Dashiell Hammett, Erle Stanley Gardner, Richard Sale, Cornell Woolrich, Frederick C. Davis....I could fill most of this column with nothing but the names of leading writers of mystery books who got their start in the pulps—some of whose best work in fact is to be found only by assiduous prowling among dusty back numbers of fiction magazines.

But I could support the campaign more vigorously if this fourth issue of *Detective Story Annual*, a collection of reprints from Street & Smith publications, were as good as its predecessors. Earlier *DSA*'s have contained distinguished novelets by Cornell Woolrich or by Ellery Queen [Frederic Dannay & Manfred B. Lee] and opuses by less well-known names worthy of such company.

This one, however, has far too many stories that illustrate the pulp weaknesses: the black-and-white characterization, the formula situations, and the total disregard of logic and fairness. Novelets by Edward S. Williams and Maurice Beam and shorts by Richard Sale and George Harmon Coxe are good (though hardly in a Hammett or Gardner class), but Mr. Nanovic

Nanovic should have guessed how very bad some of the others are by any standards above the barest hack competence.

PSEUDONYM DEPARTMENT. Whenever I am introduced to a stranger as a mystery practitioner, the conversation opens with a cry of "Well then you can tell me. Is Erle Stanley Gardner A.A. Fair?" That seems to be the burning question of the hour. I am ethically unable to answer it in public print (though any reasonable offer for a private answer will be considered), but I am able to call to your attention that Mr. Gardner was Charles J. Kenny and Carleton Kendrake. [As Boucher surely knew, Gardner was A.A. Fair also.]

Mr. Kenny's THIS IS MURDER is now available as a Bestseller Mystery (25 cents) and Mr. Kendrake's THE CLUE OF THE FORGOTTEN MURDER in the Sun Dial reprints (49 cents), both reissued under the name of Gardner. Gardner fans who may have missed them take note.

The newest guessing game is offered to the public by Stanley Hopkins Jr., who prefaces his MURDER BY INCHES with the statement: "The only completely fictitious character in this novel is the author." I have no nominations: the only internal clues are that Mr. Hopkins knows Long Island, likes cats and is not a professional mystery novelist. ["Hopkins Jr." turned out to be the daughter of bookman and pioneer Sherlockian Christopher Morley.]

Stanley Hopkins Sr., you will recall, was "a promising detective, in whose career Holmes had several times shown a very practical interest," as Watson tells us in "The Adventure of the Golden Pince-Nez." The younger Hopkins should find much in common with T. Gregson, mystery reviewer for *Harper's*. For Tobias Gregson was another inspector whom Holmes called "the smartest of the Scotland Yarders"—faint praise indeed from the Master.

RADIO DEPARTMENT. You doubtless need no prompting to listen to the *Ellery Queen* program (KPO, Thursdays, 9:30), which was for years the only radio program making an intelligent appeal to the mystery-reading audience. Now it has two rivals, both on Tuesday nights.

Suspense (KQW, Tuesdays, 6:30) is the CBS competitor to NBC's *Inner Sanctum* but far more restrained and better written. The writing in fact is frequently done by no less than John Dickson Carr. Mr. Carr is no stranger to radio (he wrote similar shockers for BBC) and handles the medium as compellingly as he does the novel, making *Suspense* a must for all whodunit aficionados.

Murder Clinic (KSFO, Tuesdays, 6:00) features even more impressive names: [G.K.] Chesterton, [E.C.] Bentley, [Agatha] Christie....It is a serial anthology, presenting each week one of the great fictional detectives in his best case. The skillful adaptations are the deft work of Lee Wright, mystery editor of Simon & Schuster.

REPRINT OF THE MONTH. INTRIGUE: THE GREAT SPY NOV-
ELS OF ERIC AMBLER (Knopf, $2.95). A wistful letter from the pub-
lisher says: "It doesn't seem to us that Ambler has ever had the attention he
deserves." If so it certainly isn't the fault of this column, where I and my
predecessor Mr. [Edward Dermot] Doyle have alike insisted that Eric Ambler is the greatest spy novelist of all time, beside whom all others are
pygmies.

Alfred Hitchcock contributes the introduction to this volume, as is most
fitting. For only a Hitchcock film can come near an Ambler novel in its
immediacy of terror, its conviction that international intrigue is not the
glamorous game of [E. Phillips] Oppenheim agents but a real and dangerous part of life which might involve you yourself at any moment.

Ambler's JOURNEY INTO FEAR (now being filmed with Orson
Welles) is likewise available this month in Pocket Books (25 cents). An-
other noteworthy current PB is H.C. Bailey's THE BEST OF MR. FOR-
TUNE STORIES, selected by Lee Wright.

WISTFUL QUERY. Does any one else know and admire the works of
Leo Perutz? Among the various authors for whom I have appointed myself
a John the Baptist, I've had even less success with Perutz than with M.P.
Shiel or Charles G. Finney. This strange Viennese writer of psychological
melodrama has his own quality—[Luigi] Pirandello writing blood-and-
thunder—which I had never found even approximated until this week, with
Chris Massie's THE GREEN CIRCLE (reviewed below).

So if you do happen to like Perutz, read Massie; and if you like the
Massie and don't know Perutz, then instantly get hold of THE MASTER
OF THE DAY OF JUDGMENT, which can be found for a dime in almost
any secondhand store, in the Boni paperback edition. Whether or not THE
MASTER is a mystery novel can be debated for hours, but certainly it is
one of the most startling novels of murder and trick psychology that I
know.

MEMO TO ALICE TILTON. Please, please bring back Cassie Price.
Life in Dalton is not the same without her. We accept no substitutes.

March 28, 1943

Remember when mystery novels used to be puzzles?   The majority of
the crop now is anything else but. There are romances, there are farces,
there are psychological studies, there are spy novels....Lord, are there spy
novels! (See the reviews below, in which half the week's crop is spy stuff.)

But the least important element in the current whodunit is the very question of who done it. Your last chapter is usually one of two things: a startling unmasking of the individual who has stood out since the first chapter
as the least suspected person, or the Eeny-meeny-miny-moe solution, in
which the detective confronts a half dozen equally possible suspects,

points at one and declaims, "Thou art the man!" Whereupon the murderer says, "My God, so I am!" and confesses.

Now I'm a conservative. I like romances and farces and spy novels (in moderation) and I revel in psychological murder studies, but what I really want is a good solid puzzle I can sink my teeth into. That's why it's always a happy month that's marked by a new book from Agatha Christie or John Dickson Carr or Helen McCloy or Nicholas Blake or Ellery Queen [Frederic Dannay & Manfred B. Lee].

For these masters, although at their best they can, purely as novelists, write rings around most of the puzzle scorners, never forget that the mystery novel is a fascinating and rigid form, and that a mystery without a puzzle is like a 13-line sonnet.

The occasion for all this didacticism is the new Ellery Queen: THERE WAS AN OLD WOMAN (Little Brown, $2). The Queen style has varied greatly through the years; it's a far cry from the top-heavy erudition of the early days when Queen was crown prince of the [S.S.] Van Dynasty to the quiet, solid American regionalism of [the 1942 Queen novel] CALAMITY TOWN. But whatever his style as a novelist, he has always been an impeccable master of formal construction and one of the most brilliant technicians in the trade.

THERE WAS AN OLD WOMAN isn't and doesn't pretend to be another CALAMITY TOWN. It's a faster, brasher, lighter work. What it's most like is an E.Q. radio program in book length: the same freakish situation, grotesque characters, rapid movement, economical dialogue, low comedy relief. And the same consummate combination of devious trickery and absolute fairness that is the Queen trademark.

What's it about? An old woman who lived in a shoe (or a mansion so called because of her fabulous fortune made in shoes) and had so many children that a cold-blooded murderer with a chilling taste in Mother Goose irony began killing them off. You may—of a Queen book I shan't say guess—you may deduce the murderer's identity if you are exceptionally alert and astute; but even if you do, I'm warning you, hold on to your seat. The surprise in the last two pages will leave you grinning groggily.

LUSITANIA DEPARTMENT. My own [1942 novel] THE CASE OF THE SEVEN SNEEZES was printed, bound and sent out to the trade before my father-in-law happened to notice that I had the Lusitania sailing the wrong way. Editors, agents, readers—nobody spotted it. It's a relief to notice that Lusitania can happen to other people too.

There's a minor one in Jefferson Farjeon's MURDER AT A POLICE STATION. The killer's alibi depends on a trick with a clock which defies the mechanism of any clock I have ever met personally.

But the gem occurs in Mabel Seeley's ELEVEN CAME BACK. One of her sub-plots deals with a young man who was once a presidential candidate. This was at a convention in 1935, and he was in his twenties at the time. Required reading for Miss Seeley and [her publisher, Doubleday] Crime Club: U.S. Constitution, Art. II, Sec. 1, Par. 5.

BLURB DEPARTMENT. Blurbs are intended to lure customers into reading a book; they should at least have the same effect on their writers. Harper's blurb on the new Ethel Lina White calls her superintendent an Inspector. Smith & Durrell describe Anthony Gilbert's Arthur Crook, an unorthodox lawyer as much an antagonist of the police as Perry Mason, as "Arthur Crooks of Scotland Yard." Granting that few copywriters can write blurbs with the enticing skill of Bennett Cerf, couldn't they at least get the facts right?

BEST DIVIDEND OF THE MONTH. The absorbing lore of the diamond trade in Robert Terrall's THEY DEAL IN DEATH. (There are fascinating facts too about the sewers of New York, which have been unjustly neglected.)

MOST INTERESTING NEW WRITER O.T.M. Hugh Addis, whose NIGHT OVER THE WOOD, uneven as it is, demands the attention of all interested in the macabre.

April 25, 1943

It's always a dreary moment in the life of a mystery fan when there's nothing new by his favorite authors, he's never heard of any of the whodunits on the shelves and the assistant librarian is on duty who doesn't know his tastes. He winds up saying eeny-meeny-miny-moe and eventually, like as not, spends a pretty terrible evening.

One remedy for this sad situation is to try picking books by publisher. Certain imprints maintain such high standards of excellence that it's practically impossible to go wrong on them; even first novels will be of the level you expect from longstanding professionals.

Three imprints are outstanding in the mystery field—a fact which I've long suspected and which my six months of complete coverage in this column have decidedly confirmed. They are Simon & Schuster (Inner Sanctum Mysteries), Duell, Sloan & Pearce (Bloodhound Mysteries), and William Morrow. Pick a book with one of those three imprints and you can't go wrong.

The quality of an imprint (and the quality of more books than their authors like to admit) depends on the editor; and one of the best in the business is Marie Fried Rodell, formerly mystery editor for Morrow and now editor of Duell's Bloodhound Mysteries, and author of the book-of-the-month within this column's scope, MYSTERY FICTION: THEORY AND TECHNIQUE (Duell, Sloan & Pearce, $2).

As editor for Morrow, Mrs. Rodell elicited some of the finest work of Carter Dickson [John Dickson Carr] and Erle Stanley Gardner. As mistress of the Bloodhounds she discovered Dorothy B. Hughes and developed

Lenore Glen Offord and Elisabeth Sanxay Holding among many others. In addition Mrs. Rodell (unique, I believe, among mystery editors) has been a practicing mystery novelist herself, producing under the pseudonym of Marion Randolph three of the most civilized and satisfactory novels of recent years.

MYSTERY FICTION is the compendium of all that Mrs. Rodell has learned of the field in her years as editor and writer, and few can ever have learned more. The book is no critico-esthetic history like Howard Haycraft's great MURDER FOR PLEASURE; it is a textbook, a how-to (or more frequently how-not-to) book, and "invaluable" is the only word in the thesaurus to fit it exactly.

It opens with the statement: "There is a legend these days that anyone can learn to write....This is nonsense—and dangerous nonsense." The chapter that follows (as also the painfully true chapter on "The Economics of Mystery Fiction") is aimed at deterring as many novices as possible. Which is as it should be: a writing career is like a marriage; if it is so weakly rooted that it can be prevented, it should be.

But if the roots are strong and you are damned well going to write a mystery or else, you'll be a fool if you try it without Rodell on your side. Here you will not learn how to write (that's up to you) but you will learn to avoid the thousand and one pitfalls that can assure the rejection of what you do write.

And even if you don't have the itch to write, you'll find MYSTERY FICTION well worth reading as a uniquely informative book on a strange and fascinating field, and as amusing and well written as it is instructive. Who writes mysteries? Who reads them? How much money do they make? How do you go about thinking one up? Are there any taboos? How many varieties of mystery novels are there?

I know from experience how many people ask these questions. Well, you'll find all the answers in Rodell, and they're the right answers. (The few very slight factual errors were probably inserted deliberately to afford pleasure to authors whom Mrs. Rodell has edited.) Rodell on Theory and Technique will stand henceforth as the Hoyle of homicide.

PURCHASE DEPARTMENT. Recommendations in this column are usually for rental rather than buying. The Rodell of course belongs on your permanent shelf, and so might the odd anthology called WORLD'S GREAT MYSTERY STORIES, edited by Dr. M.E. Speare [who is not credited in the book itself] and Will Cuppy (Tower Books, 49 cents). I say odd because I'm completely unable to figure out the standards of inclusion. It's an omnium-gatherum of everything from a straightforward [Agatha] Christie problem to a [Charles] Dickens ghost story, from a panicking [Stephen] Leacock parody to [William] Faulkner at his grimmest. Five at most of the eighteen stories are crime-mystery; the rest have nothing in common with them or each other save that they are almost without exception unusually good yarns and not too hackneyed. The gem of the collection is a subtly evil horror story by, of all people, F. Scott Fitzgerald.

Mr. Cuppy, the erratic humorist and mystery-critic, contributes an introduction in which the humorist wins hands down.

OPEN SECRET DEPARTMENT. It isn't considered ethical to announce one's discovery that, say, Mabel Seeley is really Dashiell Hammett. But when a publisher lets the cat out of the bag himself, maybe it's all right to call attention to it. So notice the back jacket of any current Dodd Mead mystery which advertises THE BRASS CHILLS by Hugh Pentecost, author of THE FOURTEENTH TRUMP.

THE FOURTEENTH TRUMP was by Judson P. Philips.

Under either name Mr. P. is one of the fastest and cleverest writers going. And the title of his latest (and perhaps best) is as above, THE BRASS CHILLS, and not, as it appeared in this column a few weeks ago, THE BRASS CHILIS.

REPRINT DEPARTMENT. Lieutenant Commander Allan R. Bosworth's FULL CRASH DIVE, which this department has previously urged upon you with wild enthusiasm, is now on the newsstands as a Crime Novel Selection (25 cents). It has been retitled, so help me, THE SUBMARINE SIGNALED ...MURDER!

June 6, 1943

The most interesting current phenomenon within the scope of this column is the extraordinary development of the spy novel. This development is most readily noticeable simply as a matter of quantity: where a season used to bring an occasional [Eric] Ambler, [E. Phillips] Oppenheim or Van Wyck Mason, the spy novels now amount to about a third of the crop. To be exact, of 103 novels I've reviewed in 1943, at least 34 have had espionage or sabotage as a dominant element.

But quantity is only half the story: the improvement in quality has been equally marked. Spy novels were formerly the literary stepchildren of the mystery trade. Only six years ago a mystery of any serious literary caliber might be a psychological study, a social satire, a horror story or what-have-you, but certainly not a spy story. Spy stuff meant, God help us, Oppenheim and [William] Le Queux.

At last Ambler came, and from his BACKGROUND TO DANGER (1937) we may date the transfiguration of the spy story. Ambler showed that human characterizations, good prose, political intelligence and above all a meticulously detailed realism, far from getting in the way of intricate spy adventures, can strengthen them and raise them to a new plane.

Many post-Ambler factors helped to continue the new high level of espionage. One was Ethel Vance, whose ESCAPE, overrated as a novel of suspense, nevertheless showed how the suspense framework could serve for a novel of character. Another was Manning Coles who, following close in Ambler's footsteps, showed that the master could damned near be beaten at his own game.

And another was the political awareness developing in England after Munich, which led almost every top-flight mystery writer to save the Empire from Fascism by the intervention of his star detective. Margery Allingham's TRAITOR'S PURSE, Nicholas Blake's THE SMILER WITH THE KNIFE, Michael Innes' THE SECRET VANGUARD brought to international espionage a literacy and skill hitherto lavished on purely private murder.

The American spy novel long lagged behind the British, for reasons that aren't hard to guess. But in the past few months we've closed up the gap.

The spy novel, in short, stands now where the strict detective story did in the late '20s. An old-established hack form, it is at last coming into its own under the leadership of a group of writers who know that humor, understanding, humanity and good prose are not amiss in any form.

It may be recognized soon as the separate form that it is. Reviewing columns may even carry one box for whodunits and another for spy-sabotage yarns. These are now indiscriminately published as mysteries or "straight" novels, the chief difference being whether the publisher wishes to charge $2 or $2.50.

Like the mystery, the spy story is a literary microcosm. It includes everything from such romantic trash as George F. Worts' OVERBOARD to the grim Hammett-like tautness of Peter Cheyney's DARK DUET. And it includes a high percentage of novels which deserve consideration as serious fiction, particularly the works of those two extraordinary young Englishmen, Geoffrey Household and Graham Greene, whose infinite professional skill makes the depth and humanity of their work only the more impressive.

Why this war should have produced such results where the last war assuredly did not is hard to explain. One factor may be one of the elements which I attributed above to Eric Ambler—political intelligence. Certainly the average reader (and the average writer) is more aware this time of underlying reasons and motivations, and certainly the spy novel can reach a higher level when its characters act out of their psychological natures than when they are simply arbitrarily on Our Side or Their Side—good vs. bad, cowboys vs. Indians.

The modern spy novel tends to probe far more deeply into moral issues than one expects of popular fiction. (Outstanding examples, aside from Household and Greene, are Dorothy B. Hughes' THE FALLEN SPARROW and Mark Saxton's THE YEAR OF AUGUST.) But this is true only on the highest level; below that level the spy novel shows a tendency to violate the prime rule of the mystery—justice.

Howard Haycraft has shown how the whodunit could not flourish under

Fascism; a Gestapo man wouldn't say "Whodunit?" but "Where's the Jew-Communist we can pin this on?" Even so our own writers are too prone to feel that once they have proved a character to be a Fascist (or even a German by race) they have done their duty. The dastard is obviously guilty as hell of murder or anything else.

But for a really vicious attitude let me commend you to Mr. Cleve F. Adams, whose UP JUMPED THE DEVIL (Reynal & Hitchcock, $2) is a grand piece of ultra-hardboiled action and dialogue in the toughest tradition and at the same time a very nasty piece of work.

Mr. Adams' aim seems to be to sow suspicion and distrust of everything connected with the war effort. Washington executives are stupid stuffed shirts; the FBI is filled with overeducated incompetents; Latin-American diplomats are Cesar Romero caricatures. Everybody is out of step but private eye Rex McBride, who pursues his own extra-legal courses.

The author has utter contempt for anyone who is not a white Nordic. Among the descriptive words employed throughout the book are wop, nigger, spig and kike. And when someone finally objects to the Gestapo-like methods of McBride (who guesses at a suspect, kidnaps him, and has him tortured until he confesses), the dick utters this ringing manifesto: "An American Gestapo is goddam well what we need!"

As Joseph Henry Jackson said of a recent pro-appeasement British spy thriller, Mr. Adams has the right to produce such a book and Reynal & Hitchcock the right to publish it. I also have the right to say what I think of it.

June 27, 1943

The prize item in this month of June, when the summer slack is beginning to set in in the murder business, turns out to be a reprint, one of those Bestseller Mysteries that are available on the news stands for a quarter. And yet not quite a reprint either, because this is its first appearance in book form.

The opus in question is Dashiell Hammett's story $106,000 BLOOD MONEY, a singularly inept title for a singularly ept, if I may coin a positive, piece of work. Most of you know that Hammett and in fact the whole hard-boiled school of detective stories started in the pulp magazines, not between book covers. *Black Mask* in the twenties exerted an influence on the course of the whodunit comparable to that of *The Strand Magazine* in the nineties, when the [Sherlock] Holmes stories were appearing.

Dashiell Hammett is unique. None of his successors in the hardboiled vein have ever attained his ironic, hardbitten authenticity, though John Spain [Cleve F. Adams] and Raymond Chandler have come close. But his unique qualities did not appeal to book editors, who doubtless looked down their refined noses and murmured "Pulp!" until 1929, when Knopf brought out RED HARVEST, that magnificent saga of gang warfare in Montana. The next two years brought three successive masterpieces: THE DAIN CURSE, THE MALTESE FALCON and THE GLASS KEY.

After a three-year gap he produced THE THIN MAN, by which he is unfortunately best known. Unfortunately because its alcoholic blitheness lacks the sting and vigor of the early works and because Nick Charles, no matter how charming he is when played by William Powell, is a pallid creature beside Sam Spade and the fat and nameless operative of the Continental Agency.

For the past nine years Hammett has been silent. This is no place to probe the reasons for that silence—which sounds much better than confessing that I haven't the slightest idea what they are.There are rumors that he is engaged on a work of serious fiction; a friend once answered the frequent question, "What's become of Hammett?" by saying, "Oh, he's sitting in the Beverly Wilshire contemplating his novel."

Publishers and devotees are alike vexed by this long silence, and the smart ones are realizing that the Hammett crop is nowise limited to the five book-form novels. The back files of *Black Mask* and later of *American [Magazine]* contain almost virgin veins of the finest Hammett ore. For years various publishers have tried to talk him into bringing out a volume of pulp reprints but he has protested that he'd have to rewrite; they're too far below his present standard.

Then his present standard is unreasonably high, as anyone knows who has read the several shorts reprinted in *Ellery Queen's Mystery Magazine* or the novelette in THE POCKET MYSTERY READER.

And now Lawrence Spivak, bless him, has persuaded the Master (by what blackmail I shudder to think) to permit the reprinting of a whole novel from those dusty back-files, and it is an opus fully worthy to rank with the established Hammett canon.

$106,000 BLOOD MONEY tells of the most daringly conceived bank robbery on record, executed right here on Montgomery Street, and of how the gangsters, imported for the stunt and later double-crossed, turn San Francisco into a gorier Chicago. The plump anonymous Continental Op is in the midst of it all, turning and twisting the plots and counterplots as best he may, and finally bringing off one of the most adroit denouements I know.

Of familiar Hammett, the story most resembles RED HARVEST. There is the same fine careless carnage, the same half-humane, half-cruel depiction of criminal types, and even more dexterity in construction and action.

PSEUDONYM DEPARTMENT. Another writer much of whose best work is lost in back pulp files is Cornell Woolrich, who made what I imagine is his radio debut recently with a yarn on Columbia's program *Suspense* (which excellent weekly chiller, by the way, has now moved to 7 P.M. Tuesdays on KQW). The odd thing is that this story of Woolrich's was identical, even to the title, with one in the recent volume I WOULDN'T BE IN YOUR SHOES, by William Irish. This will hardly surprise any who recognized in that volume the inimitable tricks of terror and suspense which only Mr. Woolrich can bring off.

A pseudonym problem that has bothered a lot of readers for a long time is: Is Francis Iles, author of BEFORE THE FACT ([the source novel for Alfred] Hitchcock's SUSPICION), the same as Anthony Berkeley, creator of Roger Sheringham? Their identity has often been stated as a fact, and still Mr. Berkeley (whose real name, to complicate matters, is A.B. Cox, under which he has also written novels from one of which that same Hitchcock lifted the handcuff sequence in THE 39 STEPS) is coy and refuses to confess.

By now, you see, this is leaving the Pseudonym Department and approaching the Department of Utter Confusion. But all the while this confusion has been growing more confounded there have been two perfectly clear bits of evidence. One Ellery Queen [Frederic Dannay] uncovered in a recent issue of his magazine: in 1934 a "Francis Iles" story was copyrighted by Anthony Berkeley Cox!

For the other I am indebted to that indefatigable scholar of mysteries, James Sandoe: also in 1934, an indiscreet year, the British firm of Hamish Hamilton published a book called O ENGLAND! The author's name appeared on the title page as A.B. Cox (Francis Iles).

The prosecution rests.

THIS IS WAR DEPARTMENT. A recent Farrar & Rinehart book, ostensibly produced under wartime paper restrictions, has 12 totally blank pages between chapters, a pure waste of 5 per cent of the book's paper.

July 25, 1943

Anthologies are the hardest of all books to review. If you dislike the selections, it's hard to protest; there's no telling what involvement of rights drove the editor to use them. And if you think the choices are perfect, you want to list a whole table of contents, with comments, and the hell with space requirements.

In the case of the Ellery Queen series of selections, however, it shouldn't be necessary to say more than: Here is a new anthology from the world's finest collection of detective short stories. It's called THE FEMALE OF THE SPECIES: THE GREAT WOMEN DETECTIVES AND CRIMINALS (Little Brown, $2.50), and contains 21 stories in 422 pages.

That should be enough. If you've ever read a Queen anthology, you're on your way to the book store now. Previous Queen works have treated the personalities of detectives (CHALLENGE TO THE READER), the history of the form (101 YEARS' ENTERTAINMENT), and crime in sports (SPORTING BLOOD). This latest—well, look at the title.

Women, even the unusual women who solve or commit crimes, have a softening influence on the Cousins Queen. The preface to this collection is written with a sort of tender whimsy normally foreign to the Queen temperament, and the stories depend much more upon character and style than upon strict detectival plotting.

The selection of stories is far from hackneyed. Six have never appeared in book form before and one is printed for the first time anywhere. You'll find the familiar females at the top of their form—[Stuart Palmer's] Hildegarde Withers, [Agatha Christie's] Miss Marple, [F. Tennyson Jesse's] Solange Fontaine, [Gilbert Frankau's] Kyra Sokratesco. But you'll also meet new heroines—Karl Detzer's astute script girl Rose Graham, H.H. Holmes' [Anthony Boucher's] surprising nun Sister Ursula, Roy Vickers' hyperbolic hypocrite Fidelity Dove (who has won my heart) and—

See? I told you. One starts in listing the whole table of contents. My only quarrel is with the omission of Violet Strange. I fear I'm in a minority on this point, but Anna Katharine Green's society girl detective seems to me to have a possibly dated but nonetheless real charm. Look her up and see what you think.

Charm is in fact the word for what all these assorted detectives and criminals have, in the midst of the direst situations; and the collection of their exploits is unqualifiedly recommended to anyone who is devoted either to crime or to women.

And who else is there?

TABU DEPARTMENT. Those critics who, like Marie F. Rodell, speak of sex tabus in the mystery novel are advised to look into the works of M. Scott Michel. Tabus? You might as well speak of the influence of the Hays Office on Krafft-Ebing, whose ghost is probably making notes for a new edition from the Michel novels.

LUSITANIA DEPARTMENT. Ever since I wrote a novel in which the Lusitania sailed the wrong way, I have been consoled to find similar boners in the truly illustrious. One of the vital clues in Ngaio Marsh's COLOUR SCHEME is the "Once more into the breach" tirade from [Shakespeare's] HENRY V (III, i), which Henry delivers before Harfleur. Miss Marsh and her erudite detective persistently refer to it as "the speech before Agincourt," which is, since the actual Agincourt speech (IV, iii) [is] also involved in the novel, pretty confusing for the amateur puzzle solver. But this, like Geoffrey Homes' curious conviction in THE HILL OF THE FRIGHTENED MONK that the president of Mexico is named "Comacho" with an o, doesn't detract from excellent work; it just makes you wonder where the editor was.

TITLE DEPARTMENT. If you see Francis Bonnamy's DEAD RECKONING (reviewed below) and think you've read it before, you haven't. You're thinking of a volume of Kenneth Fearing's poems or a [Francis] Ilesian murder novel by Bruce Hamilton, both of which (to say nothing of various magazine stories) had the same title. I don't understand this; there seems to be no legal bar to keep you from putting out another book called ONE WORLD and playing merry hell with Messrs. Simon, Schuster, [Wendell] Willkie and Walgreen.

YOU-PAYS-YOUR-MONEY DEPARTMENT. Quote from the jacket of George Harmon Coxe's MURDER FOR TWO: "No part of this book has appeared in any magazine or periodical in the United States." Quote from copyright page of the same book: "Published in *Black Mask* magazine under the title BLOOD ON THE LENS."

PULP DEPARTMENT. Readers often speak of an author "coming up" from the pulps to the dignity of book publication. In actuality a book writer often rejoices when he finally makes the pulps and begins to get a little money. And a fan who keeps a careful eye on the news stands will often find his favorite authors and characters in episodes which his rental library knows not of.

As for instance, in the current (July) *Baffling Detective Mysteries* there's a Craig Rice story about John J. Malone, splendidly on his own and uncluttered by Jake and Helene Justus, and fine reading it is, though the solution may leave you scratching your head.

In the same magazine, I'd like to bow to a colleague. The anonymous foreman of the "Jury Room" department does as succinct and tasteful a job as I know of sentencing the current whodunits. And this month's I-wish-I'd-said-that prize goes to his review of Patricia Wentworth's highly feminine THE CHINESE SHAWL: "Had I but known, I wouldn't have bothered."

August 29, 1943

AN OPEN LETTER TO DOROTHY CAMERON DISNEY. Dear Miss Disney: My readers know that I am an admirer of your work. In fact I might as well get the plug in right here and remind them that your latest, CRIMSON FRIDAY, is a highly tricky and admirably written job.

But I resent intensely your attitude as a guest reviewer for the *New York Times Book Review*. Little Brown's advertisements for the new Ngaio Marsh novel quote you as follows:

"COLOUR SCHEME has everything—style and atmosphere, humor which is never forced, a striking and unusual background, and a group of characters, English, Maori and New Zealander, who are fascinating and completely credible ....urbane....highly tooled...."

So far I'm stringing along with you. We're in complete agreement, and you put it far more infectiously than I did in my own rave, especially after a printer got through cutting it. But then you go on:

"COLOUR SCHEME is a must for everyone who wants the kind of mystery story that would bore anyone fascinated by Terry and the Pirates."

This choice specimen of tasteless snobbery leaves me as near speechless as I ever become, but I shall try to make my protest articulate. Although I feel like the editor who wrote the classic rejection slip that read:

My dear sir:

My dear sir!

Sincerely yours

In the first place, simply as a matter of fact it isn't true. Like now, take for instance me. I am fascinated (indeed that's a lukewarm word for it) by Terry and the Pirates. I know it by heart from way back, and can spend many happy hours with fellow aficionados wondering if Normandie will ever be rid of her Quisling husband, if Rouge will ever meet up with the Dragon Lady, and what happened to April when she went to India after her brother. And I'm sorry but I was not bored by COLOUR SCHEME.

In the second place, you picked a bad example for your comparison. I take it you don't read the comics. That's all right. There are nice people that don't, just as there are nice people who don't drink or smoke or who don't read mysteries. You can't have all the vices. So you don't appreciate that the comics are a microcosm, like the mystery, with a multitude of levels; and picking Terry as the type of the banal comic is a little like choosing [Eric] Ambler as a sample of the stupid spy novel.

For Milton Caniff draws exceedingly well (the equivalent in his medium of literate prose), his characters are complex and three-dimensional, his dialogue is vivid and accurate, and his action, while frankly melodramatic, depends far more on character development than on circumstance.

In the third place, your comment implies that a good mystery is too good for most people, that Miss Marsh is casting pearls before the rental library swine. And that moreover there's something oddly laudable in boring the unworthy.

Now a good mystery has no right to bore anyone except those who are conscientiously bored by all mysteries. If you're writing a mystery, you're damned well writing a mystery. The higher the literary plane to which you can raise the mystery, the better. But as long as you're writing within the mystery form, you must excel in that form as well as in your more literary pretensions.

This Miss Marsh emphatically does do. My exception is to your comment, not to her work. But others (naming no names) who try to fuse an incompetent mystery with a capable straight novel would be far more honest to abandon the small financial security of the mystery and simply write the straight novel.

My last objection goes practically into allegory, with the moral that minorities should stick together. The mystery and the comics are both commercial forms that can have noncommercial merits, and both have suffered from the attacks of snobs. (You know the kind of reviewer who from the attacks of snobs. (You know the kind of reviewer who uses "mystery novel" as a synonym for lousy hackwork.) We're in no position to start attacking each other. It is very like the far more important question of anti-Semitism among Catholics or anti-Negro feeling among Jews. You're a dope to start socking your fellow victim.

Sincerely yours,

Anthony Boucher

THIS IS WAR DEPARTMENT. My congratulations to Doubleday Doran, whose Crime Club seems to be accomplishing more in the way of paper conservation than any other house. Recent Crime Club novels have run as low as 184 pages for a full uncut text which would have made a good 300 in 1941, and this without any sacrifice of reading ease or re-bindability. The simple fact is that our pre-war books were often unpardonably padded in size, and the present emergency measures may mean a lasting reform. (Though library patrons remain incredulous and maintain that they're being cheated out of reading matter.)

RADIO DEPARTMENT. CBS's *Suspense,* by far the best mystery-thriller program created by radio, is still on the air, but KQW, the local CBS outlet, has stopped carrying it. If this news saddens you as much as it does me, you might try a protesting postcard to KQW. Mass action may turn the trick.

BITER BIT DEPARTMENT. Last month I called Morrow for a consistent error of spelling in one of their books—Geoffrey Homes' excellent THE HILL OF THE TERRIFIED MONK. I've just had a charming note from Morrow's mystery editor, admitting the error and happily pointing out that I, the old perfectionist, got the title of the book wrong in my complaint. My face has turned the exact ruddy color of the water left from cooking rhubarb chard.

September 19, 1943

Anybody wanting a nice key example of the relative importance at the box office of reviewers on one hand and a first rate theatrical personality on the other is hereby advised to investigate THE TWO MRS. CARROLLS.

This play, one of the first solid box office smashes of the fall New York season, has had a curious stage history. It was moderately sensational or at least colossal in London in 1935, when it starred Elena Miramova and Leslie Banks. That version, like the current Broadway one, was set in the south of France and written by Martin Vale.

The London hit was of course brought over to America but it died in try-outs and never reached New York. Miramova starred again, with Earle Larrimore opposite her, but this time the setting was Massachusetts and Long Island.

To complicate the picture yet further, it was revived last year in summer stock to star Edith Atwater. This time it had the American setting.

Obviously, since the original London star couldn't carry it here, THE TWO MRS. CARROLLS was not to the American taste. It belonged to a very special theatrical genre which is characteristically British: the quiet and subtle murder thriller.

Far better plays of the genre have failed in America—TEN MINUTE ALIBI [by Anthony Armstrong, 1933] for instance, or ROPE'S END [by Patrick Hamilton, 1929]. Not until very recently, with LADIES IN RE-TIREMENT [by Edward Perry & Reginald Denham, 1940] and ANGEL STREET [by Patrick Hamilton, U.S. debut 1942], has the Broadway public begun to perceive the intense theatrical pleasure of adroit suspense without the claptrap of sensation.

While the British theater produced subtle and terrifying masterpieces, the American was content with such exceedingly adept hoke as THE TRIAL OF MARY DUGAN [by Bayard Veiller, 1928] or such complete balderdash as THE BAT school [referring to the many imitations of the hit thriller play of the 1920s by Mary Roberts Rinehart & Avery Hopwood]. Except for KIND LADY [by Edward Chodorov, 1936] (which was based on an English short story [Hugh Walpole's "The Silver Mask")]) I can think of only one superlative American murder play. And that of course is ARSENIC AND OLD LACE [by Joseph Kesselring, 1941]. And now a play of the British school (though Martin Vale is an American, the widow of Bayard Veiller) is turning them away on Broadway. This seemed a phenomenon that it behooved me as a murder connoisseur to investigate.

And the first thing that my investigations turned up was that hardly a reviewer in New York had liked the play. To be exact, the only two who went on record as believing that THE TWO MRS. CARROLLS is a good play were on the *Journal-American* and the *News*—for whatever that proves.

And yet the show was selling out—murder a success in spite of itself. This I had to see.

I went with an actress. That seemed logical. Between us we ought to see what makes it tick.

And we saw.

The second Mrs. Carroll is a happy life-loving girl living with her painter husband in a villa in the south of France. Her happiness and love of life persist when she begins to suffer a mysterious ailment and even when she suspects that her husband is more than artistically interested in his latest model, but they are shaken when the first Mrs. Carroll turns up with the news that the charming painter had attempted to poison her and is now hard at work producing the mysterious ailment.

What develops from there would be almost as unfair to reveal as the solution of a mystery novel, and anyway plot-telling is not one of the more attractive ways of filling hungry space.

You can see it's a promising situation. It's not dissimilar to the classic LOVE FROM A STRANGER [by Frank Vosper, 1936, based on Agatha Christie's short story "Philomel Cottage"], save that the murderer there was a strict money-making artisan, while Geoffrey Carroll is an artist who commits his crime out of death-and-beauty obsession never made quite too clear.

Also like LOVE FROM A STRANGER, it's a long time getting under way. Until the entrance of the first Mrs. Carroll at almost 10 o'clock, the play could pass for straight drawing room stuff. And since the basic suspense plot is not begun until so late, the earlier part is relentlessly padded with small talk, manifestos on art, and digressions which sound like plot threads and come to nothing. (There's a lot about an earlier suicide in the same villa which is only slightly more relevant than the mystery of Judge Crater's whereabouts.)

Once things get going, they go. The last scene of all switches with an abrupt change of pace into the melodrama of pure physical violence and contains one dazzling *coup de theatre* that brings shrieks and clutchings from the feminine audience, including my actress.

And my actress brings me back to the answer to the play's success. It is a vehicle. It is perhaps about the most thorough-going female starring vehicle since SUSAN AND GOD [by Rachel Crothers, 1937] (and certainly no worse a play). Sally Carroll runs the gamut from Alpha quite a ways past Omega and into another alphabet. Joy, tenderness, passion, wonder, suspicion, fear, terror—oh, go get your own thesaurus and look up under emotions.

And these emotions are portrayed by Elisabeth Bergner.

Bergner has rarely appeared on the stage in America, nor anywhere for several years, but it's where she belongs. What seems a trifle too mannered in the closer view of the screen is effective and right behind the footlights.

But this is my actress's field. She says (and you see why she should remain nameless here): "It isn't great acting. It's a great bag of tricks and she's using them every minute. Frankly, it isn't a role that would tempt me; it's too shallow a character, and there's nothing to do but pull out all the tricks. But she's the girl that can do it."

I feel the same way, and I felt that a corresponding bag of tricks was just what Martin Vale needed. Why is it that people who write and direct murder plays never bother to learn anything about murder tricks?

When will there be a murder play by a major murder writer? Yes, I know Rufus King had a flop [INVITATION TO A MURDER, 1934], though it wasn't a bad play; but how about a play by Ellery Queen or John Dickson Carr for the most subtle chillers?

If a great star in a great role can carry a bad murder play, what would happen if all aspects were equally high in standard?

In discussing THE TWO MRS. CARROLLS nothing much matters but play and star. The other actors are most of the time fighting against stock roles and slow scenes and do very well. Victor Jory as the murderer does rather more than that, and Stiano Braggioti (once himself a murder victim in Katharine Cornell's DISHONORED LADY [by Margaret Ayer Barnes & Edward Sheldon, 1930]) makes a nearly human being out of a stickish faithful friend.

Reginald Denham's direction is hard to judge. Denham surely knows suspense drama; he wrote SUSPECT and LADIES IN RETIREMENT. But Hitchcock himself couldn't get excitement into that endless first act. The curiously harsh treatment on the first Mrs. Carroll, which does not help the revelation scene, must be Denham; but so must the generally excellent pacing of the last act.

The occasional odd pauses and stage waits must, I think, be attributed to the unpredictable Bergner technique; in a play that's been running since early August, the cast surely must know the script by now.

It will in all probability be running much longer. Most of the reviewers covered themselves beautifully on that. If it flopped, all right, so didn't they say it was a bad play? If it clicked, all right, so didn't they say Bergner could carry it?

She can, and seeing her do so is as spectacular a theatrical experience as there's been recently outside of the vehicles which Gertrude Lawrence not only carries but juggles in midair.

But it still hurts me as a murder fan to see such very grade B homicide wreaking havoc at the box office.

September 26, 1943

By the time this review reaches San Francisco, MURDER WITHOUT CRIME will have closed after 37 performances.

There's food for worry in this statement—worry chiefly about the current crop of Broadway reviewers. I don't intend to sound like the Shuberts (who recently struck Louis Kronenberger of *PM* off their press list because he found their revival of THE STUDENT PRINCE shoddy), nor do I agree with the disgruntled individuals who put the blame for all the theater's troubles on the shoulders of the critics.

But for an innocent drifting into New York from the West, it is hard to see just what the main stem reviewers are aiming at.

The war has given the box-office a terrific lift. It's as true in New York as it is in San Francisco that certain opuses can now run on indefinitely which would have been lucky to last a month in the thirties.

The war has also upset the reviewing situation, with many first-stringers going into the army or shifting to a war correspondent's post. Other leaders have died or retired. The stable is full of new names.

Now there are two possible attitudes for these new leaders to take in this boom time. They can recognize the tolerance of the present theater-going public and be proportionately tolerant themselves, or they can try to uphold certain fixed theatrical standards even in view of the fact that a bad show can be a sock hit nowadays.

Which they're doing I don't know and I'm not at all sure that they do. Example A: you remember LAUGH TIME, the Frank Fay-Bert Wheeler-Ethel Waters show recently tried out in San Francisco? Even the supposedly more tolerant West Coast press found a good deal to complain about in it, and most theatergoers concluded that even Frank Fay's superlative skill did not quite redeem the evening.

So it opened on Broadway, practically unchanged, to almost unanimous rave notices.

Example B is MURDER WITHOUT CRIME and brings us back at last to the lead on this story.

Last week I reported on THE TWO MRS. CARROLLS and agreed with the press that it was a very bad murder play but a splendid vehicle for Elisabeth Bergner. I had gathered from reviews that the same was true of MURDER WITHOUT CRIME—bad play but fine vehicle for Henry Daniell. And since for my money a superb Daniell vehicle sounds more promising both theatrically and murderously than a superb Bergner one, I felt I could probably put up with the badness of the play.

I took with me a notable criminal connoisseur from Random House [almost certainly editor Lee Wright, who had purchased Boucher's earliest detective novels]. At the end of the slightly awkward first scene we said, "Well, if it doesn't get any worse than this..." At the end of the first act we said, "Hey, look! This is good!" And at the end of the third act we swore, in the name of all fanciers of felony, a blood vendetta against the New York critics.

What is wrong with J. Lee Thompson's MURDER WITHOUT CRIME I confess I don't see. It is not perhaps one of the all-time great murder plays—not another LADIES IN RETIREMENT or ROPE'S END—but it is certainly very high Grade B.

Perhaps some of the difficulty is this: the average drama critic faced with a murder play is in somewhat the position of a reviewer of general fiction criticizing his first mystery novel. He doesn't know the form, he doesn't know what's good or bad about this particular example, and he simply says, "Oh well, murder..."

MURDER WITHOUT CRIME is a tautly written, economical play with a cast of only four characters—almost a chamber study in murder. It tells of Stephen, young-man-about-London, who quarrels with his mistress over the return of his estranged wife. In a scuffle he accidentally stabs the mistress, then gets panicky and attempts the amateur's clumsy cover-ups, only to realize that his landlord, Matthew, has discovered his secret.

It is Matthew who makes the play. A subtle, decadent, sadistic specimen of the impoverished aristocrat, he seems at first a trifle over-written, a size larger than life. Gradually, however, the script exposes and analyzes his motives until you finally come to accept him as repellent and vicious but evilly fascinating and thoroughly believable.

The character of the sadist who discovers murder and proves himself, by his gloating exploitation of the murderer, far the more sinister criminal of the two, is not a new one. There was a magnificent example in Patrick Hamilton's ROPE'S END (which this Thompson play resembles in several other details as well), and there is the fantastic title figure of Jules Romains' surrealist shocker VERGE AGAINST QUINETTE.

But Matthew has his own quality, his own individual tone, particularly apparent in his vein of morbid and macabre humor. This humor of Matthew's may be another factor that disconcerted the critics. It is sometimes hard to accustom your palate to what the Germans call "gallows humor." But once your palate is trained, there is a peculiar pleasure in the outrageous gag in the midst of terror, in the giggle that is half shudder.

That Henry Daniell's Matthew is (or rather, alas, was) a magnificent performance should go without saying. For my own taste, his consummate effortlessness is more entrancing to watch than all the tricks in the bags of the most pyrotechnic display artists. Bretaigne Windust's direction held the taut mood admirably and succeeded even in imparting perfect pace to the difficult scenes where laughs at once broke and heightened the tension. As an actor, Windust kept the show going skilfully in the tricky and unrewarding role of the murderer. Viola Keats made the wife quietly sympathetic and Frances Tannehill's figure was worth pages of exposition in her part as the victim.

In short, no one who savors the enjoyment of murder could have been bored at the Cort Theater. And any Coast producer who would like to try his luck with a small cast, one-set show with a great star might be wise to get in touch promptly with J. Lee Thompson and Henry Daniell. [Thompson, born in 1914, was serving with the RAF when this column was written and never saw it until I sent him a copy more than 55 years after its publication. When the war ended he worked as a screenwriter and eventually became a movie director, best known for THE GUNS OF NAVARONE and CAPE FEAR.]

September 26, 1943

Note: This column was written by San Francisco mystery writer Lenore Glen Offord while Boucher was in New York.

"Oh, just write about anything on which you have strong opinions," said the regular mystery editor airily, and left for New York.

This offers almost too much latitude. The mystery editor pro tem, here-inafter referred to as "I," has many violent prejudices ranging from maca-roni salad and people who won't use guest towels to what George Dyer calls "invertebrate sentences." It might be as well to choose one of the milder opinions for this column, though it will undoubtedly rouse the op-position of all good critics, including Mr. Boucher himself.

I hold a qualified brief for that type of mystery called the Had-I-But-Known. Nobody, of course, can defend the heroines who say that they wouldn't have gone snooping down the dark cellar stairs had they but known who waited there to bop them. That is sheer laziness on the part of an author who can't contrive incidents without making his characters into perfect fools. My defense does, however, include the little teaser sentences usually found in the first chapter of a mystery with a female narrator: "I was to find that those closed doors hid death and terror. Because of that innocent act we were to live through a hideous week of uncertainty and suspicion." You know the sort of thing. It and the antics of the witless heroines are now lumped together for blanket condemnation.

Well, try writing a detective story in the modern manner and see if you can avoid the temptation. In the old days you could start off in the midst of things, with a body in the first paragraph, a detective in the second, and a good haul of material clues not later than page 10. All the newer manuals, however, demand that before the murder takes place the reader should be introduced to your characters, especially the one who's to be bumped off. You're advised to set the stage, and describe the events leading to the crime directly rather than by flashback or questioning of suspects.

That means 30 or 40 pages of narration in which nothing much seems to happen. The author must, of course, be painting a three-dimensional por-trait of each character. He must plant as unobtrusively as possible a dozen salient facts or ideas. He must establish the mood of his story. He's plenty busy for those first two chapters; but, he wonders, will the reader stay with him?

If you are a budding Margery Allingham or Elizabeth Daly it is possible to make your early chapters so interesting that nobody notices the tardy appearance of the corpse, but that takes outstanding ability. You may also say phooey to the reader, you're going to take your time, and if you bore him at first that's his loss. That demands a superb assurance. Not many of us can muster either or both of those qualities.

Mystery writers are a diffident lot; their worst nightmare is that of a reader returning one of their books to the circulating library and saying he'd stopped at page 30 because it was too slow. He has missed the grin-ning corpse on page 52, the screams that rend the night on page 99, and all the rest of the author's carefully wrought thrills; and just one or two little-did-I-think sentences in Chapter 1 might have announced what was in store for him and lured him into continuing.

Naturally, the trick must be sparingly used. I maintain though that the novice should not be frowned upon for yielding to this temptation. No more should he (or more probably she) be called a true had-I-but-knowner, with all the awful connotations of that term.

HELP WANTED. Can any steady mystery reader remember this obscure reference? Both the regular editor and I are searching for a book published around 1936 or '37, in which two of the characters, presumably the detective and his Watson, discussed a League for the Preservation of Neglected Positives. (That means the positive form of a word never heard except in a negative connection: insomnia, inveterate, disheveled.) The detective wondered what had become of "that fine old word may" used as the positive of "dismay."

We should much like to know in what work this conversation occurred. The solution of the problem will not affect the fate of nations, but it would spare us some agonized racking of the brain.

THIS IS WAR DEPARTMENT. It's curious to see some of our top-flight writers ignoring the rules about contemporary backgrounds. Example: Craig Rice, in HAVING WONDERFUL CRIME, allowed the lovely Helene [Justus] to go tearing about New York with unlimited gasoline.

October 17, 1943

The theater is booming like anything in New York now, so much so that the number of successful exhibits threatens to exceed the number of available show houses. Every play tried out on the road is hoping for a death on Broadway to make room for it, and there is even talk of reopening theaters out of the Times Square district, converted movie palaces, and the honorable old-timers of Forty-Second Street which housed burlesque until [New York City mayor Fiorello] LaGuardia saved the city from its baser self.

The spoken drama falls chiefly into two classes—obstetrical comedy and what George Jean Nathan calls the "bomb in Gilead" plays which aim to bring the Realities of War Home to Us. The latter usually fold in a week and the former run forever, but neither contributes much to the theater either as an art form or as satisfying entertainment.

For the true life and sparkle of what will be known as the American Theater of the early 40s, you have to turn to the musical stage, and there you'll find inventiveness, charm, spirit and everything else that makes the theater something that catches your breath for a second when the houselights dim.

For pure authentic American contributions to the joy of nations I commend you to two shows of past seasons still running merrily: STAR AND GARTER and SOMETHING FOR THE BOYS.

Michael Todd's STAR AND GARTER started off to be glorified, $3.30 burlesque, back in the days when there still was burlesque. He dressed it up with such giant box office names as Bobby Clark, Margie Hart and the diamond-naveled literata herself, Gypsy Rose Lee, and gave it an orchestra and production values and a line of girls that must have roused Flo Ziegfeld from his grave.

The decline of burlesque is a sad subject and close to my heart since few things are dearer to me than burlesque unless they be locked room murders or time machines. To put it briefly, the beginning of the end was the growth of the strip tease. More and more emphasis fell on the stripper and less and less on the comics, so that when censorship finally clamped down on the strip there was nothing left.

But Michael Todd had sense enough to be very careful about the comics. Bobby Clark, that great zany, is no longer with the show, but Pat Harrington fills his shoes almost to perfection, with Larry Martin and Joe Lyons and Tiny Pearson not far behind. Result: all the classic bits of burlesque executed just a little better.

And with them Mr. Todd gives you an assortment of specialty acts chosen with a skilled taste which only Clifford Fischer might rival. Gloria Gilbert's toe-spinning, the adagio acrobatics of Wayne and Marlin, the spectacular involutions of the Hudson Wonders, Marjorie Knapp plaintively singing and, above all, the incomparable low-comedy xylophony of Professor Lamberti—these make an evening to rejoice anyone.

The best of burlesque and vaudeville in a show as satisfactory as it is unpretentious—that's STAR AND GARTER.

SOMETHING FOR THE BOYS is something else again. There's ostentation galore here. There are all the phony trappings of a Broadway musical, from the vast chorus executing with impeccable perfection routines of incredible dullness to the big spectacle scene when an Army bomber flies directly at the audience. And there's a plot which *The New Yorker* summarizes as "How Ethel Merman won the war by learning to receive radio programs through her teeth."

Nevertheless, in that absurd and accurate sentence is the key to why the evening is glowing and wonderful: the two words Ethel Merman.

It's hard to explain why I would cheerfully go to see her in anything. It's partly that fine resounding trumpet of a voice, which is certainly not musical but which does project a song and not a crooner's approximation thereof. But mostly it's the complete feckless, reckless, vulgar ease of her personality. She comes on a stage and polestar and pyramid! There's somebody there. Something's happening to you.

There's Betty Bruce, who is just about as sensational as Paula Lawrence's replacement. There are three fine screwball comedy numbers staged by Lew Kessler. And there is, thank God, Ethel Merman, who is in person the American Theater, and long may it wave.

October 31, 1943

NOTES OF A WEST COAST REVIEWER IN NEW YORK. Going East is like going back to peacetime. In New York they have taxicabs and chocolate and bourbon and eggs and butter and beer....But publishing shoptalk brings you back to the war. The big boom in war books is falling off but the boom in mysteries, bless it, goes right on soaring. Almost anything sells, and the only problems are paper and cloth for bindings. Mystery reprints continue to do wonderfully; [Erle Stanley] Gardner and [Ellery] Queen all but support Pocket Books....Everyone agrees that sale of these reprint rights is the best thing that's happened financially to whodunit writers; but in some corners there is head-shaking over What Will It Lead To?

A rough division of New Yorkers is into those who swear by *PM* and those who call it "the uptown edition of *The Daily Worker*" but both parties agree that Crockett Johnson's "Barnaby" is probably the greatest comic strip ever created. And why doesn't the *Chronicle* carry it? (Editorial department please notice.) You poor benighted Westerners who have been deprived of this great fantasy, dash to your bookstores for BARNABY in book form (Holt, $2). (Craig Rice fans: notice the peculiar spiritual identity of Barnaby's fairy godfather Jackson J. O'Malley with John J. Malone.)

Greatest problem in the mystery trade: how to get more money for the author. For because of the rental libraries, mystery novels make less money per reader than any other breed. And yet we couldn't exist without the rental libraries. One possible solution: upping mysteries to $2.50; they certainly bring in more rental income than the average $2.50 straight novel. Another solution: the Swedish rental tax stamp plan. And that is a story. Marie F. Rodell devotes a full page (p. 219) of her excellent MYSTERY FICTION: THEORY AND TECHNIQUE to a detailed description of this plan, whereby every rental must be accompanied by a tax stamp, the money for which ultimately reaches the author. It was I who first told Mrs. Rodell that Sweden had a plan for levying royalties on rentals; I don't know where I heard it or where she got the added detail of the stamps.

Baynard Kendrick, creator of blind Captain Duncan Maclain, was stimulated by the Rodell description to a brave new crusade for the adoption of the plan in America. He has been working valiantly, lining up adherents; and he and Mrs. Rodell and I arranged a lunch at the Murray Hill Hotel for a conference of war.

Now the lobster at the Murray Hill Hotel (God bless publishers' expense accounts) is of such a quality as to render a man impervious to most shocks of life, but at this luncheon it turned to Dead Sea fruit in my mouth. For Mr. Kendrick had written for details of the Swedish plan to the ex-president of the Swedish Authors' League, now in Canada. That day he had received his answer. It read:

"Dear Mr. Kendrick:

"I regret to inform you that I know of no such plan. Moreover, there are no rental libraries in Sweden."

So there's the mystery for you. Between us, Mrs. Rodell and I seem to have created a wonderful myth. Our heads hang in shame; but, we hasten to add, we still think it's a damned good idea.

Finest privilege of the trip: meeting at last the great mystery scholars of America—Edgar W. Smith of New York, Vincent Starrett of Chicago, James Sandoe of Boulder [Colorado], and above all Ellery Queen [Frederic Dannay]. Mr. Queen and I talked for ten solid hours on our first meeting and never switched from shoptalk once. He is in the truest sense a gentleman and a scholar, and his editorial achievements in *Ellery Queen's Mystery Magazine* have done more to raise the standard and the status of the mystery short story than any other single factor since Poe. As to the treasures of his library, which contains an over 90% complete collection of all detective and borderline shorts in book form, cold print can never succeed in expressing my bibliophilic raptures.

HELP RECEIVED DEPARTMENT. Last month Mrs. [Lenore Glen] Offord and I asked for the name of the fictional detective who founded the Society for the Rehabilitation of Neglected Positives. We've had answers from Mary Ellen Mannon of Ukiah and Frank W. Seineke of San Francisco, to whom our deepest gratitude.

The detective in question is James Greer, his creator is Newton Gayle, and the Society flourishes in the book called DEATH FOLLOWS A FORMULA and presumably in others.

SOCIAL CONSCIOUSNESS DEPARTMENT. Readers of [Leslie Charteris'] THE SAINT STEPS IN will be amazed to hear from Simon Templar a reasoned attack on "free enterprise" that would not displease the editors of *PM;* but that amazement will be topped by finding on p. 119 as complete and flattering a misunderstanding of [political columnist] Westbrook Pegler's position as I can imagine ....Anyone shocked by the Saint's unorthodox line may find consolation in the reassuringly naive patriotism of George Harmon Coxe's MURDER IN HAVANA, in which Yankee blood is a sure proof of innocent integrity.

November 28, 1943

This is addressed to fellow devotees of gadgetry, to those like me who love gadgets and tricks and formal puzzlement in the mystery novel, who reveled in the Baffle Books and Crimefiles and mourned their passing and who turn first to the Photocrime when they read a copy of *Look.*

This subdivision of the whodunit began, so far as I know, with an incredible little number in 1925 by Vincent Fuller called THE LONG

GREEN GAZE and subtitled "a cross-word puzzle mystery," an idol's-eye yarn which concealed its clues in cross-words constructed as execrably as the novel was written, and reached its apogee in the Crimefiles.

Since the last of these, in 1938, there hasn't been much trickery to tickle our appetites—only Will Oursler's pleasant compilations of legal documents and the Christopher Storm novels of Willetta Ann Barber and R.F. Schabelitz, excellent in their concept of an artist-detective who gives you sketches of clues, but the worst H.I.B.K. in writing and its equivalent in drawing.

Now, however, comes a real gem of gadgets: Muriel Stafford's X MARKS THE DOT (Duell, Sloan & Pearce, $2). Miss Stafford is America's most famous graphologist or, as she sometimes calls herself, "handwriting psychologist." In X she appears in her proper person as the handwriting analyst of a newspaper who is forced by circumstance first to identify an unknown corpse from a sample of his writing and eventually to trip a murderer by the same scientifico-miraculous means.

The plot, the patter on graphology and the lively picture of newspaper life are enough to make a satisfactory grade B mystery, but the window dressing lifts it to the A class. This consists of samples of the handwriting of all the characters, fascinating and containing the complete solution of the case—even for the layman. See the cut reproduced here. [The illustration is not available for reproduction in this book.] This in itself reveals the identity of the nameless corpse and contains the evidence that convicts a murderer. Can you resist a challenge like that?

The people who like tricks like this are also apt to do crossword puzzles, particularly the fiendish British variety developed by that great critic of the mystery novel, "Torquemada" (the late Powys Mathers). You may have run across such British puzzles in E.R. Punshon's THE CROSS-WORD MURDER or Dorothy [L.] Sayers' short story "The Fascinating Problem of Uncle Meleager's Will" (in LORD PETER VIEWS THE BODY).

You'll now find 55 of the "British" school, somewhat simplified for American taste, in DOUBLE-TALK CROSS-WORD PUZZLES, edited by Albert Morehead (Knopf, $1.50). In this type of puzzle, definitions are replaced by "clues," frequently puns or anagrams, or simply suggestive phrases, as when "stein" is defined as "a mug is a mug is a mug." The perfect clue in the book perhaps is "Fanaticism was rife in Zola's time." The answer is "zealotism." The clue is a quite accurate statement; it contains a straight dictionary definition of the answer ("fanaticism"), and the phrase "Zola's time" is an anagram of "zealotism."

Once you get the hang of this allusive method, you'll find it at once easier and more fun than any ordinary crosswords. And if you have any puzzle-minded friends, here is the perfect Christmas present.

GOURMET'S DEPARTMENT. It's just as well that Joseph Henry Jackson always insists, understandably, on reviewing M.F.K. Fisher's books himself. If I were ever to attempt it, I am sure the review would turn straight into a love letter. Mrs. Fisher has a passion for food and is herself a food for passion. And now she up and invades this department. All aficionados of crime are hereby urged to investigate her THE GASTRO-NOMICAL ME (Duell, Sloan & Pearce, $2.50). In this autobiography of two hungers you will find, starting on page 10, a unique and disconcerting little true murder story. After that you're on your own, but if you can stop reading after that sample of the Fisher style, there's something wrong with one of us.

THE REPRINT DEPARTMENT. From now on I intend to list here every month the outstanding recent reprints. If anything shows up here that you haven't read, you have the Boucher guarantee that it's well worth your 25 or 49 cents to investigate. For November: John August's ADVANCE AGENT (Tower, 49 cents), unusually intelligent spy thriller with sharp comments on American Fascism; Agatha Christie's POIROT LOSES A CLIENT (Tower, 49 cents), one of Christie's subtlest plot-tricks; A.A. Fair's [Erle Stanley Gardner's] THE BIGGER THEY COME (Pocket Books, 25 cents), the first and in many ways the best of the Donald Lam-Bertha Cool saga; H.F. Heard's A TASTE FOR HONEY (Mercury, 25 cents), indescribable but essential, as Mr. Jackson recently pointed out; and Ellery Queen's [Frederic Dannay & Manfred B. Lee's] THE EGYPTIAN CROSS MYSTERY, complex and absorbing first period Queen.

December 26, 1943

When I settled down to compile a best-of-the-year list, 1943 turned out to have been very good. It didn't always seem so at the time, but preparing the list meant leaving out reluctantly a dozen or so novels that could easily have been tops in another year.

Six of the 1943 crop were exceptional. They don't belong in a best-of-the-year but rather in a best-period, as permanent contributions to criminous literature. They are:

SHE DIED A LADY by Carter Dickson [John Dickson Carr]; the deductive problem at its most brilliant, plus humor and good writing.

COLOUR SCHEME by Ngaio Marsh; literate comedy of manners in New Zealand.

THE LADY IN THE LAKE by Raymond Chandler; as fine a chunk of prose as the hardboiled school has produced.

THE MINISTRY OF FEAR by Graham Greene; subtle and moving blend of melodrama and morals.

WALL OF EYES by Margaret Millar; probably the very cream of the year, it has everything, whether viewed as a straight psychological novel or a whodunit.

Three of these six are spy novels, which is not surprising. Espionage now marks a good third of the mystery field, and the news of the year is the great improvement in its quality. Almost equal to those mentioned are Michael Hardt's A STRANGER AND AFRAID, Helen McCloy's DO NOT DISTURB, Mark Saxton's THE YEAR OF AUGUST, Robert Terrall's THEY DEAL IN DEATH and Mitchell Wilson's STALK THE HUNTER.

Runners-up in non-spy fields:

The leisurely British school: DEATH OF A BUSYBODY, by George Bellairs.

The romantic Eberhart school: UNIDENTIFIED WOMAN, by (of all people) Mignon G. Eberhart.

The screwball humorous school: THE THURSDAY TURKEY MURDERS, by Craig Rice.

The school of pure terror: THE BLACK ANGEL, by Cornell Woolrich.

Psychological-novel-cum-mystery: DEATH IN THE DOLL'S HOUSE, by Hannah Lees and Lawrence Bachmann.

The borderline Francis Iles school: THE GREEN CIRCLE, by Chris Massie.

The short story [collection]: I WOULDN'T BE IN YOUR SHOES, by William Irish [Cornell Woolrich] (which is also the year's only volume of shorts).

Critique: MYSTERY FICTION: THEORY AND TECHNIQUE, by Marie F. Rodell.

True Crime: THE ART OF MURDER, by William Roughead.

Anthology: THE FEMALE OF THE SPECIES, edited by Ellery Queen [Frederic Dannay].

Best new detective of the year: Napoleon Bonaparte, the half-caste Australian inspector of Arthur W. Upfield's novels, of which the first, MURDER DOWN UNDER, still seems the best.

The year produced at least a dozen admirable new writers, who landed near the very top on first try and from whom we may well expect the absolute bests of 1944 or more probably, allowing for second-novel slump, 1945. The three novices (in fact if not in results) that I'm most anxious to see more from are Lucy Cores (PAINTED FOR THE KILL), Norbert Davis (THE MOUSE IN THE MOUNTAIN), and Matthew Head (THE SMELL OF MONEY). Watch out too for Kit Christians, Dale Clark (a pulp stand-by but, I believe, new to books), Amen Dell, and Finlay McDermid. (Bellairs, Hardt, Terrall and Upfield, mentioned above, are also 1943 debuts.)

There are twenty-five other novels whose titles I jotted down as possible candidates for a "best" list, and only the paper problem keeps me from plugging them. And then there is Michael Innes' THE WEIGHT OF THE EVIDENCE. I haven't read it but I pass on to you the recommendation of my understudy, Mrs. [Lenore Glen] Offord.

Reprint-of-the-year was the [Dashiell] Hammett novel lost in old *Black Mask* files and now published by Bestseller Mysteries as $106,000 BLOOD MONEY and by Tower simply as BLOOD MONEY. Nothing so exciting as that shows up on the December lists, but you couldn't ask much more for your quarter than THE POCKET BOOK OF FATHER BROWN, a careful selection of stories about the priest whom Ellery Queen [Frederic Dannay] calls "one of the three greatest detective characters ever invented." Also recommended: DEATH IN FIVE BOXES, by Carter Dickson [John Dickson Carr] (Bestseller, 25 cents), one of the cleverest of least-suspected-person plots; THE DEAD DON'T CARE, by Jonathan Latimer (Popular Library, 25 cents), hard-drinking, bawdy and memorable; VALCOUR MEETS MURDER, by Rufus King (Popular Library, 25 cents); and DEATH IN THE DOLL'S HOUSE (see above) (Bestseller, 25 cents).

Coming in January [1944]: CREEPS BY NIGHT (Forum, $1), an excellent and unusual supernatural anthology edited by Dashiell Hammett; [Rex Stout's] THE NERO WOLFE OMNIBUS (Forum, $1), including my own favorite Wolfe, THE RED BOX; and THE LODGER, by Marie Belloc Lowndes (Tower, 49 cents), which I am the only man in the field who doesn't think is an all-time masterpiece.

January 30, 1944

Serious novelists tempted to try the mystery-espionage field may well be discouraged by the critical reception of Kay Boyle's AVALANCHE. Both Edmund Wilson in *The New Yorker* and the nameless reviewer in *Time* have jumped upon it with the same slashing vigor with which Miss Boyle's Bastineau jumps down the chimney in the denouement.

I want to protest. It isn't fair. Mr. Wilson's review in particular is a brilliantly mordant job and gives him the opportunity for some much-needed puncturings of [Ernest] Hemingway and [John] Steinbeck, but it is criticism on a false level. It is asking of a frank and avowed melodrama the qualities of great tragedy.

In the other cases which Mr. Wilson cites there was, to be sure, an element of pretention and phoniness. There is none in AVALANCHE. Miss Boyle set out to produce a good spy meller; she achieved one of the best. To demand the non-commercial subtleties of her earlier work is to blame a Hitchcock picture for not being CRIME AND PUNISHMENT.

Perhaps Miss Boyle might have been wise to keep her public straight by publishing AVALANCHE under a pseudonym; then everybody could have been happy and an honest piece of craftsmanship received its due recognition.

Another author whose latest book should have been pseudonymous is Mary Violet Heberden. Under the epicene initials M.V., Miss Heberden has published many hard-boiled novels dealing with private dick Desmond Shannon; her latest, TO WHAT DREAD END (see below), is of the feminine atmospheric-romance school, and she seems much more at home being feminine than when she tried so valorously to be tough.

While we're on pseudonyms I'd like to know why Judson Philips often writes as Hugh Pentecost. (Note: the great villain of William Gillette's neglected THE ASTOUNDING CRIME ON TORRINGTON ROAD was named Hugo Pentecost.) Philips and Pentecost write in the same style for the same publisher, their identity is an open secret, and where such series characters as Danny Coyle and Luke Bradley are not involved, it seems a pure toss-up as to which gets the by-line.

The latest Pentecost is a taut and spirited novelette of murder among war workers, called "The Dead Man's Tale," which is the only reason why you should investigate THE FIFTH MYSTERY BOOK (Farrar & Rinehart, $2.50). The omnibus also contains a familiar [Agatha] Christie short, a hyper-slick Philip Wylie novelette, and an almost unbearably friendly and chatty story of family murder by Ethel Gayle.

The publishers say they "are proud to publish these mysteries for the first time in book form." The Christie story about Miss Marple appeared last year in Ellery Queen's distinguished anthology THE FEMALE OF THE SPECIES.

TRUE MURDER DEPARTMENT. About the only people who will be unhappy about Alexander Woollcott's posthumous LONG, LONG AGO are the devotees of murder. Their fellow aficionado has let them down badly with some bald synopses of over-familiar cases, reprinted from *Look*. Perhaps the projected volume of Woollcott letters will contain more characteristic criminous comments.

February 27, 1944

One of the chief points upon which died-in-the-wool mystery aficionados may differ bitterly is the device of the hermetically sealed room. Many will agree with Sally Benson in a recent *New Yorker* that it is a threadbare formula; others, with me loudly at their head, will maintain that it is no more threadbare than a fugue, a sonnet or any other classically restricted form.

Israel Zangwill's THE BIG BOW MYSTERY (1892) was, I believe, the first novel to make the impossible room the focus of its problem. By the 1920's it had become a standard device, exploited, often brilliantly, by [Melville Davisson] Post, [G.K.] Chesterton, [S.S.] Van Dine, [Edgar] Wallace and almost everyone else.

Then in 1930 John Dickson Carr published his first novel, IT WALKS BY NIGHT (possibly the best first whodunit ever written), and the locked room found its great interpreter. The number of locked rooms that Carr has constructed (under his own name and that of Carter Dickson), in novels, short stories and radio plays, can hardly be estimated. In 1935 he produced THE THREE COFFINS (original British title: THE HOLLOW MAN), an all-time classic in which [his detective character] Dr. [Gideon] Fell definitively analyzes the locked room situation, with examples of every possible type.

You'd think this would put an end to it, but it's only made the game harder. Now the trick is to produce a locked room which is apparently not classified by Dr. Fell. Two daring disciples, in fact (Clayton Rawson and H. H. Holmes) [the latter a pseudonym of Boucher himself], have quoted the THREE COFFINS chapter in their novels, tricking the reader momentarily into thinking that they have something new and unclassifiable.

All the easy locked rooms, it is true, are now exhausted. It's no field for the hack. But a master, and particularly The Master, can still make the locked room the most fascinating and stimulating problem possible in the field of strict deductive fiction. If you doubt this statement, investigate HE WOULDN'T KILL PATIENCE by Carter Dickson (just out from Morrow), and revel in the most absolute locked (or in this case sealed) room yet devised by man.

ART DEPARTMENT. The most delightful jacket since I started reviewing is that of Craig Rice's HOME SWEET HOMICIDE. I shan't attempt to describe it; rush at once to your bookstore and revel in it. Revel in the book itself too; it at last removes the jinx which has always hung over juvenile detectives. It's a mystery that might have been written by E. Nesbit (than which I know no higher praise) if she were an American of this decade.

PSEUDONYM DEPARTMENT. It is, I guess, an open secret by now that William (PHANTOM LADY) Irish is Cornell Woolrich. No one else could frame a story at once so implausible and so compelling, though the latest Irish (see below) may be a bit too implausible even for his fans. And do you know that the real name of this unlikely magician is, so help me, Cornell George Hopley-Woolrich?

BAKER STREET DEPARTMENT. A year or so ago I wrote here about the "lost" Holmes story recently found among the papers of the Doyle estate. Now Hesketh Pearson's CONAN DOYLE: HIS LIFE AND ART (London: Methuen, 1943) not only prints an excerpt (first rate) from that story but gives the synopsis (execrable) of another, which will complicate immensely the problems of the Conanical canon. Note: any local devotee of Holmes who knows and loves that canon with proper Irregularity will, as the lawyers say, find it to his advantage to communicate with this column.

March 26, 1944

The first time that I encountered the delicious shudder of true terror in literature was when I read M. R. James' "Canon Alberich's Scrap Book" some twenty years ago. You may recall how the Englishman Dennistoun bought in St. Bernard de Comminges the scrap-book of the unprincipled canon, containing, inter alia (a spot of Latin is inevitable when discussing James), the picture of a struggling demon exorcized by Solomon—a picture obviously drawn from life.

That night Dennistoun's "attention was caught by an object lying on the red cloth just by his left elbow. Two or three ideas of what it might be flitted through his brain....'A penwiper? No....A rat? No.... A large spider? I trust to goodness not—no. Good God! A hand like the hand in the picture!' "

Lesser writers may make their demons appear fortissimo in all their ugly horror, but no sharply unveiled monstrosity can ever terrify me as did (and does) that first glimpse of what seemed to be a spider, a rat or a penwiper.

This effect was beautifully reproduced ten years ago in THE MUMMY, one of the few intelligent horror films, but it remains characteristically M. R. James. The James enthusiast will recall similar moments: the bag of treasure which puts its arms about the hunter's neck in "The Treasure of Abbot Thomas"; the two figures glimpsed beside the road in "Count Magnus"; perhaps most brilliant of all, the very real terror of a mass of crumpled linen in "Whistle And I'll Come for You."

Montague Rhodes James, provost of Eton, authority on church architecture, specialist in the New Testament apocrypha, used to write a ghost story every Christmas for the delight and terror of his friends. These works form indisputably the finest body (if the word is not too inappropriate) of ghost stories in our language or any other that I know; and twenty-two of them (including all those just cited) are now available in BEST GHOST STORIES OF M.R. JAMES (Tower Books, 49 cents).

No half dollar (including sales tax) could ever bring you a more terrifying reward.

KEY DEPARTMENT. To return to the mystery story proper, we find it at present suffering from a surfeit of keys. There were [Dashiell] Hammett's THE GLASS KEY, [Lenore Glen] Offord's SKELETON KEY, [Frank] Gruber's THE FRENCH KEY, my own THE CASE OF THE SOLID KEY and [Earl Derr] Biggers' SEVEN KEYS TO BALDPATE. Now comes THE PARCHMENT KEY, by the engagingly pseudonymous Stanley Hopkins, Jr. This is a book which goes a step beyond even [Dorothy L.] Sayers or Nicholas Blake in turning the deductive-detective form into a vehicle for unusual psychological analysis. Who done it is obvious almost from the first, and the book's one murder is all but irrelevant; detection is devoted purely to the motives behind apparently meaningless malice. It's an out-of-the-way book, quite possibly a history-making trail-breaker. I'm sorry to add that its chief interest is to making trail-breaker. I'm sorry to add that its chief interest is to the student: the mystery fan, I'm afraid, will find it nebulous, slow and dull.

PSEUDONYM DEPARTMENT. According to [gossip columnist] Leonard Lyons, Kieran Abbey (see below) is Jim Kieran, brother to the omniscient John and to Helen (THE OPENING DOOR) Reilly. [In fact Kieran Abbey was a pseudonym for Helen Reilly herself.]....If Bobbs-Merrill really wish to keep secret the identity of Jane Beynon, author of CYPRESS MAN, they shouldn't put on the jacket the same publicity photo that they use for that admirable whodunit writer Lange Lewis. My guess would be that CYPRESS MAN is Miss Lewis' first novel, dug out of the trunk and somewhat revised; there are traces of immaturity in it, and despite war references its people and events are purely of the '30s. With all its flaws, though, I liked this novel (build-up to murder rather than a mystery) because Miss Lewis-Beynon has an almost unique ability to write the kind of young people that I in those '30s knew and (I confess) was. I read her with interest, admiration and a certain mirror-conscious embarrassment.

April 30, 1944

For a year now I've been regretting the fact that I did not bestow the most enthusiastic of my faces on Lucy Cores' PAINTED FOR THE KILL—a novel that grows even better in retrospect and now looks to me like possibly the best first mystery since Clayton Rawson's DEATH FROM A TOP HAT. The error is rectified in the listing of the new Cores below.

CORPSE DE BALLET is perhaps not strictly as good as the first; the plot is at once easily seen through and a little hard to accept. But once again Miss Cores (pronounced Cor-eez) has written a civilized and delightful novel with an unusual professional background and proved herself a, if not the, leading American contender for the English laurels of [Ngaio] Marsh and [Margery] Allingham.

(Aside: when I was last in New York I met the original of [Cores' character] Toni Ney, my favorite viewpoint heroine. Like Toni she is a former ballet dancer and body trainer, now a newspaper woman. But Miss Cores is guilty of a marked injustice in not emphasizing her cookery. Until Toni has served Captain Forrest her lobster cooked alive in tomato paste and wine the portrait is incomplete.)

ART DEPARTMENT. You may not have many chances to see a portrait painted by a Grade A murderer, so you'd better betake yourself this week to the San Francisco Museum and have a look at Thomas Griffiths Wainewright's delightfully skillful water color of Mrs. Wilson. For Wainewright's singularly callous career of murder, see Oscar Wilde's essay "Pen, Pencil and Poison," readily available in my POCKET BOOK OF TRUE CRIME STORIES (advertisement).

The "Art of Australia" exhibit, running through May 7, of which Waine-wright forms part (he was sent out to penal servitude as a forger), has another interest for the murder fan—the shrewdness of the aborigine in Dadswell's bronze bust and his biblical dignity in Dowling's "An Aboriginal Camp" may give you a fresh insight into [Arthur W.] Upfield's Inspector Napoleon Bonaparte.

BAKER STREET DEPARTMENT. In case anyone missed Mr. [Joseph Henry] Jackson's long essay on the subject (the *Chronicle's* "This World," April 9, 1944), it should be repeated here that the three glorious books of the year for all true students of the Sacred Writings are PROFILE BY GASLIGHT, edited by Edgar W. Smith (Simon & Schuster, $2.75), the first volume of Baker Street essays to be aimed intelligently at the general public rather than at the tiny group of specialists; THE MISADVEN-TURES OF SHERLOCK HOLMES, edited by Ellery Queen [Frederic Dannay] (Little Brown, $2.50), a collection of parodies and pastiches marked by the perfect taste and delightful commentaries which distinguish all Queen anthologies; and SHERLOCK HOLMES AND DR. WATSON, edited by Christopher Morley (Harcourt Brace, $2), the perfect book with which to set your children's feet upon the true path.

If after reading these volumes you feel the stirring of the Irregular spirit, remember that we have in San Francisco a branch of the Baker Street Ir-regulars, known as The Scowrers. Address yourself to me or to Mr. Jack-son. (Aside to those who have already done so: you'll hear more from us as soon as plans for a next meeting are more clearly formulated.)

HIGHER CRITICISM DEPARTMENT. All true and serious aficionados of the whodunit are urged to ask their reference librarians for Section 1 of the *Wilson Library Bulletin* for April, wherein they will find a highly provocative bibliography of the great detective stories, prepared by that most deeply versed of criminous scholars, James Sandoe. See also the May issue of *Good Housekeeping,* in which Ellery Queen [Frederic Dannay], supreme authority on the detective short stories, lists his "Golden Ten" books of shorts. I'll discuss these lists further next month, and meanwhile would be curious to hear any of your comments on them.

FUNNY COINCIDENCE DEPARTMENT. In the same week the same motive for murder, as unheard of previously as it is hard to believe, shows up in Grace Hoster's TRIAL BY MURDER and John Spain's [Cleve F. Adams'] THE EVIL STAR. One would give a pretty penny to hear the authors' comments—Mr. Spain's being doubtless the more vivid and less printable.

May 28, 1944

Ellery Queen's [Frederic Dannay's] listing of the "Golden 10" books of detective short stories in the May *Good Housekeeping* is a boon to addicts. It gives the essential background of all modern detective writing, and you can't call yourself an aficionado until you've read those 10 volumes. (You won't find them in rental libraries—try the public libraries and second-hand stores.) For your convenience, here is the list; clip it and check it.

Edgar Allan Poe's TALES, 1845.
Sir Arthur Conan Doyle's THE ADVENTURES OF SHERLOCK HOLMES, 1892.
Arthur Morrison's MARTIN HEWITT: INVESTIGATOR, 1894.
Baroness Orczy's THE OLD MAN IN THE CORNER, 1909.
R. Austin Freeman's JOHN THORNDYKE'S CASES, 1909.
William MacHarg and Edwin Balmer's THE ACHIEVEMENTS OF LUTHER TRANT, 1910.
G. K. Chesterton's THE INNOCENCE OF FATHER BROWN, 1911.
Ernest Bramah's MAX CARRADOS, 1914.
Melville Davisson Post's UNCLE ABNER, 1918.
H. C. Bailey's CALL MR. FORTUNE, 1920.

Minor dissent of course is possible. For my own money I'd rather see Freeman represented by THE SINGING BONE (1912), in which he invented the "inverted" detective story, and I wish the ten could be stretched to eleven to include M.P. Shiel's PRINCE ZALESKI (1895).

You'll notice the list stops short in 1920. That's understandable: up to the middle twenties the best detective writing was in the short story; since then the full-length novel has dominated. The reasons for this are largely economic, having to do with the rise of the rental library, the reluctance of publishers to risk books of shorts, and the change in magazine policy which offered almost no well-paying market for Class A detection up to the founding of *Ellery Queen's Mystery Magazine.*

But there still are some good books of shorts, even some possibly great ones; and I'd like to supplement the Queen list with a "Silver 13" of volumes published in the quarter century since his list closes. In chronological order:

Edgar Wallace's THE MIND OF MR. J.G. REEDER, 1925. (In U.S., THE MURDER BOOK OF J.G. REEDER, 1929).
T.S. Stribling's CLUES OF THE CARIBBEES, 1929.
F. Tennyson Jesse's THE SOLANGE STORIES, 1931.
Georges Simenon's LES 13 COUPABLES, 1932.
Agatha Christie's THE THIRTEEN PROBLEMS, 1932. (In U.S., THE TUESDAY CLUB MURDERS, 1933.)
Dorothy L. Sayers' HANGMAN'S HOLIDAY, 1933.
Margery Allingham's MR. CAMPION: CRIMINOLOGIST, 1937.
E.C. Bentley's TRENT INTERVENES, 1938.
Ellery Queen's [Frederic Dannay & Manfred B. Lee's] THE NEW AD-

VENTURES OF ELLERY QUEEN, 1940.

Carter Dickson's [John Dickson Carr's] THE DEPARTMENT OF QUEER COMPLAINTS, 1940.

William Irish's [Cornell Woolrich's] I WOULDN'T BE IN YOUR SHOES, 1943.

Raymond Chandler's FIVE MURDERERS, 1944.

Dashiell Hammett's THE ADVENTURES OF SAM SPADE, 1944.

Arguments gratefully accepted.

REPRINT DEPARTMENT. You'd hardly expect to find a Lewis Browne reprint plugged in this column, but aside from the fact that anti-Fascism is any department's business, it's a subject that has cropped up here before. It's next to impossible to draw border lines among the novels on native American Fascism, which range from such an unmistakable spy meller as Oliver Weld Bayer's NO LITTLE ENEMY, through ambiguous cases like the novels of Mark Saxton, to an unmistakable "straight" novel such as Benjamin Appel's THE DARK STAIN. If your interest in home-grown corn-fed evil has been whetted by whodunits (and the mystery writers' treatment of this problem has been a highly praiseworthy job of propaganda), you'll want to read Lewis Browne's SEE WHAT I MEAN, now available in reprint (Forum, $1) and even more timely now, with the sedition trials going on, than when it was published. You'll find it a frank, vigorous and vivid picture of the growth of a Fascist movement.

June 25, 1944

Acting on the assumption that the *Chronicle* has some readers who don't take *Good Housekeeping,* this column, like last month's, will go on discussing Ellery Queen's [Frederic Dannay's] list of "most importants" appearing therein.

In the June *G.H.* he gives "The Ten Most Important Detective Novels" as follows:

Emile Gaboriau's L'AFFAIRE LEROUGE (Paris, 1866).

Wilkie Collins' THE MOONSTONE (London, 1868).

Anna Katharine Green's THE LEAVENWORTH CASE (New York, 1878). Sir Arthur Conan Doyle's A STUDY IN SCARLET (London, 1887).

E.C. Bentley's TRENT'S LAST CASE (London, 1913).

Freeman Wills Crofts' THE CASK (London, 1920).

Agatha Christie's THE MURDER OF ROGER ACKROYD (London, 1925).

S.S. Van Dine's THE BENSON MURDER CASE (New York, 1926).

Dashiell Hammett's THE MALTESE FALCON (New York, 1930).

Francis Iles' BEFORE THE FACT (London, 1932).

The list is chosen for historical importance rather than present-day readability, with emphasis on "firsts" rather than "bests," and by that standard is largely unarguable. But I should like to register two dissents, one mild and one violent.

MILD DISSENT. BEFORE THE FACT is not, as Queen terms it, "the finest inverted detective novel ever written." It is not an "inverted" detective novel; it is the story of an undetected successful murderer who as the novel ends is about to succeed in murdering, with her own consent, the one person who has even suspected him. (I refer of course to the original book and not to the absurd ending tacked onto [Alfred] Hitchcock's film adaptation SUSPICION.) Superlative though it is as a crime novel, it is not a detective novel at all; if the list is to contain an "inverted" detective specimen, let it rather be R. Austin Freeman's MR. POTTERMACK'S OVERSIGHT (1930).

VIOLENT DISSENT. S.S. Van Dine is of no "importance" whatsoever. I know that this is a startlingly heretical statement, but it is high time that somebody said the emperor has no clothes on. The tremendous vogue of Van Dine in the '20s (THE BISHOP MURDER CASE is said to have had an advance sale of 70,000 copies!) is a fascinating phenomenon but quite irrelevant to the history and development of the detective story.

Stranger even than the popular reception of Van Dine's first stories was the esthetic exaltation of the critics. Anyone trying to reread Van Dine now, as I have recently done, will find not only that [his detective character] Philo Vance is insufferable and fully worthy of the treatment which [poetic humorist] Ogden Nash prescribed for him ("a kick in the pance") but that the characters are wooden, the plots unfair, the technique ragged, and the prose compounded of the damndest pretentious jargon of erudition (on the part of all characters) that ever tried to pass itself off as the English language.

But British and American critics joined in hallelujahs proclaiming that at last the detective story had become Literature, capital L, and all those who had scorned whodunits, according to the Chicago *Post,* "may be willing to admit that the writing of such a novel can be raised to a high art." Van Dine, said [critic] Harry Hansen, "belongs to the aristocracy of detective fiction." And those are typical of the major reviews.

This overflowing joy might be understandable if Van Dine had come earlier in detective fiction. But when the first Van Dine appeared, Dorothy [L.] Sayers, Anthony Berkeley, Philip MacDonald, Father [Ronald A.] Knox, Freeman Wills Crofts and Agatha Christie were all practicing mystery novelists. [A.A.] Milne's THE RED HOUSE MYSTERY was four years old, and [E.C. Bentley's] TRENT'S LAST CASE thirteen. [A.E.W. Mason's Inspector] Hanaud had been detecting for 16 years, and [R. Austin Freeman's] Dr. Thorndyke for almost 20.

One can only surmise that Van Dine's outrageous pretensions ensnared that horrible species, Snobbus americanus; and where Snobbus leads Boobus follows. It was a curious phenomenon, but where is its "importance"? Many of the writers mentioned above as preceding Van Dine are still practicing; all are still influential. But where is Van Dine's influence?

In the '20s he did exert an influence, but it vanished with merciful rapidity. The only important writer to show markedly Van Dinian affects was Ellery Queen himself [Frederic Dannay and his cousin and collaborator on fiction Manfred B. Lee], and even he shook the shackles off speedily. Nothing could be less Vance-like than [the 1942 Queen novel] CALAMITY TOWN.

For a long time I clung to memories and said, "To be sure, Van Dine fell off badly, and THE DRAGON MURDER CASE may well be the worst whodunit ever written; but still THE GREENE and THE BISHOP were something wonderful." If you feel that way, try to reread them. Go ahead. I dare you.

So please, Mr. Queen, delete Van Dine from your list. And in his place by all means insert Dorothy L. Sayers (representing her probably by THE NINE TAILORS), who may have gone too far in her later efforts to fuse the detective story and the straight novel, but who by those efforts has influenced at least every other current top-notcher.

ESPIONAGE DEPARTMENT. If the average detective-story writer's concept of the Gestapo is correct, there is no excuse for our not having won the war years ago. When up against stalwart American agents, the dreaded Gestapo men prove to be the veriest dolts. But rarely have they (or the reader's intelligence) been so insulted as by a passage in Hulbert Footner's recent UNNEUTRAL MURDER. Here the Gestapo obligingly leaves six complete sets of fingerprints on the scene of a murder, and the American detective explains: "The Gestapo men were either very careless, or they were unfamiliar with modern methods of detecting crime." Fingerprint identification has of course been in use in Germany for 40 years, longer than in France or England, and one of the greatest authorities on the subject, Dr. Robert Heindl, was recently and may still be Privy Councillor at the German Foreign Office.

BAKER STREET DEPARTMENT. For first-rate stimulating conversation on Sherlock Holmes, see pp. 238ff. of THE NEW INVITATION TO LEARNING (now reprinted by New Home Library, 69 cents), where Rex Stout and Elmer Davis present the Irregular view and Jacques Barzun and Mark Van Doren try vainly to cling to "factual" sanity. (For horror enthusiasts, the same volume presents a notable discussion of Henry James' "The Turn of the Screw," particularly valuable for the participation of Katharine Anne Porter.) Also see the current issue of that excellently varied and readable Free French magazine *Tricolor* for some notes on Holmes' French ancestry by Wallace Brockway.

July 30, 1944

When you see on a newsstand a fifteen-cent booklet called SLEEPY LAGOON MYSTERY by Guy Endore, you're apt to remember THE WEREWOLF OF PARIS, decide this is a reprint of an Endore thriller you've missed, and glom on to it fast.

In one way you'll be making a mistake, and I wonder how deliberately the format and title were intended to deceive. In another way you'll be making no mistake at all; for SLEEPY LAGOON MYSTERY is an exciting and important pamphlet, and the more people read it the better—even if they are trapped into reading it under false pretenses.

It is the story of and the story behind the so-called "zoot suit riots" in Los Angeles in 1942. It is the account of one of the most dubious murder trials ever held in a democracy, and an exposure of the ugly racist philosophy that made such a trial possible. It is a study of the forces which aim to foment racism in this country, from Goebbels to a certain publisher whose name cannot be mentioned in these pages even in contempt.

It is the narrative of a bitter episode, now almost forgotten (save by the 17 boys who are in San Quentin as its result) but infinitely significant as a case-history of how it happens here. I urge you to get it and read it; Mr. Endore and the facts may urge you to further action.

FANTASY DEPARTMENT. Three recommendations to the devotees of creeps and crawls. (1) Read [John] Dunninger's WHAT'S ON YOUR MIND? (Forum, $1) for accounts of telepathy just convincing enough to unsettle your most orthodox convictions, and for a fine set of telepathic laboratory tests to try on yourself and your friends. (2) Send to Arkham House, Sauk City, Wisconsin, for its fall catalog, in which the publishers of [H.P.] Lovecraft, [August] Derleth and [Clark Ashton] Smith offer the most saliva-stirring array of treats for the fantasy palate that these jaded eyes have seen in years—I wish I had space to list them all, but you can request the catalog and revel. (3) Take out a year's subscription to *The Acolyte*. This is a mimeographed quarterly, edited by Francis T. Laney and Samuel Russell, which contains such invaluable items as check-lists of books by celebrated fantasy writers, annotations (somewhat in the Baker Street Irregular manner) on the myths of H.P. Lovecraft, and sound articles surveying the works of little-known fantasists. For a year (four issues), send 50 cents to The Acolyte, 1810 N. Harvard, Hollywood 27. You won't regret it.

BAKER STREET DEPARTMENT. Frederic Dorr Steele, greatest and best loved illustrator of the Sherlock Holmes stories, died on July 6, leaving unfinished his projected complete illustration of the Canon for the

Limited Editions Club. His memory will live as long as an aquiline profile and a dressing gown survive in the popular mind—which is world without end.

BIBLIOPHILY DEPARTMENT. Note to Henry Gamadge, book expert: the perverse order of the Shakespearean plays so nearly fatal to you in Elizabeth Daly's THE BOOK OF THE DEAD, which causes you to wonder what the 1839 Harper editors had in mind, is simply that of the First Folio. What [the First Folio editors] Heminge and Condell had in mind, however, God knows.

TITLE DEPARTMENT. The current Broadway success TEN LITTLE INDIANS is—as you have gathered—[based on] Agatha Christie's AND THEN THERE WERE NONE, somewhat softened from its original rigid purism of killing off all the characters so as to allow Young Love to survive for the curtain. The play title is a reversion to or rather a paraphrase of the original English title of the novel, TEN LITTLE NIGGERS. The play was called that in London too; but in America we are careful not to offend minorities verbally, whatever else we may do with them (cf. Endore above). Two other examples are current of this reverting to British murder titles: the film GASLIGHT from the play [by Patrick Hamilton] which was called ANGEL STREET in New York, and the latest [Peter] Lorre-[Sydney] Greenstreet meller, THE MASK OF DIMITRIOS, from the finest of the superlative Eric Ambler novels, published here as A COFFIN FOR DIMITRIOS.

If this trend continues, we may recover some fine British titles changed for mysterious reasons in this country. The best example is probably Dorothy L. Sayers' THE FIVE RED HERRINGS, unaccountably altered by [her then U.S. publishers] Brewer, Warren & Putnam to the weak SUSPICIOUS CHARACTERS. Sometimes, however, title changes have been improvements; Anthony Rolls' sardonically pleasing study of a clergyman who takes up murder was published originally in England as THE VICAR'S EXPERIMENTS, but an unknown genius at Little Brown retitled it CLERICAL ERROR. (It's a little known but rewarding book, by the way, which you might well look up if you liked [Francis Iles'] BEFORE THE FACT and [C.S. Forester's] PAYMENT DEFERRED and [Richard Hull's] THE MURDER OF MY AUNT.)

August 27, 1944

When I met Will Cuppy he had been extinct for seven years. In the summer of 1941 a small blinking man emerged from some unmentionable haven of extinction and was introduced to me as the mystery reviewer of the New York *Herald-Tribune*. It was the Cocktail Hour (always capitalized and capitalized upon in the publishing business); so Mr. Cuppy had breakfast and talked about mystery novels, which he deplored, and extinction, which seemed an enviable state.

As psychoneurotics turn to the study and practice of psychiatry, so the extinct (as of August 23, 1934, he says, and he ought to know) Mr. Cuppy shows a sympathetic interest in all other forms of extinct life, from Pithecanthropus erectus (so called because he walked with a slight stoop) to Martha, the last of the passenger pigeons. He has presented his researches into the lives of his fellows, and into such other topics as Aristotle, protective coloration and perfectly damnable birds, in two classic volumes called HOW TO TELL YOUR FRIENDS FROM THE APES (1931) and HOW TO BECOME EXTINCT (1941).

People wonder sometimes (and not always politely) what mystery reviewers do with themselves in their lucid moments. With Mr. Cuppy the answer is simple: he has written the two funniest books I know. Nothing else can reduce me to such hopeless floor-rolling as Mr. C's blunt chunks of ludicrous fact. The two books (illustrated respectively by [the one-name artist known as] Jacks and [William] Steig) are now available in one volume called THE GREAT BUSTARD AND OTHER PEOPLE (Murray Hill, $1.98). You couldn't do better.

Mr. Cuppy has lately become incensed (and I join him) about a matter of protective coloration in book publishing, to wit: Coward-McCann's curious decision to publish Michael Venning's JETHRO HAMMER as a straight novel. The slim and bearded Mr. Venning has written two good mysteries under his name and a dozen under a much more famous one [Craig Rice]. He is a mystery writer, and there is no doubt in the reader's mind after four pages that JETHRO HAMMER is a mystery novel. An unusual one to be sure; a rich, complex, expanded one; an experimental mystery to please the admirers of, say, [Raymond Postgate's] VERDICT OF TWELVE. But it is a formal, technical mystery novel about Venning's usual detective Melville Fairr; and there is not a word on the jacket blurb that would lead you to suspect that it contains so much as a crime, much less an elaborate job of strict detection.

You can see Coward-McCann's reasoning: mystery novels are sure of a reasonably small sale but can never hit the jackpot; straight novels may sell nothing at all but there is no limit to their possible success. For Venning's sake I hope the trick pays off. But the result may also be the irritation of deluded straight-novel readers and the deprivation of whodunit fans, who'll read that blurb and think: Not for me.

Don't let the blurb deceive you. JETHRO HAMMER is the mystery fan's meat. And, as Mr. Cuppy says of the ermine's attempt to look like snow: "Who do they think they're fooling anyway?"

POLICE DEPARTMENT. While reviewing [Jean Mayer Liebeler's] YOU, THE JURY (see below) I was summoned for jury duty in Berkeley and thus happened to hear what I trust was a highly untypical bit of courtroom dialogue. The case turned on whether or not the culpable driver in an auto accident was drunk at the time. After a discussion of such reasonable sobriety tests as picking a match off the floor while standing on one foot, the judge asked the policeman who had booked the defendant whether any exemplars were taken of his handwriting at the time. Policeman: "No. I asked him to write out a statement but he refused." Defense attorney: "You realize he was within his constitutional rights in so refusing?" Policeman (with a condescending laugh): "There are lots of constitutional rights but that wasn't a court there."

WASTE NOT WANT NOT DEPARTMENT. If you read William Irish's DEADLINE AT DAWN a few months ago and wondered why it sounded so familiar, that was because it is an 80,000-word version of the 10,000-word short "Of Time and Murder," by Cornell Woolrich, in a 1941 *Detective Fiction Weekly*. (It is hardly likely that Mr. Woolrich will sue Mr. Irish.) And if John Dickson Carr's latest [TILL DEATH DO US PART] (reviewed below) gives you the same effect, that's because it's an expansion of one of the grand radio shows he wrote last year for CBS's *Suspense* program.

September 24, 1944

In 1928 Vincent Starrett edited for the Modern Library a volume called FOURTEEN GREAT DETECTIVE STORIES, which Ellery Queen [Frederic Dannay] has justly termed "the first really distinguished (mystery) anthology, from the standpoint of quality of selection, by an American author." The collection is still in print and still worth your 95 cents, although it now inevitably seems a bit dated. A lot has happened to the detective story in the years since 1928, and it's been a constant mystery why no publisher has ever asked Mr. Starrett to compile another anthology.

Now at last a publisher has had that good sense, and the result is all that one might hope for and more. The new Starrett is WORLD'S GREAT SPY STORIES (Tower, $1) and it is, to put it succinctly, a landmark. There has never been a specialized collection of espionage stories in America before (and only one in England); and one might have doubted if there were enough good material in the way of short spy stories to fill a volume.

The answer is yes! with an exclamation point. Mr. Starrett has rounded up 25 stories, from short-shorts to novelettes, that will thrill, perplex and delight you—and even (once in a great while) give you a pretty shrewd idea of what international espionage is really like. There are the established spy specialists such as [W.] Somerset Maugham and Eric Ambler (both in top form) and E. Phillips Oppenheim (in what I guess is about his top form too). There are the detective story writers like [John Dickson] Carr and

[Frank] Gruber and [Sir Arthur Conan] Doyle and me and Starrett himself, who have had fun turning from everyday crime to sinister international involvements. There are the big names from Joseph Conrad (who has a nice ironic way with anarchists) to Pearl S. Buck (who shows how a Nobel Prize winner can get away with slick hack work if she sets it in China). And I guarantee that there are hardly a half dozen stories out of the 25 which even an aficionado will know.

Mr. Starrett can not only choose the perfect anthology, he knows how to give it form with his own comments. If you've ever read any of his bookish essays, you know his charm and skill; if not, you'll succumb to him at his most charming and skillful introductions to these stories.

WORLD'S GREAT SPY STORIES is a classic in the anthology field, one of the best specialized anthologies ever edited—and all at only $1 for 445 well-filled pages.

FANTASY DEPARTMENT. You have certainly encountered in anthologies the two masterpieces of Fitz-James O'Brien, "The Diamond Lens" and "What Was It?" If you want to know more about this short-lived Irish-American screwball, take a look into Francis Wolle's FITZ-JAMES O'BRIEN: A LITERARY BOHEMIAN OF THE EIGHTEEN-FIFTIES (University of Colorado, $2)—an academic treatise with the vices and virtues of its kind.

October 1, 1944

Last Friday the annual crime season opened at the War Memorial Opera House. For honest whole-hearted reveling crime an opera season can be equaled only by a season of Shakespearean repertory. Factual court annals have never indicated that criminality predisposes one to lyrical outbursts, but composers of opera have always found it difficult to work their characters up to quite the proper pitch without a murder or two.

But murder is only a part of the record. If you wonder why a reviewer supposedly hardened by a weekly diet of mystery novels is still somewhat aghast at the goings on at the Opera House, consider the following list of crimes and criminals as they are to occur in the season.

In AIDA [by Giuseppe Verdi, 1871] we have espionage (Amonasro and Aida), high treason (Rhadames) and attempted murder (Amonasro).

In LA FORZA DEL DESTINO [by Verdi, 1862], manslaughter (Don Alvaro) and sororicide (Don Carlo).

In MARTHA [by Friedrich Flotow, 1847], a clear-cut case of fraud (Harriet and Nancy) in entering into and receiving money for contracts which they have no intention of fulfilling.

In LAKME [by Leo Delibes, 1883], sacrilege (Gerald and his friends), attempted murder (Nilakantha) and suicide (Lakme).

In MANON [by Jules Massenet, 1884], card-sharping, a pitiful attempt at a jail delivery (Lescaut and Des Grieux) and prostitution (in which a gentleman names no names).

In LUCIA DI LAMMERMOOR [by Gaetano Donizetti, 1835], a forced marriage (Enrico), murder (Lucia) and suicide (Edgardo).

In SALOME [by Richard Strauss, 1905], incest (Herod and Herodias) and suicide (Narraboth). (The killings of Iokanaan and Salome can hardly be considered murders since they are ordered by the Tetrarch.)

In FALSTAFF [by Verdi, 1893], pocket-picking and all forms of petty knavery (Falstaff and his companions).

In RIGOLETTO [by Verdi, 1851], abduction (the courtiers), rape (the Duke) and murder (Sparafucile), the last crime made doubly despicable by fraud.

In FAUST [by Charles Gounod, 1859], necromancy (Faust), murder (Mephistopheles) and infanticide (Marguerite), plus another fruitless attempt at jail delivery.

In UN BALLO IN MASCHERA [by Verdi, 1859], necromancy (Ulrica), assassination (Renato) and subversive activities (Sam and Tom).

In LES CONTES D'HOFFMANN [by Jacques Offenbach, 1881], fraud (Spalanzani), breaking and entering—or more correctly here, entering and breaking (Coppelius), and shadow-stealing (Dapertutto). The activities of Dr. Miracle are a bit hard to define criminologically.

And in CARMEN [by Georges Bizet, 1875], smuggling (Carmen and her associates), desertion (Don Jose) and—guess what—murder.

The only clean bills go to LA BOHEME [by Giacomo Puccini, 1896], where nothing more criminous happens than the minor frauds played upon the landlord and Alcindoro, and IL SEGRETO DELLA SUSANNA [by Ermanno Wolf-Ferrari, 1909], where nothing happens at all.

What wounds me as a mystery novelist is the spectacle of all this crime and no detection. The closest approach to a detective that you'll find in all these operas is the baritone Don Carlo in FORZA. As a private operative he sets out to track down the murderer of his father (only it wasn't really a murder because you see all Don Alvaro was trying to do was steal the old boy's daughter only the father pulled a gun on him and when it fell and hit the floor—well, anyway, as I was saying) and pursues him all over Spain and Italy and back to Spain again, with occasional truly detectival tracking down of clues. (He wears disguises too.)

But where murder is emotional, detection is rational; and it's hard to conceive a closely reasoned aria. Though I'd like to see it attempted some day. The ideal subject is of course The Master—Sherlock Holmes, who has been featured as protagonist of a song cycle and a violin and piano suite (both by Harvey Officer) but never as a singing dramatic role. He should be a baritone, naturally (if only because acting ability seems generally confined to the lower registers of the male voice), with Watson as a bass.

The only composer I know of who tackled the task of setting a police investigation to music was Umberto Giordano. The first act of his FEDORA [1898] is almost nothing but a routine series of examinations of successive witnesses by a police officer. The result, it must be admitted, is a little less than enthralling.

But for pure ripe murder without detection there are a good many operas the crime fancier might like to see added to the season. L'AMORE DEL TRE RE [by Italo Montemezzi, 1913] has a magnificent if probably impractical poisoning method. PAGLIACCI [by Ruggero Leoncavallo, 1892] of course has about as theatrical a murder as has ever been contrived (although Queena Mario went it one better in her [1934 novel] MURDER IN THE OPERA HOUSE by having Nedda [a character in the opera] actually murdered in a play within a play within a play). And [Franco] Leoni's L'ORACOLO [1905], based on a Chester Bailey Fernald story, has a fine strangulation by a pigtail right here on [San Francisco's] Grant Avenue.

Even without these, however, the season is rich enough. And if you're one of those who truly relish the enjoyment of murder, you'll forget all about mystery novels and radio and class B movies this month and betake yourself to the Opera House. That's where crime is burgeoning.

October 29, 1944

This month the firm of Duell, Sloan & Pearce, inspired by its astute and admirable mystery editor Marie F. Rodell, launched something new in criminous publishing: the Regional Murder series (irreverently known in the trade as The Rivers of Blood of America).

The first volume, edited by Ted Collins (producer of the Kate Smith [radio] program and evidently quite a murder fancier), is called NEW YORK MURDERS. Now you may think, if you know your [Edmund] Pearson and your [Alexander] Woollcott and your [Russell] Crouse, that you are already familiar with Manhattan murderers; but Mr. Collins and his collaborators have dug up surprises for you.

Do you know for instance the strange tale of Charles Jeffords, who was acquitted in 15 minutes for one murder, framed for another by the same evidence which acquitted him of the first, and sentenced to death under a non-existent statute? Or have you ever met Fred Scahrn, who at 18 was all but convicted of murder because he smoked cigars and finally freed because his dead sister liked pears?

These stories are here recounted respectively by those first-rate mystery novelists Kurt Steel and Lawrence Treat, and there are other cases, equally unknown and rewarding, told by Baynard Kendrick, Edward D. Radin and Inspector Thomas Byrnes. But the find of the volume is Angelica Gibbs, of

The New Yorker, whose subacid account of a suburban killing places her beside [Janet] Flanner and [Dorothy L.] Sayers among the few great female criminographers.

Seven essays plus a calendar and a bibliography of New York murders add up to a noble $2.75 worth to start the series. Later volumes are to include CHICAGO MURDERS, edited by Sewell Peaslee Wright, and SAN FRANCISCO MURDERS, edited by Joseph Henry Jackson.

LIBEL DEPARTMENT. A few months ago I was rash enough to remark in print that a certain biographical subject deserved the treatment of "an American Hesketh Pearson," which provokes the following comment from Mr. Pearson himself:

"The enclosed cutting is actionable. The bare suggestion that there could be an American Hesketh Pearson is criminally libellous. It is like suggesting that there is an Eskimo William Shakespeare. And indeed there is far more likelihood of there being a Zulu Hesketh than a Yankee one. To improve on an aphorism of Oscar [Wilde], we have nothing whatever in common with the Americans, least of all language. Tell the San Francisco *Chronicle* that we will accept a million dollars and an issue of the paper devoted exclusively to an elaborate apology, with articles by all the leading American writers proving conclusively that nothing in the least resembling Hesketh has ever been seen within the same hemisphere with the American continent."

The cash settlement is of course on its way, but because of the paper shortage this brief apology will have to replace the complete issue of the *Chronicle*. And if we may not have an American Hesketh Pearson, I may at least join my voice to Mr. [Joseph Henry] Jackson's in plaintively demanding why we may not have an American edition of Mr. Pearson's excellent CONAN DOYLE: HIS LIFE AND ART.

ART DEPARTMENT. DRAWN AND QUARTERED, the collected cartoons of the macabre master Charles Addams, is now available in a reprint edition (World, $1.49). A bat without a belfry, a vampire without a coffin, a haunt without a house is better off than a library without this grimoire of grotesque gaggery.

CHAOS DEPARTMENT. On the back of the jacket of the top-drawer GREEN FOR DANGER by Christianna Brand is a list of current and coming Dodd Mead mysteries. Among them is GREEN FOR DANGER by Susannah Shane.

November 26, 1944

I owe a profound apology to the Scowrers, to all those loyal devotees of Sherlock Holmes who have expressed their eagerness to join a San Francisco branch of the Baker Street Irregulars. One unpredictable misfortune after another has forestalled a general meeting of the Scowrers.

But now, come hell and/or high water, we are resolved to hold a session on Friday, January 5, 1945, to coincide with the irregular annual meeting of the Society in New York. You will receive details of time and place when they are decided upon; and in the meantime I'd be happy, just to get a rough idea of attendance, to hear from any of you who would enjoy an evening devoted to such momentous questions as the identity of the second Mrs. Watson and the correct nomenclature of the sinister brothers Moriarty.

(Any Scowrers, actual or prospective, who will be in New York on January 5 are urged to get in touch with Edgar W. Smith, Buttons-cum-Commissionaire of the Irregulars, at 1775 Broadway, New York 19.)

I trust this delay has not put too great a strain upon your patience, but as the Master himself remarked in "The Adventure of the Veiled Lodger": "The example of patient suffering is in itself the most precious of all lessons to an impatient world."

RISUS SARDONICUS DEPARTMENT. All followers of the Bookman's Notebook have certainly by now invested in Bennett Cerf's collection of anecdotes, TRY AND STOP ME (Simon & Schuster, $3). But I might nevertheless point out that Mr. Cerf's taste should appeal particularly to readers of this column. For their special delight he has included stories about Sir Arthur Conan Doyle and Lizzie Borden, about Quentin Reynolds' classic reaction to a throat-slitter, and sundry other criminous comicalities, plus a notable collection of eerie episodes from oral traditions entitled "The Trail of the Tingling Spine." (In typing copy I left out the r in the second word but that makes a good title too.)

BIBLIOGRAPHY DEPARTMENT. If you are polite to the detective librarian, she will show you the H.W. Wilson *Bulletin of Bibliography* for May-August 1944 (Vol. 18 no. 4), which contains James Sandoe's "Contributions Toward a Bibliography of Dorothy L. Sayers"—a needed and useful work which will leave you impressed alike by the versatility of the subject and the assiduity of the compiler.

ERRATUM. The proofreader who knows what I mean better than I do is a fairly constant source of confusion, though I've never been "corrected" quite so fabulously as my colleague Joel W. Hedgpeth, whose review describing an archaic romance was printed as "an armchair romance." Now I must apologize to Craig Rice, the reprint of whose excellent THE WRONG MURDER (Tower, 49 cents) was listed here, with a certain appropriateness, as THE WRONG NUMBER.

FANTASY DEPARTMENT. Arkham House, the small publishing company run single-handed by August W. Derleth, has succeeded in refuting definitively the long-established legend that there is no book-buying market for pulp fantasy. The earlier Arkham collections of Derleth, H.P. Lovecraft and Clark Ashton Smith are now out of print; the current volumes of Donald Wandrei, Smith, and Henry S. Whitehead are doing fine; and the firm is clearly in the black. Arkham plans for 1945 include books of shorts by Robert Bloch, Frank Belknap Long, Derleth, and Robert E. Howard; an omnibus of the novels of William Hope Hodgson, one of the great English fantasists even if unknown in America; and a series of $2.50 novels including Fritz Leiber's superlative CONJURE WIFE and Arkham House's first unpublished manuscript, WITCH HOUSE, by Evangeline Watson. When plans such as these flourish under present circumstances, you can bet that there'll be no holding Arkham House back after the war: good news to those of us who've kept maintaining that the fantasy pulps are the current successors to the American tradition of [Charles] Brockden Brown, [Edgar Allan] Poe, Fitz-James O'Brien and [Ambrose] Bierce.

December 10, 1944

As a man who loves murder and the theater almost equally, I keep going to murder plays. I went to RAMSHACKLE INN [by George Batson] despite the warnings of the New York critics. I do not entirely trust those gentlemen, who love murder not at all and whose love for the theater might provide an interesting footnote for Krafft-Ebing.

I am incurably hopeful, but there is something very strange about the American murder play. It isn't so much that it doesn't make much sense, that it is loosely plotted, that it seeks to cover the lack of psychological action with an inordinate deal of physical action. The set of RAMSHACKLE INN has no less than eleven practicable exits. (Whenever you see that many exits you can always remember that there's yet another one, leading onto Geary Street.) I think the chief trouble is that the American murder play simply doesn't give a damn about murder.

There have been exceptions, of course. The American theater has produced KIND LADY [by Edward Chodorov, 1935, based on a story by Hugh Walpole] and MARGIN FOR ERROR [by Clare Boothe, 1939] and SMALL MIRACLE [by Norman Krasna, 1934] and the superbly unclassifiable ARSENIC AND OLD LACE [by Joseph Kesselring, 1941]. But the school to which RAMSHACKLE INN belongs started in the twenties with THE BAT [by Mary Roberts Rinehart and Avery Hopwood, 1920, based on Rinehart's 1908 novel THE CIRCULAR STAIRCASE], which was not at all bad, and went on to THE CAT AND THE CANARY [by John Willard, 1922], THE WOODEN KIMONO [by John Floyd, 1926], THE GORILLA [by Ralph Spence, 1925], THE SKULL [apparently never performed on Broadway], THE MONSTER [by Crane Wilbur, 1922] and a dozen others, getting progressively worse. The school mercifully faded (at about the same time, by coincidence, that the American mystery novel was coming into its own) but still persists. Every Broadway season sees several flops of this nature and occasionally, as with RAMSHACKLE INN, a hit.

These plays depend on the lights going out and a lot of people running about, and differ from an Avery Hopwood farce only in that they revolve around a corpse instead of a bed. A mystery novel even of the fastest, brashest sort depends to some extent upon characterization and action and writing; these plays rely on eleven practicable exits (as in RAMSHACKLE INN) and a good man at the switchboard.

British murder plays are apt to equal or excel the best mystery novels in psychological and literary skill. They are also apt to fold quickly on Broadway. They take murder seriously even if sometimes sardonically; they are concerned with the whys and what nexts of crime, not with irrelevant physical motion.

And they find their mystery in the human character, the who and how and why of a murderer, not the mere mechanics of who is going to turn out to be somebody unexpected.

The Broadway season of 1943-44 produced three murder plays. One, MURDER WITHOUT CRIME [by J. Lee Thompson], was an intelligent, adroit British specimen starring Henry Daniell. One, THE TWO MRS. CARROLLS [by Martin Vale], was a feeble and inept imitation of the British starring Elisabeth Bergner. The third, RAMSHACKLE INN, was the American school at its worst starring ZaSu Pitts.

The first closed almost at once. The second is still running on Broadway. The third is here with us now.

The moral would seem to be that the public which supports the better mystery novels just doesn't care about the theater.

December 31, 1944

I'm afraid, in summing up the crop, that this wasn't so good a year as 1943. It offered no such absolute topnotchers in our field as [Margaret Millar's] WALL OF EYES, [Raymond Chandler's] THE LADY IN THE LAKE or [Graham Greene's] THE MINISTRY OF FEAR, nor any such gratifying debuts as those of Lucy Cores, Arthur W. Upfield or George Bellairs.

It did furnish a couple of trends, however. One, and disappointing, was a marked dropping off in production this fall: only 77 faces in the column for the second half of 1944, against 169 this spring and 105 and 155 for fall and spring of 1934. The paper problem and the manpower shortage among writers seem the likeliest answers. There's certainly no falling off of demand; witness the ever-increasing number of cheap reprints.

The other trend lies in those cheap editions, which are beginning to offer more and more frequently not strictly reprints but first book-appearances of magazine material at 25 or 49 cents. These range from superlative, as in the collections of shorts by [Dashiell] Hammett (Bestseller) and [Raymond] Chandler (Avon), through a book like Ken[dell Foster] Crossen's

THE CASE OF THE CURIOUS HEEL (Eerie Series), at least as good as the cloth-bound average, to stuff that is, if possible, even worse than the book trade will tolerate.

You can see the possibilities. There could be more profit for both author and publisher in fifty readers buying a 25-cent book than in a hundred renting a $2 one.

Trends and all, it wasn't a really bad year. I even had some trouble choosing among rival candidates for the "bests" which follow.

Pure detective novel (puzzle-cum-writing): HE WOULDN'T KILL PATIENCE, by Carter Dickson [John Dickson Carr] (Morrow).

Atmosphere-romance: TO WHAT DREAD END, by M.V. Heberden (Doubleday Crime Club).

British patience: JACK-IN-THE-BOX, by J.J. Connington (Little Brown).

American ditto: CASE OF THE GIANT KILLER, by H.C. Branson (Simon & Schuster).

Humor and humanity: HOME SWEET HOMICIDE, by Craig Rice (Simon & Schuster).

Novel of manners: CORPSE DE BALLET, by Lucy Cores (Duell, Sloan & Pearce).

Espionage-pursuit: THE DARK TUNNEL, by Kenneth Millar (Dodd Mead).

Fast action: THE CASE OF THE CROOKED CANDLE, by Erle Stanley Gardner (Morrow).

Hardboiled: THE NEEDLE'S EYE, by Edward Lee (Doubleday Crime Club).

Adventure: THE LAST SECRET, by Dana Chambers (Dial Press).

Gentle-and-scholarly: BRIDE'S CASTLE, by P.W. Wilson (Farrar & Rinehart).

Borderline murder: CRYING AT THE LOCK, by Adeline Rumsey (Simon & Schuster).

Short stories: THE ADVENTURES OF SAM SPADE AND OTHER STORIES, by Dashiell Hammett (Bestseller).

Anthology: WORLD'S GREAT SPY STORIES, edited by Vincent Starrett (Forum).

Holmesiana: THE MISADVENTURES OF SHERLOCK HOLMES, edited by Ellery Queen [Frederic Dannay] (Little Brown); PROFILE BY GASLIGHT, edited by Edgar W. Smith (Simon & Schuster).

Best new detective: lively, likeable Red Blake in the novels of Edward Lee.

Best new Watson (the best in fact in years): Sancho, the basic-English-speaking Lengua Indian in Dana Sage's THE MOON WAS RED.

Most of the year's best debuts were in the hardboiled school—where they're much needed. Edward Lee and Leigh Brackett were outstanding, with Bruno Fischer, N.R. de Mexico, and the team of North Baker and William Bolton also deserving your future attention. From England we got Simon Harvester and James Warren, who, British though they may be, are not without a touch of Hammett too. Dana Sage's Pan-American detection is something unique and promising and Hilda Lawrence shows an aptitude for chilling atmosphere. A borderline novel from Australia, SINNERS NEVER DIE, revealed a very fresh and real feeling for people in its author, A.E. Martin.

I'd say, "Watch for these names next year"; but I didn't do so well on that last December. Cores, to be sure, topped herself in 1944, and Upfield and Bellairs have produced regularly and satisfyingly; but of the other debutants I tapped, where are Norbert Davis, Matthew Head, Kit Christians, Amen Dell, Finlay McDermid, Michael Hardt and Robert Terrall?

Maybe their draft boards know the answer.

January 28, 1945

Westerns and mysteries are often bracketed together in reading surveys and such, and there are certain points of marked resemblance: both are "escape" literature; both are rented from libraries or bought in magazines and reprints rather than purchased as standard trade books; both consist of internal variations on a relatively fixed series of external formulas.

But though reviewers occasionally cover both fields, they share few fans in common; and I for one am almost completely ignorant of the writers of Westerns. So when such an authoritative aficionado of murder as William Targ edits a WESTERN STORY OMNIBUS (Tower, 49 cents) it seems a good chance to get acquainted.

I don't intend to climb out on a limb, as certain critics have done in regard to the mystery, and write a psycho-sociological history of the Western after this brief dip into its literature. But it does seem from Targ's choices that the Western is far more formula-ridden and far less capable of intelligent literary variation than the mystery. The best stories come from writers not strictly in the field (O. Henry, William C. White, Edwin Corle, Maxwell Struthers Burt), while the pulp headliners exhibit a great competence rather than the creative vigor of a [Dashiell] Hammett or a [Raymond] Chandler. Even a hack whodunit seems to offer some solidity of characterization and ingenuity of plot beside these stereotypes.

And yet such a pure pastiche of all your boyhood screen-memories as Clarence E. Mulford's "Riding With the Mail" or Frank Gruber's "The Marshal of Broken Lance" has its own evocative charm. You feel you've read it before, but it's well done and it's still fun to read. Perhaps, since the murder novel is apt to involve cultural problems and the fantasy of the future has metaphysical implications, this is the purest and most satisfactory of all escape literature.

I've a feeling the true Western fan might object to Harry Sinclair Drago's "The Drifting Kid Moves On" as introducing a touch too much of Depression-period realism. I know that fans I've spoken to bitterly protest the omission of Eugene Manlove Rhodes. Myself, I might object to the inclusion of Charles W. Webber's "Gonzaleze Again" as representing in intensified concentration the worst aspect of the Western—the contemptible racism of Nordic supremacy. But from what I know of Targ in my own field I'm sure this is a just and representative anthology, and well worth your attention, either for pleasure or for education, in one of the most popular but critically least studied fields of fiction.

REPRINT DEPARTMENT. Alfred Knopf publishes three of the greatest modern mystery masters: [Eric] Ambler, Chandler and Hammett. To honor this trio, Knopf has launched a new reprint line of Black Widow Thrillers, attractive, well-made books at $1.75 each; the first three volumes are [Ambler's] A COFFIN FOR DIMITRIOS, [Chandler's] THE BIG SLEEP and [Hammett's] THE MALTESE FALCON. At such a price Knopf is obviously not competing with the regular reprint lines; these are intended as permanent library volumes, and such works as these deserve that status.

RADIO DEPARTMENT. Recommended listening: *The Saint* series (KPO, Thursday, 9:30 p.m.); since the original author, Leslie Charteris, has a hand in the writing, the result is something far more recognizable to us book-readers than most radio adaptations of book characters. Also recommended, and strongly: the *Sherlock Holmes* series (KFRC, Monday, 8:00 p.m.); Miss Edith Meiser has fortunately been replaced as script-writer by the team of Denis Green and Bruce Taylor, who have a taste for the Canon and an ingenuity all their own in furnishing forth such untold tales as those of James Phillimore or the Gryce Pattersons on the island of Uffa. (Taylor is the pseudonym of a well known mystery novelist and hagiographer.) [In fact Taylor was the pseudonym of Boucher himself.]

February 25, 1945

Mystery novelists die too (though to the best of my knowledge not one has ever been murdered), and 1944 saw several reductions in the ranks. Herewith is a brief necrology, with gratitude to all of them for the pleasure they have given fans and a prayer that they may rest in peace.

Margaret Armstrong (died July 18, 1944) was a serious scholar and biographer (most noted for her excellent TRELAWNEY) who turned in her seventies to the production of whodunits. Her several mysteries were of varying merit: myself, I have a very soft spot for MURDER IN STAINED GLASS (Random House, 1939), a work rich in scholarly charm and in the curious lore of an almost lost craft.

Irvin S. Cobb (died March 10, 1944) was capable, in the best tradition of American humorists, of being bitterly unfunny. His famous Judge Priest has occasionally functioned as a pure detective; but more murderously memorable are a few terrible short stories of death and crime, mostly collected in the volume FAITH, HOPE AND CHARITY (Bobbs-Merrill, 1934).

Hulbert Footner (died November 25, 1944) was one of the most productive of American mystery novelists, and many connoisseurs swear by [his series character] Mme. Rosika Storey as a subtle and charming detective. See the box below for a note on the posthumous Footner novel, with its [Christopher] Morley preface.

Stephen Leacock (died March 28, 1944) was a strong fan, an ardent defender and a brilliant parodist of the whodunit. His commonsensical enjoyment was a relief among all the highfalutin theories on the Place of the Mystery Novel, and no finer reductio ad absurdum has been achieved than when he in FURTHER FOOLISHNESS (John Lane, 1916) composed a complete whodunit in precisely 250 words.

A more uncertain obit is that of Maurice Leblanc, reported to have died shortly before the liberation of France. Circumstances of the report were vague, and one remembers that the great French bibliography, the Catalogue Generale, once listed Leblanc as having died in 1923. It is to be hoped that the creator of the gentleman-burglar Arsene Lupin, a figure of almost Holmesian greatness never quite justly appreciated in this country, may be capable of as many resurrections as his protagonist. (Many of the Lupin stories, by the way, are available in good fifty cent Canadian reprints at the French book store in Normandie Lane at the City of Paris.)

MAGAZINE DEPARTMENT. The latest (March) issue of *Ellery Queen's Mystery Magazine* ranges as usual over all the excellences of the mystery form, from a surprisingly unfair problem by Nicholas Blake to the best product yet of Mr. Queen's [Frederic Dannay's] prodigy-protege, the teen-age James Yaffe. Of special interest to *Chronicle* readers are the debut of another astonishing apprentice, 17-year-old Ralph Norman Weber of Oakland and Berkeley (who is hereby invited to get in touch with this department for dinner to celebrate his coming out), and something of a masterpiece (with a San Francisco setting) by Miriam Allen deFord. A lesser story perhaps than her unforgettable "Mortmain" (*EQMM*, March 1944), Miss deFord's "Something To Do with Figures" lays one of the most startling pitfalls for the reader that I've encountered outside of [Agatha] Christie, and I'm not ashamed to admit I pitched into it head first.

March 25, 1945

For an interesting taste of the earliest form of crime fiction in English, you might try the recent pocket edition of Daniel Defoe's TALES OF PIRACY, CRIME AND GHOSTS, edited by Carl Withers (Penguin, 25 cents).

Defoe lived in one of the golden ages of British crime, when Jack Sheppard's Houdinesque jail breaks and the unparalleled villainy of the thief-taker Jonathan Wild (who played Holmes, Moriarty and Fagin all at once) interested the public far more than foreign politics or court affairs. Straight reporting of contemporary history was an unborn art, but the public wanted to read about its dastardly heroes. So Defoe, with the same persuasive factuality with which he transmuted Selkirk into [Robinson] Crusoe, produced "first-hand" and often "first-person" accounts of their exploits.

Mr. Withers has gathered here from sundry sources the Sheppard and Wild narratives, a long "autobiography" of the pirate Avery, and a series of ghosts, real and fake. Some of the matter (especially the Avery story) is tedious; some of the anecdotes (particularly the episode of the Quaker, the hams, the burglar and the devil) are delightful. All are intensely interesting as representing the earliest days of fiction when it was still ashamed to reveal its fine imaginative nakedness and hid behind the veil of supposed authenticity.

And it's worth plowing through a great many pages of drab "factuality" to hit upon the sly touches of deadpan humor which are so characteristic of Defoe.

The whirligig of time, it has been pointed out, brings in its revenges; and now, over two centuries later, crime fiction is again disguising itself as fact. *Master Detective Magazine*, under the intelligent editorship of Clayton Rawson, creator of The Great Merlini, is currently inaugurating a series of stories (two or three to the issue) which bear the note:

"This story is based on fact, but, except when otherwise noted, fictitious names, which bear absolutely no relation to the real characters and places involved, have been used."

This leeway enables the writers to combine the conviction of true detective narration with the formal structure, suspense and surprise of the fictional detective story.

April 29, 1945

It doubtless seemed a very sound idea to A.S. Burack, editor of the Boston publication *The Writer*, to assemble in book form a sort of symposium of essays on WRITING DETECTIVE AND MYSTERY FICTION (The Writer, $3.75). The principle of compilation was good too—partly scissoring out standard commentaries by [Dorothy L.] Sayers, [Howard] Haycraft, [S.S.] Van Dine, etc., partly commissioning new essays by leading practitioners (even though a few of the practitioners chosen seem something less than authoritative).

All that's lacking is an over-all editorial plan. Instead of a series of essays on various phases of mystery writing, you have an amalgamation of articles, each of which sets out to cover all the phases. The result is endless repetition of basic principles, plus occasional specific directions which usually boil down to not "how to write" but "how I write"—which is all one can expect.

For the serious aficionado there's great interest in the personalia of such notable figures as Craig Rice, Richard Lockridge, Lee Wright or Q. Patrick. But as an essential or even useful text on whodunit writing, this will never push off the shelf the works of Marie F. Rodell or Howard Haycraft.

BORDERLINE DEPARTMENT. Margaret Millar's THE IRON GATES is being promoted by Random House as a straight novel and was reviewed as such by Mr. [Joseph Henry] Jackson himself. It more than deserves such prestige (and the additional sales which it implies); two years ago, in WALL OF EYES, Mrs. Millar had already established herself as a first flight psychological novelist. This note is just a reassurance to mystery fans that Mrs. Millar has not abandoned them; in addition to all its other virtues THE IRON GATES is a perfectly plotted and admirably intelligent detective story, with subtle, ironic Inspector Sands at his best. Whatever you look for in a novel—atmosphere, character study, good prose, clever plot-tricks or what-have-you—you'll find it in Millar.

FANTASY DEPARTMENT. SUPERNATURAL STORIES OF H.P. LOVECRAFT (Tower, 49 cents) is the first reasonably full inexpensive selection of the work of the Master, selected by his disciple August Derleth, who contributes a sound foreword. For anyone at all interested in the fiction of imagination and terror, this is the buy of the year.

May 27, 1945

It's almost four years now since Ellery Queen [Frederic Dannay] founded his Mystery Magazine and proved despite all scoffing that there's a large and hungry public for consistently first-rate short detective fiction. Now at last other publishers have corralled enough material and paper to follow his example; and you'll find currently on the stands the first issues of three "class" detective magazines.

Each of them costs a quarter. From there on they differ markedly.

Mystery Book Magazine (Standard) uses new material only, no reprints. First issue contains short novels by Brett Halliday (at his best) and Dorothy B. Hughes (a trifle below hers). Later issues will use all lengths. Trimming includes an ingenious if elementary "crossword mystery" by Margaret Petherbridge and reviews of current novels by Will Cuppy, who seems to have received quite different texts from those I read under the same titles.

The Saint's Choice (Bond-Charteris) is all reprint—a long Saint novelette and four short stories, all good but mostly familiar to aficionados. What makes it highly readable, however, is the long editorial introductions by Mr. [Leslie] Charteris (or by the Saint—the two characters have reached a point of perfect fusion). I shall never protest the familiarity of the Saint's selections if he continues this amusing and provocative commentary (though I must protest his unpardonable typography).

Rex Stout Mystery Quarterly (Avon) has a reprinted Nero Wolfe novelette, seven reprinted short stories and one new one (a sound toughie by Bruno Fischer). The reprints are reasonably unhackneyed and cover the widest range of mystery rather than strict crime fiction. Mr. Stout contributes only a brief general introduction. Louis Greenfield is listed as managing editor. Trimming here includes assorted page-filling quotes and a "Sherlock Holmes Quiz" the answers to which are very nearly 100 per cent wrong. I assume this is Mr. Stout's way of thumbing his nose at the Baker Street Irregulars for their reception of his thesis that "Watson Was a Woman."

To sum up: every one of the mags offers enough entertainment to be worth your quarter. They have the advantage over the Queen magazine in that their policies allow for novelettes as well as shorts. If their rates are satisfactory and their editors perceptive, they should be able to get as good new originals as Queen (and the Charteris and Stout ventures will surely increase their original content if the Authors' Guild has anything to say about it).

But only a scholar like Queen with a library like Queen's could equal his amazing finds in unheard-of and excellent reprint material. Turn Vincent Starrett loose in the Ned Guymon collection and you might achieve it.

REPRINT DEPARTMENT. Hardly to be listed as "best buys" but still gratifying are Knopf's reissues of the four [Raymond] Chandler novels in uniform format (Black Widow Thrillers, $2 per volume). No reader of this department needs to be reminded of the qualities of Chandler writing or of Knopf book-making; and Mr. Knopf is certainly right in thinking that his star stable (Chandler, [Dashiell] Hammett, [Eric] Ambler) deserves permanent library editions as well as cheap reprints.

June 24, 1945

TRUE CRIME. The Rivers of Blood of America, more formally known as the Regional Murder Series, flows gorily on, tinged a more brilliant and satisfying crimson than ever in its second volume, CHICAGO MURDERS (Duell, Sloan & Pearce, $2.75).

The first volume, NEW YORK MURDERS (Duell, Sloan & Pearce, 1944), was an intelligent collection of interesting cases, but only Angelica Gibbs' essay on the Wilkins case achieved individual distinction as a criminous classic. The Chicago volume, edited by Sewell Peaslee Wright, bristles with classics; and it's hard to tell where to start in describing its riches.

My own favorite is Otto Eisenschiml's treatment of the pathetic Orpet-Lambert affair. If you've read Mr. Eisenschiml's WHY WAS LINCOLN MURDERED? and his more recent brochure "The Case of A.L., Aged 56," you know him as one of the most thorough and intellectual analysts of physical evidence. Since he is by profession a chemist, the highly complicated chemical evidence in the Orpet trial is peculiarly his meat; and its involutions become for the first time lucid and absorbing. It's an exposition worthy of [R. Austin Freeman's scientific detective character] Dr. Thorndyke, combined with one of the most pitiful human stories ever unfolded in a trial. Result—a murder essay to stand with the best.

Vincent Starrett deploys all of his scholarship and not a little of his charm to investigate the neglected American career of the poisoner Neill Cream, and incidentally to revaluate his somewhat overrated British practice. He uncovers a story curious in its own right and invaluable in view of later events—and no reader of criminal matters needs to be reminded of the felicity of Starrett's style.

Craig Rice, handicapped in her speculations by the danger of libel suits when treating a recent case, still makes the macabre Wynekoop killing as perversely vivid as any trial handled by [her lawyer-detective character] John J. Malone—at the same time miraculously resisting the fiction writer's temptation to embroider on fact.

Nellise Child succumbs to that same temptation, dressing up her account of the murder of Joseph Bolton with more revelation of the murderess' hidden thoughts than a[n Edmund] Pearson-[William] Roughead aficionado is apt to accept. The story is still sound and readable; and more than readable is reporter Leroy F. McHugh's racy account of the singular experience of Dr. Silber C. Peacock, whose sterling character remained untarnished even by his murder.

It is not the fault of Elizabeth Bullock (my opposite number on the Chicago *Sun* and now mystery editor of Farrar & Rinehart) that her account of the Rock Island Express murder is one of the lesser essays; she's done a solid piece of research on a rather clumsy, commercial and uninspired episode.

It probably is John Bartlow Martin's fault that his account of that master murderer H.H. Holmes adds little save a few inaccuracies (including the consistent misnaming of the last victim) to the already published accounts. But the bulk of the essays adds up to as fine a murder volume as America as produced since the death of Pearson.

July 29, 1945

Today this generally profound and scholarly commentary turns into a pure society gossip column. Two weeks ago at the Beverly Hills Hotel a cocktail party in honor of Lee Wright was proffered, or thrown, by Simon

& Schuster's Western representatives, Messrs. [Raymond J.] Healy and [J. Francis] McComas.

If you know anything at all about the status of the modern mystery novel, you know who Lee Wright is—and are thereby one up on many of the guests, because free drinks are free drinks. Miss Wright is the editor of Inner Sanctum Mysteries and possessor of a combination of detached critical intelligence and shrewd commercial good sense which makes her unique in her own (or almost any other) field.

Mystery writers and students—perspicacious souls—flocked to sit at Miss Wright's feet. Ned Guymon, who possesses the finest scholarly library of and on the whodunit ever assembled, drove up from San Diego; H.H. Holmes [the pseudonym Boucher himself used for his Sister Ursula whodunits], who is praying that the new Leo McCarey picture [THE BELLS OF ST. MARY'S] will start a boom in nuns even as detectives, flew down from San Francisco.

And the Los Angeles area, of course, contributed a colossal all-star cast. Craig Rice arrayed herself completely in black, even to an almost invisible hat without one accent of color (see? you get fashion notes yet) in honor of her next [Jake & Helene] Justus-[John J.] Malone novel, due this fall, entitled GOOD MOURNING. [The novel was actually published as THE LUCKY STIFF.] Raymond Chandler sat on a sofa and wondered mildly where all the people came from, while the people wondered mildly at the almost embarrassed quietness which has produced the finest bitter toughness of our times.

Then there were Finlay McDermid, who once wrote an excellent first mystery and is now making a good living instead, and Michael Venning [one of the pseudonyms of Craig Rice], whose silky beard offered the only evidence that West Coast writers can be hirsutely masculine as well as Greenwich Villagers, and Geoffrey Homes, who is temporarily abandoning detection for a straight psychological murder novel which I eagerly await, and Latin-American specialist Dana Sage, who seemed perplexed by these mores and only partly present, and Daphne Sanders [another Craig Rice pseudonym], who was a pretty if somewhat silly child.

There was a handful of the better scientifiction pulpists— Cleve Cartmill, Webb Marlowe and the masterful A. E. Van Vogt—from whom the criminous crew is trying to lure a murder or two.

There were the Jobilies and the Garyulles and then of course there were a few small shots—petty celebrities like [ventriloquist] Edgar Bergen and [radio writer] Norman Corwin. Nobody noticed them much. Murder is not only a profession; it is almost a way of life, and the party was devoted to it.

I am reluctant to inform the over-expectant public that these crime devotees spent their time eating and drinking and talking like any other cocktail party. But it is a regrettable fact that the afternoon (and evening) (and night) did not contain one single killing. It is at least consoling to reflect that the motives for one or two were probably planted. After all, cocktail parties are—but that is a sentence to which I have never yet found the predicate.

PROPHECY DEPARTMENT. Miles Burton's [John Rhode's] latest novel, NOT A LEG TO STAND ON, is dated in an odd manner. Its events obviously take place shortly after the complete end of the war; peace reigns and detective Desmond Merrion is "late of the Naval Intelligence and now once more a gentleman of leisure." The story opens on "Wednesday, October 18." That date fell on Wednesday in 1944; the combination will not recur until 1950. Mr. Burton may be a pessimist, or he may simply be judging the probable progress of the war by his own leisurely sense of tempo.

August 29, 1945

If you read this department regularly, you have doubtless by now found yourself practically bludgeoned into reading *Ellery Queen's Mystery Magazine*, which I never tire of plugging; and once bludgeoned, you have undoubtedly succumbed hopelessly to the appeal of the best regular selection of detective stories ever edited.

Now I want to urge you to try writing for that magnificent market. Queen [Frederic Dannay] has announced a $5000 detective-crime short story contest, running from now to December. Any type of story is eligible, from deductive puzzlement to atmospheric terror, and amateurs and professionals are equally urged to compete. The judges will be the criminous connoisseur Christopher Morley, the historian of horror Howard Haycraft, and the erudite editor, Ellery Queen himself.

Rules in brief: length should be between 5,000 and 10,000 words. You may submit as many stories as you want—all typed of course ("or legibly written," the rules say, but I'd advise against it), with your name and address on each entry and a stamped return envelope enclosed. First prize, $2000, with six awards of $500 each. Manuscripts must be received before December 3, 1945 by first-class mail, addressed to EQMM $5,000 Detective Short Story Contest, Ellery Queen's Mystery Magazine, 570 Lexington Avenue, New York 22, N.Y.

You can't lose, since all worthy manuscripts not receiving an award will still be purchased at the magazine's regular rates—which keep going up. So whether you're a professional who feels like outdoing himself or just a guy that's always had an idea for a mystery story, here's your chance.

Another prize contest announcement is addressed exclusively to the Scowrers. The Speckled Band, the Boston chapter of the Baker Street Irregulars, offers a prize of one $100 War Bond for the best paper elucidating the various difficulties in "A Scandal in Bohemia."

These difficulties are manifold; the dates given are, in true Watsonian fashion, manifestly incorrect, and there are peculiarly suggestive details in the description of Irene Adler's hasty marriage. Most significant is Holmes' own narrative of his actions as a witness: "I was half-dragged up to the altar, and before I knew where I was, I found myself mumbling responses which were whispered in my ear, and vouching for things of which I knew nothing..."

In the Church of England marriage service the only responses are uttered not by witnesses but by the principals themselves. From which one is all but driven to conclude that....

But I leave the rest of the speculation to Scowrers who may wish to enter the contest. Papers must not exceed 3,000 words, must be typed double-spaced, and postmarked not later than February 1, 1946. Contestants must be members of the Baker Street Irregulars or one of its affiliates (meaning here The Scowrers), and should address their papers to the Executive Officer of their society (meaning here me).

If you seriously contemplate such a paper, please get in touch with me for further notes on the "difficulties" referred to.

RADIO DEPARTMENT. The *Sherlock Holmes* program returns to the air Monday, September 3 (KFRC, Mutual, 8 p.m.). Among the first shows will be "The Problem of Thor Bridge" (one of the few strict detective puzzles in the Canon, and shamefully plagiarized by S.S. Van Dine in THE GREENE MURDER CASE) and many specimens from the box at Cox, including the fascinating episode of Colonel Warburton's madness.

September 20, 1945

As Bennett Cerf says, "The customers always write," and the soundest idea for a column in some while turns up in a letter from "an undying mystery and detective story fan" in Fairfax who wants some notes on the by now almost numberless series of 25 cent mystery editions. He's noticed how much these vary in quality and he wants some guide to assure him of getting a good one.

He's got the right approach. In the two-bitters just as in the two-buckers, publisher's imprint is, next to a detailed knowledge of all authors in the field, the most nearly certain guide to a good book.

The successful initiator of the 25-cent reprint business in America was Pocket Books, Inc., and they still lead the field in the matter of careful intelligent selection. Mysteries are only a part of Pocket Books' activities, but their whodunits are probably the most meticulously chosen of any and are always uncut.

Penguin Books were, in England, the originators of the whole cheap-paper-reprint idea, and their American affiliate (with the same name) holds up the high standards of the original British series. Penguin mysteries are well chosen and uncut.

Popular Library and Dell specialize in what used to be called rental fiction, without the broader scope of Pocket Books and Penguin. But in the mystery field they are among the leaders. Their choices are good, they are not cut, and they often have useful additions—photographs and biographical notes in the case of Popular, well worked out maps and casts of characters with Dell.

Lawrence Spivak publishes three series of mystery reprints: Mercury, Bestseller and Jonathan. All are extremely well selected but in most cases are cut. (The copyright page tells you if they are.) Spivak's series are especially notable for having rescued from pulp files (under the editorship of Ellery Queen [Frederic Dannay]) many excellent [Dashiell] Hammett stories never before printed in book form.

Avon has done some important rescuing too, in its volumes of novelettes by Raymond Chandler. Its whodunit reprints are not many, but good and uncut; and its frequent short-story collections often include important mystery material. (The current AVON STORY TELLER for instance offers a hitherto unreprinted Chandler.)

Bond-Charteris, which has up to now specialized in reprinting [Leslie] Charteris with amusing new prefaces by the author, is branching out into general reprints. Among other treasures it now controls the exclusive reprint rights on Craig Rice. Its future activities will be worth watching; though the books will chiefly be cut, the editorial standard will be high; and there's even hope for improvement of the wretched Bond-Charteris typography.

I think I've mentioned all of the first-rate mystery reprinters (I'll get indignant letters if I haven't). Some, notably Eerie Series, have gone in for pulp stories which never appeared in book form—some of which are well worth attention. Mostly, outside of the names above, you're taking your chances unless you know the author in question.

Myself, I want to start a reprint house specializing in pulp horror. I've got to found it, because I have the perfect name—the ideal imprint for a firm turning out the grisliest oogy-boogy. It will be called Charnel House.

RACE RELATIONS DEPARTMENT. Dorothy B. Hughes once remarked that the low-comedy colored stooge in a novel of Bertram Millhauser's had set back the cause of the Negro in America a good twenty years. Now Mrs. Hughes has more than redeemed the honor of the mystery by offering in her DREAD JOURNEY the character of James Cobbett, Pullman porter—possibly the first Negro in detective fiction to be written straight, as a man of intelligence and dignity. I know the exact counterpart of Mr. Cobbett, and it warms my cockles to see my friend written so sympathetically and deftly. That clinking you hear way off in Santa Fe, Mrs. Hughes, is my toast to you.

October 28, 1945

I've said before that the safest way of picking a mystery, if you know nothing of the author, is by imprint—that is, by the name of the publisher. If you've liked most of a publisher's choices in the mystery field, the odds are you'll also like the new one you've never heard of.

Publishers think this is a good method too, but they know that there's a certain unexplained inertia which usually keeps the lay reader from remembering publishers' names. So some of the houses that specialize in whodunits have developed catch-names for their mystery lines on the sound principle that a customer will remember an advertising gadget where he won't recall a plain firm name.

Some of them even have picture trademarks. The terrified little man (his name is McCurdle) who denotes Inner Sanctum Mysteries and the sniffing beast of Bloodhound Mysteries have become sure guides to good detection for many readers.

So here's a little quiz for you. Undoubtedly, as a steady mystery reader, you've become aware of these trade catch-names; but have you ever noticed who publishes which lines? Here is a list of eight standard series of mysteries. The answers will be found on Page 16. Anyone getting the publishers of all eight right is hereby awarded the degree of D.C.S. (Doctor of Criminous Scholarship).

1. Armchair Mysteries
2. Bloodhound Mysteries
3. The Crime Club
4. Fingerprint Mysteries
5. Gargoyle Mysteries
6. Inner Sanctum Mysteries
7. Murray Hill Mysteries
8. Red Badge Detective Stories

BAKER STREET DEPARTMENT. Excellent news is the promised appearance in January of *The Baker Street Quarterly*, a 72-page journal of Sherlockiana dedicated to the enlightenment and amusement of the B.S.I., the members of its scion societies. The annual subscription fee of $5.00 may be sent to the publisher, Ben Abramson, 3 West 46th Street, New York 19.

REPRINT DEPARTMENT Addenda to my recent listing of recommended reprint series: the several "classic" lines— Detective Novel Classics, Thriller Novel Classics, etc.—are usually cut but almost invariably well selected. And the Collins White Circle reprints, published in Canada but frequently available on local news stands, contain much interesting matter by British authors whose works have not otherwise appeared in this country. I'm often asked where one finds the reprints I list in my column. Most of them are pretty widely distributed; the largest selection of current reprints that I know is displayed by the news stand in the East Bay Terminal.

MAGAZINE DEPARTMENT. Strongly recommended to aficionados: Ken[dell Foster] Crossen's mystery column in *Pic*—not only for its succinct and acute reviews but for its unique notes on inside gossip and shoptalk of the mystery trade.

ANSWERS TO QUIZ:

1. David McKay Company
2. Duell, Sloan & Pearce
3. Doubleday, Doran & Company
4. Ziff-Davis
5. Coward-McCann, Inc.
6. Simon & Schuster
7. Farrar & Rinehart
8. Dodd, Mead & Company

November 25, 1945

I have just spent an invalid weekend reading almost nothing but mysteries of the hard-boiled school. My impression at the moment, from which I may perhaps to some extent recover, is that an infinite weight must rest upon the consciences of Dashiell Hammett, for what he fathered, and Raymond Chandler, for what he furthered.

God knows Hammett was welcome in the stuffy [J.S.] Fletcher-[S.S.] Van Dine '20s. God knows his own works and those of his best disciples are still admirable. God knows that the softer mystery novel has benefited by the hard-boiled influence—witness for instance [Rex Stout's] Archie Goodwin, who saves Nero Wolfe from offensive pretension.

But nothing like reading a flock of hard-boiled novels in succession can so thoroughly expose Mr. Chandler's contention in his by now famous [essay] "The Simple Art of Murder" that they represent the sole tendency toward truth in the mystery novel.

Chandler says in effect that Hammett took murder away from the vicar's rose garden and gave it back to the people "who are really good at it." But a mobster, a gunman (and when by the way will the tough boys learn that a gunsel does not mean a gunman?), is not good at murder—simply at killing. [Nineteenth-century essayist Thomas] De Quincey rightly insisted that there was more to murder than two blockheads and a dark lane; and the true murders that survive over centuries and still exercise their fascination are precisely those that stem from the vicar's rose garden.

The hard-boiled novel (and I mean the school—the masters are smarter) offers not murders but killings unworthy of any writing beyond the police blotter. It also offers an appalling mental and spiritual vacuum, in which people think solely with their muscles and love solely with their gonads. Add an almost fascistic contempt for democratic processes and exaltation of private force, and you have their sickeningly empty world.

Truth? Ask yourself—you, the average reader. You know people somewhat like those you meet in all the other mysteries save the top-bracket ones. Have you ever met these characters that drink five quarts without showing it and receive three beatings daily without noticeable effect? Is this realism or is it the wild romanticism of a world compounded equally of sadism and over-compensation?

The reality of murder? Have you ever personally known a professional gunman? But that clever amusing amateur that was at your last dinner party—was she very different from [the 1920s murderess] Ruth Judd?

FANTASY DEPARTMENT. I've recommended before that unusually good amateur magazine *The Acolyte*. I particularly recommend the current Fall issue, which is devoted almost exclusively to a long, perceptive and definitive article on M.R. James, the greatest of ghost-story writers, by Samuel D. Russell. Single copies at 15 cents or a four-issue subscription for 50 cents may be obtained from Francis T. Laney, 1005 West 35th Place, Los Angeles 7.

MISPRINT DEPARTMENT. Children's Book Week apparently drove the typographers mildly mad around here. Most of the typos that befell me were reasonably self-explanatory, but I do feel I owe Christopher Hale this explanation of how the veddy-veddy socialite family in his admirable RUMOR HATH IT came—doubtless to its shocked horror—to be called a socialist family.

REPRINT DEPARTMENT. Cheap reprints are excellent things, but the major classics in the field should be kept in print in regular trade editions. One step in that direction is Knopf's Black Widow Thrillers. Another, newly announced, is Little Brown's European Espionage Novels. Attractively printed and bound and uniformly priced at $2, this series starts off with Ethel Vance's ESCAPE, Helen MacInnes' ABOVE SUSPICION, Martha Albrand's NO SURRENDER and Geoffrey Household's ROGUE MALE. The first three need no bush, but there may be some unfortunate souls who have not yet discovered Household. This young Englishman (author of two novels, a book of short stories and a juvenile—and last heard of in the North African campaign) is for my money one of the startlingly good writing talents of our day; and ROGUE MALE (which you may recall on the screen as MAN HUNT) is his most cohesive and successful work.

December 30, 1945

When I first began my annual post mortem survey, it looked as though the last war-time year of the mystery novel had not been too victorious a one. But a year is not unmemorable that produces four novels which, I prophesy, should appear with fair regularity on all future reading lists of the whodunit.

These four are Margaret Millar's powerful study in psychology and irony, THE IRON GATES (Random House) (that ferrous pun was accidental but inevitable); Joel Townsley Rogers' macabre tour de force, THE RED RIGHT HAND (Simon & Schuster); Axel Kielland's high-spirited melodrama of the Norwegian underground, SHAPE OF DANGER (Little Brown); and A.E. Martin's uniquely human treatment of carnival freaks, THE OUTSIDERS (Simon & Schuster).

To round out an even baker's dozen of Best of 1945, take Marten Cumberland's meticulous STEPS IN THE DARK (Doubleday Crime Club), Doris Miles Disney's realistic MURDER ON A TANGENT (Doubleday Crime Club), Christopher Hale's Mary-Pettyish RUMOR HATH IT (Doubleday Crime Club), Matthew Head's sardonic THE DEVIL IN THE BUSH (Simon & Schuster), Dorothy B. Hughes' vividly spun DREAD JOURNEY (Duell, Sloan & Pearce), Michael Innes' eruditely witty APPLEBY'S END (Dodd Mead), Baynard Kendrick's compelling OUT OF CONTROL (Morrow), Ellery Queen's [Frederic Dannay & Manfred B. Lee's] compassionate THE MURDERER IS A FOX (Little Brown), and Lawrence Treat's trail-breaking V AS IN VICTIM (Duell, Sloan & Pearce); and you have solid evidence that the year was much more rewarding than it seemed at times to an omnivorous reviewer.

Further honors:

Short stories: Dashiell Hammett's THE CONTINENTAL OP (Bestseller) and THE RETURN OF THE CONTINENTAL OP (Jonathan), both edited by Ellery Queen [Frederic Dannay].

Bibliography: Edgar W. Smith's BAKER STREET INVENTORY (Pamphlet House).

Anthology: Ellery Queen's [Frederic Dannay's] ROGUES' GALLERY (Little Brown).

New detectives: working policemen Mitch Taylor and Jub Freeman in Treat's V AS IN VICTIM; Berkeley professor Gregor Sergeyevitch Pavlov in Jessica Ryan's THE MAN WHO ASKED WHY (Doubleday Crime Club).

New novelists of promise in addition to Rogers and Ryan include Mary Plum (STATE DEPARTMENT CAT, Doubleday Crime Club), Julius Fast (WATCHFUL AT NIGHT, Farrar & Rinehart), William L. Stuart (THE DEAD LIE STILL, Farrar & Rinehart), and the team of Bettina and Audrey Boyers (MURDER BY PROXY, Doubleday Crime Club). And Edmund Crispin, despite an uneven and irritating first book (OBSEQUIES AT OXFORD, Lippincott), is a man to watch.

True Crime literature was enriched this year by three volumes of permanent interest: Lillian de la Torre's classic ELIZABETH IS MISSING (Knopf); the excellent collection of CHICAGO MURDERS (Duell, Sloan & Pearce); and Joseph Henry Jackson's definitive THE PORTABLE MURDER BOOK (Viking).

Sales of mystery novels (especially in pocket editions) and income of mystery novelists were probably higher this year than ever before—though the latter is still not proportionate to the former. Mystery films have graduated more and more into the "A" category, and radio whodunits are innumerable. (And it was not six years ago that the pioneer *Ellery Queen* program went long unsponsored.)

Murder is now a major industry, and I'm more than curious to see how reconversion affects it.

January 27, 1946

"Mystery novelists are the most interesting writers I have; they can always talk about something else besides their own shop." This flattering dictum comes from an important New York editor, who adds the less gratifying suggestion that a good mystery novelist is usually a man who can write well but has nothing to say. But let us disregard the unsettling implications of the second dictum and consider the truth in the first.

It is true that I have not (with one major exception) met a mystery novelist of any distinction who was not absorbed in and absorbing on some other topic as well. Some of these extracurricular interests have become by now well publicized. Every fan knows for instance that Baynard Kendrick is an authority on the rehabilitation of blind veterans; that Dorothy L. Sayers is a leader in the intellectual renascence of Anglican Catholicism; that H. F. Heard is a mystical philosopher (but have you heard that his detective stories are composed by automatic writing?); and that Nicholas Blake is an important poet.

Here are a few more for the collection.

Craig Rice composes words and music—extraordinarily good cocktail-hour songs. (Whenever [in one of her Jake Justus-John J. Malone novels] a few lines are quoted from a song at Jake's Casino, you may be sure the entire song exists and is wonderful.)

Kurt Steel is an authoritative expert on Neo-Thomist philosophy.

Ken[dell Foster] Crossen and Bruce Elliot are noted practicing magicians.

Leslie Charteris knows almost all there is to know on the theory and practice of East Indian cooking.

Dorothy B. Hughes is the primo half of a magnificent hot piano team—
and two-piano playing strictly ad lib is something that awes me even more
than the lady's narrative suspense.

Stuart Palmer is one of the few men willing to admit that he actually saw
a sea serpent.

Kenneth Millar is a virtuoso of the limerick.

Mystery novelists, in short, are a little of everything. Sometimes, as with
Rice and Crossen, their outside interests filter into their work; sometimes,
as with Steel or Hughes, the other personality comes as an astonishing
shock. But the perverse variety of their interests is undoubtedly one factor
that keeps the whodunit forever interesting even to a reviewer.

February 24, 1946

As you may have been noticing, the mystery novel of the past few years
has become less and less characterized by "criminal investigation"—to
take my text from the title of this column. In fact it's even becoming less
and less characterized strictly by mystery.

To be sure, a few old masters still produce formal deductive problems—
and it's paradoxical to note that such deductionists as [Ellery] Queen
[Frederic Dannay & Manfred B. Lee] and [Agatha] Christie are at the top
of the sales lists. But the trend is toward emotion, excitement, suspense—
away from whodunit and toward "what is going to happen to this protagonist?"

Now emotion, excitement, suspense are all legitimate qualities of the
"straight" novel, while the one distinctive feature of the mystery is the
more and more neglected puzzle element.

So publishers (and reviewers) are coming up against a problem: where
does one draw the line between "mystery" and "straight" novels?

The problem might be unimportant if it weren't for an economic factor.
Mysteries, with their assured rental-library sales, will always sell enough
copies to pay for the cost of printing, but they will never hit the top sales
figures. (The all-time advance sale on a mystery was the 75,000 of [S.S.
Van Dine's] THE BISHOP MURDER CASE. More typical is the fact that
now, at the height of the mystery boom, Mrs. [Mary Roberts] Rinehart's
THE YELLOW ROOM sold over 40,000—fabulous among mysteries but
far from epochal among novels.)

A straight novel on the other hand can sell into six figures, but it can also
sell as few as 250 copies.

Hence the problem: should one of these border-line suspense novels be
sold as a mystery, with assured small profits, or as a novel, with a gamble
on the big money?

Some quasi-mysteries have successfully hit the jackpot with pure
"straight" novel promotion. [Daphne DuMaurier's] REBECCA was the

great example of successfully deluding the public that thinks it doesn't read mystery novels. In other cases publishers have, with varying success, tried to straddle both markets by inventing new classifications, such as (a vile word) "psycho-thrillers."

This month Simon & Schuster launches its own solution to the problem—Inner Sanctum Mystery Specials, which will appear at irregular intervals in addition to the regular monthly publication of Inner Sanctum Mysteries. The meaning of this "Special" qualification has been well explained by S&S editor Lee Wright:

"It marks a novel of suspense, a novel of crime and punishment rather than crime and detection.

"During the past 25 years the mystery novel has been gradually but steadily widening its scope. Today it can be as much a reflection of life as a riddle about death.

"We believe that the audience for this type of modern mystery story can be and should be as big as it is for other kinds of fiction. Therefore this special trademark, to set apart what we think is a distinguished novel of suspense."

The first Special is Elisabeth Sanxay Holding's THE INNOCENT MRS. DUFF. It would be a pity to tip off any of the plot of this study in how respectability, boredom and drink gradually lead to murder; and I've expatiated many times on Mrs. Holding's magical excellence. I'll merely say that it's hard to see how S&S's new series could have got off to a better start, and you'd best get in on the ground floor of what is certain to be an important series of borderline suspense stories.

March 31, 1946

Mystery Writers of America, Inc., has proposed to make an annual award for the most inept mystery criticism of the year, to be reverently known as the Edmund Wilson Memorial Award. My nomination for the award in 1946 will tactfully go not to any of my colleagues but to part of a symposium on 25-cent reprints in the *Free World Magazine* for March.

The chairman of this symposium was Atwood H. Townsend of New York University, presiding over the only other member, Victor Weybright, editor of Penguin Books. Mr. Weybright's remarks are a nice blend of practicality and idealism, but Townsend's portion qualifies him admirably for the coveted award.

What largely perturbs him is that the greater bulk of the reprint business is given over to mystery stories, to the neglect of "other titles less consciously aimed at the lowest common denominator." The climax of many injured references to this fact comes in the following paragraph:

"At a time when the real world is full of real problems demanding solution, it is not a healthy thing for the literate portion of the most powerful nation on the earth to turn away from bothersome reality toward such es-capist fantasies as are retailed by the millions in comic strips, radio serials, Hollywood romances, and now the quarter 'whodunits.' "

I submit that this sentence is hogwash. Its academic snobbishness is ap-parent, from its reference to the "literate portion" to its meticulous placing of "whodunit" within quotes.

The whodunit is later referred to as "commercial pandering to our semi-literates....one more opiate for the people." A person with the background in economics which such striking phraseology indicates must surely realize that it is the whodunit which has made the whole two-bit reprint field fi-nancially feasible. That the field should expand, that it is trying to expand is undeniable; but the whodunit is still the solid seller which makes possi-ble more advanced publishing.

The false logic involved in the premise that the reading of whodunits implies a turning away from reality needs no demonstration. Many of the readers of this column are my fellow workers in local politics. And the Utopia envisioned by Mr. Townsend, in which a healthy and literate nation has finally turned away from escapist fantasies bravely to consider only real problems, is an aseptically terrifying one.

By this blunt condemnation of all forms of popular entertainment Mr. Townsend performs a serious disservice to his own cause of education. The people, literate or semi-literate, of America are not going to waver in their devotion to comic strips, movies, soap operas and two-bit murders. Far more to the point is to encourage the good (socially and esthetically) and discourage the bad within those fields. I know that there are good comic strips, good movies and good whodunits; I am even told that there are good soap operas.

And if Mr. Townsend wishes truly to improve the educational effect of the two-bit reprint lines, he would do far better by the selective intelligence of praising such sound editing as that of the Pocket Books or Penguin, among others, and condemning the endless, taste-lowering output of cheap opportunists.

To say that all mysteries are "consciously aimed at the lowest common denominator" is precisely as true as to say that professional educators are smug prigs.

April 28, 1946

"Why don't you edit an anthology not of great detectives but of great Watsons?" a publisher's representative once asked me.

After a moment's excitement I had to confess the project was impossi-ble—there just aren't any.

In the detective short story there is of course Watson himself, the au-thentic John H., and after him....who? Possibly Agatha Christie's social hanger-on Mr. Satterthwaite, in the Harley Quin stories (and in one Poirot novel); possibly the splendid French criminal Flambeau, when he assists [G.K. Chesterton's] Father Brown; possibly that exquisitely limned minor aristocrat Squire Randolph, in Melville Davisson Post's fine Uncle Abner legends. But who else?

Nor is the situation much happier in the novel form; Mrs. Christie's Dr. Ernest Sheppard (in THE MURDER OF ROGER ACKROYD) has indeed his peculiar claim to the title of "a great Watson." Patrick Quentin's Peter Duluth was an admirable Watson before he set up in later novels as a detective in his own right. And the modern American mystery novel has produced two Watsons of the first water, worthy to be named immediately after John H.—Rex Stout's Archie Goodwin and Francis Bonnamy's Francis Bonnamy.

But by and large, mystery novels and short stories fall into one of three classes. (A) They dispense with the Watson entirely—a trend most noticeable in the hard-boiled school. (B) The Watson is nebulous and characterless—the case usually in the formal-problem British school but reaching its nadir of nebulousness in S.S. Van Dine's S.S. Van Dine, a character written in disappearing ink. (C) The Watson is replaced by a wife or secretary, thus rendering obvious and manifest the latent sexual significance of the Holmes-Watson relationship.

(C) is possibly the most prevalent modern solution. But it is interesting to notice that two of these charming sex-cum-humor teams actually form, as teams, a sort of joint Watson to a real detective. Craig Rice's Jake and Helene Justus and the Lockridges' Mr. and Mrs. North function as double-Watsons to the detection respectively of John J. Malone and Lieutenant Bill Weigand.

If you like Watsons, if you regret the failure of the detective form to develop worthily one of its most interesting possibilities, you will welcome as loudly as this department the return this week of Mr. Julius Ricardo. Mr. Ricardo, the little man of impeccable taste and utter emptiness, has been used by his creator in only five novels and one short story in the space of 36 years. Connoisseurs of A.E.W. Mason argue as to whether THE HOUSE OF THE ARROW or AT THE VILLA ROSE is the better work (I am inclined to submit a minority report for THE PRISONER IN THE OPAL). The new novel, THE HOUSE IN LORDSHIP LANE, is not, I'm afraid, in that class; but it does present the great Hanaud in all his idiomatic splendor, and it offers that rarest of gifts—an indisputably great Watson.

UNCLASSIFIABLE DEPARTMENT. You may have read in *Time* and elsewhere that [political journalist] Walter Duranty is starting a service whereby you subscribe so much and receive a weekly letter from him on unspecified subjects. Well (I don't know how to break this to you more gently), a similar service is now being offered by Mr. Leslie Charteris, more generally known (especially in his own subconscious) as The Saint.

You only have to send a dollar a month or $10 for a year to Mr. Leslie Charteris, 314 North Robertson, Hollywood 35.

May 26, 1946

Far too little has appeared in print on the subject of The Detection Club of London. The following letter from E.R. Punshon is released by The Macmillan Company to celebrate THERE'S A REASON FOR EVERY-THING, Mr. Punshon's "fourth book to appear in the United States" (by which, with the usual bibliographical solipsism of publishers, Macmillan means his fourth book to be published by Macmillan.)

"The London Detection Club was founded some years before the war with the idea of bringing together those writers of detective stories who were willing to aim at as high a literary standard as their gifts permitted, and to avoid the easy, the trite, and the conventional. For instance, the homicidal maniac, for whose actions no reasoned explanation is required, and, in general, those tricks Mr. Bernard Shaw has classified as the 'all the time' stunt, by which he meant the trick of, for example, introducing and describing an old man with a long beard, and then explaining in the last chapter that it was 'all the time' the handsome young hero in disguise.

"The subscription to the club is nominal, the expenses are provided by communal effort, as, for example, by the publication of books to which various members contribute—such as THE ANATOMY OF MURDER, brought out before the war.

"For the ceremony of initiation Miss Dorothy L. Sayers provided us with an amusing formula. In this, Eric, the club's mascot, a skull provided for eyes with electric bulbs that glow terrifyingly at critical moments, is produced, and on Eric the candidate proclaims his willingness to do his best to live up to the club's standards, invoking upon himself in failure such dire penalties as the wrath of critics, the neglect of publishers, and a plethora of misprints on every page of every book.

"I myself was inducted by the late G.K. Chesterton, at that time president of the club. Alas, that these grim days of war and peace have put an end for the time to this sort of social fooling that does so much to bring people together and break down the barriers of distance and mistrust...."

It is not purely out of laziness that I have let Mr. Punshon write most of my column this month. America long had nothing comparable to The Detection Club. Now we have Mystery Writers of America, Inc.; and that is indeed comparable but largely in terms of contrasts.

MWA also tries to raise the standards of the mystery novel; MWA also will finance itself by books by its members; but MWA is primarily concerned with its ringing battle-cry: "Crime Does Not Pay—ENOUGH!"

Where the English organization is clearly a gentlemen's club, the American is more nearly a trade union.

The space allowed to this column forces me into a cliff-hanging technique. This month you get Mr. Punshon on The Detection Club; coming next month, by special airmail to the *Chronicle* from New York, a detailed report on the nature and activities of Mystery Writers of America.

Don't miss this next breathtaking episode!

June 30, 1946

Mystery Writers of America, Inc. has announced its first annual awards of "Edgars" for the best work in the mystery field in 1945.

Edgars, or more formally "Edgar Allan Poe Awards of Merit," are copies of a special limited edition of Viking's THE PORTABLE POE. This year they go to:

Julius Fast for WATCHFUL AT NIGHT (Rinehart), best first mystery novel.

Dick Powell, star; Edward Dmytryk, director; Adrian Scott, producer; John Paxton, writer, and Raymond Chandler for MURDER, MY SWEET (based on Chandler's FAREWELL, MY LOVELY), best motion picture of a mystery nature.

Frances and Richard Lockridge and Ellery Queen [Frederic Dannay & Manfred B. Lee] respectively for *Mr. and Mrs. North* and *Adventures of Ellery Queen*, best radio mystery programs.

And to this column for best mystery criticism.

Scrolls are being awarded to RKO Pictures, makers of the winning film, and to the producers and agencies of the two radio shows. Honorary Mention scrolls go to THE HOUSE ON 92ND STREET among films and *Suspense* in radio.

I had intended to devote this column to a complete picture and history of Mystery Writers of America, but now is not the right time. The entire question of MWA's activities and particularly its relation to the Authors' Guild is in a state of flux at the moment, and the story is best postponed until the picture is clearer. Meanwhile any mystery writers (in any field) resident in this area are urged to get in touch with me as Regional Vice President.

One thing is certain: there has never been more active interest among writers in the broad problems of organization and self-protection. MWA is only one of a group of recent signs of this interest, which also include the militant Committee for Action now forming within the Authors' Guild, and the American Authors' Authority, propounded by James M. Cain as an over-all body to look after matters of copyright and literary property.

Writers are coming more and more to realize that the size of their checks depends on the solidarity of the craft as well as on the individuality of the artist. We may even soon become worthy of the legislative attention of the Honorable Clarence Lea.

GOSSIP COLUMN. The chief topic of conversation in New York mystery circles remains the recent visit of Craig Rice—possibly the most disturbing descent recorded since that of Sennacherib.... Random House has treated David Duncan of Berkeley to a honey of a jacket for his THE SHADE OF TIME, to appear this fall....Marie F. Rodell, the wholly admirable editor of Duell's Bloodhound series, has abandoned the pseudonym "Marion Randolph," under which she published three first-rate whodunits; a forthcoming slick detective short will bear her own name.

Leo Margulies plans to turn *Startling Stories* into a magazine of high-grade intelligent fantasy along the lines of the lamented *Unknown Worlds*, featuring such names as L. Sprague de Camp, Cleve Cartmill and Fletcher Pratt....The 25-cent book and magazine market is suffering a marked recession; bandwagons never play their best when too many tootlers climb aboard.

That greatest of all detective plays, Sophocles' OEDIPUS [TYRANNUS] (wherein the detective tracks down as the criminal—himself), proved so deservedly successful in the Old Vic production that mobs were actually storming the doors at the performance I attended....David Dodge of San Francisco has joined Simon & Schuster's Inner Sanctum stable; and I don't know whether to congratulate editor Lee Wright on getting such an author or Dodge on getting such an editor....When S&S's entrancing maid-of-all-work Elinor Green was informed that the firm's newest prize was leaving for Central America, she observed: "Well, that's the way it is—here today, Guatemala."

July 28, 1946

This is about The Bloodhound. Some seven years ago the then-new firm of Duell, Sloan & Pearce resolved, among other intelligent editorial policies, to have a first-rate mystery department. They went about it not by finagling names away from other publishers' lists but by putting the department under a first-rate editor, Marie Fried Rodell (whose recent trip to this coast so brightened the lives of Bay Region murdermongers).

From the start The Bloodhound, symbol of DS&P murder books, has kept his nose keenly to the trail of good writers. Few publishers in this country have achieved such a high standard of excellence in the mystery field. The Bloodhound discovered Dorothy B. Hughes, Lawrence Treat and Manning Long. The Bloodhound achieved proper recognition for Elisabeth Sanxay Holding and Francis Bonnamy. The Bloodhound nosed out the idea of the Regional Murder Series, which has thus far produced a notable group of volumes on New York, Chicago and Denver murders, with Los Angeles, San Francisco and Detroit coming up next year.

And now two new Duell books along somewhat different lines are emphatic musts for readers of this department.

One of these is the first official publication of Mystery Writers of America, Inc., the anthology called MURDER CAVALCADE (Duell, Sloan & Pearce, $3).

For this collection 20 members of MWA have contributed material gratis, with all royalties to go to the treasury of the organization (an idea suggested by the successful books of the English Detection Club).

The result is a fine gallimaufry of gore, most of it appearing for the first time in book form. The contents range from short-shorts by Kurt Steel and Percival Wilde to novelettes by Helen McCloy and Phoebe Atwood Taylor; from low comedy by Richard Burke to the higher criticism by [Ellery] Queen [Frederic Dannay] and [Howard] Haycraft; from tricky fiction by Ken[dell Foster] Crossen to even trickier fact by Q. Patrick (with a stop-over at that fascinating new form, "Fact-Fiction.")

My own favorites are a highly-charged pulp story by Robert Arthur, a heart-breaking study in murder by Dorothy B. Hughes, and a highly ingenious piece of fact-fiction by William [Lindsey] Gresham. But whatever your murderous taste may be, you'll find something admirably suited to it here—plus a witty preface by Richard Lockridge and interesting anonymous notes.

The other Duell book that rates the highest stamp of approval is John Schwarzwalder's WE CAUGHT SPIES (Duell, Sloan & Pearce, $3). Mr. Schwarzwalder entered the Army in 1941 as a buck private. He rose to be a major in charge of Counter Intelligence Corps activity in northern Germany. Obviously he was good at his job, and by a fortunate freak of luck he is equally good as a writer.

I know no other book on espionage which combines so felicitously as this a series of fascinating true stories with a quietly effective style, a clean sharp mind, perceptive irony, and a keen political acumen.

MYSTERY MEDLEY. Clayton (The Great Merlini) Rawson is now editing whodunits for Ziff-Davis....Lawrence (T As in Titles) Treat is junketing on this coast....Craig (Anything Can Happen) Rice is in Chicago, covering the Heirens-Degnan case....Leslie (The Brighter Buccaneer) Charteris receives one of the great ribbings of mystery history in the current (August) *Ellery Queen's Mystery Magazine*, but it's nothing compared to the ribbing he's taking from friends (and from himself) on his current screen assignment—the master of suave slick dialogue is now scripting a Tarzan picture.

August 25, 1946

The average mystery novelist, in order to eat, must produce at least a book a year and preferably two or three. You'd expect that a successful first novel would betoken a forthcoming flood of whodunits with the same by-line.

But oddly, that just doesn't happen. I've been looking over back issues of this column, checking on the writers whom I've annually tapped as best-first-of-the-year; and the result is a very where-are-the-snows-of-yesteryear mood.

My figures for 1942, when I started reviewing, are incomplete, and 1945 is too close to judge yet. But let's look at 1943 and 1944.

In 1943 three writers made brilliant debuts and followed through. Lucy Cores, George Bellairs and Arthur W. Upfield are now among the top names in their respective schools. But the others who had me so excited?

Dale Clark, Norbert Davis and Matthew Head have each produced one more book. (Head was on government service in Africa.) And not a further word has been heard from such superlative debutants as Robert Terrall, Michael Hardt, Kit Christians, Amen Dell or Finlay McDermid. McDermid is a story editor in Hollywood; as to the others....

Again, three of the 1944 first novelists have established themselves nicely. Hilda Lawrence and A.E. Martin are names to utter reverently, and Bruno Fischer, despite a passion for changing publishers, is building a solid place for himself. But the year produced two unusually entertaining British writers in James Warren and Simon Harvester, four much-better-than-average hard-boilers in Edward Lee, Leigh Brackett, N.R. de Mexico and the team of North Baker and William Bolton, and something new and unclassifiable in the Latin-American Dana Sage.

Here is a project for criminal investigation. What has become of all these people? Some are probably writing for pictures. Some, God help them, may be writing for radio. Some are undoubtedly not writing at all and doing very well thank you.

Some probably had their second novels rejected and became discouraged. (It is almost traditional in the business that second novels are bad.) Others became discouraged upon realizing that a published book does not mean finding that pot of gold.

But I'm curious as to why people with that much talent abandon a typewriter. If you have any information, let me know. And meanwhile you could do far worse than go back and reread any one of these admirable firsts.

TWO BIT DEPARTMENT. Though the bottom is said to have dropped out of the two-bit market, new things keep happening in it. One is the growing trend toward original publication in paper-back form— note the [Bruno] Fischer and [Dwight V.] Babcock books listed in the adjacent column.

Another item is the curious pair of magazines now on the stands from Anson Bond, publisher. In addition to his well-chosen (and badly designed) line of reprints, Mr. Bond offers the *Craig Rice Crime Digest* and the *Movie Mystery Magazine*.

I am frankly not quite sure who wants to read novelizations of crime movies or 20,000 word outlines of 80,000 word mystery novels, nor am I at all sure of my own reactions to them. But you might try them and see what you think.

September 29, 1946

A major plaint of all radio writers (ranking practically with sponsors who have read [Frederic Wakeman's then best-selling novel] THE HUCKSTERS and decided if Evan Llewellyn Evans gets away with it so can they) is the impermanence of their work. You can write the best show you're capable of writing, and one minute after air time it's gone for ever. Which is especially true of radio mysteries.

Radio plays by a [Norman] Corwin, a[n Arch] Oboler, a[n Archibald] MacLeish finally achieve the permanence of publication. And there have been a few attempts at publication of radio mysteries. *Ellery Queen's Mystery Magazine* frequently runs Queen radio scripts and the excellent John Dickson Carr *Suspense* shows. THE CASE BOOK OF ELLERY QUEEN (Bestseller, 1945) contains three radio adventures, and Frank Owen's MURDER FOR THE MILLIONS (Frederick Fell, 1946) and Queen's [Frederic Dannay's] THE MISADVENTURES OF SHERLOCK HOLMES (Little Brown, 1944) each include one radio script in an anthology of short stories. The most ambitious yet was THE SAINT'S CHOICE OF RADIO CRIME, recently reviewed here.

But the public is not too enthusiastic about reading stories in script form. The public is used to the normal format of narrative fiction. And so simultaneously two different sources come up with the same solution to this problem of evanescence: rewrite the radio plays into standard short stories.

One is Queen himself, who as the pioneer of radio mystery deserves to be likewise the pioneer of this new departure. For the next year each issue of *EQMM* will carry one short story based on a Queen radio show. Each story will be tied plot-wise into the month of issue and the whole will form eventually a CALENDAR OF CRIME. [In fact the task of converting twelve Queen radio scripts into short stories took several years, and CALENDAR OF CRIME was not published until 1952.]

The other is the recently founded Hollywood firm of Editorial Associates, which is a sort of Available Jones of the publishing business. For a price, the Associates will do anything from styling a publisher's books to ghosting for his authors. Their first major venture is the new magazine *Suspense*, which should hit the stands in a week or so, and which will consist entirely of short-story adaptations of the best past programs of that top-ranking radio chiller, CBS's *Suspense*.

This business of turning radio plays into short stories isn't so easy as it sounds. Some recent "film-novelizations" have been mere transcripts of a shooting script, and John Steinbeck successfully sold two plays as novels chiefly by rearranging their typography; but Ellery Queen and Editorial Associates have a little more conscience than that. They realize that different media demand different approaches, and that the only way to make a short story out of a radio play is to know the play by heart and settle down to writing a short story on the same plot.

Queen's current experiment, "The Adventure of the Dead Cat," is particularly successful; he has transformed a good routine radio plot into a first-rate short by adding elements of ironic subjective commentary impossible to radio. The writers at Editorial Associates (Cleve Cartmill, Roby Wentz and others) are equally adroit—Wentz for instance makes a palatable short out of the Robert E. Lee-Irving Reis "Fury and Sound" which of all *Suspense* shows seemed originally to have been conceived in pure radio terms.

Look up these adventures in a new transformed medium. I think you'll find them provocative—and highly entertaining.

October 27, 1946

As the romantic novel has had its Daisy Ashford and the Western its David Statler (whose delightful ROARING GUNS you may recall), so it was inevitable that the mystery novel should in time produce a startlingly precocious master.

This master is Leslie W. Morris II, a 12-year-old Kentuckian, whose "The Municipal Murders" is the most entrancing item to cross this desk in years. In 38 pages Mr. Morris and his detective Austin Christe cover everything from The Perfect Alibi to The Least Suspected Person and in an unforgettable style.

Mr. Morris is a master of the mot injuste, the illuminatingly wrong word. The discovery of the corpse will give you the idea.

"Jonathan Gilbert Christe, wealthy, retired broker, was the latest victim of this savage ravenger....He was stretched across his diffused desk....and the dislodged receiver of a telephone was dangling flaccidly at his feet. A thin red stream was flowing from an ugly hole in his forehead and disseminating and absorbing on some bibulous paper beneath his head."

If you can henceforth ever dislodge from your vocabulary the superb portmanteau word "ravenger," you are a strong man. Persevere in the story and you will find the bibulous paper matched in the Inspector's office by an indispositioned desk and an intimate ash tray. And these are only random samples of the delights awaiting you.

Send 40 cents (cash or money order) to the publisher, Worth Estes, 215 Irvine Road, Lexington 30, Kentucky. You'll find no more rewarding money's-worth in this year's crop of murder.

SARTOR RESARTUS DEPARTMENT. This department has often had occasion to quarrel with Mr. Edmund Wilson, who once achieved the magnificent suggestion that the publication of mystery novels be suppressed in a time of paper shortage. By now Mr. Wilson undoubtedly agrees with me that, as of the making of books there is no end, so also is there no end in sight when the question arises of suppressing them. [Wilson's MEMOIRS OF HECATE COUNTY was being prosecuted for obscenity.] Whatever we may think of each other, Mr. Wilson and I know that we are not islands to ourselves. Our interests are common, and on the solution to Mr. Wilson's current plight depends the future of our profession.

PROMOTION DEPARTMENT. The firm of Julian Messner is launching a new series of whodunits to be known as "Recommended Mysteries"—each complete with advance raves from assorted celebrities who recommend. For myself, I am not given to caring markedly what Sir Cedric Hardwicke or Mary Margaret McBride thinks of a mystery, but it will be interesting to see the sales effect of this promotional method. It will also be interesting to see if the books of the series are as outstanding as the first (David Goodis' DARK PASSAGE) or as tawdry as the second (Dana Wilson's MAKE WITH THE BRAINS, PIERRE).

COLOPHON DEPARTMENT. Another new mystery list, that of Farrar & Straus, is henceforth to be embellished with the lethal sketch reproduced herewith. [The sketch of the colophon that accompanied Boucher's article is omitted from this collection.] Such unpartnerly conduct between F and S seems slightly inauspicious, but I shall be content if F&S mysteries live up to the high standards set by the first, Wade Miller's DEADLY WEAPON.

RESURRECTIONIST DEPARTMENT. Yet another new or at least renovated mystery line is that of Ziff-Davis, now edited by Clayton ("The Great Merlini") Rawson (and the only firm so far to accept the Mystery Writers of America contract). Its first book is the new Michael Shayne [by Brett Halliday].

November 24, 1946

"Poe said: Let there be a detective story; and it was so; and when Poe created the detective story in his own image, and saw everything that he had made, behold, it was very good; and he cast the detective story originally in the short form, and that form was, and is, and forever will be the true form. Amen."

Thus Ellery Queen [Frederic Dannay] (not so much with sacrilege as with true religious fervor) concludes his introduction to THE QUEEN'S AWARDS (Little Brown, $2.75), the first of an annual series of volumes containing each year's winners in the *EQMM* short story contest.

(The title, by the way, throws me. I could understand QUEEN'S AWARDS, THE QUEEN AWARDS or THE QUEENS' AWARDS. THE QUEEN'S AWARDS I find puzzling.)

The multiplication of anthologies in recent years, the increase (particularly in the 25-cent market) of books of one author's shorts and novelettes, and above all the success of *EQMM* itself seem to indicate that the public is at last coming to share Queen's belief that the short story is the true detective story.

And whether you share that belief or not, you'll not easily find a better batch of detectival reading than this collection of the Queen prize-winners. They include the first short story appearances of such celebrated sleuths as [Manning Coles'] Tommy Hambledon, [Anthony Gilbert's] Arthur Crook, [Ngaio Marsh's] Roderick Alleyn, [Frances Crane's] the Abbotts, and [Clifford Knight's] Huntoon Rogers—and if the first four are not quite up to their best books, the two last are perhaps preferable in miniature.

Other stories range from pure detection (with such astonishing new detective types as Manly Wade Wellman's Amerindian and Helen McCloy's Cossack) to fine underplayed studies in murder by Philip MacDonald and Q. Patrick.

But look: the only way to do justice to the book would be to devote a paragraph to each story, and there isn't space. Main point is you'd better get it. You'll have fun arguing with the awards (one of my own favorites, the Kenneth Millar, is in the last category); you may even enjoy the cute family-joke story which rounds out the collection; and above all you'll have the pleasure of several solid hours spent with the detective story at its best.

BAKER STREET DEPARTMENT. Three pamphlets (hardly totaling more than 50 pages among them) have recently appeared that demand inclusion on all Irregular book shelves.

Adrian Conan Doyle's "The True Conan Doyle" (Coward-McCann, $1) was written in warm indignation as a reply to Hesketh Pearson's CONAN DOYLE: HIS LIFE AND ART. Adrian, one of the two Doyle heirs who bestride the Holmesian world like a Siamese colossus, felt that Mr. Pearson's shrewdly perceptive work was irreverent. His answer is touchingly filial, even in its absurd attempt to prove that Doyle himself was his own prototype for Holmes. But it is regrettable that this small piece of familial piety should find a publisher when the important biography which it attacks has not yet appeared in America.

More welcome to the habitue of Baker Street are Helene Yuhasova's "A Lauriston Garden of Verses" (Pamphlet House, $1.50) and J.A. Finch's "Flashes by Fanlight" (The Fanlight Press, 50 cents). The first contains six sonnets and a ballade, all equally delightful as skilled verse and as warmly felt Sherlockiana. The second is a series of jottings (originally published in a Chicago paper which will get no publicity here) on such topics as the nicotinic versatility of Holmes and his awareness of telephones and finger-prints.

The Yuhasova may be ordered from the Argus Book Shop, 3 West 46th Street, New York 19, and the Finch from Jay Finley Christ, 9551 Longwood Drive, Chicago 43.

December 29, 1946

Report on 1946.

Outstanding trend: greater output of criminous literature. For the last half of 1946, whodunits and their near relatives have been appearing at the rate of almost one a day, the greatest frequency since before the war.

Other trends: growing prevalence of the $2.50 price for mysteries—a long-needed raise, though I believe Duell [Sloan & Pearce] and Ziff-Davis are the only firms which split the increase 50-50 with their authors. Increase of specialized mystery editing—important new mystery lines established by Ziff, Messner, and Farrar Straus, with similar setups rumored from Harper, Appleton [Century Crofts] and others. Gradual elimination of the marginal two-bit reprints, with the field settling down to a half dozen well-edited and soundly financed firms.

Oddest aspect of the year: the number of startling original new variants of plot and technique in a field that has threatened to exhaust itelf for the last 20 years. Helen Eustis' THE HORIZONTAL MAN (Harper), Pat McGerr's PICK YOUR VICTIM (Doubleday Crime Club) and Wilson Tucker's THE CHINESE DOLL (Rinehart) all presented tricks in their way as historic as [Agatha Christie's] THE MURDER OF ROGER ACKROYD or [Anthony Berkeley's] THE POISONED CHOCOLATES CASE. And Carol Kendall's THE BLACK SEVEN (Harper), Samuel Rogers' YOU LEAVE ME COLD! (Harper) and Doris Miles Disney's WHO RIDES A TIGER (Doubleday Crime Club) were, if less successful, very nearly as original.

Gratifying aspect: 1946 was a fine year for firsts, especially in contrast to 1945. Of the six novelty items just listed, all but the Rogers were first mysteries, and the Eustis HORIZONTAL MAN is not only unquestionably the best first of this year but a permanent addition to the list of crime classics. Almost as impressive debuts were those of David Goodis (DARK PASSAGE, Messner), Lewis Padgett (THE BRASS RING, Duell, Sloan & Pearce), and the team of Edwin Rolfe and Lester Fuller (THE GLASS ROOM, Rinehart).

England is doing well too, sending us admirable first novels from Sybil Ericson (THE CURATE'S CRIME, Mystery House), Robert Player (THE INGENIOUS MR. STONE, Rinehart), Maureen Sarsfield (GREEN DECEMBER FILLS THE GRAVEYARD, Coward-McCann), and Margot Bennett (TIME TO CHANGE HATS, Doubleday Crime Club).

Jot down in your records too the names of debutants Thomas B. Black, Lester Dent, Robert Finnegan, John Gearon, Alexander Irving, M.S. Marble, Peter Mortimer, Anthony Quayle and Showell Stiles, any one of whom might have copped top honors for firsts in a lesser year.

Further gratification: it was a good year for old masters. Agatha Christie's THE HOLLOW (Dodd Mead), H.C. Bailey's THE LIFE SENTENCE (Doubleday Crime Club), John Dickson Carr's HE WHO WHISPERS (Harper) and Carter Dickson's [John Dickson Carr's] MY LATE WIVES (Morrow) all rank among their authors' best products.

Other outstanding items.

[Mary Roberts] Rinehart-atmosphere school: THE PAVILION by Hilda Lawrence (Simon & Schuster).

Suspense novel: THE INNOCENT MRS. DUFF by Elisabeth Sanxay Holding (Simon & Schuster).

Satire: WHAT HAPPENED AT HAZELWOOD? by Michael Innes (Dodd Mead).

Hard-boiled: TIGER BY THE TAIL by Lawrence Goldman (McKay).

Murder novel: THE MAN WHO WATCHED THE TRAINS GO BY by Georges Simenon (Reynal & Hitchcock).

Factual murder: DENVER MURDERS, edited by Lee Casey (Duell, Sloan & Pearce).

Spy-adventure: THE ASSASSINS by Hildegarde Tolman Teilhet (Coward-McCann).

Factual espionage: WE CAUGHT SPIES by John Schwarzwalder (Duell, Sloan & Pearce).

Short stories: DR. SAM: JOHNSON, DETECTOR by Lillian de la Torre (Knopf).

Anthology: TO THE QUEEN'S TASTE, edited by Ellery Queen [Frederic Dannay] (Little Brown).

Criticism: THE ART OF THE MYSTERY STORY, edited by Howard Haycraft (Simon & Schuster).

Most interesting dividend: WHERE THERE'S SMOKE by Stewart Sterling (Lippincott).

Most curious atmosphere: THE WHITE MAZURKA by Bettina Boyers (Doubleday Crime Club).

Most delightful novelty: "The Municipal Murder" by Leslie W. Morris II (Estes).

Oddest book of the year: THE DEADLY PERCHERON by John Franklin Bardin (Dodd Mead).

And for the straight detective novel, well-conceived, well-written and well-plotted (an item that becomes increasingly hard to find in its pure form), special welcome to Christianna Brand's THE CROOKED WREATH (Dodd Mead), Patrick Quentin's PUZZLE FOR FIENDS

(Simon & Schuster), and Lawrence Treat's H AS IN HUNTED (Duell, Sloan & Pearce).

January 26, 1947

NEW YORK. In my last column of 1946 I mentioned the trend toward the $2.50 price for mysteries as a major phenomenon of the year. The trend is growing and may soon be all-inclusive, but not for the original reason advanced by Mystery Writers of America, which was that mysteries are worth as much to rental libraries as the average straight novel and should pay their way for their authors.

Now, just as mysteries are going up to $2.50, many straight novels are going to $3 and even beyond; for publishers have been trapped between the devil of decreasing sales and the blue sea of fabulously rising production costs.

Book publishing held the line against inflation better than almost any other industry. Now it is forced into inevitable rises; and the question is, how will we the reading public react?

It's a situation that has many publishers in a jittery state of contemplating the windows of their nice tall buildings, and it is of course hardly the ideal moment for such a militant organization as Mystery Writers of America to approach them on the subject of authors' rights. But MWA remains vigorous and active. It has had reasonable success on contract negotiations, it is possibly within shouting distance of settling its problems with the Authors' Guild, and its regional organizations are at last beginning to burgeon and flourish. (Watch for announcement of a San Francisco meeting in February.)

The 25-cent market, so important to the mystery field, has been seriously hit by the current condition of the business; but even there a few signs of life are evident, particularly the rejuvenation of Street & Smith's *Shadow* as a bimonthly featuring such authors as [Cornell] Woolrich and Miriam Allen deFord in addition to its regular Shadow novel, and the excellent series of short story collections to be published by Lawrence Spivak and edited by Ellery Queen [Frederic Dannay]. This distinguished list will start off with Stuart Palmer, whose Hildegarde Withers shorts have never before been collected, and go on to Roy Vickers, John Dickson Carr and other masters.

AWARDS DEPARTMENT. MWA is now tallying the ballots on its 1946 awards. This department's votes went unqualifiedly for Helen Eustis' THE HORIZONTAL MAN for first novel, Howard Haycraft for criticism, and *Pat Novak for Hire* for radio—and at least the first two are, I'd prophesy, sure of a landslide victory. Further prophecy: for the criticism award for 1947, watch James Sandoe's recently inaugurated column in the Chicago *Sun*.

POLITICS DEPARTMENT. Add mystery writers in politics: Veronica Parker Johns, who ran for the Connecticut legislature last fall on the Democratic ticket. Did she win? No!

SAN FRANCISCO DEPARTMENT. Two whilom San Franciscans have brightened my stay enormously. One was ex-mystery writer Gelett Burgess, who delighted me with unprintable rhymes at the Wednesday Culture Club, an informal organization which lunches on Fridays and devotes itself to such important topics as limericks and the Oxford theory of Shakespearean authorship. The other was Ina Claire. It is strictly no business of this department, but I can't help reporting, with a loud Calloo Callay, that Miss Claire in [George] Kelly's FATAL WEAKNESS and Bert Lahr in the revival of BURLESQUE present the two finest performances I've seen this year—or any other year in recent memory. (This does not include certain interesting performances at meetings of MWA.)

February 23, 1947

The March issue of *Ellery Queen's Mystery Magazine*, now on sale, contains the editor's four-page report on the magazine's second annual short-story contest.

Get it and read it, for this contest has become a highly significant phenomenon in the detective story field. Queen [Frederic Dannay], despite the sales in the millions of his mystery novels [written in collaboration with his cousin Manfred B. Lee], has always maintained that the short story is the true and perfect detective form; and first in his magazine and now in his contest he has made his point—developing new short story writers, luring established novelists into the shorter form, attracting figures from other literary fields, and in general raising the detective short to a startling new standard of excellence.

(Though this devotion to the short story is becoming almost a monomania with Queen—his list of female detectives on page 52 of the current magazine casually ignores all those who have appeared only in novels.)

Contest winners this time range from England to the Antipodes, and California can boast the capture of the $3000 first prize (H.F. Heard) and two of the $500 second prizes (Philip MacDonald and Leslie Charteris). (The fact that all California winners are of British origin somewhat baffles me.)

Mr. Heard's first-prize story, "The President of the United States, Detective," appears in the current issue, and I've a strong feeling that a tempest may rage about this award.

And Queen himself has similar fears; he devotes a two-page afterword to a defense of the choice, which I at least find totally unconvincing.

If a story of the future in which a character averts world catastrophe by superlatively daring scientific reasoning is a detective story, then 50 per cent of the contents of *Astounding Science-Fiction* should be regularly reprinted in *EQMM*, and no list of detective story writers would be complete without the classic names of A.E. Van Vogt, L. Sprague de Camp and Robert Heinlein.

This is not to decry Mr. Heard's story, which is admirable science-fiction (though I may doubt the advisability of the Yellow Peril as a fictional theme). But after this award (plus the reprinting some months ago of Horace Fish's supernatural fantasy "The Wrists on the Door,") I do wonder what is happening to the Queen editorial policy.

Mr. Queen's case, that the detective-short has attracted some of the best writers and best writing, can stand by itself; there is no need to strengthen it by trying to prove that every conceivable form of fiction is, properly regarded, a detective story.

MWA DEPARTMENT. The first meeting of the Northern California chapter of Mystery Writers of America, Inc., will take place this Friday, February 28—an organizational meeting at which the regional vice president [Boucher himself] will explain the objectives and current problems of MWA and try to get the local ball rolling.

Those objectives, very simply stated, are more money and a better understanding (both by writers and by the public) of the craft. While the first must largely be handled by the national organization, we hope that the regional groups can contribute importantly to the second—and incidentally have fun.

If you are a professional writer in the mystery field—book form, pulps, slicks, radio or what-have-you—and have been overlooked in the invitations, don't feel slighted. You are hereby invited (this first meeting is open both to members and to nonmembers) and urged to get in touch with me for details.

March 30, 1947

Alva Johnston's THE CASE OF ERLE STANLEY GARDNER (Morrow, $1.50) marks an epoch. So far as I know it's the first time that a living mystery novelist has ever been honored by a biography.

The choice of subject is a good one. Gardner is not only one of the more fabulous personalities in a not precisely prosaic profession, he's also a singular phenomenon in sales and popularity.

Myself, I'm a Gardner fan. I read him with avidity and pleasure. I'd even read him if I weren't reviewing, than which I have no higher praise. But he's oddly hard to defend against the articulate minority who charge that his characters are sticks and his dialogue is wooden. You can only protest that his tempo and plotting are such that you don't care (and perhaps add that [Gardner's pseudonym] A. A. Fair seems curiously more able at both character and dialogue).

Mr. Johnston makes both his virtues and his flaws a plausible part of his character, as the trick-brilliant lawyer who realized that his ingenious mind was a commercial commodity to be peddled more profitably in other markets than the courts.

Johnston's volume is not so much a book as an unreorganized reprint of magazine articles. He skirts over some of the more interesting aspects of his subject (such as Gardner's unique relations with his publisher). But he presents vividly a character and career; he adds photographs and an unusually detailed bibliography; and above all he provides a multitude of stories of Gardner's own courtroom days, when his achievements threatened to parallel a Bill Fallon or an Earl Rogers.

PUZZLE DEPARTMENT. If you're the puzzle-minded type of mystery devotee (a dying species, I sometimes fear), you'll enjoy two new puzzle books, both far above the caliber of the average opus appearing on this side of the Atlantic. One is a new edition of W.W. Rouse Ball's classic MATHEMATICAL RECREATIONS AND ESSAYS, revised by H.S.M. Coxeter (Macmillan, $2.95). This is chiefly designed for post-graduate puzzlers with sound mathematical backgrounds, but even the laity will enjoy such sections as those on how to find your way through any maze or on the strange history of mathematical prodigies. Simpler but still worthy of your keenest efforts is Geoffrey Mott-Smith's MATHEMATICAL PUZZLES FOR BEGINNERS AND ENTHUSIASTS (New Home Library, 69 cents)—probably the most lucid, ingenious, accurate and admirable popular puzzle book I have ever seen.

POLICY DEPARTMENT. The spring of '47 has been the heaviest mystery-publishing season since I started reviewing five years ago. For months I've been running seven reviews a week; at the moment of writing I'm 21 volumes behind, and things'll doubtless be worse by the time you read this. So this department is starting a new policy.

Henceforth, if I feel at the end of 50 or 100 pages that there is no point in my finishing a book and little reason why you should begin it, I'll simply stop. Farewell to this conscientious business of reading through everything that comes over the desk. The books that hold me, for better or worse, I'll review as before; the others will be listed, as in the adjacent column, under "Other Books Received."

It seems the only way, paper and time being what they are, to assure you of a reasonably complete coverage of the crop. If you have any other suggestions, I'd be glad to hear them.

April 20, 1947

One hundred and six years ago tomorrow the detective story was born, with the publication in *Graham's Magazine* of "The Murders in the Rue Morgue"—that classic opus in which Edgar Allan Poe established all the precedents, from the impossible situation to the omniscient detective, from the last-minute title change to the underpaid author.

Now in 1947 the detective story is enjoying for the first time a nation-wide birthday celebration. This is Mystery Book Week, and the *Chronicle* book section joins other literary publications all over the country in wishing the whodunit a long life, speckled with frequent and profitable deaths.

Major event of the week's celebrations will be the awarding, at banquets in New York and Hollywood, of the Edgars, the annual Edgar Allan Poe awards bestowed by Mystery Writers of America, Inc.

This year these tokens will take the shape of porcelain busts of Mr. Poe (recipients are asked to provide their own ravens) specially modeled for the occasion by Peter Williams, noted ceramist, limerick fancier, and husband to mystery novelist Manning Long (whose latest, DULL THUD, warmed this department's cockles). These Edgars, plus special presentation copies of Howard Haycraft's invaluable THE ART OF THE MYSTERY STORY, will be awarded to:

Helen Eustis for THE HORIZONTAL MAN (Harper), best first mystery novel.

William Weber for "The Criminal Record" by Judge Lynch, in *The Saturday Review of Literature*, best criticism of mysteries.

William Spier, producer, and Bob Tallman and Jason James, writers, for *The Adventures of Sam Spade* (CBS, Sunday nights), best mystery radio program.

Mark Hellinger, producer, Robert Siodmak, director, and Anthony Veiller, scenarist, for THE KILLERS (Hellinger-Universal), best mystery film.

These awards were voted by a nation-wide ballot of MWA members.

The New York Poe Awards Dinner will feature the induction into MWA of four honorary members: Dr. Thomas Gonzalez, chief medical examiner of the City of New York; Dr. Alexander S. Wiener, chief serologist and "blood detective" of the Medical Examiner's office; Dr. Frederic Wertham, psychiatrist, criminologist and author of DARK LEGEND: A STUDY IN MURDER (one of the all-time masterpieces in the field of crime writing); and Christopher Morley.

(MWA is flourishing locally in San Francisco, I should add; and any mystery writers we may have overlooked in invitations are urged to get in touch with the secretary, Lenore Glen Offord, at 611 Euclid Avenue, Berkeley.)

June 29, 1947

A first-rate anthology of the detective story is a hen's tooth for scarcity. When it does occur, its distinction may come from any of several causes. It may be notable for the critical intelligence of its comments, like the [S.S.] Van Dine and [Dorothy L.] Sayers collections. It may be outstanding in the absolute excellence of its choices, like Vincent Starrett's FOURTEEN GREAT DETECTIVE STORIES or Ellery Queen's [Frederic Dannay's] definitive 101 YEARS' ENTERTAINMENT. Or it may be distinguished by the originality and interest of its pattern, like Kenneth Macgowan's SLEUTHS with its Who's Who biographies of detectives, or the various specialized Queen anthologies.

The last angle is the most promising for the modern anthologist. It's late in the day to come up with such stimulating and inclusive criticism as is contained in the Van Dine or Sayers prefaces. The masterpieces of the genre have become too familiar for an editor to attempt a general anthology on a basis of pure excellence.

But new patterns and slants are still possible—as evidence of which this month of June brings to the fortunate 'tec-reader two brand new and wholly admirable collections.

One is Raymond T. Bond's FAMOUS STORIES OF CODE AND CIPHER (Rinehart, $3.50). Cryptanalysis and the puzzle-whodunit share a similar appeal, and it's not unnatural that they've often been combined since Poe's immensely overrated "The Gold-Bug." The combination doesn't always work (the most intelligent treatment of ciphers that I can recall in a modern novel was in Helen McCloy's PANIC—and it all but ruined the novel); but Mr. Bond has, with impeccable taste, chosen just precisely the stories in which the blend came off.

Many of the stories are reasonably familiar, but they assume a fresh interest when placed together and compared from this new viewpoint and illuminated by Mr. Bond's informative and often provocative comments. It's a book assured of a permanent place on the select shelf of Grade-A specialized anthologies.

Another completely new anthological idea makes its appearance in MURDER BY EXPERTS (Ziff-Davis, $3.50), edited by Ellery Queen and 20 other members of Mystery Writers of America.

As Queen explains at length in an entertaining preface, there was some dissatisfaction with the higgledy-piggledy nature of MWA's first anthology. It was decided that this time each of 20 top-notch American murder-mongers should select his one favorite detective story and write an editorial introduction explaining why. All "Red-Headed Leagues" and "Purloined Letters" were to be barred as too familiar—and all royalties of course were to go to the organization.

The result should prove as much of a benefit to the detective story fan as to the MWA treasury. The stories are, by definition, of extraordinary high quality, but even more fascinating are the introductions and choices.

It will surprise no one that Clayton Rawson picks a John Dickson Carr (whose most eminent disciple he is), or that Baynard Kendrick, creator of blind Captain Duncan Maclain, selects a story about blind Max Carrados (and writes a somewhat belligerent preface). Nor that critics so respected as Howard Haycraft and Vincent Starrett choose authors of such generally underestimated perfection as Melville Davisson Post and Frederick Irving Anderson.

But it may fascinate you to find such an intellectualized author as Helen McCloy picking an admirable short by the crude hard-hitting Brett Halliday [who was McCloy's husband at the time], or so humorless a recounter of society emotions as Helen Reilly choosing a delightful farce by Patrick Quentin, or Leslie Charteris prefacing (with the book's best introduction) a [G.K. Chesterton] Father Brown story.

Whether you want a group of 20 detective stories, all guaranteed outstanding, or whether you want a revealing insight into the mental workings of your favorite detective story writers, MURDER BY EXPERTS is a volume you cannot possibly afford to miss.

BAKER STREET DEPARTMENT. Hesketh Pearson's invaluable CO-NAN DOYLE: HIS LIFE AND ART, the publication of which was circumvented in this country by a series of unpleasant and unprintable maneuvers, has now been reprinted in England in a one shilling edition by the British Publishers Guild, a co-operative venture. No Holmesian collection is remotely complete without this excellent study of Watson's literary agent; and while you're ordering books from England, you might add Guy Warrack's distinguished and tasteful monograph SHERLOCK HOLMES AND MUSIC (Faber & Faber, 7s 6d).

FANTASY DEPARTMENT. Two important critico-bibliographical works will soon be available to the collector (possibly three, if the long-promised PILGRIMS THROUGH TIME AND SPACE ever materializes). THE CHECKLIST OF FANTASTIC LITERATURE (Shasta Publishers, 1713 East 55th Street, Chicago 15) promises to contain full, detailed, cross-indexed bibliographical information on over 5000 titles. ENTER GHOST: A STUDY IN WEIRD FICTION by Paul W. Skeeters and Samuel D. Russell (Carcosa House, 774 Caliburn Drive, Los Angeles 2) is scheduled to include not only the "most complete bibliography ever assembled on this special subject" but also over 100,000 words of critical history. Each book is listed at a prepublication price of $5; since both editions are strictly limited and the prices are more than apt to rise later, collectors and fans are strongly urged to send advance orders to the respective publishers at once.

August 31, 1947

Almost exactly five years ago I took over this department from your old murderous mentor, Edward Dermot Doyle. Now Mr. Doyle is back from the wars, and this is my farewell column.

I don't need to spend any of it in introducing Mr. Doyle, whom every San Francisco crime enthusiast remembers with delight. (I can testify myself to his unerringly perceptive judgment; he always raved about a Boucher book.)

My five-year tenure here has been a lustrum not without luster. It's a span that has covered the rise and decline of the boomingest period in the history of the mystery novel—the only period during which the average mystery novelist made approximately decent money.

Those days are dying now. Sales are falling to prewar levels, with production costs still more than twice as high as prewar. The once wildly spawning reprint market has contracted to a handful of established lines. The publication of a mystery novel is beginning to be a dubious economic venture for either publisher or author; and while the spate of previously-contracted-for books still continues, there's some question as to how many whodunits Mr. Doyle may be reviewing here a year from now.

But I don't want to depart on so mournful a note of Götterdämmerung. I would rather look back on the joys of a job which proffered such wonderful moments as the time an indignant author wired a hundred words cross-continent to the editor of the *Chronicle*, demanding my instant dismissal for having failed to rhapsodize over his prize-winning novel, or the unbelievable occasion on which Scribners set an all-time high in mystification by neglecting to print the last chapter of a mystery novel.

Reading every whodunit published can be something less than thrilling, but there is a peak-in-Darien thrill about those moments when you suddenly realize that look, you are reading the first novel of a major contender. I'm happy that my five years included the debuts of such figures as Helen Eustis, Hilda Lawrence, Lewis Padgett, George Bellairs, A.E. Martin and Arthur W. Upfield—among many others, includeing Robert Finnegan, whose death this month meant the loss to the mystery field of one of its most up-and-coming new practitioners. (I shan't speak here of the loss he meant in other fields, as [labor union activist] Mike Quin. Under all his names, may he rest in peace.)

I've had a good time, and I'd like to extend my thanks to a great many people who made it possible: to Lenore Glen Offord, for her frequent and invaluable understudying; to James Sandoe of the Chicago *Sun*, for his unfailing help with critical research problems; to Mystery Writers of America, for honoring this column with the first of its awards for mystery criticism; to the *Chronicle*, for giving me a completely free rein in comment and thought; to Orphelia Stull, who sets in the Book Department a standard which will make life hideous for any secretary I ever employ privately; to Joseph Henry Jackson, who managed to rub off on me some of his boundless knowledge of the technique of book reviewing.

And above all to you, for reading the column.

I'll still be around, issuing my dicta on fantasy and science fiction and sundry other topics; but to the strict connoisseurs of crime and devotees of dereliction, I now bid good-bye—and good hunting.

VOLUME II

THE WEEK IN MURDER

Weekly Columns

1942

October 11, 1942

H.F. Heard, MURDER BY REFLECTION (Vanguard, $2). Miss Ibis finds her life in meticulous re-creation of the past and her death in a startling new method from the future. Some superscientific detection may qualify this as a whodunit. The psychological build-up to murder is the finest since [Francis Iles' 1932 novel] BEFORE THE FACT. Caviar, but high grade. (Note to Heard fans: No Mr. Mycroft.)

Kelley Roos, THE FRIGHTENED STIFF (Dodd Mead, $2). Haila and Jeffrey Troy rent an ex-speakeasy in the Village [i.e. New York's Greenwich Village] and find the garden complete with naked corpse. Very bright fast stuff, up to the neat title, with some nice ribbing of the H.I.B.K.'s ["Had I But Known" romantic suspense novels in the tradition of Mary Roberts Rinehart] and a tricky plot way above the average of the murder-can-be-fun school.

G.D.H. & Margaret Cole, TOPER'S END (Macmillan, $2.50). Superintendent Wilson comes in late on a confusing pair of poisonings in a country house crowded with academic refugees. Characters good, action nil. Quietly solid stuff, if a bit too much of it.

Clifford Knight, THE AFFAIR OF THE SPLINTERED HEART (Dodd Mead, $2). The nebulous Huntoon Rogers watches several murders in post-Pearl Harbor Hawaii and finally makes possible the success of the Marshall and Gilbert raid. As a spy thriller, dull. As mystery, painfully unfair.

October 18, 1942

Helen McCloy, CUE FOR MURDER (Morrow, $2). Psychiatrist Basil Willing cracks the murder of a stage corpse in a [19th-century French playwright Victorien] Sardou revival. Admirable writing and meticulously intricate plotting—but what less would you expect from McCloy?

Jerome Barry, LEOPARD CAT'S CRADLE (Doubleday Crime Club, $2). Soda chef Chick Varney helps frustrate a murderer who scatters cat's cradle symbols. Surprising if badly motivated solution, amusing drugstore patter, plus encyclopedic and fascinating dope on string tricks.

A.R. Hilliard, OUTLAW ISLAND (Farrar & Rinehart, $2). Young D.A. Jerry Carver is foiled by an eccentric group who play games around murder; sage and monumental Judge Manfred provides the tricky solution. Gratifyingly three-dimensional writing—and a brand-new motive for murder.

George Harmon Coxe, THE CHARRED WITNESS (Knopf, $2). News photographer Kent Murdock uncovers some new variations on the burned-corpse theme. Hard, fast movement and a double twist.

Richard Hull, AND DEATH CAME TOO (Messner, $2). Sergeant Scoresby makes the grade without calling in the Yard. Good British routine, but a far cry from [Hull's 1934 novel] THE MURDER OF MY AUNT—save for a brilliantly Hullian curtain line.

October 25, 1942

Virginia Rath, POSTED FOR MURDER (Doubleday Crime Club, $2). Michael Dundas (of Gisele's on [San Francisco's] Post Street) takes to the Berkeley hills to clear his favorite cousin of a charge of wife-killing. Good local color and suave detection.

A.A. Fair [Erle Stanley Gardner], BATS FLY AT DUSK (Morrow, $2). Remember Donald Lam joined the Navy? So now Bertha Cool flounders alone through an intricate mess of blind beggars, music boxes and pet bats, with Donald offstage as armchair detective—if armchairs are G.I. at Vallejo. Just about the best Fair yet; and the best Fair is the best fare.

Judson P. Philips [also known as Hugh Pentecost], THE FOURTEENTH TRUMP (Dodd Mead, $2). Danny Coyle, the Lloyds of New York, sees through a routine killing to a fifth column plot. Clever dope on bridge rackets, grade A Broadway dialogue, a swell Marie Wilson blonde and a sock surprise.

Frederick C. Davis, DEEP LAY THE DEAD (Doubleday Crime Club, $2). More spy stuff, this time with Rig Webb, snowbound in Pennsylvania, frustrating the Axis quest for our just-perfected unbreakable cipher. More emphasis on people and emotion than on spyduggery, and a good job too.

Agatha Christie, THE MOVING FINGER (Dodd Mead, $2). Miss Marple, the omniscient spinster, finds a new reason for poison-pen letters. Passable second string Christie.

November 1, 1942

Jeffery Farnol, VALLEY OF NIGHT (Doubleday Doran, $2.50). Bow Street Runner Jasper Shrig tangles with Cornish wreckers, a nonagenarian villainess and a skull that nods. Fine romantic period stuff, and a colorful change from modern murder.

Phoebe Atwood Taylor, THREE PLOTS FOR ASEY MAYO (Norton, $2). One gem, "The Swan Boat Plot," and two minor novelets. The Mayo-Taylor charm functions better at full length.

Philip Mechem, AND NOT FOR LOVE (Duell, Sloan & Pearce, $2). Cynthia Coveney's bon vivant Uncle Eldred untangles murders and emotions in the Colorado mountains. Cynthia's individual and subacid narration makes up for a conventional and confusing plot.

Robert Portner Koehler, HERE COME THE DEAD (Phoenix, $2). Pecos Appleby, the Law West of Asey Mayo, solves the stabbing of a tourist during the San Ysidro rain dance. Pecos is agreeable, but plot and solution take a lot of believing.

M.V. Heberden, MURDER MAKES A RACKET (Doubleday Crime Club, $2). Desmond Shannon, than whom they don't come tougher, breaks up a racket preying on refugees. The hard-boiled effect is marred by the author's conviction that all levels use the impersonal "one."

W.T. Ballard, SAY YES TO MURDER (Putnam, $2). Studio yes-man William Lennox solves Hollywood murders to save his neck and the studio's reputation. The plot is old hat, the writing lurid, glamorous and painful.

November 8, 1942

Dorothy Cameron Disney & George Sessions Perry, THIRTY DAYS HATH SEPTEMBER (Random House, $2). New collaborating team produces extraordinary novel of murder in the Connecticut summer colony. Skill, suspense and psychological subtlety.

John Spain [Cleve F. Adams], DIG ME A GRAVE (Dutton, $2). Confidential agent William Rye breaks up blackmail and murder in L.A. politics. Authentic hard school—as close to Hammett himself as anything in many years.

John Dickson Carr, THE EMPEROR'S SNUFF-BOX (Harper, $2). Dr. Dermot Kinross, criminal psychologist, clears a beautiful and suggestible woman of murder charges in pre-war France. Admirable characterization, precise plotting and a flawless surprise solution to bring you out of your chair.

Walbridge McCully, DEATH RIDES TANDEM (Doubleday Crime Club, $2). Kathleen King takes a secretarial job and finds love, hate and hyoscine. A tricky alibi and lots of romance, but wordy.

Vivian Connell, THE CHINESE ROOM (Dial Press, $2.50). As a psychological experiment, British banker Bude writes anonymous threats to himself; he gets more than he writes. This promising mystery is subordinate to the gratifying development of Bude's sex life. Turgid and tumescent writing.

November 15, 1942

No column was published this week.

November 22, 1942

Craig Rice, THE SUNDAY PIGEON MURDERS (Simon & Schuster, $2). Bingo and Handsome, street photographers, start out with well-meaning blackmail and acquire a fine collection of living friends plus a mere four corpses. A must, but impossible to describe or classify; who expects a mystery's main virtue to be its cockle-warming charm?

Kathleen Moore Knight, BELLS FOR THE DEAD (Doubleday Crime Club, $2). The Thorntree castle on Lake Tsanitlan, Guatemala, houses a strange matriarchy where suspicion and terror await a young American bride. Atmosphere and excitement, plus unusually clean and credible romantic writing.

Mignon G. Eberhart, WOLF IN MAN'S CLOTHING (Random House, $2). Nurse Sarah Keate returns as sensible and peppery as ever to solve a brace of murders, straighten out a snarled romance, and strike a blow for democracy. The mistress of the [Mary Roberts] Rinehart school at the top of her form.

Charlotte Murray Russell, MURDER STEPS IN (Doubleday Crime Club, $2). Noah Harper, retired Iowan shoe manufacturer, and wife Louella, befriend a desolate girl in Miami and plunge into murder, which Noah's horse sense and knowledge of shoes unravel. Highly pleasing new detective team lost in unconvincing romance.

Frank Gruber, THE GIFT HORSE (Farrar & Rinehart, $2). Book salesmen Johnny Fletcher and Sam Cragg inherit a horse—and could anything happen to those two without involving a few corpses? Padded action and fuzzy plot, not up to Gruber standard.

November 29, 1942

Harriet Rutland, BLUE MURDER (Smith & Durrell, $2). Novelist Arnold Smith, bombed out of London, takes refuge in a household where murder is about to pop. Short on detection and surprise but long on the quiet psychological chills of the best British school.

H. Donald Spatz, DEATH ON THE NOSE (Phoenix, $2). Columnist Jeff Quentin defends his life and his virtue while solving gruesome series of murders in big time radio. Careless but brashly amusing.

Margaret Tayler Yates, DEATH BY THE YARD (Macmillan, $2). Navy wife Davvie McLain goes through a lot to foil the Japanese raid on Pearl Harbor. Entertaining, if a bit flippant, but history has most unfairly tipped the ending.

December 6, 1942

Ruth Fenisong, MURDER NEEDS A FACE (Doubleday Crime Club, $2). Sergeant Gridley Nelson and the incomparable Negress Sammy find puppets, paupers and murders on a low-income housing project. Novel background and admirable writing recommend this to every type of fan.

Elisabeth Sanxay Holding, KILL JOY (Duell, Sloan & Pearce, $2). Maggie was only 19 and the sad-eyed Miss Dolly seemed tragically glamorous to her, but there was no glamor to the tragedies that maid and mistress found in the old boathouse on the swamp. Another beautiful study in the subtle and miasmic horror of emotions such as only Mrs. Holding can bring off.

Katherine Wolffe, THE ATTIC ROOM (Morrow, $2). Small town postmistress goes herb gathering and finds corpse of golden haired stranger; Captain Courtney Brade astutely pigeonholes him and his murderer. Friendly if hackneyed story, told in disconcerting mixture of simplicity and Fine Writing.

M. Scott Michel, THE X-RAY MURDERS (Coward-McCann, $2). It took two years to murder the X-ray specialist. It takes Shamus Extraordinary Wood Jaxon three days to solve the murder, with time out for three killings on his own. Slick, sexy and synthetic.

Edith Howie, MURDER'S SO PERMANENT (Farrar & Rinehart, $2). Lieutenant Worrall, the Max de Winter of detectives, rescues the fair librarian from murderers, saboteurs and aristocrats. Pleasingly realistic library patter, but otherwise strictly for romance addicts.

Miles Burton [also known as John Rhode], DEATH AT ASH HOUSE (Doubleday Crime Club, $2). Inspector Arnold plods through the problem of the bashed secretary and at last catches up with the reader. Relentlessly painstaking—and giving.

December 13, 1942

Whitman Chambers, BRING ME ANOTHER MURDER (Dutton, $2). Reporter Will Randall gets tangled in elections, blackouts, love killings and a Hollywood ex-wife. His city editor, "The Duchess," uncovers a murderer and the year's most unusual motive. Scene: A mythical West Coast city. Medium-boiled and satisfying.

Ione Sandberg Schriber, A BODY FOR BILL (Farrar & Rinehart, $2). Sabotage in an Akron rubber plant imperils the fair secretary in a singularly confused story, rather like an Alice Tilton farce offered seriously. "In all my life," complains Lieutenant Bill Grady, "I have never run into such a bunch of assorted idiots." I'm not arguing.

December 20, 1942

H.C. Branson, THE PRICKING THUMB (Simon & Schuster, $2). Bearded John Bent relentlessly breaks down the hocus pocus of a brilliant triple murder. Quietly convincing detective and unusually interesting murderer duel in a solid and rewarding work of a kind rare in the American mystery. For fans of [Freeman Wills] Crofts and [Georges] Simenon.

Charles L. Leonard [M.V. Heberden], THE STOLEN SQUADRON (Doubleday Crime Club, $2). Hardbitten detective Paul Kilgerrin joins the Fifth Column to find planes boldly stolen direct from the factory. A wryly realistic story; despite a confusing start, much the best of the season's crop of sabotage novels.

H.F.S. Moore, MURDER GOES ROLLING ALONG (Doubleday Crime Club, $2). Major Peters, provost marshal at Fort Bragg, tackles corpses in the Medical Corps; perky Janet Masters narrates and solves the case—with mirrors. A sprightly, pleasing yarn, in spite of military snobbery and a strained solution. (And ideal escape fiction: Fort Bragg worries less about the war than any civilian locale in months.)

Willetta Ann Barber & R.F. Schabelitz, MURDER ENTERS THE PICTURE (Doubleday Crime Club, $2). Christopher Storm, sketching sleuth, meets murder in his bride's Connecticut family. Scads of corpses, [Mabel] Seeleyesque atmosphere, and plentiful pictures that hold the essential clues—Storm signals to the wary eye.

Kerry O'Neil, DEATH AT DAKAR (Doubleday Crime Club, $2). American girl reporter foils Nazi quest for death ray formula in Rio and Dakar. The local color is hot from the guidebook, and the preposterous dialogue makes the Rover Boys sound like Clifford Odets. Perfect ammunition for the snobs who claim mysteries are execrable writing.

December 27, 1942

No column was published this week.

1943

January 3, 1943

Jeune Inconnu [French for "an unknown young man"], THE MURDER OF ADMIRAL DARLAN (San Francisco Chronicle, $0.05 daily). A connoisseur's item, possibly deserving to rank with such historical masterpieces as THE MURDER OF LORD DARNLEY, attributed to Mary Stuart (Edinburgh, 1567), and THE MURDER OF SIR EDMUND GODFREY, revised and edited by Titus Oates (London, 1678). No novelist has ever succeeded in surrounding a victim with so many suspects and with such variously cogent motives. [Jean-Francois Darlan, a pro-Nazi and one of the highest-ranking officials in France's Vichy government, was assassinated in North Africa on December 24, 1942.]

Frances Crane, THE YELLOW VIOLET (Lippincott, $2). Detective Pat Abbott postpones his marriage to narrator Jean Holly to smash an Italian spy ring in San Francisco. A Spanish diseuse, a dachshund named Pancho and too many corpses are involved in the frantic if somewhat inconclusive goings on.

January 10, 1943

Lawrence Goldman, FALL GUY FOR MURDER (Dutton, $2). Framing Johnny Saturday for murder was only the start of a plot that went on to include a phonily hung jury, a strange religious sect, a brand new trick in drug distribution and even an eclipse of the sun, with another murder timed for total darkness. First rate pulp; incredible, maybe, but fast and skillful and totally enthralling.

Richard Powell, DON'T CATCH ME (Simon & Schuster, $2). Andy and Arab Blake investigate a fake Chippendale and dive into a fabulous complex of antique rackets, Tommy guns and Nazis. Bright and attractive new pair in the damndest goings on since [Elliot Paul's] Homer Evans left Paris.

Erle Stanley Gardner, THE CASE OF THE SMOKING CHIMNEY (Morrow, $2). Frank Duryea, staid, sensible D.A. of Santa Delbarra, again finds his domestic and professional life disrupted by his wife's incorrigible grandfather. Gramps Wiggins (remember THE CASE OF THE TURNING TIDE?) is as racily refreshing as ever, especially on the joys of plain cooking and fancy drinking, but the dull and simple case which he solves is worthy neither of him nor of his creator.

January 17, 1943

Arthur W. Upfield, MURDER DOWN UNDER (Doubleday Crime Club, $2). U.S. debut of Australia's leading mystery writer. Half-caste Inspector Napoleon Bonaparte solves the dual problem of Mr. Jelly, who vanishes regularly and profitably, and Mr. Loftus, who vanished once and fatally. Unusual and timely setting, good puzzle, and unique detective. Long and slow but richly rewarding.

Charlotte Armstrong, THE CASE OF THE WEIRD SISTERS (Coward-McCann, $2). Rich youth has three sisters, respectively blind, deaf and one-armed; one of them is in a hurry to murder him. Quietly effective MacDougal Duff does better than solve the murder; he prevents it. Blend of romance, wit, terror, detection and skilled writing is more engrossing than any dozen corpses.

Garland Lord, MURDER PLAIN AND FANCY (Doubleday Crime Club, $2). Bit actress stranded in Wisconsin looks up her long-lost aunt, to find the aunt a corpse and herself the heir and chief suspect. A fellow actor protects her, but next door lives an enigmatic man....Love story, with occasional murders and no detection.

Louis Trimble, DATE FOR MURDER (Phoenix, $2). Service station man Mark Warren solves lurid killings on Coachella date ranch, featuring unique collection of bedroom-and-bath alibis. Spicy-detective.

January 24, 1943

Elizabeth Daly, NOTHING CAN RESCUE ME (Farrar & Rinehart, $2). Malevolent joker inserts ominous quotations in manuscript of wealthy amateur's novel; Henry Gamadge scents evil and smokes it out after two murders. Interesting people in a civilized and literate novel, with slightly fuzzy solution.

Baynard Kendrick, BLIND MAN'S BLUFF (Little Brown, $2). Blind Captain Duncan Maclain cracks the case of the blind victim and the little mankiller who wasn't there. The usual fascination of Maclain's character and methods, plus a diabolically brilliant and simple new murder device.

Anthony Abbot [Fulton Oursler], THE SHUDDERS (Farrar & Rinehart, $2). The publishers have with great solemnity sworn reviewers not to reveal a word of the plot of this one—a wise gesture of self-protection. You wouldn't believe me if I told you, just as I couldn't believe Mr. Abbot. But Commissioner Thatcher Colt is his usual soigne, capable and pleasing self in this his most perilous and least plausible adventure.

January 31, 1943

George Harmon Coxe, ALIAS THE DEAD (Knopf, $2). Tony Kenyon hires out as substitute for an accidental corpse, not bargaining on deaths that are no accident. Something of a [Cornell] Woolrich shocker, something of straight Hammett, something of a spy meller, and never quite what you think it is.

Van Siller, ECHO OF A BOMB (Doubleday Crime Club, $2). To free from terror the girl he loves, foreign correspondent Bryan Sloane must solve a murder in Virginia and a more tragic death-in-life in a London blitz. Skilled build-up better than crowded explanation; but the publishers don't err in labeling this "a distinguished first."

Peter Cheyney, DARK DUET (Dodd Mead, $2). Three brutally believable novelettes of British counter-espionage, centering around hard Michael Kane and erratic free-Belgian Ernest Guelvada. [E. Phillips] Oppenheim material, but Hammett treatment.

Melba Marlett, ANOTHER DAY TOWARD DYING (Doubleday Crime Club, $2). Ex-schoolteacher Sarah O'Brien sees a murder, but even her policeman husband disbelieves her until she stakes herself out as murder-bait. Clumsy solution and far too much foreboding, but interesting style and details—especially in presentation of the world's first pregnant detective.

Bernard Dougall, THE SINGING CORPSE (Dodd Mead, $2). Politics and swing music make a lethal combination, investigated by publicist Steve Borden. More interesting for backstage gossip on how name bands are born than for its story.

Amelia Reynolds Long, MURDER TO TYPE (Phoenix, $2). Professional Southerner Stephen Carter fights the law to solve murder by blood transfusion. Flat and unprofitable.

February 7, 1943

Carter Dickson [John Dickson Carr], SHE DIED A LADY (Morrow, $2). Suicide pact in 1940 England proves to be murder—if the murderer could have stood on thin air; the great H.M. [Sir Henry Merrivale] investigates, in a wheel chair and a Roman toga. Movingly human story woven around as pyrotechnically dazzling a plot as even Mr. Dickson has ever conceived. Collector's item.

Norbert Davis, THE MOUSE IN THE MOUNTAIN (Morrow, $2). Strand a group of Yanqui tourists in the Mexican hamlet of Los Altos and anything can happen, from casual south-of-the-border killings to a series of cold-blooded murders. Plump and venal detective Doan sorts things out, but the real star is his Great Dane Carstairs. Action, fun, satire and first-rate light writing.

Stewart Sterling, DOWN AMONG THE DEAD MEN (Putnam, $2). Sterling's specialty is the lesser known police squads, here the N.Y. Harbor Police, whose Lieutenant Steve Koski is as hard and shrewd a man as the Finest boasts even in fiction. A torso murder, a ship magnate's family and the submarine menace blend into a biting yarn, fast and tough and terrific.

A.B. Cunningham, THE AFFAIR AT THE BOAT LANDING (Dutton, $2). Deer Lick sheriff Jess Roden solves murder by left-handed stobs [wooden plugs used to keep water out of boat bottoms]. Convincing backwoods people and realistic emotional atmosphere plus Roden's uniquely effective sleuthing. Absorbing despite hold-out of evidence.

Susannah Shane [Harriette Ashbrook], LADY IN A WEDDING DRESS (Dodd Mead, $2). The wedding guests waited impatiently, while the bride bloodily imbrued her wedding dress, finding a freshly murdered body. Tensely emotional story told at furious tempo with adept cinematic technique.

Arthur M. Chase, PERIL AT THE SPY NEST (Dodd Mead, $2). Timid Mr. Purdy tangles with dreadful Nazi saboteurs while the eagle screams. Naive.

February 14, 1943

Matthew Head, THE SMELL OF MONEY (Simon & Schuster, $2). Mrs. Jimson was rich, and collected odd individuals who amused her. The smell of money does something to people, even amusing ones....Singularly well-written and understanding work, with its own bitter honesty and grotesque horror; a major first novel. [San Francisco] Bay Region setting.

Michael Venning [Craig Rice], MURDER THROUGH THE LOOKING GLASS (Coward-McCann, $2). Pulp writer learns abruptly that he has long had a split personality, and his other self is wanted for murder. Quiet, sad, gray detective Melville Fairr helps him reconstruct his alternate life and produces one of the season's most startling surprise solutions to the murder. Intricate and fascinating.

William Francis, BURY ME NOT (Morrow, $2). Corpse vanishes and freshly murdered body replaces it in coffin. Private eye Anthony Martin drinks and leches his way to a solution of sorts. At times very funny; in [Jonathan] Latimer's absence this may do.

February 21, 1943

David Keith [Francis Steegmuller], A MATTER OF ACCENT (Dodd Mead, $2). T.S. Weaver (who was once involved in [Keith's 1940 novel] A MATTER OF IODINE), has his quiet art-dealing life disrupted again, by short wave propaganda and the counterplots of Free French and Vichy-ites. Civilized, unsensational and deeply convincing, this is probably the best spy novel yet with an American setting.

Cornell Woolrich [also known as William Irish and George Hopley], THE BLACK ANGEL (Doubleday Crime Club, $2). Inexperienced girl undertakes to clear her husband, convicted of murder; a word more would be unfair to the book's constantly unfolding surprises. Even Mr. Woolrich has never written a tenser, more jolting novel; if your heart goes no farther than your throat, you're lucky.

William Brandon, THE DANGEROUS DEAD (Dodd Mead, $2). Sam Ireland takes a blackmailing case, is hired by the suspected blackmailer to investigate a murder attempt, and ends up learning how a corpse murdered a mink. Clever plot, convincing atmosphere of winterbound Vermont, good people, and general satisfaction.

Leslie Ford, SIREN IN THE NIGHT (Scribner, $2). When Grace Latham travels, she finds murder the way some people find Burma Shave ads. When she visits S.F. [San Francisco] and General deWitt orders a blackout....well! Colonel Primrose on hand in almost supernaturally good form, but little of Sergeant Buck. Chills, romance, gallantry and humor.

Vera Kelsey, SATAN HAS SIX FINGERS (Doubleday Crime Club, $2). The Ethel Lina White of the Good Neighbor Policy plunges an American heroine into Rio and the terror surrounding a diamond called Satan's Sixth Finger. Cricketers may protest multiple-guilt solution, but there's fine local color and scads of excitement.

Stanley Hopkins, Jr., MURDER BY INCHES (Harcourt Brace, $2). Trojan Horse on Long Island frustrated by affable amateurs. Main novelty, an extraordinary new wartime use for cats. Unassumingly pleasant.

February 28, 1943

Mark Saxton, THE YEAR OF AUGUST (Farrar & Rinehart, $2.50). Adult novel of political intrigue, with no clearcut triumph of virtue and not a single sinister Nazi but with a terribly convincing picture of the threat of the anti-German American fascist. Required reading for more than its very marked values as a subtle thriller.

Chris Massie, THE GREEN CIRCLE (Random House, $2.50). A madman and a murderess tell each other their lives through a long night in which reality and illusion blend inseparably. Extraordinary psychological tour de force, leaving you with a haunting uneasiness.

Alice Tilton [Phoebe Atwood Taylor], FILE FOR RECORD (Norton, $2). Leonidas ("Bill Shakespeare") Witherall escapes from a bread hamper to act as warden in an alarm during which a Mr. Haymaker is murdered in his study with the Samurai sword of the great-great-great-grandfather of the five Lately boys. After that, things begin to get complicated. The fun is wearing a trifle thin in this latest Tilton, but only by comparison with her own best; she's still miles ahead of any competitors in murderous lunacy.

Herman Petersen, THE D.A.'S DAUGHTER (Duell, Sloan & Pearce, $2). Lydia is about 17 and Hank isn't much older, and they're very nice and real young people just like anybody else. Except that Lydia is the D.A.'s daughter, and when the widow who fancies Hank is killed, Lydia starts her own investigation. Novel notion that doesn't quite come off.

March 7, 1943

Vera Caspary, LAURA (Houghton Mifflin, $2.50). Murdered woman comes to life as seen through [Alexander] Woollcott-like friend and the detective who finds himself falling in love with her image. Publishers call this a "psychothriller," vile word, but meaning in this case a connoisseur's item, for those who rejoice in [Raymond] Postgate, [Oscar] Wilde, or [Kenneth] Fearing. Subtle, sinister and swell.

Hannah Lees & Lawrence Bachmann, DEATH IN THE DOLL'S HOUSE (Random House, $2). Six-year-old Mimsy sees her parents shot; resultant psychic block seals up her knowledge. Dr. Black Farragon has a double problem: to clear his best friend of murder and to save the child from a permanent psychosis. Intelligent and exciting.

Dale Clark, FOCUS ON MURDER (Lippincott, $2). Ex-news photog Johnny Kendall shoots small town ax murder for sheriff and finds himself in so deep he has to solve it. Fresh and lively story, novel in plot and technique, with absorbing snatches of killer's diary tucked into narrative. Firstrate first.

Lange Lewis, JULIET DIES TWICE (Bobbs-Merrill, $2). Gigantic Lieutenant Tuck tracks down murderer of campus actress at "Southwest U.," hampered by escaped loonies, amateur and pro psychologists, and a baffling professor of drama. For U.S.C. alumni a grand roman a clef, for others that rarest of mysteries—a really good novel with a university setting.

Jeanette Covert Nolan, FINAL APPEARANCE (Duell, Sloan & Pearce, $2). Lace White attends historic ceremony for dope for novel on Doppelites, but stays to solve murder of Father Moonstone. Interesting background of descendants of typical 19th-century socialist experiment, but first-person is unconvincing as detective and wordy as novelist.

Lawrence Lariar, DEATH PAINTS THE PICTURE (Phoenix, $2). Cartoonists MacAndrew and Bull solve "suicide" of artist for continuity of true-crime comic strip. Commercial art patter affords chief interest in crude opus by *Collier's* cartoonist.

March 14, 1943

Hugh Addis, NIGHT OVER THE WOOD (Dodd Mead, $2). Halfback takes summer job as gardener for unearthly family and bodies start cropping up in the wood. Ordinary plot made fascinating by strange characters and stranger writing, alternating narrative of amateur purple with dialog of eery brilliance. Uneven, but macabre and compelling; watch Mr. Addis!

E.X. Ferrars, NECK IN A NOOSE (Doubleday Crime Club, $2). Toby Dyke and his factotum George (a Lugg [meaning the hulking sidekick in Margery Allingham's novels about Albert Campion] with brains) solve the problem of the corpse without a murder and the murder without a corpse. Pretty puzzle with English setting but American directness.

Aaron Marc Stein, THE CASE OF THE ABSENT-MINDED PROFESSOR (Doubleday Crime Club, $2). Archeologists Tim Mulligan and Elsie Mae Hunt expose academic scandals to save friend who's been framed into believing himself a homicidal maniac. Vitriolic picture of university—which I'm glad I don't recognize.

Philip Wylie, CORPSES AT INDIAN STONES (Farrar & Rinehart, $2). [Clarence Budington] Kellandish archeologist Agamemnon Plum excavates murderer (and love) at swank resort. Slick and smooth, with only flashes of author's attitude to this Generation of Vipers.

Hulbert Footner, DEATH OF A SABOTEUR (Harper, $2). Plump Amos Lee Mappin foils Latvian fascists. Plot has timely angles, but cliche-ridden style and flagrant unfairness make this seem a survival from the 20's.

March 21, 1943

Timothy Fuller, THIS IS MURDER, MR. JONES (Atlantic-Little Brown, $2). Emerson West, the poor man's [Alexander] Woollcott, fakes solution to 100-year-old murder and thereby provides method for his own death. Harvard's Jupiter Jones solves both killings, aided by nitrous oxide and a coast-to-coast hookup. Swift, satiric and satisfying.

Anthony Gilbert, DEATH IN THE BLACKOUT (Smith & Durrell, $2). Shrewd, vulgar Arthur Crook starts with nothing but a mislaid monstrosity of a hat but proves too much for over-clever killer. Realistic study in middle-class murder, with grotesque London characters, sinister suspense and tricky twists.

Christopher Hale, MURDER IN TOW (Doubleday Crime Club, $2). Lieut. Bill French visits Florida for convalescence, but his aunt fishes up a corpse. Nice people, perilous action and bright atmosphere; St. Petersburg Chamber of Commerce should sponsor a reprint edition.

Mabel Seeley, ELEVEN CAME BACK (Doubleday Crime Club, $2). Power-mad, evil woman dominates party at ranch in Grand Teton country. (Twelve ride up mountain for moonlight excursion, and eleven....)

Crammed with excitement and "terror," but as artificial and contrived as it is skilful. Far from another [THE] WHISPERING CUP [also by Seeley, 1940].

Jefferson Farjeon, MURDER AT A POLICE STATION (Bobbs-Merrill, $2). Poetic Sergeant Pork finds stranger's corpse dumped in his charge room; his father Jeremy helps him rattle through the gentry's skeletons to the answer, in dialect that may prove thick going for American readers.

March 28, 1943

Robert Terrall, THEY DEAL IN DEATH (Simon & Schuster, $2). Spanish Relief Administrator Alexander Barker returns to N.Y. for rest, finds himself trapped in Nazi intrigue. But this isn't the same old material; it's new and fascinating stuff on traffic in industrial diamonds, with an approach as fresh as the subject matter. Unusually long, but you're sorry when it's over; for here is the closest there is (?) to an American [Eric] Ambler.

Giles Jackson [also known as Dana Chambers], COURT OF SHADOWS (Dial Press, $2). Semi-pro agent Nile Boyd of G-2-B risks life, limb and love to expose Nazi spy ring in Brooklyn. No novelty or subtlety here, but just an unusually good job of straight formula cops-n-robbers, with everybody turning out to be somebody else. Fun.

R.A.J. Walling, A CORPSE BY ANY OTHER NAME (Morrow, $2). Body burned in blitzed building bears bullet in brain. Mr. Tolefree (now of Special Branch) elucidates with leisured skill and concealed evidence.

Ethel Lina White, PUT OUT THE LIGHT (Harper, $2). Capricious tyranny of village Queen Elizabeth asks for murder and gets it (on p. 221); plodding Superintendent Pye nabs killer, with his sister's [Miss] Marple-ish aid. Solid if soporific.

Ida Shurman, DEATH BEATS THE BAND (Phoenix, $2). Maleficent maestro murdered at mike; doghouse-slapper Jack Coler solves transparent problem. Swing shoptalk sole distinction in hack job.

April 4, 1943

D.B. Olsen [Dolores Hitchens], CATSPAW FOR MURDER (Doubleday Crime Club, $2). Septuagenarian Miss Rachel Murdock and cat Samantha venture into mountains back of San Berdoo to save distinguished heroine from mysterious menace; solid Lieutenant Mayhew has to follow to save Miss Rachel. Usual high-grade Olsen blend of perverse psychology, crawling terror and homey familiarity.

M.P. Rea, DEATH OF AN ANGEL (Doubleday Crime Club, $2). Dunbarton, MacGregor's department store has a new series of murders, this time in the Christmas rush; Lieutenant Powledge sifts the staff's varied emotions to a pretty thin solution. Formula, but pleasantly readable.

Elizabeth Jordan, HERSELF (Appleton-Century, $2.50). Rich young idler probes mysterious epidemic in small town. Date of action is given as 1938—surely a misprint for 1908, when such dull and dated drivel might possibly have been bearable. "Solution" passes belief; my critical ethics have never been so strained as by the desire to reveal that....Well, it isn't that the butler did it; what is the other unpardonable sin?

April 11, 1943

Hugh Pentecost, THE BRASS CHILLS (Dodd Mead, $2). Saboteur uses murder as weapon to plant fear and dissension at Pacific naval repair base; Lieutenant (formerly Inspector) Luke Bradley traps him after frustrated Jap raid. Sharp, fast, exciting yarn, vivid with a refreshingly realistic patriotism.

Margot Neville, LENA HATES MEN (Mystery House, $2). Wealthy voyeuse poisoned by her collection of gilded youth; Inspector Grogan of the Sydney C.I.B. guesses the culprit. Interest of Australian setting and some unusual characters balanced by amateurish writing and feeble construction.

Clifford Knight, THE AFFAIR OF THE JADE MONKEY (Dodd Mead, $2). Or, The Rogers Boy in Yosemite, where Huntoon R. tracks a murderous traitor, finally reads his name in a spy list and thereby deduces his identity. Foot-stirring descriptions of mountain scenes and hikes almost redeem slovenly plot and the season's clumsiest love-relief.

Sada Cowan, BITTER JUSTICE (Doubleday Crime Club, $2). Rich, handsome Latin M.D. framed for chorine's murder; gallant Portia, torn between Latin and husband, clears him in long and unlikely trial. A "glamorous," snobbish, vulgar book, literarily and emotionally on the True Confession level.

April 18, 1943

Craig Rice, HAVING WONDERFFUL CRIME (Simon & Schuster, $2). The irrepressible Justuses (Jake & Helene) and the indispensable Malone (John J.) descend on New York to find a bridegroom in name only and a bride wearing someone else's severed head. The Finest will never be the same again. Rice fans need no urging—and is there any benighted soul who isn't one?

Harriette R. Campbell, MAGIC MAKES MURDER (Harper, $2). Practitioner of serious magic meets "accident" in blitz crater; sleepy, gentle Simon Brade solves pattern with his porcelain clues and then faces moral dilemma. Horror, humanity and logic satisfactorily blended.

Kurt Steel, AMBUSH HOUSE (Harcourt Brace, $2). Hank Hyer, usually as honest as he is mercenary, has to frame a victim to save his fair client. What counts though isn't the plot, nicely twisted as it is, but Angelica, Hank's 9-year-old Spanish refugee, who brings an oddly successful note of sentiment into the hard-boiled Hyer saga.

H.C. Bailey, MR. FORTUNE FINDS A PIG (Doubleday Crime Club, $2). To be exact, Reggie never does find the pig, but in the search he unearths a typhus epidemic among evacuees, a scurrilous London scandal sheet, a survival of pre-Roman worship, and assorted murders, all put to use by a diabolical Quisling. Cryptically sinister.

A.B. Guthrie, Jr., MURDERS AT MOON DANCE (Dutton, $2). Old man Cawinne's boy West comes back from the East to clean up them thar rustlers and breeds. How this routine Western ever got published as a mystery must remain a secret between Dutton and God.

April 25, 1943

Frances & Richard Lockridge, DEATH TAKES A BOW (Lippincott, $2). Jerry North introduces expatriate lecturer on "That Was Paris" only to find lecturer dead from morphine; Pam North and Lieutenant Weigand take over from there. Even meatier and more amusing than most of the superlative North cycle.

Robert Reeves, CELLINI SMITH, DETECTIVE (Houghton Mifflin, $2). Murder in L.A. hobo jungle with tense investigation covering Skid Row—flophouses, B-girls, spielers, burlesque and all. Well in the top bracket of the hard-boiled school; a book as lean and tough and strong as its detective.

Amen Dell, JOHNNY ON THE SPOT (Mystery House, $2). Mistaken identity plunges machinist Johnny Angel into murders and home-grown fascism in Greenwich Village. Solution a let-down, but story is fast, amusing and strongly pro-labor—a rare and needed note in whodunits.

Robert Portner Koehler, STEPS TO MURDER (Phoenix, $2). Isabel Marsh tries to help childhood friend in domestic tangle and witnesses murder of friend's ex-husband. Isabel's suitor, Captain Branson, saves her in nick of time from killer with cleverly simple alibi. Good routine.

Merlda Mace, HEADLONG FOR MURDER (Messner, $2). Christine Anderson, an impetuous dope distinguished even among had-I-but-known heroines, pries into murder and finds romance after an understandable number of attempts on her life and a solution that must have surprised the author.

May 2, 1943

Helen McCloy, DO NOT DISTURB (Morrow, $2). When WAACandidate Edith Talbot heard sobs and then a scream behind the hotel door, she disregarded the "Do Not Disturb" sign; and from that moment her life became a nightmare of flight and terror and distrust. Cannily and sensitively written, with a Hitchcockian sense of the looming menace of everyday details, this startling departure from Miss McCloy's straight detective stories is as exciting a chase novel as has come my way since [Geoffrey Household's] ROGUE MALE.

Anne Hocking, DEATH LOVES A SHINING MARK (Doubleday Crime Club, $2). Sympathetic Oxonian Inspector William Austen, C.I.D., is now Major of Security Police in wartime Cairo, where he encounters the bitter problem of the woman who needed killing and the 2-year-old who didn't. Quietly intelligent story in unfamiliar and vivid setting.

John Rhode, DEAD ON THE TRACK (Dodd Mead, $2). Superintendent Hanslet (testily heckled by Dr. Priestley) patiently breaks down an accident and a suicide into two clever murders. Devotees of ultra-British detection will find a pleasantly solid job (despite dubious statements on ballistics); others beware.

Peter Cheyney, FAREWELL TO THE ADMIRAL (Dodd Mead, $2). Slim Callaghan, the Sam Spade of London, arranges solution to "suicide" that provides him with three fees and a private revenge. Fair ersatz Hammett (more convincing if a single female had a less than superb figure), but not so original as previous Cheyney opuses.

Anne Nash, SAID WITH FLOWERS (Doubleday Crime Club, $2). Two spinster florists in Carmel-like town find friend murdered by nationally famous maniac and begin to wonder about their strange young assistant. Freshness of floral background relieves familiar and feminine story.

Daphne Sanders [also known as Craig Rice and Michael Venning], TO CATCH A THIEF (Dial Press, $2). First episode in the dual career of John Moon, thief-detective, who is a little like [Leslie Charteris'] The Saint, a little like [Maurice Leblanc's] Arsene Lupin, more like [Thomas W. Hanshew's] Cleek of the Forty Faces, and a lot like Superman, only less realistic.

May 9, 1943

Manning Long, FALSE ALARM (Duell, Sloan & Pearce, $2). False alarms play prelude to cyanide on N.Y. ARP Post C-21; redhead Liz Parrott and cat I-Am carry on without husband Gordon (now in G-2). Clever puzzle, surprising if slightly intuitional solution, and invaluable picture of life in March 1942, all in the crisp, sardonic, human and delightful style that's characteristically Long.

Eaton K. Goldthwaite, YOU DID IT (Duell, Sloan & Pearce, $2). When meek Homer (Milquetoast) Adkins' wife ran off with a gangster, the worm turned and planned the perfect crime. What seems at first a middle-class American before-the-fact novel of murder turns and twists itself to include G-men, counterfeiters, crooked boxing and much also not foreseen by Homer, all related with a dryly effective realism. Unusual and absorbing.

Dorothy Dudley & Juanita Sheridan, WHAT DARK SECRET (Morrow, $2). Femme fatale stabbed in practice blackout in pre-war Hawaii; spinster orthodontist helps and hinders charming Chinese sleuth Angie Tudor in delving answer out of past. Humor and atmosphere blend in promising debut, marred only by weak motivation.

Mignon G. Eberhart, THE MAN NEXT DOOR (Random House, $2). Murder, spies, wartime color and romance in Washington. Devout Eberhartians will doubtless revel in this emotion-laden yarn, but Nurse Keate's tart common sense would have been welcome in it.

Eustace L. Adams, DEATH CHARTER (Coward-McCann, $2). Nazi spy charters Diesel yacht for sinister rendezvous off Bahama but is bloodily thwarted by American skipper. Mr. Adams is noted for his adventure stories for boys.

May 16, 1943

Arthur W. Upfield, WINGS ABOVE THE CLAYPAN (Doubleday Crime Club, $2). Mysteriously drugged girl in unpiloted airplane engages attention of half-caste Inspector Napoleon Bonaparte, aided by bush witch doctor Illawalli. More confused and less ingenious plot than MURDER DOWN UNDER, but even richer in fascinating Australian local color.

Erle Stanley Gardner, THE CASE OF THE BURIED CLOCK (Morrow, $2). A clock set to sidereal time, a clever new assistant D.A. and a client who won't talk even to Mason himself add up to Perry Mason's most troublesome case in some time. Pretty slow getting started, but winding up with a courtroom scene quite up to the best Gardner standards.

Jonathan Stagge [also known as Patrick Quentin], THE SCARLET CIRCLE (Doubleday Crime Club, $2). Murderer with passion for graves and moles (which he decorates with lipstick) trapped in New England storm by Dr. Westlake and daughter Dawn, who hasn't grown a month nearer puberty in six years. Overslick writing and simple problem mark a certain falling off in the Stagge line.

McKnight Malmar, NEVER SAY DIE (Coward-McCann, $2). One of those Long Island house parties ends as usual with the murder of hostess; heroine battles gallantly to clear her enigmatic husband. Writing and people pleasing enough to deserve a less cliche-ridden plot.

May 23, 1943

Finlay McDermid, GHOST WANTED (Simon & Schuster, $2). Knifing of blackmailing agent makes suspects of half of Hollywood; Lieutenant Bernal (a West Coast Weigand) tracks trickily simple killer, helped by writer and actress (swell people) and hampered by distractions of December 7, 1941. Bitterly accurate Hollywood milieu, with dialogue and characterization well above average.

George Bellairs, DEATH OF A BUSYBODY (Macmillan, $2). Prying spinster drowned fittingly in vicar's cesspool; Inspector Littlejohn unearths the murderer, and with him all the scandals of Hilary Magna plus a highly respectable religious racket. Unusually adroit and delightful specimen of the English whodunit.

George Childerness, MURDER IN FALSE FACE (Phoenix, $2). Publisher Kent and stooge Phelps (reminiscent of [Rex Stout's Nero] Wolfe-[Archie] Goodwin team) tangle with gangsters, civic reform, blondes and murder. Lively entertainment up to the explanation, which leaves everything a deeper mystery than before.

May 30, 1943

Lucy Cores, PAINTED FOR THE KILL (Duell, Sloan & Pearce, $2). Murder under mudpack in ultra swank Fifth Avenue beauty salon solved by balletomane Captain Torrent and the season's most pleasing amateur stooges. A gay and charming book, filled with well-sketched people, unobtrusively good plotting, and entrancing catty details on the beauty business.

Charles L. Leonard [M.V. Heberden], THE FANATIC OF FEZ (Doubleday Crime Club, $2). Paul Kilgerrin, the most complex character among hard-boiled private eyes, undertakes perilous quest for gas formula in pre-Invasion French Africa. Convincing color, fine plots and counterplots of Gestapo, Ovra, and de Gaullists, and vigorous action. Strong stuff.

Constance & Gwenyth Little, THE BLACK RUSTLE (Doubleday Crime Club, $2). Marina Hays week ends with strange family who set to killing each other off while a rustling ghost walks. Wacky enough, but not especially believable.

Richard Burke, BARBARY FREIGHT (Putnam, $2.50). Mate Bill Mason discovers clever Nazi plot to take over his ship and spends 12 frantic hours frustrating it. Lots of factitious suspense and none of the humor that enlivened Mr. Burke's Quinny Hite stories.

June 6, 1943

Dorothy Cameron Disney, CRIMSON FRIDAY (Random House, $2). Brutal murder of servant and disappearance of garishly mysterious harpist torment close-knit New England family. Dr. Traphaven, connoisseur of crime, dredges up past murders to explain present. Domestic emotions in best Disney manner, plus good new variants on standard tricks.

C.W. Grafton, THE RAT BEGAN TO GNAW THE ROPE (Farrar & Rinehart, $2). Plump young lawyer Gil Henry's first detective case leaves him the most soddenly beaten pulp in fiction, but triumphant over an intricate web of wills, women, murders and cost accounting. For fast, ingenious and humorous action, this Mary Roberts Rinehart prize winner is nominated for junior partner in the legal firm of [Erle Stanley] Gardner & [his pseudonym A.A.] Fair. [C.W.'s daughter Sue Grafton is one of today's best-known mystery writers.]

Cecile Hulse Matschat, MURDER AT THE BLACK CROOK (Farrar & Rinehart, $2). Honeymooning Andrea and David Ramsay (of MURDER IN OKEEFENOKEE) solve needling of heavy in meller revival. Nazis and Japs and orchids and impersonation and oil hijacking and a sinister Major named Cassius are all entangled in a dull and evolved (?) story, with opulent New Orleans atmosphere. Heavy going.

George F. Worts, OVERBOARD (Kinsey, $2). Hyper-slick hammock romance masquerading as spy novel, with transparent plot, fabulous coincidences, lush Hawaiian glamor and a grub-into-butterfly heroine—named, so help me, Zorie Corey.

June 13, 1943

Raymond Postgate, SOMEBODY AT THE DOOR (Knopf, $2). Unpleasant Councillor murdered with poison gas, apparently administered (and it can be done) in a crowded railway carriage. Mr. Postgate dissects the lives of the occupants of the carriage, leading to a logical solution by character. Not quite another VERDICT OF TWELVE, but a penetrating and sometimes brilliant tour-de-force in character study.

Guy Elwyn Giles, TARGET FOR MURDER (Morrow, $2). Stolen jewels, wealthy blondes, an African explorer with a lecture-platform voice, and a grisly series of murders by arrow add up to a headache for insurance investigator Brice Kent, one of the more light-hearted members of the hard-drinking school. Featherweight, but good fun.

June 20, 1943

George Harmon Coxe, MURDER FOR TWO (Knopf, $2). Crusading woman columnist shot—but is it professional or private murder? News photog Flash Casey uses camera and wits to find out, aided by capable Lieutenant Logan and a disconcerting charming AWVS girl. Fast and smooth and tricky.

Lilian Lauferty, THE HUNGRY HOUSE (Simon & Schuster, $2). The House dominates the lives of the Holdens, inbred New England aristocrats, and when Matt Holden proposes to sell the House, he dies. So in turn do his brothers until convalescing prosecutor Tim Dodd learns who is the House's instrument. Grand romantic reading with none of the H.I.B.K. vices, up to denouement that takes a lot of believing.

Amelia Reynolds Long, DEATH WEARS A SCARAB (Phoenix, $2). Mighty Southern Steve Carter investigates maternity claim for wealthy collector of Egyptian items, and the murders begin. There's a mummy's curse mixed up in it too, but you don't need to worry about your blood pressure.

June 27, 1943

Lenore Glen Offord, SKELETON KEY (Duell, Sloan & Pearce, $2). Murder of warden in blackout drags forth all the skeletons in a tight little group in the Berkeley hills and puts another spirited Offord heroine through merry hell. Beautifully intricate murder set-up, well-woven love story and charm and humor in the telling.

Ruth Fenisong, THE BUTLER DIED IN BROOKLYN (Doubleday Crime Club, $2). Accidental killing followed by elaborate murder brings suave Sergeant Gridley Nelson and Negress Sammy to investigate affairs of Manhattan family transplanted to Brooklyn. Pleasantly written novel about nice people, with somewhat chancy solution.

Kathleen Moore Knight, TRADEMARK OF A TRAITOR (Doubleday Crime Club, $2). Young American couple in Panama accidentally become bearers of secret message and frustrate Fascist plot to take over Central America, straightening out their tangled romance the while. Good local color but otherwise pretty familiar.

July 4, 1943

Elizabeth Daly, EVIDENCE OF THINGS SEEN (Farrar & Rinehart, $2). Henry Gamadge, usually the impersonal expert, can hardly be impersonal when the evidence seems to prove either that his wife is mad or that lean brown ghosts can kill. Miss Daly's always skilled writing carries an extra emotional punch in this uncanny tale, cannily told.

A.B. Cunningham, THE GREAT YANT MYSTERY (Dutton, $2). The problem of why anyone should poison a saintly and dying woman is one that Sheriff Jess Roden meets with his usual skill, humanity and understanding of his mountain people. Cunningham's studies in Americana are unique in the mystery field; don't let the corny title scare you off from a high-grade job.

Oliver Weld Bayer, PAPER CHASE (Doubleday Crime Club, $2). Lawyer Jeff Piper investigates death of a client though five states and two affairs, and learns how liverwurst on a roll may mean murder and a uniquely brilliant Nazi plot. The blithest of the season's intrigue yarns, marred only by the tame finale and by the insistence of the whodunit-writing heroine that it's all too unlikely for one of her books.

M.V. Heberden, MURDER GOES ASTRAY (Doubleday Crime Club, $2). Tough Desmond Shannon sets out to trace a missing girl and finds himself up against an entire city—a Jersey burg which is one compact crime ring. Little mystery but lots of excitement in a powerfully sinister set-up.

July 11, 1943

M. Scott Michel, SWEET MURDER (Coward-McCann, $2). Wood Jaxon takes only two killings and one seduction to solve the case of the raped corpses and the stag pictures in Nazi code. Fast, able and entertaining, but a bit strong for some stomachs.

Eden Phillpotts, FLOWER OF THE GODS (Macmillan, $2.25). Eccentric English botanist disappears upon receipt of rare Andean flower; after a year or so a solution is reached, with infinite talk and no action. A doctor's prescription should be required for this powerful soporific.

July 18, 1943

Ngaio Marsh, COLOUR SCHEME (Little Brown, $2.50). Shabby-genteel family running New Zealand spa amasses curious group of guests, from a remittance man to a great actor. Theft of Maori treasures, fifth-column activity and conflict of personalities build to murder in boiling mud-hole, ably solved by one Septimus Falls (who won't go long unrecognized by Marsh fans).

Rufus King, A VARIETY OF WEAPONS (Doubleday Crime Club, $2). Ann Ledrick visits isolated Adirondack esate to photograph ocelots and finds an encore of a 20-year-old murder. Slyly shifting suspense, deft characterization and a convincing aura of diamond-as-big-as-the-Ritz wealth, plus a puzzle of Kingly dexterity.

Eunice Mays Boyd, MURDER BREAKS TRAIL (Farrar & Rinehart, $2). Congressional party on air tour of Alaska marooned in mysteriously abandoned ghost town; Arctic winter brings tension and murder. Ex-grocer F. Millard Smyth elucidates past and present mysteries. Unique setting and pleasant detective in long, slow and none too believable story.

Walbridge McCully, DOCTORS, BEWARE! (Doubleday Crime Club, $2). Psychoanalyst strangled while suicidal glamor girl bares all on confessional couch; D.A. Carey Galbreath investigates. All right if you dote on hospital details and don't mind singularly inefficient medical and police work.

Milton Propper, THE BLOOD TRANSFUSION MURDERS (Harper, $2). Profuse and unlikely gore in Philadelphia hospital, with detective Tommy Rankin as surprised as anybody by the outcome. Impossible in style and substance.

July 25, 1943

Geoffrey Homes, THE HILL OF THE TERRIFIED MONK (Morrow, $2). Ben Logan arrives in Tucson to exploit opening of theater and gets deeply entangled in murder of its ratty manager. Highly attractive people, sun-fresh atmosphere, suave sleuthing by Jose Manuel Madero, incisive humor and sock surprises add up to an unqualifiedly swell job.

Richard Lakin, THE BODY FELL ON BERLIN (Putnam, $2.50). Corpse stowed in bay of Sterling bomber and dumped out over Wilhelm-strasse; RAF Intelligence officer Jasper Doyle follows psychological clues to astonishing solution, with interludes of romance and flight. A first novel by an RAF officer, this is presumably as authentic as it is intelligent, fresh, well written and thoroughly rewarding.

Francis Bonnamy, DEAD RECKONING (Duell, Sloan & Pearce, $2). Murder in the august precincts of the Library of Congress involves maps, pirate treasure and the strange creatures that haunt reading rooms. Sound detection by criminologist Peter Shane, some memorable characters and effective subacid wit, with pseudonymous author Bonnamy as the season's most entertaining Watson.

Cortland Fitzsimmons, TIED FOR MURDER (Lippincott, $2). Helpless "victim" of first-aid class has throat slit in blackout; psychologist Percy Peacock unravels motives in Southern California community. Good enough routine.

Lawrence Lariar, HE DIED LAUGHING (Phoenix, $2). Murderous she-nanigans in animated cartoon studio solved by comic strip artists MacGre-gor and Bull. Inside picture of the home of "Benny the Bear" may hold interest despite formula writing and characters.

August 1, 1943

Agatha Christie, TRIPLE THREAT (Dodd Mead, $2.50). Not a new Christie (as the jacket might suggest), but an omnibus reprint of three books of short stories. [POIROT INVESTIGATES (1925), PARTNERS IN CRIME (1929), and THE MYSTERIOUS MR. QUIN (1930).] The 1924 investigations of M. [Hercule] Poirot creak a little by now; but the half-symbolic interventions of Harley Quin are still vivid, and the adventures of Tommy and Tuppence [Beresford] are still topnotch parodies of the great (including Poirot). Essential classics for your library.

Susannah Shane [Harriette Ashbrook], LADY IN A MILLION (Dodd Mead, $2). Insouciant amateur Christopher Saxe solves case involving a pair of Quiz Kids, a girl who turned down a million dollars, and murder in Times Square on New Year's Eve. Swift and spirited, with likable people and trick solution.

Ruth Darby, MURDER WITH ORANGE BLOSSOMS (Doubleday Crime Club, $2). Bride drops dead en route to altar but fortunately has invited ex-detective Peter Barron and narrator-wife Janet to wedding. Long Island society stuff, slick and relentlessly amusing.

F.V. Morse, BLACK EAGLES ARE FLYING (Doubleday Crime Club, $2). British family inherits Ohio estate plus legacy of revenge and murder, all recounted by nominally male had-I-but-knowner. Insipid writing and corny plot add up to amateurish job.

August 8, 1943

Lawrence Treat, O AS IN OMEN (Duell, Sloan & Pearce, $2). Psychologist Carl Wayward foresaw murder in the week-end party but couldn't guess that the only witness would be a girl who saw it the day before it happened. Psychology, extra sensory perception and good novel writing combined in an odd, fascinating and sometimes disturbing story.

Marion K. Sanders & Mortimer S. Edelstein, THE BRIDE LAUGHED ONCE (Farrar & Rinehart, $2). Stabbing of playboy at ski resort astutely solved by Dr. Seth Noble. Unique among recent debuts in that it's not a farce nor a thriller nor a study in psychology but just a thoroughly sound detective story in the classical mold. Strongly recommended to the formally puzzle-minded and to fans of winter sports.

August 15, 1943

Anna Mary Wells, MURDERER'S CHOICE (Knopf, $2). If your cousin, a diabolically clever mystery novelist, told you he was planning a suicide which would frame you for his murder and then died an apparently natural death, what would be your next move? The answer, a book for fans of Raymond Postgate and Francis Iles, contains highly literate writing, a dazzling triple-reverse solution and an exceptional portrait of a not-too-bright man of good will.

August 22, 1943

Harry Stephen Keeler, THE CASE OF THE TWO STRANGE LADIES (Phoenix, $2). There's no describing a Keeler novel. But if you like him, you'll want to know that his thirty-ninth is shorter than most, is about beheaded corpses and a sage Chinese book, and has the damndest dazzling problem and solution of the year.

Manning Coles, WITHOUT LAWFUL AUTHORITY (Doubleday Crime Club, $2). Amateur cracksman and cashiered British officer join forces for unofficial counterespionage, heckling and helping Tommy Hambledon of the Foreign Office. Amusingly and well written, if episodic and fabulously coincidental, their exploits make a good light meller, miles removed from the magnificent first two Coles novels. [DRINK TO YESTERDAY (1940) and A TOAST TO TOMORROW (1940).]

Sara Elizabeth Mason, MURDER RENTS A ROOM (Doubleday Crime Club, $2). Murders at guest-home of old Alabama family solved by shrewd Sheriff Bill Davies. Not much as a mystery, but a pleasant romance about nice people in a timeless Southern setting.

Monte Barrett, MURDER AT BELLE CAMILLE (Bobbs-Merrill, $2). House party stranded by river rising is confronted with murder and voodoo. Full of Southern atmosphere, wooden characters and every cliche in the trade.

Martha Albrand, WITHOUT ORDERS (Little Brown, $2.50). Captured American officer comes to in Italian sanitarium to find himself identified as insane Veronese aristocrat. Promising idea, totally muffed by purportedly "European" novelist who has a tourist's knowledge of Italy and a hammock's knowledge of writing.

Harry Stephen Keeler, THE CASE OF THE TWO STRANGE LADIES (Phoenix, $2). There's no describing a Keeler novel. But if you don't like him, you'll want to know that his thirty-ninth has three barely connected actions, all execrably written and peopled with stock characters talking phonetically spelled dialects.

August 29, 1943

Vera Kelsey, THE BRIDE DINED ALONE (Doubleday Crime Club, $2). Dana Madison was a charming, spoiled, rationalizing woman who drifted into murder with the same easy grace with which many heroines glide onto the primrose path; but her third husband, even richer than the others, was also harder and wiser. Not strictly a mystery, though as exciting as any such, but rather in the Wilkie Collins tradition of intricate plot-counterplot between strong characters, and not unworthy of the Master.

A.A. Fair [Erle Stanley Gardner], CATS PROWL AT NIGHT (Morrow, $2). Donald Lam is in the South Pacific now, proving as fatal to Japs as he ever was to murderers; and Bertha Cool is entirely on her own, without even his offstage aid. Clumsily, lustily, she cracks her first solo case. The plot's a bit hard to follow and less brilliant than some Donald handled, but Bertha has never been better.

Grace Hoster, GOOD-BYE, DEAR ELIZABETH (Farrar & Rinehart, $2). Lecherous school superintendent dies "natural" death while contemplating phallic flower; teachers present unravel it without police. Odd novel, with picture of small town high school and laudable attempt at multidimensional characters. Nebulous, inconclusive, sometimes corny, but more than a little promising.

Van Siller, GOOD NIGHT, LADIES (Doubleday Crime Club, $2). Lieutenant Pete Rector admitted there are too many women in Washington, but he didn't approve of killing them off and planting them in his bedroom. Some interesting characters, capable writing, and good picture of wartime capital (without spies!) don't quite atone for an unusually banal and unbelievable plot.

September 5, 1943

Kit Christians, DEATH AND BITTERS (Dutton, $2). Stranger in Chicago bar knifed by one of cast of new hit radio show; barkeep Cowboy Peterson uses professional knowledge of drinking habits to spot killer. Familiar basic plot skillfully dressed up with likable people, inside knowledge of radio and bars and unforced brightness. Grade A entertainment.

Octavus Roy Cohen, SOUND OF REVELRY (Macmillan, $2). Dance instructors Steve Harrison and Judy Morgan find love and business a confusing mixture, which gets all the more complicated when you add Nazis, blondes, G-men and assorted murders. Pleasant lightweight mystery-romance.

September 12, 1943

Margaret Millar, WALL OF EYES (Random House, $2). Criminous counterpoint between Toronto underworld and decadent family of wealth deftly resolved by ironic Inspector Sands. Fine psychological novel, rich in subtle overtones and admirable writing, culminating in inevitable but breath-taking solution. More serious in tone than Mrs. Millar's earlier ones, this is equally noteworthy for literary quality and brilliant trickery.

Dorothy B. Hughes, THE BLACKBIRDER (Duell, Sloan & Pearce, $2). Juliet never knew friend from enemy on her terrified flight from New York to Santa Fe; she knew only that she must reach the Blackbirder, legendary smuggler of refugees, and that men who helped her died. Mrs. Hughes turns to her own Southwest for the setting of an ethical melodrama almost as deeply moving as [her 1942 novel] THE FALLEN SPARROW and if anything even more intricately exciting.

Cyril Hare, TRAGEDY AT LAW (Harcourt Brace, $2.50). Threats and accidents dog His Majesty's Judge of Assize on the Southern Circuit and lead to murder in London, solved by Inspector Mallett. Slow, quiet, cumulative novel, distinguished by legal ingenuity, sound characterization and an absorbingly ironic picture of the panoply of British justice.

Brett Halliday, BLOOD ON THE BLACK MARKET (Dodd Mead, $2). Mike Shayne, inexplicably a widower and harder boiled than ever, breaks up the gasoline-rubber racket in Miami. Familiar formula of high-grade tough action.

Mary Reisner, SHADOWS ON THE WALL (Dodd Mead, $2). Fatal "accident" at New England house party solved by chance and D.A. John Dillon. Pretentiously "literary" novel, full of ham emotions, sophomoric philosophy and other excess wordage.

September 19, 1943

George Bellairs, MURDER WILL SPEAK (Macmillan, $2). Twenty-three-year-old murder crops up to complicate Inspector Littlejohn's Christmas vacation. Remember [Bellairs' previous novel] DEATH OF A BUSYBODY? This one has the same meticulous thoroughness, strong characterization, local color and quiet [Angela] Thirkellish wit which put Mr. Bellairs and his Littlejohn well in the top rank of the Scotland Yard school.

Nap Lombard [Pamela Hansford Johnson & Neil Stewart], THE GRIN-NING PIG (Simon & Schuster, $2). Lovely-legged Agnes Kinghof and husband, Captain Andrew (on leave during Sitzkrieg), follow their 'satiable curiosity into the grisly mess of murders committed by one calling himself the Pig-Sticker. Sometimes very funny and/or macabre, but a little long, a little forced and more than a little unbelievable in plot.

Kerry O'Neil, NINTH FLOOR: MIDDLE CITY TOWER (Farrar & Rinehart, $2). Jerry Mooney is the modern Robin Hood of Philadelphia, which is nice work if all your antagonists are dolts and every coincidence breaks in your favor. This episode is something about a ruby and a murder and is as foolish as it is unfair.

September 26, 1943

Note: This column was written by guest reviewer Lenore Glen Offord while Boucher was on a visit to New York.

Ruth Sawtell Wallis, TOO MANY BONES (Dodd Mead, $2). Prize mystery by notably competent newcomer. Against background of anthropology museum whose director is liberally hated by all the employes, intelligent heroine struggles first with enmity, then with suspicion and terror. Gruesome details about preparation of bones aren't stressed but neither are they minimized. Well-prepared climax, literate writing and some authentic shivers.

Norbert Davis, SALLY'S IN THE ALLEY (Morrow, $2). This one's plot is "a trail of mayhem and confusion" (publisher's description; accurate). It's also slick, funny and fast as a good roller-coaster ride. Characters include the dog Carstairs, his reluctant owner Doan, and others, some of them villainous but all goofy. If you take comedy with your thrills, this is your dish.

Lee Thayer, HANGING'S TOO GOOD (Dodd Mead, $2). Notorious meanie found strung up in Connecticut stable. Suicide setup doesn't fool veteran Peter Clancy who, aided by invaluable man Wiggar and likable elderly narrator, rescues the innocent and forces surprise confession. For those who like straight mystery, minus thrills or dividends.

M.P. Rea, BLACKOUT AT REHEARSAL (Doubleday Crime Club, $2). Old photograph album furnishes material for blackmail and before you know it blackmailer dies, surrounded by curious objects. Woman narrator, co-operating with Chief of Police Wilson, learns significance of poultry needle, unsmoked cigarettes and homemade furniture polish. Smooth and straightforward, but explanation thin.

D.B. Olsen [Dolores Hitchens], CAT'S CLAW (Doubleday Crime Club, $2). Miss Rachel Murdock, adventurous spinster, witnesses attack on mysterious stranger, afterward found dead. Lieutenant Mayhew can't keep her from participation in sinister events that follow. Mystery neatly solved, but preview of coming events is so dramatic that their actual performance falls flat.

October 3, 1943

Note: This column was written by guest reviewer Lenore Glen Offord while Boucher was on a visit to New York.

Michael Innes, THE WEIGHT OF THE EVIDENCE (Dodd Mead, $2). Somebody in Nesfield University drops a meteorite on Professor Pluckrose, who once dyed a bust of the Vice-Chancellor bright green. His colleagues, no less eccentric, are subjects of four-star detection by Inspector Appleby, that scholar among Scotland Yarders. As always, comedy and wit are pointed up by suave complexities of Innes style. Required reading for connoisseurs.

Virginia Perdue, HE FELL DOWN DEAD (Doubleday Crime Club, $2). Married in haste, attractive heroine repents in terror as repeated attempts on husband's life gradually reveal that his enemies' hatred is abundantly justified. Expertly handled suspense, sound characterization, fine economy of writing make this a recommended item.

Erle Stanley Gardner, THE CASE OF THE DROWSY MOSQUITO (Morrow, $2). Against desert background, Perry Mason takes his customary liberties with the letter of the law, while solving riddles of wealthy mining man's will, arsenic, gunshots and curiously unenterprising mosquitoes. Usual Gardner slickness, sudden plot twists and bewildering speed; unusually rewarding dividends about lost mines.

Marion Holbrook, WANTED: A MURDERESS (Dodd Mead, $2). Salem Peabody, nice girl so courageous as to be almost foolhardy, gets mixed up in sinister events on island in Lake Champlain. No dull moments, what with threats, military secrets, abductions and five violent deaths. Sheriff Bone arrives at correct solution and resigns his job; read it and see why.

H.F.S. Moore, DEATH AT 7:10 (Doubleday Crime Club, $2). Unpleasant woman dies of slow-acting poison. Inquisitive amateur Mark Kent reconstructs fatal last day of her life and traps killer through clairvoyance rather than logic, while police stand by marveling. Interesting device presented in unconvincing language.

Isabel Waitt, DEATH A LA KING (Phoenix, $2). Who poisoned the novocaine just before Grandma King had a tooth extracted, or do you care? Mystery-writer Victor Quade manages to discover answer after second murder occurs. Poverty-stricken writing does nothing to help this one.

October 10, 1943

Leslie Charteris, THE SAINT STEPS IN (Doubleday Crime Club, $2). The ungodly are now at work sabotaging the rubber program, but they reckon without a Saint who has all his old dash and skill plus a new political maturity. As colorful and exciting as any Saint story, and most interesting as evidence that Times Like These can make even Simon Templar grow up.

Lange Lewis, MEAT FOR MURDER (Bobbs-Merrill, $2). Vegetarian Hollywood phony's eccentricities lead to mass murder, unraveled by bulky Lieutenant Tuck. At times a bit strained, but fantastic and fascinating, with one of the year's most ingenious poisoning setups.

John Spain [Cleve F. Adams], DEATH IS LIKE THAT (Dutton, $2). The entire surviving cast of [the 1942 Spain novel] DIG ME A GRAVE, starring cynical Bill Rye, tangles with more L.A. politics and murder; the cast will be much smaller next time. Better-than-average hard stuff, but more routine than the unforgettable first Spain.

Anthony Gilbert, THE WOMAN IN RED (Smith & Durrell, $2). The woman in red is an evil eccentric who hires a girl as secretary, then tries to change her identity and drive her mad. Shifting viewpoints and anticlimactic explanations sap the magic that a [Cornell] Woolrich could have given to the idea. But solid, vulgar Arthur Crook remains one of the most interesting modern detectives.

Merlda Mace, MOTTO FOR MURDER (Messner, $2). This is one about the arrogant matriarch and the snow-bound family avid for her money. The hack formula has rarely been handled with less distinction.

October 17, 1943

Mitchell Wilson, STALK THE HUNTER (Simon & Schuster, $2). I hate to say a word about the plot of this one because from page five on you're in for a series of the finest coups de theatre that ever left you groggy. Let's just say that it's about the Gestapo vs. the Czech underground in New York, and that Mr. Wilson knows how to write and how to fill the perils of his heroine with a magic of terror that will make you shudder anew every time you see an art museum or a record shop or a starlit beach.

Ursula Parrott, ISLAND OF FEAR (Dodd Mead, $2). Two gilded parasites, kidnaped by Nazis on Vichy-held Caribbean island, grow to emotional and patriotic maturity. Economical novelet with no purple patches; decidedly above-average hammock romance.

Marion Strobel, ICE BEFORE KILLING (Scribner, $2). Teen-age Chicago skater suspected of poisoning her father's mistress, saved by murderer's obliging confession. Amateurish job crowded with unpleasant people and unbelievable events but notable for a good deal of adolescent understanding and an occasional jolt of pure nightmare horror.

George Harmon Coxe, MURDER IN HAVANA (Knopf, $2). Engineer Andy Talbot makes valiant singlehanded try at curbing Axis activities in Cuba. Highly professional job, but about as original and imaginative as its title.

Robert Portner Koehler, SOME TRY MURDER (Phoenix, $2). Pecos Appleby hunts smuggled aliens at New Mexico border and finds disappearing corpses. Pretty neat in plot, but something less than abForBhidips Oppenheim, MR. MIRAKEL (Little Brown, $2). This mad marvel starts with the usual well-groomed espionage, plunges into Lotos Land fantasy and ends up with a world cataclysm. Written by talents as diverse as Michael Innes or M.P. Shiel it could have been something to cheer about; written by Oppenheim it turns out pure nonsense, with much choice if unintended comedy.

October 24, 1943

Peter Cheyney, THE STARS ARE DARK (Dodd Mead, $2). Cumulative episodes in the undercover, unofficial secret service of Britain, with perceptive illumination of the lives of the men and women working in it, all tautly and brilliantly written by the only successful British follower of Hammett. Even better than [his previous thriller] DARK DUET, this puts Mr. Cheyney right up there with the best of Manning Coles.

Herman Petersen, OLD BONES (Duell, Sloan & Pearce, $2). Discovery of long-dead bones in old mill starts fresh murders and general hell, which sagacious Doc Miller puts an end to. The most exciting and satisfying of Mr. Petersen's adeptly written pastorals.

Mary Collins, THE SISTER OF CAIN (Scribner, $2). Arrival of pregnant Navy wife in S.F. [San Francisco] precipitates murders among her in-laws, a set of sisters beside whom the Papins [a pair of sadistic French murderesses who are the subject of an essay in Boucher's 1943 anthology THE POCKET BOOK OF TRUE CRIME STORIES] radiate innocent charm. All-female cast, aside from lawyers and hard-working detective Cassidy. Modernized [Mary Roberts] Rinehart and excellent, up to unpardonable chance solution.

Ethel Lina White, THE MAN WHO WAS NOT THERE (Harper, $2). Reunion of college group (quaintly self-titled Seven Sullied Souls) dampened by evil genius bent on indiscriminate murder. Set in grisly confines of private zoo, this gets off to a fine start but peters out in long series of anti-climaxes.

Clifford Knight, THE AFFAIR OF THE FAINTING BUTLER (Dodd Mead, $2). A glamorous slick writer, a literarily minded butler and poisoned vitamin pills start murder popping right in Huntoon Rogers' back yard. More lively and readable than most Knight, but the nebulous Mr. Rogers' solution is as pure guesswork as ever.

Alfred Eichler, MURDER IN THE RADIO DEPARTMENT (Gold Label, $2). Murder and sex in radio dept. of large advertising agency, straightened out by copywriter Martin Ames. Ames' approach to murder through sales technique is interesting; otherwise straight run-of-the-mill.

October 31, 1943

Phoebe Atwood Taylor, GOING, GOING, GONE! (Norton, $2). The first full-length Asey Mayo in far too long starts out about an auction in which a corpse turns up. From then on it involves commandos, ration boards, pink seashells and general Cape Coddments, in such a vein of sprightly madness that one suspects the collaboration of [her pseudonym] Alice Tilton. Completely delightful—enough so even to make me forgive a shamelessly suppressed vital clue.

Phyllis A. Whitney, RED IS FOR MURDER (Ziff-Davis, $2). The lives, loves and deaths of the display department of a large Chicago department store, straightened out by Sylvester Hering, store detective. Transparently familiar as a mystery but highly readable as the blithely told inside story of a mad profession.

Garland Lord, MURDER WITH LOVE (Morrow, $2). Family reunion sours into murders for which our heroine gets framed. Well-sketched characters, lively dialog and lots of love; fine fare for romance readers who can overlook slovenly detection and multiple-guilt plot.

Sax Rohmer, SEVEN SINS (McBride, $2.50). No Fu Manchu, but mummies, murder, roulette, spies and mysticism make a heavy brew for fighting French detective Gaston Max. Nonsense but fairly good fun.

Amelia Reynolds Long, THE TRIPLE CROSS MURDERS (Ziff-Davis, $2). Ted Trelawney investigates highly complex insurance fraud among Philadelphia medicos. Admirably intricate plot marred by characterless writing and careless deductions.

November 7, 1943

Raymond Chandler, THE LADY IN THE LAKE (Knopf, $2). No plot summary can do justice to a Chandler. So Philip Marlowe, L.A. shamus, takes another case and has his troubles and cracks it. What matters is the insight you get into the places he sees and the people he meets and the magnificent clean prose in which it's all told. Chandler has taken the best of Hammett and added a touch of a poet like Kenneth Fearing. You won't find a better hard-boiled mystery novel this year—nor many better novels, unqualified.

Muriel Stafford, X MARKS THE DOT (Duell, Sloan & Pearce, $2). Drab little stranger murdered in a newspaper office; victim identified and murderer trapped through all but superhuman abilities of handwriting analyst Stafford. Passable story, adorned with specimens of all characters' handwriting and fascinating lore of graphology. The best piece of trick gadgetry since the Crimefiles.

Arthur W. Upfield, THE MYSTERY OF SWORDFISH REEF (Doubleday Crime Club, $2). Halfcaste Inspector Napoleon Bonaparte deserts the bush to track a murderer at sea. More about swordfishing than murder, but salty, detailed and full of surprising new side lights on the most interesting of recent detectives.

Patricia Wentworth, MISS SILVER DEALS IN DEATH (Lippincott, $2). The assorted inhabitants of Vandeleur House flats have quite enough problems of love, finance and character to hold the interest without murder, but murder enters, and with it spinsterish Miss Silver. Pleasant English sentimental novel, with slightly foolish mystery plot.

Jo Eisinger, THE WALLS CAME TUMBLING DOWN (Coward-McCann, $2). Acidulous gossip-scribe D'Arcy turns sleuth to avenge murder of aged priest; fair damsel, sinister henchman and rare Bibles are involved. Uneven, but well plotted and rising to frequent heights in both tough action and sardonic dialogue.

Theodora Du Bois, THE WILD DUCK MURDERS (Doubleday Crime Club, $2). Anne and Jeffrey McNeill chase murderous fifth columnists in university. Singularly unexciting spy story, with a plot as muddled as its ideology and a solution involving no less than three separate murderers.

November 14, 1943

John Stephen Strange, LOOK YOUR LAST (Doubleday Crime Club, $2). There are three novels here: one, a world-wide web of intrigue involving cartels, Rudolf Hess, the Moscow trials and our own Fascists; two, the private murder tying in to the vast supermurder, which Barney Gantt cracks efficiently; and three, a picture of those days in 1941 when there was so little time to look your last on all things lovely. All three are high-grade stuff.

Mignon G. Eberhart, UNIDENTIFIED WOMAN (Random House, $2). Murders past and present disrupt wedding and army routine at Florida training camp; ex-D.A. Major John Campbell handles both love interest and detection satisfactorily. Puzzle, glamor, terror and romance blended into admirable dish.

Carey Magoon, I SMELL THE DEVIL (Farrar & Rinehart, $2). Medievalist Adelaide Stone borrows Cyprian's sermons from Cowabet College rare book room and murders ensue until Sergeant Morningstar traps killer. Slow pleasant story of spinsters in graduate research, with unexplained occult overtones and the year's most unbelievable murderer.

Philip M. Fisher, VANISHING SHIPS (Mill, $2.50). Eighteen cargo ships vanish into thin air; Lieutenant (j.g.) Bill Devon scents the answer but uncovers an even more fabulous plot than he expected. Some banal writing (including a weird new theory of the Jap accent) counterbalanced by stirring action, imaginative villainy and a splendid set of deep-dyed heavies.

Ione Sandberg Shriber, INVITATION TO MURDER (Farrar & Rinehart, $2). Wealthy retired Lieutenant Bill Grady finds startling solution to poisoning affair among wealthy Clevelanders, as related by wealthy and wordy heroine, who just will tell lies to the police, but comes forth with such truths as "I had the sick sensation that I was behaving like every foolish heroine in any detective story."

November 21, 1943

Dashiell Hammett, BLOOD MONEY (Tower, 49 cents). First clothbound edition of the 1927 pulp novel resurrected earlier this year as a Bestseller paperback. Setting: San Francisco. Detective: the Continental Op. Subject: bank robbery and murders innumerable. Authentic vintage Hammett, topping 99% of the 1943 hard-boiled school.

Allison Holt, BIER FOR A HUSSY (Phoenix, $2). Murders in Jersey shore colony solved by affable Lieutenant Fitzpatrick. Unassumingly pleasant if a bit nebulous in its detection.

Miles Burton [also known as John Rhode], WHO KILLED THE DOCTOR? (Doubleday Crime Club, $2). The squire knew very well the doctor was murdered, but hang it, the johnny was a foreigner and investigation might upset the gentry. The second victim is a lady, however, so Inspector Arnold and Desmond Merrion find the murderer, who obligingly belongs to the lower classes. Ammunition for Anglophobes.

Kootz, PUZZLE IN PAINT (Crown, $2). Pint-sized Jason Emory investigates murders and fake Cezannes. Novel: alternate layers of glib art patter and somewhat sickening drunken sex. Mystery: I cannot recall in the $102^1/_2$ years of the mystery story such a flagrant example of the total suppression of all evidence until after the denouement.

November 28, 1943

Craig Rice, THE THURSDAY TURKEY MURDERS (Simon & Schuster, $2). Bingo and Handsome, those most innocent of city slickers, whom you'll remember from THE SUNDAY PIGEON MURDERS, land in an Iowa small town and fall victim to everything from escaped convicts to the farmer's daughter—incidentally solving a few murders and picking up two grand. Joyous cause for thanksgiving—what might happen if [William] Saroyan had plot sense.

Boris Karloff (editor), TALES OF TERROR (Tower, 49 cents). Tower Books set a bogyman to catch bogymen, with excellent re-sults—mixture of sound classics ([Ambrose] Bierce, [Bram] Stoker, [Oliver] Onions) and first-rate novelties ([Philip] MacDonald, [Robert Hugh] Benson, [Helen A.] Hull), plus intelligent and stimulating introduction.

Will Cuppy (editor), WORLD'S GREAT DETECTIVE STORIES (Tower, 49 cents). Conservative collection of exploits of great detectives. Choice sometimes rather dubious (e.g., [Dorothy L.] Sayers) or overfamiliar (e.g., [Dashiell] Hammett), but on the whole a good selection—if it's your first detective anthology.

December 5, 1943

Ruth Fenisong, MURDER RUNS A FEVER (Doubleday Crime Club, $2). White-headed Sergeant Gridley Nelson, one of this department's favorite gentleman coppers, solves murder of radio commentator and breaks up minor spy ring by rediagnosing a case of encephalitis. Pleasant people and easy skillful story-telling, if based on a couple of pretty fearful coincidences.

Dean Hawkins, WALLS OF SILENCE (Doubleday Crime Club, $2). After 200 Victory-format pages of Southern atmosphere and talk about a six-year-old murder, crammed with every cliche of plot and style, our hero tells each of five suspects that his guilt is discovered and he'd best commit suicide, so one of them does and that's that.

December 12, 1943

Elisabeth Sanxay Holding, THE OLD BATTLE-AX (Simon & Schuster, $2). The latest of the superlative Holding studies in psychological suspense involves a widow of staid integrity, an amoral returned expatriate, a macabre masquerade, and the most subtly horrible killer since Miss Holding's own [1938 novel] THE OBSTINATE MURDERER. Terrifying and terrific.

Helen McCloy, THE GOBLIN MARKET (Morrow, $2). American correspondent in banana republic investigates death of predecessor and unearths oil cartels and Falangists. McCloy brings to spy meller the same meticulous plotting and intelligent writing that mark her straight whodunits.

A.L. Furman (editor), THE MYSTERY COMPANION (Gold Label, $2.75). Unusual collection of pulp material never before published in book form, ranging from the purest hack to small masterpieces by Cornell Woolrich and Geoffrey Homes. A set of stories with Spanish "color" are unfalteringly illiterate but are balanced by first rate American by [Robert] Bloch, [Dale] Clark, [Fritz] Leiber and [Vincent] Starrett. The season's most uneven but also most unhackneyed anthology.

December 19, 1943

Margaret Echard, BEFORE I WAKE (Doubleday Crime Club, $2). Invalided Guadalcanal hero finds his lost memory in unraveling the secret of woman writer's sudden death and sinister life. Interesting people, unusual psychology and sound picture of Southern California suburb.

Doris Miles Disney, A COMPOUND FOR DEATH (Doubleday Crime Club, $2). Leisurely, detailed story of New England murder investigation (one victim is named Steve Fisher! [author of I WAKE UP SCREAMING and other noir thrillers]) by capable county detective Jim O'Neill. Publishers call it a "chess puzzle," but the reader is asked to play blindfolded. (Deepest mystery: the meaning of the title.)

Christopher Hale, HANGMAN'S TIE (Doubleday Crime Club, $2). Lieutenant Bill French stooges for domineering female politician in routine murder episode. Competent but unexciting; the Lieutenant has done better in solo efforts.

Garnett Weston, THE MAN WITH THE MONOCLE (Doubleday Crime Club, $2). Young archaeologist with marked resmblance (especially mental) to Superman pursues the Papers, the Girl, and a 1917-vintage Prussian. The setting is labeled America but is obviously Ruritania. Naive and glamorous.

December 26, 1943

No column was published this week.

1944

January 2, 1944

Frances Crane, THE APPLEGREEN CAT (Lippincott, $2). You expect murder on an English week-end party, but imagine killing the maids with the servant problem what it is! Marine Intelligence officer Pat Abbott intervenes ably. Nice quiet writing, interesting people and a well-conceived murder.

E.P. Fenwick, THE INCONVENIENT CORPSE (Farrar & Rinehart, $2). Columnist brings his mistress to reunion of old school friends, who embarrass him by hammering her skull in. Easy to read, unconvincing in characterization and solution.

January 9, 1944

Elizabeth Daly, ARROW POINTING NOWHERE (Farrar & Rinehart, $2). Henry Gamadge answers cryptic appeals of unknown "client," held prisoner in a respectable New York family, and murders ensue. Slow development, intuitional detection and hard to swallow plot pull this somewhat below Miss Daly's usual high standard, but she still writes politely and well.

January 16, 1944

Kathleen Moore Knight, DESIGN IN DIAMONDS (Doubleday Crime Club, $2). Dutch diamonds and German agents in a Mexican setting that rings true, with Margot Blair as narrator (topnotch) and detective (fallible). Vivid and startling spy meller.

Roman McDougald, THE DEATHS OF LORA KAREN (Simon & Schuster, $2). A guilt fixation, a menacing midget and a lethal dose of atropine make an eerie problem for Philip Cabot. Confusing start and somewhat sketchy characterization are more than atoned for by admirably tricky plot and sense of lurking terror.

Marion Bramhall, MURDER SOLVES A PROBLEM (Doubleday Crime Club, $2). Doctor's daughter and clean, strong young professor meet, love, part and are united after a couple of intrusive murders are crudely cleaned up.

January 23, 1944

Kay Boyle, AVALANCHE (Simon & Schuster, $2.50). So you didn't expect Kay Boyle in this department? Neither did I; but this story of an American girl caught up in the Gestapo vs. Underground duel in the French Alps is simple, moving and beautiful, and at the same time as suspensefully contrived as the best professional thrillers. One of the most distinguished espionage novels to date.

Georges Simenon, ESCAPE IN VAIN (Harcourt Brace, $2.50). Two short novels of retribution by futility. Murder (in THE LODGER) and petty rackets (in ONE WAY OUT) only rivet men more firmly to their sordid existences. Drab, pitiful and deeply moving, told with all the skill of Simenon's economical realism. (Translated by Stuart Gilbert.)

J.J. Connington, JACK-IN-THE-BOX (Little Brown, $2). A cursed Viking hoard, a Liberian occultist and three splendid new murder methods make a pretty puzzle for Sir Clinton Driffield. Flawless specimen of detailed British school.

Robert Goffin, THE WHITE BRIGADE (Doubleday Doran, $2). Belgium's leading mystery novelist offers the saga of the Belgian Underground, a stirring story weakened by the awkward treatment which is half-novel, half-documentary. Valuable and authentic, but the same material was much better handled in Katharine Roberts' PRIVATE REPORT. (Translated by Charles Lam Markmann.)

H.W. Roden, YOU ONLY HANG ONCE (Morrow, $2). Public relations counsel John Alden Knight finds corpses and gangsters in his office but drinks his way out. Capable if conventional hardboiled job, tainted by the author's contempt for what he calls "yids."

Amelia Reynolds Long, DEATH HAS A WILL (Phoenix, $2). Steve Carter draws a will and solves the murders it causes. Routine job; plot fairly good, writing fairly bad.

January 30, 1944

Michael Brandon, NONCE (Coward-McCann, $2.50). One of the strangest of murder novels, with an uncondensable plot involving witchcraft and an eerie new motive and written with a fury that carries you into weird regions of sex and madness. Unclassifiable, violent and compelling.

Kelley Roos, SAILOR, TAKE WARNING! (Dodd Mead, $2). Murder in the Central Park model boat coterie solved by Jeff and Haila Troy, at the present moment this department's favorites in the Bright Young Couple race. Airtight puzzle, convulsingly plausible dialogue and grand fun for all.

M.V. Heberden, TO WHAT DREAD END (Doubleday Crime Club, $2). External tension of blitz and internal tension of emotional conflict build to murder in English doctor's household. First-rate character study and love story distinguish deliberately simple mystery.

Susannah Shane {Harriette Ashbrook], THE BABY IN THE ASH CAN (Dodd Mead, $2). Christopher Saxe finds an heiress, a baby, a corpse and, in due time, a murderer. Featherweight and fast, with amusing action and morally dubious denouement.

Constance & Gwenyth Little, THE BLACK HONEYMOON (Double-day Crime Club, $2). Medical murders in mad menage, solved by nurse-heroine and an unlikely lout named Kelly. Many people find the Littles hilarious.

February 6, 1944

Donald Henderson, MR. BOWLING BUYS A NEWSPAPER (Random House, $2). Mr. Bowling, a failure as a musician and as a man, finds success in a complexly motivated series of apparently motiveless murders. Sardonic study in personalities and wartime life which only the hard-to-swallow ending keeps from a place, not so much beside Francis Iles as beside Jules Romains' Quinette episodes—fictional murder more terribly true than [true crime writer William] Roughead.

Frances & Richard Lockridge, KILLING THE GOOSE (Lippincott, $2). Lieutenant Weigand finds himself working on two cases at once until Pam North proves they're one. Rather more sober and even sinister than most North episodes (though panickingly perverse in spots), with an excellent murderer, a frantic finale, suggestive political overtones and a slightly muddy plot.

Erle Stanley Gardner, THE D.A. CALLS A TURN (Morrow, $2). Thanksgiving Day "accident" means murder to Doug Selby, who can always pick a murderer but still can't choose between the girl reporter and the lady lawyer. A bit too much luck in the solution, but the usual fine Gardner counterplots and superb tempo.

E.R. Punshon, THE CONQUEROR INN (Macmillan, $2). Unidentified corpse and 2000-pound notes lead Inspector Bobby Owen to black market and I.R.A. plots. Pretty slow going, but rewarding for its solid construction and the distinguished characterization of an Irish "patriot."

BEST BUYS IN REPRINTS. John Dickson Carr, THE CROOKED HINGE (Popular Library, 25 cents); Freeman Wills Crofts, TRAGEDY IN THE HOLLOW (Popular Library, 25 cents); Dashiell Hammett, RED HARVEST (Pocket Books, 25 cents); Dorothy B. Hughes, THE FALLEN SPARROW (Dell, 25 cents).

February 13, 1944

Carter Dickson [John Dickson Carr], HE WOULDN'T KILL PA-TIENCE (Morrow, $2). Two young magicians assist H.M. [Sir Henry Mer-rivale] in investigating the murder of a zoo director and nearly lose their own lives in the snake house. The murder happens in positively the most hermetically sealed room on record, and the solution is as dazzlingly sim-ple as the snake scenes are nerve-twisting. There's love too, and gags, and the Blitz—in short, just about everything, if the snakes aren't too much for you.

Irene Cleaton, THE OUTSIDER (Little Brown, $2). That rarest find, a period mystery novel, set in murky, reeky 1820 Edinburgh, where a gay London girl finds her dour Scots relatives enmeshed in tragedies recalling such great Scottish names as William Burke and Deacon Brodie. Excellent atmosphere and period sense lift run-of-the-mill plot and writing to a col-lector's item.

Frederick C. Davis, LET THE SKELETONS RATTLE (Doubleday Crime Club, $2). Cy Hatch's honeymoon leads him into a deadly family set-up in Pennsylvania, where the natural deaths are even more terrible than the murders. More bucolic and human than Hatch's New York epi-sodes but just as spirited.

Anthony Gilbert, A SPY FOR MR. CROOK (Barnes, $2). M.P.'s battle for constituent's pension leads him into spy plot; his doughty secretary and Arthur Crook get him out. The plot on reflection makes little sense, but it swings along rapidly and the satiric sidelights on Parliament and war-time bureaucracy are a joy.

H.C. Bailey, THE QUEEN OF SPADES (Doubleday Crime Club, $2). The strongest admirers of Mr. Bailey's short stories are more reserved about his novels, and even those who like the [Reggie] Fortune novels may hesitate about those starring Joshua Clunk. This current Clunker is some-thing about spies and black market and many murders, all pretty confused. (English title: SLIPPERY ANN.)

Colin Curzon, THE CASE OF THE EIGHTEENTH OSTRICH (Mac-millan, $2). Another long and frantic spy farce by "the leading humorist of the R.A.F.," in which Mark Antony and Tinka, abetted this time by an American officer, pursue stuffed ostriches with The Papers in them. The R.A.F.'s taste in humor, as befits men of action, is practical, elementary and heartless.

BEST BUYS IN REPRINTS. Nicholas Blake, THE BEAST MUST DIE (Black Cat, 25 cents); John Dickson Carr, THE THREE COFFINS (Bestseller, 25 cents).

February 20, 1944

Craig Rice, HOME SWEET HOMICIDE (Simon & Schuster, $2). This is about a woman mystery novelist with three pseudonyms and three children and any resemblance to Craig Rice and her offspring is purely photographic. Except that the younger Rices never lived next door to a murder and solved it while marrying Mother off to the detective lieutenant. Children as lovable as your own and as infuriating as the ones next door (or vice versa) in a story that will warm every last cockle in your heart.

James Norman, AN INCH OF TIME (Morrow, $2.50). American jade merchant tracks down heroin smuggling in occupied China, helped and hampered by a Mexican guerrilla, a beautiful Eurasian named Mountain of Virtue, and a puppet General who collects (and eats) 100-year-old eggs. Local color vivid, characterizations subtle, plots intricate—Eric Ambler cum Milton Caniff.

Carl Randau & Leane Zugsmith, THE VISITOR (Random House, $2). Murder victim returns to life—or is he an impostor? Even the boy's own mother has her doubt, while the divided opinions of his friends and the citizenry build up what is at once a pleasing small town novel and a clever trick mystery. Sort of Murder in Our Town [referring to the play by Thornton Wilder]—an agreeable novelty.

Brett Halliday, MICHAEL SHAYNE'S LONG CHANCE (Dodd Mead, $2). Mike Shayne moves to New Orleans to guard a lush heiress who is promptly murdered. Crooked police, sex rackets, Louisiana color and lots of cognac add up to the fastest and trickiest Shayne opus yet.

Denis Scott, MURDER MAKES A VILLAIN (Bobbs-Merrill, $2). Whimsical Mike James encounters murder of a Borgian actress while trailing a fake Menander manuscript. Pleasantly written, but a bit clumsy in plot and humor.

Pelham Groom, MOHUNE'S NINE LIVES (Liveright, $2). Squadron Leader Peter Mohune (pronounced, of course, Moon) crashes in Europe, foils the Gestapo, escapes to England, exposes the fifth column, frustrates Hitler's second invasion attempt and wins a lovely Czech. Naive and amateurish but rather appealingly so, with authoritative descriptions of operations rooms and dog fights.

BEST BUYS IN REPRINTS. William Irish [Cornell Woolrich], PHANTOM LADY (Tower, 49 cents); Gypsy Rose Lee [ghosted by Craig Rice], MOTHER FINDS A BODY (Tower, 49 cents).

February 27, 1944

Dana Chambers, THE LAST SECRET (Dial Press, $2). Jim Steele, now hush-hush Government agent, is dragged into Nazi schemes to trap scientist who has at last harnessed atomic power. Part spy story, part deductive mystery, part science fiction, part anti-appeasement propaganda; breath-less, bloody and beautiful in all departments.

North Baker & William Bolton, DEAD TO THE WORLD (Doubleday Crime Club, $2). Intern Danny Michaels recognizes a floater in the Chi-cago morgue, thereby exposing a complex mesh of fraud, gangsters and leprosy. At once hard-boiled and human, lively and likable, this is the most interesting debut so far this year. More Michaels, please!

Jerome Barry, LADY OF NIGHT (Doubleday Crime Club, $2). "Dame de Noche" was the name of a best-seller, a perfume and an apparent mur-deress; ex-soda-jerk Chick Varney tells the story in glib drugstore patter, with strange dope on Philippine customs. Bright as a new penny, and just about as deceptive.

Bruno Fischer, THE HORNETS' NEST (Morrow, $2). Ex-reporter Rick Train has to discover which of three well-curved claimants inherits an es-tate and which is trying to murder him; he succeeds amid plentiful carnage from New York to Florida. Satisfactory new entry for medium-tough stakes.

William Irish [Cornell Woolrich], DEADLINE AT DAWN (Lippincott, $2). Small-town boy and girl have three hours to escape from New York and clear themselves of murder of total stranger, without police and almost without clues. The author's most contrived and least believable story yet, and still magically exciting almost against one's judgment.

Helen Reilly, THE OPENING DOOR (Random House, $2). Inspector McKee solves another killing among the rich, pampered and emotional. Murder-romance complete with sinister foreshadowings, strange ethics and half-witted heroine.

March 5, 1944

Raymond Chandler, FIVE MURDERERS (Avon, 25 cents). Not a re-print but first book-appearance of five novelets from *Black Mask*, concern-ing an assortment of private eyes and many more than five killers. Some of the most hardbitten writing and memorable carnage you're apt to find anywhere, with at least one story ("Nevada Gas") fully on the level of the Chandler novels.

Leigh Brackett, NO GOOD FROM A CORPSE (Coward-McCann, $2). Bashing of night-club singer starts long chain of murders; private eye Ed-mond Clive loved and avenges her. Something less than Chandler but much above average in the hard school, with believably real Los Angeles setting.

Harry Stephen Keeler, THE CASE OF THE LAVENDER GRIPSACK (Phoenix, $2). America's foremost craniophile has produced another wild phantasmagoria about the adventures of a skull, this time in a most irregu-lar Chicago courtroom. The manuscript has apparently been hacked by the publisher [in fact the novel only seemed cut because it was part of a tetralogy whose previous installments—THE MAN WITH THE MAGIC EARDRUMS (1939), THE MAN WITH THE CRIMSON BOX (1940) and THE MAN WITH THE WOODEN SPECTACLES (1941)—dated before Boucher's reviewing years]; what remains still displays the incredibly fertile imagination and equally incredible bad writing of all Keeler. For devotees only (which includes, I confess, me).

Dorothy B. Hughes, THE DELICATE APE (Duell, Sloan & Pearce, $2.50). This happens 12 years after the end of this war, in a world in which no technological advances have taken place since 1940, in which most of Africa is a great independent black democracy, and in which Russia has no voice in the United Nations' control of Germany. If you can accept all that, you may enjoy the ever artful Hughes suspense technique as Piers Hunt saves the papers from the Germans.

John Rhode, DEATH INVADES THE MEETING (Dodd Mead, $2). Dr. Priestley discovers gadgetish murder method in "natural" death of chairman of local invasion committee. Typical Rhode, much of it absorbing in its stodgy way, but marred by an oddly inconclusive solution.

Lee Thayer, A PLAIN CASE OF MURDER (Dodd Mead, $2). Murder of New Jersey draft board chairman (bad week for chairmen at Dodd Mead) involves Peter Clancy and valet Wiggar with draft dodgers, knife-throwing Nazis and one of the year's less credible alibis. For Clancy fans.

BEST BUYS IN REPRINTS. Selwyn Jepson, KEEP MURDER QUIET (Mercury, 25 cents); Ellery Queen [Frederic Dannay & Manfred B. Lee], THE FOUR OF HEARTS (Pocket Books, 25 cents); Craig Rice, HAVING WONDERFUL CRIME (Tower, 49 cents).

March 12, 1944

Babs Lee & Clare Castler Saunders, MEASURED FOR MURDER (Scribner, $2). Murder at Fifty-Fifth Street fashion show leads cocky Argus Steele to unmask the Zaharoff of South America. [Basil Zaharoff was a notorious European arms dealer of the 1930s.] Fast, blithe, gossipy and gratifyingly unpadded.

Howard Swiggett, MOST SECRET MOST IMMEDIATE (Houghton Mifflin, $2). Authoritative, intelligent and often exciting novel of attempts to supply American materiel to European undergrounds in 1941. Author is Deputy Director General of British Supply Mission. Scenes of espionage abroad are so vividly convincing that one grudges space devoted to Washington love story, well written though it is.

John August, THE WOMAN IN THE PICTURE (Little Brown, $2.50). Success of American fascist clique depends on destroying girl who knows secret of past murder; liberal writer Scott Warner sets out to save her and democracy. Lots of stirring plot-counterplot (much of it happening, appropriately, in Hitchcock, Wyoming) and sound ideology—a little muffled at the end when personal melodrama oversimplifies the true issue.

Katharine Hill, DEAR DEAD MOTHER-IN-LAW (Dutton, $2). Bothersome biddy bashed at bridge tea; realtrix Lorna Donahue finds suburban murderer. Nasty but vivid victim is polished off too soon and ending is very weak, but there's an agreeable [Helen] Hokinsonish picture of commuting Connecticut.

Dornford Yates, AN EYE FOR A TOOTH (Putnam, $2.50). [Jonah] Mansel, [Richard] Chandos & Co. brave machinations of Duke Saul of Varvic to solve and avenge murder of Englishman in pre-war Austria. Road-company [John] Buchan, a bit too heavy-handed and black-and-white to be as exciting as its incidents could justify.

Jimmy Starr, THE CORPSE CAME C.O.D. (Murray & Gee, $2.50). Sleazy, sexy Hollywood murder tale by a film columnist, as full of star names as a movie magazine and somewhat less literate. The Hollywood firm of Murray & Gee is a new imprint in mysteries; they seem to have lots of paper.

BEST BUYS IN REPRINTS. Agatha Christie, THE SECRET ADVERSARY (Mercury, 25 cents); Jonathan Latimer, THE LADY IN THE MORGUE (Pocket Books, 25 cents).

March 19, 1944

Leslie Charteris, THE SAINT ON GUARD (Doubleday Crime Club, $2). Two long novelettes, one of the iridium black market in New York, one of saboteurs and spies in Galveston, with Simon Templar in his new and likable role as self-appointed defender of democracy. Fast and flamboyant fun.

Arthur W. Upfield, WINDS OF EVIL (Doubleday Crime Club, $2). Inspector Napoleon Bonaparte traps a mad strangler who strikes only in dust storms. As rich in Australian atmosphere and character as any Upfield, with a new quality of horror and a more clear-cut plot than usual.

Ruth L. Yorck, SIXTY TO GO (Messner, $2.50). Not a thriller but a spy story which is also a novel of people and a political allegory, this tells of a kind of underground fresh to fiction: the once-gilded expatriates of the Riviera, working their passage into the new people's world. Despite awkward construction and occasional inept English, this book by a German refugee has irony, pathos and an intuitive perception of the European mind which makes American novels on similar themes seem like cardboard.

Marjorie Fischer, EMBARRASSMENT OF RICHES (Random House, $2). Professor on Caribbean cruise suddenly finds on his hands $2,000,000, a blonde, a brunette and some murderous Nazis. Pleasantly told and warmly human light spy stuff.

C.W. Grafton, THE ROPE BEGAN TO HANG THE BUTCHER (Farrar & Rinehart, $2). Fat, persistent little Gil Henry gets into even more trouble as a lawyer on his own than when he was a junior partner, climaxed by one terrible night when he finds three successive corpses on the same spot. Spirited and amusing, if long, but based on so ancient and hackneyed a plot that the fan who hasn't solved it all by page 30 should hand in his resignation.

Stanley Hopkins, Jr., THE PARCHMENT KEY (Harcourt Brace, $2). Private Peter Marrell investigates not a murder but a series of petty malicious incidents which lead to unmasking the fascist psychology in private life. Long Island setting but purely British tempo in a novel that is interestingly experimental but, I regret to say, pretty thoroughly unexciting.

BEST BUYS IN REPRINTS. Helen McCloy, DANCE OF DEATH (Dell, 25 cents); D.B. Olsen [Dolores Hitchens], THE CAT SAW MURDER (Dell, 25 cents).

March 26, 1944

H.C. Branson, CASE OF THE GIANT KILLER (Simon & Schuster, $2). Sedulous, bearded John Bent untangles a finely woven mesh of embezzlement, bribery and murder. The best Branson yet, a flawless job to delight the purist who does not insist on extraneous excitement, and demonstrating (a) that the Simon-pure detective story still lives and (b) that the so-called rules of detective fiction were made to be broken—but only by one who understands them as well as Mr. Branson.

Dale Clark, THE NARROW CELL (Lippincott, $2). Lieutenant Kenmore of the San Diego police fights political corruption to solve current murders in civilian defense and a past one in the Marine Institute. Intricate, vivid and satisfying in plot and writing.

Dana Lyon, IT'S MY OWN FUNERAL (Farrar & Rinehart, $2). This opens with the hero trapped inside a coffin and flashes back to his finding the freshly murdered corpse of his six-month-dead wife. The toughness is at moments synthetic and you may get impatient with the slow-witted characters, but the fine and fabulous plot is the closest thing I know to [Cornell] Woolrich and [his literary alter ego William] Irish.

Kieran Abbey [Helen Reilly], BEYOND THE DARK (Scribner, $2). Boy meets girl when spies shoot at them; from then on it's one long chase. Absurdly bad and unbelievable story made highly enjoyable by its terrific pace and the bright color of its crooks' tour of Manhattan.

Peter Cheyney, YOU CAN'T KEEP THE CHANGE (Dodd Mead, $2). Mr. Cheyney writes two kinds of books: superlative hard-bitten spy novels (THE STARS ARE DARK) and pot-boiling imitations of the American tough school. This is one of the latter, about a jewel robbery and many wenches, all exquisitely lush, and Slim Callaghan.

BEST BUYS IN REPRINTS. John Dickson Carr, THE BURNING COURT (Popular Library, 25 cents); Dorothy B. Hughes, THE DOROTHY B. HUGHES MYSTERY READER (Forum, $1); Mabel Seeley, THE CRYING SISTERS (Mercury, 25 cents).

April 2, 1944

Margaret Millar, FIRE WILL FREEZE (Random House, $2). The old situation of the haphazard group of strangers isolated under tension receives bang-up fresh treatment from Mrs. Millar when she strands the passengers of a Canadian "Sno-bus" in an ancient chateau inhabited by a moron (magnificently depicted) and her keeper. Vivid characters, taut suspicion and a fine vein of macabre humor make this a distinguished job.

Leslie Ford, ALL FOR THE LOVE OF A LADY (Scribner, $2). More Washington murders for Colonel Primrose and Grace Latham, this time tied in with cartels and International Mystery Men. Chatty and romantic as ever, with everything told you three times (in anticipation, happening and retrospect) and the first murder never explained at all.

BEST BUYS IN REPRINTS. Agatha Christie, THE PATRIOTIC MURDERS (Pocket Books, 25 cents); David Frome [Leslie Ford], THE HAMMERSMITH MURDERS (Dell, 25 cents).

April 9, 1944

Oliver Weld Bayer, NO LITTLE ENEMY (Doubleday Crime Club, $2). Liberal political cartoonist Tom Bonbright embarks on a bond-selling caravan tour which would (and I trust will) gladden the heart of Alfred Hitchcock, with murders, chorus girls, sabotage, enigmatic "hero" and final exposure of home-grown American fascism. As fast and entertaining as [Bayer's 1943 novel] PAPER CHASE, and a good deal meatier in characters and ideas.

Eric Traviss Hull, MURDER LAYS A GOLDEN EGG (Doubleday Crime Club, $2). Spirited Sally Stewart dreads an island week end with her husband's first wife and family and ends up by solving a brace of murders. Pleasant realism in the telling and a touch of real terror in the denouement make a better-than-average first novel.

Lawrence Lariar, THE MAN WITH THE LUMPY NOSE (Dodd Mead, $2). Mr. Lariar is a successful cartoonist who took to whodunits, publishing with Phoenix two novels banal in writing and plotting but interesting for their first-hand backgrounds of commercial art. The leap from Phoenix to the $1000 [Dodd Mead] Red Badge Prize is unheard of, but this prize novel is more of the same—a dull and unconvincing fifth column story starring Homer Bull, dressed up with a good patter about cartoonists and illustrated with cartoons by the characters (all of whom, oddly, draw like Lariar).

Mary Loveland Burns, MURDER AT CRAWFORD NOTCH (Humphries, $2). Unbelievably evil novelist murdered at New Hampshire inn; handsome young lawyer Peter Van Allyn traps killer. Cliche-ridden but unassuming and harmless.

Eli Colter, THE GULL COVE MURDERS (Mill, $2). Patrick Campbell, "the biggest detective in Los Angeles County," takes on the muddled and murderous affairs of a wealthy family in what might be Pacific Palisades. Familiar and flat tough stuff set in good seacoast scenery.

Sidney E. Porcelain, THE PURPLE PONY MURDERS (Phoenix, $2). Wealthy amateur Stephen Clay solves shooting in New York racing circles. Clever plot-trick stifled by implausibilities and total ineptness of characterization and humor.

BEST BUYS IN REPRINTS. Agatha Christie, MURDER IN THREE ACTS (Tower, 49 cents); Rufus King, MURDER CHALLENGES VALCOUR (originally THE LESSER ANTILLES CASE) (Dell, 25 cents).

April 16, 1944

M.M. Mannon, MURDER ON THE PROGRAM (Bobbs-Merrill, $2). Women's Club board meeting at Black Bart Inn means a murder problem for slow, shrewd Sheriff George White, complicated by a fabulous alibi, a beneficent impostor and a child medium. Thoroughly satisfactory, whether as an unguessably fair mystery or as a literate, satiric and human novel.

E.H. Clements, CHERRY HARVEST (Messner, $2.50). After a hundred peaceful and charmingly British pages of life at half-term in an evacuated girls' school, this suddenly turns thriller, complete with murder, spies and secret weapon—and still in the same delightfully quiet and witty style. An [E. Phillips] Oppenheim plot that happened to wander into an [Angela] Thirkell novel, it should prove a joy to readers of either school.

Mary Reisner, THE HOUSE OF COBWEBS (Dodd Mead, $2.50). Identical twins, an evil and beautiful woman, a golden singing bird and a split-second murder add up to a glamorous romance for the [Daphne] Du-Maurier fans, if not to the psychological novel which Miss Reisner seems at aim at.

Garnett Weston, POLDRATE STREET (Messner, $2.50). Murder is one of the more normal manifestations of life on Poldrate Street (just off Undertakers' Row in Los Angeles), where nymphomania, voyeurism and necrophily make it seem tame. A gentleman-tramp named Old Highway metes out his own deductive justice. Fantastically over-perverse (a poor man's KINGS ROW), the novel is almost funny but never for a second dull.

Eunice Mays Boyd, DOOM IN THE MIDNIGHT SUN (Farrar & Rinehart, $2). Retired grocer F. Millard Smyth, the Mr. Pinkerton of Alaska, again encounters and solves murders in the North. Mrs. Boyd has a pleasing detective and virgin territory, which she describes well; an editor who would bluepencil her endless padding and discipline her guesswork solutions could easily push her into the front rank.

Sax Rohmer, BIMBASHI BARUK OF EGYPT (McBride, $2.50). Lots of lush and lurid Oriental color is the only redeeming feature of these unbelievable, unfair and ridiculous episodes in the detection of spies and murderers by Bimbashi (Major) Mohammed Ibrahim Brian Baruk of the Camel Corps.

BEST BUYS IN REPRINTS. Nicholas Blake [C. Day Lewis], THERE'S TROUBLE BREWING (Popular Library, 25 cents); William Irish [Cornell Woolrich], PHANTOM LADY (Pocket Books, 25 cents).

April 23, 1944

Edward Lee, A FISH FOR MURDER (Doubleday Crime Club, $2). The first case of likable young Red Blake, who is in turn fishing-barge attendant, apprentice detective, professional gangster and candidate for murder—all under the tutelage of private eye Dan Wheeler, who neatly solves assorted killings. Medium-boiled and fast, with good Southern California beach city color.

Ruth Fenisong, JENNY KISSED ME (Doubleday Crime Club, $2). Gwen Mattice had infinite sex appeal and a bright new racket based on it; the combination meant murder, which Joseph Wheaton, the Fact Photographer, solves with intelligence and humanity. Deftly characterized, suspensefully plotted, compassionately written.

Dana Sage, THE MOON WAS RED (Simon & Schuster, $2.50). A brand-new kind of Pan-American mystery novel, starring Donald O'Keefe Adams III (Don O'K), New England industrialist, who knows both Americas intimately, and his incomparable bodyguard Sancho, Lengua Indian, who speaks basic English and basic sense. At times a bit too prosaically educational, but on the whole a good mystery with grand new detectives and a vividly communicated understanding of South America. (It's a pity that this of all books should suffer from exceedingly slipshod proofreading in its Spanish.)

Raymond Knotts, AND THE DEEP BLUE SEA (Farrar & Rinehart, $2). Kidnaping of heiress starts series of murders in Miami, cleared up by Chicago newspaperman Jim Hale. Not always believable (especially a crucial episode with a phonograph record), but light-hearted, amusing and readable.

Nancy Rutledge, BEWARE THE HOOT OWL (Farrar & Rinehart, $2). Another of those isolated and involuted family groups killing each other off because of a freak will. Muzzy plotting and an inconsistently conceived heroine pull down a story which is nevertheless an unusually fresh and sprightly sample of Had-I-But-Knowning.

Anthony Wynne, EMERGENCY EXIT (Messner, $2). Locked-room problem of financier killed in snow surrounding air raid shelter elucidated by Dr. Eustace Hailey. Studious and static.

BEST BUYS IN REPRINTS. Erle Stanley Gardner, THE CASE OF THE DANGEROUS DOWAGER (with Perry Mason) (Pocket Books, 25 cents); Rufus King, MURDER BY THE CLOCK (with Lieutenant Valcour) (Popular Library, 25 cents).

April 30, 1944

Lucy Cores, CORPSE DE BALLET (Duell, Sloan & Pearce, $2.50). The great Izlomin (a sort of Nijinsky-Lifar blend) went mad the last time he danced his "Phoebus"; this time he vanishes and turns up dead. Toni Ney, now a newspaperwoman, solves his murder and her own emotional problems but just escapes death in a bubblebath by the intervention of intelligent, ballet-loving Police Captain Torrent. Wit, skill, charm and balletomania—all in generous portions.

Elizabeth Dean, MURDER A MILE HIGH (Doubleday Crime Club, $2). Antique dealer Emma Marsh answers urgent summons of friends at Colorado summer opera festival and finds a dominant nonagenarian, gold bricks, and two tenors—one murdered. High-spirited, lively and very funny, in a a warmly quiet way.

Cleve F. Adams, THE CROOKING FINGER (Reynal & Hitchcock, $2). Crooked conniving and copious carnage in Nevada gambling town bring Rex McBride closer than ever to death. Rattling, slugging, explosive prose from one of the five best post-Hammett tough practitioners.

D.B. Olsen [Dolores Hitchens], THE CAT WEARS A NOOSE (Doubleday Crime Club, $2). Miss Rachel Murdock and cat Samantha meet up with everything from a poisoned canary to a luminous werewolf before they end the series of murders in a Los Angeles family. None of Miss Murdock's recent adventures has equaled her almost [Mabel] Seeley-like [1939 novel] THE CAT SAW MURDER, but they remain highly readable.

Grace Hoster, TRIAL BY MURDER (Farrar & Rinehart, $2). Insufferably self-sufficient Norse girl gets framed for murder in Idaho; acquitted after one of fiction's odder trials, she finally traps the killer by chance. Tortuous and heavy, neither straight novel nor mystery—though I have a hunch Miss Hoster might do well at either if she would once make up her mind.

Patricia Wentworth, THE CLOCK STRIKES TWELVE (Lippincott, $2). If you tell your family you know who stole the papers and will wait alone in the study for his confession, you can jolly well expect to be murdered. This is only the first of the cliches encountered by mousy Miss Silver as she straightens out an alibi and two romances.

BEST BUYS IN REPRINTS. Lawrence G. Blochman, MIDNIGHT SAILING (Dell, 25 cents); Geoffrey Homes, THE MAN WHO DIDN'T EXIST (Dell, 25 cents).

May 7, 1944

No column was published this week.

May 14, 1944

Dashiell Hammett, THE ADVENTURES OF SAM SPADE AND OTHER STORIES (with an Introduction by Ellery Queen [Frederic Dannay]) (Bestseller, 25 cents). The three shorts about devil-faced Sam Spade (of THE MALTESE FALCON), plus four assorted crime stories and a first-rate Queen introduction. Almost all have been previously reprinted in Queen publications, but as the first collected edition of short Hammett this merits loud huzzahs.

Alice Tilton [Phoebe Atwood Taylor], DEAD ERNEST (Norton, $2). A moving finger, a deep freeze and a blonde birthday present are a few of the factors involved in this latest exploit extraordinary of Shakespeare-bearded Leonidas Witherall, to whom things happen. Daffy delight.

Jefferson Farjeon, GREENMASK (Bobbs-Merrill, $2). John Letherton dreamed wild exploits, like [James] Thurber's Walter Mitty, but his vacation in Wales surpassed any dreams, with an innful of scoundrels, two damsels in distress, assorted corpses and emeralds and the ghost of a green-masked highwayman. Not so much mystery as adventure-fantasy, and as such, despite a weak ending, most enjoyable.

Octavus Roy Cohen, ROMANCE IN THE FIRST DEGREE (Macmillan, $2). Discharged veteran of Tunisia finds love and adventure and peril in New York theater circles and black market. Light and fast and pleasantly romantic.

John Spain [Cleve F. Adams], THE EVIL STAR (Dutton, $2). Police department politics, a cursed sapphire and beautiful triplets make life miserable for Lieutenant Stephen McCord of Los Angeles. Capable enough, but commonplace and uninspired for Spain.

Richard Burke, THE FRIGHTENED PIGEON (Putnam, $2.50). American dancer smuggles papers out of Vichy; her run-ins with the Gestapo (which surely can not be quite so bunglingly stupid) change her from ivory towerist to patriot. Routine spy chase stuff.

BEST BUYS IN REPRINTS. Eric Ambler, A COFFIN FOR DIMITRIOS (Tower, 49 cents); Vera Caspary, LAURA (Sun Dial, $1); Agatha Christie, DEATH ON THE NILE (with Hercule Poirot) (Avon, 25 cents).

May 21, 1944

Darwin L. Teilhet, ODD MAN PAYS (Little Brown, $2.50). The basic outline of this sounds banal: American officer on leave in London runs afoul of spy group, foils them with the help of British Intelligence, and wins an English girl. But Captain Teilhet has enriched this material with a fine firsthand picture of a nation at war, a keen understanding of English and American character and, above all, a hazy cryptic nightmare style of telling which gives the story a vivid unreality more terrible and immediate than any realism. An unusual dish, for palates that relish [Graham] Greene or [Geoffrey] Household.

Mignon G. Eberhart, ESCAPE THE NIGHT (Random House, $2). Murder, terror and romance among a well-bred and inbred little group on the Monterey Peninsula. California atmosphere admirably captured and though some may dissent from the kind of highly feminine and emotionalized mystery which Eberhart writes, none can deny that she does it exceedingly well—and rarely better than this time. (Serialized as THE SISTERS.)

Jerome Odlum, THE MORGUE IS ALWAYS OPEN (Scribner, $2). Sam Booker and Jimmy Webb, new detective firm, disappointed when their first case is divorce routine, but it blossoms into a fine web of bigamy, imposture and multiple murder. Fast, hard-boiled and highly readable.

Brenda Conrad, GIRL WITH A GOLDEN BAR (Scribner, $2). Initiation of an army nurse, complete with authentic-sounding hospital and barracks routine, sinister spy plot and skillfully handled quadrangle. Despite its wild coincidences, this is the most agreeable light-summer-romance-with-spy-trimmings to reach this column in a long, long time.

Rufus King, THE CASE OF THE DOWAGER'S ETCHINGS (Doubleday Crime Club, $2). Grande dame opens her mansion to war workers. Result, a corpse in the shrubbery and involvement in an international plot. Mr. King's recent aristocratic romances are among the best of their kind, slick, deft, atmospheric (though the denouement of this one is slightly foolish and more than slightly snobbish), but this department for one would welcome the return of [King's series character] Lieutenant Valcour.

Miles Burton [also known as John Rhode], THE SHADOW ON THE CLIFF (Doubleday Crime Club, $2). Espionage, black market and murder in seacoast town solved by Desmond Merrion of Naval Intelligence, whose specialty is clearing the aristocracy and proving that crime is a property of commoners. Pretty heavy going. (English title: FOUR-PLY YARN.)

BEST BUYS IN REPRINTS. Ellery Queen [Frederic Dannay & Manfred B. Lee], MYSTERY PARADE (containing THE SIAMESE TWIN MYSTERY and THE GREEK COFFIN MYSTERY) (Forum, $1); Percival Wilde, MYSTERY WEEK END (Mercury, 25 cents).

May 28, 1944

Erle Stanley Gardner, THE CASE OF THE CROOKED CANDLE (Morrow, $2). The rarely mentioned civil side of Perry Mason's practice yields a pretty problem of oil and karakul, which quickly develops into murder. All the Gardner virtues of brilliant pace and absorbing courtroom scenes, plus an intricate puzzle of tide movements which would delight Freeman Wills Crofts—making this one of the very top items in America's best selling mystery series.

Manning Long, BURY THE HATCHET (Duell, Sloan & Pearce, $2.50). That grim and lively redhead Liz Parrott gets herself stranded with husband Gordon and cat I-Am on an island far up the Hudson where odd individuals go in for Indian quaintness and the hatchet is buried in other people's skulls. Plot and solution have their unbelievable moments, but the sardonic sprightliness of Liz's narration is a unique and abiding joy.

Charles L. Leonard [M.V. Heberden], THE SECRET OF THE SPA (Doubleday Crime Club, $2). Paul Kilgerrin didn't need to solve the first murder; he committed it. But there were plenty more to follow and some new problems for the curious Kilgerrin ethics before he could track down the fifth column distribution of dope. Hard, ironic and exciting.

Richard Shattuck, SAID THE SPIDER TO THE FLY (Simon & Schuster, $2). To escape spies, Rocky Smith confesses to murder, but instead of being safely jailed he finds himself among his "victim" 's family, offspring of a Mormon prophet's several wives, compared to whom the Sycamores in [George S. Kaufman's play] YOU CAN'T TAKE IT WITH YOU are sane and reasonable. A little forced and confused compared to earlier Shattuck, but still about as wacky as they come and kind of wonderful.

Gilbert Coverack, ATS MYSTERY (Macmillan, $2). Two ATS girls (British WACs) murdered by bombing and strangulation; Inspector McBride has his troubles with their officious commander (a masterfully malicious portrait) but doggedly tracks down the murderer. Solid and well characterized job which should please everybody but the unflatteringly presented ATS.

John Roeburt, JIGGER MORAN (Greenberg, $2). Bashing of Yorkville doctor uncovers mess of American rackets and German propaganda, investigated by intellectual-taxidriver Jigger Moran. Odd and not quite successful mixture of harsh realism, melodrama and character novel.

BEST BUYS IN REPRINTS. Margery Allingham, POLICE AT THE FUNERAL (with Albert Campion) (Bestseller, 25 cents); Patrick Hamilton, HANGOVER SQUARE (Tower, 49 cents).

June 4, 1944

Charles G. Booth, MR. ANGEL COMES ABOARD (Doubleday Crime Club, $2). Modern version of the Mary Celeste episode (which the author insists on calling Marie) opens a fast, colorful, romantic story of contraband gold, hijacking and neurotics in Havana. Little mystery but lots of adventure in the grand manner.

E.R. Punshon, NIGHT'S CLOAK (Macmillan, $2). Murder of malicious magnate makes latest case for Inspector Bobby Owen and involves Japanese daggers, poisoned chocolates, some sidelights on the Common Wealth movement and many unobtrusively well-drawn characters. Able and admirable British detection, though not for the impatient.

George Harmon Coxe, THE GROOM LAY DEAD (Knopf, $2). Medically discharged marine finds himself involved in murders, sun cults and wineries in upstate New York—hardly ideal for convalescence, but he fights through to a double-barreled solution and the realization that he's ready for combat again. Fast and good.

Vincent Starrett, THE CASE BOOK OF JIMMIE LAVENDER (Gold Label, $2.50). A derelict in the Gulf Stream, a house that vanished and a blood-gorged raven are among the matters that engross Chicago detective Jimmie Lavender. Twelve skillful problems in the classic tradition (most of them now first gathered between covers) by the great bibliophile, mystery critic and Sherlockolater.

George Childerness, TOO MANY MURDERERS (Phoenix, $2). Three voluntary confessions to the same murder are too much for the police, but not for the publisher ("Nero") Kent and secretary ("Archie") Phelps. Stoutly amusing narration may compensate for chaotic plot.

Kootz, PUZZLE IN PETTICOATS (Crown, $2). Style-stealing in the ladies' garment trade leads to murder, solved by diminutive, ithyphallic Jason Emery. Something more bearable than the first Kootz (PUZZLE IN PAINT): Jason's sex life is more nearly restrained and the details of Seventh Avenue background are interesting, though Kootz has still not the faintest idea of how to construct a whodunit.

BEST BUYS IN REPRINTS. Joseph Shearing, THE STRANGE CASE OF LUCILLE CLERY (Tower, 49 cents); Rex Stout, TOO MANY COOKS (with Nero Wolfe) (Dell, 25 cents).

June 11, 1944

Richard Powell, ALL OVER BUT THE SHOOTING (Simon & Schuster, $2). If you read [Powell's 1943 novel] DON'T CATCH ME (and who didn't?) I trust you know that Andy Blake is a nice, quiet guy married to the unpredictable and incomparable blonde Arab (for Arabella), who likes guns and love and trouble. You can imagine a little of what happens when the Blakes hit Washington and stumble on a ring of spies who co-ordinate loose talk. Joyously daffy melodrama plus a cogent lip-zipping message— as sweetly coated a propaganda pill as has yet been concocted. (Appeared in *American Magazine* as DEATH TALKS OUT OF TURN.)

Zelda Popkin, SO MUCH BLOOD (Lippincott, $2). Long Island home of legendary shipbuilder becomes a shambles as first a dog and then a psychiatrist bleed to death. Navy doctor Sam Tate traces the deaths to dicoumarin and thence to a well-concealed murderer. Quite the goriest book of the season and one of the trickiest and most entertaining.

John Rhode, MEN DIE AT CYPRUS LODGE (Dodd Mead, $2). Psychic investigator killed by booby trap in haunted house where spies foregather; Inspector Waghorn does all the work but Dr. Priestley knows the answer. At his best, nobody can touch Rhode for ingenious murder gadgets and few can top him for meticulous unraveling; he's very close to his best in this one.

Agatha Christie, TOWARDS ZERO (Dodd Mead, $2). Complex upper-class family emotions provide long build-up to the zero hour of murder, when Inspector Battle intervenes with stolid brilliance. The plot-trick is not a new one but the Christie skill is in full evidence.

William Targ, THE CASE OF MR. CASSIDY (Tower, 49 cents). Private killer horns in on exploits of mass-murderer but is frustrated by bibliomaniac Hugh Morris and a first [edition] of TAMERLANE. First published in 1939 (as by Targ and Lewis Herman) and now brought up to date, this creative venture by the editor of the superlative Tower and Forum reprint lines is a passable mystery, marred by endless recapitulations; as a picture of Chicago's literary and bibliophilous circles, with [Vincent] Starrett, [A.C.] Spectorsky and Ben Abramson among the characters, it's a bookman's delight.

Amelia Reynolds Long, SYMPHONY IN MURDER (Ziff-Davis, $2). Nasty Philadelphia symphony conductor shot in the coda; Trelawney solves all. Unbelievable murder method, wooden characterization and unconvincing musical background add up to one of Miss Long's poorer efforts.

BEST BUYS IN REPRINTS. Agatha Christie, AND THEN THERE WERE NONE (Pocket Books, 25 cents); Dorothy B. Hughes, THE CROSS-EYED BEAR MURDERS (Dell, 25 cents).

June 18, 1944

Geoffrey Homes, SIX SILVER HANDLES (Morrow, $2). Murder in the San Joaquin valley, involving a fruit tramp, a framed soldier and Confederate $1000 bills, keeps Humphrey Campbell moving in his five days before induction. Well above average as a hard, fast whodunit, and often threatening to turn into the rich and compassionate straight novel which Mr. Homes is surely bound to produce in time.

Dorothy B. Hughes, JOHNNIE (Duell, Sloan & Pearce, $2.50). Texan PFC on leave in New York takes his first subway ride smack into the middle of a mythical kingdom spy plot full of decadent nobility, glamorous duchesses and sinister Prussians. Pure light-hearted fantasy, as full of delight as it is free of conventions.

Cornell Woolrich, THE BLACK PATH OF FEAR (Doubleday Crime Club, $2). Love and murder, terror and sanctuary blend in a nightmare flight through Havana that starts in Sloppy Joe's and ends in an opium den. The consciously colorful atmosphere robs this of some of the impact Woolrich can get from drab American cities, but it's nonetheless exciting. (Reservation: Far more lenient moralists than the Hays office may be bothered by its frank glorification of private revenge-killing.)

Carlyn Coffin, DOGWATCH (Farrar & Rinehart, $2). Connecticut matron finds vanishing corpse, FBI men and saboteurs to enliven her round of war work and record collecting. Familiar story, often slipshod in details (see p. 78 for a curious estimate of San Francisco drinking habits), but disarmingly pleasant and real in the telling.

Anne Nash, DEATH BY DESIGN (Doubleday Crime Club, $2). The flower-shop heroines of [Nash's 1943 novel] SAID WITH FLOWERS are again involved in murder 100 miles down the coast from here and again San Franciscan Mark Tudor clears it up. Agreeably gossipy yarn up to the end, which involves coincidences, accomplices and a courtroom scene that sets a new high in implausibility.

Hulbert Footner, UNNEUTRAL MURDER (Harper, $2). Amos Lee Mappin runs the Underground in Lisbon in a story banal in style, episodic in action and based on the premises (a) that all Portuguese automatically hate Germans and love Americans, (b) that American espionage in Portugal is understandable and welcome while German activities are a dastardly violation of neutrality, and (c) that the Gestapo is drafted exclusively from the ranks of congenital idiots.

BEST BUYS IN REPRINTS. Peter Cheyney, THE LONDON SPY MURDERS (originally THE STARS ARE DARK) (Avon, 25 cents); Frances & Richard Lockridge, MURDER OUT OF TURN (with Lieutenant Weigand & the Norths) (Mercury, 25 cents).

June 25, 1944

H.F.S. Moore, SHED A BITTER TEAR (Doubleday Crime Club, $2). Before-the-fact story of a meek mouse who found courage for murder but made three mistakes. One was not reading the will, one was not allowing for Major Carey Peters (of MURDER GOES ROLLING ALONG), and the third provides an ironic ending to a cynically amused chronicle of crime in the Atlanta cotton aristocracy.

Marion Bramhall, BUTTON, BUTTON (Doubleday Crime Club, $2). Antiques, real estate and personal problems blend for murder among Boston suburb button collectors. Much lighter and faster than the first Kit Acton novel (MURDER SOLVES A PROBLEM) and full of sufficient absorbing lore on the fine art of button collecting (yes, honest) to atone for its clumsy denouement.

BEST BUYS IN REPRINTS. Agatha Christie, THE BOOMERANG CLUE (with Lady Frankie Derwent) (Dell, 25 cents); Elspeth Huxley, MURDER ON SAFARI (with Superintendent Vachell) (Prize Mystery, 25 cents).

July 2, 1944

Kerry O'Neil, DEATH STRIKES AT HERON HOUSE (Farrar & Rinehart, $2). Private dick Jerry Mooney, who loves to play Robin Hood, plans a benevolent fur fraud which somebody turns into murder. For a wartime book this has a lot of white paper but not quite enough. There's still plenty of prose most resembling Corey Ford writing about the Rollo Boys. (Published in *Blue Book* as MOONEY MAKES WITH MURDER.)

BEST BUYS IN REPRINTS. Raymond Chandler, RAYMOND CHANDLER'S MYSTERY OMNIBUS (containing THE BIG SLEEP and FAREWELL, MY LOVELY) (with Philip Marlowe) (Forum, $1); Agatha Christie, THE MAN IN THE BROWN SUIT (with Colonel Race) (Bestseller, 25 cents); Erle Stanley Gardner, MURDER UP MY SLEEVE (with Terry Clane) (Tower, 49 cents); Van Wyck Mason, THE RIO CASINO INTRIGUE (with Major Hugh North) (Tower, 49 cents).

July 9, 1944

Amelia Reynolds Long, MURDER BY TREASON (Phoenix, $2). A rainstorm drives Steve Carter into a meeting of the Front of Democracy where he finds and fights treason and murder. Barely passable routine in familiar Long manner, with American-Fascism theme left pretty much undeveloped.

BEST BUYS IN REPRINTS. Rufus King, MURDER BY LATITUDE (with Lieutenant Valcour) (Detective Novel Classic, 25 cents); Gypsy Rose Lee [ghosted by Craig Rice], MOTHER FINDS A BODY (with Biff Brannigan) (Popular Library, 25 cents); Richard Sale, PASSING STRANGE (with Daniel Webster) (Tower, 49 cents); Robert Terrall, THEY DEAL IN DEATH (with Mr. Katz) (Books Inc., 49 cents).

July 16, 1944

Elizabeth Daly, THE BOOK OF THE DEAD (Farrar & Rinehart, $2). The old volume of Shakespeare was the Harper 1839 edition, quite uninteresting to bibliophiles; the man had died a natural death from leukemia, which can't be faked. But out of those two drab facts grows Henry Gamadge's most absorbing and dangerous case. The season has offered few more engrossing experiences than watching Gamadge create a coherent pattern out of the baseless fabric of a singularly insubstantial pageant, and even Miss Daly has rarely written more skillfully.

Hake Talbot, RIM OF THE PIT (Simon & Schuster, $2). Snowbound group in North Woods is haunted by a Czech magician, a Provencal ghost, a wendigo and a murderer; gambler Rogan Kincaid finds the rational answer. Talbot belongs among the very few (with [John Dickson] Carr, [Melville Davisson] Post and [Clayton] Rawson) who can build a horrifying and supernatural situation and then explain it without a let-down. Whether you want eerie chills or brilliant jiggery pokery, this is your dish.

August Derleth, MISCHIEF IN THE LANE (Scribner, $2). Petty vandalism leads to oxalic acid poisoning in Sac Prairie. Judge Ephraim Peck finds the least suspected murderer. Solid conventional job.

BEST BUYS IN REPRINTS. John Dickson Carr, THE BLIND BARBER (with Dr. Gideon Fell) (Penguin, 25 cents); Matthew Head, THE SMELL OF MONEY (Tower, 49 cents); Chris Massie, THE GREEN CIRCLE (Tower, 49 cents); Lenore Glen Offord, SKELETON KEY (with Todd McKinnon) (Books Inc., 49 cents).

July 23, 1944

Amber Dean, DEAD MAN'S FLOAT (Doubleday Crime Club, $2). Three spinsters find that the nice people at their summer resort include a murderer and assorted victims. Debit side: careless editing and leaky "solution." Credit: agreeably chatty style, good feminine details, and the year's best discovery of a corpse (by an INNOCENT VOYAGE 5-year-old).

Jeremy Lane, DEATH TO DRUMBEAT (Phoenix, $2). A drum fixation, aconite poisoning, nymphomania and Indian legends form the problem for psychiatrist Whitney Treat. Toxicologically dubious; otherwise readable, if routine.

Kathleen Moore Knight, INTRIGUE FOR EMPIRE (Doubleday Crime Club, $2). Pat Torreon stumbles on a clue in Morocco which leads him through Cuban adventures to Mexico City to expose the menace of Hispanidad. Miss Knight's style is eminently slick and enjoyable but her melodrama is based on cliches and coincidence and her politics on errors of fact and psychology. And one may doubt how much Good Neighborliness is created by a novel in which all Latins are heavies, all good characters are at least half Yanqui, and the FBI runs internal Mexican affairs. The novel is itself a specimen of an imperialism as deplorable as that it attacks.

BEST BUYS IN REPRINTS. Dorothy Cameron Disney & George Sessions Perry, 30 DAYS HATH SEPTEMBER (Bestseller, 25 cents); Georges Simenon, MAIGRET TRAVELS SOUTH (containing THE MADMAN OF BERGERAC and LIBERTY BAR) (with Inspector Maigret) (Tower, 49 cents).

July 30, 1944

P.W. Wilson, BRIDE'S CASTLE (Farrar & Rinehart, $2.50). Archdeacon relates to American troops the intricate and curious story of murders in noble English family in 1743, 1875 and 1893. Leisurely, erudite, complex and slyly humorous, reminiscent both of Wilkie Collins and Stanley Casson—a book that may prove boring to the impatient but a rare treasure to the connoisseur.

Ruth Sawtell Wallis, NO BONES ABOUT IT (Dodd Mead, $2). Cousin Mattie, the old witch, knew too many things about too many people, and one member of her close-knit New England family preferred murder to her disclosure; romantic Swedish copper Eric Lund detects. Good sketching of people and houses, well-integrated and suspenseful narrative, fine period flavor of 1932, and not a single Had-I-But-Known make this a leading entry in the atmosphere-romance stakes.

Ken[dell Foster] Crossen, THE CASE OF THE CURIOUS HEEL (Eerie Series, 25 cents). "Impossible" murders pile up around fabulously successful and obnoxious ex-pulp writer (whose identity is fun to guess); First Grade Detective Jason Jones, the poor man's Nero Wolfe, pursues Mycroftian methods in solving it all. Not a reprint as its pocket-format would indicate, but first book appearance of a high-grade pulp yarn.

Hugh Addis, DARK VOYAGE (Dodd Mead, $2). All the principals of an ancient killing turn up on a Honolulu-S.F. boat trip and murder starts again; detective Gregory reaches a surprise solution which is neither unexpected nor holeproof. Much more conventional than Mr. Addis' unevenly brilliant NIGHT OVER THE WOOD and lacking its macabre humor, this is probably a better book than his first but certainly a duller.

BEST BUYS IN REPRINTS. Frank Gruber, THE LAUGHING FOX (with Fletcher & Cragg) (Penguin, 25 cents); Will Oursler, FOLIO ON FLORENCE WHITE (with Philip Strong) (Mercury, 25 cents); Ellery Queen [Frederic Dannay & Manfred B. Lee], HALFWAY HOUSE (with Ellery Queen) (Pocket Books, 25 cents).

August 6, 1944

Queena Mario, DEATH DROPS DELILAH (Dutton, $2). Young love, spy stuff and corpses galore in a straw-hat opera school (based on that run by the author). Too many murders and too little detection, but Miss Mario's inside knowledge of opera is as entertaining as ever.

Marten Cumberland, THE KNIFE WILL FALL (Doubleday Crime Club, $2). Revenge-murderer terrorizes prewar Paris with playing-card warnings before he strikes; Commissaire Saturnin Dax tracks him down. The book is overlong and the plot is a dated cliche of the 20's, but much of the detailed working-out is first-rate, and there's a certain pleasure in an opus that's just a plain honest-to-get detective story with no trimmings.

Sara Elizabeth Mason, THE HOUSE THAT HATE BUILT (Doubleday Crime Club, $2). Long rankling family feuds build to murder in Southern town; patient Captain Gardner traps mad killer. Minutely detailed small-town novel; smooth enough, but a little less than absorbing.

BEST BUYS IN REPRINTS. Carter Dickson [John Dickson Carr], THE RED WIDOW MURDERS (with Sir Henry Merrivale) (Jonathan, 25 cents); David Frome [Leslie Ford], MR. PINKERTON GROWS A BEARD (with Evan Pinkerton) (Popular Library, 25 cents); Anthony Gilbert, DEATH TAKES A REDHEAD (originally DEAR, DEAD WOMAN) (with Arthur Crook) (Arrow, 25 cents).

August 13, 1944

E.P. Fenwick, MURDER IN HASTE (Farrar & Rinehart, $2). Most evil boy in private school vanishes; quest for him, led by Sheriff Thad Shaw, turns up ugly skeletons, literal and figurative. Disquieting story of odd psychologies and obscure menaces, not unworthy of Elisabeth Sanxay Holding. In fact, you might call it the first novel of the Holding school, hitherto represented solely by Mrs. H.; and a fine foundation for a school it is.

R.A.J. Walling, THE CORPSE WITHOUT A CLUE (Morrow, $2). Mystery man disappears and clueless corpse turns up in 1942 London; Mr. Tolefree sees the connection and follows it to a solution which should astonish and may grieve you. Standard make; will neither alienate nor win over new Tolefree fans.

BEST BUYS IN REPRINTS. John Dickson Carr, THE CORPSE IN THE WAXWORKS (with Henri Bencolin) (Avon, 25 cents); Erle Stanley Gardner, THIS IS MURDER (with Sam Moraine) (originally published as by Charles J. Kenny) (Tower, 49 cents); George Worthing Yates, THE BODY THAT WASN'T UNCLE (with Hazlitt Woar) (Dell, 25 cents).

August 20, 1944

Hilda Lawrence, BLOOD UPON THE SNOW (Simon & Schuster, $2). Private detective Mark East is "mistakenly" hired as secretary in a curious isolated household; his true profession comes in handy when somebody starts killing off the servants. Icily atmospheric and deftly plotted debut, notable for its three-dimensional handling of the below stairs characters usually snubbed by novelists (and for its odd conviction that the Basques live in Switzerland).

David Dodge, BULLETS FOR THE BRIDEGROOM (Macmillan, $2). S.F. tax accountant James Whitney slips off to Reno for a pre-induction honeymoon, but everyone he meets there is either a Jap spy or a disguised G-man. Long-standing Dodge fans may think Whit's murder cases were more original than this espionage episode, but there's grand Nevada color, furious action, and the zestful, biting Dodge prose.

Arville Nonweiler, MURDER ON THE PIKE (Phoenix, $2). Jon Ramsay, instructor at U. of Wisconsin, gets curious about "natural" death of great scientist; abetted by his Claudia-ish [referring to the heroine of Rose Franken's popular novel] twin Dee, he investigates, with almost fatal results. Basically clumsy plot and awkward start but a good deal of freshness in the telling.

BEST BUYS IN REPRINTS. Erle Stanley Gardner, THE D.A. CALLS IT MURDER (with Doug Selby) (Pocket Books, 25 cents); Baynard Kendrick, THE IRON SPIDERS (with Stan Rice) (Tower, 49 cents).

August 27, 1944

John Dickson Carr, TILL DEATH DO US PART (Harper, $2). May I for once give no synopsis of a plot? The twists and turns of this story, set in an English village in 1939, are so ingenious from page 1 on that you'd do best not even to read the publisher's blurb. It's enough to say that the novel is 100-proof Carr; fine atmosphere, skillful interplay of character, brilliant manipulation of suspicion, another superlative locked room, and Dr. Gideon Fell bumbling magnificently through it all.

Samuel Michael Fuller, THE DARK PAGE (Duell, Sloan & Pearce, $2.50). Circumstance traps newspaper editor into committing murder, then into watching his star reporter track him down while circulation soars. Romantic, [Ben] Hechtic picture of newspaper life, fine Bowery local color, and sensational pace. [In the late 1940s Fuller became a movie director.]

Jean Mayer Liebeler, YOU, THE JURY (Farrar & Rinehart, $2). The defendant, charged with murder in the art museum, is obviously too handsome and well-bred to be a killer, so Holly Phillips spends her days on the jury rooting for him and finally solves the case. This cogent argument for all-male juries and the painfully obvious surprise solution are the only blots on an otherwise notable first mystery with better-than-average courtroom transcription; Mrs. Liebeler may well be a comer in the glamor-romance school.

Frances Crane, THE AMETHYST SPECTACLES (Random House, $2). Pat Abbott is back in New Mexico on convalescent leave from the service, with enough vigor left to solve the murder of a fellow marine and sundry others. At the end the book bogs down into 70 pages of clumsy and implausible explanations, but up until then it's a delight, with a very real charm in its Southwest atmosphere and in the persons of Pat and his narrator-wife.

Mary Fitt, CLUES TO CHRISTABEL (Doubleday Crime Club, $2). Childhood friend of British novelist tries to piece together her life to understand her death. Revealing character by piecemeal indirection can be a rewarding idea, but Christabel seems to have had very little to reveal. The device as used here is pretentious and inconsistent, resulting in an unfortunate hybrid that is neither whodunit nor straight novel.

September 3, 1944

A.B. Cunningham, THE CANE-PATCH MYSTERY (Dutton, $2). The sugar-cane harvest, the ways of the aristocracy and voodoo complicate Sheriff Jess Roden's quiet relentless investigation of brutal murder. Like all Cunninghams this offers memorable writing and fine regional flavor, and in so distinguished a book who's going to quibble about loose ends of plot?

Christianna Brand, GREEN FOR DANGER (Dodd Mead, $2). Murders in British military hospital under blitz ably solved by cocky little Inspector Cockrill. A bit wordy, but recommended to those who relish (a) Kildarish details of hospital routine or (b) a reverse-English solution that legitimately made my eyes pop for the first time in long months.

Paul Whelton, DEATH AND THE DEVIL (Lippincott, $2). Hard-drinking reporter Garry Dean tangles with mobsters, dope-peddlers, wealthy malefactors and naked mantraps. Mr. Whelton is a new entry in the hard-boiled field who seems to have every virtue save individuality.

BEST BUYS IN REPRINTS. Nicholas Blake, SHELL OF DEATH (with Nigel Strangeways) (Penguin, 25 cents); Raymond Postgate, VERDICT OF TWELVE (Triangle, 49 cents); Craig Rice, THE THURSDAY TURKEY MURDERS (with Bingo & Handsome) (Detective Novel Magazine, 15 cents).

September 10, 1944

Francis Bonnamy, A ROPE OF SAND (Duell, Sloan & Pearce, $2.50). Peter Shane, the good gray detective, probes to learn whether espionage or private passion is behind the murders in a curious colony on the Lake Michigan sand dunes. Skillful, witty, understanding job, as delightful for the spinsterish irony of Bonnamy's narration as for the solid intricacies of plot and motivation.

H.W. Roden, TOO BUSY TO DIE (Morrow, $2). The little man walked into Johnny Knight's publicity office and paid $2000 to get his name in the papers; he got in all right, as a corpse, and Johnny and private eye Sid Ames need all their drinking and leching capacity to find his murderer. Smoother, faster and brighter than Roden's first, with a chilling denouement.

Ben Hecht, I HATE ACTORS! (Crown, $2.50). Hecht's Hollywood is a Never Never Land full of Pharaonic producers, nudes with snakes, cockney Swamis, cockeyed reporters, and every known breed (all illegitimate) of actors—in short, a photographic piece of naturalism. But murder is real even in Hollywood, and the resolute killing off of actors, understandable though it may be, makes grim counterpoint to a fabulous farce. Fine rowdy fun.

Rex Stout, NOT QUITE DEAD ENOUGH (Farrar & Rinehart, $2). In the title novelette, Archie (now Major) Goodwin has to frame himself for murder to lure Nero Wolfe into the services of G-2. In "Booby Trap" Nero exposes murder and corruption within G-2 itself. The wartime Wolfe may bother accustomed fans, but the stories are fast, funny, tricky and exciting, and the sketches of Military Intelligence, coming from the chairman of the Writers' War Board, are presumably as authoritative as they are enjoyable.

BEST BUYS IN REPRINTS. Agatha Christie, SAD CYPRESS (with Hercule Poirot) (Bestseller, 25 cents); Erle Stanley Gardner, THE CASE OF THE SULKY GIRL (with Perry Mason) (Triangle, 49 cents).

September 17, 1944

A.E. Martin, SINNERS NEVER DIE (Simon & Schuster, $2). Murder, blackmail and petty passions in a small Australian town around 1895, told by the most satisfactorily unpleasant first person since [Richard Hull's 1934 novel] THE MURDER OF MY AUNT. A beautiful job, in which the warmth of common humanity comes through (despite alien locale and nasty narrator) to combine with a pure gift of storytelling reminiscent of Wilkie Collins. Significant debut in the borderland of the mystery novel.

Virginia Perdue, ALARUM AND EXCURSION (Doubleday Crime Club, $2). Oil tycoon suffers amnesia in sabotage "accident" and regains his senses in mental sanitarium. His efforts to reconstruct his life, his personal relationships and his all-important war research make a violent moving novel, filled with physical and psychological action and building to a series of murders that evoke an almost Aristotelian sense of pity and terror.

Samuel Rogers, DON'T LOOK BEHIND YOU! (Harper, $2). Mass murder attempts by maniac on university faculty solved (and something more than solved) by young psychologist. Good talk about murder, some fine chilling moments and a uniquely brilliant psychological plot.

A.A. Fair [Erle Stanley Gardner], GIVE 'EM THE AX (Morrow, $2). Donald Lam is back from the Navy! So he drops in at the office to see Bertha and before he gets to bed that night he's deep in a murder case, with blackmail and the shady deals of automobile attorneys for trimming. The case itself is perhaps less stimulating than the last two which Bertha handled on her own, but the hero's return still brings loud huzzahs from this department.

Roy Vickers, DATE WITH DANGER (Vanguard, $2). Cute British redhead barges into spy-muddle and murder and finds herself working for the Secret Service and besieged by fascinatingly enigmatic men. Pleasant enough routine escapade but a far cry from Mr. Vickers' great short stories.

BEST BUYS IN REPRINTS. Amen Dell, JOHNNY ON THE SPOT (with Johnny Angel) (Green Dragon, 25 cents); Dashiell Hammett, THE MALTESE FALCON (with Sam Spade) (Pocket Books, 25 cents).

September 24, 1944

Kenneth Millar, THE DARK TUNNEL (Dodd Mead, $2). Detailed knowledge of ASTP [the WWII Army Specialized Training Program] is valuable to the German High Command, so spies and murder invade the peace of a Michigan university. Remarkable debut, noteworthy alike for its intelligent and varied portrayals of Germans, the ingenuity of its murder methods, the pulsating power of its suspense writing and its curious academic toughness—a style blended of equal parts Raymond Chandler and Michael Innes, and effective as hell. [After the war Millar became much better known as private-eye novelist Ross Macdonald.]

Lenore Glen Offord, THE GLASS MASK (Duell, Sloan & Pearce, $2.50). Murder years ago in a small-town patriarchy in the Sacramento valley absorbs the attention of pulp-writing Todd McKinnon, whose probing all but results in fresh killing. Little overt action but plenty of subtle tension, with all the expected Offord charm and intelligence and a wonderful 8-year-old (Todd's stepdaughter-elect).

Theodora Du Bois, THE CASE OF THE PERFUMED MOUSE (Doubleday Crime Club, $2). The Ivory Tower was a Connecticut refuge which a Lady Bountiful had established for repairing shattered talents, but rats gnawed at the inmates and a 13-year-old seemed to be going mad. Anne and Jeffrey McNeill clean up the gruesome problem with their usual medical and human dexterity. Highly satisfactory and somewhat off-the-beaten-track.

George Bellairs, THE MURDER OF A QUACK (Macmillan, $2). Old-style bone setter hanged on his own pulleys in quiet English village; Inspector Littlejohn ably delves into background of secrets and crimes. Very little mystery, but you'll like the village, the Inspector and the private woes of Constable Mellalieu.

Harry Stephen Keeler, THE CASE OF THE 16 BEANS (Phoenix, $2). This installment in the case history of Mr. Keeler's dementia is still about that compendium of Chinese wisdom, "The Way Out," this time involved with a legacy of 16 beans and a fantastic kidnaping plot. I enjoyed it in a dazed sort of way.

Francis & Marian Cockrell, DARK WATERS (Tower, 49 cents). War-shocked heroine visits kin in dread Louisiana swamps, where someone (is it the cryptic fat man?) tries to drive her mad. The film is to star Merle Oberon.

October 1, 1944

Emery Bonett, OLD MRS. CAMELOT (Blakiston, $2.50). British government worker suspected of murdering her benefactress clears herself by unearthing family skeleton. Familiar enough story but exceptionally good telling of it in best leisurely English manner, with admirable portrait of a world that doesn't know it's dead. (English title: HIGH PAVEMENT.)

Wyatt Blassingame, JOHN SMITH HEARS DEATH WALKING (Bart House, 25 cents). Instead of book-reprints like other 25-cent publishers, Bart House specializes in first-book appearances of unreprinted magazine material. It's an admirable policy but the editors couldn't have chosen worse stuff than this lurid nonsense, which seems more like a movie serial of the Clutching Hand days than like good honest pulp.

BEST BUYS IN REPRINTS. Timothy Fuller, HARVARD HAS A HOMICIDE (with Jupiter Jones) (Dell, 25 cents); Dorothy B. Hughes, THE BLACKBIRDER (Tower, 49 cents); Manning Long, INVITATION TO MURDER (originally FALSE ALARM) (with Liz Parrott) (Arrow, 25 cents).

October 8, 1944

M.V. Heberden, MURDER OF A STUFFED SHIRT (Doubleday Crime Club, $2). The evil weakness of cafe society and the evil strength of a draft-dodging racket keep Desmond Shannon busy amid ceaseless carnage. Tough, ironic, hard-paced, with a fine flair for phonies of any class, this is about the best Shannon story yet.

Gene Hurley, HAVE YOU SEEN THIS MAN? (Bobbs-Merrill, $2). Daring bank robberies with incidental murders seem to be work of a man some years dead; press agent Tim Flaherty absorbs plenty of punishment and liquor in tracking him down. You should solve the puzzle on page 14, but you'll find the telling of it brisk, brash, lively and likable.

L.A.G. Strong, ALL FALL DOWN (Doubleday Crime Club, $2). Crabbed bibliophile [crushed to death] with his own books; Inspector Ellis McKay, one of the Yard's odder exhibits, displays a many-faceted personality until the killer confesses. Mr. Strong is a prominent novelist, poet, dramatist, biographer and record-collector; his whodunit will be praised by those who feel that lack of action must indicate high literary quality.

Andrew I. Albert, THE MAORI MURDER CASE (Vulcan, 25 cents). Did sinister Maoris or more sinister politicians dispose of the civic crusader? Hotel manager Paul Decker finds the killer and cleans up the city. Passable lightweight.

George Sanders [ghosted by Craig Rice & Cleve Cartmill], CRIME ON MY HANDS (Simon & Schuster, $2). When an anonymous extra is killed on location, George Sanders discovers that real-life amateur detection is a very different matter from playing The Saint. Mr. Sanders' writing debut is a competent professional job, though some of the running gags wear as thin as the solution.

BEST BUYS IN REPRINTS. Virginia Perdue, HE FELL DOWN DEAD (Mercury, 25 cents).

October 15, 1944

Lee Thayer, FIVE BULLETS (Dodd Mead, $2). Psychology-class experiment in Florida university turns to murder; Peter Clancy is on hand to solve it. Never much doubt as to the killer but a lot of nicely plotted complications in ballistics.

D.G. Hastings, DEATH AT THE DEPOT (Harper, $2). Petty-minded gossips in a north Vermont town decide that the cultured stranger is a sinister spy; since they turn out to be perfectly right I don't know what it proves about gossip except that telling an entire story through second-hand chatter makes an interesting experiment and a dull book.

BEST BUYS IN REPRINTS. E.C. Bentley, TRENT'S LAST CASE (with Philip Trent) (Pocket Books, 25 cents); Leslie Charteris, THE SAINT IN MIAMI (with Simon Templar) (Triangle, 49 cents); Ellery Queen [Frederic Dannay & Manfred B. Lee], THE GREEK COFFIN MYSTERY (with Ellery Queen) (Tower, 49 cents).

October 22, 1944

Helen McCloy, PANIC (Morrow, $2). This is a mixture of two novels: one almost supernatural, about the literally Pan-ic terror that comes upon dwellers in lonely cottages; the other severely rational, about the cryptanalysis of an "unbreakable" cipher. Each is close to topnotch, but the blend of the hyperemotional and hyperintellectual is less than successful.

Margaret Echard, IF THIS BE TREASON (Doubleday Crime Club, $2). Underground railway for Italian PW's brings our heroine (pursued by an eyepatch) to conflict of love and duty; the author attains suspense chiefly by the simple method of withholding facts. Nice Southern Oregon atmosphere and good enough writing, but a disapppointment from the usually unusual Miss Echard.

Robert Portner Koehler, CORPSE IN THE WIND (Phoenix, $2). Murder of a Milquetoast involves imposture, fraud and a brilliant alibi, cracked by ex-copper Les Ivey and [Pam] North-ish wife Lia. Most agreeably readable of Koehler novels to date.

BEST BUYS IN REPRINTS. C.W. Grafton, THE RAT BEGAN TO GNAW THE ROPE (with Gil Henry) (Triangle, 49 cents); Ellery Queen [Frederic Dannay & Manfred B. Lee], THE ROMAN HAT MYSTERY (with Ellery Queen) (Jonathan, 25 cents); Marion Randolph, BREATHE NO MORE (with Jeremy Gaunt) (Tower, 49 cents).

October 29, 1944

Van Siller, UNDER A CLOUD (Doubleday Crime Club, $2). Captain Pete Rector recuperates from Tunisia by investigating sinister series of accidents at Montana dude ranch complicated by casual Western reaction to violent deaths. Unusual and good despite much loose talk on strikes which makes you want to rub the author's nose in some statistics.

Brett Halliday, MURDER AND THE MARRIED VIRGIN (Dodd Mead, $2). Virgins of any sort are scarce enough in Michael Shayne's career, but the suicide of a wedded one starts his New Orleans practice off with a bang. Clever locked-room murder method and typical Halliday hard-paced action make up for tall coincidences and hazy characters.

BEST BUYS IN REPRINTS. Nicholas Blake, THE SMILER WITH THE KNIFE (with Georgia Strangeways) (Popular Library, 25 cents); Raymond Chandler, FAREWELL, MY LOVELY (with Philip Marlowe) (Tower, 49 cents); J.H. Wallis, ONCE OFF GUARD (Mercury, 25 cents; as THE WOMAN IN THE WINDOW: Tower, 49 cents).

November 5, 1944

Bruno Fischer, QUOTH THE RAVEN (Doubleday Crime Club, $2). Grocer Sam Tree was a quiet respectable citizen of Queens, but when murder and blackmail threatened his foolish but well-loved wife, he turned (quietly and respectably) into a tower of strength—and a Grade A detective. Nice counterpoint of bourgeoisie and tough eggs, plus a startling if guessable solution.

Anthony Gilbert, THIRTY DAYS TO LIVE (Smith & Durrell, $2). Odd will of murdered eccentric makes innocent spinster logical next victim, but crude crafty Arthur Crook saves her after a bookful of attempts. Too little Crook and too many red herrings drag a good idea a trifle below the high Gilbert standard.

BEST BUYS IN REPRINTS. Noel Burke [Dolores Hitchens, also known as D.B. Olsen], THE SHIVERING BOUGH (Bart House, 25 cents); Craig Rice, THE WRONG MURDER (with John J. Malone & the Justuses) (Tower, 49 cents); Phoebe Atwood Taylor, GOING, GOING, GONE! (with Asey Mayo) (Triangle, 49 cents).

November 12, 1944

Erle Stanley Gardner, THE CASE OF THE BLACK-EYED BLONDE (Morrow, $2). A blonde-socking wolf and a baby-snatching mother could mean complications enough but Perry Mason's real trouble on this murder is that Sergeant Holcomb is back on Homicide and out for Mason's scalp. Rapid and readable as ever.

Arthur W. Upfield, NO FOOTPRINTS IN THE BUSH (Doubleday Crime Club, $2). Half-caste Inspector Napoleon Bonaparte almost meets his match in an egomaniac half-caste murderer whose psychology only he can understand. No mystery but rather a duel between detective and quarry—a bit too long but full of adventure, Australian scenery and aboriginal magic.

Thomas B. Dewey, HUE AND CRY (Jefferson House, $2). Marijuana for minors and the naked corpse of a beautiful schoolmarm raise havoc in the small-town hotel owned by Singer Batts, who would rather solve Elizabethan murders. With Joe Spinder as legman-narrator, the shyly dominant Batts makes a good debut in the fast and fairly hardboiled school.

Anne Rowe, TOO MUCH POISON (Mill, $2). Hysterical patient of Park Avenue doctor fakes suicide at party, then is really killed by cobra venom; polo playing Cliff Mallory rescues doctor's wife from suspicion—and from the doctor. Mildly foolish murder puzzle but engagingly narrated feminine romance.

Clifford Knight, THE AFFAIR OF THE DEAD STRANGER (Dodd Mead, $2). Professor Huntoon Rogers of UCLA has an infallible formula for success as a detective: pick a picturesque locale, calmly watch a series of murders committed under his nose, and finally, after 60,000 words, accuse a suspect who obligingly confesses all. The locale this time shifts between Taxco, Mexico and Westwood, Los Angeles. I keep reading Rogers' exploits in the hope that some day a murderer will coolly say, "O.K., Hunt; now prove it."

Kerk Rogers, WITH INTENT TO DESTROY (Mill, $2.50). This murder-spy-meller-with-deeper-meanings opens with a scene in which a clergyman is ousted from his pulpit by the wealthy vestrymen because of his sermons attacking New Deal bureaucracy. In between shootings and chases there seems to be a lot more imaginative political reasoning (including something like Tiffany Thayer's theory of the war and sinister references to "the unwashed") which would probably make the book worth denouncing if it possessed the slightest skill or clarity.

BEST BUYS IN REPRINTS. Margery Allingham, KINGDOM OF DEATH (with Albert Campion) (Bestseller, 25 cents); George Harmon Coxe, NO TIME TO KILL (Triangle, 49 cents).

November 19, 1944

Patrick Quentin, PUZZLE FOR PUPPETS (Simon & Schuster, $2). Peter Duluth, now a Lieutenant j.g., finds that his wife Iris looks like her socialite cousin, which abruptly plunges him into a mess involving Turkish baths, roses, circuses, puppetry, a drunken criminologist and an astonishing denouement. The San Francisco setting is treated with more affection than accuracy. Fine fast reading, made especially notable by an [Edmund Lester] Pearson-like essay on the case by one of the characters.

H.C. Bailey, THE CAT'S WHISKER (Doubleday Crime Club, $2). To this set of German agents in England, routine spying was incidental to their real object: the fomenting of ill will between British and American troops. The hands-across-the-sea team of Reggie Fortune and G-man Waldo Rosen break up the racket. Novel idea and meticulous intricacies make this one of the best full-length Fortunes.

Simon Harvester, EPITAPH FOR LEMMINGS (Macmillan, $2.50). The Lemmings, who perish in an attempt to return to a a past that isn't there any more, are symbols of the fifth columnists, whose sabotage of food dumps in 1941 England is here frustrated by counter-espionage agents Murray and Fleming. Chinaware, Cornish tramps, the continental cinema, Stonehenge and an unfair number of lovely women come into this novel, which for terseness and intelligence recalls Peter Cheyney's "Dark" series.

Lawrence Treat, THE LEATHER MAN (Duell, Sloan & Pearce, $2.50). Mr. Treat here abandons his lettered detective stories (as O AS IN OMEN) for a curious tale of murder and neuroses among Connecticut suburbanites, with a hero who is never quite certain whether or not he killed his ex-mistress. The authentic folklore of the Leather Man, interpreted as a guilt-symbol, lends novelty to a complex and interesting book.

Denis Muir, DEATH DEFIES THE DOCTOR (Phoenix, $2). Manchester millionaire Dan Forrester and spinster secretary Florence D'Este find multiple murder and maleficent magic in the depths of New Guinea. Unusual atmosphere and perceptive phrases alternate with jerky narration and crude plotting. Uneven, but the most literate book which its publishers have yet sent to this column.

BEST BUYS IN REPRINTS. Richard Burke, HERE LIES THE BODY (with Quinny Hite) (Tower, 49 cents); Agatha Christie, N OR M? (with Tommy & Tuppence Beresford) (Jonathan, 25 cents).

November 26, 1944

Georges Simenon, AFFAIRS OF DESTINY (translated by Stuart Gilbert) (Harcourt Brace, $2). In NEWHAVEN-DIEPPE a signalman watches murder from his tower, tries to profit by it and winds up as a futile murderer himself. THE WOMAN OF THE GRAY HOUSE tells how a respectable and inflexible matriarch can get away with murder and end her days in inflexible respectability. Both are Grade A Simenon, which means studies in murder at its most chilling and convincing.

William Irish [Cornell Woolrich], AFTER-DINNER STORY (Lippincott, $2). Irish is the name on this book but there's no use trying to preserve pseudonymity when the stories all appeared in pulps as by Cornell Woolrich. There couldn't be a mistake anyway; most of these stories are first-rate specimens of that master of the suspense and terror of the commonplace. If you liked [the 1943 Irish collection] I WOULDN'T BE IN YOUR SHOES, you'll be equally engrossed by this—even if one or two may strike you as a bit too patly ironic.

Edith Howie, CRY MURDER (Mill, $2). Successful prodigals return to midwest Little Theater group and the blood starts flowing. Ross Langdon doubles as love interest and detective, if you call it detection. Good reading for the romance public if you don't insist on three dimensions to your characters.

Granville Church, RACE WITH THE SUN (Mill, $2). Murder of Asiatic authority in a private museum sends his son hightailing it over the globe to learn vital secret of Japanese underground. As travelogue, convincing; as footnote to history, suggestive; but as novel, pretty much non-existent.

December 3, 1944

Edward Lee, THE NEEDLE'S EYE (Doubleday Crime Club, $2). Remember Red Blake in [Lee's previous novel] A FISH FOR MURDER— the youngest, freshest, liveliest private eye in some seasons? He's growing up now, he's learning more about crime—and when a rich man's son is murdered in a Leftist labor center he begins to learn something about the world he lives in. Not only one of the strongest recent tough whodunits, this is a vigorous social argument, not impartial (Mr. Lee would rightly answer "Who could be?") but stating truths so bluntly that it is sure to be branded in some quarters as controversial.

Constance & Gwenyth Little, GREAT BLACK KANBA (Doubleday Crime Club, $2). Amnesiac American finds herself crossing Australia in an express train with assorted strange relatives, two fiances and a murderer. There's lots of good scenery and the humor is, for the Littles, pleasingly unstrained; it's a nice book if you're willing to waive all notions of human behavior and motivations.

BEST BUYS IN REPRINTS. Leigh Brackett, NO GOOD FROM A CORPSE (with Edmond Clive) (Handi-Books, 15 cents); Brett Halliday, BLOOD ON THE BLACK MARKET (with Michael Shayne) (Dell, 25 cents); Van Wyck Mason, THE WASHINGTON LEGATION MURDERS (with Captain Hugh North) (Bestseller, 25 cents); Margaret Millar, FIRE WILL FREEZE (Tower, 49 cents).

December 10, 1944

John Creasey, THE LEGION OF THE LOST (Stephen Daye, $2.50). This is Mr. Creasey's 40th novel and yet so far as I know his first published in the U.S. He turns out to be a sound addition to the spy field—not of its newest school but rather like Dennis Wheatley or a more modern and intelligent [E. Phillips] Oppenheim. This tale of the smuggling of valuable intellects out of Europe by Dr. Palfrey and his Anglo-Russo-American aides is twice as long as the average, but once you get into it it's as gory and surprising a meller as you could wish.

Ione Sandberg Shriber, PATTERN FOR MURDER (Farrar & Rinehart, $2). Ill-starred December-May wedding in Cleveland society brings on a brace of murders. Major Bill Grady is on hand but bridesmaid Kate Sturtevant finds the killer for him. Shriber's best in some time: high-grade glamor-romance with well concealed clue.

BEST BUYS IN REPRINTS. Elizabeth Daly, MURDERS IN VOLUME 2 (with Henry Gamadge) (Penguin, 25 cents); A.A. Fair [Erle Stanley Gardner], SPILL THE JACKPOT (with Bertha Cool & Donald Lam) (Triangle, 49 cents); William Sloane, TO WALK THE NIGHT (Penguin, 25 cents). NOTE: Not a true detective story, though it uses the framework of the form, but one of the most subtly and persuasively chilling horror novels of this generation.

December 17, 1944

Ellery Queen [Frederic Dannay], editor, BEST STORIES FROM ELLERY QUEEN'S MYSTERY MAGAZINE. As Queen admits in his introduction, "Each issue of EQMM is the cream of the crop; this collection is the cream of the cream." This superlative selection, possibly the finest assortment of the modern detective story yet to appear between covers, is at present available only as a dividend to readers of The Detective Book Club; it is listed here in the hope that public pressure will demand the wider circulation it so imperatively deserves.

James Warren, SHE FELL AMONG ACTORS (Doubleday Crime Club, $2). Great old-school actor drowned in cold bath; Detective Sergeant James Warren follows twisted clues of character to a murderer with almost Simenonian motives. British setting and dexterity plus American tempo and conciseness make an unusual and highly welcome first novel.

Melba Marlett, ESCAPE WHILE I CAN (Doubleday Crime Club, $2). Insanity festers in once-wealthy Michigan family, bringing creeping terror to new bride. A certain feeling of familiarity and the year's worst H.I.B.K. opening might put you off this one, which would be a pity. You'd miss some original intelligent treatment of stock situations and a few brand new chills.

Patricia Wentworth, THE KEY (Lippincott, $2). Refugee inventor murdered in typically typical English village; gentle Miss Maud Silver investigates, although it's hard to see why since the solution is brought about without her. Pleasing period collection of cliches.

BEST BUYS IN REPRINTS. Helen McCloy, THE DEADLY TRUTH (with Dr. Basil Willing) (Detective Novel Magazine, 15 cents).

December 24, 1944

Will Crowell, MURDER IN MOCKING VALLEY (Eerie Series, 25 cents). The Eerie Series of two-bit paperbacks has the interesting policy of publishing not book reprints but pulp novels new to book form. The current specimen however isn't much—a pretty chaotic yarn of multiple murders entangled with spiritualism, folklore and scalping, solved after a fashion by D.A. Tony England and reporter Karen Midnight. Lurid.

BEST BUYS IN REPRINTS. Rufus King, A MURDERER IN THIS HOUSE (originally SOMEWHERE IN THIS HOUSE) (with Lieutenant Valcour) (Detective Novel Classic, 25 cents); Richard Powell, THE CASE OF THE CURIOUS CHAIR (originally DON'T CATCH ME) (with Arab & Andy Blake) (Handi-Books, 15 cents).

December 31, 1944

N.R. de Mexico, MADMAN ON A DRUM (Cavalcade, 25 cents). The best non-reprint paperback yet is this nightmare of Larry Graham, who found his girl vanished and all the forces of New York, animate and inanimate, linked to drive him mad. You may have some unanswered whys at the end, but you won't care as you whirl along in one of the tensest pursuit-terror episodes outside of [Cornell] Woolrich.

K. Alison La Roche, DEAR DEAD PROFESSOR (Phoenix, $2). Roseview College for Girls had a skeleton in the closet of the lecture room and plenty more among the faculty—all of which leads of course to murder. Police chief Rufus Albert Jones finds a killer and a bride. Lightweight and amusing.

Ernestine Malan & Alma K. Ledig, COBWEBS AND CLUES (Dorrance, $2). Skulduggery in private hospital involves rubber cobwebs and trick photography; Dr. Phil Barrow detects. And so this column winds up 1944 with the dullest and most amateurish whodunit of the year, to be read only during tomorrow's hangover when nothing matters anyway.

BEST BUYS IN REPRINTS. Frank Gruber, THE TALKING CLOCK (with Johnny Fletcher & Sam Cragg) (Penguin, 25 cents); Lawrence Treat, O AS IN OMEN (with Carl Wayward) (Mystery Novel Classic, 25 cents).

1945

January 7, 1945

Agatha Christie, DEATH COMES AS THE END (Dodd Mead, $2). Wealthy clergyman brings home lush young wife whose presence evokes all the worst in his large family, including homicidal mania; quiet, astute secretary Hori finally traps murderer. That sounds like and is a thoroughly good standard Christie product, but its strange distinction lies in the fact that it is set in Egypt of the Twelfth Dynasty, circa 2000 B.C. One of 1944's oddest and most interesting whodunits, reviewed here so belatedly because DYKTAWO? (which is the fine coinage of Sergeant P.J. Ackerman, meaning Don't You Know There's a War On?).

BEST BUYS IN REPRINTS. Agatha Christie, APPOINTMENT WITH DEATH (with Hercule Poirot) (Dell, 25 cents); J.B. Priestley, BLACKOUT IN GRETLEY (Penguin, 25 cents); Percival Wilde, TINSLEY'S BONES (Mercury, 25 cents).

January 14, 1945

Francis Beeding, SPELLBOUND (Tower, 49 cents). Black magic in an Alpine lunatic asylum is as much of a plot outline as it's fair to give of this superlative thriller, originally published in 1928 as THE HOUSE OF DR. EDWARDES. A little-known, neglected book, but crammed with ingenious horror, solid characters and vivid visualizations. It's the best Beeding I've read, and I'm grateful to the forthcoming [Alfred] Hitchcock film for prompting this reissue.

Richard Foster [Kendell Foster Crossen], THE LAUGHING BUDDHA MURDERS (Vulcan, 25 cents). Stabbing of a politician-Orientalist and theft of a one-ton gold Buddha solved by Tibetan lama Ching Kwang Kham. Alternately adept and amateurish, averaging a readable B minus.

Marjorie Carleton, CRY WOLF (Morrow, $2.50). This is another of the Gothic-[Charlotte] Bronte-[Daphne] DuMaurier derivatives, with the young bride (this time in name only) visiting the sinister family, and with it the school reaches its nadir. No G-B-DuM heroine ever before exhibited quite so little sense, and it's hard to say whether the author's notions of criminal psychology or her ideas of novelistic prose are more pitiful. How did this happen to Morrow of all firms?

BEST BUYS IN REPRINTS. Dashiell Hammett, THE ADVENTURES OF SAM SPADE AND OTHER STORIES (Tower, 49 cents); Lange Lewis, JULIET DIES TWICE (with Lieut. Tuck) (Dell, 25 cents); Cornell

Woolrich, THE BLACK ANGEL (Avon Murder Mystery Monthly, 25 cents).

January 21, 1945

Elliot Paul, I'LL HATE MYSELF IN THE MORNING and SUMMER IN DECEMBER (Random House, $2.50). "Summer in December" is a fine full-blooded story set in Chile, about rotos (migratory workers) and flamenco dancers and German storm tourists, with Brett Rutledge (author of [Paul's pseudonymous 1940 novel] THE DEATH OF LORD HAW-HAW) frustrating the latter; it's rich and vigorous and in all the most authentically Latin of the many recent spy stories set in Latin America. The other short novel in this two-decker is a Homer Evans story, and I don't know whether Homer is falling off or I've simply lost my taste for him. He's never seemed the same since he left Paris. This one is studiedly mad and religiously amoral and you may enjoy it as much as I did the fabulous [1939 Paul novel] MYSTERIOUS MICKEY FINN.

TIME OUT FOR MURDER (Quick Reader, 10 cents). The unnamed anthologist has selected good and reasonably unhackneyed stories of the pure chess puzzle type, by [R. Austin] Freeman, [Dorothy L.] Sayers, [Ellery] Queen and [Ben Ames] Williams. Well worth your dime.

Carter Dickson [John Dickson Carr], SCOTLAND YARD: DEPARTMENT OF QUEER COMPLAINTS (with Colonel March) (Dell, 25 cents); Hugh Pentecost, CAT AND MOUSE (Quick Reader, 10 cents); Mitchell Wilson, STALK THE HUNTER (Tower, 49 cents).

January 28, 1945

Elisabeth Sanxay Holding, NET OF COBWEBS (Simon & Schuster, $2). The trouble with reviewing Mrs. Holding lies in her greatest virtue: her murderers are so well conceived, so terribly plausible, that you want to talk about them and to hell with the mystery, cleverly contrived though it be. But since ethics forbid my expatiating on what will probably prove the most interesting killer of 1945, I can only say that this is another Holding masterpiece of suspense—a little different this time in that it has a male protagonist—that it fascinatingly treats the borderline of sanity, and that you must read it.

Marcos Spinelli, ASSIGNMENT WITHOUT GLORY (Lippincott, $2). What starts out as a fairly routine counter-espionage novel about Brazilian-American Peter Costa of G-2 in quest of German radio stations in Brazil turns into something special when the quest takes him into the jungle depths of the Matto Grosso. Here, among muleteers, missionaries and rubber workers, is so absorbing and authentic a picture of a strange world that you're glad to forgive the author his occasional cliches of plot and prose.

Patrick Laing [Amelia Reynolds Long], IF I SHOULD MURDER (Phoenix, $2). This is the one about the killing off, one by one, of the jury that hanged an innocent man, with the mad killer somewhat belatedly trapped by blind Professor Patrick Laing. In the '20s certain technical ingenuities would have commended it; in the '40s it seems badly dated in matter and manner.

February 4, 1945

Ellery Queen [Frederic Dannay & Manfred B. Lee], THE CASE BOOK OF ELLERY QUEEN (Bestseller, 25 cents). In addition to the expected reprints from THE ADVENTURES [OF ELLERY QUEEN] (1934) and THE NEW ADVENTURES [OF ELLERY QUEEN] (1940), this paperback presents three hitherto unprinted radio plays, making it for the collector a Queen first and for the fan a fascinating study, with Ellery as three different characters in three different prose styles, but always unriddling an impeccably constructed problem.

Dorothy Cameron Disney, THE 17TH LETTER (Random House, $2). As a fan of Miss Disney's straight mysteries I'm sorry she felt she had to follow the trend toward the spy novel. It isn't her metier; she slips over the border between a Hitchcock chase and a Keystone [Kops] one, and coincidence waves more long arms than a Hindu god. But there's agreeable writing here and a vivid picture of wartime Halifax; you may enjoy Paul and Mary Strong as they trap saboteurs with a program of [Ibsen's play] "The Wild Duck."

BEST BUYS IN REPRINTS. Erle Stanley Gardner, THE PERRY MASON OMNIBUS (containing THE CASE OF THE DANGEROUS DOWAGER and THE CASE OF THE SHOPLIFTER'S SHOE) (Forum, $1, uncut); Clayton Rawson, DEATH FROM A TOP HAT (with The Great Merlini) (Dell, 25 cents, uncut); Rex Stout, THE RED BULL (originally SOME BURIED CAESAR) (with Nero Wolfe) (Dell, 25 cents, uncut).

February 11, 1945

Michael Innes, APPLEBY'S END (Dodd Mead, $2). On his way to investigate an odd business of petrification Inspector John Appleby meets the Ravens, the epigones of a family of Victorian minor artists. From then on his case becomes a strange bookish farce involving sinister blind men, corpses in the snow and even Love, all somehow entangled with the stories of that lesser Wilkie Collins, Ranulph Raven. It all makes sense (though of a kind that may disappoint some fans) in the end, but the important thing is the telling: that erudite macabre wit which is so peculiarly Innes' own. Caviar of the finest sort, with just enough pungent minced onion.

Manning Coles, GREEN HAZARD (Doubleday Crime Club, $2). This opens with Tommy Hambledon's death but Scowrers will know how properly to evaluate the death of a detective in Switzerland. Circumstances and a beard force Tommy to live in Berlin as an explosive expert on explosives, and his activities there among the higher Nazis make the best Hambledon adventure since A TOAST TO TOMORROW—a long and fertilely invented spy story, with an oddly convincing inside picture of wartime Berlin.

Agatha Christie, REMEMBERED DEATH (Dodd Mead, $2). Rosemary had been dead for a year but remembrance was still keen in all who knew her, and when they gathered for another party at the scene of her "suicide"....Colonel Race investigates the fresh (and apparently impossible) murder, with unexpected aid in his deductions. For devotees of the pure puzzle this is the finest Christie in years—intricate, fair and unguessable.

Peter Cheyney, THEY NEVER SAY WHEN (Dodd Mead, $2). In between his superlative "Dark" spy stories, Mr. Cheyney insists on turning out little numbers like this, in which fraud, blackmail and murder enable Slim Callaghan to meet an unlikely quantity of blondes, brunettes and bottles. Hard boiled and hard going.

February 18, 1945

Hilda Lawrence, A TIME TO DIE (Simon & Schuster, $2). In that fine first mystery BLOOD UPON THE SNOW, private detective Mark East found terror in a mountain resort in winter. Now he revisits the same resort for his summer vacation and encounters an even more curious web of psychopathic evil. A church supper, a stolen arrow and a tin of truffles make the summer heat oppressively chilling in a novel which may be overlong but is certainly rich, intelligent and rewarding.

George Harmon Coxe, THE JADE VENUS (Knopf, $2). The Jade Venus was a lousy picture but a clue to the hiding place of Italian art treasures, so when it reached Boston too many people wanted it. Result: a series of murders for photographer (now Captain) Kent Murdock. Maybe not the best Murdock story but grand for pace and action.

Baynard Kendrick, DEATH KNELL (Morrow, $2). Murder of novelist's mistress involves gunsmiths, carillons and spaniels, and teaches Captain Duncan Maclain a few new truths about himself and people. For a Kendrick this is pretty loosely plotted, but the blind Captain grows in stature with every book—one of the few great and inexhaustible latter-day detectives. (Serialized as PRIVATE INVESTIGATOR MACLAIN.)

Mignon G. Eberhart, WINGS OF FEAR (Random House, $2). The libel waiver on this spy-pursuit story is unusually sweeping: "Nothing in this book derives from anything that ever happened." Most readers will agree heartily but the loyal Eberhartians may achieve sufficient suspension of disbelief to enjoy the glamorous people, the colorful Mexico City locale and the smooth competence of the telling.

BEST BUYS IN REPRINTS. A.B. Cunningham, THE GREAT YANT MYSTERY (with Sheriff Jess Roden) (Detective Novel Classic, 25 cents, cut); Carter Dickson [John Dickson Carr], THE WHITE PRIORY MURDERS (with Sir Henry Merrivale) (Jonathan, 25 cents, cut); Veronica Parker Johns, SHADY DOINGS (with Judge Prentiss) (Atlas, 25 cents, cut).

February 25, 1945

Mary Plum, STATE DEPARTMENT CAT (Doubleday Crime Club, $2). George Stair stroked the cat named Trouble, bad-luck mascot of the State Department, and from then on had his hands full of spies, beautiful and otherwise, South American pro-Fascists, and their equivalents in the Department itself. Likable people, a highly convincing inside-Washington atmosphere and lots of action make you more than willing to overlook some pretty wild coincidences.

Sam Merwin, Jr., KNIFE IN MY BACK (Mystery House, $2). Young Boston banker loses the stuffing from his shirt when he tangles with murder, paperweight collecting and cigar-smoking Amy Brewster. Rapid, easy storytelling makes up for a somewhat unedited effect in plot and writing.

Nancy Rutledge, BLOOD ON THE CAT (Farrar & Rinehart, $2). Hard-bitten small-town editor Killian McBean finds himself, his pressman and his cat so deep in murder that he has to fight his way out to a solution. The unassuming readability of the book may outweigh the character cliches and some quite unbelievable details of plot.

Hulbert Footner, ORCHIDS TO MURDER (Harper, $2). Christopher Morley's six-page obit on Footner is a touching tribute to a friend and a typical piece of Morleyana which should make this book an important collectors' "first." The volume also contains Footner's last mystery novel (about Amos Lee Mappin), no better and no worse than the thirty-odd others, on which Mr. Morley and this department do not see eye to eye.

Laurelle Miller, THE HEN LAYS MURDER AND OTHER STORIES (Jupiter, 25 cents). Odd melange of mysticism and amateur writing trying to pass itself off as a two-bit murder book. This is fair warning.

March 4, 1945

Raymond Chandler, FIVE SINISTER CHARACTERS (Avon, 25 cents). Four novelettes from *Dime Detective* and a short from the [*Saturday Evening*] *Post*, about detective John Dalmas and others, collected for the first time in book form and possibly even better than [the 1944 Chandler collection] FIVE MURDERERS. If in prose, characterization, psychology, moods and sense of locale Mr. Chandler doesn't top nine out of any ten contemporary serious novelists, may I be Edmund Wilson.

Axel Kielland, SHAPE OF DANGER (translated by Carolyn Hannay) (Little Brown, $2.50). Wealthy Norwegian playboy becomes drunkenly entangled with the Underground and gradually, through a series of high adventures, learns the full meaning of life in these times. This Norwegian novel (first published in Sweden), combining the high-hearted humor of Manning Coles with the bitter reality of Peter Cheyney, makes one of the liveliest melodramas of the war, by an author new to the U.S. from whom I want more as soon as possible—and through the same unbelievably readable translator.

Austin Ripley, PHOTOCRIME (Garden City, 50 cents). Thirty of the best of the picture problems about Inspector Hannibal Cobb, which have been appearing in *Look* since 1937, including guest contributions by Alfred Hitchcock (fine) and Orson Welles (fuzzy). For the puzzle-minded, ideal—and not bad either for devotees of cheesecake.

Simon Stone, KNIGHT MISSING (Macmillan, $2). Hypocritical philanthropist gets his in pre-war Manchester. Sir Brian Conway clears RAF trainee of suspicion. The characters, if you can call them that, alternately discuss alibis and go on abrupt chases; any proposed Union Now will have to do something about this sort of thing.

George F. Worts, FIVE WHO VANISHED (McBride, $2). Young S.F. engineer, traveling by convoy to the Islands, runs afoul of the machinations of a tyrannical Hawaii family. Glamor romance, with first-reader characterizations and a solution simply contrived by withholding all evidence.

BEST BUYS IN REPRINTS. Carl Randau & Leane Zugsmith, THE VISITOR (Tower, 49 cents, uncut); Craig Rice, THE SUNDAY PIGEON MURDERS (with Bingo & Handsome) (Banner, 25 cents).

March 11, 1945

Ngaio Marsh, DIED IN THE WOOL (Little Brown, $2). Rumors of espionage bring Roderick Alleyn to investigate a year-old murder on a New Zealand sheep ranch; his subtle probings into past and present stir the murderer to fresh action. Largely a detailed reconstruction of the victim's character from numerous narratives, handled with such impeccable skill that it's hard to say why this seems a lesser Marsh—which still means a novel well above the crowd.

Herbert O. Yardley & Carl Grabo, CROWS ARE BLACK EVERYWHERE (Putnam, $2.50). Espionage and counterplot among all nations and colors in 1940 Chungking, culminating in a frustrated attempt to destroy the Generalissimo [Chiang Kai-Shek]. Not precisely distinguished as a novel (the conversion to right thinking of the protofascist American heroine is pretty hard to take) but full of excellent color, detail and action, plus some intricate cryptanalysis worthy of Major (BLACK CHAMBER) Yardley.

Edmund Crispin, OBSEQUIES AT OXFORD (Lippincott, $2). Murder in a repertory company at Oxford brings about a fine interplay of the theatrical and the academic, resolved by English professor Gervase Fen. Very young and very erudite, this is the first novel of a new author, strongly influenced by [John Dickson] Carr and [Michael] Innes, who may easily hit the top ranks as soon as he rubs off a few rough edges.

BEST BUYS IN REPRINTS. Charlotte Armstrong, THE CASE OF THE WEIRD SISTERS (with MacDougal Duff) (Mercury, 25 cents, cut); H.H. Holmes [Anthony Boucher], NINE TIMES NINE (Penguin, 25 cents, uncut).

March 18, 1945

Anthony Gilbert, DEATH AT THE DOOR (Smith & Durrell, $2). Ancient curse causes modern murders in noble family; lawyer Arthur Crook himself finds the first body—and the murderer. Excellent atmosphere (of wartime London and a morbid little village), solid writing, and the superbly vulgar Crook in his longest role to date make this the best Gilbert since [the 1942 novel] MYSTERY IN THE WOODSHED—as British as [Angela] Thirkell and as suspenseful as [Cornell] Woolrich. (English title: HE CAME BY NIGHT.)

Vera Kelsey, FEAR CAME FIRST (Doubleday Crime Club, $2). It was a queer household, that group of oddly related women clustered about the lovely Seattle heiress, and the tension mounted through fatal accidents to culminate in a freak blizzard and a powerful revelation of character tragedy. One of the best of the slow-sinister novels this season, with a believable validity rare in the school.

Inez Oellrichs, AND DIE SHE DID (Doubleday Crime Club, $2). Wealthy neurotic doubly murdered by arsenic and blunt instrument; milkman Matt Winters untangles the affairs of her unpleasant family. Despite a somewhat chaotic plot it's agreeable reading, and the resolutely homespun Matt is welcome back after three years' absence from the field.

Kathleen Moore Knight, STREAM SINISTER (Doubleday Crime Club, $2). Mass murder in wealthy Mexican family, complete with romance, ghosts, a long-lost heir and characters cut out of the very best slick pasteboard. The total effect is readable and the trick solution is almost as startling as the number of loose ends it leaves.

Walbridge McCully, BLOOD ON NASSAU'S MOON (Doubleday Crime Club, $2). Anyone's first novel may be bad and a second novel is proverbially so. But Miss McCully's third makes it clear that she has settled down to a career of illiterate naivete. This one is about a nurse who is framed for murder in the Bahamas but inherits a million dollars and marries a navy officer. The mastermind is Lieutenant Swansdown, a creation of which S.J. Perelman could be proud.

Cecile Gilmore, FEATHER OF DOUBT (Curl, $2). The complex and lushly described loves of the American Bureau of Information staff in Tunis, noted here only because the publisher's blurb tries to make out that it's a spy-intrigue story. (Published in *Cosmopolitan* as TENSION IN TUNIS.)

March 25, 1945

A.E. Martin, THE OUTSIDERS (Simon & Schuster, $2). Blackmail and murder among Australian carnival freaks, including giant, midget, starving man and tattooed lady, quietly handled by spruiker (spieler to you) Pel Pelham. Unlike last season's superlative SINNERS NEVER DIE, this Martin is a formal detective story, but it has all the same qualities of humor, irony, tenderness and warmth, plus the strangest (and most human) cast of characters that ever surrounded murder. Unique and admirable.

Charlotte Armstrong, THE INNOCENT FLOWER (Coward-McCann, $2). Murder in a family with seven children leads MacDougal Duff into odd bypaths where his personal fears and emotions all but obfuscate his keenly analytic mind. A fine and unusual novel, rich in subtlety and indirections—not for the action fans but a treat for the connoisseur. And the children are swell.

Frances Crane, THE INDIGO NECKLACE (Random House, $2). Murders in New Orleans Creole family, with curare, crypts and a hint of voodoo. Pat Abbott and his wife are as charming as ever, but the real attraction is gourmet Captain Jonas, who discusses murder over the finest meals that ever stimulated deduction. (Warning: Pay no heed to the elaborate ground plans; they seem to have been drawn without reference to the text, which they flatly contradict.)

Amelia Reynolds Long, DEATH LOOKS DOWN (Ziff-Davis, $2). Discovery of manuscript of "Ulalume" starts series of Poesque murders in Poe seminar at Philadelphia college; detective Ted Trelawney contrives an equally Poesque denouement. The writing is on the flat side but the imagination and lore of the plot make this the best of Miss Long's many books—which is more polite than saying the first bearably good one.

Octavus Roy Cohen, DANGER IN PARADISE (Macmillan, $2). Smuggled cigars, seditious subversion and sinuous sirens make a murder plot for advertising man Jimmy Drake to rescue his beloved from. So very slick and glamorous that you can hardly believe its author used to write about gold-toothpicked Jim Hanvey.

Harry Stephen Keeler, THE CASE OF THE IVORY ARROW (Phoenix, $2). I've given up trying to describe Keeler novels. Either you like them or you don't. This one is like all the others, plus a certain new vein of self-conscious satire on publishing, and a character named Herman Hierony-mous, the Kraut King, which may give you an idea. His fabulous fertility could make Keeler the greatest writer in the business—if he could only write.

April 1, 1945

Lange Lewis, THE BIRTHDAY MURDER (Bobbs-Merrill, $2). Holly-wood Class B producer poisoned by exact method described by his wife in her best-selling novel; huge, sensitive Richard Tuck guides the investiga-tion to a subtly startling end. Shrewd plotting, acute observation and ingen-ious (if slightly overstressed) psychological delvings make possibly the best of Miss Lewis' admirable novels.

Marten Cumberland, STEPS IN THE DARK (Doubleday Crime Club, $2). Blind Parisian stumbles into spy plot; Commissaire Saturnin Dax, the French Inspector French [referring to Freeman Wills Crofts' detective character], meticulously untangles the multiple murders of a series of bril-liant young officers. A sterling job in the finest tradition of the simon-pure police novel.

D.B. Olsen [Dolores Hitchens], CATS DON'T SMILE (Doubleday Crime Club, $2). Murders in Sacramento boarding house absorb Miss Ra-chel Murdock, aided by her cat Samantha—which is only fair since an-other cat is one of the victims. Miss Rachel is getting awfully cute—especially without Lieutenant Mayhew to clarify things.

Louis Trimble, MURDER TROUBLE (Phoenix, $2). S.F. newsman Tom Holland finds haunts, corpses, bosoms and black markets in northeast Washington. Lively yarn, with strong macabre passages (which some readers may find too callous) and a plot that's almost too intricate to fol-low.

Merlda Mace, BLONDES DON'T CRY (Messner, $2). Christine Ander-sen thought herself lucky to get an apartment in Washington but there was a blonde corpse in the dumb waiter and a naked man on the davenport. Reasonably readable up to an ending which makes a minimum of sense.

Jimmy Starr, THREE SHORT BIERS (Murray & Gee, $2). Murders of midgets in Hollywood studio add zest to the liquor and loving of reporter Joe Medford. Unparalleled in the cheap vulgarity of its characters and its wit. (The publishers will probably quote that as "Unparalleled in...its wit. S.F. Chronicle.")

April 8, 1945

A.B. Cunningham, DEATH VISITS THE APPLE HOLE (Dutton, $2). Shotgun killing of rural lecher goes down as Sheriff Jess Roden's worst failure; the story behind it culminates in a unique scene between detective and murderer. If you know Cunningham, no more words are needed; if you don't, this is as good a book as any in which to meet an unclassifiable master.

E.P. Fenwick, TWO NAMES FOR DEATH (Farrar & Rinehart, $2). Successive "suicides" in Boston suburb expose a nasty tangle of middle-class family possessiveness for Lieutenant Eggart. Simply and subtly written, with knowable characters and plausibly complex motivations, this won't disappoint those who recognized Fenwick in MURDER IN HASTE as a possible major contender.

Leslie Charteris, THE SAINT MEETS THE TIGER (Bond-Charteris, 25 cents). A somewhat rewritten new edition of the first (1929) Saint story, MEET THE TIGER. Fascinating as a period piece and quite able to hold its own with the current crop. (Note: The minute typography is not so illegible as it looks. It couldn't be.)

Whitman Chambers, ACTION AT WORLD'S END (Dutton, $2). Mining engineer Ken Lowrie tried to fight Falangism in Mexico and got a bullet for his pains. Four years later he returns to Acapulco as lieutenant on a destroyer to finish the job, and incidentally straighten out his love affairs and frustrate the Japanese invasion of Mexico. Good action thriller.

Leslie Ford, THE PHILADELPHIA MURDER STORY (Scribner, $2). Threatened scandal in Main Line family leads to murder in lobby of *Saturday Evening Post*; trust Grace Latham and Colonel Primrose to be on hand. Regulation Ford, with more attention to family problems than to the backstage glimpses of the Curtis Publishing Co.

Ken[dell Foster] Crossen, THE CASE OF THE PHANTOM FINGERPRINTS (Vulcan, 25 cents). Forty-eight guests and 49 sets of fingerprints turn murder of Broadway producer into an Impossible Situation right up the alley of First Grade Detective Jason Jones. Ingratiating story (not a reprint), which would rate higher if its "impossible" gimmick weren't exactly the same as in one of Carter Dickson's [John Dickson Carr's] best novels.

BEST BUYS IN REPRINTS. Hugh Pentecost, THE BRASS CHILLS (with Luke Bradley) (Popular Library, 25 cents, uncut); Craig Rice, THE WRONG MURDER (with John J. Malone & the Justuses) (Popular Library, 25 cents, uncut).

April 15, 1945

Craig Rice, THE LUCKY STIFF (Simon & Schuster, $2). At the hour when Anna Marie officially died in the electric chair, her lively and fleshly ghost began to haunt Chicago politicians, bringing plentiful fresh crimes for John J. Malone to untangle. Jake and Helene Justus are around too, and if their participation seems this time a litttle forced, Malone is still wonderful and so is Miss Rice's Chicago.

Elisabeth Sanxay Holding, DARK POWER (Black Cat, 25 cents). This reprint of an early (1930) and almost forgotten Holding merits listing as a new book, which it will be to most fans, who'll find in this story of a young girl, an old house and a strange family all the succinct neurotic terror which Mrs. Holding has made peculiarly (and I mean peculiarly) her own.

August Derleth, NO FUTURE FOR LUANA (Scribner, $2). Murder of nasty star of traveling tent-show proffers perverse method and motive for Judge Ephraim Peck. Too large a cast for the reader to keep straight, but brilliant background and neatness of problem make this the best of the leisurely atmospheric Sac Prairie mysteries.

Joe Barry, THE FALL GUY (Mystery House, $2). Invasion of S.F. gangsters in pursuit of idol's-eye emeralds brings good old days back to Chicago; private detective Rush Henry maneuvers through the carnage to a tidy solution. Good fast reading.

Alice Campbell, NO LIGHT CAME ON (Scribner, $2). Jewel robbery and murders in pre-war Paris torment the life of American Gay Ripley, who sets a new all-time record as a suffering and fainting heroine.

BEST BUYS IN REPRINTS. James M. Cain, LOVE'S LOVELY COUNTERFEIT (Tower, 49 cents, uncut); Will Oursler, THE TRIAL OF VINCENT DOON (with Strong & Matthews) (Mercury, 25 cents, uncut); Rex Stout, BLACK ORCHIDS (with Nero Wolfe) (Tower, 49 cents, uncut).

April 22, 1945

Frances & Richard Lockridge, PAYOFF FOR THE BANKER (Lippincott, $2). It's a major marvel how the Lockridges can consistently turn out books that are at once delightful zany comedies, sensitive novels of moods and manners and perfectly plotted detective stories. This newest, played largely among the Long Island set, is ideal in each respect, with the Norths and Lieutenant Weigand all at their best. And it includes the funniest single sequence I've read since I started reviewing.

Lavinia R. Davis, EVIDENCE UNSEEN (Doubleday Crime Club, $2). Saboteurs, grandes dames and gallant hotel managers bring murder and romance into the Atlantic City vacation of antique dealer Nora Hughes. Loosely plotted but promisingly written—with Nora head and shoulders above the average heroine in intelligence and credibility.

Rufus King, THE DEADLY DOVE (Doubleday Crime Club, $2). Once the gentle kindly Dove is hired for a murder he can't be stopped even when his employer loses his motive. This premise makes for a deftly contrived and callous farce of death among the wealthy and their sycophants in the Catskills. Condensed in *Redbook* as THE ADVENTURE OF THE IN-

CAUTIOUS GUEST—despite which it sounds oddly like a novelized play.

Eunice Mays Boyd, MURDER WEARS MUKLUKS (Farrar & Rinehart, $2). Timid Fairbanks grocer F. Millard Smyth finds, in perverse order, a ghost, a corpse and a murderer. Full of Alaskan local color and as endless as a Northern night.

H.G. Coulter, DEATH COMES TO CASANOVA (Manthorne & Burack, $2). Bashing of lupine artist in Southern California small town enables dramatist Anthony Frayne to stage startling denouement. Passable enough if you can take the singularly pedantic prose.

Lelia di Benedetto & Jules E. Harris, MURDER SHRIEKS OUT (Field-Doubleday, $2). Groom shot on wedding morn; are spies involved? Adolescent twins share the narration, hard-drinking Grandmother Carey detects. It's all too cute for words—and to think it took two authors to do it!

April 29, 1945

Ruth Sawtell Wallis, BLOOD FROM A STONE (Dodd Mead, $2). American girl archeologist, exploring primitive caves in French Pyrenees, discovers first a 20,000-year-old body—and then a nice fresh one. Fine emotional tensions, well-conceived characters and locale, fascinating scientific dividend and superlative economy of narration make this a honey.

Kelley Roos, THERE WAS A CROOKED MAN (Dodd Mead, $2). The odd population of a boarding house near Columbia University makes a fine background for murder and for the deft investigations of Jeff and Haila Troy. Interesting people, bright dialogue, smooth [narration] and a neat plot-trick add up to a typically satisfactory Roos opus.

Freeman Wills Crofts, ENEMY UNSEEN (Dodd Mead, $2). Murder by stolen Home Guard explosives involves a mystery novelist and a crossword puzzle expert—which affords Chief Inspector French an even more intricate puzzle than usual. For the patient only, but for them a rewarding treasure.

Anne Rowe, FATAL PURCHASE (Mill, $2). Unique Japanese art treasures, collector's mania, espionage and a little matter of illegitimacy weave terror around art dealer heroine. Good light reading up till a long section of explanatory anticlimax.

Marion Holbrook, CRIME WIND (Dodd Mead, $2.50). This is the one about the American girl who takes a job at a Latin American embassy, innocently carries The Papers, is pursued by sinister characters, and eventually by pure chance overhears a conversation and frustrates the Nazi plans for hemispheric dominion. It's a smooth and capable job, ripe with Yankee imperialism, of a story which did not precisely cry out to be written once again.

Robert Portner Koehler, TREAD GENTLY, DEATH (Phoenix, $2). Murder and murderous attempts in aristocratic Virginia family solved by Al and Isabel Branson. Passable routine.

May 6, 1945

Dashiell Hammett, THE CONTINENTAL OP (with an introduction by Ellery Queen [Frederic Dannay]) (Bestseller, 25 cents). Four long short stories (three of them in book form for the first time) about the nameless but immortal private operative who is San Francisco's greatest contribution to detective literature. Grade A Hammett, with a provocative introduction which is Grade A Queen.

Doris Miles Disney, MURDER ON A TANGENT (Doubleday Crime Club, $2). 20-year-old secret provokes murder among the social workers at Ida Talbot Community Service House; county detective Jim O'Neill sleuths ably even when emotionally involved. This has just about everything: a novel background admirably observed, some fine detailed detective work, unglamorous reality of people and atmosphere and even a refreshingly believable love story.

Dennis Allan, BORN TO BE MURDERED (Mill, $2). Unpleasant publisher, a born murderee, killed by 18-inch dart; colorful Neil O'Brien and his blind brother Larry fit the pieces together. Good solid straight mystery with agreeably fallible detectives.

Bennett Barlay [Kendell Foster Crossen], SATAN COMES ACROSS (Eerie Series, 25 cents). Fabulous mastermind Satan II kidnaps, sabotages and murders with impunity until novelist Larry Donald outwits Scotland Yard and FBI to trap him. Modernized Edgar Wallace and good fun—if not unguessable. (Not a reprint.)

Helen Reilly, MURDER ON ANGLER'S ISLAND (Random House, $2). The evidence proves so conclusively that the lovely WAC Pfc. must have murdered her lover's wife that Inspector Christopher McKee sets out to clear her. You may be a little surprised by the Inspector's free use of listening devices, but a WAC uniform doesn't in the least alter the standard Reilly heroine.

Charlotte Murray Russell, NO TIME FOR CRIME (Doubleday Crime Club, $2). The indomitable Jane Amanda Edwards is a war-worker now but her best stay-on-the-job resolutions can't keep her out of murder, especially when it happens next door and involves Burmese rubies. The Sherumund dust-jacket is fine but the contents seem to mistake confusion for comedy.

May 13, 1945

Joel Townsley Rogers, THE RED RIGHT HAND (Simon & Schuster, $2). This logical nightmare is completely undefinable and incapable of synopsis. Let's say that Mr. Rogers (a long-standing pulp master new I believe to book form) has taken the terrible tension of [Cornell] Woolrich-[William] Irish, the fertile plot imagination of [Harry Stephen] Keeler, the technical ingenuity of [Agatha] Christie and the stern deductions of [John Dickson] Carr and a timeless twisted stream-of-consciousness narrative method of his own and produced something unique and exciting.

Helen Woodward, MONEY TO BURN (McKay, $2). Arsonous robbery leads to murder in big furniture store; bonding corporation investigator Dan King breaks down the killer. Ingenious scientific detection, well realized characters and intimately studied details of store life add up to more than satisfactory debut of new imprint (Armchair Mysteries) and new author.

Gordon Meyrick, BODY ON THE PAVEMENT (Mystery House, $2). Cockney sneak-thief, mysterious hunchback, deserted houses and series of murders weave peril for Inspector Rex Haig. Agreeable lightweight thriller despite plot cliches and overglib hero.

H.W. Roden, ONE ANGEL LESS (Morrow, $2). Private investigator Sid Ames exposes murder and corruption in small city run by sinister undertaker. Sid's incredible ability to take physical punishment is more impressive than his detection. Able but chiefly for sadists.

Marty Holland, FALLEN ANGEL (Dutton, $2). Petty heel Eric Stanton finds his schemes have landed him as chief suspect in a murder case which he has to solve to save his neck. Ersatz [James M.] Cain, with its toughness about as authentic as its geography of San Francisco, and an ending which was a terrific smash surprise in 1908.

May 20, 1945

Bennett Cerf (editor), THREE FAMOUS MURDER NOVELS (Modern Library Giant, $1.45). Mr. Cerf's collection of three undisputably immortal masterpieces deserves the classic permanence of the Modern Library. The novels are Francis Iles' BEFORE THE FACT, E.C. Bentley's TRENT'S LAST CASE (about journalist Philip Trent), and A.E.W. Mason's THE HOUSE OF THE ARROW (about Inspector Hanaud). You can't possibly do better.

Margery Allingham, PEARLS BEFORE SWINE (Doubleday Crime Club, $2). After four years Albert Campion returns at last, tempered by the war, to find too many minds left in England who understand neither the causes nor the effects of the conflict. Murders and a brilliant plot for abstracting national art treasures (including, early Allingham addicts will be pleased to note, the Gyrth Chalice) engage his detectival talents satisfactorily, but the reader will be even more absorbed by the succession of wonderfully sketched bit roles and the comments on the Fascist mentality, non-German variety.

John Rhode, TOO MANY SUSPECTS (Dodd Mead, $2). Poisoned vegetable marrow starts a trail of almost unbelievably ingenious false clues; Inspector Jimmy Waghorn solves this one on his own with only a little needling from Dr. Priestley. Solidly detailed project for Rhode scholars.

Bertram Millhauser, WHATEVER GOES UP (Doubleday Crime Club, $2). Body adrift on advertising balloons reveals murder plot at mansion near S.F. to gastronomous Seth Ross. Light, fast and coyly amusing, but not helped by a transparent plot, the year's wildest coincidences, and a Negro stooge drawn in the blackest burned cork.

May 27, 1945

Ellery Queen [Frederic Dannay & Manfred B. Lee], THE MURDERER IS A FOX (Little Brown, $2). Ellery Queen returns not only to the scene but to the mood and manner of [the 1942 Queen novel] CALAMITY TOWN when he revisits Wrightsville to save the sanity of a veteran by cracking a 12-year-old closed murder case. Highly satisfactory combination of astonishing technical tour de force with warmly human novel.

Eaton K. Goldthwaite, SCARECROW (Duell, Sloan & Pearce, $2.50). Shattered hulk of veteran returns to upset plans of many individuals in Connecticut mill town; shrewd, capable Lieutenant Joseph Dickerson solves the resultant murder. Mr. Goldthwaite has the rare faculty of getting better with every book, but this one has so many virtues of psychology, locale, characterization and plotting that it's hard to see how much longer he can go on improving.

Erle Stanley Gardner, THE CASE OF THE GOLDDIGGER'S PURSE (Morrow, $2). Black goldfish and a possibly black-hearted golddigger trap Perry Mason into a position where he's about to be arrested as accessory to murder. For a Gardner surprisingly slow and talky, but with some pretty legalities and extralegalities.

Lee Thayer, ACCIDENT, MANSLAUGHTER OR MURDER? (Dodd Mead, $2). Two painters, an ex-dancer and a mysterious hermit confuse Peter Clancy in this Maine murder-by-iceboat. Unusual setting and narrative structure place it a notch above standard Clancy.

June 3, 1945

Elizabeth Daly, ANY SHAPE OR FORM (Farrar & Rinehart, $2). Curious relationship of elderly eccentric to her twin stepchildren and a rustic god arouses Henry Gamadge's interest; murder does not diminish it. Fascinating character problems and delicate subtlety of plot treatment make another bullseye for the completely admirable Daly (even if she does let perfectionist Gamadge misquote Shakespeare).

Dana Chambers, DARLING, THIS IS DEATH (Dial Press, $2). A mummy-faced Government agent, a Fascist-minded publisher and a white lipstick shape a plot that fetches Ashley Rawdon from snowbound New England to Florida and almost to death. The fast, exciting Chambers narration fetches you along willingly despite coincidences and a fairly muddy finale.

Gerald Brown, MURDER IN PLAIN SIGHT (Phoenix, $2). Aristocratic Boston decadents get away with plenty but Duke McCale keeps them from quite getting away with murder of bridegroom. A little less obvious underlining of characters and psychology might push Mr. Brown into the real competition.

Patricia Wentworth, SILENCE IN COURT (Lippincott, $2). Innocent heroine on trial for life; stranger appears out of nowhere and clears her. Writing: alternately pleasant and dull. Plotting: the most outrageous offering of unfairness and false logic since the palmiest days of J.S. Fletcher.

June 10, 1945

Richard Powell, LAY THAT PISTOL DOWN (Simon & Schuster, $2). Pistol-packing Arab and peace-pursuing Andy Blake find themselves enmeshed in something about antique pistols and a fabulous new steel process. Padded and repetitive in spots but mostly frantic, furious and funny, with dialogue crisp as water chestnuts.

Richard Keverne, CORONER'S VERDICT: ACCIDENT (McKay, $2). "Accidental" drowning of painter leads to exposure of blackmail ring. As diffuse, disjointed and endless a specimen of the solidly dull school as has been printed in this country in years, despite a modicum of charm about old inns. The publishers label it, so help me, as "Terror and Suspense"; I'm afraid they scare a lot easier than I do.

BEST BUYS IN REPRINTS. Clyde B. Clason, GREEN SHIVER (with Theocritus Lucius Westborough) (Popular Library, 25 cents, uncut); H.H. Holmes [Anthony Boucher], ROCKET TO THE MORGUE (with Sister Ursula) (Phantom, 25 cents, uncut); Van Wyck Mason, THE BUDAPEST PARADE MURDERS (with Captain Hugh North) (Bestseller, 25 cents, cut).

June 17, 1945

Phoebe Atwood Taylor, PROOF OF THE PUDDING (Norton, $2). I know there exist otherwise sane and pleasant people who don't care for Asey Mayo. Myself, I like the Codfish Sherlock better with every book, and I dote on the absurd goings on that plague his Cape Cod life. This time they center around a square plum pudding, so help me, and are if anything better than ever. A joyous job of japery.

Helen Douglas Irvine, 77 WILLOW ROAD (Doubleday Doran, $2). Young lodger in Cambridge rooming house discovers curious collection of papers revealing sinister family tragedy. [Wilkie] Collinsian documentary method excellently employed to relate tender and terrible story.

Jean Leslie, ONE CRIED MURDER (Doubleday Crime Club, $2). Pulp-purveying professor Peter Ponsonby unravels murder, blackmail, espionage and his own love affairs at a Southern California university. Ponsonby'd be the first to admit he's a feeble detective, but he's a swell guy, and you'll want more of him and of Miss Leslie's admirably observed academic background.

Marion Bramhall, TRAGEDY IN BLUE (Doubleday Crime Club, $2). Muscarine poisoning of charming dipso leads nurse's aide Kit Acton into bosom of decadent Boston family. Hospitals and blue bloods usually mean H.I.B.K. at its worst, but Miss Bramhall brings the stock material to life with a lively fresh treatment.

Hugh Holman, TROUT IN THE MILK (Mill, $2). The great Thoreau dictum on circumstantial evidence leads homely, shrewd Sheriff John Ewell Macready to his murderer. Convincing picture of Southern mill-town, easy readability and likable (if slightly overwritten) new detective.

A. Fielding, POINTER TO A CRIME (Mystery House, $2). Brutal murder in Lincolnshire, motiveless "suicide" in London—Chief Inspector Pointer adds them up with the aid of an air raid. Good routine specimen.

June 24, 1945

Carter Dickson [John Dickson Carr], THE CURSE OF THE BRONZE LAMP (Morrow, $2). Ancient Egyptian curse operates in English Gothic mansion to effect the most impossible of all lady-vanishments; Sir Henry Merrivale proves himself the master of even this jiggery-pokery. Oddly devoid of the chills which its author would have provided 10 years ago, but a brilliant and flawless blend of humor, deception and logic.

Oliver Weld Bayer, AN EYE FOR AN EYE (Doubleday Crime Club, $2). Half-private, half-political vendetta among French refugees in New York enmeshes a curiously assorted series of lives—and deaths. Economical, vivid, off-formula and satisfying.

Manning Long, SHORT SHRIFT (Duell, Sloan & Pearce, $2.50). Still husbandless and this time even catless, Liz Parrott sallies into Virginia to find callous murder in a respectable Southern family. For the blend of humor and chills, for assiduous and acidulous observation of people, this department wants but Manning here below and wants that Manning Long.

Martha Albrand, NONE SHALL KNOW (Little Brown, $2). Espionage, counter-espionage and love in the Swiss mountains. The details of smuggling children for the Underground are interesting; the rest is routine but slick and capable.

Sara Elizabeth Mason, THE CRIMSON FEATHER (Doubleday Crime Club, $2). Subtle "accidents" in Alabama family prove to be murder under the shrewd inspection of Sheriff Bill Davies while pneumonic heroine finds true love. Satisfactory family atmosphere weakened by proofless solution.

Manning Lee Stokes, THE WOLF HOWLS MURDER (Phoenix, $2). Murder in the Illinois Mound country takes on sinister supernatural Indian trimmings which don't fool resolute private eye Barnabas Jones. Basically good story and background marred by sloppy editing.

July 1, 1945

William Irish [Cornell Woolrich], IF I SHOULD DIE BEFORE I WAKE AND OTHER STORIES (Avon, 25 cents). First book appearance of six novelettes and shorts, selected by the author and mostly as first printed by Cornell Woolrich. Various in quality but containing at least two of the finest Woolrich-Irish opuses—which is about as fine as terror-suspense comes currently.

P.W. Wilson, BLACK TARN (Farrar & Rinehart, $2.50). The author of BRIDE'S CASTLE produces another leisurely period piece about the genealogical oddities of an old family and the architectural oddities of its abode, ably expounded by Sir Julian Morthoe. Not for impatient modernists but rich in scholarship, wit and quiet charm.

George Bellairs, CALAMITY AT HARWOOD (Macmillan, $2). Poltergeist activities build up to murder of housing speculator; Inspector T. Littlejohn uncovers spy ring amid record mortality of suspects. Mr. Bellairs' dry satire and casual convincingness can make me forgive a number of sins, which in this case include a deliberate refusal to play fair and (astonishing in an avowedly anti-Nazi book) what the Writers' War Board calls "perpetuation of a racial stereotype."

Anne Nash, CABBAGES AND CRIME (Doubleday Crime Club, $2). Dodo Trent and Nell Witter take a vacation from their flower shop only to find themselves nursemaids to a vast kennel of dogs and intimate onlookers at murder. Lively and delightful story, full of good characters and amusing incidents—and all but ruined by the season's most unprepared and disappointing anticlimax.

Miles Burton [also known as John Rhode], NOT A LEG TO STAND ON (Doubleday Crime Club, $2). One-legged flyer disappears leaving his artificial limb behind him; amateur Desmond Merrion helps Inspector Arnold track him down, living or dead. Somewhat ingenious puzzle lifts this a bit above the abysmal run of Burton novels.

BEST BUYS IN REPRINTS. Agatha Christie, MURDER IN RETRO-SPECT (with Hercule Poirot) (Jonathan, 25 cents, cut); Mabel Seeley, THE WHISPERING CUP (with Sheriff Eric Maland) (Popular Library, 25 cents, uncut).

July 8, 1945

Royce Howes, THE CASE OF THE COPY-HOOK KILLING (Dutton, $2). Impaling of newspaper receptionist leads hard, efficient Captain Ben Lucias through a fine cross-section of the city's crackpots—all potential killers. Deft, tough and off the beaten track.

Francis Allan, FIRST COME, FIRST KILL (Reynal & Hitchcock, $2). Peculiar will of Westchester tycoon turns a house of mourning into a house of terror for his bereaved daughter; detective John Storm rescues her. Some highly involved and ingenious puzzlement but all a little on the unbelievable side.

Ed Doherty, THE CORPSE WHO WOULDN'T DIE (Mystery House, $2). Freelance reporter Dan Fallon interviews boat arrivals and discovers corpse. From then on things spin into a frantic chaos.

BEST BUYS IN REPRINTS. Ngaio Marsh, ARTISTS IN CRIME (with Inspector Roderick Alleyn) (Bestseller, 25 cents, cut); Georges Simenon, MAIGRET TO THE RESCUE (contains THE GUINGUETTE BY THE SEINE) (with Inspector Maigret) (Mercury, 25 cents, uncut); Jonathan Stagge [also known as Patrick Quentin], MURDER BY PRESCRIPTION (with Dr. Hugh Westlake) (Popular Library, 25 cents, uncut).

July 15, 1945

Vera Caspary, BEDELIA (Houghton Mifflin, $2.50). Quietly convincing details and gentle tension build up a terrifying study of a female Landru in 1913 New England. Not quite another LAURA but a chillingly beautiful job.

C.P. Donnel, Jr., MURDER-GO-ROUND (McKay, $2). Remember the rumors of a Nazi negotiated peace? Mr. Donnel presents an ingeniously horrible possibility behind those rumors, frustrated by Tony Costello of the State Department. Plenty of action and murders, lively international movement and able writing make this a well above average first spy novel.

BEST BUYS IN REPRINTS. Erle Stanley Gardner, THE CASE OF THE SHOPLIFTER'S SHOE (with Perry Mason) (Tower, 49 cents, uncut); Helen McCloy, DO NOT DISTURB (Tower, 49 cents, uncut); Kurt Steel, THE IMPOSTOR (Tower, 49 cents, uncut).

July 22, 1945

E.X. Ferrars, I, SAID THE FLY (Doubleday Crime Club, $2). Murders and jewel rackets in Little Carberry Street ably analyzed by patient Inspector Cory. Excellent sense of locale, real and unusual characters, mounting suspense and appealingly human detective put Ferrars well among the top British entrants.

Christopher Hale, MIDSUMMER NIGHTMARE (Doubleday Crime Club, $2). Assorted murders and arson on millionaire's estate near Grand Rapids solved by Lieutenant Bill French and a U.S. Senator, no less. Jerky narrative and trite and unbelievable solution put it a bit below the Hale standard, but there are not one but two full-fledged love stories—if that helps.

Eden Phillpotts, THEY WERE SEVEN (Macmillan, $2.50). Because he has a reputation as a serious novelist, critics invariably treat the mysteries of Eden Phillpotts with reverent awe. His characters are wooden, his dialogue is unspeakable, his books are endless and actionless and his plots are stupidly unfair; and this latest product of the Grand Old Man (now 83) differs from others only in being even longer. It will undoubtedly meet with a chorus of tactful praise, but I still say the Emperor has no clothes on.

BEST BUYS IN REPRINTS. Blanche Bloch, THE BACH FESTIVAL MURDERS (Mercury, 25 cents, cut); Hugh Pentecost, CANCELLED IN RED (with Inspector Luke Bradley) (Popular Library, 25 cents, uncut).

July 29, 1945

Hildegarde Tolman Teilhet, THE DOUBLE AGENT (Doubleday Doran, $2.50). This is another one about the young couple fleeing for their lives across picturesque countrysides pursued by sinister spies—in this case the Nach-Niederlage Nazis [i.e. survivors of Hitler's Third Reich] who have gone underground in France. But even if the pattern and much of the detail is overfamiliar, the people are so interesting, the action so deftly developed and the workmanship of such caliber that any escape-addict is in for a fine time.

Allison Burks, TIGHT ROPE (Duell, Sloan & Pearce, $2.50). Lone lorn girl, hired to impersonate heiress, becomes focus of elaborate murder scheme carefully worked out to include every cliche of plot and prose. Unique instance of the Duell Bloodhound following a false trail.

BEST BUYS IN REPRINTS. Leslie Charteris (editor), THE SAINT'S CHOICE, VOLUME 2 (Bond-Charteris, 25 cents); Rufus King, MURDER IN THE WILLETT FAMILY (with Lieutenant Valcour) (Popular Library, 25 cents, uncut).

August 5, 1945

Charles L. Leonard [M.V. Heberden], EXPERT IN MURDER (Double-day Crime Club, $2). Taut hard Paul Kilgerrin visits Morocco to trap the Nazi-subsidized holy man who is preaching a jehad against the whites. Convincing local color, tough action (even to a minor war), seasoned with the bitter realism of the Kilgerrin outlook.

Bettina & Audrey Boyers, MURDER BY PROXY (Doubleday Crime Club, $2). Here is an all but indescribable dish—not so much a mystery as the story of how the delightful Austrian wife of a best-selling novelist learned that sudden wealth and Hollywood fame may mean living in subtle terror among twisted minds. Far from any beaten track and well worth a side trip to investigate.

John Rhode, SHADOW OF A CRIME (Dodd Mead, $2). Ingeniously framed road accident proves murder to Inspector Jimmy Waghorn. Work-manlike but one of the duller Rhode opuses, redeemed only by an unex-pected glint of humor in the very last paragraph.

John Dow, THE LITTLE BOY LAUGHED (Mystery House, $2). The demons of love and drink bring murder to a Connecticut week-end but the real demon is the callous, crime-avid child Eddie, beyond doubt the most repellent detective ever created. The author at least earns a citation for nonconformity even if his weird device fails to come off.

BEST BUYS IN REPRINTS. Leslie Charteris, ALIAS THE SAINT (Bond-Charteris, 25 cents); M.M. Mannon, HERE LIES BLOOD (Croy-don, 25 cents, cut).

August 12, 1945

Leslie Charteris (editor), THE SAINT'S CHOICE OF TRUE CRIME STORIES (Bond-Charteris, 25 cents). It will surprise no one to learn that the Saint's taste in crime runs to the colorful and even lurid, both in inci-dent and in narration. You'll find none of the irony, scholarship or signifi-cance of a [William] Roughead or [William] Bolitho here, but you'll have grand fun with [Baynard] Kendrick, [Craig] Rice and others. There's a good if typical [Edmund] Pearson, a highly readable first-hand narrative by San Diego's Lieutenant Dieckmann, and Charteris' own nose-thumbing account of the true case on which he constructed the Saint novelet "The Sizzling Saboteur."

Margaret Yates & Paula Bramlette, THE WIDOW'S WALK (Dutton, $2). Murder of the usual lush femme fatale involves lots of nice people in Nantucket until Professor Horace Carter, a coy intellectual, traps the killer. Much real fresh charm and some excellent background color annoyingly marred by the worst H.I.B.K. mannerisms.

BEST BUYS IN REPRINTS. John Dickson Carr, THE FOUR FALSE WEAPONS (with Henri Bencolin) (Detective Novel Classic, 25 cents, cut); Anthony Gilbert, THE WOMAN IN RED (with Arthur Crook) (Mercury, 25 cents, cut); Hake Talbot, RIM OF THE PIT (with Rogan Kincaid) (Thrilling Mystery Novel, 15 cents, cut).

August 19, 1945

Samuel Rogers, YOU'LL BE SORRY! (Harper, $2). Sadistic kidnaping on Wisconsin summer estate unfolds a plot of Jacobean murk and terror as analyzed by Professor Paul Hatfield. Mr. Rogers is developing a horror-suspense style of his own almost as chilling as [Cornell] Woolrich or [Elisabeth Sanxay] Holding, but one might wish that this magnificently evil plot (am I right in thinking it was suggested by a play of [Elizabethan dramatist Thomas] Middleton's?) had been fully developed in a straight murder novel rather than cramped into the solution-section of a mystery.

Ken[dell Foster] Crossen, MURDER OUT OF MIND (Five Star, 25 cents). Murder during an experiment in extrasensory perception poses a pretty problem for [Alexander] Woollcottian lecturer Chairman Fosdick Van Dyke. Interesting dividend of E.S.P., smart venom and ingenious puzzle mark this hasty first draft of a possibly very good book.

BEST BUYS IN REPRINTS. Frances Crane, THE TURQUOISE SHOP (with Pat Abbott) (Popular Library, 25 cents, uncut); Carter Dickson [John Dickson Carr], THE UNICORN MURDERS (with Sir Henry Merrivale) (Tower, 49 cents, uncut); Ngaio Marsh, DEATH AT THE BAR (with Roderick Alleyn) (Pocket Books, 25 cents, uncut).

August 26, 1945

Dashiell Hammett, THE RETURN OF THE CONTINENTAL OP (with an introduction by Ellery Queen [Frederic Dannay]) (Jonathan, 25 cents). One novelette and four short stories (including the classic "The Gutting of Couffignal") about the plump nameless operative who is San Francisco's great gift to detection. Collector's item.

Baynard Kendrick, OUT OF CONTROL (Morrow, $2). Marcia knew the perfect murder method. It had worked before, and when her security as the wife of Tennessee's leading gubernatorial candidate was threatened she felt no qualms about using it again, but she underestimated the harmless blind house-guest next door. An "inverted" detective story with new and startling twists, and probably the best yet of the excellent Captain Duncan Maclain series.

Francis Bonnamy, THE KING IS DEAD ON QUEEN STREET (Duell, Sloan & Pearce, $2.50). Dominating extrovert breaks his neck—accident, murder or good clean fun? Bonnamy, this department's favorite Watson, does most of the work himself in this story of wartime Alexandria, with gray Peter Shane adding the finishing touches. I may be prejudiced in his favor because he features two small boys who might have been modeled on my own, but Mr. Bonnamy seems to me one of the most amusingly civilized mysterymongers extant.

Peter Cheyney, SINISTER ERRAND (Dodd Mead, $2). Himmler's External Section is at work charting the accuracy of buzz bombs—which means tense and tricky days for Michael Kells and his colleagues in counter-espionage. Grim, taut, convincing story, with only the implausibly high average of female beauty to remind you of Mr. Cheyney's [Slim] Callaghan potboilers.

BEST BUYS IN REPRINTS. Raymond Chandler, THE HIGH WINDOW (with Philip Marlowe) (Tower, 49 cents, uncut); Dorothy L. Sayers, STRONG POISON (with Lord Peter Wimsey) (Tower, 49 cents, uncut). Note to Wimsey fans: This is the one in which he meets Harriet.

September 2, 1945

Richard Lockridge & G.H. Estabrooks, DEATH IN THE MIND (Dutton, $2.50). Can a man be hypnotized into treacherous actions repugnant to his waking mind? The answer is so startling as to be incredible if co-author Estabrooks weren't a professor of psychology and author of a book on hypnotism. This detailed and absorbing dividend is excellently dovetailed into a well above average spy story, rather on the hardboiled side, to make an unusually rewarding thriller.

Ruth Fenisong, THE LOST CAESAR (Doubleday Crime Club, $2). The accessory business, song-writing and a native Fascist plot shape the background to murder, cracked by Detective Sergeant Gorse. Colorful and warm, with knowledgeable details and likable people.

Elma K. Lobaugh, SHE NEVER REACHED THE TOP (Doubleday Crime Club, $2). Dangerously evil woman breaks neck on haunted stairs in a house party on the Lake Michigan sand dunes. Unusually good first novel (despite questionable ending), rich in character and atmosphere and unique in its sense of the petty boredoms attendant on murder.

Valentin Mandelstamm, V. 5 (Brentano, $1.50). There's no danger that this romance of spies and robot bombs in Hollywood will ever be translated into English. In its present form it will appeal chiefly to those who want to see what Rover Boys prose sounds like in French.

BEST BUYS IN REPRINTS. Allan R. Bosworth, FULL CRASH DIVE (with Admiral Wetherbee) (Death House, 25 cents, cut); Leslie Charteris, PAGING THE SAINT (originally published as WANTED FOR MURDER) (with Simon Templar) (Bond-Charteris, 25 cents, uncut); D.B. Olsen [Dolores Hitchens], THE ALARM OF THE BLACK CAT (with Miss Rachel Murdock) (Bestseller, 25 cents, uncut).

September 9, 1945

L.A.G. Strong, MURDER PLAYS AN UGLY SCENE (Doubleday Crime Club, $2). Dictatorial principal of acting school strangled at annual matinee; Inspector Ellis McKay traps the murderer by his knowledge of people and ancient phonograph records—and by withholding his essential clue from the reader. Despite this sin a most agreeable book, full of well-drawn likable people and excellent theater-school atmosphere. (But if I may challenge McKay's discographic scholarship: a Tamagno record numbered DR100 could not possibly be a single-sided disc.)

Amber Dean, CHANTICLEER'S MUFFLED CROW (Doubleday Crime Club, $2). The gory sport of cock-fighting (for which the reader may not share the characters' enthusiasm) leads to a grisly murder in rural New York State. Too many loosely knit plot threads and much annoying why-I-did-thus-and-so-I-shall-never-know keep this from quite fulfilling the promise of Miss Dean's first novel.

BEST BUYS IN REPRINTS. Francis Bonnamy, DEAD RECKONING (with Peter Shane) (Death House, 25 cents, cut).

September 16, 1945

A.B. Cunningham, MURDER BEFORE MIDNIGHT (Dutton, $2). Murder of a good girl leads Sheriff Jess Roden to some very bad big-business moonshiners—and, of all things, to The Woman. The solid reality of Cunningham's backwoods setting is as admirable as ever; even in love Roden functions superlatively, and perhaps under the circumstances you can forgive him for leaving one murder pretty much unexplained.

Patrick Quentin, PUZZLE FOR WANTONS (Simon & Schuster, $2). Wealthy hostess attempts reconciliation party of estranged mates but some ironic person begins polishing off the wives. The garish Reno setting and the light-hearted sleuthing of Peter and Iris Duluth are alike delightful and the ever-skilled Quentin technique is an object lesson to any aspirant— particularly in the problem of handling an unusually large cast with perfect clarity.

September 23, 1945

Margaret Scherf, THE OWL IN THE CELLAR (Doubleday Crime Club, $2). A vagrant owl, a pink blanket, a green mask and assorted corpses happily complicate the lives of some of the daffiest people you've ever hoped to meet. Miss Scherf's own brand of zany murder has been missing for too long from the bookstalls; if you like your crimes blithe and screwy, this is your dish.

H.C. Bailey, THE WRONG MAN (Doubleday Crime Club, $2). American colonel tracking down a lost British comrade uncovers a nest of fences, adulterers, impostors and murderers; psalm-singing Joshua Clunk sets all to rights—for a sizable cut. Elaborately ingenious puzzle if you can abide Clunk's character and the repetitions and indirections of the Bailey style.

Leslie Charteris, LADY ON A TRAIN (Bond-Charteris, 25 cents). The amusing foreword (the only bit of prose in the book that sounds Charterian) is worth your attention; from then on you'll doubtless be better off at the Deanna Durbin movie than with this hastily thrown together paraphrase.

BEST BUYS IN REPRINTS. Anthony Boucher, THE CASE OF THE SOLID KEY (with Fergus O'Breen) (Popular Library, 25 cents, uncut); Carter Dickson [John Dickson Carr], THE READER IS WARNED (with Sir Henry Merrivale) (Pocket Books, 25 cents, uncut); Finlay McDermid, GHOST WANTED (with Lieutenant Bernal) (Tower, 49 cents, uncut).

September 30, 1945

Dorothy B. Hughes, DREAD JOURNEY (Duell, Sloan & Pearce, $2.50). With such a masterpiece of suspense as this it would be unfair to detail any more of the plot than that it deals with the growing tension of terror around a film star on the eastbound Chief who knows she is about to be murdered. For fascinating interplay of character, for vivid sketching of brilliant-hued people, for the mounting menace of petty detail, for the magical power with which she achieves suspension of disbelief, this is Mrs. Hughes' finest book to date and not to be missed under any circumstances. You heard me.

Erle Stanley Gardner, THE CASE OF THE HALF-WAKENED WIFE (Morrow, $2). Oil-lease finagling leads Perry Mason to a yachting party, a murder and his most spectacular public blunder. The book starts on the slow side but builds to some of the most exciting and satisfactory legal maneuvering that even Gardner has contrived. (No, the title doesn't mean what you might think, you cur.)

Theodora Du Bois, DEATH SAILS IN A HIGH WIND (Doubleday Crime Club, $2). When Anne and Jeffrey McNeill buy a sloop, you can be sure murder is brewing among the Connecticut boating crowd. Lots of action and knowledgeable scenes of life afloat don't quite atone for a banally obvious murderer nor for Anne's snobbery, which grows less endurable book by book.

Anthony Gilbert, THE SCARLET BUTTON (Smith & Durrell, $2). Bludgeoning of spidery blackmailer brings Arthur Crook to defense of accused RAF veteran. Transparent mystery, excessive (if amusing) padding and unusual feebleness of Crook's efforts add up to very minor Gilbert—but still enjoyable to fans who value the author's quietly satiric manner.

E.E. Halleran, THIRTEEN TOY PISTOLS (McKay, $2). Veteran Bob Ferguson sets up in Jersey resort town as lawyer-detective to track a fugitive; he finds him, plus a fee, a murderer and love, among some of the year's dimmest characters and flattest humor.

October 7, 1945

Roy Vickers, FOUR PAST FOUR (Jefferson House, $2). Shooting of the husband of a great actress leads private detective James Segrove into the intricate confusion of a radio alibi, a jewel theft and a judicial murder. Meticulous puzzle-piece in the finest British tradition, told with literacy and irony.

Van Siller, SOMBER MEMORY (Doubleday Crime Club, $2). Montana dude ranch in winter makes a sinister setting for brooding over a past murder and building to a fresh one. Cumulatively powerful job featuring nicely ambiguous characters, excellent atmosphere and a startling finale.

A.L. Furman (editor), THE THIRD MYSTERY COMPANION (Gold Label, $2.75). Twenty detective and crime stories, from short shorts to novelettes, most of them (if not, as the preface claims, all) appearing for the first time in book form, plus twelve pages of biographical notes and Raymond Chandler's absorbingly argumentative article on "The Simple Art of Murder." [Margery] Allingham, [John] Collier, [Stuart] Palmer, [Vincent] Starrett, [Cornell] Woolrich are among the all-star cast, and I was especially happy at last to see one of Richard Sale's screwball-fantasy Captain McGrail stories in a book.

Willetta Ann Barber & R.F. Schabelitz, THE NOOSE IS DRAWN (Scribner, $2). As illustrator-detective Christopher Storm returns from the wars, his wife finds a corpse on the terrace. First-hand details of Red Cross drives and the literary business, mounting terror and a double-twist solution make this the most enjoyable Storm I've weathered. (Two minor dissents: the always fascinating sketches include not only the true solution but a quite unexplained false trail. And nobody ever had such an untroublesome pregnancy as Storm's narrator-wife.)

Lawrence Lariar, THE GIRL WITH THE FRIGHTENED EYES (Dodd Mead, $2). Returned veteran seeks vanished sister of dead comrade and finds himself neck-deep in art-racketeering and murder; comic-strip writer Homer Bull extricates him. Fast-paced yarn with good background of N.Y. art circles; the best Lariar to date, though Bull's deductions must be taken largely on trust.

Jerome Odlum, THE MIRABILIS DIAMOND (Scribner, $2). Pursuit of legendary million-dollar diamond leads private eye John Steele a dangerous chase between Hollywood and Baja California. Good routine toughie—possibly first rate if you've never read [Dashiell Hammett's] THE MALTESE FALCON.

BEST BUYS IN REPRINTS. Nicholas Blake, THE CORPSE IN THE SNOWMAN (with Nigel Strangeways) (Popular Library, 25 cents, uncut); Ngaio Marsh, ENTER A MURDERER (with Roderick Alleyn) (Tower, 49 cents, uncut).

October 14, 1945

Ellery Queen [Frederic Dannay] (editor), ROGUES' GALLERY: THE GREAT CRIMINALS OF MODERN FICTION (Little Brown, $3). You know by now that the annual Queen anthology is one of the major events of the year in the criminous field. That fabulous critic and scholar always manages to find excellent and unfamiliar stories, to arrange and annotate them with ingenuity and taste, and to produce that rarest book—an anthology which is a creative job. It's enough to say that this highly immoral collection of the exploits of successful criminals is up to the Queen standard; there are no higher superlatives.

Julius Fast, WATCHFUL AT NIGHT (Farrar & Rinehart, $2). "Accidental" killing on rifle range forces medical lab Sergeant Clark into detection—by which he learns that friends can be murderers and Americans can be fascists. Vivid sense of locale and vigorous prose mark an unusually well-written and often terrifying first novel.

Maurice Walsh, NINE STRINGS TO YOUR BOW (Lippincott, $2). Irish Con Madden settles into a Scottish village to clear up a year-old murder—and straighten out a love life or two. Leisurely enjoyable narrative, distinguished more for its rhythmic idiomatic dialogue than for its detection.

Katharine Hill, CASE FOR EQUITY (Dutton, $2). Realtrix-actress Lorna Donahue finds a vanishing corpse, a possible Nazi, a summer stock company and young love—and all but gets killed for her pains. A slightly foolish story but pleasant reading.

BEST BUYS IN REPRINTS. John Dickson Carr, THE MAD HATTER MYSTERY (with Dr. Gideon Fell) (Popular Library, 25 cents, uncut); Kenneth Fearing, DAGGER OF THE MIND (Bestseller, 25 cents, uncut); Georges Simenon, MAIGRET RETURNS (with Inspector Maigret) (Jonathan, 25 cents, uncut).

October 21, 1945

Leslie Charteris (editor), THE SAINT'S CHOICE OF HUMOROUS CRIME (Bond-Charteris, 25 cents). Mostly a long and funny novelette by the editor, plus familiar [Mark] Twain and O. Henry, less familiar [Robert] Benchley and Saki [H.H. Munro], and an outrageous Saint parody by Cam-

Cameron Blake. The selections are amusing enough, but the editor's notes are the cream of the jest and not to be missed.

Marjorie Alan, DARK PROPHECY (Mill, $2). The standard British house-party murder (this time at a masked ball) is handled freshly and effectively by a new author who manages to combine the chess-puzzle appeal with an adroit feminine emotionalism that never gets out of hand. Good solid stuff. (Published in England as MASKED MURDER.)

Arthur W. Upfield, DEATH OF A SWAGMAN (Doubleday Crime Club, $2). Inspector Napoleon Bonaparte gets himself jugged for vagrancy to solve a murder puzzle involving such disparate factors as the swagmen's chalk code, windmill gazing and the kidnaping of a charming child. Slow start but lots of rewarding tension in the end, with Bony in top form.

D.B. Olsen [Dolores Hitchens], BRING THE BRIDE A SHROUD (Doubleday Crime Club, $2). Professor A.L. Pennyfeather plunges in to save his G.I. nephew from assorted harpies and finds he has to solve a murder to do it. Good setting of California town, ingenious variations on clue planting and absence of Miss Rachel and cat set this a notch above recent Olsens.

Constance & Gwenyth Little, THE BLACK EYE (Doubleday Crime Club, $2). Eugenia borrowed the apartment for a rest; she didn't bargain on an amorous sergeant to share it nor on mummified corpses under the bed. All very frantic, which Little fans seem to find synonymous with funny.

Kathleen Moore Knight, PORT OF SEVEN STRANGERS (Doubleday Crime Club, $2). Small group of tourists stranded in Vera Cruz hotel find romance, excitement and murder. Sheerly improbable actions of murderer, standardly stupid heroine and careless editing lessen enjoyment of brightly written story.

BEST BUYS IN REPRINTS. Erle Stanley Gardner, THE CASE OF THE LUCKY LEGS (with Perry Mason) (Tower, 49 cents, uncut); Vera Kelsey, THE BRIDE DINED ALONE (Mercury, 25 cents, cut); Ellery Queen [Frederic Dannay & Manfred B. Lee], THE TRAGEDY OF Y (originally published as by Barnaby Ross) (with Drury Lane) (Pocket Books, 25 cents, uncut).

October 28, 1945

Lawrence Treat, V AS IN VICTIM (Duell, Sloan & Pearce, $2.50). Routine hit-and-run case ties freakishly in with murder; plodding third grade detective Mitch Taylor and intellectual lab technician Jub Freeman dovetail the answer. In this contrasted team Mr. Treat has created the most believable police professionals in American detective fiction; in its unpretentious way this may be an epoch-making book, marking a fresh new realistic approach to police procedure. Add the skill at puzzle construction and the deftness of psychological characterization that have always marked

Treat's work and you have a grand book that will leave you hungry for more Taylor-Freeman collaborations.

Roman McDougald, THE WHISTLING LEGS (Simon & Schuster, $2). The first murder was to be only a build-up to a framed suicide; private detective Philip Cabot's job was to guess not only the murderer (whose legs whistled) but the victim. A noble and intricately woven problem-structure plus plenty of character, atmosphere and action.

Babs Lee, PASSPORT TO OBLIVION (Scribner, $2). Spying and killing in Lisbon, with Argus Steele solving the pressing problem of the allergic refugee. Familiar enough stuff (the reader who doesn't beat Steele to the answer by 100 pages will be disbarred), but ingratiatingly lively and colorful in the telling.

Bruno Fischer, THE DEAD MEN GRIN (McKay, $2). Family feuds in upstate New York lead to multiple murders, disentangled by ex-cop Ben Helm. Good small-town background and solid—if also somewhat stolid— narration.

November 4, 1945

August Derleth, IN RE: SHERLOCK HOLMES: THE ADVENTURES OF SOLAR PONS (with an introduction by Vincent Starrett) (Mycroft & Moran, $2.50). A superlative collection of Holmesian pastiches, presenting Mr. Solar Pons and Dr. Parker, successors in Praed Street to the immortal team of Baker Street. Delightful in concept and execution, these twelve tales will prove a rich find to all those who have long regretted that Watson recorded only sixty of the Master's cases.

Jessica Ryan, THE MAN WHO ASKED WHY (Doubleday Crime Club, $2). Gregory Sergievitch, professor of Slavic languages at U.C. [University of California], has a 'satiable curiosity which leads him, in the best of recent detective debuts, into a fine mess of dope-addicts, composer-conductors, anti-Semites, Mormons and murderers. In all, as literate and satisfactory a first mystery as the season has produced, and if Miss Ryan is a local girl (as she must be from her knowledgeable details of S.F. and Berkeley), the drinks are on Boucher whenever she wants them.

Elinor Chamberlain, APPOINTMENT IN MANILA (Dodd Mead, $2). Philippine philanthropist murdered by Quisling; artist Olivia Brander detects and romances through Japanese invasion. Highly satisfactory first half, rich in well-absorbed local color; but after December 8, 1941, the reader finds it hard to sustain interest in the small private murder. And if three suspects are all traitors, who cares which of them actually struck the blow? An imperfectly balanced book but one promising good things to come from this Red Badge prize winner.

Frank Gruber, THE SILVER TOMBSTONE (Farrar & Rinehart, $2). Those ingeniously improvident book salesmen Johnny Fletcher and Sam

Cragg are at it again; this time their corpse-finding, sucker-fleecing routine involves Hollywood hotels and Arizona silver mines. For his first book in three years Gruber has practically dropped even the pretense of writing a mystery story. It's pure chaotic farce, it makes no sense at all and it's kind of wonderful.

Mary Roberts Rinehart, THE YELLOW ROOM (Farrar & Rinehart, $2.50). When Carol opened the Maine summer house she discovered the charred corpse of a total stranger; fortunately her next-door neighbor was ex-G-man Major Jerry Dane. All the familiar Rinehart ingredients of romance, society and terror are blended to the taste of her fans. Mrs. Rinehart has still of course not bothered to learn the first principles of honest whodunit construction; after almost forty years of success without them, why should she?

Milton M. Raison, NOBODY LOVES A DEAD MAN (Murray & Gee, $2). Murder of fading star involves drama critic Tony Woolrich in endless Hollywood escapades. The author achieves an unguessable solution by the simple method of basing it on no facts whatsoever. The action involves two murders, a suicide, assorted love affairs, a gambling raid, a kidnaping, a sinister cult ritual and a dash of homosexuality; and the jacket blurb says "Raison ought to get a special Oscar for restraint."

November 11, 1945

Christopher Hale, RUMOR HATH IT (Doubleday Crime Club, $2). Mr. Cornelius Den Hof Izonga quietly collected all the private scandals of the best people in his Michigan town and doled out shrewd advice in return—which made him a singularly useful and dangerous man when the murders started. Lieutenant Bill French is as efficient as ever but it's Mr. Izonga's book—and a highly satisfying full-bodied one, far above the general run of slick socialite-family opuses.

Robin Grey [Elizabeth Gresham], PUZZLE IN PORCELAIN (Duell, Sloan & Pearce, $2.50). Bumptious parvenue in old Virginia poisoned by rattlesnake venom; tinkerer Hunter Lewis pieces together a shattered statue and the murder puzzle. A mite coy but nonetheless a pleasing debut, with some agreeable fresh angles.

William Gray Beyer, EENIE, MEENIE, MINIE—MURDER! (Mystery House, $2). Jewel theft and gunplay complicate private murder for unorthodox Philadelphia shamus Cornelius Duffy. Active but chaotic.

BEST BUYS IN REPRINTS. Agatha Christie, DEATH COMES AS THE END (with Hori) (Grosset & Dunlap, $1, uncut); Erle Stanley Gardner, THE CASE OF THE SHOPLIFTER'S SHOE (with Perry Mason) (Pocket Books, 25 cents, uncut); James R. Langham, SING A SONG OF HOMICIDE (with Sammy Abbott) (Popular Library, 25 cents, uncut).

November 18, 1945

Matthew Head, THE DEVIL IN THE BUSH (Simon & Schuster, $2). I trust you all remember Mr. Head's uniquely ironical THE SMELL OF MONEY—one of the half dozen best first mysteries in my reviewing experience. (Don't ask me to list the others—I don't know—though they'd certainly include Lucy Cores, Kenneth Millar and Joel Townsley Rogers.) This, his second, is no anti-climax. Set in the Congo bush which Head knows at first hand, it presents living, confused, fascinating people in a finely woven mesh of semi-civilized emotions against a background of vivid primitive atmosphere. For his psychology, his economy and his bite, Mr. Head is hereby proclaimed the American [Georges] Simenon.

Helen McCloy, THE ONE THAT GOT AWAY (Morrow, $2). Hunt for escaped P.W. [prisoner of war] on Scottish moors ties into complex family problems—and murder; Captain Basil Willing appears on the scene late but clears matters up efficiently. Some readers (meaning at least me) may find the solution a bit hard to swallow, but on readability, intelligence and impeccable craftsmanship Miss McCloy still remains well ahead of the field.

George Harmon Coxe, WOMAN AT BAY (Knopf, $2). Paul McKinnon, one of our less infallible secret service operators, visits Havana to recover the secret diary of a Vichy official from the official's widow who happens to be McKinnon's divorced wife if you're still following. Possibly good novelette relentlessly padded to book length.

November 25, 1945

M.V. Heberden, VICIOUS PATTERN (Doubleday Crime Club, $2). Upstate New York town, completely taken over by gangsters, makes the serious mistake of tangling with Desmond Shannon. Miss Heberden's ear for colloquial speech is still fairly faulty but she can tell a good story—and this is one of the goriest since [Dashiell Hammett's] RED HARVEST.

William L. Stuart, THE DEAD LIE STILL (Farrar & Rinehart, $2). Centre Street and the FBI are helpless against Jap-inspired murders until artist Sam Talbot takes over. Highly effective debut in the sadistic and ultra-objective hardboiled school.

Brett Halliday, MARKED FOR MURDER (Dodd Mead, $2). Michael Shayne returns to Miami to clean up a murderous gambling racket and avenge a friend. Standard Shayne, with some ingenious twists involving an endless series of blonde twists.

Anne Damer & Jack Denton Scott, TOO LIVELY TO LIVE (Doubleday Crime Club, $2). Murders and espionage in British ministry solved by American journalist Elwyn Mills. Ministry background and characters excellent, but the resolute brightness and ultimate chaos of this effort may make you see some good in the dull but craftsmanlike British school.

Robert Portner Koehler, MURDER EXPERT (Phoenix, $2). Murder at a gathering of mystery writers cracked by Al and Isabel Branson. Too much question-and-answer but an ingenious final plot-twist.

Sam Merwin, Jr., MESSAGE FROM A CORPSE (Mystery House, $2). Manuscript biography of dead tycoon leads to chain of murders; Brahmin vulgarian Amy Brewster is featured, with a minimum of detection. Amusing in spots, though the key clue (supposedly a cryptogram) is the year's most offensive fraud on the reader.

December 2, 1945

Alfred Hitchcock (editor), SUSPENSE STORIES (Dell, 25 cents). Excellent anthology, admirably balancing familiar stories (Pierce, [James M.] Cain, [Wilbur Daniel] Steele) with little-known gems (Fraley, Outerson, Straus). Detection, espionage, folk lore, fantasy and fact jostle excitingly; and there's a foreword on "The Quality of Suspense," by Mr. Hitchcock—who knows.

Anne Rowe, UP TO THE HILT (Mill, $2). Blackmail and murder in glittering N.Y. theater and literary circles. Foolish plot of coincidence and wrong guesses but lightly and agreeably told.

BEST BUYS IN REPRINTS. John August, THE WOMAN IN THE PICTURE (Popular Library, 25 cents, uncut); Raymond Chandler, THE HIGH WINDOW (with Philip Marlowe) (Pocket Books, 25 cents, uncut); Agatha Christie, EASY TO KILL (with Luke Fitzwilliam) (Pocket Books, 25 cents, uncut); Carter Dickson [John Dickson Carr], THE PLAGUE COURT MURDERS (with Sir Henry Merrivale) (Jonathan, 25 cents, cut).

December 9, 1945

H.C. Branson, THE FEARFUL PASSAGE (Simon & Schuster, $2). Seemingly simple murder-robbery yields murky secrets of motivation as John Bent investigates. Like all of Branson's works this is a civilized and distinguished contribution to the serious literature of the detective story, and there's a peculiar ironic aftertaste to this one.

Austin Ripley, MINUTE MYSTERIES (Sleuth House, 25 cents). This latest collection of the ingenious puzzles about Professor Joseph Fordney shows that their author is, understandably enough, beginning to feel the strain. Many of them are repetitious and a few unfair. But there are still several satisfactorily neat brain crackers, and Warren King's illustrations have a pleasing mammary implausibility.

BEST BUYS IN REPRINTS. Francis Bonnamy, DEAD RECKONING (with Peter Shane) (Death House, 25 cents, cut); Allan R. Bosworth, FULL CRASH DIVE (with Admiral Wetherbee) (Death House, 25 cents, cut).

December 16, 1945

Patricia Wentworth, SHE CAME BACK (Lippincott, $2). Titled Englishwoman returns from the grave after three years—or is she an impostor planted as an enemy agent? The question is answered by a murder or two and the intervention of Miss Maud Silver. Never much mystery, but somehow the most enjoyable of the quiet Miss Silver books to reach this department.

BEST BUYS IN REPRINTS. Lilian Lauferty, THE HUNGRY HOUSE (Tower, 49 cents, uncut); Charles L. Leonard [M.V. Heberden], ASSIGNMENT TO DEATH (originally THE FANATIC OF FEZ) (with Paul Kilgerrin) (Thriller Novel Classic, 25 cents, cut); Lawrence Treat, THE LEATHER MAN MURDERS (originally THE LEATHER MAN) (Mystery Novel Classic, 25 cents, cut).

December 23, 1945

Jonathan Stagge [also known as Patrick Quentin], DEATH, MY DARLING DAUGHTERS (Doubleday Crime Club, $2). A legendary American family, international medical secrets, sex repression and silver polish combine into a devilish puzzle for Dr. Hugh Westlake. Slick, satiric, surprising and satisfactory.

BEST BUYS IN REPRINTS. Anthony Berkeley, TRIAL AND ERROR (with Ambrose Chitterwick) (Pocket Books, 25 cents, uncut); Agatha Christie, THE MURDER OF ROGER ACKROYD (with Hercule Poirot) (Pocket Books, 25 cents, uncut); Georges Simenon, THE PATIENCE OF MAIGRET (with Inspector Maigret) (Bestseller, 25 cents, one novelette uncut).

December 30, 1945

Stuart Towne [Clayton Rawson], DEATH FROM NOWHERE (Yogi Mysteries, 25 cents). Two fantastic novelettes, hitherto unreprinted, about magician-detective Don Diavolo and murder among Swamis and circuses. The writing is amusing if hasty and the plots are sterling specimens of the [John Dickson] Carr-[Clayton] Rawson impossible situation school.

BEST BUYS IN REPRINTS. Baynard Kendrick, THE LAST EXPRESS (with Captain Duncan Maclain) (Dell, 25 cents, uncut); Lenore Glen Offord, SKELETON KEY (with Todd McKinnon) (Dell, 25 cents, uncut).

1946

January 6, 1946

E.R. Punshon, SECRETS CAN'T BE KEPT (Macmillan, $2). Disappearance of amateur blackmailer causes Inspector Bobby Owen to unearth all the secret scandals of Wychshire—and eventually a corpse or two. Nineteen forty-six starts off well with this specimen of the leisurely detailed school at its soundest, with an ending which, if somewhat chancy, may yet chill your blood.

January 13, 1946

No column was published this week due to a business trip Boucher took to New York.

January 20, 1946

Hilda Lawrence, THE PAVILION (Simon & Schuster, $2). She came to the old house as a refugee only to find that the death of its owner had turned it into a haunted palace. There among the aged survivors of two curious clans and the memories of her own childhood began the quest into the past for motives of madness and murder. In its emotional impact, its domestic detail, its subtle terror, its aura of aristocracy (and even, I must admit, in its possibly excessive length), this novel to me succeeds in authentically possessing all the qualities generally attributed to the synthetic [Mary Roberts] Rinehart school.

Anthony Gilbert, DEATH LIFTS THE LATCH (Smith & Durrell, $2). Young nurse asks one question too many about "natural" death of patient and the web of suspense and peril starts weaving around her—severed at last of course by resourceful Arthur Crook, who perhaps deserves even better than [Edgar Wallace's character] J.G. Reeder the epithet of "the man with the criminal mind." Solidly intricate and humorously terrifying— definitely one of the better Gilberts. (Published in England as DON'T OPEN THE DOOR.)

January 27, 1946

Marjorie Bonner, THE SHAPES THAT CREEP (Scribner, $2). Stanford botanist Vaughan Proudfoot and wife Sally set out for a sabbatical on the Vancouver coast and encounter a series of corpses—plus a cryptic will, a flood and a treasure. Erudite but human, gentle but suspenseful—in all a charming book, with attractive new sleuths and a vivid fresh setting.

Richard Foster [Kendell Foster Crossen], THE INVISIBLE MAN MURDERS (Five Star, 25 cents). Impossible-situation murders in Hollywood studio solved by Tibetan private eye Chin Kwang Kham. Agreeable detective in amusing story marred by one sadistic scene and a certain implausibility in the solution. Not a reprint.

Jeremy Lane, MURDER MENAGERIE (Phoenix, $2). Clever new murder method raises hell among research biologists until psychiatrist Whitney Wheat solves the puzzle of the tiger, the termites and the termagant. Good enough.

Lois Eby & John C. Fleming, THE CASE OF THE MALEVOLENT TWIN (Dutton, $2). Is the bold buccaneering financier himself or his sinister twin? Is Zachary Stone the great private detective or an impostor? Is the secretary as harmless as he seems? Will love conquer all? And unnumbered other questions including How did this get published?

BEST BUYS IN REPRINTS. Elizabeth Daly, EVIDENCE OF THINGS SEEN (with Henry Gamadge) (Bantam, 25 cents, uncut); Matthew Head, THE SMELL OF MONEY (Mercury, 25 cents, uncut); Rufus King, MURDER ON THE YACHT (with Lieutenant Valcour) (Popular Library, 25 cents, uncut).

February 3, 1946

Manning Coles, THE FIFTH MAN (Doubleday Crime Club, $2). For once Tommy Hambledon is eclipsed; here he plays second fiddle to Anthony Colemore, a man after Tommy's own heart, who leads at least a quintuple life in a brilliant gammoning of the German secret service. Pure fantasy spiced with luck, impossibility and high humor—and grand fun every page of the way.

Doris Miles Disney, DARK ROAD (Doubleday Crime Club, $2). Hazel had a drunken husband, a wealthy lover, a beautiful face and a shrewdly petty mind which could contrive the perfect accidental murder but could neither foresee nor endure its aftermath. Not a mystery but a well-plotted and well-written novel of murder, ironic and moving.

E.C.R. Lorac, MURDER BY MATCHLIGHT (Mystery House, $2). Silent murder in a London park involves bicycles, air raid wardens, magicians and Sinn Feiners—none of which daunt patient, intelligent Chief Inspector Macdonald. Old-line British detection, with more humor and characterization than most.

Harriette R. Campbell, CRIME IN CRYSTAL (Harper, $2). Black market clothes, a gypsy seeress and an oddly saintly chief suspect make a murder puzzle for Simon Brade. Slow start redeemed by ingenious solution and good interplay of characters.

Roy Huggins, THE DOUBLE TAKE (Morrow, $2). Seemingly simple case of identity leads private eye Stuart Bailey into tangled web of gangsters, socialites, sadists and unnumbered lovelies. Mr. Huggins adds nothing to the established hardboiled formula but he does an unusually able job within its possibly over-familiar frame.

Edith Howie, NO FACE TO MURDER (Mill, $2). Murder of janitor and choir singer uncovers choice scandals among the parishioners of St. Thomas' Cathedral, Episcopal. Randolph Garrison is more efficient as a lover than as head of homicide, but the telling and the churchly background (even to an agreeable bishop) are pleasing.

BEST BUYS IN REPRINTS. Geoffrey Household, ROGUE MALE (Bantam, 25 cents, uncut); Mabel Seeley, THE LISTENING HOUSE (Popular Library, 25 cents, uncut).

February 10, 1946

Frances & Richard Lockridge, MURDER WITHIN MURDER (Lippincott, $2). Miss Gipson was doing research for a book of true murders; was she killed (and in the 42nd Street library at that) because she had researched too well or because she was primly playing hob with her family's happiness? Lieut. Bill Weigand and the Norths turn up the answer; you should beat them to it by many pages but those pages are written with such wit, charm and humanity that you won't mind.

George Bagby [Aaron Marc Stein], DEAD ON ARRIVAL (Doubleday Crime Club, $2). Unlikely murders in a brownstone in the East Fifties provide footsore Inspector Schmidt with a household of madmen, a cryptogram, and a heroine who leaves her panties on corpses. Schmidt's ghost Bagby has been missing for years; his peculiar blend of wacky humor, sound logic, good writing and O'Malleyesque directness [referring to the cop character created by William MacHarg] is hereby welcomed back with a huzzah.

Charlotte Armstrong, THE UNSUSPECTED (Coward-McCann, $2.50). Ex-flyer stages marital masquerade which frustrates murderous plots of sinister theater director and awakens ugly-duckling heiress. I seem to be in a minority in thinking that Miss Armstrong's excellent detective stories had stronger novelistic values than this deliberately contrived borderline effort, but it's still a satisfactory job in the increasingly important suspense-without-mystery school.

Peter Mortimer, IF A BODY KILL A BODY (Mystery House, $2). Smalltown girl reporter Kerry Brooks covers her first murder trial and unearths evidence to prove the confessed murderer innocent. No great shakes for excitement, but in its background and people somehow very likeable.

Martha Albrand, REMEMBERED ANGER (Little Brown, $2). American soldier assumes identity of dead Frenchman to track down Underground traitor now flourishing in liberated France; love complicates his quest. Hitch-pullet. (Pullet: the immature and feminine relative of the cock.)

Miles Burton [also known as John Rhode], ACCIDENTS DO HAPPEN (Doubleday Crime Club, $2). A famous editor once said, "No American mystery can be so dull as a dull British, and no British so bad as a bad American." Mr. Burton gives her the lie. Not only is his latest dull, endless and snobbish; its ending (one can hardly say solution) provides the most incompetent detecting (by Desmond Merrion) of the past decade—bad enough to make the brashest American quickie seem well-plotted. (Published in England as EARLY MORNING MURDER.)

February 17, 1946

A.E. Martin, DEATH IN THE LIMELIGHT (Simon & Schuster, $2). Has-been American actor visits Sydney and finds himself up to the neck in a murder plot eventually solved by Inspector Gormley. Closer to a straight whodunit than earlier Martins but with all the Australian color, the vivid knowledge of show business and the quiet pleasure in humanity that we've come to expect from one of the prime contenders in the field.

Valentine Williams, COURIER TO MARRAKESH (Houghton Mifflin, $2.50). USO ballad-singer risks her life and love in high adventure from Morocco to besieged Rome, always opposed by the sinister superhuman figure of Dr. Adolf Grundt, better known as Clubfoot. It's so long since there's been a Clubfoot story, I'd all but forgotten what fine grisly fun he provides. As to his spectacular death at the end of this—well, one of the characters observes, "It's not the first time that the worthy Doktor Grundt has been officially dead and buried." Nor, I pray, the last.

Octavus Roy Cohen, LOVE HAS NO ALIBI (Macmillan, $2). Strange things start happening to Kirk Douglas, from an anonymous $100,000 deposit in his account to the murder of a total stranger (female) in his apartment. Kirk figures the puzzle neatly if not surprisingly, with assists from Lieut. Max Gold and (in all too brief a scene) Jim Hanvey. The most ingenious and agreeable yet of Mr. Cohen's slickly glittering Manhattan mysteries.

Amber Dean, CALL ME PANDORA (Doubleday Crime Club, $2). When Abbie Harris bought an apartment house she hardly expected to take over a beauty shop as well—nor yet a well-stabbed blonde corpse. Pleasant specimen of the matronly-narrator school, with humor, beauty-background, young love and not too weak a plot.

Francis Sill Wickware, DANGEROUS GROUND (Doubleday Crime Club, $2). While the jury deliberates Serena's fate, her lawyer and the doctor who loves her go over all the events that led to the murder charge and find, in this mesh of abnormal psychology and smalltown narrowness, the key to free her. Highly readable and professional job, all but ruined by an unbelievable, unethical and unpardonable denouement.

Duane W. Rimel, THE CURSE OF CAIN (McKay, $2). Carl knew he'd committed the first of the murders but now another killer was at work, intent on wiping out the whole family. It's hard to say what is worst in this story—the flat writing, the dull heel offered as protagonist or the completely silly "solution." And will Mr. Rimel (and the editor of McKay mysteries) please look up the effects of arsenic in any toxicology?

BEST BUYS IN REPRINTS. Margery Allingham, THE FASHION IN SHROUDS (with Albert Campion) (Pocket Books, 25 cents, uncut); R. Austin Freeman, MR.POLTON EXPLAINS (with Dr. Thorndyke) (Popular Library, 25 cents, uncut); William Irish [Cornell Woolrich], DEADLINE AT DAWN (Tower, 49 cents, uncut).

February 24, 1946

Dana Chambers, DEATH AGAINST VENUS (Dial Press, $2). Subtle methods of driving a girl mad prove not enough so plotters turn to murder; Dr. Richard Vine achieves his own reintegration from dipsomania by cracking the plot. Diffusion of guilt may irritate purists but Chambers' high-tension readability holds up right along the line.

Frances Crane, THE SHOCKING PINK HAT (Random House, $2). Conveniently present when an automobile complete with corpse smashes up on a San Francisco hill street, Patrick Abbott and his wife Jean investigate a mystery seriously involving one of their friends. Atmosphere and local color excellent; minor characters drawn with admirable vividness; the solution, however, might have offered a more original and personal murder motive than the one so frankly revealed by the jacket blurb. (Review by Lenore Glen Offord.)

John Rhode, THE SECRET OF THE LAKE HOUSE (Dodd Mead, $2). Meticulous Scotland Yard work by Jimmy Waghorn (now a Superintendent) all but hangs the wrong man; Dr. Priestley emerges to the rescue. Slightly shopworn plot-gambit but thoroughly solid piece of work.

Hugh Holman, SLAY THE MURDERER (Mill, $2). OPA [Office of Price Administration] investigator framed for murder in Southern town but cleared by shrewdly rustic Sheriff Macready. Not a crystal-clear plot, but the likeable sheriff has my best wishes in his campaign for re-election.

Vincent Starrett, MURDER IN PEKING (Lantern Press, $2). Killings among expatriates in pre-war China investigated by Hope Johnson. Slathers of vivid local color, but such a connoisseur of detection as Mr. Starrett should know better what can and cannot be done in the form.

Lee Thayer, A HAIR'S BREADTH (Dodd Mead, $2). Berkeley (whose homicide rate is as high in fiction as it is low in fact) offers the setting for the latest deductive exploits of Peter Clancy and valet Wiggar. Action centers around a war show in the stadium. Clancy fans will not be disappointed.

March 3, 1946

Erle Stanley Gardner, THE D.A. BREAKS A SEAL (Morrow, $2). White gardenias, a great criminal lawyer and a very pretty will-breaking case set the background for the murder which Doug (now Major) Selby walks into on leave. Gardner formula—but a formula which his fans (including me) see no good reason to tire of. (But is anyone else getting very tired of Morrow's wide-eyed jackets?)

Allan MacKinnon, MONEY ON THE BLACK (Doubleday Crime Club, $2). Detective-Sergeant David Stanners spends his leave from the Royal Navy in semi-official investigation of the black market in London; ensuing murders require all the best leg-and-brain-work possible from him and Gaelic-swearing Inspector Duncan MacCallum. Novel and welcome blend of British routine and American forthrightness.

Alfred Eichler, DEATH AT THE MIKE (Lantern Press, $2). Sudden death of a participant threatens the success of the Mr. Anthony-like "Road to Happiness" program, but agency director Martin Ames uses everything from teratology to phonetics to flush out a murderer and send up the program's Hooper. Fast and knowledgeable.

Ann T. Smith, DEATH IN THE CARDS (Phoenix, $2). Grisly events from black magic to felidicide surround murder in Boston rooming house; Paul Redfern cracks case to save his suspected wife. Much exciting story material, not too well digested.

Leonard H. Nason, CONTACT MERCURY (Doubleday, $2.50). Lieutenant Colonel Eadie wasn't G-2; he just had a routine job to do, but before he finished it he had invaded Paris single-handed and rescued the atomic bomb from Germany. Eadie is likeable, the somewhat plotless confusion is probably typical of actual events in liberated France, and the sections on the bomb have the virtue of bearing no indiscreet relation to fact.

BEST BUYS IN REPRINTS. Agatha Christie, THE BODY IN THE LIBRARY (with Miss Marple) (Pocket Books, 25 cents, uncut); Graham Greene, THE MINISTRY OF FEAR (Penguin, 25 cents, uncut).

March 10, 1946

Elizabeth Daly, SOMEWHERE IN THIS HOUSE (Rinehart, $2). My Webster says that a solander is an eczymatous eruption of a horse's hind leg but Elizabeth Daly asserts it is a book made into a cigarette box. And so intense is my devotion to Mrs. Daly that I shall henceforth look upon Webster with suspicion. Solanders and all, she has here accomplished another of her beautiful jobs of laying bare all the terror of criminality while never raising her voice above a genteel whisper. Henry Gamadge is in his usual perfect form and you'll be pleased to know that David Malcolm, last met as a suspect, is coming along promisingly as an assistant.

Ellery Queen [Frederic Dannay & Manfred B. Lee], DRURY LANE'S LAST CASE (Little Brown, $2). Last of the reissues of the Drury Lane novels, originally published as by Barnaby Ross—a classic specimen of the elaborately formal deductive problem, with a dividend of Shakespeare-ana (horrifying to us Oxonians) and a unique solution.

Lavinia R. Davis, BARREN HERITAGE (Doubleday Crime Club, $2). Decadent aristocracy in the New Jersey pine barren country means terror to a girl trapped in it. The plot is hackneyed enough but for once the Crime Club designation of "character and atmosphere" means just what it says.

Verne Chute, FLIGHT OF AN ANGEL (Morrow, $2). Jamie-Boy Raider, one of the more clinically anomalous of the current spate of amnesia victims, gets in and out of unnumbered beds and shooting scrapes both here and in Los Angeles in quest of his true identity. Highly professional performance in that peculiarly phony blend of coincidence, naivete and sentimentality which passes as hardboiled realism.

BEST BUYS IN REPRINTS. Frank Gruber, THE LAUGHING FOX (with Johnny Fletcher) (Penguin, 25 cents, uncut); Ellery Queen [Frederic Dannay & Manfred B. Lee], THE DEVIL TO PAY (with Ellery Queen) (Tower, 49 cents, uncut); Richard Sale, PASSING STRANGE (Jonathan, 25 cents, uncut).

March 17, 1946

John Roeburt, THERE ARE DEAD MEN IN MANHATTAN (Mystery House, $2). Jigger Moran, cabby and disbarred lawyer, knows all the angles—and needs to know them as he tangles with gangsters, sadists and an Albany-minded D.A. Even one of the oldest cliche solutions doesn't keep this from being a highly individual and effective variant on the hardboiled school.

Peter Yates, DEATH IN THE HANDS OF TALENT (Five Star, 25 cents). Reporter Sandy Blunt starts out for a feature series on the peculiarly varied clients of the world's oddest agent and finds himself deep in murders, disappearances—and celluloid animals. Good lightweight fun. Not a reprint.

Rex Stout & Louis Greenfield (editors), RUE MORGUE NO. 1 (Creative Age, $2.75). This first volume of a projected annual series is a welcome but exceedingly spotty anthology. Credit: all of the stories are new to book form; they include a small masterpiece by John Van Druten and several good fantasies and capable yarns. Debit (aside from the startling omissions, which are doubtless on non-aesthetic grounds): the editors seem to have chosen at least half the stories by pure chance—pulling them out of a hack, you might say.

Wenzell Brown, MURDER SEEKS AN AGENT (Five Star, 25 cents). The Murder Machine lethally assaults the Manhattan literary and theatrical world, with mild Professor Peter Aswell caught in the middle. Humor and fast action, both of a fairly elementary sort. Not a reprint.

M. Scott Michel, THE PSYCHIATRIC MURDERS (Mystery House, $2). Red-headed psychiatrist Job Cleveland lets the corpses fall wildly about him while he investigates blackmail and hypnotism. Interesting plot-gadget lost in a book less sexy than Michel's previous efforts but no more coherent or convincing.

Sidney E. Porcelain, THE CRIMSON CAT MURDERS (Phoenix, $2). Harriet led a hard enough life without suffering after death the padded and pointless investigations of detective Stephen Clay. A novel and fantastic murder method is the sole bright spot in this welter of dull confusion.

BEST BUYS IN REPRINTS. Mary Collins, THE FOG COMES (with Sheriff Wade) (Bantam, 25 cents, uncut); Ngaio Marsh, COLOUR SCHEME (with "Mr. Septimus Falls") (Pocket Books, 25 cents, uncut).

March 24, 1946

Michael Innes, THE UNSUSPECTED CHASM (Dodd Mead, $2). Another of Mr. Innes' wonderful melodramas in Cloud Cuckoo Land, wherein he abandons Inspector Appleby to relate how textual critic Richard Meredith quoted [Dr. Samuel] Johnson to a tobacconist and thereby set out to expose the nefarious International Society for the Diffusion of Cultural Objects, from the Scottish Isles to Florida. An incredible and delightful blend of [John] Buchan and early [Aldous] Huxley, of [Robert Louis] Stevenson and Norman Douglas, of T.S. Eliot and L. Frank Baum.

Donald Henderson, A VOICE LIKE VELVET (Random House, $2). Raffles Psychoanalyzed; or, If You're Disappointed in Yourself, Become a Cat Burglar. Inspector Hood unravels the double life of Ernest Bisham, B.B.C. announcer, bringing about an unexpected denouement. This might be called a leisurely novel with a modicum of suspense, but slow parts are redeemed by subacid humor and the scenes in the broadcasting studio are wonderful. (Review by Lenore Glen Offord.)

Katherine Wolffe, DEATH'S LONG SHADOW (Five Star, 25 cents). Murder of obscure recluse in Minnesota leads Captain Courtney Brade to New England in cross-country quest of long-dead motives. Quietly satisfactory job. Not a reprint.

Peter Cheyney, I'LL SAY SHE DOES! (Dodd Mead, $2). Shenanigans in Paris and London by Federal agent Lemmy Caution, who tells it all in his own peculiar patter. Pretty good story if you can wade past the smart-cracking smokescreen.

Gerald Butler, KISS THE BLOOD OFF MY HANDS (Farrar & Rinehart, $2.50). For a hundred pages the author does a stunning job of portraying Bill Saunders as one of the most vicious and brutal petty criminals since [Graham Greene's 1938 novel] BRIGHTON ROCK; for another hundred he depicts him as one of nature's noblemen under the love of a good woman. Murder and sex are commonplaces in both sections, the extremely able writing of which proves that the English can be just as tersely tough as the Americans—and just as phony.

Lee Hirsch, MURDER STEALS THE SHOW (Fell, $2). Murder starts in suburban theatricals and crashes Broadway, as narrated by Sergeant Keff and solved by psychiatrist Doc Bart. Inconsistent in style and unbelievably chaotic in form but sometimes agreeable in its theatrical background.

BEST BUYS IN REPRINTS. Freeman Wills Crofts, THE CASK (with Georges La Touche) (Penguin, 25 cents, uncut); Dorothy L. Sayers, BUSMAN'S HONEYMOON (with Lord Peter Wimsey) (Pocket Books, 25 cents, uncut).

March 31, 1946

Robert Finnegan, THE LYING LADIES (Simon & Schuster, $2). Hitchhiker framed for murder; reporter Dan Banion rips into the local political and economic setup to turn up the real killer. Long full-bodied story, rich in well-sketched characters and vigorous action; Banion emerges a major new detective with a sense of social responsibility unique in the field.

Mary Plum, SUSANNA, DON'T YOU CRY! (Doubleday Crime Club, $2). Pair of disabled veterans return to home town to find a welter of financial chicanery, political skulduggery and deftly concealed murder. Their success in setting things to rights (and in concluding two love affairs) makes an unassumingly delightful book.

Leslie Charteris (editor), THE SAINT'S CHOICE OF IMPOSSIBLE CRIME (Bond-Charteris, 25 cents). The fifth volume of the Saint's eccentric anthology runs over into the scientifictional borderline of criminology with fatal fantasies of the future by [Fredric] Brown, [Oscar J.] Friend, [Henry] Kuttner and [Frank Belknap] Long, and a more nearly realistic novelette by Charteris himself. All this plus the usual genial (in either sense) and linguigenal Charteris commentaries makes an interesting and off-beat quarter's worth.

Joe Barry, THE TRIPLE CROSS (Mystery House, $2). The vogue for amnesiacs gets a new twist in this one, with private eye Rush Henry, himself a victim of amnesia, scrambling madly to solve a tricky imposture case out of the vacuum of his memory. Good new gimmick (plus another fresh twist at the end) handled with unsubtle vigor.

Theodora Du Bois, MURDER STRIKES AN ATOMIC UNIT (Double-day Crime Club, $2). Dr. Jeffrey McNeill has his hands unusually full what with solving a clever murder, rescuing his wife Anne from spies, and above all protecting the secrets of the early stages of U-235 research. Well-told and highly readable, but Miss Du Bois knows much better than to plot so carelessly, and the usual statement that the characters are imaginary is for once very easy to believe.

Vera Kelsey, WHISPER MURDER! (Doubleday Crime Club, $2). Two mysterious arsons lead to murder and general fireworks in small Midwest city. Slow and suspenseless item, unworthy of so generally excellent a writer as Miss Kelsey.

BEST BUYS IN REPRINTS. C.W. Grafton, THE RAT BEGAN TO GNAW THE ROPE (with Gil Henry) (Mercury, 25 cents, cut); Elisabeth Sanxay Holding, NET OF COBWEBS (Bantam, 25 cents, uncut).

April 7, 1946

Rafael Bernal, UN MUERTO EN LA TUMBA (DEAD MAN IN THE TOMB) (Mexico: Editorial Jus, $3.50 Mexican). The best-characterized, meatiest and funniest whodunit yet produced in Latin America, with fasci-nating sidelights on archeology and politics and shrewd detection by tauto-logical Don Teodulo Batanes. Noted here in the hope that local Spanish bookstores may stock it—a must for connoisseurs.

Sibyl Ericson, THE CURATE'S CRIME (Mystery House, $2). Bluff squire-parson overtaken by mushrooms and arsenic; unorthodox Alastair MacAlastair of the Yard takes over. Quiet humor, perceptive characteriza-tion and admirably deceptive blend of direct and "inverted" method make Miss Ericson the most welcome British discovery since George Bellairs. More, please!

A.B. Cunningham, DEATH RIDES A SORREL HORSE (Dutton, $2). Well-contrived fake riding accident methodically exposed by Sheriff Jess Roden against curious background of "sorority house" for mountaineer girls. Not the most outstanding Cunningham, but any A.B.C. is, in its pa-tience and integrity, outstanding among the usual crop.

M.V. Heberden, MURDER CANCELS ALL DEBTS (Doubleday Crime Club, $2). Murder in a smug group of "sophisticates" provides opportunity not only for some capable sleuthing by Commander Rick Venner but also for an inspired critique of a type of American civilization. (Suggestion to Crime Club: For such atmosphere novels as this and [the 1944 Heberden novel] TO WHAT DREAD END, so different from the Desmond Shannon rough stuff, wouldn't it make sense to use the author's full name—Mary Violet Heberden?)

Thomas B. Black, THE WHITEBIRD MURDERS (Reynal & Hitch-cock, $2). Familiar ingredients of crooked politics, white slavery, mobsters and lush hairpins add up to near-fatal dish for private eye Al Delaney. But despite the familiarity, Black knows how to put it over; his fast vigor marks one of the better recent hardboiled debuts.

Edmund Crispin, HOLY DISORDERS (Lippincott, $2). Necromancy and Nazism raise hell, literally and figuratively, in a cathedral town; anomalous Professor Gervase Fen contributes a tightly reasoned solution. If this doesn't quite add up to a perfect blend of John Dickson Carr, Michael Innes and M.R. James, it isn't for want of trying.

April 14, 1946

Lester Dent, DEAD AT THE TAKE-OFF (Doubleday Crime Club, $2). The lives (and deaths) of most of the passengers and crew of the great transcontinental airliner were singularly interwoven in a strange pattern involving everything from gangsters to senators, from love to high finance. In his first clothbound effort an acknowledged pulp master proves that fabulous coincidences and occasional infelicities of writing matter hardly at all if you possess the inborn gift of telling a rattling story.

A.A. Fair [Erle Stanley Gardner], CROWS CAN'T COUNT (Morrow, $2). A pretty pattern of emerald smuggling, a tame crow and a spendthrift trust sends Donald Lam as far as Colombia in quest of a typically ingenious answer. Bertha Cool's role is small this time. Since [New York *Herald-Tribune* mystery reviewer] Will Cuppy has up and said in print that Mr. Fair is "Erle Stanley Gardner as ever was," I wonder now why I have so long respected Mr. Gardner's request to keep the fact quiet; but I may add that Mr. Fair not only is Mr. Gardner—he's usually even better than Gardner.

Wolfe Kaufman, I HATE BLONDES! (Simon & Schuster, $2). S&S likes an occasional whodunit from a figure in show business; former press agent and *Variety* mug Kaufman proves himself, if not quite so gifted as Gypsy Rose Lee, at least much better than George Sanders. The story's about milk-swilling private eye Dick Anderson commuting between Boston and New York on a very nasty murder-cum-blackmail case, and its lean hardness manages to avoid all the pitfalls of the tough school save for a somewhat fuzzy solution.

Kathleen Moore Knight, THE TROUBLE AT TURKEY HILL (Doubleday Crime Club, $2). Miss Knight momentarily abandons Latin America to return to Penberthy Island and selectman Elisha Macomber, whose homespun acuity unravels the murder web woven about three returned servicemen. The narrator contributes most of the standard spinster-cliches but it's all agreeable reading.

Carol Kendall, THE BLACK SEVEN (Harper, $2). The Twiggs were a curious and evil family but the depths of their evil (and the secret of the seven niggerbabies) might never have been known if they'd steered clear of Roderick (Drawers) Random—a 12-year-old blend of Quiz and Dead End Kid, who makes the season's oddest detective. Interesting try that doesn't quite come off—not so much Drawers' fault as that of the quite unbelievable problem he has to solve.

Marjorie Boniface, WINGS OF DEATH (McBride, $2). Murders at New Mexico tourist lodge—do they stem from espionage, pigeon-training, art-thievery or just plain personal emotions? Texan sheriff Hiram Odom straightens it all out. Harmless.

BEST BUYS IN REPRINTS. Erle Stanley Gardner, THE D.A. DRAWS A CIRCLE (with Doug Selby) (Pocket Books, 25 cents, uncut); E.C.R. Lorac, CHECKMATE TO MURDER (with Inspector Macdonald) (Bart House, 25 cents, uncut).

April 21, 1946

Geoffrey Homes, BUILD MY GALLOWS HIGH (Morrow, $2.50). Ex-detective Red Bailey had built himself a good life in the Sierra, a clean life in which he could forget he had once killed a man. But the threat of exposure drove him into a frameup for a new murder and ultimately into a tragedy Elizabethan in its inevitability and its copious carnage. Not a whodunit but a brief novel of murder in the [James M.] Cain tradition, with all Cain's tense vigor and an added humanity and honesty.

Robert Player, THE INGENIOUS MR. STONE (Rinehart, $2). Adroit poisoning of obnoxious schoolmistress affords fine matching of wits between the fabulous Lysander Stone and dowager Bertha Bradford, all narrated in assorted British and Scottish settings through a Wilkie Collins series of first-person documents. Notable modern job in a splendid old tradition.

Will Creed [also known as Peter Yates], DEATH WEARS A GREEN HAT (Five Star, 25 cents). A green Homburg is the only clue to the murderer of a N.Y. gossip columnist; cryptic Inspector Day astutely probes among Manhattan's sophisticates. Solution is ethically debatable but puzzle and narration are smoothly entertaining. (Not a reprint.)

Dorothy Foster Brown, GRIMM DEATH (Smith & Durrell, $2). Deacon pitchforked in New England barn; Sergeant Archer Brett plods wordily along to a solution as unlikely as it is unfair. Soporific.

BEST BUYS IN REPRINTS. Richard Hull, KEEP IT QUIET (Mercury, 25 cents, cut); Georges Simenon, THE PATIENCE OF MAIGRET (containing A BATTLE OF NERVES and A FACE FOR A CLUE) (with Inspector Maigret) (Penguin, 25 cents, uncut).

April 28, 1946

A.E.W. Mason, THE HOUSE IN LORDSHIP LANE (Dodd Mead, $2.50). Mr. Julius Ricardo first assisted at the criminal investigations of the great Hanaud of the Surete in 1910; 36 years later both Watson and detective are in the same excellent form as they inquire into the "suicide" of a financier and its repercussions on a great shipping firm and on the Nazi-subsidized dope traffic. The novel itself unfortunately is overlong and none too clearly planned, but the hand of an unforgettable master is still happily in evidence.

Franklyn Pell, HANGMAN'S HILL (Dodd Mead, $2). The [G.K.] Chestertonian principle of hiding a corpse in a battle is used to good effect in polishing off an unsavory war correspondent during the retaking of Alsace; Lieutenant Schneider and newsman Larry Shanahan collaborate on uncovering the culprit and a black market racket. Knowledgeable and fascinating details of censorship and other angles of war reporting make up for almost total lack of characterization. (Winner of $1000 Red Badge prize) Mildred Gordon, THE LITTLE MAN WHO WASN'T THERE (Doubleday Crime Club, $2). Deputy sheriff Bucky Johnson is one of those resolutely plucky and chipper girls who keep finding corpses and never being quite murdered. The scene of her activities is a swank Arizona rancho and your reaction will depend on just how much girlish charm you can take.

BEST BUYS IN REPRINTS. Francis Bonnamy, DEAD RECKONING (with Peter Shane) (Penguin, 25 cents, uncut); Carter Dickson [John Dickson Carr], NINE—AND DEATH MAKES TEN (with Sir Henry Merrivale) (Pocket Books, 25 cents, uncut).

May 5, 1946

Raymond Chandler, RED WIND (Tower, 49 cents). Five novelettes about assorted detectives in the topflight early manner (1933-39) of the undisputed contemporary master of the hardboiled school. All of them have previously appeared in the Avon paperback collections but this, their first clothbound publication, is nonetheless vigorously welcomed.

Arthur W. Upfield, THE DEVIL'S STEPS (Doubleday Crime Club, $2). Australian Napoleon Bonaparte is unusually useful in tracking down undercover Fascists, who by their very nature never suspect that the half-caste may be a police inspector. This brings him into more "civilized" settings than Bony usually frequents, where he observes the murder of a Nazi general. The upshot involves more chance and guesswork than is agreeable, but devotees of one of the greatest figures of modern detection won't mind too much.

Paul Whelton, CALL THE LADY INDISCREET (Lippincott, $2). Reporter Garry Dean spots peculiar byplay at a bank and follows it up on various levels of mayhem, sex and murder. Interesting opening situation fades promptly into familiar formula (including the inevitable nympho), but it's all very readably told.

Patrick Laing [Amelia Reynolds Long], MURDER FROM THE MIND (Phoenix, $2). Hypnosis of amnesia victim reveals details of past murder and starts current series in psychology faculty; blind professor Patrick Laing fingers the killer. Plot ingenuity is a touch above the flat writing, but just one more amnesia-victim whodunit is going to cause a serious trauma in this reviewer's psyche.

BEST BUYS IN REPRINTS. Hilda Lawrence, BLOOD UPON THE SNOW (with Mark East) (Pocket Books, 25 cents, uncut); Craig Rice, HOME SWEET HOMICIDE (with the Carstairs family) (Pocket Books, 25 cents, uncut).

May 12, 1946

Lee Casey (editor), DENVER MURDERS (Duell, Sloan & Pearce, $2.75). The murders included in Duell's New York and Chicago volumes could largely have happened in any metropolis, but with this Denver collection the Regional Murder series hits its full regional stride. From a drunken frontier shooting to an absorbing problem in Indian affairs, these killings could hardly have happened elsewhere; and the Colorado-assembled staff of writers has done admirably by them. Brett Halliday, William MacLeod Raine and Clyde Brion Davis are the most nationally known names, but you'll find the various Denver newspapermen equally adept. It's a pity that Denver's greatest murder (remember the spider man in the attic in 1942?) receives the least satisfactory treatment, but the book as a whole is a distinguished work both as crime reporting and as Americana.

M.S. Marble, EVERYBODY MAKES MISTAKES (Rinehart, $2). Throat-slitting is a standard Hollywood indoor sport, but when someone starts practicing it literally, it means hell for a press-agent and his clients. Enigmatic private detective Craig McKenzie saves a few lives and reputations. This has all the ingredients of run-of-the-mill tough stuff, but Miss Marble adds something in her writing that makes even her Hollywood lovelies into believable, knowable people. A fresh, good first, hereby joyfully welcomed.

Richard Sale, BENEFIT PERFORMANCE (Simon & Schuster, $2). Actor's double murdered in error; actor takes over real-life role of double to crack crime—an action far more plausible in the novel than it sounds in summary. Little in fact of the fabulous Hollywood goings-on in this opus would be plausible in summary but it's all kind of wonderful at the time, intricately plotted and told with that sharp-phrased glitter which marks Sale's best work.

Leslie Charteris (editor), THE SAINT'S CHOICE OF HOLLYWOOD CRIME (Saint Enterprises, 25 cents). Hollywood is one of the most frequently used locales for fictional murder, and the mystery often consists in where on earth the author got his idea of what Hollywood is like. The Saint has wisely chosen stories only by men who have lived in and known this borough of Bedlam—Steve Fisher, Frank Gruber, Robert Leslie Bellem, and a couple of Hollywood hangers-on called Boucher and Charteris. Result: an interesting and unhackneyed collection of criminous cinemas.

Thomas Kyd, BLOOD IS A BEGGAR (Lippincott, $2). Professorial dullard shot during lecture; toughly human Sam Phelan has his troubles with the academic atmosphere but snags the killer. Able writing and some adroitly fair misrepresentation make an intelligent first mystery.

BEST BUYS IN REPRINTS. John Buchan, THE THREE HOSTAGES (with Richard Hannay) (Bantam, 25 cents, uncut).

May 19, 1946

Joe Csida, CRIME IS OF THE ESSENCE (Five Star, 25 cents). Murders and romance in the perfume business solved by human relations counsellor Mr. Tinney. Two-dimensional and unfair, but amusing in its easy pace and its background of radio and perfumery.

William G. Bogart, THE QUEEN CITY MURDER CASE (Mystery House, $2). A prison break, blackmail, nightclubs and a singular episode in auctioneering spell plentiful bloodshed and a problem for Johnny Saxon. Good fast pulp action petering out in a shapeless solution.

Raymond Marshall [also known as James Hadley Chase], BLONDES' REQUIEM (Crown, $2). Tough dick Marc Spencer starts off on an interesting problem in corrupt small-town politics but the story keeps getting bloodier and more diffuse until it winds up in total incredibility. Fairly able standard-tough style.

BEST BUYS IN REPRINTS. Margery Allingham, DEATH OF A GHOST (with Albert Campion) (Penguin, 25 cents, uncut); Dorothy B. Hughes, JOHNNIE (Tower, 49 cents, uncut); Craig Rice, 8 FACES AT 3 (with John J. Malone & the Justuses) (Bond-Charteris, 20 cents, cut).

May 26, 1946

No column was published this week.

June 2, 1946

John Dickson Carr, HE WHO WHISPERS (Harper, $2). This is Carr in excelsis, constructed with such admirably chilling suspense from the first word that I decline even to outline the kinds of impossible murder, supernatural terror and abnormal psychology with which Dr. Gideon Fell is confronted. In many ways it marks a return to middle period Carr (the era of THE THREE COFFINS [1935] and THE CROOKED HINGE [1938]), and that means the formal detective story at its highest point of ingenuity and literacy.

E.R. Punshon, THERE'S A REASON FOR EVERYTHING (Macmillan, $2). No fictional policeman deserves professional advancement more than solid, intelligent Bobby Owen. It's gratifying to learn that he's now deputy chief constable of Wychshire and equally gratifying to know that his promotion doesn't keep him from investigating such absorbing problems as this, involving a haunted house, a recurrent bloodstain, a vanished Vermeer and a plethora of twins. Overlong, but admirable in characters and detail.

Maurice Leblanc, THE CASE OF THE GOLDEN BLONDE: SHERLOCK HOLMES VERSUS ARSENE LUPIN (adapted into English by J.B.) (Atomic Books, 25 cents). This new translation (the fourth into English) of the Leblanc classic is only passable in style and far too freely and carelessly cut, but it is good to have this delightful adventure-parody back in print in English. This is moreover the first edition, English or French, which frankly gives the name of Arsene Lupin's adversary as Sherlock Holmes rather than Herlock Sholmes or Holmlock Shears. Definitely an item for Baker Street collections.

John Newton Chance, DEATH STALKS THE COBBLED SQUARE (McBride, $2). An ambiguous character named Chance visits a lonely inbred English town on an equally ambiguous errand, undergoes some of the season's wildest adventures, and somehow saves England from the atom bomb. Nine parts agreeably lurid nonsense plus one part pure nightmare terror. (Published in England as SCREAMING FOG.)

Fulton Oursler, THE HOUSE AT FERNWOOD and THE WAGER (Pony Books, 25 cents). Two novelettes in the REBECCA or young-bride-learns-dread-secret pattern, the first conventional, the second involving a novel supernatural variant. Both are written with a slick haste below Mr. Oursler's (or [his mystery-writing pseudonym] Anthony Abbot's) best standards, but "The Wager" belongs in any fantasy-borderline collection. (Not a reprint.)

June 9, 1946

Margot Bennett, TIME TO CHANGE HATS (Doubleday Crime Club, $2). Murder in a village of evacuees involves a Shakespearean actress, a cow-milking alibi and a murderer who leaves visiting cards—all jam to blithe young John Davies. In character and dialogue this is the brightest find of the season, unobtrusively witty, sly and delightful; in plotting it has the English endlessness of a Miles Burton and an anything but watertight solution. With mixed feelings this department hereby chants a Te Deum for its charm and a charm against its tedium.

Jean Leslie, TWO FACED MURDER (Doubleday Crime Club, $2). Disappearance of faculty wife exposes academic scandals, providing perilous problem for pulping professor Peter Ponsonby. Authentic background, ingenious puzzle, suspenseful finish and deft light charm make up a completely pleasing book.

Marion Strobel, KISS AND KILL (Scribner, $2). Murder at an Adirondacks resort sets a problem for A. Lincoln Lacy, but murder itself seems clean beside the petty viciousness of human relations depicted. In this as in her ICE BEFORE KILLING, Miss Strobel's plotting is, to be polite, peculiar, and she can be more elusively cryptic than [H.C. Bailey's detective character] Reggie Fortune. But irritating though her books can be, she has a sense of evil, an ability to portray poisonous people and a talent for writing—which does not, however, seem well adapted to the mystery novel.

Don[ald Clough] Cameron, DIG ANOTHER GRAVE (Mystery House, $2). Manhattan newsmen, racketeers and cafe society find that blackmail leads to murder and kidnaping, all unraveled by reporter Martin King, who knows a least suspected person when he sees one. Acceptable.

Harry Land, THE CORPSE ON THE HEARTH (Macrae-Smith, $2). Eccentric hermit, covetous family, golden nest-egg....murder! All happening an hour north of San Francisco and solved by D.A.'s investigator Feisty Frick. Elementary and not always too believable, but fast and reasonably amusing.

Kathleen Sproul, DEATH LISTENED IN (Phoenix, $2). Casual curiosity leads Helen Allan spang into the peculiar household of a half-mad psychiatrist—and into a fistful of murders. Passable enough up to the ending, which hinges upon a device of such monstrous impossibility that it makes Buck Rogers look strictly scientific.

BEST BUYS IN REPRINTS. Vera Caspary, LAURA (Bestseller, 25 cents, uncut); Manning Long, BURY THE HATCHET (with Liz Parrott) (Bart House, 25 cents, uncut).

June 16, 1946

Alexander Irving, BITTER ENDING (Dodd Mead, $2). Dr. Tony Post, as thorough a heel as ever refrained from fooling himself, has to turn detective in self-protection when the man he has cuckolded turns up as a corpse in the dissecting room. Unusually interesting first, highly recommended for its skill and intelligence and especially for its honest and ironic presentation of unsympathetic protagonists. (Minor complaint: Why do writers who've probably seldom been west of Buffalo set novels in the San Francisco region?)

Mignon G. Eberhart, FIVE PASSENGERS FROM LISBON (Random House, $2). The hospital ship Magnolia picks up passengers from a lifeboat; one was murdered, all are possible murderers. Colonel Josh Morgan, ambulatory patient, skillfully handles romance and detection. Against this unusual background the familiar basic plot develops new highlights and the Eberhart skill with atmosphere appears at its best. (Review by Lenore Glen Offord.)

Lucy Cores, LET'S KILL GEORGE (Duell, Sloan & Pearce, $2.50). Brilliant second-rate writer, confused by many with God, is finally polished off in his Connecticut home; attractive actress-protege suffers suspicion from the police and peril from the killer. The satiric comedy-of-manners tone of Miss Cores' earlier novels is replaced here by a more routine innocence-terror-romance pattern. But it's her own business if she'd sooner be a second [Mignon G.] Eberhart than a second [Margery] Allingham; she remains an intelligent and charming writer in any school.

Denis Scott, THE BECKONING SHADOW (Bobbs-Merrill, $2). Family feuds over mining property lead to ingenious series of murder attempts including poisoning by dynamite; detective Michael James has to turn courtroom lawyer to break the case, among the features of which is a time-table alibi to rejoice [Freeman Wills Crofts'] Inspector French himself. Plot of British intricacy treated with American warmth and humor; somewhat overloaded but good.

Patricia Wentworth, PILGRIM'S REST (Lippincott, $2). Murders past and present in English country house demand the intervention of Miss Maud Silver, who has done neater jobs of untangling. Recommended to those with endless time and a fondness for gentle un-excitement.

Milton M. Raison, THE GAY MORTICIAN (Murray & Gee, $2). Drama critic Tony Woolrich, covering an operetta premiere in San Francisco, finds himself knee-deep in bank robbers, reward frame-ups, wenches and coffins. The best whodunit that Murray & Gee has yet published—and the best is none too good.

BEST BUYS IN REPRINTS. Philip MacDonald, THE RASP (with Anthony Gethryn) (Penguin, 25 cents, uncut); Ellery Queen [Frederic Dannay & Manfred B. Lee], THE DOOR BETWEEN (with Ellery Queen) (Tower, 49 cents, uncut).

June 23, 1946

Mitchell Wilson, THE PANIC-STRICKEN (Simon & Schuster, $2). Four characters, a yacht and a sense of evil are all Mr. Wilson needs to sketch a taut story of a young man coming of age under terror. Tour de force of economical suspense technique—yet somehow just a little too coldly precise in its skill.

Richard Powell, SHOOT IF YOU MUST (Simon & Schuster, $2). The Blakes—Arab and Andy—are at it again. I could add details about Renaissance jewelry, sinister Argentinians, machine pistols and a pair of characters who may or may not be Adolf Hitler and Benvenuto Cellini, but all you need to know is that it's a typical Blake phantasmagoria, even wilder than most in action and even funnier in dialogue.

John Franklin Bardin, THE DEADLY PERCHERON (Dodd Mead, $2). Psychiatrist George Matthews draws a peculiar patient who has direct and practical dealings with leprechauns—a pleasing fantasy which turns abruptly into shocking nightmare. I do not believe a word of the ultimate solution, but the goings-on along the way make up the most astonishing and unputdownable first mystery in years.

Lloyd S. Thompson, DEATH STOPS THE SHOW (Crown, $2). Murder of producer at S.F. premiere of epic involves drama critic Phil French and police lieutenant Greenway in everything from high-pressure press agents and bosomy stars to secret weapons and Nazi agents. Excellent atmosphere of S.F. and show business plus good fast wisecracks—almost good enough to mask the wild incoherence of the plot.

BEST BUYS IN REPRINTS. E.C. Bentley, TRENT'S LAST CASE (with Philip Trent) (Tower, 49 cents, uncut); Ellery Queen [Frederic Dannay & Manfred B. Lee], THERE WAS AN OLD WOMAN (with Ellery Queen) (Pocket Books, 25 cents, uncut).

June 30, 1946

No column was published this week.

July 7, 1946

Note: This week's column was written by Lenore Glen Offord.

E.X. Ferrars, CHEAT THE HANGMAN (Doubleday Crime Club, $2). All the evidence points to one woman as the murderer of the man upstairs. Alice Church, a guest at the party below, can't believe it. Her own evidence, gathered from talks with the other guests, turns the scale. Quiet and slow-paced, this literate English item is nevertheless oddly satisfying.

Axel Kielland, DANGEROUS HONEYMOON (Little Brown, $2.50). One of the most charmingly funny heroines in years, Ann Dickson, tells how she married a chance-met Swede in order to escape from Germany with crucial information. The fast and exciting plot isn't as convincing, somehow, as that of the memorable [previous Kielland novel] SHAPE OF DANGER; but with such good entertainment, who are we to complain?

Helen MacInnes, HORIZON (Little Brown, $2.50). Peter Lennox, planning escape from a prison camp, finds himself released and drafted into the Underground instead. A period of inaction in the Tyrol leaves him nearly hopeless until he learns that his friends work quietly and well. Novels of resistance haven't yet lost their thrill. The sober approach to this story gives it new interest.

John Evans [Howard Browne], HALO IN BLOOD (Bobbs-Merrill, $2). Twelve Chicago ministers officiate at the funeral of an unknown murder victim. Paul Pine, one of those indestructible detectives, finds his new job tied in with this bizarre arrangement, also with innumerable gunsels and gamblers. This item is well enough constructed if lacking in novelty after the opening.

Sue Brown Hays, GO DOWN, DEATH (Scribner, $2). One decayed Southern mansion can provide plenty of ghosts, legends, rats, secret rooms and murders. Three decayed mansions are almost too much. John Benson, private operative, arrives late and does singularly little to relieve the horrors surrounding Lacey Randall, narrator. Lively if none too credible.

July 14, 1946

Hildegarde Tolman Teilhet, THE ASSASSINS (Doubleday, $2.50). Gordon Allgrove was a quiet linguistic scholar and all he wanted was to re-establish the family rug factory in postwar China, but the counterpoint of other men's melodrama changed the shape of his world. Possibly nothing save the best by [Eric] Ambler has ever given quite so completely the this-could-happen-to-me feeling of the ordinary man caught up in plots of violence; this reality, plus the living characters, the absorbing local color and the general excellence of technique, puts THE ASSASSINS well toward the top of this year's spy-adventure heap.

William Irish [Cornell Woolrich], THE DANCING DETECTIVE (Lippincott, $2). Eight novelettes and short stories, mostly originally published as by Cornell Woolrich and some of them retitled for this edition, add up to a bibliographer's nightmare. Nightmares of a more masochistically pleasant nature await the reader who recognizes in Irish-[George] Hopley-Woolrich the great living master of what the psalmist calls "the noonday devil"—the infinite terror of prosaic everyday detail.

Charles L. Leonard [M.V. Heberden], PURSUIT IN PERU (Doubleday Crime Club, $2). Murder of U.S. agent and abduction of girl fetch Paul Kilgerrin to the jungles of Peru, where fascists and piranhas compete in menace. Kilgerrin seems oddly mellowed since earlier books but his adventures are still taut, hard, believable and exciting.

Jonathan Stagge [also known as Patrick Quentin and Q. Patrick], DEATH'S OLD SWEET SONG (Doubleday Crime Club, $2). Music-minded murderer tries to carry out the mystical words of "Green Grow the

Rushes-O" in a series of fantastic killings in a New England town. Well-sketched background and people and some pretty misdirections, but Dr. Hugh Westlake's detection is all but non-existent.

H.W. Roden, WAKE FOR A LADY (Morrow, $2). Publicist Johnny Knight acquires a gorgeous gal (outrageously named Gorgeous) who wants to make Hollywood; the murderous proclivities of her little friends take all the best skills of private eye Sid Ames. The book you've been seeing in the Acme beer ads makes lively entertainment —if your suspension-of-disbelief quotient is high.

Alice Campbell, WITH BATED BREATH (Random House, $2). Surrounded by sinister characters in a gloomy English country house, Avis Marriott plays a courageous if imprudent part in solving multiple crimes. Afterward Dr. Camden Bruce explains. This brave try at creating breathless suspense is spoiled by over-complicated plotting and a style that leaves no time for effects to sink in. (Review by Lenore Glen Offord.)

BEST BUYS IN REPRINTS. Nicholas Blake, MALICE IN WONDERLAND (originally published as THE SUMMER CAMP MYSTERY) (with Nigel Strangeways) (Penguin, 25 cents, uncut); Timothy Fuller, THREE THIRDS OF A GHOST (with Jupiter Jones) (Popular Library, 25 cents); Emmett Hogarth, THE GOOSE IS COOKED (with Marty Cohen) (Bond, 25 cents, uncut).

July 21, 1946

Bettina Boyers, THE WHITE MAZURKA (Doubleday Crime Club, $2). Anthony Coldwell set out quixotically to find an unknown girl; he found two, and more than two murders, in the strange village of St. Andreae—a Polish community transplanted outlandishly into the midst of Connecticut. A novel of curious atmospheric charm and psychological subtlety; after this and last year's intelligent MURDER BY PROXY, Bettina Boyers goes on the Must Watch list.

Will. Cuppy (editor), MURDER WITHOUT TEARS: AN ANTHOLOGY OF CRIME (Sheridan House, $3). Unusual and largely laudable anthology, comprising (a) a first rate selection of true murders by [Edmund] Pearson, [William] Roughead, [Stewart H.] Holbrook and others (including [James] Thurber!); (b) 125 pages of edifying amusement from the Newgate Calendar; and (c) a group of 14 mostly off-trail short stories, some familiar and some rejoicingly unhackneyed. I suppose the only thing that keeps me from an unqualified rave is Uncle Will's coy introduction, which set my teeth so firmly on edge that I didn't recover until Grant Allen's superbly subacid "Curate of Churnside" on page 505. Maybe you better start backwards.

Dorothy Gardiner, BEER FOR PSYCHE (Doubleday Crime Club, $2). Arsenic in the beer disrupts family picnic; Wilbertine Darren, whose name is commonplace beside those of her relatives, struggles through comic chaos to an answer. Absurd and mildly amusing.

Marie Blizard, THE LATE LAMENTED (Mystery House, $2). Murder of charming rich girl bares past secrets of Connecticut small town and slowly reveals the evil behind her charm; Eve MacWilliams and G-man Mac Bronson share the sleuthing. Agreeable enough up to a pretty uneven solution.

Clifford Knight, THE AFFAIR OF THE CORPSE ESCORT (McKay, $2). Hollywood publicity dream backfires into multiple murder; Professor Huntoon Rogers is on hand. With Knight's usual excellence at locale and some amusing Hollywood gags this is one of his most entertaining books, but I've yet to see that Rogers has any function as a detective beyond sitting around for 70,000 words and then bluntly accusing a man who kindly confesses.

Leonard Q. Ross [Leo Rosten], THE DARK CORNER (Century, 25 cents). A novelization of the current film about how private eye Bradford Galt was framed for murder by a sinister art dealer—if, that is, you take novelization to mean a shot-by-shot description of the machine-made picture. Worth noting as a curiosity only because of the renowned byline attached.

July 28, 1946

Patrick Quentin, PUZZLE FOR FIENDS (Simon & Schuster, $2). All fans in good standing know Peter Duluth—which gives us an advantage over Peter, who wakes from an accident to find himself surrounded by a strange new family (complete with luscious bedfellow) who insist that he is Gordon Friend III for motives many, complex and murderous. This is the best Duluth story since the legendary PUZZLE FOR FOOLS—so good that I'm driven to quoting the publishers' blurb: "Right up in the top drawer with the prestissimo, pluperfect practitioners."

Frank Diamond, MURDER RIDES A ROCKET (Mystery House, $2). Agents of all nations comb Manhattan for new portable rocket-gun while corpses drop right and left; the incredible Ransome V. Dragoon and the fetching Vicky Gaines are of course in the thick of it. Nonsense if you're going to be stuffy about it, but to my taste highly agreeable nonsense, with a fantastic absurdity not unlike some of the brighter moments of the [Leslie Charteris] Saint saga.

Leslie Allen, MURDER IN THE ROUGH (Five Star, 25 cents). "Accidental" death on golf course involves the prodigious Napoleon B. Smith in financial tangles and murder plots. Lightweight, fast and often funny. (Not a reprint.)

D.B. Olsen [Dolores Hitchens], CATS DON'T NEED COFFINS (Doubleday Crime Club, $2). Three wisteria seeds, a murdered fuchsia and the ghost of a buried doll are some of the elements in the mystery ghost of a buried doll are some of the elements in the mystery unraveled by Miss Rachel Murdock. The elements are good, but Miss Rachel, who has been 70 for seven years now, gets cuter with every book.

Milton K. Ozaki, THE CUCKOO CLOCK (Ziff-Davis, $2). Amorous Chicago beautician stabbed in fairly elementary Locked Room; Bandy Brinks executes the legwork on eight sexy suspects while Professor Caldwell solves all by psychological technique. Sometimes brashly amusing (Bandy), often prosily top-heavy (the professor).

Lois Eby & John C. Fleming, BLOOD RUNS COLD (Dutton, $2). Murder of a screen gossip columnist is a laudable idea, but the wildness of the action and the brightness of the humor may overpower you a bit before reporter Tommy Marvel tracks down the exceedingly least-suspected killer.

BEST BUYS IN REPRINTS. Ellery Queen [Frederic Dannay & Manfred B. Lee], THE TRAGEDY OF Z (originally published as by Barnaby Ross) (with Drury Lane) (Pocket Books, 25 cents, uncut); Darwin L. Teilhet, THE FEAR MAKERS (Pocket Books, 25 cents, uncut); Percival Wilde, DESIGN FOR MURDER (Jonathan, 25 cents, uncut).

August 4, 1946

Elma K. Lobaugh, SHADOWS IN SUCCESSION (Doubleday Crime Club, $2). Chicago girl visits New Orleans for a vacation full of color; she gets a bit too much of it, with love, murder, madness and voodoo whirling around her in a Vieux Carre nightmare. Miss Lobaugh's first mystery was unusually good; her second puts her in the category of first-rank challengers, with atmosphere, ease, wit, passion and a subtle and complex [sense] of character.

Raymond Chandler, SPANISH BLOOD (Tower, 49 cents). Five masterly crime novelets by the incomparable master, all previously reprinted in paperbacks, make their exceedingly welcome first appearance between boards.

Garnett Weston, THE HIDDEN PORTAL (Doubleday Crime Club, $2). Undersea passage to Gibraltar motivates murderous muddle among Americans, British, Nazis and Falangists in Spanish Morocco—where I hope the Moroccan color is more accurate than the author's Spanish. The mythical passage offers a few spots of [H. Rider] Haggardesque imagination in the midst of a long and routine romantic melodrama.

Susannah Shane [Harriette Ashbrook], DIAMONDS IN THE DUMPLINGS (Doubleday Crime Club, $2). Jewel theft on Connecticut esate leads to murder; debonair Christopher Saxe covers many miles and pages in following tortuous back-trails. It is highly regrettable that this is the posthumous last book by Susannah Shane (nee H. Ashbrook); it's also regrettable that it's far from her best.

Charles G. Booth, MURDER STRIKES THRICE (Bond, 25 cents). Three interrelated novelets of murder and political corruption revolving around punishment-absorbing private eye McFee. Good enough run-of-the-mill toughies.

Marjorie Bonner, THE LAST TWIST OF THE KNIFE (Scribner, $2). House party murder in Laguna Beach, so familiar, so padded, so eventless and so incredibly badly ended that it seems as though it could never possibly have come from the author of the delightful SHAPES THAT CREEP.

August 11, 1946

Ellery Queen [Frederic Dannay] (editor), TO THE QUEEN'S TASTE (Little Brown, $3). The subtitle reads: "The first supplement to [Queen's 1941 anthology] 101 YEARS' ENTERTAINMENT, consisting of the best stories published in the first four years of *Ellery Queen's Mystery Magazine.*" I couldn't write a stronger rave than that. 101 YEARS was the finest detective anthology ever published; this is a fully worthy supplement. And the best stories from *EQMM* means the best stories, period. The essential book of the year for all permanent libraries of detection.

Showell Styles, TRAITOR'S MOUNTAIN (Macmillan, $2.75). Henry Todd, a proper civil servant, stumbles over a corpse and is catapulted into espionage and high adventure in England, Egypt and Wales. The plot is elementary and somewhat absurd but you won't in the least mind as you follow a charming bunch of people making excellent bright conversation among spectacular scenery. Especially recommended to those with a fondness for either mountaineering or [Lewis Carroll's poem] "The Hunting of the Snark."

George Sanders [ghosted by Leigh Brackett], STRANGER AT HOME (Simon & Schuster, $2). Wealthy Hollywoodian returns after four lost years to find out which of his closest friends tried to murder him; his probing brings on more murders, adroitly handled by Detective Lieutenant Joe Trehearne. Menacing and somber in tone, subtle and skillful in characterization, this is so far a cry from the flip first Sanders novel that it's hard to attribute them to the same typewriter.

Bruno Fischer, THE SPIDER LILY (McKay, $2). The jury acquitted him on an "unwritten law" defense but that isn't enough when you know you're innocent and have to learn who framed you. Well constructed melodrama, solid small-town background and some noble poker playing add up to Fischer's best yet.

Lawrence P. Bachmann, THE KISS OF DEATH (Knopf, $2.50). Fine brain of DaVincian genius crudely splattered on wall; Dr. Stanley Garrison uses psychological test methods to trap killer while straightening out his own emotional life. Odd combination of [Edwin Balmer & William MacHarg's] Luther Trant and [Max Brand's] Young Dr. Kildare. (Aside:

Neither Trant, the first psychological detective, nor any of his successors has solved the problem of how to detect by psychological methods while playing fair with the lay reader.)

Erle Stanley Gardner, THE CASE OF THE BACKWARD MULE (Morrow, $2). Past murder and present jailbreak demand Terry Clane's immediate attention on his return to San Francisco from the contemplative Orient. Clane is an interesting try at a novel type of detective, fusing Western and Eastern civilizations; but I doubt if he will quite appeal to followers of either Perry Mason or [the writer on Asian philosophy] Gerald Heard.

August 18, 1946

Leslie Charteris (editor), THE SAINT'S CHOICE OF RADIO THRILLERS (Saint Enterprises, 25 cents). Look, I'll admit I'm prejudiced; I write radio mysteries. But prejudiced or not, I feel that the first comprehensive anthology of radio crime plays is a major event in mystery publishing. Too few such shows have been reprinted, but here you'll find excellent choices from familiar shows ([*Ellery*] *Queen*, [*Sherlock*] *Holmes, Suspense, The Saint,* and *Calling All Cars*) and individual masters ([Norman] Corwin and [Arch] Oboler), plus the expected entertaining Charteris commentary. Definitely a buy.

Wade Miller [Robert Wade & Bill Miller], DEADLY WEAPON (Farrar Straus, $2). Burlesque house and marihuana racket shape background to San Diego murder starring private eye Walter James and police lieutenant Austin Clapp. Machine-gun tempo, tight writing, unexaggerated hardness and unorthodox and overwhelming ending mark highly satisfactory debut of new publishers and new writing team.

Ruth Fenisong, DESPERATE CURE (Doubleday Crime Club, $2). Self-sufficient woman doctor at last finds love in her thirties but with it came tragedy and murder, in which her own life and those of her patients are curiously interwoven. Not so much a mystery novel as a case-history study in murder, and an unusually adroit and perceptive one.

Aaron Marc Stein, ...AND HIGH WATER (Doubleday Crime Club, $2). Wandering archaeologists Tim Mulligan and Elsie Mae Hunt invade the Mississippi lead-mining country in search of a pre-Columbian fragment; instead they find a terrifying flood, peculiar people and murder. Humor, warmth, intelligence and a nice study in unusual folkways make a delightful book.

Clarence Mullen, THEREBY HANGS A CORPSE (Mystery House, $2). Framed fights, assorted other rackets and a lush wench or two shape a parlous puzzle for private operatives Eddie Wright and Tony Lantz. Tony is not too impressive as the brains of the team but Eddie is a fast, vigorous legman-narrator and the author's pugilistic background makes the traditional hard-boiled punishment-taking more believable than usual.

Carolynne & Malcolm Logan, ONE OF THESE SEVEN (Mystery House, $2). Artist-autobiographer shot in locked room to which seven celebrities hold keys; ex-prodigy Justus Drum pins down the killer. Reasonably sound and ingenious story, but atmosphere of cultured sophistication rings spurious.

BEST BUYS IN REPRINTS. H.C. Branson, I'LL EAT YOU LAST (with John Bent) (Bond, 25 cents, cut); Manning Coles, DRINK TO YESTERDAY (with Michael Kingston) (Tower, 49 cents, uncut); Robin Grey [Elizabeth Gresham], PUZZLE IN PORCELAIN (with Hunter Lewis) (Bart House, 25 cents, uncut).

August 25, 1946

No column was published this week.

September 1, 1946

Lawrence Treat, H AS IN HUNTED (Duell, Sloan & Pearce, $2.50). Framed as a traitor by the Nazis, Bill returned to find the one man who could clear him murdered and himself the chief suspect. Sound routine work by lab technician Jub Freeman and detective Walter Ivy blends with nightmarish adventure to achieve a new suspense. It's high time somebody up and said that Lawrence Treat is in the very top flight of American mystery writers, so I'm hereby saying it. H as in Honey!

Van H. Cartmell & Bennett Cerf (editors), FAMOUS PLAYS OF CRIME AND DETECTION (with an introduction by John Chapman) (Blakiston, $3.75). The full texts of 13 criminous plays, ranging in time from [William Gillette's] SHERLOCK HOLMES to [Patrick Hamilton's] ANGEL STREET and in mood from the farce of [George M. Cohan's] SEVEN KEYS TO BALDPATE to the tragedy of [Jeffrey Dell's] PAYMENT DEFERRED, from the overt excitement of [George Abbott & Philip Dunning's] BROADWAY to the covert chills of [Edward Chodorov's] KIND LADY. A superlative collection which can't be too strongly commended to your permanent shelves.

Kenneth Millar, TROUBLE FOLLOWS ME (Dodd Mead, $2). From Pearl Harbor to Tijuana (via Detroit and San Diego), murders pursue Ensign Sam Drake as he tries to track down fascist subversion among Negroes. Tense well plotted story which blends liberal politics, love and melodrama with a God-given ability to write which has no serious business striking twice in the Millar family. [The author, later and much better known as Ross Macdonald, was married to crime novelist Margaret Millar.]

George Harmon Coxe, DANGEROUS LEGACY (Knopf, $2). Ex-flyer Spence Rankin inherits the estate and the obligations of his murdered Filipino friend—which means a tense battle against obvious forces of evil and some less obvious. Strong melodrama, Philippine color and good characterizations make one of Coxe's best.

Bruno Fischer, KILL TO FIT (Five Star, 25 cents). Middle-aged love may provoke bitterness and murder, especially when politics and gangsters are involved; gun-wise Rick Train plays all the angles to a shrewd solution. The standard houseparty set-up handled with a fresh warmth and solidness; good buy at any price. (Not a reprint.)

Dwight V. Babcock, HANNAH SAYS FOUL PLAY (Avon, 25 cents). Gossip columnist shot during Palm Springs' fantastic Circus Week; Hannah Van Doren, that gorgeous ghoul, smells murder. Fast action, tricky solution and lots of gags, mostly as funny as they are broad. (Not a reprint.)

Z.H. Ross, THREE DOWN VULNERABLE (Bobbs-Merrill, $2). Not the [bridge expert Ely] Culbertsonian crime the title indicates but multiple murder among a group of has-been actors snowbound in the Nevada mountains; the somewhat cute team of Beau Smith and Pogy Rogers investigates. Passable.

Jane Layhew, RX FOR MURDER (Lippincott, $2). Dope smuggling in the curio business motivates a murder investigated by nurse Mollie Thompson and chemist Larry Stone. These young Canadians are highly agreeable people who may learn in time that a series of endless conversations does not constitute a novel.

Frances Crane, THE CINNAMON MURDER (Random House, $2). Beautiful Brenda Davison, who wasn't born into penthouse society, is scared of her in-laws. Patrick and Jean Abbott take her case, rattling family skeletons, discovering corpses and being chased around New York by interesting characters. The Crane style of underwriting, usually commendable, gives this tale a curiously perfunctory tone. (Review by Lenore Glen Offord.)

Leslie Ford, HONOLULU STORY (Scribner, $2). In pleasantly authentic atmosphere Grace Latham does all the observing, overhearing and sympathizing with young love that this yarn requires. Colonel Primrose already knows the secrets of the disembodied face, the hula dancer and the dead shot aunt from Maui. Ford fans would be disappointed if Grace didn't hinder him. Ford fans won't be disappointed. (Review by Lenore Glen Offord.)

Constance & Gwenyth Little, THE BLACK STOCKING (Doubleday Crime Club, $2). If you find necrophilia a side-splitting subject, you may revel in this account of maniacal merrymaking in a hospital. I can only agree with the publisher's blurb that the Littles' "wacky handling of murder is practically indescribable."

BEST BUYS IN REPRINTS. Geoffrey Homes, NO HANDS ON THE CLOCK (with Humphrey Campbell) (Bantam, 25 cents, uncut); Anthony

Gilbert, DEATH IN THE BLACKOUT (with Arthur Crook) (Bantam, 25 cents, uncut); Cornell Woolrich, BLACK ALIBI (Jonathan, 25 cents, cut); Elizabeth Daly, NOTHING CAN RESCUE ME (with Henry Gamadge) (Bantam, 25 cents, uncut); Christopher Hale, HANGMAN'S TIE (with Lieutenant Bill French) (Bart House, 25 cents, uncut); Peter Storme, THE THING IN THE BROOK (with Henry Hale) (Bond, 25 cents, cut).

September 8, 1946

Paul Cain, SEVEN SLAYERS (Saint Enterprises, 25 cents). First book publication of seven hardboiled shorts from *Black Mask*, distinguished by absolute objectivity, sharp melodramatic twists and a tight taut toughness hard to parallel outside of the best Hammett and Chandler.

Marten Cumberland, A DILEMMA FOR DAX (Doubleday Crime Club, $2). Crippenesque corpse in deserted villa enlists the most minute efforts of Commissaire Saturnin Dax and his Paris police associates. Somewhat disappointing solution but a lot of fine detail work along the way.

Gerald Butler, MAD WITH MUCH HEART (Rinehart, $2). Detective James Wilson has three conflicting duties: to catch a mad killer, to prevent his lynching and to console his beautiful blind sister. Many critics praise Mr. Butler's simplicity and compassion; this minority report finds him synthetic in both style and emotion.

Anne Rowe, DEADLY INTENT (Mill, $2). The loves of an interior decorator, the emotions of a sub-deb and the problems of a penthouse pushover motivate a series of murders resolved by spinster-narrator Mertie Farwell. Pleasant if rather lax.

Elizabet M. Stone, POISON, POKER AND PISTOLS (Sheridan House, $2). Curare-coated toothbrush murders New Orleans medico; frightfully blithe girl reporter Margaret Slone solves all. Foolish and tiresome.

BEST BUYS IN REPRINTS. John Dickson Carr, THE EMPEROR'S SNUFF-BOX (with Dermott Kinross) (Pocket Books, 25 cents, uncut); Richard Lakin, THE BODY FELL ON BERLIN (with Jasper Doyle) (Detective Novel Classic, 25 cents, cut); James R. Langham, A POCKETFUL OF CLUES (with Sammy Abbott) (Saint Enterprises, 25 cents, cut).

September 15, 1946

Lillian de la Torre, DR. SAM: JOHNSON, DETECTOR (narrated as from the pen of James Boswell) (Knopf, $2.75). If you know Miss de la Torre's masterly ELIZABETH IS MISSING or have read any of the Johnson stories in *Ellery Queen's Mystery Magazine,* you need only be told that this volume contains nine detectival exploits of the great lexicographer (three hitherto unpublished) and that Knopf has made it probably the most attractive book of detective shorts ever published. If de la Torre is new to you, I envy you as you discover these magical eighteenth-century pastiches, conceived and written with an ideal blend of scholarly precision and the delightful will to entertain.

William Roughead, NOTHING BUT MURDER (Sheridan House, $2.75). There is not much to be said in reviewing a new Roughead. The elderly Scottish Writer to the Signet is the dean and paragon of the narrators of true crime and each new collection of his perceptively ironic essays is a cue for dancing in the streets. Especially to be noted in the new volume are his fine analysis of the murder of Sir Thomas Overbury and his exhaustive "familiar survey" of the practice of poison in Scotland.

Leslie Edgley, FEAR NO MORE (Simon & Schuster, $2). This latest variation on the Lady Vanishes theme plays between San Francisco and Hollywood and involves a ceramics collector, a girl being driven mad, several disappearing corpses and an intelligent young skip tracer named Jay Rogers. For macabre tension and quietly satisfactory writing it's one of the best yet within a formula which constantly threatens to prove exhausted.

David X. Manners, MEMORY OF A SCREAM (Mystery House, $2). Ex-doctor Robert Galt, framed for malpractice, achieves rehabilitation by solving friend's murder. Human insight into odd people and effectively nightmarish style lend distinction to a somewhat familiar basic plot. Good debut.

Phoebe Atwood Taylor, THE ASEY MAYO TRIO (Messner, $2). In three novelettes Asey Mayo encounters murder in, respectively, a private school, an astronomical observatory and a moving house. None of the stories is within hollering distance of the best Mayo novels but they'll do for those who (like me) can never get quite enough of the Codfish Sherlock and the freakish humor of his creator.

Richard Burke, THE FOURTH STAR (Mystery House, $2). Sculptress murdered in deserted First Avenue mansion; Times Square detective Quinny Hite cannily covers New York to catch the killer. Quinny is as always a [Damon] Runyonesque delight, but his latest exploit seems to have been written and edited with careless haste.

Will F. Jenkins, THE MURDER OF THE U.S.A. (Crown, $2). The publishers insist on promoting this as a mystery novel. As such it is unspeakable; for a more sympathetic review see next week's fantasy-and-science-fiction column. [That column will be included in the third volume of THE ANTHONY BOUCHER CHRONICLES.]

BEST BUYS IN REPRINTS. Craig Rice, HOME SWEET HOMICIDE (with the Carstairs family) (Tower, 49 cents, uncut).

September 22, 1946

Kenneth Fearing, THE BIG CLOCK (Harcourt Brace, $2.50). Magazine tycoon murders his mistress; ramifications of his cover-up spread through-out his unique editorial organization. Off-beat murder study, ironic and compelling, distinguished by some of the sheerly best writing in several years' crops of mysteries—or, for that matter, novels.

Norbert Davis, OH, MURDERER MINE (Handi-Books, 20 cents). The beauty business and the academic life meet startlingly. Result: assorted murders for plump detective Doan and his bored Great Dane Carstairs. Homicidal humor is a matter of personal taste, but to me Mr. Davis is one of the very few writers besides Alice Tilton [Phoebe Atwood Taylor] who can be exceedingly funny in the midst of murder. (Not a reprint.)

Rufus King, MUSEUM PIECE NO. 13 (Doubleday Crime Club, $2). Midwest newspaper publisher collects rooms which have witnessed mur-der; this with his other peculiarities drives his latest wife into a Bluebeard nightmare. The oddest and possibly the best of Mr. King's curious experi-ments in the slick-macabre. (And it's rank ingratitude on my part to long for the return of [King's series character] Lieutenant Valcour.)

Dana Chambers, THE CASE OF CAROLINE ANIMUS (Dial Press, $2). A baby owl's quill, a nonagenarian dowager and a parody of the Rubaiyat [of Omar Khayyam] turn Florida into a battlefield of wits and bullets for Jim Steele. Chambers has achieved his own synthesis of the hardboiled and the slick-magazine schools, and this latest Steele adventure (though far from another LAST SECRET) should prove exciting to devo-tees of either.

Amber Dean, WRAP IT UP (Doubleday Crime Club, $2). The peculiar habits of painters and excisemen and the milder forms of sex provide a puzzle in murder in the Finger Lakes district; spinster Abbie Harris nar-rates. Miss Dean's books have their weaknesses (in this case including the year's most transparent plot) but they have also a fresh simple likability which is disarming.

Michael Stark [Lawrence Lariar], RUN FOR YOUR LIFE! (Crown, $2). Murder on a train full of nuclear physicists leads private eye Steve Ericson into a welter of wenches and killings. Good tempo and interesting data on atomic murder methods (not all so novel as the author supposes) help out an otherwise routine but capable toughie.

BEST BUYS IN REPRINTS. John Dickson Carr, DEATH WATCH (with Dr. Gideon Fell) (Bestseller, 25 cents); Michael Venning [Craig Rice], MURDER THROUGH THE LOOKING GLASS (with Melville Fairr) (Mercury, 25 cents).

September 29, 1946

Van Siller, ONE ALONE (Doubleday Crime Club, $2). Amorous caprice of a radio writer sends him on a round-robin nightmare from Arizona to Montana to Washington, tormented by a fascinating woman who may well be a subtle murderess. Somewhat disappointing in its denouement but up to then an unusual and effective suspense item.

Lee Wilson, THIS DEADLY DARK (Dodd Mead, $2.50). San Francisco reporter Matt Foster, wantonly blinded in petty robbery-killing, devotes his blacked-out life to minute study of the people involved—and winds up with the answer and his own reintegration. Not too successful in characterization or plot-technique but striking and moving in concept. (Winner of this fall's $1000 Red Badge contest.)

Samuel Rogers, YOU LEAVE ME COLD! (Harper, $2). Tensions in odd household build to bacteriological murder prompted by the most shocking motive in the history of the crime novel. Personally I found the criminological voyeurism of Professor Paul Hatfield even a bit more shocking. Literate but not quite good enough to carry off its subject.

Hilea Bailey, BREATHE NO MORE, MY LADY (Doubleday Crime Club, $2). Cryptic telegram sends narrator Hilea to tourist camp near war plant where the murders pile up until the great Hilary Bailey III is forced to intervene. Interesting gimmicks on monoxide poisoning and surplus property reconversion scattered in a diffuse and very long story.

Dennis Allan, DEAD TO RIGHTS (Mill, $2). Sinister machinations of octopoid newspaper monopoly involve framed strikes, a series of murders and the attentions of elderly satyr Count Blaise de Brincourt. Good story idea, not helped by flat writing and some just-barely-legitimate tricks of deception.

BEST BUYS IN REPRINTS. Chris Massie, THE LOVE LETTERS (Bantam, 25 cents, uncut); Arthur Train, TUTT AND MR. TUTT (with Ephraim Tutt) (Bantam, 25 cents, uncut).

October 6, 1946

Lewis Padgett [Henry Kuttner], THE BRASS RING (Duell, Sloan & Pearce, $2.50). The father had a brass fetishism and the son dementia praecox—a family ideally shaped for murder, but retired detective Seth Colman wanted no part of it. Seth's glittering wife Eve had her own ideas, and the result is an excellent psychology-cum-action whodunit plus some shrewd commentaries on other husband-and-wife detecting teams. Mr. Padgett, currently top man in science fiction, threatens in this debut to take over the mystery field with equal success.

Agatha Christie, THE HOLLOW (Dodd Mead, $2.50). Dominant medico finds three women more than even he can handle at one week-end party; it is fortunate that Hercule Poirot lives nearby to puzzle out the deceptively simple murder problem which ensues. A Grade-A plot combined with a much solider novel than usual makes this the best Christie in years—which increases one's regret for a typical British Jew caricature complete with lisp. (Serialized as THE OUTRAGED HEART.)

Georges Simenon, BLIND ALLEY (translated by Stuart Gilbert) (Reynal & Hitchcock, $2.50). Pointless life of Riviera rich builds petty tensions culminating in murder—and in a unique murderer's atonement. For the first half both Simenon's technique and that of his translator seem a little less certain than usual, but the closing scenes are among the author's finest achievements in this borderland between the "straight" and the murder novel.

R.T.M. Scott, THE AGONY COLUMN MURDERS (Dutton, $2). A severed finger, a beaten dog and a psychical seance cause the corpses to pile up around Aurelius ("Secret Service") Smith and his assorted assistants—not one of whom has aged a month in the past 20 years. By modern standards a fairly absurd piece of work, but if you'd like to see what the whodunit was like in the middle '20s, you'll find this restful and readable.

Ione Sandberg Shriber, THE LAST STRAW (Rinehart, $2). Lieutenant Bill Grady, convalescing in San Diego, discovers murder and love rampant among the better people of La Jolla. How Grady reached his solution managed to escape me; otherwise this is not a bad specimen of the lushly social school.

Julius Fast, THE BRIGHT FACE OF DANGER (Rinehart, $2). Girl hospital technician, convinced of her amnesiac guilt in a murder, drives herself through wild paths of terror to final clearance—and love. Somewhat unconvincing formula job, far removed from the easy reality of Fast's excellent first, WATCHFUL AT NIGHT.

BEST BUYS IN REPRINTS. Dorothy B. Hughes, THE BAMBOO BLONDE (Pocket Books, 25 cents, uncut); Hilda Lawrence, BLOOD UPON THE SNOW (with Mark East) (Pocket Books, 25 cents, uncut).

October 13, 1946

Edward D. Radin, 12 AGAINST THE LAW (Duell, Sloan & Pearce, $2.75). Mr. Radin is the dean of the modern American fact-detective school, which means that he tells a story easily, with fictional readability, smooth tempo and emphasis on the details of police work. Some may find his approach a let-down from the literary irony of [Edmund] Pearson or [William] Roughead; others may find its direct freshness a marked relief. Either way, no connoisseur of crime can afford to miss a collection of twelve such unhackneyed cases so ably treated.

Thomas B. Dewey, AS GOOD AS DEAD (Jefferson House, $2). Living revenant stirs small-town curiosity; philosophic hotel proprietor Singer

Batts investigates, to find everything from corpses to buried treasures to Chicago gangsters. Basic plot weak and confused but smooth, tight and fast in the telling.

Mignon G. Eberhart, THE WHITE DRESS (Random House, $2). Recipe for Eberhart novel: one beautiful heroine suspected of murder; one slick-haired gentleman and one rugged one, rivals; professional detective (Captain Manson); other suspects to taste; fold into routine plot; flavor with atmosphere (Miami, including hurricane); and garnish with evidences of material wealth. This one's perfectly cooked, admirably served. (Review by Lenore Glen Offord.)

Inez Haynes Irwin, THE WOMEN SWORE REVENGE (Random House, $2). The eighteenth-century poltergeist, resuming activities in the old More house in Satuit, at first does little but scare the family. Then Lizbeth More is stabbed and nearly everyone in town turns amateur detective, making the darndest discoveries you ever heard of. Chief Patrick O'Brien, a nice fellow, is allowed in on the arrest. (Review by Lenore Glen Offord.)

Robert Sidney Bowen, MAKE MINE MURDER (Crown, $2). Gerry Barnes doesn't need the money. That plus a passion for exclamation points and being struck by lightning makes him distinguishable from other smart-cracking lecherous operatives. His first case involves buried treasure and killings galore and its telling is a professional if shoddy job.

George Harmon Coxe, FLASH CASEY...DETECTIVE (Avon, 25 cents). Four undistinguished and almost indistinguishable novelettes about the murder-photographing activities of newspaper cameraman Flash Casey—quite a cut below Mr. Coxe's novels about his colleague Kent Murdock, or even the Dr. Standish shorts. (Not a reprint.)

Manning Lee Stokes, GREEN FOR A GRAVE (Phoenix, $2). Blackmail and nicotine poisoning make a lethal mixture in the hard-drinking and -loving Missouri set, analyzed by private detective Barnabas Jones. Passable.

October 20, 1946

David Goodis, DARK PASSAGE (Messner, $2). Parry was an unimportant guy who got framed for murder and eventually escaped from San Quentin. You'll have to take it from there yourself; I'm not going to try to synopsize the details of his escape, his adventures and his ultimate vindication. I'll only say that here is the most notable writing talent to emerge in the field in a long time. Mr. Goodis has an originality of naturalism, a precise feeling for petty lives, a creatively compelling vividness of detail that you might perhaps match if you could combine top [Cornell] Woolrich with early [Clifford] Odets. This is the goods.

Maureen Sarsfield, GREEN DECEMBER FILLS THE GRAVEYARD (Coward-Mccann, $2.50). Somebody starts poisoning off the old retainers around the quiet village; enigmatically alluring sculptress suspected until Inspector Lane Parry makes some neat deductions. Miss Sarsfield has the British faults of excessive length and mild snobbery; she also has the virtues of the best British school—trim plotting, intelligently sketched atmosphere, attractive gentleman-sleuth, and a wittily civilized polish that is highly gratifying. Chalk up a discovery for Coward-McCann's Gargoyle.

George Bagby [Aaron Marc Stein], THE ORIGINAL CARCASE (Doubleday Crime Club, $2). The antique furniture business provides a complex murder problem for sore-footed Inspector Schmidt, who manages on the side to solve another problem of young love vs. class prejudice. To the average reader a delightfully told story; to the mystery technician a model of precisely how to integrate a love motif, an absorbing dividend and a perfectly plotted problem. Recommended to novices for study and to all for pleasure.

Sam Merwin, Jr., A MATTER OF POLICY (Mystery House, $2). Mild [Clarence Budington] Kelland-type hero finds himself knee-deep in murder and love when someone anonymously insures his life for half a million; cigar-smoking tycooness Amy Brewster and other odd characters achieve the payoff. Featherweight but rowdily entertaining.

A.L. Furman (editor), THE FOURTH MYSTERY COMPANION (Lantern Press, $2.75). The Furman formula remains unchanged: mostly crime and detection, a few supernatural stories; chiefly first time in book form, all previously unanthologized; and maybe half of them worth anthologizing. Which adds up to nearly 400 pages of relatively good reading, this time distinguished by [Elisabeth Sanxay] Holding, [William] Irish-[Cornell] Woolrich and Louis Paul.

Curtiss T. Gardner, BONES DON'T LIE (Mill, $2). Corruption and murder in huge steel plant exposed by "General" U.O. Flint, the first big-business detective on record. Flint is a novelty and the mechanical details of steel manufacture are endlessly fascinating--and deserving of a better story.

Roman McDougald, PURGATORY STREET (Simon & Schuster, $2). Does the plastic surgery hide a returning war hero or a murderous impostor, and which does Mona love—or both? Wordy, pretentious, hysterical and synthetic, this is a brilliantly precise job of hitting exactly on the nose a certain current fashion in mysteries. It is undoubtedly Mr. McDougald's worst book and will probably make his fortune.

October 27, 1946

H.C. Bailey, THE LIFE SENTENCE (Doubleday Crime Club, $2). Release of [Florence] Maybrick-like "murderess" starts new series of crimes, resolved by Reggie Fortune. I usually dislike the Bailey novels as much as I admire his short stories, but here is a full-length Fortune with all of the qualities of cleverness, suspense amd compassion which have distinguished the shorts. An important book and (despite Reggie's mannerisms) often a moving one.

Brett Halliday, BLOOD ON BISCAYNE BAY (Ziff-Davis, $2.50). Before Michael Shayne left Miami, he thought he'd easily have time to settle a gambling debt for a friend, but that simple project turned into a singularly complex affair of blackmail, divorce and murder. Possibly the best of the fast-paced Shayne novels.

James Nelson (editor), THE COMPLETE MURDER SAMPLER (Doubleday Crime Club, $2.50). Mr. Nelson has devised a new kind of classified anthology, with all of the Crime Club's symbols on the excellent Vera Bock jacket and every conceivable type of crime story neatly labeled inside. Some of the choices (such as [Robert Barr's character] the British-satiric Eugene Valmont to represent the French detective) are at least questionable, but the novel scheme and generally unhackneyed quality make this one of the better buys in anthologies.

John Rhode, DEATH IN HARLEY STREET (Dodd Mead, $2). Dr. Priestley and colleagues establish that the death of the great gland specialist was (to use the publisher's grammar) neither accident, suicide nor murder. One of the year's most ingenious criminal plots handled with Rhodian precision but buried in endless static talk.

Lee Thayer, THE JAWS OF DEATH (Dodd Mead, $2). The Florida swamps, a giant crocodile and a stolen dinosaur egg provide an interesting background for the investigations of Peter Clancy, whose charm lures his fans into overlooking his little habit of suppressing evidence.

Carolyn Thomas, PROMINENT AMONG THE MOURNERS (Lippincott, $2). Multiple murders on Midwest campus lead publicity director Susan Byerly into endless perils, mostly her own damned fault. Miss Thomas has sufficient charm and ease of writing to make one hope that she'll learn to plot more sharply and to slice relentlessly her heroine's persistent prattling.

Dana Wilson, MAKE WITH THE BRAINS, PIERRE (Messner, $2). Maybe you can swallow the muddled sentimentality that so often passes for tough-mindedness in fiction. Maybe you aren't tired of sagas of Hollywood sex. Maybe you can even believe in a French hero who complains of his difficulties with American psychology and language but writes in strictly ersatz James [M.] Cain. But if you can gulp down all of these elements at once you're a stronger man than I am.

BEST BUYS IN REPRINTS. Francis Bonnamy, A ROPE OF SAND (with Peter Shane) (Penguin, 25 cents, uncut); Craig Rice, THE RIGHT MURDER (with John J. Malone & the Justuses) (Popular Library, 25 cents, uncut).

November 3, 1946

Christopher Morley (editor), MURDER WITH A DIFFERENCE (Random House, $2.75). To connoisseurs of murder I need only mention that this volume contains Richard Hull's THE MURDER OF MY AUNT, H.F. Heard's A TASTE FOR HONEY and Patrick Hamilton's HANGOVER SQUARE—three offbeat opuses, all otherwise out of print, which are absolute masterpieces of criminous irony. If any bush were needed to such vintage products, Mr. Morley's preface provides precisely the proper boscage.

David Duncan, THE SHADE OF TIME (Random House, $2). To prove his innocence of a past crime, Sebastian Sands reconstructs it and apparently commits murder again—by the same impossible method. Chief Quigley of Monterey explains the "atomic displacement" in terms of human cunning. Few real people talk like these characters but then few plots are as fresh and well constructed as this one.

Lester Dent, LADY TO KILL (Doubleday Crime Club, $2). A damsel in distress, a hireling murderer and airline executive Chance Molloy make an explosive combination for a transcontinental train trip, with complex deals in surplus property hinging on the outcome. Fast, medium hard and highly readable.

Elizabeth Daly, THE WRONG WAY DOWN (Rinehart, $2.50). Mysterious maneuvers with a rare aquatint lead Henry Gamadge into devious paths of spiritualism, deceit and murder. Far from one of Miss Daly's best plots but related with her accustomed suavity and charm.

M. Scott Michel, THE BLACK KEY (Mystery House, $2). This is yet another amnesia-victim mystery but psychiatrist Alexander Cornell's investigation of wanton wastrels and medical murders has a few new twists. The best of Mr. Michel's persistent attempts to combine psychiatry and detection.

W.T. Ballard, MURDER CAN'T STOP (McKay, $2). Skull Lake is a Sierra resort where the vacationing film colony and the Old West meet; the result is the highest homicide rate in recent fiction, with movie troubleshooter Bill Lennox hard at work saving his skin. Unlikely motivation and frequent cliches mar a fast-paced and generally enjoyable meller.

Audrey Gaines, OMIT FLOWERS, PLEASE (Messner, $2). Reporter and screwball girlfriend complicate murder among Washington bluebloods and gamblers; suave Inspector Major straightens things out. Brief spots of light amusement in an otherwise pretty routine job.

BEST BUYS IN REPRINTS. Raymond Chandler, THE LADY IN THE LAKE (with Philip Marlowe) (Pocket Books, 25 cents, uncut); Helen McCloy, CUE FOR MURDER (with Dr. Basil Willing) (Tower, 49 cents, uncut).

November 10, 1946

Carter Dickson [John Dickson Carr], MY LATE WIVES (Morrow, $2.50). I have by now run out of superlatives for the works of Mr. Dickson (and/or Mr. Carr). I'll say only that this latest exploit of Sir Henry Merrivale deals with the tracking down of a mass murderer of the Brides-in-the-Bath school, that its background ranges from the London theater to a gruesomely contrived testing ground for army nerves, and that writing, humor and misdirection are as always alike incomparable.

Rex Stout, THE SILENT SPEAKER (Viking, $2.50). The characters and institutions are of course imaginary, but by one of those literary coincidences the action resembles what might have happened if OPA [Office of Price Administration] head Chester Bowles had been murdered at a NAM [National Association of Manufacturers] banquet—which gives Mr. Stout a chance at some telling political comment as well as his w.k. [well known] deftness at murdermongering. This is the first full-length Nero Wolfe novel in six years; and if the Old Maestro's "deductions" consist chiefly in finding and hiding one essential piece of evidence, his character emerges more vividly and validly than in any other Wolfe story I recall. Archie Goodwin is in top form and all in all it's Old Home Week with a grand time for all—including Stout's lucky new publishers.

Christianna Brand, THE CROOKED WREATH (Dodd Mead, $2.50). Sir Richard should have known better than to change his will with all of his nervously charming grandchildren gathered around him; Inspector Cockrill clears up the inevitable result with an assist from a flying bomb. The will-changing is the only familiar facet in this fresh and intelligent mystery. Miss Brand writes with the social comedy of a [Margery] Allingham and the plot technique of an [Agatha] Christie—a rare reminder of those noble days in the '30s which John Strachey called the Golden Age of English Detection.

Stella Ryan, DEATH NEVER WEEPS (Coward-McCann, $2). Lucy Presgile is a convincingly evil woman, meticulously and viciously destroying her husband and her daughter, with the waves of her corruption spreading through her aristocratic family until the inevitable murder (and not of Lucy) results. And Stella Ryan is a solid, rewarding novelist who presents interesting and well-shaded characters in a series of beautifully built crises and terrors which you won't soon forget.

Doris Miles Disney, WHO RIDES A TIGER (Doubleday Crime Club, $2). Death of octogenarian leaves trunkful of diaries which great-niece investigates, slowly piecing together the astonishing tragedy behind the old lady's long and warped life. Solution takes a bit of believing but most of the book is warm, full-bodied, well-written reconstruction of the past.

Edith Howie, THE BAND PLAYED MURDER (Mill, $2). Jewel thefts, love and marihuana tie into murders of two girl vocalists with big-time band; assorted musicians and sole remaining girl combine to trap crazed killer. Colorful, unassuming and pleasant.

Kathleen Buddington Coxe [Amelia Reynolds Long & Edna McHugh], MURDER MOST FOUL (Phoenix, $2). Catastrophic carnage on college campus collated by cute co-ed and psychology professor Francis Thrush. Lightweight readability might be agreeable (if coyly cloying) if the characters weren't such stock cardboard, from the spinster gossip to the blackface comics.

BEST BUYS IN REPRINTS. Richard Powell, ALL OVER BUT THE SHOOTING (with Arab & Andy Blake) (Popular Library, 25 cents, uncut); Richard Sale, LAZARUS NO. 7 (Jonathan, 25 cents, uncut).

November 17, 1946

Michael Innes, WHAT HAPPENED AT HAZELWOOD? (Dodd Mead, $2.50). Sinister butler, secrets from Australia, the blunt instrument and the bad baronet dead in his study—for once Mr. Innes provides all the strictly traditional elements, with his plot veering into fantasy only in a somewhat eyebrow-raising solution. But conventional though the set-up may be, the irony and delight of the Innes style is in evidence as fully as ever—perhaps even intensified by contrast. Inspector Cadover ably understudies the cryptically absent Appleby.

Joel Townsley Rogers, LADY WITH THE DICE (Handi-Books, 20 cents). Gambler-murderer haunted by fate finds the sinister number 12 pursuing him as he marches relentlessly from one crime to the next and finally to his diabolically contrived end. Tremendously intricate plot, sensational if sometimes over-pulpy style and chilling supernatural overtones make a short novel not unworthy of the author of THE RED RIGHT HAND. (Not a reprint.)

Edwin Rolfe & Lester Fuller, THE GLASS ROOM (Rinehart, $2.50). Big-shot bookie, framed for wife's murder, doubles as hunter and hunted as he at once evades pursuit and tracks the true killer through the vicious wilds of American Fascism. The drive and punch of a first-rate toughie with the added virtues of rare literary skill and political awareness plus a truer painting of the color of Los Angeles than any other mystery I can recall. Even the possible complaints about character-consistency are compliments: the book is so good you wish it were perfect.

Thomas B. Black, THE 3-13 MURDERS (Reynal & Hitchcock, $2). Yogi-ish cult, prominent banker and the dope racket make up private eye Al Delaney's most dangerous case. Good dialogue, credible toughness, solid plotting and plentiful excitement mark a far above average hardboiled novel.

Leslie Charteris, THE SAINT SEES IT THROUGH (Doubleday Crime Club, $2). New York niteries and their hag-ridden habitues provide the background for Simon Templar's latest tilt against the ungodly. Can you imagine The Saint seriously in love and uninterested in boodle? Or his creator writing as frequently like [Ernest] Hemingway as like Charteris? It's all a little disconcerting but highly readable and, as a change, welcome.

Anne Nash, UNHAPPY RENDEZVOUS (Doubleday Crime Club, $2). Three totally unconnected young girls disappear; as their corpses start turning up, Thorne Westcott ranges from Berkeley to Carmel to forestall the final killing. Pleasant enough telling of completely incredible story.

Edwin Lanham, SLUG IT SLAY (Harcourt Brace, $2). Millionaire publisher murdered in a curious New York which seems to have only two rival newspapers; city editor Arthur Leslie tumbles to a solution and a romance. Wild guesswork and feeble characterizations add up to a thoroughly second-rate book, surprising on Harcourt Brace's small and generally distinguished mystery list.

BEST BUYS IN REPRINTS. Lange Lewis, MURDER AMONG FRIENDS (with Lieutenant Tuck) (Bart House, 25 cents, uncut); D.B. Olsen [Dolores Hitchens], THE CLUE IN THE CLAY (with Lieutenant Mayhew) (Bart House, 25 cents, uncut).

November 24, 1946

Note: This week's column was written by Lenore Glen Offord.

Dorothy B. Hughes, RIDE THE PINK HORSE (Duell, Sloan & Pearce, $2.50). To Sailor, in pursuit of the Senator, the fiesta seems a series of obstacles to the ill-fated meeting with his enemy. To the reader it is a dreamlike mixture of beauty and terror. Nobody but Dorothy Hughes can cast suspense into such an uncanny spell, and she's never done it better.

Joseph T. Shaw (editor), THE HARD-BOILED OMNIBUS (Simon & Schuster, $3). *Black Mask* could pick 'em back in the thirties. Of these fifteen novelette-length stories, at least eleven appear masterly even to a non-aficionado such as I. Action usually takes the place of detection and there's more blood than you can shake a stick at. There's also some very effective writing.

Frances & Richard Lockridge, DEATH OF A TALL MAN (Lippincott, $2). The doctor found murdered in his private office isn't cold before Pamela North muscles in on Lieutenant Weigand's investigation. Through subsequent deaths, escapes and menaces, Pam backs her intuition against the evidence. All Lockridge items are fun to read and well constructed but some former ones have been more solidly satisfying.

A.B. Cunningham, ONE MAN MUST DIE (Dutton, $2.50). Jacob Reaf didn't die in combat as reported but came home to find himself superfluous to everyone—his wife, her new husband, her mother and several old friends. Sheriff Jess Roden nearly dies himself before he solves Reaf's murder. Quietly excellent in the Cunningham manner.

Eaton K. Goldthwaite, CAT AND MOUSE (Duell, Sloan & Pearce, $2.50). Are the screaming cat and dead mice warnings of death in Christopher Eliot's suburban circle? Himself suspected and threatened, he tries to place the guilt for his mistress' death, but it's Lieutenant Joseph Dickerson who watches the parcel locker and analyzes the kiss. Detective and author do equally good jobs.

Michael Blankfort, THE WIDOW MAKERS (Simon & Schuster, $2.50). Those Fascists are after The Papers again. This time three children possess the evidence, a legacy from their father. How can they judge whom to trust or how best to conceal the secret? This admirable situation, filled with suspense in early chapters, works out to a disappointingly soft conclusion.

Hugh Holman, UP THIS CROOKED WAY (Mill, $2). Our homespun sheriffs seem usually to do good detecting jobs. Carolinian John Macready is no exception as he invades university circles to discover who stabbed the landlord. Routine but pleasantly unpretentious.

BEST BUYS IN REPRINTS. Ruth Fenisong, MURDER NEEDS A NAME (with Sgt. Gridley Nelson) (Bond, 25 cents, cut); Agatha Christie, MR. PARKER PYNE, DETECTIVE (Bestseller, 25 cents, uncut); Mitchell Wilson, FOOTSTEPS BEHIND HER (Mercury, 25 cents, uncut).

December 1, 1946

Note: This week's column was written by Lenore Glen Offord.

Ellery Queen [Frederic Dannay] (editor), THE QUEEN'S AWARDS, 1946 (Little Brown, $2.75). The Queens are acknowledged leaders in encouraging the production of good short detective stories. It seems their generous awards aren't wasted. The 14 prize winners in this volume display almost uniform excellence. You may even prefer some of the runners-up ([William] Faulkner, [Manning] Coles, [Helen] McCloy) to the top-ranker, but don't miss any of them.

P.W. Wilson, THE OLD MILL (Rinehart, $2.50). Two men in Skeltdale die "as no man was ever killed before," and then the Unknown Malady stops short. Science is baffled to the end but Sir Julian Morthoe, connoisseur and expert on curious deaths, knows the solution. These Westmoreland period pieces continue to prove completely charming.

Vera Caspary, STRANGER THAN TRUTH (Random House, $2.50). Noble Barclay's magazines peddle a curious variety of Truth, for John Ansell, studying an obscure unsolved murder, is constantly thwarted and nearly dies himself. The reader may guess what is Truth sooner than these assorted narrators, but he'll still be interested in Miss Caspary's style and underlying indictment.

Erle Stanley Gardner, THE CASE OF THE BORROWED BRUNETTE (Morrow, $2.50). There was a charming brunette waiting on each corner down the street as far as Perry Mason could see. This time it's his own curiosity which involves him in a typically lively Gardner plot, working up to the usual threat of disbarment. Guess who wins.

Octavus Roy Cohen, DANGEROUS LADY (Macmillan, $2.50). Seems this lovely heiress arrives in Cherokee and right away is involved in three murders. She won't talk even to convince her lover that she's innocent. The hero and detective Bernie Williams solve her dilemma. Smooth, thoroughly readable, easy to forget about.

Marjorie Alan, RUE THE DAY (Mill, $2). Psychoses and jealousies fill the atmosphere of Matthew Kane's gloomy English household, and then what do you think? The Master decides to change his will. Take it from there as Inspector Lacey does. Pleasant, literate and undistinguished, this is good run-of-the-mill.

George Bellairs, DEATH IN THE NIGHT WATCHES (Macmillan, $2). The terms of Mr. Worth's will didn't please his heirs so the murders began. Inspector Littlejohn of Scotland Yard traps the criminal with some straightforward and good-humored detection. It seems I'm in a minority in finding Bellairs' characters two-dimensional and his style (though not his subject) reminiscent of the [Horatio] Alger books.

BEST BUYS IN REPRINTS. Elizabeth Jenkins, HARRIET (Bantam, 25 cents, uncut); Mary Collins, DEAD CENTER (Bantam, 25 cents, uncut).

December 8, 1946

Dale Clark, THE RED RODS (Messner, $2). Civic corruption, the dope racket and vanity publishing weave several plot threads into a net of persistent peril for private investigator Gillian Baltic. Terse, cryptic, effective— one of the strongest, solidest toughies of the year.

Wilson Tucker, THE CHINESE DOLL (Rinehart, $2.50). Apparently pointless commission leads private eye Chuck Horne into a welter of gamblers, murderers and beautiful Chinese. Some fascinating facts on the Fantasy Amateur Press Association are badly integrated into the story, but the writing is sound and the plot exciting and the surprise ending turns on a trick which Agatha Christie might well envy.

Robert K. Brunner (editor), SHOCKING TALES (Current Books, $2.95). A collection of "grim tales in which some atrocity is not only committed by the hero but also endorsed by the author"—the editor's definition, and one which certainly fails to apply to much of the contents. A peculiar volume, ranging from the hackneyed to the obscure, from the dull to the dazzling.

James Crockett, LULLABY WITH LUGERS (Crown, $2). Airline tycoons, big-time gangsters, Nazi agents and free-shooting heiresses complicate life for engineer Wilberforce D. James. Careless but carefree; formula but funny.

Schuyler Broocks, MURDER MAKES A MARRIAGE (Mystery House, $2). Does murder of war correspondent involve military secrets or private emotions? Realtor Cham Thorne is more adept than most at handling a love affair while investigating murder. Agreeable enough up to pretty muzzy conclusion.

Helen Holley, BLOOD ON THE BEACH (Mystery House, $2). Grande dame of fine old Georgia family settles down for Florida sojourn which includes murders and suspicion for all her friends and relations. Richly redolent of all the charm of the Old South including magnolia blossoms, young love, the caste system and the glorification of extra-legal killing.

Louis Trimble, GIVE UP THE BODY (Superior, $2). Oregon millionaire bisected by cleaver; girl reporter Adeline O'Hara tears apart his philanthropies and philanderings to find a murderer. Harmless quickie.

BEST BUYS IN REPRINTS. Dorothy B. Hughes, DREAD JOURNEY (Tower, 49 cents, uncut); Richard Powell, LAY THAT PISTOL DOWN (with Arab & Andy Blake) (Bantam, 25 cents, uncut).

December 15, 1946

Phoebe Atwood Taylor, PUNCH WITH CARE (Farrar Straus, $2.50). Ever since [Taylor's pseudonym] Alice Tilton moved into the household she's exerted more and more influence on Miss Taylor's Cape Cod detective stories. These started out as reasonably straight regional detection, but this latest gorgeous gallimaufry of quizzes, soap operas, secret rooms, progressive education and railroad hobbying is distinguishable from a Tilton farce only by the presence of Asey Mayo. Maybe there are too many plums in the pudding and maybe you won't quite understand the solution but you won't find many downright funnier whodunits this season.

Van Wyck Mason, SAIGON SINGER (Doubleday, $2.50). Ex-mistress of a Japanese tyrant now reigns as glamorous opera star in French Indo-China where Major Hugh North fences with her, flirts with her and ultimately solves her murder. The gallant major's return is highly welcome after five years, the Annamite local color is fascinating, and even howlers in opera and chemistry do not keep this from being one of the best of the North novels.

Cromwell Murray, DAY OF THE DEAD (McKay, $2). Irish-Mexican anti-Fascist Angel Obrion returns to Lake Patscuaro to frustrate a Sinarquista coup planned for the Day of the Dead—and incidentally to rescue a beautiful blonde turista. Simple but vigorous plot, effectively told with sound local color.

Raymond Knotts, MEETING BY MOONLIGHT (Doubleday Crime Club, $2). Famous aviatrix plays hob (sexual, political and financial) with too many lives, but oddly it is not her murder which Chicago editor Jim Hale has to solve. Too many improbabilities and too much routine pile up toward the end but the first half is fresh and promising.

Anthony Gilbert, THE BLACK STAGE (Smith & Durrell, $2). One of those English families develops a murder (in the library of course) and Arthur Crook, of all people, indulges in a last-act reconstruction of the crime. The jacket quotes a rave about an earlier Gilbert from "Anthony Boucher, noted English mystery critic." As just punishment the publishers can quote nothing from me on this surprisingly dull routine job.

Marco Page [Harry Kurnitz], THE SHADOWY THIRD (Dodd Mead, $2.50). Violin kidnaping leads to murder in New York musical circles, solved by lawyer David Calder, who detects in alternate spasms of rudeness and cuteness. The narrative technique is irritatingly similar to that of a class B screen whodunit. In a very small minority I didn't care much for Mr. Page's highly touted [1938 novel] FAST COMPANY—which is all that keeps me from being seriously disappointed in this comeback.

Charlotte Murray Russell, THE BAD NEIGHBOR MURDER (Doubleday Crime Club, $2). Jane Amanda Edwards, one of mystery fiction's more nebulously conceived protagonists, has an imbecile brother who finds a female corpse on his bed; and if the chaotic goings-on that follow are not side-splittingly funny, it isn't for want of trying.

December 22, 1946

E.C.R. Lorac, FIRE IN THE THATCH (Mystery House, $2). Death by arson heightens conflict between Devonshire landed gentry and invaders from London; credit solution to Chief Inspector Macdonald, whom the jacket justly calls "Scotland Yard's most likable detective." Quiet, solid, satisfactory.

Sam D. Cohen, ONE HUNDRED TRUE CRIME STORIES (with an introduction by Lewis J. Valentine) (World, $1.49). True crime narration in the short-short length doesn't leave much room for literary grace or psychological nuances, but Mr. Cohen can pack a lot of story into 1500 words, and most of his cases (which range from San Francisco to Soviet Russia) are interesting and unhackneyed. (Not a reprint.)

William Gray Beyer, DEATH OF A PUPPETEER (Mystery House, $2). Sadistic web-spinning dramatist murdered by gun explosion; Cliff Parks Parks, firearms expert and amateur psychologist, maneuvers the solution. Lightweight, fast and readable, with dividend of extensive gun-lore.

THE AVON MYSTERY STORY TELLER (Avon, 25 cents). Patternless anthology by unnamed editor but a solid quarter's worth of crime stories, ranging from an overfamiliar but excellent [Craig] Rice to an obscure but unreadable [J.S.] Fletcher. Chief discovery is Francis Cockrell's detective Joe Mudd, who sounds more like [William MacHarg's character] O'Malley than that copper himself.

Edmund Crispin, THE MOVING TOYSHOP (Lippincott, $2). Noted poet revisiting Oxford walks in on a corpse which promptly vanishes; erudite, eccentric, egregious Gervase Fen takes a hand. The expenditure of Mr. Crispin's unquestioned gifts of wit, poetry and scholarship on his confused plots, crass low comedy and unbelievable detective is the saddest example of conspicuous waste in the detective field.

Marty Holland, THE GLASS HEART (Messner, $2). Hard-boiled heel stumbles onto murder set-up, blackmails crazy old harridan, but is redeemed by love and a small miracle. Tough creampuff, very soggy inside.

December 29, 1946

No column was published this week.

1947

January 5, 1947

Pat McGerr, PICK YOUR VICTIM (Doubleday Crime Club, $2). Aleutian-isolated Marines find torn newspaper story of murder, naming murderer but not murderee; ex-flack Pete Robbins tells all he knows about the Washington bureaucracket in which the killing happened, and marine Joe Morris, by one of the all-time great feats of armchair detection, picks the victim. Without its gimmick the book would stand up excellently as a satiric novel of uplift and enterprise; the unique towhomdunit angle makes it the find of the season.

Margot Bennett, AWAY WENT THE LITTLE FISH (Doubleday Crime Club, $2). Pornographic murdermonger tomahawked at auction sale; aspirant-detective John Davies gropes among peculiar personalities, with his own emotions not so uninvolved as a detective might wish. As delightfully rich in wit and indirection as the author's first, TIME TO CHANGE HATS, and far better plotted; too long, to be sure, and too digressive, but a good thing is a good thing even if there's too much of it.

Stewart Sterling, WHERE THERE'S SMOKE (Lippincott, $2). Mr. Sterling's specialty in his too infrequent books is the detailed study of the detective activities of little-known squads of the city of New York—in this instance the Bureau of Fire Investigation. Simply as a straight medium-boiled novel of murder in radio this would be good; add a complete authentic documentation on fire control, some thrilling fire scenes and the hard-bitten character of fire marshal Ben Pedley and the result is an off-the-trail honey.

Lavinia R. Davis, TASTE OF VENGEANCE (Doubleday Crime Club, $2). New England small town life seemed a friendly, warming thing to Nora and Larry Blaine; even the fatal accidents seemed a part of the human birth-and-death pattern until the death came that could not be accident. Quiet, cumulative novel, written with skill and great warmth.

Bruno Fischer, THE PIGSKIN BAG (Ziff-Davis, $2.50). Adam Breen led the ordinary suburban life of any mildly successful salesman, complete with well-loved wife and daughter, until chance brought him the pigskin bag whose mysterious contents were worth any number of lives—even those of suburban daughters. Excellent first half of domestic suspense, falling off into more routine if still effective gangster melodrama.

Dorothy Park Clark, ROLL JORDAN ROLL (Doubleday Crime Club, $2). Fine old southern family's domestic round of bourbon and horseflesh is startlingly interrupted by assorted murders. Ambitious attempts at atmosphere and character ineptly handled.

Frank Gruber, BEAGLE SCENTED MURDER (Rinehart, $2). The balance on a Gruber book is usually pretty evenly weighted by his vices of haste, carelessness and chaos and his virtues of pace and interesting dividends (in this case dime novels); his humor may fit in either scale. But this time nothing could outweigh Otis Beagle and Joe Peel, the most unredeemedly repellent characters ever to appear in a book—petty, stupid chiselers whose viciousness Mr. Gruber seems to find blithely amusing.

January 12, 1947

Dashiell Hammett, HAMMETT HOMICIDES (edited by Ellery Queen [Frederic Dannay]) (Bestseller, 25 cents). First collected book appearance of a Grade-A novelette and three short stories about The Continental Op plus two other shorts by Hammett and an introduction and notes by Queen. Do I need to say more?

Margaret S. Marble, THE LADY FORGOT (Harper, $2.50). I keep swearing off of amnesia novels and they keep appearing, and it's even all right with me if they're as intelligent as this study of a neurotic girl who, acquitted of murdering her lover, tries to recover her sanity by discovering the truth behind her amnesia of the murder-moment. It's all a little self-consciously psychiatric, and you may resent the precise psychological diagramming of every motion and motive, but it makes an unusual and solid novel.

Kathleen Moore Knight, FOOTBRIDGE TO DEATH (Doubleday Crime Club, $2). Off-islanders bring a complex of personal problems and a whiff of international intrigue to Penberthy Island where selectman Elisha Macomber stands sturdily ready to solve everything. Small weaknesses in solution but by and large one of the more readable specimens of mystery-cum-romance.

Addison Simmons, DEAD WEIGHT (Phoenix, $2). Radio plotman uses real small-town history as stuff for his soap opera; result, murder—which his ulcer-riddled collaborator Ed MacIntyre solves largely by dreams. Passable writing and quite a bit of ingenuity.

BEST BUYS IN REPRINTS. Oliver Weld Bayer, AN EYE FOR AN EYE (Tower, 49 cents, uncut); Craig Rice, THE THURSDAY TURKEY MURDERS (with Bingo & Handsome) (Tower, 49 cents, uncut).

January 19, 1947

David Dodge, IT AIN'T HAY (Simon & Schuster, $2). You remember that hard-fighting C.P.A. James Whitney and you remember his creator's tight vigorous prose; they're among S.F.'s better products. This time Whit gets involved in the marijuana racket, which results in copious mayhem (largely in his and my favorite local restaurant) and nearly breaks up his marriage. Tough, colorful story, admirably and terrifyingly told.

Antonio Helu, LA OBLIGACION DE ASESINAR (COMPULSION TO MURDER) (Albatros, $3 Mexican). Occasionally a foreign language book is important enough to mention here and send you to the polyglot bookstores to find it. Helu is the great precursor of the Mexican detective story and founder of what is becoming a notable school, and these short stories, chiefly about the delightful criminal-detective Maximo Roldan, have a wit and ingenuity that make them a must for your collection. Xavier Villaurrutia's prologue is worth noting too, as possibly the first serious Mexican essay on the art of the whodunit.

William Irish [Cornell Woolrich], IF I SHOULD DIE BEFORE I WAKE AND OTHER STORIES (Avon, 25 cents). Six more shorts and novelettes, most of them originally published [as] by Cornell Woolrich— and to watch the Old Master of suspense technique at work is worth anybody's two bits.

Robin Grey [Elizabeth Gresham], PUZZLE IN PEWTER (Duell, Sloan & Pearce, $2.50). Curious theft of chessmen leads to madness and murder; that amiable tinker Hunter Lewis (whom the jacket astonishingly calls Homer) puts the pieces together. A bit hard to follow in spots but told with a great deal of placid charm.

Will Creed [also known as Peter Yates], DEATH COMES GRINNING (Five Star, 25 cents). Nurse in wealthy Pittsburgh family suspects murder; doctor opposes her but she makes her point when the entire family is wiped out. Wildly sensational ending to dullish tale. (Not a reprint.)

Dornford Yates, WERE DEATH DENIED (Putnam, $2.50). Those British stalwarts Richard Chandos and Jonah Mansel, idling about France as usual, have a run-in with some peculiarly nasty crooks and bluntly decide to exterminate them—which they do after 250 pages of involved strategic diagrams and dubious ethical attitudinizing.

BEST BUYS IN REPRINTS. John Dickson Carr, IT WALKS BY NIGHT (with Henri Bencolin) (Jonathan, 25 cents); Patrick Quentin, PUZZLE FOR PUPPETS (with Peter Duluth) (Pocket Books, 25 cents).

January 26, 1947

Note: This week's column was written by Lenore Glen Offord.

Arthur W. Upfield, THE BONE IS POINTED (Doubleday Crime Club, $2). Months after an unpleasant character disappeared in the Queensland bush, Inspector Napoleon Bonaparte sets out to find the body by his unique aboriginal methods. Some really wonderful stuff on bush magic, with a completely new reason for concealing a death, make this a heartily recommended item.

David Kent, A KNIFE IS SILENT (Random House, $2.50). The film producer's Carolina estate boasted Haitian servants. Was there a touch of voodoo in his beautiful star's murder? Luckily Jason Burr is on hand to untangle the mystery and save a likable narrator from several dangers. Nice detection and writing in spite of a top-heavy explanation.

Allan MacKinnon, HOUSE OF DARKNESS (Doubleday Crime Club, $2). Chased over England and Scotland by resourceful traitors, Colin Ogilvie must save his country by next Saturday. He's strong on romance and Commando tactics but only medium on brains; still there are no slow moments in this blend of [John] Buchan and [Manning] Coles with its not unpleasant flavor of naivete.

Helen Reilly, THE SILVER LEOPARD (Random House, $2.50). This heroine's engaged to a man with a fractured skull, loves another who behaves suspiciously throughout, and is framed for murder. New York's Inspector McKee does some astute work in solving puzzles and combatting her unseen enemy. Perfect example of the [Mignon G.] Eberhart formula, done with smooth competence.

John A. Saxon, LIABILITY LIMITED (Mill, $2.50). Interesting and realistically tough set-up—insurance adjuster Sam Welpton seeking clues in a third-rate gin mill—continues with Sam suspected of murder and entangled with venal policemen and ends in a welter of coincidence. Fast-moving and readable enough.

Adam Ring, KILLERS PLAY ROUGH (Crown, $2). Mrs. Blanding guessed there was some secret about her filigree necklace and was murdered after hiring a repellent private detective, Jim Pierce. The usual hoods and wicked nightclub proprietors, with other highly improbable villains, impede his labors. Little liquor, no luscious ladies; just slug, sap and shoot.

February 2, 1947

Note: This week's column was written by Lenore Glen Offord.

Marjorie Carleton, THE SWAN SANG ONCE (Morrow, $2.50). Taynor and Iris Harrison, an apparently loving couple, are quietly plotting each other's destruction. One of them is abundantly justified, but if evil were brought to justice his own integrity would be lost. Suspense is perfectly handled in this superior item which for my taste has about everything.

William Gilmore Beymer, THE MIDDLE OF MIDNIGHT (Whittlesey House, $2.50). Occupation forces in Dortheim battle a new German underground which uses such spectacular weapons as man-eating dogs, a secret laboratory in the castle and appalling "sky music." If this is corn it's been distilled to pack a real wallop. Roderick Braun is gallant beyond the call of duty.

Freeman Wills Crofts, DEATH OF A TRAIN (Dodd Mead, $2.50). The saboteurs must be traced without exciting their suspicions so Inspector French hides his usual painstaking methods behind some brilliant chicanery. The railroading details may bewilder you somewhat but the detecting won't. The Old Master never did a better job.

Paul Whelton, ANGELS ARE PAINTED FAIR (Lippincott, $2). The Reutler murder covered up a more sinister racket and prominent officials muzzled the papers. Reporter Garry Dean leaves his job and enlists the barkeep's gorgeous daughter to help in breaking the case. Action aplenty, solid detection, wisecracks on every page—maybe a few too many.

Peter Cheyney, UNEASY TERMS (Dodd Mead, $2.50). Why the Cheyney "Dark" novels should be so excellent and his others so middling nobody seems to know. Anyway here are the murdered stepfather; the secret; the good sister, the bad one and the young one, all beautiful; and Slim Callaghan slugging his way to a not-unexpected finish.

Lois Eby & John C. Fleming, HELL HATH NO FURY (Dutton, $2.50). Los Angeles' lady detective Pat O'Leary keeps postponing her wedding to pursue the playboy heir's murderer. Except for one slugging match the bridegroom seems helpless; little Pat outthinks him, the police and the criminal. This book is a powerful addition to the case against feminine sleuths.

February 9, 1947

Note: This week's column was written by Lenore Glen Offord.

Jack Iams, THE BODY MISSED THE BOAT (Morrow, $2.50). Forget about the mystery, nobody liked the American consul to French Equatorial Africa, anyway; served him right to be poisoned and put in the empty gorilla cage. Concentrate on the genuinely funny events and wonderful characters and read this just for laughs. Can't name the detective, he's a chief suspect.

George Harmon Coxe, THE FIFTH KEY (Knopf, $2). Photographer Kent Murdock, covering a radio show in New York, drinks doped whisky, awakens beside the corpse of the show's author, finds that someone has photographed him. Detecting thus becomes mandatory. Slick work with actors, agents, blackmailers and that extra key, and Coxe's firm economical style.

E.R. Punshon, IT CAN LEAD ANYWHERE (Macmillan, $2.50). Mousy man, follower of religious fanatic, is bludgeoned to death. Acting Chief Constable Bobby Owen investigates this and other dramatic events in village of Chipping Up. Good characterization, gentle humor, logical working out somehow can't save this from seeming ponderous.

Marie Blizard, THE MEN IN HER DEATH (Mystery House, $2). The guests and hangers-on of Hester Bruce ("Hollywood's Most Beautiful Brain") had reason to detest their hostess. Eve and Tom MacWilliams, who discovered her body, move into the Maine murder cottage and find the clues to the mystery. Coherent, light and pleasantly feminine.

Eli Colter, CHEER FOR THE DEAD (Mill, $2.50). Agreeable millionaire found bopped in swimming pool. His heirs, half-sisters who'd never met, do their utmost to get murdered also despite efforts of L.A. private eye Pat Campbell. Solution comes by elimination and surprise ending seems rather unfair, but the story's readable.

Victor Patrick, THREE TO MAKE MURDER (Mystery House, $2). Nasty millionaire found shot in study. Family and members of houseparty lie and hide evidence; so does ex-G.I. Peter Ames, who thus gets himself involved. Chief Conklin and others detect. Shifting viewpoint and vague characterization make this yarn hard to follow.

February 16, 1947

Ellery Queen [Frederic Dannay] (editor), 101 YEARS' ENTERTAINMENT (Modern Library Giant, $1.95). So definitive is Queen's great anthology and so unusual (and welcome) is the intrusion of the whodunit into the distinguished ranks of Modern Library Giants that this event deserves more than a casual listing as a reprint. Get it.

Frederick C. Davis, THURSDAY'S BLADE (Doubleday Crime Club, $2). A murderer at large in N.Y. radio with a set of days-of-the-week razors makes a worthy antagonist for ingenious Professor Cy Hatch. Dexterous plotting, some unusual motivations and realistic radio background.

Aaron Marc Stein, WE SAW HIM DIE (Doubleday Crime Club, $2). The several peculiarities of Balkan nobility, Southern California cultists and the nursing profession weave a problem as intricately menacing as it is funny for archeologists Tim Mulligan and Elsie Mae Hunt. Lively characterization and (rare in whodunits) some really sound cryptanalysis atone for a somewhat hurried ending and the irritating confusion of two characters named Elsie and Elise.

Edward Ronns [Edward S. Aarons], TERROR IN THE TOWN (McKay, $2). Mass murders in New England fishing village build terror for young bride Verity Farland—who displays a courage and good sense rare among terrified heroines. Basic plot weakly motivated but local color and readability make for solid enjoyment.

Henry Kane, A HALO FOR NOBODY (Simon & Schuster, $2). A jewel racket and some more personal murders provide occupation for Peter Chambers, a private eye who thrives on drink, wenching and coincidences. Reasonably good toughie, at once more literate and more confusing than most, but the publisher's blurb of "a worthy successor to Dashiell Hammett" is hard to swallow.

Amelia Reynolds Long, MURDER BY MAGIC (Phoenix, $2). Fraudulent occultism and a locked-room murder frame a puzzle for attorney Stephen Carter. Ingenious plot and gimmickry deserve better writing and characterization.

Z.H. Ross, OVERDUE FOR DEATH (Bobbs-Merrill, $2.50). Murder and high finance in a Seattle electric shaver company, investigated by one of those spirited heroines. Somewhat more readable than the last Ross but marred by unlikely business maneuvers, nonsensical cryptography and a solution that explains nothing.

BEST BUYS IN REPRINTS. W. Somerset Maugham, ASHENDEN; OR, THE BRITISH AGENT (Tower, 49 cents, uncut); John Rhode & Carter Dickson [John Dickson Carr], FATAL DESCENT (with Dr. Horatio Glass) (Popular Library, 25 cents, uncut).

February 23, 1947

Note: No new books were reviewed in this week's column.

BEST BUYS IN REPRINTS. Leslie Charteris, FOLLOW THE SAINT (with Simon Templar) (Tower, 49 cents, uncut); Phoebe Atwood Taylor, THE PERENNIAL BOARDER (with Asey Mayo) (Penguin, 25 cents, uncut).

March 2, 1947

Stuart Palmer, THE RIDDLES OF HILDEGARDE WITHERS (with an introduction and critical notes by Ellery Queen [Frederic Dannay]) (Jonathan, 25 cents). The jacket quotes me as saying "Hildegarde Withers is incomparable and inimitable"—which I'll stick to, and add that Major Palmer is fair-to-middling incomparable himself in the astuteness with which he blends blithe humor and neatly contrived plots. This is the first collection of his short stories, most of them new to book form—which makes it a must for first-edition collectors but even more of a must for any reader fond of charm and dexterity.

Percival Wilde, P. MORAN, OPERATIVE (Random House, $2.50). Nothing is rarer in the mystery field than the truly humorous detective story—the story, that is, in which not only characters and dialogue but even the basic plot is inherently comic. And no series of such stories has been more uniformly successful than the adventures of P. Moran, correspondence school detective. Here, collected for the first time, are seven of those exploits, mostly from *Ellery Queen's Mystery Magazine* but a few new even to Moran's most loyal devotees. Result: joy unalloyed.

Hilda Lawrence, DEATH OF A DOLL (Simon & Schuster, $2.50). Hope House, home for working girls, looked like a haven for Ruth, but it was there that murder overtook her in the guise of a masked doll. Mark East undertakes so sensitive and sympathetic an investigation that he seems hardly to need the pair of quaint old maids wished on him as stooges. Delicate perception of character and quiet shudders worthy of a naturalistic M.R. James make a distinguished book.

Hugh Lawrence Nelson, THE TITLE IS MURDER (Rinehart, $2). Braxton's was S.F.'s most exclusive bookstore before the murders—nice grisly murders too, in the course of which Detective Lieutenant Steve Johnson managed to learn quite a bit about the book business and to fall in love with a possibly murderous book clerk. A bit short on detection but very long on human warmth, good writing and admirably observed shop background.

Frank Owen (editor), THE FIRESIDE MYSTERY BOOK (Lantern Press, $2.50). There's a little of everything here: true crime (including an interesting excerpt from the N.Y. Folklore Society), fantasy (especially a fascinating oddment by Norman McGlashan), an Ellery Queen radio play, and assorted magazine crime stories by [John] Collier, [Richard] Sale, [Cornell] Woolrich and others.

Dorothy Quick, THE FIFTH DAGGER (Scribner, $2). We won't talk about this. In five years of reviewing I have not seen a more subliterate novel from a major publishing house.

John Franklin Bardin, THE LAST OF PHILIP BANTER (Dodd Mead, $2.50). Last season Mr. Bardin made his debut with THE DEADLY PERCHERON, a fantastic novel at once wonderful and outrageous, which combined many features of the best and the worst of the year. Now he follows up with another psychiatric fantasia which has neither the virtues nor the vices of the first. Huckster finds manuscript purportedly by himself, prophesying his next 24 hours—and it starts to come true. Promising start, but lackadaisical plotting and verbose self-analysis by all characters make a book which is neither good nor bad but plain dull.

March 9, 1947

John Dickson Carr, THE SLEEPING SPHINX (Harper, $2.50). A year-old murder presents a returning Army officer with a complex emotional problem and Dr. Gideon Fell with a puzzle made up of such oddments as a collection of murderers' masks, a child's printing set and a juggling game with coffins. Even Mr. Carr has rarely proffered such an admirably intricate lesson in plotting—while showing the newer school that he can use some elements of the "psychological" novel as well.

Mignon G. Eberhart, ANOTHER WOMAN'S HOUSE (Random House, $2.50). Myra loves Richard, Richard plans to divorce Alice who's serving a life sentence for murder, Alice is unexpectedly pardoned and the trouble starts. For once our heroine isn't unjustly suspected on the flimsiest evidence and her adventures are convincing. Applause to Mrs. Eberhart for forgetting her own formula. (Review by Lenore Glen Offord.)

William Irish [Cornell Woolrich], BORROWED CRIME AND OTHER STORIES (Avon, 25 cents). The excellence of the Woolrich-Irish pulp novelettes is now so widely recognized that the mere announcement of this latest collected volume should send you scurrying to a newsstand.

Erle Stanley Gardner, TWO CLUES (Morrow, $2.50). Two novelettes about shrewdly likable Sheriff Bill Eldon, who has his troubles with local politics but makes short shrift of city-bred murderers. Second-string Gardner but enjoyable.

Ruth Sawtell Wallis, COLD BED IN THE CLAY (Dodd Mead, $2.50). Petty irritations of small-college faculty life blossom into murder; G-man Eric Lund is fortunately on hand. Strained writing and weak plot place this one below Miss Wallis' high standards.

Peter Stirling, STOP PRESS—MURDER! (Phoenix, $2). Murder of his city editor produces publicity problems and peril for publisher Edward Harper. Short, fast, acceptable time-killer.

Elihu Adams, OPERATION HOMICIDE (Mill, $2.50). Curious professor witnesses inexplicable murder which remains fairly inexplicable after 250 more pages of assorted killings and talk. Professor is named Agricola John Ispenwill and his style is about what you might imagine from that.

BEST BUYS IN REPRINTS. Bruno Fischer, QUOTH THE RAVEN (Bestseller, 25 cents, cut); Erle Stanley Gardner, THE CASE OF THE ROLLING BONES (with Perry Mason) (Tower, 49 cents, uncut).

March 16, 1947

Anthony Gilbert, BY HOOK OR BY CROOK (Barnes, $2). Miss Martin was old and unwanted but a chance observation of hers (plus the persistence of Arthur Crook) was the one factor that ruined a perfect murder. There's little mystery in this relentless study of middle-class murder but there is a reality, an understated bourgeois terror, that makes it far more chilling than a dozen violent thrillers. Gilbert—and Crook—at their best.

Francis Bonnamy, PORTRAIT OF THE ARTIST AS A DEAD MAN (Duell, Sloan & Pearce, $2.50). When an artist has painted his self-portrait as a hanged man, is his actual hanging suicide or murder? This nice esthetico-criminal question leads Peter Shane and the inestimable Bonnamy through mazes of art theory, Washington society and international fascism with all the subtlety of characterization and irony of intelligence that a Bonnamy fan expects.

Franklin James, KILLER IN THE KITCHEN (Lantern Press, $2). The black market and other Chicago rackets make life exciting for Mickey

Richards, a female entry in the hardboiled handicap. Familiar enough, but in its brisk brash way far from unreadable.

Cledwyn Hughes, HE DARED NOT LOOK BEHIND (A.A. Wyn, $2). Wife of small-time dentist has beauty, charm...and an artificial leg; growing jealousy of the leg drives husband to dentally contrived murder for which the leg finds its own revenge. I'm not at all certain whether this is intended as a psychological study in remorse-delusions or as a supernatural retribution-fantasy; in either case it's a disappointingly superficial handling of a superlative idea.

Van Siller, THE CURTAIN BETWEEN (Doubleday Crime Club, $2). Our hero marries a mysteriously fascinating girl who may be going mad; endless problems and murders ensue chiefly because everybody, in musicomedy fashion, refuses ever to say one simplifying word. In its slick glib way I suppose this isn't really bad; trouble is I've come to expect so much better and solider work from Van Siller.

Constance & Gwenyth Little, THE BLACK GOATEE (Doubleday Crime Club, $2). The old gambit of the disappearing corpse plays itself out in a resolutely eccentric family. Strictly for Little fans.

BEST BUYS IN REPRINTS. Elspeth Huxley, THE AFRICAN POISON MURDERS (with Superintendent Vachell) (Popular Library, 25 cents, uncut); Paul McGuire, A FUNERAL IN EDEN (with George Buchanan, Sultan of Kaltai) (Penguin, 25 cents, uncut).

March 23, 1947

Wilkie Collins, THE WOMAN IN WHITE (World, $1.49). This classic mystery melodrama, three times as long as the average modern whodunit and 30 times as rewarding, appears at last in a well-printed, readable, one-volume edition which should win countless new enthusiasts to the magnificent villainies of Count Fosco and the consummate technical mastery of his creator.

Fredric Brown, THE FABULOUS CLIPJOINT (Dutton, $2.50). A drunken printer is slugged and rolled in an alley—apparently the drabbest and most insoluble of murders, but the victim's brother and son team up to unearth not only the killer but a curious new motive. Despite occasional purpleness this is a singularly effective job of portraying people as they are and murder as it is—a sordidly compelling story.

Manly Wade Wellman, FIND MY KILLER (Farrar Straus, $2.50). Ex-M.P. Jackson Yates joins the J.D. Thatcher detective agency and finds J.D. a very charming girl up to her lovely neck in a locked-room murder and a peculiar will. It's a pity that the plot turns on some recently exploded aspects of the paraffin test; but Wellman's first novel, if less original than his many shorts, is vigorous, medium-hardboiled and likable.

D.B. Olsen [Dolores Hitchens], GALLOWS FOR THE GROOM (Doubleday Crime Club, $2). A bird sanctuary, a beautiful girl, assorted suitors and a set of apostle spoons (complete with Judas) weave a pattern of terror for mild Mr. A.L. Pennyfeather. Nice blend of ordinariness and chills (and absence of quaint old ladies) makes this the best Olsen in years.

Thomas Kyd, BLOOD OF VINTAGE (Lippincott, $2.50). Cleverly contrived "accident" among the bluest of blue-bloods calls for the talents of Sam Phelan, as intelligent as he is unpolished. Indirections of character and careful study of stagnant aristocracy make a good book—but badly flawed by bold-faced cheating of the reader.

Knight Rhoades, SHE DIED ON THE STAIRWAY (Arcadia House, $2). It's the old lady who wants to change her will again but this time she's not the murderee. Instead an unexpected murder pattern evolves around her, the mystification of amateur magician Lieutenant Price Price, S.F.P.D. Lightweight but ingenious and often amusing.

Roy Vickers, THE WHISPERING DEATH (Jefferson House, $2.50). You never know what to expect from Mr. Vickers, who ranges from the criminous comedy of Fidelity Dove through the well plotted stolidity of FOUR PAST FOUR to the realistic irony of the Department of Dead Ends. This time his publishers have seen fit to dredge up a 15-year-old serial in the manner of Edgar Wallace—sensational, hackneyed, ridiculous...and mildly entertaining.

BEST BUYS IN REPRINTS. Charlotte Armstrong, THE INNOCENT FLOWER (with MacDougal Duff) (Pocket Books, 25 cents, uncut).

March 30, 1947

Maurice Richardson (editor), NOVELS OF MYSTERY FROM THE VICTORIAN AGE (Pilot Press, $3.95). If space allows I'll take this up at length later; at the moment I'll simply note that it contains three incomparable classics—[Wilkie Collins'] THE WOMAN IN WHITE, [J. Sheridan LeFanu's] CARMILLA, and [Robert Louis Stevenson's] DR. JEKYLL AND MR.HYDE—plus an extraordinary "lost" detective story of 1862, THE NOTTING HILL MURDER, an utterly absorbing incunable which is alone worth the price of the volume.

Mary Collins, DEATH WARMED OVER (Scribner, $2.50). When the murders start in a singularly unpleasant L.A. boarding house, Janey Jeffries can eavesdrop and get conked as well as any Had-I-But-Known heroine—with the difference that Janey has a fine salty spirit of her own and that her creator conceives murder as a real and unglamorous fact. Vigorous character-humor and excellent evocation of atmospheric detail make Mrs. Collins' belated return a joyous event.

Robert Finnegan, THE BANDAGED NUDE (Simon & Schuster, $2.50). Methodical destruction of the paintings of a Bohemian S.F. artist leads to destruction of the artist himself plus a few bystanders—almost including Dan Banion, whose investigation is prompted as much by an odd sense of human fellowship as by his duties as a reporter. Mr. Finnegan has something affirmative and warming to say about people and he says it here even better than before; watch this man as a contender for top honors.

Roger Bax [also known as Andrew Garve], DISPOSING OF HENRY (Harper, $2.50). Denise (nee Daisy) knew what she wanted and resolutely got it up to and including a wealthy and unobservant husband; then came Trant, who appealed equally to the erogenous zones of her body and the thanatogenous zones of her mind. The resultant murder plot, its apparent perfection, its inescapable flaws and final disastrous collapse create an absorbingly understated melodrama revolving around three extremely well-realized characters.

Manning Coles, WITH INTENT TO DECEIVE (Doubleday Crime Club, $2). Meek retired merchant switches lives with Argentinian swashbuckler, to his own peril and pleasure and the total confusion of the Yard. Far from the best Coles (Tommy Hambledon plays a passive role and the awkward structure involves telling most events twice over) but still a nice exercise in good-humored implausibility.

ALSO RECEIVED. Kate Clugston, A MURDERER IN THE HOUSE (A.A. Wyn, $2.50); Jay L. Currier, CARGO OF FEAR (Messner, $2); John Rhode, EXPERIMENT IN CRIME (with Dr. Priestley) (Dodd Mead, $2.50); Clare Casler Saunders, DESIGN FOR TREACHERY (with Dr. F. Lance Henry) (Scribner, $2).

BEST BUYS IN REPRINTS. Anthony Gilbert, DEATH AT THE DOOR (with Arthur Crook) (Bantam, 25 cents, uncut); Craig Rice, THE SUNDAY PIGEON MURDERS (with Bingo & Handsome) (Pocket Books, 25 cents, uncut).

April 6, 1947

James Keddie, Jr. (editor), THE SECOND CAB: FIFTEEN SHER-LOCKIAN ESSAYS, ONE SONNET AND A QUIZ (The Speckled Band, $3). The Boston scion society of the Baker Street Irregulars has produced a book second only to PROFILE BY GASLIGHT in the varied charm and intelligence of its offerings, from such old masters as [Edgar W.] Smith, [Vincent] Starrett, [P.M.] Stone and [James] Keddie, Sr., and such welcome newer names as Henry C. Clark and Mandel E. Cohen. (May be ordered from the editor, 6 Beacon Street, Boston.)

Doris Miles Disney, APPOINTMENT AT NINE (Doubleday Crime Club, $2). Shooting of doctor produces complex problems of jealousy and paternity ably resolved by county detective Jim O'Neill. Nice intricate puzzling, tempered by strong human values and an unusually sympathetic investigator.

Lenore Glen Offord, MY TRUE LOVE LIES (Duell, Sloan & Pearce, $2.50). Noel had scarcely fallen in love when the corpse turned up in the plaster works and her new true love was a leading suspect, but Inspector Aloysius Cletus Geraghty maneuvered adroitly through the wilds of S.F. Bohemia to a neatly twisted solution. Balanced helpings of romance and murder, served in style but with regrettably less of the off-beat Offord individuality than usual.

George Bagby [Aaron Marc Stein], THE TWIN KILLING (Doubleday Crime Club, $2). The coming young stars of baseball and the wise money of Times Square make a murderous combination—which at least justifies Inspector Schmidt (whose attitude toward shoes agrees with that of this department) in spending most of his official time at the ball park. A trifle loose in solution but as fresh, lively and agreeable a sports whodunit as has turned up in years.

Dana Chambers, ROPE FOR AN APE (Dial Press, $2.50). A quiet Connecticut week end for Niles Boyd entails lush damsels, ghastly bashings and an escaped orang-outang—all adding up to a well constructed (if weakly motivated) puzzle, told with that easy readability and high-geared tempo which makes it so painful to announce that this is the late Mr. Chambers' last book.

Wade Miller [Bob Wade & Bill Miller], GUILTY BYSTANDER (Farrar Straus, $2.50). Ex-detective Max Thursday pulls himself out of alcoholism to rescue the kidnaped son he has never seen, tangling with every sinister aspect of the San Diego underworld to do it. Less startling than Miller's first but a sound, meaty hardboiled novel.

BEST BUYS IN REPRINTS. Richard Lockridge & George H. Estabrooks, DEATH IN THE MIND (with Johnny Evans) (Tower, 49 cents, uncut); A.E. Martin, SINNERS NEVER DIE (Bestseller, 25 cents, cut).

April 13, 1947

Richard & Frances Lockridge, THINK OF DEATH (Lippincott, $2.50). Lawyer Martin Brooks, late a major in the OSS, goes on a Westchester weekend with theatrical people, finds his divorced wife anew and becomes a leading suspect in her second husband's murder. Synopsized thus it sounds a pretty routine story—which it is anything but when clothed with the graces and subtleties of the Lockridges' narration. Full-bodied characters and a convincingly delicate sense of the impact of murder provide an object lesson in the revitalizing of a familiar situation.

Hugh Holman, ANOTHER MAN'S POISON (Mill, $2.50). White-supremacy Congressman purged with cyanide; Sheriff Macready shrewdly mingles detection and politics to solve an "impossible" crime. Able detective story in interesting (and nondidactic) political setting.

M.S. Marble, DIE BY NIGHT (Rinehart, $2). Joe Gaylord, a private eye with a good deal of unprofessional charm, visits his aunt's eccentric L.A. household to find that the people next door are even screwier: they think they're Greek gods and goddesses and they murder each other. Some of the season's most agreeable writing wasted on one of the season's most incoherent plots.

Julius Long, KEEP THE COFFINS COMING (Messner, $2). Planted as a spy inside a successful American Fascist front, Charles Rinehart shoots his way through the year's most persistent carnage to learn the identity of the secret backer. Alternately tough and talky, astute and oversimplified— a sort of [Sinclair Lewis political novel] IT CAN'T HAPPEN HERE as a [Humphrey] Bogart starring vehicle.

Wenzell Brown, MURDER SEEKS AN AGENT (Arcadia House, $2). Here's a unique publishing phenomenon: a $2 reprint of a novel which originally appeared a year or two ago as a 25-cent paperback. It's still a mildly amusing meller about lurid N.Y. criminality and hesitant Professor Peter Aswell.

Henry E. Helseth, THE CHAIR FOR MARTIN ROME (Dodd Mead, $2.50). A farrago of cliches and claptrap, worth noting only as the most arrant romantic sentimentalizing over a criminal since [Sir Edward] Bulwer-Lytton's EUGENE ARAM. Recommended to the educators who denounce radio thrillers, just to give them something really to worry about.

April 20, 1947

Ngaio Marsh, FINAL CURTAIN (Little Brown, $2.50). Agatha Troy Alleyn undertakes a commission to paint the Grand Old Man of the English theater—and Inspector Roderick Alleyn, back from the wars, finds his wife a principal witness in the first murder case to greet him. A brand new poison, a surprise murderer and a fabulously eccentric family with the theatrical background the author draws so well—all add up to a performance so adroit, so literate, so charming that only later reflection reminds us that Miss Marsh has left her inspector without a shred of proof and that her characters this time are the purest stock—if dressed in far better taste than the average stock company can afford.

Manning Long, DULL THUD (Duell, Sloan & Pearce, $2.50). My beloved Liz Parrott is now running a rental library, God help her, but blackmail and murder among an assorted group of young women in an East Side walk-up better display her peculiar talents. There are many mystery-mongers whom I highly esteem for various weighty reasons but there are few indeed who are more sheer fun to read than the brusquely ironic Manning Long.

Leslie Edgley, FALSE FACE (Simon & Schuster, $2). Biographer Evan Beatty witnesses an accident and finds himself unwittingly in love with the perverse personality of the dead victim; his quest for her true nature ranges from Washington politics to Chicago gangsterism. Partly awkward, partly obvious, but at its best a compelling study in obsession.

M.V. Heberden, THEY CAN'T ALL BE GUILTY (Doubleday Crime Club, $2). Desmond Shannon cleans up a corrupt New York municipality where the leading industrialist, the Democratic machine bosses, the cops and the liquor runners are all members of the Communist Party. If you can accept this novel Cloudcuckooland, you may enjoy this tough action-crammed story—up to a finale in which Miss Heberden's usually sharp sense of plotting follows her feeling for probability out of the window.

Joseph L. Bonney, LOOK TO THE LADY! (Lippincott, $2.50). The jacket blurb and the author's foreword hinted at some startling technical ingenuity so I hopefully plodded through all of this dim and dull rehash of the HAMLET theme, only to find that the promised tantalizing query at the end resolved itself simply to, "Who cares?" An ingenious promotional job of dressing up a completely uninteresting manuscript.

ALSO RECEIVED. Minna Bardon, BLOOD-RED DEATH (with G.I. Antwerp) (Phoenix, $2); Libbie Block, BEDEVILED (Doubleday Crime Club, $2); Barbara Frost, THE UNWELCOME CORPSE (with Jane MacDevitt) (Coward-McCann, $2.50). Tom Van Dycke & Ben Kerner, NOT WITH MY NECK (with Johnny Greer) (Messner, $2).

BEST BUYS IN REPRINTS. Francis Iles [also known as Anthony Berkeley], BEFORE THE FACT (Pocket Books, 25 cents, uncut); Ellery Queen [Frederic Dannay & Manfred B. Lee], THE ADVENTURES OF ELLERY QUEEN (Tower, 49 cents, uncut).

April 27, 1947

John Dickson Carr, DR. FELL, DETECTIVE AND OTHER STORIES (with an introduction by Ellery Queen [Frederic Dannay]) (Mercury, 25 cents). Five short stories and three radio plays, mostly about the fabulous figure of Dr. Gideon Fell (plus an unusually interesting Queen preface), form a volume to make a reviewer regret that there are no new superlatives. Here is the detective story at its puzzle-purest, written with rare distinction and literary skill—and all in first edition for one silver quarter.

David Partridge (editor), CRIMES OF PASSION (Garden City, $1.49). In his brief introduction Mr. Partridge seems to assert that the only interesting motive for murder is lust. He can't mean this seriously (for comprehensive rebuttal, see [William] Bolitho's MURDER FOR PROFIT or [F. Tennyson] Jesse's MURDER AND ITS MOTIVES) but the result is a certain triangular monotony in the stories chosen. Individually however the distinguished excerpts from such names as [William] Faulkner, [Arthur] Schnitzler, Sherwood Anderson and John Collier and the extraordinary items from such lesser lights as Ellis St. Joseph and Nathan Asch (plus a bawdy [Honore de] Balzac blackout) assure the murder bawdy [Honore de] Balzac blackout) assure the murder fancier some absorbing moments.

J. Lane Linklater, SHADOW FOR A LADY (Mill, $2.50). Silas Booth is a reasonably unique private eye—he works without a license throughout this introductory adventure and he makes the guilty defray the expenses of clearing the innocent. Otherwise he's familiar enough, but his intervention in blackmail and murder in L.A. and the adjoining smudge-laden orange country is told with a fast easy pace which suggests a Grade A professional of the [Erle Stanley] Gardner school.

Jean Leslie, THREE CORNERED MURDER (Doubleday Crime Club, $2). Harmless househunting leads Professor Peter Ponsonby into the midst of murky municipal politics where he finds himself a candidate first for a murder-frame and then for murder. Too many characters and somewhat diffuse plotting weaken a valuable political story told with charm and the conviction of first-hand observation.

Frank Gruber, THE HONEST DEALER (Rinehart, $2). Death Valley and Las Vegas are the latest arenas of adventure for those money-making murder-magnets Johnny Fletcher and Sam Cragg. A more than usually cohesive story and some frantic and fantastic gambling episodes make this one of their best exploits.

Willetta Ann Barber & R.F. Schabelitz, DRAWBACK TO MURDER (Scribner, $2.50). Strange practices, private and professional, of New York sculptors build a murder case for sketchpad detective Christopher Storm, who spends most of his time rescuing his peculiarly submoronic sister. Excessive length and Had-I-But-Knowning balanced by interesting (and eyebrow-lifting) background of art profession and Storm's always fascinating gimmick of clue-sketching.

Hammond Innes, FIRE IN THE SNOW (Harper, $2.50). British screen writer in Dolomites crosses the trail of international crooks and Fascists, all intent on hidden hoard of gold. Excellent [Eric] Ambleresque start of underplayed melodrama in Alpine ski setting, degenerating into implausible violence and violent implausibility. (Published in England as THE LONELY SKIER.)

May 4, 1947

No column was published this week.

May 11, 1947

Stuart Palmer, MISS WITHERS REGRETS (Doubleday Crime Club, $2). Hildegarde Withers had sincerely promised to retire from meddling, but when murder in a Long Island swimming pool parallels the sinister events in her tank of tropical fish she's back on the trail, to the mingled grief and relief of Inspector Oscar Piper. It's been six long parched years since the last novel about the horsefaced schoolteacher and it's high time that the Grand Old Man of the humorous detective story returned to demonstrate to the modern upstarts just how it's done.

John Godey, THE GUN AND MR. SMITH (Doubleday Crime Club, $2). A Long Island house-party of the Better People, from the music critic host to minor royalty, turns into nightmare as a political plot emerges and the charming pianist-heroine finds herself faced with vicious physical terror. Unsatisfactory plot synopsis, I know; but that's because the plot is so admirably constructed and so chillingly elusive. Let's simply say that Mr. Godey's debut is one of the most satisfactory melodramas in some time, adorned with a keen sense of effect and a fine gift of storytelling.

Mary Fitt, DEATH AND THE PLEASANT VOICES (Putnam, $2.50). Tensely the British county family awaited the new heir who proved to be first half colored, second an impostor and finally a corpse. Multiple weaknesses of motivation and detection detract from quiet charm and skilled writing.

Storm Jameson, BEFORE THE CROSSING (Macmillan, $2.75). Murder of Socialist M.P. leads David Renn, novelist and secret agent, into exploration of Fascist decay in prewar England. One would like to welcome the whodunit debut of a novelist usually so distinguished as Miss Jameson, but the present work is largely as a novel ineffectual and as a melodrama dull.

Margaret Echard, THE DARK FANTASTIC (Doubleday, $2.50). Ruthless woman murders to attain a marriage which in its turn causes her own death. In a post-Civil War setting, Miss Echard treats a peculiar series of phenomena (traditional in her own family) which she explains as part psychological, part paranormal, part supernatural—an interesting idea mangled by wordiness, inconsistency and a singularly unsympathetic lot of characters.

James M. Fox, THE LADY REGRETS (Coward-McCann, $2.50). Kidnaping and murder in family of L.A. tycoon implicate John and Suzy Marshall, whose adventure gets off to a lively promising start but bogs down in confusion.

ALSO RECEIVED. Patrick Laing [Amelia Reynolds Long], THE SHADOW OF MURDER (Phoenix, $2); Dorothy Mayor, IT'S AN ILL WIND (Mill, $2.50); Patricia Wentworth, LATTER END (with Miss Maud Silver) (Lippincott, $2.50).

BEST BUYS IN REPRINTS. Francis Bonnamy, THE KING IS DEAD ON QUEEN STREET (with Peter Shane) (Penguin, 25 cents, uncut); Frances & Richard Lockridge, MURDER OUT OF TURN (with Mr. & Mrs. North) (Pocket Books, 25 cents, uncut).

May 18, 1947

Anthony Thorne, SO LONG AT THE FAIR (Random House, $2.50). As far as plot goes this is the oldie about the Paris Exposition and the girl whose companion vanishes, but the hackneyed legend has never before been remotely so well told. Mr. Thorne shifts his emphasis from suspense and terror to the dazzled awakening of an English miss in Paris, and he tells it liltingly. The economy and precision of his writing, the pure warmth of his people, the singing sense of youth and joy—all make this as enchanting a piece of light fiction as has crossed this desk in years.

V. Sackville-West, DEVIL AT WESTEASE (Doubleday, $2.50). "Straight" novelists condescending to the whodunit are apt enough to fall flat on their faces but Miss Sackville-West's narrative of murder and disappearance in one of those hidden-away villages is a joy and a delight. The experienced fan should have no trouble figuring the answer (though he'll hardly anticipate the beautiful twist it receives) but the leisurely charm and ease of the telling provide an excellent evening's diversion.

Louisa Revell, THE BUS STATION MURDERS (Macmillan, $2). Stabbing of an admiral's overbearing widow involves ex-Latin teacher Miss Julia Tyler in the intimate scandals of all levels of the city of Annapolis. Wild coincidence and a solution devoid of detection do not lessen the appeal of this attractive book, which manages to blend the romantic and local-colorful elements of Leslie Ford (Miss Julia's favorite author) with an agreeably humorous perception of its own snobbish garrulity. Even those allergic to spinster-narrators may well want more of Miss Julia.

Patrick Quentin [also known as Q. Patrick and Jonathan Stagge], PUZZLE FOR PILGRIMS (Simon & Schuster, $2.50). It was not enough that Peter Duluth should lose his wife's love; he had to protect her lover from a murder charge—and then himself fall in love with the other chief suspect. One of the most tangled emotional situations on record, fused with an adroit puzzle-plot and a vivid Mexican background.

Baynard Kendrick, MAKE MINE MACLAIN (Morrow, $2.50). Three novelettes about blind Captain Duncan Maclain and the murders he solves among Hollywoodites, opera singers and (most interesting) the odder denizens of Staten Island. Somewhat sketchy, less firm in plot or character than the Maclain novels, but still welcome to all devotees of one of the greatest of modern sleuths.

Leslie Ford, THE WOMAN IN BLACK (Scribner, $2.50). Production genius Enoch B. Stubblefield was being touted as presidential timber; he should have known that his career would be blighted by murder when he met Grace Latham. Colonel Primrose is in the hospital (measles), but it doesn't matter since the murderer obligingly stops and confesses all when the proper length has been reached. There's some agreeable nastiness on

Washington society, some good scenes for Sergeant Buck and an unusually aggravating nitwitted heroine.

Clement Wood, DOUBLE JEOPARDY (Arcadia House, $2). The oddities of upstate New Yorkers make a good background for murder but Inspector Skelton Kyne's investigation is hampered by an endless trial scene and the year's most hackneyed and transparent plot.

ALSO RECEIVED. Robert Bloomfield, THE SHADOW OF GUILT (Doubleday Crime Club, $2); Gavin Holt, SEND NO FLOWERS (with Ritzy Tyler) (Howell Soskin, $2.50).

BEST BUYS IN REPRINTS. Helen Eustis, THE HORIZONTAL MAN (Grosset & Dunlap, $1); Mystery Writers of America, Inc., MURDER CAVALCADE (World, $1.49, uncut).

May 25, 1947

C.S. Forester, PAYMENT DEFERRED (Mercury, 25 cents). This is, to be sure, a reprint; but Mr. Forester's early novel, which for me yields only to the works of Francis Iles among ironic commentaries on middle-class murder, is so important and neglected a work that you're strongly urged to see to it, for your own great pleasure, that in this latest edition (uncut) it at last achieves the success it long deserved.

Michael Morgan, NINE MORE LIVES (Random House, $2.50). Movie stunt man Bill Ryan is framed for the blonde's murder for the Papers while hiding from the police. Fairly obvious plot, more than offset by pace and unusual background. For once the hero's marvelous escapes are credible, and no less marvelous for that. (Review by Lenore Glen Offord.)

Octavus Roy Cohen, DON'T EVER LOVE ME (Macmillan, $2.50). Formal announcements of your death might be only a grisly joke, but when the joker finally aims at you and kills your escort—well, it worries a girl. Mr. Cohen has tied up another Manhattan package in such glittering gift-wrapping that the contents don't much matter.

Alfred Eichler, ELECTION BY MURDER (Lantern Press, $2). Reactionary publisher backs Fascist revolution to take over 48 elections; radio executive Martin Ames solves his resultant murder by advertising methods. Worthy idea and fast action but all just a little too sensational and black-and-white to be effective as either novel or propaganda.

BEST BUYS IN REPRINTS. John Dickson Carr, THE LOST GALLOWS (with Henri Bencolin) (Pocket Books, 25 cents, uncut); Kenneth Fearing, DAGGER OF THE MIND (Bantam, 25 cents, uncut); Hugh Pentecost, I'LL SING AT YOUR FUNERAL (with Inspector Luke Bradley) (Popular Library, 25 cents, uncut).

June 1, 1947

Shelley Smith, COME AND BE KILLED! (Harper, $2.50). This is the story of a murderess-by-profession, an elderly woman who preys Landru-like on her weaker sisters—of her early life and how it shaped her, of her triumphs at the height of her career, and of the trap which a victim's sister laid for her. It's a beautifully solid, ironic, intelligent job; only some need-lessly contrived fireworks in the finale keep it from the very foremost rank of the great English murder tradition.

Brett Halliday, COUNTERFEIT WIFE (Ziff-Davis, $2.50). The last Shayne case happened in 24 hours; this one takes place in the next 24 im-mediately following, which must establish a sustained-action record even for the private practice of Michael Shayne, who is here involved in murder, counterfeiting and kidnaping. Unusually complex and ingenious plot plus the Halliday brand of hard fast violence— all highly satisfactory (except that the title bears no relation to the book).

Virginia Rath, A SHROUD FOR ROWENA (Ziff-Davis, $2.50). In 1939 Rowena walked out of this world in a Dundas-designed dress; in 1946 something returned—a ghost, an impostor or Rowena?—and it was up to Michael Dundas to design a solution. Interestingly complicated plot, well-tailored to display S.F.'s couturier-detective at his most charmingly shrewd.

Robert Portner Koehler, THE HOODED VULTURE MURDERS (Phoe-nix, $2). Photographer-correspondent vanishes in southern Mexico; detec-tives Avery Gregg and Tony Ellis track down his corpse, his sinister past and his murderer—who gave me my first solid surprise in some time. Pleasant narration and agreeable local color off the standard tourist trail.

Nancy Rutledge, THE PREYING MANTIS (Doubleday Crime Club, $2). The Society of the Mantis is the most fantastic Sinister Organization since the fruitiest days of [Sax Rohmer's] Fu Manchu, and its bejeweled gold emblem leaves a Trail of Death through elaborate and terrifying pur-suit scenes. A somewhat preposterous pastiche but an excitingly enjoyable one.

Miriam-Ann Hagen, PLANT ME NOW (Doubleday Crime Club, $2). Tensions of the multiply-married on a transcontinental train and at a con-vention in S.F. result in murder with hepcats Jamie Chase and Jimmy Wells acting as a jive chorus. Singularly poor plotting and construction regrettably weaken the first jivetalk whodunit—at its best so fresh and lively that even an icky square like Boucher succumbs completely.

Gene Goldsmith, MURDER ON HIS MIND (Mill, $2.50). Eminent N.Y. psychiatrist murdered apparently by patient; colleague Dr. Dan Damon intervenes to reach the truth. Damon is a personable new sleuth, though he reaches his solution without using his psychiatric knowledge or any other visible means.

ALSO RECEIVED. Alan Pruitt, THE RESTLESS CORPSE (with Don Carson) (Ziff-Davis, $2.50).

BEST BUYS IN REPRINTS. Vera Caspary, BEDELIA (Popular Library, 25 cents, uncut); Michael Venning [Craig Rice], JETHRO HAMMER (with Melville Fairr) (Jonathan, 35 cents, cut).

June 8, 1947

Bill Goode, THE SENATOR'S NUDE (Ziff-Davis, $2.50). The naked wench strangled in the senator's bed is only the symbolic prelude to a welter of Washington scandals investigated and elucidated by old-school reporter Stoney Hawk. Mr. Goode is a find; his blend of bawdry, politics, melodrama, farce and satire (with a sharp undertone of bitter reality) has the life and freshness of early [Ben] Hecht-[Charles] MacArthur and his rapid-fire agile technique provides just the vehicle for it in the brightest debut so far this year.

Stewart Sterling, DEAD WRONG (Lippincott, $2.50). A framed suicide, a phoney private eye, a fabulous estate and a murdered maid add up to homicidal headaches for Gil Vine, chief security officer of a vast Manhattan hotel. Good hard melodrama, fascinating in its details of hotel mechanism related with that minute authenticity which is Sterling's trademark.

Lee Thayer, MURDER STALKS THE CIRCLE (Dodd Mead, $2.50). You would expect a murder in Hartford, Conn., to have an insurance angle, but Peter Clancy polishes off many another facet including the forging exploits of an American, Thomas Wise. Elaborately plotted and full of bibliophilic lore; the most satisfactory Clancy-Wiggar story I can remember.

Armstrong Livingston & Captain John O. Stein, THE MURDERED AND THE MISSING (Stephen-Paul, $2.75). Memoirs of the retired head of N.Y.'s model Missing Persons Bureau, properly devoted more to typical routine than to sensation (though the chapter on the Grace Budd case is an extraordinary criminous narrative) and leaving you with a deep respect for the intelligent precision of the MPB and for the warm sensibility of Captain Stein.

John Evans [Howard Browne], IF YOU HAVE TEARS (Mystery House, $2). San Bernardino bank manager finds adultery leads to embezzlement and murder. Reasonably able job in the [James M.] Cain tradition, with some good sordid realism, but it's hard to prepare to shed your tears for Mr. Evans' facile irony and shallow characters.

STRANGER THAN FICTION: GREAT STORIES OF TRUE CRIMES (Howell Soskin, $3). An abridged reprint of a long ago British collection, this hardly fulfills the jacket promise of "seldom told tragedies." Instead they're mostly familiar stand-bys in highly uneven treatments—oddly best not in murders but in such peculiarities as the bigamy of the Duchess of

Kingston or the wondrous imposture of the Princess Caraboo. Writers include Edgar Wallace, Sir John Hall, Max Pemberton and many others.

BEST BUYS IN REPRINTS. Erle Stanley Gardner, THE CASE OF THE HAUNTED HUSBAND (with Perry Mason) (Tower, 49 cents, uncut); Craig Rice, THE LUCKY STIFF (with John J. Malone) (Tower, 49 cents, uncut).

June 15, 1947

Craig Rice (editor), LOS ANGELES MURDERS (Duell, Sloan & Pearce, $3). Previous volumes in the Rivers of Blood series have started well back in the last century; this one begins brashly in 1921 and proceeds to relate not so much the great crimes of the Southland as the production numbers built up around them. Los Angeles may not be, like San Francisco or Edinburgh, a city which breeds great murderers, but it certainly knows how to exploit what talent it can find. A half-dozen first-rate crime novelists and a member of the D.A.'s staff have collaborated to treat the most celebrated cases, from the fortunate Mrs. Obenchain (ably handled by Berkeley's Mary Collins) to the repetitious Mrs. Peete, with results to fascinate the connoisseur—of murder or of southern California.

Lawrence Treat, Q AS IN QUICKSAND (Duell, Sloan & Pearce, $2.50). He should have stayed clear of the rich lock-making Gobelins but he learned too late that they were The Enemy—the Other Ones who use and distort men. By the time he understood, there was blood and a job for professionals like Jub Freeman and Mitch Taylor. Mr. Treat remains incomparable in his understanding blend of the realism of police procedure and the reality of human beings.

Richard Powell, AND HOPE TO DIE (Simon & Schuster, $2.50). Florida is the setting of the latest adventure of Andy and Arabella Blake— Florida, that lovely vacation land filled with 12-year-old psychopathic liars, sinister blackbirders and men who throw barbed fish-gigs at you. You may not believe that Arab goes through the book without handling a gun, but you'll readily agree that fishing can be at least as violent as shooting if it involves Arab and as rowdily entertaining as any other adventure ruefully related by Andy.

Christopher Bush, THE CASE OF THE MISSING MEN (Macmillan, $2). Overbearing British whoduniteer trapped and killed by one of his own intricate plots; Ludovic Travers quietly and smoothly unravels it all. It's good to have Mr. Bush back after too long an absence; as usual he presents the simon-pure jigsaw-puzzle detective story with unobtrusive competence.

BEST BUYS IN REPRINTS. Erle Stanley Gardner, THE CLUE OF THE FORGOTTEN MURDER (originally published as by Carleton Kendrake) (with Sidney Griff) (Pocket Books, 25 cents, uncut).

June 22, 1947

Alice Tilton [Phoebe Atwood Taylor], THE IRON CLEW (Farrar Straus, $2.50). It started with three brown paper parcels and went on to involve a dinosaur footprint, a monkey who ate pistachio ice cream, a newsboy with a chauffeur and above all the old octopus of fate. In other words this is another freewheeling fantasia about Leonidas Witherall, who created William Shakespeare and looks like Lieutenant Haseltine or am I a little dizzy by now? In any event you couldn't ask for a finer merry-go-round to get dizzy on.

Margaret Erskine, THE VOICE OF THE HOUSE (Doubleday Crime Club, $2). The Melafaunts of Cornwall ran to witch's blood in the past and murderer's blood in the present; it was a happy touch of white magic which brought humorously sensitive gentleman-Inspector Septimus Finch to their dark and curse-ridden house. Slow, cumulative, eery and well-plotted—a model British baffler.

Donald Hamilton, DATE WITH DARKNESS (Rinehart, $2.50). Lieutenant Philip Branch, USNR, spends his last uniformed leave in the first action he's seen, accidentally trapped in the violent maneuvers of Vichy-ites and Resistants operating undercover in Maryland. Underplayed harsh melodrama written with an appalling contempt for the callous viciousness of all its characters.

Hilda Lewis, STRANGE STORY (Random House, $2.50). Twin baby girls in lower middle class English family grow up into highly divergent people but their lives remain oddly intertwined until one accidentally kills the other. 111 pages of completely admirable build-up and character interplay followed by 180 pages of astonishingly wordy and repetitious study in remorse and retribution, leading you to wish for once that the murder had never happened and the straight novel been allowed to run its course.

Fredric Sinclair, DROP ONE, CARRY FOUR (Doubleday Crime Club, $2). American war correspondent learns too much about a racket in China; after his "accidental" death his sister goes in peril of her life, in Calcutta and Cairo, from the murderer, one of a group of indistinguishable correspondents. Varied and detailed local color almost saves foolish and familiar plot.

Theodora Du Bois, THE FOOTSTEPS (Doubleday Crime Club, $2). Suspicion of family crime drives heroine to auditory hallucinations; Dr. Jeffrey McNeill and wife Anne intervene to save her sanity and expose a murderer. Miss Du Bois invades the fast-staling "psychological" school with a plot and characters so unbelievable as to be embarrassing. (And when will she return to the vein of such a small masterpiece as [her 1940 novel] DEATH COMES TO TEA?)

ALSO RECEIVED. Muriel Bradley, AFFAIR AT RITOS BAY (Doubleday Crime Club, $2).

BEST BUYS IN REPRINTS. Dana Lyon, IT'S MY OWN FUNERAL (Prize Mystery, 25 cents, uncut).

June 29, 1947

No column was published this week.

July 6, 1947

Margery Allingham, THE CASE BOOK OF MR. CAMPION (edited by Ellery Queen [Frederic Dannay]) (Mercury, 25 cents). There are few detectives so quietly understanding as Albert Campion and few mystery writers so tastefully civilized as his creator. Mr. Queen has here gathered seven Campion stories for their first U.S. book appearance, with a preface explaining Mr. Campion's bibliographic history (which is only a little less perplexing than the changes in his character since the earliest chronicles of his adventures). Result: a trove for bibliophiles and a superb evening for devotees of delicate detection.

Agatha Christie, THE LABORS OF HERCULES (Dodd Mead, $2.50). Twenty-two years ago Hercule Poirot retired, only to run into his greatest case when Roger Ackroyd was murdered. Now retirement tempts him again (as well it might—he is something over 80 by my figures), and he resolves as a final gesture to accept twelve cases which will parallel the Labors of his heroic eponym. The twelve resultant adventures make a uniquely shaped book, richly devious and technically brilliant—by far the best volume yet of Poirot shorts.

Inez H. Oellrichs, MURDER HELPS (McKay, $2). Ill-assorted family running roadside diner engages the attention of Matt Winters, ex-milkman-sleuth, now a candy salesman; ensuing murders demand all of Matt's admirable quiet common sense. Underplayed, well characterized and effective.

Harry Stephen Keeler, THE CASE OF THE BARKING CLOCK (Phoenix, $2). Petty Polish gangster framed for murder; only mathematico-criminologist Tuddleton T. Trotter can save him. But before the pretty puzzle is presented to T.T.T. the Keeler inventiveness goes on some of its wildest rampages, even somehow interpolating a complete short story by Mrs. K. Wonderful if you can take it.

July 13, 1947

Cary Lucas, UNFINISHED BUSINESS (Simon & Schuster, $2). Kenneth Marsh went to Mexico simply to sell and repair pumps but the disappearance of his office manager plunged him and his lovely Irish-Mexican secretary into the thick of subversive politics and melodrama. Aside from a touch of conventionality in the pay-off, S.F.'s Mr. Lucas makes a startling debut with a vivid, vigorous, solid novel, packed with realism, excitement, acute perception and deft dialogue. Anybody in the market for what may prove to be the American [Eric] Ambler?

Charlotte Murray Russell, LAMENT FOR WILLIAM (Doubleday Crime Club, $2). Murder in small town's dominant family involves gambling, tombstones, show dogs and a puzzle for police chief Homer Fitz-maurice Fitzgerald. The relentlessly Irish Uncle Homer is certainly a change from Miss Russell's usual spinster-sleuth but I'm not sure how welcome a one.

ALSO RECEIVED. Mary Richart, MURDER IN THE TOWN (with Mr. Dixon) (Farrar Straus, $2.50).

BEST BUYS IN REPRINTS. John Dickson Carr, THE PROBLEM OF THE GREEN CAPSULE (with Dr. Gideon Fell) (Bantam, 25 cents, un-cut); Erle Stanley Gardner, THE D.A. DRAWS A CIRCLE (with Doug Selby) (Tower, 49 cents, uncut).

July 20, 1947

Bruno Fischer, MORE DEATHS THAN ONE (Ziff-Davis, $2.50). Ten-tative loves of frugal virgin provoke series of small-town murders, re-solved with Maigret-like tenacity and humanity by Ben Helm. I've felt for some time that Bruno Fischer after a series of largely admirable novels was about due to hit the jackpot; he's done it this time, with a novel out-standing for its middle-class realism, its understanding of the petty com-plexity of human emotions, its adroit handling of a Freudian motive, and above all for its full-length, three-dimensional characterization of a woman not unworthy of [then well-known playwright] George Kelly.

Raymond Chandler, FINGER MAN AND OTHER STORIES (Avon, 25 cents). Curiously mixed collection containing two second-string but craftsmanlike tough novelets, the much-reprinted article on Chandler's provocative theories of murder fiction and—most welcome—his only pub-lished supernatural story, the excellent "The Bronze Door."

Elinor Chamberlain, MANILA HEMP (Dodd Mead, $2.50). Here they are again—the governess, the cryptically charming widower, the dread secret buried in the mysterious household—just as they've been ever since Currer Bell discovered the formula; but Miss Chamberlain's intimate knowledge of the Philippines (with earthquakes, volcanos, local politics and surviving Japs) manages to lend an appearance of freshness to what would seem in any other setting a padded piece of pasteboard.

Kathleen Moore Knight, THE BLUE HORSE OF TAXCO (Doubleday Crime Club, $2). Troy, who always got what she wanted, had rigged the jewelry-designing contest to snare an errant lover; it took terror and deaths against the placid background of Taxco to teach her human humility. Miss Knight bypasses a good solid novelistic theme to go careening off on some not too plausible melodrama, but it's all performed with infinite smoothness.

Frances Crane, MURDER ON THE PURPLE WATER (Random House, $2.50). Drunken gent stabbed on charter fishing boat off Key West. Captain's niece, a nightclub singer, acts suspiciously; Jean and Pat Abbott act obscurely to solve case. Constant shift between first and third persons confuses narration. Good points: Florida atmosphere and several mouthwatering recipes. (Review by Lenore Glen Offord.)

Frank Kane, ABOUT FACE (Mystery House, $2). Plastic surgery, rackets and movie-making merge in a problem which will puzzle the reader much less than it does private eye Johnny Liddell. One of the sleaziest specimens yet of the bosoms-and-brandy school.

July 27, 1947

No column was published this week.

August 3, 1947

Marten Cumberland, HATE WILL FIND A WAY (Doubleday Crime Club, $2). Luscious corpse in Salome costume starts a murder trail leading through Parisian cinema, art and vice, ably followed by rational Commissaire Saturnin Dax and his delightful aide, Brigadier Felix Norman. Another of Mr. Cumberland's highly successful efforts to enliven the best features of the solid British school with a deft touch of Gallic irony.

Sylvia Tate, NEVER BY CHANCE (Harper, $2.50). Girl's accidental death drives her musician-lover to seek her true character in the tangled mystery of her past—a search that culminates in witchcraft and murder. Miss Tate writes clearly, observantly and interminably; this could have been an outstanding first novel at one-third its present exhausting length.

Mickey Spillane, I, THE JURY (Dutton, $2.50). Private eye Mike Hammer swears revenge for the murder of his best friend and tracks the killer through some of the season's strongest scenes of sex and sadism to private execution. Able if painfully derivative writing and plotting in so vicious a glorification of force, cruelty and extra-legal methods that the novel might be made required reading in a Gestapo training school.

Perry D. Westbrook, HAPPY DEATHDAY (Phoenix, $2). I shall never know my final opinion of this narrative of detective Sam Cutting and the corpse in the university library because on page 225 it suddenly turned into something called GUNS OF POWDER RIVER. Up to that point it seemed to contain a little genuine and pleasing academic humor buried in a dull, confused story.

Milton M. Raison, MURDER IN A LIGHTER VEIN (Murray & Gee, $2.50). This latest exploit of Tony Woolrich, drama critic and detective, is in plot and writing simply down to Mr. Raison's standard; I list it only to warn you that this (to quote the jacket) "intimate, behind-the-scenes tale of big-time radio" does not even have the virtue of reasonable accuracy in depicting the industry.

August 10, 1947

Dashiell Hammett, DEAD YELLOW WOMEN (edited by Ellery Queen [Frederic Dannay]) (Jonathan, 35 cents). Four middling-to-long stories about The Continental Op (including one of my top favorites, "The Golden Horseshoe") plus two shorter Hammett crime items make up what Queen justly calls "the final volume in the most important pentalogy of detective-crime short stories assembled in our time."

Alan Wyke, PURSUIT TILL MORNING (Random House, $2.75). The lives of two half-brothers—one a sensitive introvert, the other a vicious hypocrite—culminate in a night-long nightmare of pursuit which can end only in death. The quasi-[James] Joycean style, at times strained and obtrusive, achieves in the long run the terrible compelling poetry of motive and murder.

Hugh Lawrence Nelson, THE COPPER LADY (Rinehart, $2). Dominating manufacturer and collector of copper meets curiously staged death in his own shop; S.F. detective lieutenant Steve Johnson sorts out the tangles of the odd group involved. Sprightly civilized writing plus a knowledge of copper as detailed as the background of the book business which Mr. Nelson offered in THE TITLE IS MURDER—and somewhat unconvincing solution and motivation.

Paul Tabori, HE NEVER CAME BACK (Dutton, $2.75). High-ranking Nazi assumes false identity to escape and continue the Master Plan, slickly fools the Allied occupation forces (who seem to average a mental age of 5) and is finally destroyed by, of all things, his own conscience. Central character well-drawn but surrounded by mere props; story neither believable nor especially exciting. (Published in England as THE LEAF OF A LIME TREE.)

Elizabeth Kyle, MALLY LEE (Doubleday Crime Club, $2). American girl inherits Scottish house and with it a domineering aunt and a 40-year-old murder mystery. Stock characters and obvious plot written with plodding competence.

Andrew Lyttle, A NAME FOR EVIL (Bobbs-Merrill, $2.50). Miasma of evil surrounds old southern mansion in what may be either a ghost story or a study of a mind's disintegration. Whatever it is, it is recounted in some of the most distinguished bad prose that I have ever met with.

August 17, 1947

Edmund Crispin, DEAD AND DUMB (Lippincott, $2.50). Oxford revival of [Richard Wagner's opera DER] MEISTERSINGER results in "impossible" hanging of obnoxious basso; Grouchonian Gervase Fen intervenes. For the first time I'm wholly converted to Mr. Crispin, whose fourth book—whether for light romance, absurd humor, shop talk on English opera or technical ingenuity—is right up there with the best.

Helen Reilly, THE FARMHOUSE (Random House, $2.50). Murder among her friends, lights in the graveyard, menace to her person and tangled love affairs vex Nell Shevlin's stay at the old family home until Inspector Christopher McKee enters. This familiar setup is vastly enhanced by new twists including a smash surprise at end and superb competence in telling. (Reviewed by Lenore Glen Offord.)

Kenneth Millar, BLUE CITY (Knopf, $2.50). Veteran son of dead mayor returns to midwest city to clear up his father's murder and expose municipal corruption. Routine enough in concept and in much of its plot, but Mr. Millar is to be congratulated on his sharp prose, his absorbing tempo and above all on his ability to create a hardboiled hero who is not a storm trooper.

Hildegarde Tolman Teilhet, THE TERRIFIED SOCIETY (Doubleday, $3). American Fascist leader, framed and double-crossed, escapes to strange involvement in Central American affairs, manipulated behind the scenes by Mr. Samuel Hook. Mrs. Teilhet has attempted a fascinating, difficult and all but impossible task: presenting the plausible and likable side of an inherently evil man; the result is confusion of sympathy and diffusion of interest in a book markedly disappointing after [Teilhet's previous novel] THE ASSASSINS.

William Rollins, Jr., THE RING AND THE LAMP (Simon & Schuster, $2.50). All ex-Sergeant Larry Ross tried to do was deliver a note in Paris for a comrade but he found himself thick in the complots of the Paris underworld, an escaped war criminal and the sinister cartels. Weak in character, slow in action and routine in plot—surprisingly below the Inner Sanctum standard.

August 24, 1947

Roy Chanslor, HAZARD (Simon & Schuster, $2.75). Ellen was running away—first figuratively when gambling provided the gratification she'd never known from love, then literally when she welched on her debt and found private eye John Doe Storm on her trail. In the start a superlative study in the psychology of a gambling obsession, later somewhat softened by the necessities of plot and love, but written throughout with a succinctness, a bite, a tension to leave you breathless. Mr. Chanslor, though an individualist and no mere disciple, presents as serious a challenge as James M. Cain has yet had to face.

Mary Fitt, A FINE AND PRIVATE PLACE (Putnam, $2.50). Enigmatic John Thorneycroft walks in on a strange garden party and promptly finds himself involved with Roman treasure troves, burial vaults, burglary, young love and murder. Leisurely charm of the best British school and singularly adroit misdirection make you willing to overlook a glaringly unfair solution.

Aaron Marc Stein, DEATH TAKES A PAYING GUEST (Doubleday Crime Club, $2). Peacetime creates a serious technological unemployment among spies—which results in peculiar goings on implicating Washington decayed gentility, the State Department and archeologists Elsie Mae Hunt and Tim Mulligan. Highly agreeable lighthearted entertainment.

Roy Huggins, TOO LATE FOR TEARS (Morrow, $2.50). Jane knew what she wanted, and when her husband was so dully conventional as to try to tell the police about the hot $40,000 that accidentally fell in their laps, his death was inevitable. Nice portrait of a casually vicious woman, told with economic realism and taut melodrama.

E.C.R. Lorac, MURDERER'S MISTAKE (Mystery House, $2). Cryptic thefts from North Country cottage lead Chief Inspector Robert Macdonald to combine a Lancashire outing with unraveling a petty crook's murder. Lorac and her inspector are as usual intelligently agreeable, but this time the story is dull and groping.

June Truesdell, BE STILL, MY LOVE (Dodd Mead, $2.50). Femme psych prof has never Known Life; when it does intrude on her neurotic cloisterdom it drives her to murder—after which comes True Love and a battle of conscience. Pretentious, superficial and glibly written, but easily readable—if almost as a parody of the "psychological thriller."

Mary Reisner, THE FOUR WITNESSES (Dodd Mead, $2.50). Sterling New England aristocrat casually murders ill-bred outsider; nasty New York dick, who has obviously never been to a good school, unpardonably tries to pin it on him. Stiff and lifeless manifesto on the unalienable right of the gentry to bump off bounders.

August 31, 1947

Lewis Padgett [Henry Kuttner], THE DAY HE DIED (Duell, Sloan & Pearce, $2.50). Girl pulpwriter finds herself pursued by her ex-husband, accused of plagiarism, involved in murders and cultism, and above all oppressed by a sense of a ghastly incubus in her apartment. Mr. Padgett more than fulfills the promise of his memorable first with this novel, whose lively portrayal of N.Y. writing circles combines with its cumulative, all-but-supernatural power and terror to lift it far above the by now formularized conventions of the "suspense novel."

Robert Bloch, THE SCARF (Dial Press, $2.50). Peculiar case-history reveals how to combine the careers of best-selling author and fetichistic mass-murderer. Bloch, like Padgett, has long been one of my favorite pulp fantasy authors; his first novel is a generally effective essay in the macabre though wilder and looser than the best of his mordant short stories.

Frank Gruber, THE WHISPERING MASTER (Rinehart, $2). So book salesmen Johnny Fletcher and Sam Cragg are back at the Forty-Fifth Street Hotel and once again threatened with the evicting French key when a platter sails in the window—a master record which has motivated murder. More notable for Fletcher's fantastic financial finagling than for its thinnish mystery plot.

Frederick C. Davis, DETOUR TO OBLIVION (Doubleday Crime Club, $2). One of America's foremost art collections, stored for the duration, vanishes completely; the corpses pile up while Professor Cy Hatch figures out the gimmick of its disappearance. Interesting puzzle and background marred by singularly heavy and graceless style far from Mr. Davis' blithe early manner.

David X. Manners, DEAD TO THE WORLD (McKay, $2). Mystery writer Jim Hunt, strangled while playing real-life detective, finds his spirit backtracking in time to unravel the secrets of his murder. Laudably novel concept handled with a disappointing minimum of ingenuity, consistency or wit.

VOLUME III

A BOOKMAN'S BUFFET

Longer Reviews

MISCELLANEOUS REVIEWS, 1942-48

October 4, 1942

John Alden Knight, MOON UP—MOON DOWN (Scribner, $2.50).

Edmund Pearson tells how Charles Fort, that noble science-heckler of the Bronx, once had occasion to look up one of his own books in the [Manhattan] 42nd Street library. Out of curiosity he asked an attendant what the call number meant, since the book might have been equally well classified under astronomy, physics or even philosophy. "Oh, that," he was told. "That means Eccentric Literature."

It's a useful classification, that, for your own library; but remember that the pioneer always seems eccentric. You'd put in your Eccentric division the opuses on pyramidology and Anglo-Israelitism; but you might have put there, when it first appeared [in 1927], [J.W.] Dunne's EXPERIMENT WITH TIME. And your ancestor would possibly have thought it just the right shelf for [Charles Darwin's] THE ORIGIN OF SPECIES.

Mr. Knight's book belongs tentatively in your Eccentric collection. It is a partial exposition (entwined rather confusingly with a running autobiography) of the solunar theory, according to which there are definitely predictable periods in each day when all animal activity (including that of the human animal) is heightened by some as yet undefined external cause.

Mr. Knight's researches began with the purely practical purpose of finding out when fish bite. They may well end by having efficiency experts regulate factory output by solunar periods.

If you like unusual data and don't mind muddled theorizing, if you enjoy spectacular fishing narratives, if you have an enquiring mind and like to get in on the ground floor of something new, try MOON UP—MOON DOWN. It may not stay on your Eccentric shelf forever. (White)

October 11, 1942

Michael Innes, THE DAFFODIL AFFAIR (Dodd Mead, $2).

English mystery novelists, heedless of the example of Wordsworth's nuns, have a way of fretting at their narrow room. They forever seek to widen the limits of the form and sometimes end by passing those limits entirely. But their publishers may ignore the fact, and a brilliant "straight" novel may thus be addressed solely to the somewhat baffled fan of whodunits.

The case in point is this latest Michael Innes. Mr. Innes himself once described his novels as "on the frontier between the detective story and the fantasy." (You may recall those magnificent variations on a theme by [the

16th-century Scottish poet William] Dunbar called LAMENT FOR A MAKER [1938] or the entrancingly [John] Buchanesque THE SECRET VANGUARD [1941].) Now, in THE DAFFODIL AFFAIR, that frontier has been definitely crossed.

The story starts out from New Scotland Yard, but on such a quest as [Freeman Wills Crofts' character] Inspector French never knew. There are missing (a) a counting horse named Daffodil, (b) a Cockney girl with three distinct personalities, (c) a young and authentic witch from Yorkshire, and (d) a haunted house (once investigated by Dr. [Samuel] Johnson) stolen with piecemeal plausibility during a series of blitzes.

It is Inspector Appleby's Mycroftian aunt who puts him onto the pattern of these thefts. Appleby, the delightfully civilized protagonist of the other Innes novels, and the splendidly somber Inspector Hudspith set out in pursuit, and wind up in the jungles of the Amazon as guests of the charming and horrible Mr. Wine. This gentleman has his own peculiar plans for postwar reconstruction, in which Daffodil and the haunted house are equally essential.

The macabre intellectuality of the fantasy, the almost outrageous skill of the writing, the brilliance of the concept and treatment make this one of the finds of the season. The true mystery fan may frown more than a little, but the readers of Norman Douglas, Evelyn Waugh, John Collier or the early [Aldous] Huxley will acclaim a new treasure. (Boucher)

October 18, 1942

Hans Reichenbach, FROM COPERNICUS TO EINSTEIN (translated by Ralph B. Winn) (Philosophical Library/Alliance Book Corp., $2).

"Truth," [the 19th-century German philosopher Arthur] Schopenhauer said, "is allowed only a brief interval of victory between the two long periods when it is condemned as paradox or belittled as trivial."

That interval is an exciting time to live in, when we can savor the beauty of truth fresh-minted and not yet dulled by daily handling, and Dr. Reichenbach's purpose in this volume is to make us realize that we live in just such an interval.

For despite its comprehensive title, this book is predominantly a study of the new truths of the universe as revealed by [Albert] Einstein—or rather it is both more and less than a study, it is almost an esthetic appreciation.

An opening chapter takes us hastily from Copernicus through [Tycho] Brahe and Galileo to Newton. The rest of the book is a simple and lucid exposition of the theory of relativity and its implications.

Don't let all the loose newspaper talk about the incomprehensibility of Einstein fool you. His mathematics, it is true, are only for the specialists, and not for all of them, but the broader outlines of his ideas have a clarity and grace that will appeal to any sensitive mind.

Perhaps that last sentence sounds more like the review of an art exhibit than of a scientific treatise, but that's the way Dr. Reichenbach affects you. He stresses throughout the pleasure and beauty of thought rather than the stern formulas which support it, and the result is a work at once stimulating and enjoyable.

The translation is satisfactory despite occasional echoes of German prose. The proofreading unfortunately is markedly below standard. (White)

October 25, 1942

C. K. Ogden (editor-in-chief), THE GENERAL BASIC ENGLISH DIC-
TIONARY; GIVING MORE THAN 40,000 SENSES OF OVER 20,000
WORDS, IN BASIC ENGLISH (W.W. Norton, $2.50).

The eventual world state that so many hope for presupposes a practical world language, and basic English is the most prominent candidate so far. This new basic tool might best be described as an English-Basic diction-ary, as one says English-French; it defines a large vocabulary of words in Basic English.

Two advantages to this, even for those not concerned with learning Ba-sic: it avoids the run-around method of definition, wherein A is defined by B and B by A, and it makes for clarity and a fresh understanding of words you've known all your life.

One aspect will annoy Americans: only the British spelling, with no al-ternative, is given for words of the "center-centre" and "honor-honour" groups. (Unsigned; carbon in Lilly Library)

Willy Ley, SHELLS AND SHOOTING
(Modern Age Books, $2.50).

Writing in book form on present day artillery, Mr. Ley says, is "like try-ing to paint a battle scene on canvas while the battle is going on." The lay-man's guide to the latest is always outdated by the time it reaches the bookstores.

Mr. Ley has therefore laid his major stress upon historical background and general principles of artillery, and the result is an enthralling and, if the word doesn't seem too out of place in so grim a context, a delightful book.

Readers of THE LUNGFISH AND THE UNICORN or BOMBS AND BOMBING know Mr. Ley as that rare creature, an authentic polymath. Take what subject you will, from the borderlines of zoology to the history and technique of science fiction, Ley knows whatever there is to know and can tell it to you, charmingly and with a wealth of incredible detail.

If he has a specialty, it is weapons. He has written on them for Government scientific publications and contributes a regular column on the subject to [the liberal newspaper] *PM*. Here he gives you his authoritative knowledge.

Do you know what kinds of rockets Francis Scott Key watched redly glaring? (No, Constance, not signal rockets.) Do you know what is the biggest gun ever built? (No, not Big Bertha, nor anything in the last five hundred years.) Do you know that the shells of the Paris gun attained the greatest height ever reached by a man-made object, equivalent to some five Everests?

You should know about artillery. Napoleon said "Le feu est tout," and almost every authority but [air power advocate General Alexander de] Seversky still concedes that wars are finally won on the ground and by firing power. Even the airplane is largely important as flying artillery.

But if the duty of knowing artillery doesn't move you, you should still read SHELLS AND SHOOTING for the rare privilege of contact with a curious and communicative mind. (Unsigned; carbon in Lilly Library)

November 8, 1942

Storm Jameson, THEN WE SHALL HEAR SINGING: A FANTASY IN C MAJOR (Macmillan, $2.50).

"It was five years after the war, and it was spring, the one rebellion the Dictator could not put down."

Not that he had had to contend with a real rebellion in the Protectorate as yet. But there was danger in men like Vacslav, the solid intelligent leader; danger in men like Andrej and Matthew, who planned to escape by the Underground Railroad; danger in boys like Milan, who foresaw a new future.

"Then we shall hear singing. Then we shall run out of our houses, and run home from the fields, and we shall see our men come in marching and laughing."

So Dr. Hesse was given the Protectorate for his experiments. Hesse, who saw himself as lonely and as great a man as the Dictator, had discovered a method of destroying the higher functions of the brain without affecting the body in any way. It was simple: a trifling injury to the forebrain, an electrical disturbance a thousandth of a thousandth of a volt too powerful, and the people of the Protectorate would be nothing more than useful animals.

This is the framework about which Miss Jameson has built her allegory; and it is appropriate that a novel of the Czechs should involve a fantastic plot suggesting Karel Capek. Around the framework she has written a moving and often beautiful story, but one that is apt to renew the controversy touched off by [John Steinbeck's] THE MOON IS DOWN.

The resemblance goes further than the historical situation or the pointless device of naming no nations. Miss Jameson's thesis is the same as Steinbeck's: that the cards are stacked against the tyrants, that their little victory is but an instant in time, that the deep roots of the people are ineradicable.

It is futile to revive the battle. This is just a warning that your reaction to THEN WE SHALL HEAR SINGING will depend largely on your stand in the Steinbeck war. With the difference that this is a novel, not a play transmuted by typography, and a singularly sensitive and lovely one.

With one objection from the Capek-fantasy point of view: that the victims of Dr. Hesse are well-written, but as promising Cro-Magnons rather than as lower animals. Or perhaps this too has its allegorical significance: that the greatest triumphs of cruel ingenuity can never drag man down from his post a little lower than the angels. (White)

Roger Sherman Loomis & Henry W. Wells (editors), REPRESENTATIVE MEDIEVAL AND TUDOR PLAYS (adapted and translated with an introduction by the editors) (Sheed & Ward, $2.50).

This anthology aims "to focus attention on the intrinsic power of the medieval dramatic tradition," and should succeed in that sensible aim.

The plays chosen run from the unintended but wonderful farce of the twelfth century "St. Nicholas and the Virgins" through the mixture of grotesquerie and sublimity in the Hegge mystery cycle on to the fine rowdy fooling of the interludes of the pre-Elizabethan John Heywood (whom the jacket blurb confounds with the later and very different Thomas) is enough modern appeal in these plays themselves without, for instance, carefully translating "thou" to "you." Both in verse structure and in stage technique these old mysteries frequently anticipate the latest developments in experimental theater. (APW)

November 15, 1942

Clark Ashton Smith, OUT OF SPACE AND TIME
(Arkham House, $3).

Clark Ashton Smith is the sort of obscure and admirable artist that California has a way of producing. He was born in Long Valley in the [18]90's, has lived and worked around the state (in San Francisco for a while), and now lives at Auburn. He has been a fruit picker, a painter, a hardrock miner, a sculptor, a windlasser and a poet.

In the last role he has published four volumes, was a protege of George Sterling, and has been praised by William Rose Benet. There his story might stop, and he would seem just another talented individual of chiefly local reputation. But in 1930 he took up another career: that of a pulp fantasy writer.

Pulp fantasy, best represented by the magazine *Weird Tales* (for which Smith does most of his work) and *Unknown Worlds*, is a unique and largely misunderstood genre. Fantasy of any sort, humorous or horrible, is frowned on by most magazine markets. I remember an editor of the *Saturday Evening Post* telling me, "The *Post* has only three editorial tabus: sex, religious controversy and fantasy-except-by-Stephen-Vincent-Benet."

But fantasy is an essential part of the tradition of the English short story—see any anthology for proof. It has its writers and its readers, and the general editorial opposition has driven them, the supercilious might say, underground, into a few pulps. Don't be too hasty to sneer at the word "pulp." These pulps provide the only steady market that would publish the work of a latter-day [Ambrose] Bierce or [Arthur] Machen or [Edgar Allan] Poe.

Outside of anthologies, these often excellent pulp stories have been unknown to the book-buying public until August Derleth, the Wisconsin [William] Saroyan and himself a noted pulp practitioner, founded Arkham House for the express purpose of giving permanent form to the pick of the pulp crop. Arkham House has so far published a selected volume of Derleth and a titanic complete volume of the master, H.P. Lovecraft; now it offers this mouth-watering collection of the best of Clark Ashton Smith.

Smith's fantasy is possibly the purest now going, and for that very reason sometimes less effective than it might be. Where Machen or Lovecraft make you feel that the world is a horrible and uncertain place, Smith transports you to horrible and uncertain worlds—Hyperborea before the ice age, the medieval French land of Averoigne, or Zothique, the last continent on earth. They are strange and beautiful, these worlds, but they do not impinge upon your own; there is rarely the later-than-you-think sensation of "This could happen to me."

Much of Smith, perhaps too much, is strongly under the influences of Lovecraft and [Lord] Dunsany, adorned with the arabesques of his own fantasy and poetic prose. Where his originality shows most clearly is in a peculiar blend of horror and irony, a fantasy so extreme that you hang poised between the shudder and the smile. Such a memorable classic as "The Monster of the Prophecy" is pure Smith, and incomparable.

If you are an aficionado of pulp fantasy, you need no urging; OUT OF SPACE AND TIME is just what you've been waiting for. If the field is strange to you, this volume might well make a convert. Here is a poet singing dark and unmentionable horrors, while the ironic sparkle in his eye provides the one ray of light through monstrous gloom. (Boucher)

Anita Boutell, CRADLED IN FEAR (Putnam, $2.50).

Miss Boutell deserts the mystery novel, in which she had made an important experimental place for herself, to compete for the [Daphne Du-Maurier bestseller] REBECCA public—and that's a break for the latter.

Here are all the ingredients of romantic terror: the gallant young bride, the enigmatic husband, the strange old ladies in the storm-girded New England house, the mysterious death in the past, the hovering of madness and more deaths to come.

They're blended with the Boutell skill, plus a dash of morbid psychology that's more [William] Faulkner than DuMaurier. Result: first-rate romance-cum-creeps. (AB)

January 17, 1943

J.H. Wallis, THE NIECE OF ABRAHAM PEIN
(Dutton, $2.50).

A refugee Jew, a twisted, persecuted Old Testament type, moves into a secluded and inbred New Hampshire valley, and his business acumen rouses the bitter anti-Semitism so close to the surface in too many Americans.

When his pretty niece disappears, community opinion at once decides that "the Jew murdered her," possibly for a Protocols-of-Zion ritual (didn't Henry Ford say they do that?). The most honest American judicial traditions can hardly effect a fair trial under such circumstances, especially when the evidence....

But the evidence is part of Mr. Wallis' plot, which is highly ingenious and not to be revealed. (Any readers who find it incredible should know that it is by no means unprecedented in the history of murder trials.)

This is almost two novels—a clever murder story and a study in racial prejudice, and it must be admitted that the two get somewhat in each other's way. The picture of the persecution of the Jew might be more impressive if the trick circumstances were not such that a white Protestant Nordic might have suffered almost as much.

But the realistic restraint with which the poison of race hatred is depicted is more plausible and infinitely more terrifying than any amount of emotional preaching on the subject, and the murder trial (which occupies almost half the book) is one of the most convincing in fiction. (AB)

February 7, 1943

Alden Brooks, WILL SHAKSPERE AND THE DYER'S HAND (Scribner, $5).

Will Shakspere was a bumptious card who escaped from the boredom of Stratford and his shotgun marriage to make his way in London. He began by holding horses in front of the theater and in no time was running the horse holding concession. He had an effective low gag sense and a natural instinct for "good theater" plus a countryman's brashness and shrewdness and a fine capacity for guzzling Rhenish wine and pickled herrings with the boys.

He soon found a more profitable concession: acting as a play-broker, a primitive Samuel French, who could commission a play from Kit [Christopher] Marlowe, call in Tom Nashe for additional dialog, and peddle the result to the players for a cut.

Sir Edward Dyer was a gentleman of the court, dear friend to Southampton and Essex, noted for his retiring nature, his scholarship, and his secretive practice of alchemy and literature. When the Countess of Pembroke suggested a series of historical plays, both for political reasons and to purge the theater of barbaric writing, he roughed out a sketch and hired Shakspere's stable, [Thomas] Kyd and Marlowe and the rest, to do the writing on HENRY VI.

More and more the theater came to absorb him. Earlier court plays in which he had taken some hand he refurbished and sold, through Shakspere, to the players. The Stratford man's practical theatrical sense recognized his abilities and demanded his revision on old standbys such as Kyd's HAMLET. And as Dyer's financial situation became more than precarious, his writing passed from an esthetic interest to a means of livelihood.

The [Walter] Winchells of the day had a strong suspicion that someone important was behind the stable. There was a uniform quality to the Dyer-written or Dyer-rewritten plays. But the gossips (like so many critics to come) suspected Southampton.

When that clever young noble left England in a scandal, Dyer needed another stalking-horse. Only in safe anonymity could he continue his political allegories. And who so fine a stalking-horse as the pushing Stratfordian, who already looked on the stable's plays almost as his own?

So Will Shakspere of Stratford became William Shakespeare, dramatist, the most celebrated pseudonym of all time.

A tremendous amount of spadework and ingenuity has gone into Mr. Brooks' concoction of this theory. Less ingenuity could have made it more convincing. In 200 pages it might have been startling and arresting. These 700 pages are filled with exaggerated and often ridiculous over-proof.

Mr. Brooks does an admirable job of attacking the stupid errors of Stratfordians and Baconians, only to stumble himself into the same pitfalls of bad logic, "parallel passages," assumption of conjecture as fact, and deliberate misinterpretation.

A not unfair sample occurs in his treatment of the political allegory in VENUS AND ADONIS: "The love-sick queen possesses 'golden' hair. [Queen] Elizabeth's hair, to be sure, was red, but the suggestion of similarity is there."

Much of the time Mr. Brooks combines the most perverse qualities of a Ph.D. candidate and an interpreter of Nostradamus. But there remains sufficient evidence to make his the most nearly satisfactory non-Stratfordian Shakespeare theory yet and possibly the only one that does not do violence to everything we know of the workings of the Elizabethan theater and of the professional creative mind.

The book has a thorough index but no notes and no bibliography. (White)

February 21, 1943

Constance Frick, THE DRAMATIC CRITICISM OF GEORGE JEAN NATHAN (Cornell University Press, $2).

Scholarly attempt to discover the underlying critical credo in 30 years of Nathan's writings on the drama. That the attempt fails surprises no one, least of all Miss Frick or Mr. Nathan, but the book offers some deft comments on and a valuable anthology of the most inconsistent, the most exasperating and the least boring man in the American theater. (APW)

Curt Siodmak, DONOVAN'S BRAIN (Knopf, $2).

Inhumanly ardent scientist steals dead tycoon's brain and grows it to superhuman proportions. Bodiless brain waxes powerful and takes over scientist by telepathic possession. Slowly he realizes that the brain is mad....

Published as a mystery but strictly science fiction. The idea may seem novel to the book public but pulp addicts will find it old stuff, not helped by dull prose and much psychoneurological patter. (AB)

Howard Lindsay & Russel Crouse, STRIP FOR ACTION (Random House, $2).

What happens when a troupe (burlesque) invades a troop (army), or The G-String Marauders. Why the Broadway production recently closed is a mystery: it must have been even funnier to see than this printed version is to read, and that is devastating enough, especially if your low past can supply the missing effects of burlesque ritual.

Messrs. Lindsay and Crouse wrote LIFE WITH FATHER and produced ARSENIC AND OLD LACE. This opus may not equal the warm humanity of the first or the outrageous fantasy of the second, but it's right up there with them on laughs. (APW)

March 14, 1943

Ivy Litvinoff, MOSCOW MYSTERY
(Coward-McCann, $2.50).

Recently, as an amateur drama critic, Ivy Litvinoff scoffed at [the famous Russian playwright Anton] Chekhov for writing about three sisters who spent three acts not going to Moscow. Now, as an amateur mystery novelist, Mme. Litvinoff tells of the Moscow procurator Nikulin, who spends 22 chapters not solving a murder.

The setting is Moscow, 1926. The corpse is that of a bourgeois bon vivant whose death is small loss to the state. The suspects include a dentist, a manicurist and a ballerina. The investigation involves a White Russian plot, a racket in platinum, the "wild boys of the 20's" and other irrelevancies until the murderer, tired of all the delay, tries to kill the procurator and then obligingly confesses.

You will find many interesting details on how "wild boys" are reformed and how spring comes to Moscow. But Mme. Litvinoff's reference to [Alexander] Rimsky [Korsakov]'s "song out of 'The Prophet' " (which is like saying "Schubert's song out of 'The Serenade' ") and her flat statement that "Napoleon set Moscow alight" give you less than perfect confidence in her accuracy.

The publishers recommend (and price) this as a straight novel rather than a mystery, though its intention is certainly the latter, and add "no work of fiction has ever before been written in English about Soviet life"—a statement possibly true when the book was new, but misleading now.

For the novel was written and published in England as HIS MASTER'S VOICE, by Ivy Low, around 1930. To bring it up to date the author has added eight pages on how different it would be now. She doesn't mention any change in the Russian police but it would be disloyal to our allies not to believe that they've improved. (Boucher)

March 21, 1943

A.L. Whall (editor), THE GREEK READER
(Doubleday, $5).

This reader is a comprehensive anthology of the entire body of Greek literature, with copious selections of epic, lyric and dramatic poetry, history, philosophy, oratory and Alexandrian poetry. To get all this into even a thousand-page book is impossible, and the result is a mosaic of "gems."

History and the lyric can stand this treatment better than the epic, the drama or the philosophical dialogue. Snatches torn from context and adorned with the editor's personalized titles give only the crudest idea of the great works which they represent.

The translations are confusingly various. A hundred pages of Homer coming in brief gusts from ten translators with ten distinct styles give an odd notion of the epic. Such distinguished modern translators as H.D. [Hilda Doolittle] and Dudley Fitts are completely ignored.

There has possibly never before been so much of Greek literature in one volume. But the reading of one entire play or one unmolested Platonic dialogue might offer a clearer picture of Greek literature. (APW)

April 18, 1943

William Roughead, THE ART OF MURDER (with a foreword by Joseph Henry Jackson (Sheridan House, $2.75).

A taste for murder is a curious thing. It is present in almost every individual but it manifests itself in diverse ways. There are the gore-hounds, who revel in a gangster massacre as purveyed by a tabloid or a B [movie] producer. There are the whodunit addicts, who take their murders sugar-coated with puzzle and romance.

And then there are the true aficionados of murder who read William Roughead.

These last need only the announcement that THE ART OF MURDER contains eight Roughead essays never before published in America. But the other devotees of this great art, as peculiarly human as laughter or love, should know something of the pleasures which await them in this masterly volume.

Mr. Roughead brings to the study of murder a thorough legal knowledge, an intimate first hand acquaintance with Scottish crime, a deep understanding of and interest in the more unusual variations of human behavior, a wit of the sort usually known as pawky, an immense scholarship, and a mastery of the prose style of the Scottish (as opposed to the less sonorous English) language.

In this latest volume he applies these qualities to the cases of Mr. John Williams, most brutal of murderers, who was previously celebrated by [the 19th-century essayist Thomas] De Quincey; Mrs. Lucretia Chapman, who might have poisoned her husband without suspicion if she had not also poisoned the neighbor's ducks; Mrs. Adelaide Bartlett, who demonstrates that a good defense counsel is worth a dozen clear consciences.

These are the lesser characters. The finest chapters are devoted to three of the greatest women in criminous annals: Constance Kent (my own dearest beloved), who at the age of sixteen proved herself the most subtle and complicated murderess in history; Madam Elizabeth Branch, whose refinements of sadism would make Captain Bligh blanch; and Mlle. Henriette Deluzy-Desportes, who later became Mrs. Henry M. Field.

These then are the waxworks to be seen in this gallery of the greatest of Tussaud's, the works of William Roughead. Enter and rejoice. Item: THE ART OF MURDER carries an introduction by the *Chronicle*'s Joseph Henry Jackson, long a Roughead enthusiast. (Boucher)

Frank Baker, SWEET CHARIOT (Coward-McCann, $2.50).

Good fantasy is perhaps the rarest of all kinds of fiction. It is usually to be found only in a few children's books, a very few pulp magazines and the publications of Henry Holt and Company.

Two years ago Frank Baker published his first novel, MISS HARGREAVES, the story of two young Englishmen who created a female as mythical as Mrs. Harris [Mrs. Gamp's imaginary friend in Dickens' MARTIN CHUZZLEWIT] and then found her on their hands. And the devotees of fantasy knew that here was their man.

For Mr. Baker understands fantasy like no one since Max Beerbohm and E. Nesbit. He knows that the most fantastic situation has its own inherent laws and must abide by them. He knows people and he knows music and he knows—oh, how he knows!—how to write a novel.

There's no point in telling the plot of a fantasy. A good fantasy starts out "Supposing that...."; and granted your outrageous supposition, you must work it out truly and consistently in terms of understanding people.

So Mr. Baker supposes that a mild teacher in a cathedral choir school might change places with his guardian angel, and so perfectly is the notion carried out that you end up feeling, "Well, now I know just what would happen if I tried it." Which you probably won't care to.

Here is a book as witty as Beerbohm, as tender as [James] Hilton and as awful (for fantasy isn't all fun) as a vision by [the Old Testament prophet] Ezekiel. Go to it. (AB)

Herman Ullstein, THE RISE AND FALL OF THE HOUSE OF ULLSTEIN (translated by James Stern) (Simon & Schuster, $3).

The personal history of the development of the greatest German publishing house and its destruction under Hitler, told in easy journalese. Of especial interest for its sketches of personalities in German publishing and for its detailed picture of the pre-1933 phases of Nazism, it is also an unconscious but thorough refutation of those who would wipe out the total of German being and culture; for the Ullsteins, though Jews, are emphatically German, and one likes and admires them for their very Germanness. The volume badly needs an index. (APW)

April 25, 1943

Douglas Reed, DOWNFALL: A PLAY IN THREE ACTS (Appleton-Century, $2).

Douglas Reed was German correspondent for the London *Times* and wrote the best-selling INSANITY FAIR and an absorbing history of the Reichstag fire. Here he turns his inside knowledge of German politics into the form of a play forecasting the fall of Hitler and the method of that fall.

According to Mr. Reed, 1943 is 1918. Again the people will rebel, the Junkers and the capitalists seek peace, and the Wehrmacht, holding always the long view, begins its preparations for the next stage of war. Hitler will be persuaded to disappear and the United Nations will be kind to a Hitler-less Germany.

To judge DOWNFALL as a play would be unfair. It is a prophecy which prays against its own fulfillment, a warning picture of one of the possible tricks that may be played against us. As such it is ominously plausible. (APW)

Marie Belloc Lowndes, WHAT OF THE NIGHT?
(Dodd Mead, $2.50).

This thoughtfully varied collection of wartime stories contains almost everything: a love story, a revenge story, a dog story, a cat story—but, to the regret of Lowndes devotees, no murder story. The little details of domestic life under bombings are vividly and convincingly pictured, but the stories themselves are the purest maize (which, as word lovers know, is the British for corn). (AB)

May 9, 1943

Max Shulman, BAREFOOT BOY WITH CHEEK (with illustrations by Will Crawford) (Doubleday, $2).

Ladies and gentlemen, a new zany!

Max Shulman was editor of *Ski-U-Mah*, the college humor magazine of the University of Minnesota. He is now in the Army, having doubtless been ousted from Minnesota for violating all university traditions by making the college humor magazine funny. What he must be doing to the Army one shudders to contemplate.

BAREFOOT BOY WITH CHEEK (for keeping tongue in) is, as much as it is anything, the chronicle of Asa Hearthrug's first year at the University of Minnesota (which, as a cautious note points out, is wholly imaginary). Its intent, as much as it has any, is a satire on college life, with even a touch of seriousness when it ribs the futility of a "liberal" education.

As satire it's only fair. Subsidized athletes, fraternity finances, campus politics—we've heard about them before. And the section on the faculty misses fire completely. Shulman isn't a satirist but a zany of purest ray serene, and he comes into his own when he forgets the framework completely and embarks on such an insert as the story of his father's cousin May Fuster, who eloped to South America with a Chippewa and was forced into inter-American relations with the natives to keep body and soul together. May's sultry Northern beauty brought her a large and varied clientele but she turned from this activity to become a female bullfighter, with a draped cape and a gored sword.

"Shulman proudly states," says the blurb, "that no one has influenced his style of humor." That's nonsense. The long interpolated anecdotes are pure Joe Cook and the fine mad sense of the cliche is vintage [S.J.] Perelman. But absolute originality isn't so important as the fact that Shulman at his best is as ramblingly absurd as Cook or as precisely insane as Perelman. He may be influenced, but he can meet his masters on their own ground.

The artistically selected French chapter headings, the breathless burlesques of Hemingway's purpler spasms, the portrait of the 40-year-old youth leader, the exceedingly apt tailpiece which closes the book—all are things of lunatic beauty, and Will Crawford's pictures keep matching or topping them. For a sample take Asa's physical examination.

"My next stop was the weighing room. I stepped on the scale, my weight was recorded, and a doctor said, 'You make friends easily. You are a good worker although you are a little inclined to put things off. You are going to make a long trip on water.'

"I gave him a penny and proceeded to the abdominal clinic."

See? (White)

May 23, 1943

Graham Greene, THE MINISTRY OF FEAR (Viking, $2.50).

Arthur Rowe was a murderer. "Mercy killer," the papers had said. "Mad," the court had decided, and sentenced him to an asylum, from which he was soon released. Rowe was not so certain of the nature of his act. He knew only that he was a murderer, and by that fact not quite part of mankind.

Not until he accidentally won a cake at a bazaar for the Mothers of the Free Nations—a cake that should have gone to a man who could undermine the safety of those nations.

What happens from there on could very easily have been just another story of spies and intrigues. The plot is clever and the setting realistic enough to raise it above the [E. Phillips] Oppenheim level. It might, say, have been on a par with Eric Ambler.

But Graham Greene is even more than such a brilliant romancer as Ambler. He is something so close to a great novelist that it is hard to see the difference; perhaps there is none.

The fine storytelling, the craftsmanlike construction are never relaxed, but beneath them Mr. Greene is concerned with problems of ethics and character wider in implication than any plot, the ageless problems of man's relationship to his God and to his fellow man.

It is possible that Greene probes deeper into humanity here than even [John] Steinbeck has with his angry sentiment or [William] Saroyan with his indiscriminate love. But because his plot is that of a thriller, and a damned good thriller, it is unlikely that the moral philosophers of the Book-of-the-Month Club will be particularly concerned.

Labeling Greene as just spy stuff is a little like labeling [Fyodor] Dostoyevsky as just blood and thunder. But don't shy off for that reason; if it's just spy stuff that you want, you won't find any better than this. And you find in it to boot an unexpected nourishment. (Boucher)

May 30, 1943

Philip Van Doren Stern (editor), GREAT TALES OF FANTASY AND IMAGINATION (Doubleday, $3);
Whit Burnett (editor), TWO BOTTLES OF RELISH: A BOOK OF STRANGE AND UNUSUAL STORIES (with illustrations by Carlotta Petrina) (Dial Press, $3).

Most anthologies of the supernatural and fantastic have stressed what are known in the trade as "creepy-crawlies," stories of terror and menace which portray the world as a dire and uncertain place where it is later than you think.

Here for contrast are two collections devoted to the blithe and pleasant side of fantasy. The world depicted in them is still an uncertain one, wherein a weary postman may plant himself as a tree and a petty clerk work miracles, but it is a pleasing uncertainty. It is in fact earlier than you think.

Philip Van Doren Stern, whose recent THE MIDNIGHT READER is probably the finest collection to date of creepy-crawlies, is a man of impeccable taste in fantasy. Whether in these specialized anthologies or in the miscellaneous readers which he has edited for Pocket Books he has yet to indorse a story of less than the highest rank.

Which does not mean that you will find nothing in his volume but established classics. You'll find those of course: [Robert Louis] Stevenson's "The Bottle Imp" and [Max] Beerbohm's "Enoch Soames" and [Rudyard] Kipling's "Wireless," and very fine re-reading they make. At the moment the last named seems to me one of the six finest fantasies ever written, and I don't know what the other five are.

But you'll also find lesser known gems: F. Scott Fitzgerald's brilliant free improvisations on the theme of great wealth, "The Diamond as Big As the Ritz"; Oliver Onions' beautiful and indescribable warp in space time, "Phantas"; and Stephen Vincent Benet's "The Curfew Tolls" with its inescapably true picture of the life of Napoleon if he had been born 32 years earlier.

Whit Burnett seems a trifle surprised that a volume of fantasy should come from the pages of *Story*, where each of these "strange and unusual stories" in his TWO BOTTLES OF RELISH first appeared, but he admits that he is as editor unable to resist pure imagination. An editor would be a sorry realist indeed who could resist the stories Mr. Burnett has collected here.

Story fantasy differs somewhat from the classic tradition as represented by Mr. Stern's selections. It does not attempt to make even fantastic sense. It simply says "Supposing that...." and goes on from there for a while and then stops. There's no effort to make the assumption plausible nor to carry it out to its conclusions. I don't know that this is in accord with the modern revolt against the "well-made" story but I'm not sure that slice-of-life fantasy is a possible form.

Despite this reservation, the volume is full of delightful suppositions and enchanting (or even enchanted) writing.

In these two volumes are almost a thousand pages of joyous imaginings. Unhappy is the man who cannot find in them escape of a singularly pure and vivid kind. (Boucher)

June 20, 1943

Howard B. Rand, THE CHALLENGE OF THE GREAT PYRAMID: A SCIENTIFIC REVELATION TO A SCIENTIFIC AGE (Destiny Publishers, 50 cents).

Few fields can be so diverting as good honest crackpottery, but is pyramidology honest? Pyramidology (the belief that the geometric structure of the great pyramid of Cheops outlines the history of the world from Adam, 4000 B.C. to the millennium, 2001 A.D.) seems inevitably to entail Anglo-Israelitism; and Anglo-Israelitism (the belief that the Anglo-Saxon races are the lost tribes of Israel and inheritors of all biblical prophecy) invariably if illogically means anti-Semitism. Even so brief an outline of pyramid theory as this contains its accusations against the Jews as origin of all the world's troubles. Communists (Jew-inspired of course) come in for their share of the attack, and Fascists are never mentioned. That these doctrines are couched in terms of high-falutin nonsense does not make them any the less poisonous. (AB)

August 8, 1943

Katharine Roberts, PRIVATE REPORT (Doubleday, $2.50).

Katharine Roberts' second book, like her first, deals with anti-Nazi activity in Belgium, but where CENTER OF THE WEB was frankly a spy meller, if of superior quality, PRIVATE REPORT is a straight novel, and an absorbing one.

Major Paul Denyn, an engineer in civilian life, deserted from the Belgian army rather than surrender to the Germans, assumed a false name and went underground. This is the slow, detailed story of the birth and growth of the underground movement, of which Paul became one of the most important leaders.

It is also the story of Paul's wife and her child and the impotent Nazi captain who coveted children, but above all it is the story of the Belgian people—of the Flemings and Walloons who forgot sectional enmity, of the judges who struck rather than prostitute the bench, of the clown and the grocer and the union leader and the bawd who made their peculiar talents count for Belgium's freedom.

Belgium's situation differs from that of most occupied territory. The king's surrender and imprisonment (a gesture that may seem far wiser in retrospect than it did in 1940) has prevented the formation of a puppet government. There is no successful Belgian Laval or Quisling. Nor has Belgium been so annihilatingly trodden under as Poland; there still exists a polite fiction of maintaining the normal civil life.

Miss Roberts apparently knows thoroughly the magnificent work that is being done undercover in Belgium (her book carries the indorsement of the Free Belgian Commissioner of Information) and knows moreover how to shape her knowledge into a tender and moving novel.

PRIVATE REPORT may be read as an historical document, a love story or an understanding book about people. Whichever you want, you won't be disappointed. (Boucher)

Joshua Trachtenberg, THE DEVIL AND THE JEWS:
THE MEDIEVAL CONCEPTION OF JEW AND ITS RELATION TO
MODERN ANTI-SEMITISM
(Yale University Press, $3.50).

Modern anti-Semitism rests chiefly on social and economic fables rather than the supernatural myths prevalent in the Middle Ages. Hardly the most ignorant today outside of Germany can be persuaded that a Jew is the literal offspring of the devil, who wears horns, practices sorcery and drinks Christian blood in his ritual.

But the folk mind has a most retentive memory, and its recollection of the days when it believed all this and more makes it peculiarly receptive to the more "scientific" anti-Semitism of today.

A study of those medieval concepts is therefore intensely interesting now, and Rabbi Trachtenberg's thoroughgoing scholarship could hardly be bettered. This is a book at once fascinating and repellent, dangerous perhaps, and deeply encouraging.

It is fascinating for its wealth of incredible medieval lore, decked out with contemporary woodcuts, as richly informative as a Montague Summers work on witchcraft and somewhat more rational. It is repellent for its inescapable picture of the depths to which Christian conduct can sink.

It is possibly dangerous (a consideration which its author realized) because we have fools and knaves among us who will mutter knowingly: "Well, where there was so much smoke...."

But there is hope and encouragement in the contrast between those times and today. Weak and stupid though we are, we have come a long way from the days when the most vicious anti-Semitism was the norm of Western civilization, when even the sensible and charitable dicta of popes went unheeded by clergy and laity alike, when Chaucer and [Christopher] Marlowe, [St. Thomas] Aquinas and Shakespeare could casually utter phrases that now could come only from [Nazi propagandist] Julius Streicher. Here is one consoling bit of evidence that man can grow up a little. (White)

I.A. Richards, BASIC ENGLISH AND ITS USES
(Norton, $2).

Never before our time has the world so sorely needed a lingua franca, a common language through which all people may enjoy the minimum essentials of communication. The world has grown too small for the babble of Babel; the Chinaman and the Bulgar are neighbors. They have things to say to each other and need a language in which to say them.

Of all the applicants thus far for the position of that lingua franca, no other is so strikingly adapted to the post as is Basic English. Basic, with its deftly selected limited vocabulary, its brilliantly simplified grammar, its flexibility and adaptability and above all its naturalness, offers a hope for world understanding possible through no existing unmodified language nor any artificial compound of the Esperanto type.

That seems like a large statement but you will find that I.A. Richards justifies it in this compact and rewarding book. In part this is an explanation, from the ground up, of the nature and purpose of Basic; in part it is a reasoned defense against the polemic attacks of critics whose scorn is equaled only by their inaccuracy.

Basic English has two purposes: to serve as a universal secondary language and to function as a stepping stone to the learning of English proper. Its suitability to these purposes is due chiefly to certain astoundingly perceptive discoveries of C.K. Ogden as to the nature of English which enabled him to develop from the mother tongue this fine functional tool.

It is quite possible that Mr. Ogden's discoveries are as important to the future of the world as any of the most startling advances in physical science or military strategy. Certainly anyone remotely interested in post-war planning must know the possibilities which Basic can offer.

And those possibilities could not be better expounded than they have been by Mr. Richards, whose clarity, precision and wit, as much as the importance of his subject matter, make this an essential book. (White)

August 22, 1943

Arthur Train, YANKEE LAWYER: THE AUTOBIOGRAPHY OF EPHRAIM TUTT (Scribner, $3.50).

For 24 years Ephraim Tutt, with his stogies, his salmon, his stovepipe hat and his keen-witted benevolence, has been probably the best known lawyer in the United States. As his publishers point out, there are probably a thousand people that know Mr. Tutt for every one who can name the present chief justice of the Supreme Court.

But readers heretofore have known Mr. Tutt only through his Boswell, Arthur Train, who has regrettably if understandably emphasized only the superficial aspects of the Tutt character best suited to commercial magazine work and has cluttered up even those with love stories and other demands of the market.

Now in this long and wise autobiography we at last get Ephraim Tutt at first hand in all his sage and mellow humanity, and with him a fine survey picture of the last forty years of American law.

Mr. Tutt was born in Vermont 74 years ago (one would have thought him even older) and his long career has covered a wide range—Tammany prosecutor, country lawyer, corporation attorney, and of course highly individual practitioner in the firm of Tutt & Tutt.

Three things unify the various portions of his career—the warm influence of Esther Farr, whom Tutt has loved for 46 years but could never marry; an unflagging passion for salmon fishing; and a devout quest for the means of reconciling law and justice.

Much of the book is devoted to good shop talk, illustrated with pertinent cases on this problem of the letter of the law and the spirit of human justice. To Tutt it is a lawyer's duty not to enforce the law but to force the law to serve humanity. And this end he has finally been able to attain in the peculiar practice of Tutt & Tutt. (Mr. Train, it seems, has sadly underestimated [Mr. Tutt's law partner] Samuel, who often breeds the rabbits which Ephraim pulls out of his stovepipe hat.) He has even (see the case which Train recounted as "Mr. Tutt Stages a Rodeo") brought about equitable changes in the law itself.

The book is not all law nor even all Tutt. The old lawyer has known many interesting men and women in his long career and he is adept at giving vivid glimpses of them. The anecdotes of his boyhood friend Calvin Coolidge are particularly illuminating. Theodore Roosevelt, William Travers Jerome and many others appear, along with Bonnie Doon and the other assistants of Tutt & Tutt, and Squire Hezekiah Mason and the other inhabitants of Pottsville, Tutt's favorite upstate retreat.

And Ephraim Tutt writes at least as well as he has practised, whether he is spinning yarns of his early days in Pottsville, expounding his soundly liberal philosophy, or narrating the true facts of the cases which Arthur Train has perverted for the *Saturday Evening Post*.

Minor slips are inevitable in a work covering so much material. Ephraim Tutt first met Samuel (see page 312) in 1925, yet on page 397 he tells how "Tutt and I" were assigned to a case in 1919, and Train's first narratives of the firm appeared in the same year. And one gathers on pages 339-340 that Mr. Tutt believes Seattle to be in California.

The book is complete with photographs and a thorough index which round out its quality of solid satisfaction. An old Boston lawyer advised the young Tutt: "Take the law as you find it and twist it to your ends—so long as they be good ones." Readers will find this moving and fascinating volume of legal reminiscences one of the very best ends to which even Eph Tutt could twist the law. (Boucher).

August 29, 1943

Donald A. Wollheim (editor), THE POCKET BOOK OF SCIENCE-FICTION (Pocket Books, 25 cents).

This Pocket Book is no reprint but an original and much needed anthology of a singularly imaginative and stimulating field. If you think that science-fiction is of the level of Superman and Buck Rogers, investigate this collection. The names of [Stephen Vincent] Benet, [Ambrose] Bierce, [John] Collier and [H.G.] Wells are an assurance of quality, and you'll learn new names too, for most of the stories here have never appeared before in book form. (Unsigned but clearly by Boucher)

September 19, 1943

Helen Jones Campbell, THE CASE FOR MRS. SURRATT (Putnam, $3).

Few political killings hold the least interest for murder fanciers. Whatever their historical significance, they are usually devoid either of mystery or of psychological complications. But the assassination of [President Abraham] Lincoln is inexhaustibly absorbing.

Both victim and assassin are far more complex characters than is usually the case, and the full mystery of the attendant circumstances will probably never be unraveled. Otto Eisenschiml has propounded a beautiful Least Suspected Person solution, revealing Lincoln's own Secretary of War [Edwin Stanton] as the man behind the murder; but even if one assumes that as the answer to the ultimate guilt, there remains the question of the relative culpability of the eight persons tried for the conspiracy, and tried under such dubious circumstances of military hugger-mugger that their conviction proves nothing.

Miss Campbell has taken up her cudgel in this book to establish the complete innocence of Mary Virginia Surratt, at whose Washington home many of the conspirators met. The highly unsatisfactory evidence before the military commission certainly did not justify the sentence of hanging, and it is the author's theory that Mrs. Surratt was railroaded by Stanton, who feared she might know too much of his connection with [the trigger-man John Wilkes] Booth.

The theory is not implausible but the book does nothing to substantiate it. This is a thoroughly unscholarly job, largely written in a quasi-novelistic style so that it is impossible to distinguish any new evidence the author may have from her free conjectures and reconstructions. There are no notes, no index, no bibliography—nothing, in short, to suggest anything more substantial than a pious memorial to a probably martyred woman. (Boucher)

Florence Ryerson & Colin Clements, HARRIET:
A PLAY IN THREE ACTS (Scribner, $2).

The dramatized life of the author of UNCLE TOM'S CABIN may be somewhat wooden as a serious historical document (complete with analogies for our times) but it is pure cockle-warming delight as an irreverent farce spoofing the earnestly crusading Beecher family. And how fortunate it is that the authors' research convinced them that they could depict Harriet Beecher Stowe simply by writing Helen Hayes! (APW)

September 26, 1943

Kenneth Fearing, AFTERNOON OF A PAWNBROKER AND OTHER POEMS (Harcourt Brace, $2).

Once Kenneth Fearing wrote a purported mystery novel, DAGGER OF THE MIND. It was probably the finest prose writing on murder of its year, an amazing literary tour-de-force, but it simply was not a mystery novel (after 200 pages the killer just decided to confess) and most of the specialist critics indignantly rejected it.

There are other specialists who claim that Mr. Fearing doesn't write poetry either, noting that his verse has no analyzable form, no poetic philosophy, above all no emotion recollected in tranquillity.

The fact is, all Fearing's work is of a piece, whether it comes out as poems or whodunits or even the conventional war bond appeal on the jacket; and DAGGER OF THE MIND and AFTERNOON OF A PAWNBROKER are closer to each other than either is to the main body of mysteries or poetry.

There's a term popular now in the cant of painting: "magic realist." It seems to mean an artist who takes as much care with meticulously accurate *trompe l'oeil* detail as any Dutch master but who arranges these vividly real details to form a new and heightened surreality.

That's what Fearing does with words. His eye is as sharp as William Steig's, his ear as keen as Ring Lardner's. And his precise observations, carefully selected and juxtaposed, make a picture that has all the sharp clean beauty of a nightmare.

You probably know Fearing from *The New Yorker*. If not, pick up this latest collection in some bookstore and look at "Elegy in a Theatrical Warehouse" or the opening "Continuous Performance." Or "Art Review" if you want a crooked smile, or "Thirteen O'Clock" if you want a slight chill. If a fresh and almost painfully vivid glimpse of your world means anything to you, you won't walk out of that bookstore empty-handed. (Boucher)

October 24, 1943

Charles de Coster, THE GLORIOUS ADVENTURES OF TYL ULENSPIEGL (translated by Allan Ross Macdougall) (with an introduction by Camille Huysmans and illustrations by Frans Masereel) (Pantheon, $3.50).

Katharine Roberts' excellent and authoritative novels of the Belgian underground make constant reference to the modern political significance of Tyl Ulenspiegl. It is Ulenspiegl who tweaks the noses and undermines the dignity of the conquerors. It is Ulenspiegl who lightens the hearts of the oppressed. It is Ulenspiegl, in short, who is the comic genius of rebellion.

This is a very different Tyl from the familiar Eulenspiegel of the German jest-books and the Richard Strauss tone poem. He is still an incorrigible rascal but his rascality is ennobled by a higher moral purpose. And he is as purely Flemish as the other is German.

Which is the original Tyl, Flemish or German, is a problem for scholars in folklore. In either nation he goes back to the earliest chapbooks. But his development in Flanders, his new and significant dignity, stems from the great picaresque novel of Charles de Coster, the beginning of Belgian literature according to Camille Huysmans, written in 1869 and now first presented to the American public in a popular trade edition.

De Coster's TYL ULENSPIEGL is a fundamental Belgian classic, but like the works of Nostradamus it has always achieved its greatest popularity in wartime. That is because de Coster has fused Tyl's merry pranks with the war for independence which the Lowlands waged against Philip II and his Duke of Alva and made of the prankster of folklore a living symbol of popular resistance which glows today with a new vigor.

This is a vast, sprawling, all-inclusive book and yet a singularly well-organized one. Its first 150 pages are largely a rewriting of folk material, full of those peculiarly dull practical jokes which the sixteenth century found side-splitting. But even in this opening section we find overtones of something beyond the early jest-books. There is the infinitely pathetic mad wife Katheline, Tyl's neighbor, and there are the frequent brief scenes of the maturing of Philip, even more chilling than the glimpse we get of him in [G.K. Chesterton's poem] "Lepanto."

Then Tyl's father Claes falls victim to the Spaniards and their Quislings and the rogue becomes transformed into a man of purpose. He loses none of his wit and grace in the transformation but henceforth he is the avenger of Claes, whose ashes beat on his heart, and the liberator of Belgium.

Largely the novel from then on is the story of the sixteenth century Belgian underground, which might with the change of a name or two be a contemporary narrative. But there are other elements—the superb tale of Katheline and her demon lover (so closely parallel to "A Mirror for Witches"), the tender love of Tyl and Nele, the terrible episode of the werewolf, the mystic element of Tyl's vision and the symbols which he cannot interpret, and above all the magnificent figure of Lamme Goedzak, Tyl's Sancho, whose lusty relish for food is as infectious as the thirst of [John] Steinbeck's paisanos.

Much of the book is inevitably devoted to attacks upon Catholicism (which de Coster does not always understand too well; at least once he becomes hopelessly enmeshed in a confusion on the church calendar), and the attacks, if exaggerated, are understandable in view of the period, when such a staunch Catholic as John Heywood was assailing similar abuses in England. But de Coster understands what Tyl himself does not—the economic and political causes underlying the apparent religious war.

As a battle cry of freedom the story of Tyl has its limitations. It is a cry for a narrow sort of freedom, for certain Flemish Protestants only, and it is embellished with petty hatreds: Lutheran against Calvinist, Fleming against Walloon, and everybody against the Jews.

But even with these limitations de Coster's TYL ULENSPIEGL remains one of the most welcome books of the year. Astonishingly well translated, beautifully printed and admirably illustrated with a hundred fine woodcuts, it is a masterpiece worth any reader's while as a study in the folk psychology of one of our allies, as a textbook on the conduct of an underground movement, or simply as an absorbing and vigorous piece of storytelling. (Boucher)

C.S. Lewis, OUT OF THE SILENT PLANET
(Macmillan, $2).

Clive Staples Lewis, don of Magdalen, is best known in America as the author of THE SCREWTAPE LETTERS, those sardonically scintillant bits of advice from an elderly devil to his apprentice nephew on how best to entrap the modern human soul.

Mr. Lewis is still preoccupied with moral and theological values and still capable of precise ironic prose, but he has chosen a different medium this time. He has calmly up and written a novel of interplanetary travel.

This is, needless to say, no Buck Rogers yarn. It is not even to be classed with such more literate exponents of scientifiction as Philip Wylie, Michael Arlen or R.C. Sherriff. But neither is its fantasy element a mere peg on which to hang a didactic satire as in [Samuel Butler's] EREWHON or [Edward Bellamy's] LOOKING BACKWARD.

It is at once a full-fledged and admirable science fiction melodrama and a profound and disturbing allegory of human morals.

Plot: Cambridge philologist is shanghaied to Mars by human heavies, escapes from them, wanders through adventures among the various races of Mars and ends up receiving, with the heavies, the justice administered by the god (and yet not quite a god) of the planet.

Allegory: There are three races on Mars, or Malacandra as it calls itself: the hunting and poetry-making *hrossa,* the scientific *seroni,* and the artisan *pfifltriggi.* All these races recognize each other (and man as well) as *hnau,* or intelligent beings. The bond of being *hnau* is greater than any racial distinction.

There are entrancing digressions on Martian philology. There are fascinating speculations on a solution (in interplanetary terms) of the age-old problem of evil on Earth (known to Martians as Thulcandra, the silent planet). And there is always a fine running narrative, told in quiet and perfect prose.

Mr. Lewis, bless him, has raised the imaginary voyage to a new level of literacy. (White)

George Jean Nathan, THE THEATRE BOOK OF THE YEAR 1942-1943: A RECORD AND AN INTERPRETATION (Knopf, $3).

This is the first volume of the most valuable series of theatrical annals projected since Burns Mantle conceived his BEST PLAYS. It is a complete listing of all the season's productions, with dates, casts and a full critique. It is an almost perfect reference work (it would be perfect if it consistently gave length of run and credits for direction, sets, etc.); and because it is by Mr. Nathan it is a pure joy to read.

The critiques are not just reprints of spot reviews. They are fully developed essays, with afterthoughts, comparisons, reminiscences and occasional digressions on such subjects as great curtain lines and immortal low comedy skits. When you've read the book you know, as you can never know from Mr. Mantle's combination of straight statistics and dubious tabloids, what the season was like; and in this case it isn't a pretty picture.

Nathan may infuriate you with his eccentric prose, his all-out judgments or his endless self-contradiction, but you cannot ignore him. Though at times he seems to you the most erratic drama critic in America, there are other times when he seems the only drama critic—an oasis of scholarship and judgment in a desert of journalists.

May the gods of the theater grant vast sales to this THEATRE BOOK and long life to its author, that our grandchildren may imbibe good sense and great drama from THE THEATRE BOOK OF THE YEAR 1992-1993. (AB)

November 14, 1943

Sally Benson, WOMEN AND CHILDREN FIRST
(Random House, $2).

Long before Sally Benson made Book-of-the-Month and bestsellerdom with JUNIOR MISS and MEET ME IN ST. LOUIS she had a smaller but intensely loyal public who knew her as one of the most cruel and accurate analysts of human emotions and motivations, an artist of dissection whose scalpel could lay bare almost as much in a few pages as you would find in an entire Anne Parish novel.

That public, which has been following Miss Benson in *The New Yorker* and in her first collected volumes, PEOPLE ARE FASCINATING and EMILY, with a sort of agonized admiration felt cheated when she went all sweetness and light in her nostalgic chronicles of youth. It was as though Jonathan Swift should admit that after all he rather intended to share William Saroyan's view of humanity.

But now that public may rejoice. Here is Miss Benson back again at the peak of her old form in a volume made up of 38 stories collected from the past five years of *The New Yorker*.

How these stories may strike her larger and more recent public I don't know. Some of them may shudder a little and wonder how that sweet Miss Benson can possibly be so horrid. Others may feel a kind of chilled fascination, as though they were to look into a distorting funfair mirror and suspect that it told the truth.

It is not a nice world that Miss Benson presents here. It is a world of possessiveness and pretension and petty cruelty, a cat-eat-cat existence. It is a world that you will recognize and remember.

If you read of them in *The New Yorker*, you will not have forgotten the young minister's wife gaily twitting her husband for his sudden awareness of his ministry, or the man who hated everything and married a wife in whom to concentrate his hates, or the mother who found consolation for her son's marriage in the memory that he had never worn out any of his toys.

They're all here, and whichever of Miss Benson's publics you belong to, you'll have to go far to find a more skillful collection of stories. (White)

November 21, 1943

George Herbert Clarke (editor), THE NEW TREASURY OF WAR POETRY: POEMS OF THE SECOND WORLD WAR (Houghton Mifflin, $3).

A quarter of a century ago Professor Clarke had a great success with his TREASURY OF WAR POETRY, and if history repeats itself why shouldn't Clarke? But if this collection truly represents the best poetry of this war, it does not flatter the vision of our poets. Instead of any deep realization of the true issues at stake there is a tendency to prove that our cause it is just because (a) our nations have produced such great men in the past or (b) we have such beautiful scenery. Many big names are represented (and as many omitted, among them Stephen Vincent Benet and C. Day Lewis) but the effect of the whole is that of a conservative, tasteful Sanity in Art exhibit of the Royal Academy, where neither form nor content will disturb the patriotic reactionary. (APW)

Lola Wyman, BETTER MEALS IN WARTIME
(Crown, $1);
Alice Bradley, THE WARTIME COOK BOOK
(World, 49 cents).

Here are two clear, sensible, useful and cheap guides to rationed cookery but very different in approach and results. Miss Bradley's WARTIME COOK BOOK is arranged according to the seven basic groups of foods stressed by the National Nutritional Council, written with extreme lucidity for housewives hitherto strangers to the kitchen, and devoted chiefly to the soybean-and-peanut school of recipes. Miss Wyman's BETTER MEALS IN WARTIME assumes some familiarity with cooking and more interest in a well-flavored meal than in a dietetic chart. Her attitude if not her style recalls M.F.K. Fisher's blend of gourmetism and common sense. Both books contain excellent hints on point economy. You'll get more vitamins out of the WARTIME COOK BOOK and better meals out of BETTER MEALS. (APW)

Faye Henle, AU CLARE DE LUCE: PORTRAIT OF A LUMINOUS
LADY (Stephen Daye, $2.25).

Of all the public figures of our time, certainly Clare Boothe Luce has asked for and deserved a thorough going over. She is beautiful and clever and prominent; some call her dangerous. But the job calls for a second Clare Boothe to do it justice, and Faye Henle is far from that. She sweats valiantly to make like Mrs. Luce but the result is simply a hack resume of facts already known to most of the public, spiced with a wit which consists chiefly of unending puns upon [the] words time, life and fortune. You will not understand Miss Boothe any the better after this opus but you will have a fairly interesting, if unconscious, self-portrait of Miss Henle trying to convince herself that those translucent grapes are really sour. (APW)

November 28, 1943

George Agnew Chamberlain, KNOLL ISLAND
(Bobbs-Merrill, $2.50).

Spies and saboteurs get into everything nowadays. A few years ago this would have been the story of an orphan girl who goes to work as a boy on a Delaware farm and discovers her true womanhood in the love of the virile Merchant Marine son of the household. Now it winds up in a literal blaze of glory with the destruction of a sub landing saboteurs, but spies and war never distract the author for long from the titillating temptations of transvestism. (AB)

Moss Hart, WINGED VICTORY: THE AIR FORCE PLAY (Random House, $2).

This play, surprisingly published before its Broadway opening, was commissioned by General [Henry "Hap"] Arnold himself [then chief of the Air Force] and will, by the time this review appears, have been produced for the benefit of the Army Relief Fund. Moss Hart ate, slept and flew with the Air Force and covered 28,000 air miles in his research (presumably, to judge from his play, constantly singing "Off we go into the wild blue yonder"). The result is a competently executed recruiting poster in primary colors. The OWI [Office of War Information] documentary short narrated by Clark Gable gave you a more vivid picture of Air Force training without the inevitable cliches of love, death and pregnancy. The Broadway reviewers who judge a play by its contribution to the war effort will undoubtedly welcome WINGED VICTORY loudly, while George Jean Nathan resignedly points out that there used to be higher standards of criticism. (APW)

December 5, 1943

Michael MacDougall, DANGER IN THE CARDS
(Ziff-Davis, $2.50).

Like Percival Wilde's fictional Bill Parmelee, Mickey MacDougall is a detective specializing in gambling. While other private eyes may study fingerprints or hotel registers, MacDougall finds the palmed card, the capped dice or the shill—and one less sharper is at large. His reminiscences combine in one book an encyclopedia of crooked gambling methods, a cynical study in human psychology (dividing mankind into swindlers and suckers), and an exciting collection of detective stories. You'll have a grand time reading it and you'll know what to watch for the next time you're tempted into a friendly little game. (AB)

H.P. Lovecraft, BEYOND THE WALL OF SLEEP (edited by August Derleth & Donald Wandrei) (Arkham House, $5).

Howard Phillips Lovecraft (1890-1937) was the most influential and in many respects the most interesting American fantasy writer of this century. From hints in [Ambrose] Bierce and [Arthur] Machen and particularly [Robert W.] Chambers he built up an enormous self-consistent mythology of horror (the "Cthulhu Mythos") which dominated pulp fantasy during his lifetime and achieved an independent reality of its own almost comparable to that of the [Sherlock] Holmes saga. The major works of this cycle were collected by Derleth and Wandrei in THE OUTSIDER AND OTHERS (Arkham House, 1939).

The current volume, BEYOND THE WALL OF SLEEP, contains further miscellaneous Lovecraftiana: two novels (one hitherto unpublished), poems, minor short stories, collaborations with other authors, and biographical and autobiographical notes, plus two misguided attempts at humor (mercifully lacking from most Lovecraft) and an invaluable glossary to the Cthulhu mythology by Francis T. Laney.

It is a huge book in minute type, and for the Lovecraft aficionado it is a treasure trove; but the layman who does not know the fantastic and terrible wonders of Cthulhu is advised (and indeed urged) to start with THE OUTSIDER, a few copies of the limited edition of which are still available, and would make excellent Christmas presents to those who might relish the unknown chill of outer space in the midst of holiday festivity. (AB)

December 12, 1943

Benjamin Appel, THE DARK STAIN (Dial Press, $2.75).

A liberal, intelligent Jewish policeman in Harlem is forced to kill a murderous Negro psychopath. At once the facts of the case cease to be important and only prejudice counts. Either "A Gestapo cop killed a colored man" or "This'll teach those niggers to know their place."

The vicious hatred of white for Negro, of gentile for Jew (and in both cases vice versa), is always dangerously near the surface, and the Harlem shooting offers a perfect opportunity for an American Fascist organization to use that hatred for its own ends.

THE DARK STAIN depicts the intricate mechanism of that organization and the policeman's lone-wolf crusade to unmask it. At its worst the novel is lurid and overdrawn but always exciting melodrama; at its best it is a bitter and terrible fictional counterpart of UNDER COVER [John Roy Carlson's account of the four years he spent in the American Nazi underworld] and [Gustavus Myers'] THE HISTORY OF BIGOTRY [IN THE UNITED STATES]. (AB)

December 19, 1943

Otto Eisenschiml, THE CASE OF A.L., AGED 56:
SOME CURIOUS MEDICAL ASPECTS OF LINCOLN'S DEATH AND
OTHER STUDIES
(Abraham Lincoln Book Shop, $3.50).

Why was Lincoln shot in the left side of the head when [his alleged assassin John Wilkes] Booth stood on his right? Why do the autopsy reports give two opposing descriptions of the course of the bullet? Minor questions perhaps, but no aspect of the most fascinating of political murders is without interest. This short but scholarly pamphlet makes a valuable pendant to Mr. Eisenschiml's longer Lincoln studies. (AB)

January 23, 1944

Stephen Gilbert, THE LANDSLIDE (Knopf, $2.50).

Landslide on Irish coast frees strange beasts of past age; small boy and grandfather learn their unhuman and lovely way of life. Fantasy of shimmering green beauty, written with tenderness, perception and just the right amount of allegory. (Boucher)

Jules Romains, WORK AND PLAY
(translated by Gerard Hopkins) (Knopf, $3).

The eleventh double volume of MEN OF GOOD WILL is for aficionados only. Here and there in the series has come a self-contained section, a VERDUN or QUINETTE'S CRIME, that could attract the casual reader; but the reading of WORK AND PLAY demands patience, attention and an already aroused interest.

Its period is the winter of 1923-24, its setting Paris and the mountain district of Haute-Loire. Its subject matter and tone most nearly resemble those of the fourth volume, THE WORLD FROM BELOW. As with that volume, half of it is devoted to political machinery as seen by Jerphanion, not a mere secretary this time but himself a candidate for the Chamber of Deputies.

The other half is devoted more explicitly than any other section of the whole cycle to the meaning of the title: How can the "Men of Good Will" find each other and act together for the good of the world? Romains has been obsessed with the concept of the order. The Masons, the Jesuits, the Communist party, the mysterious organization to which Laulerque once belonged—all these, which have been treated extensively in earlier episodes, now begin to be seen as prototypes of the great order—that of the Men of Good Will.

How fully this theme will be developed remains to be seen. But it is more than probable that WORK AND PLAY, like the earlier WORLD FROM BELOW, will appear, when the colossal work is completed, as one of the essential key volumes. (AB)

February 27, 1944

Sydney S. Baron, ONE WHIRL (illustrated by George Grosz) (with an
introduction by Mortimer Hays) (Lowell, $1);
Vernon Bartlett, TOMORROW ALWAYS COMES (Knopf, $2); Dorothy
B. Hughes, THE DELICATE APE
(Duell, Sloan & Pearce, $2.50).

Stories of the future are usually pure escape. They are exercises in
speculation, fascinating but as unrelated to our immediate problems as
though they took place so many centuries in the past instead of the future.

But there is a rarer sort of future story—the hortatory legend, the tale of
warning which says, "Here, God help you, is your future...unless you do
something about it now."

[Jack] London's THE IRON HEEL and [Sinclair] Lewis' IT CAN'T
HAPPEN HERE (the one now as sadly neglected as the other was over-
rated) were warnings of Fascism. [Homer] Lea's [1909 military analysis
THE] VALOR OF IGNORANCE was a warning now too well understood.
And the three books listed at the head of this review are warnings against
the all but inevitable stupidities of the peace to come.

Mr. Baron is a publicity man, a liberal and a cynic. In brash broad
strokes of devilish acuteness he pictures the peace conference or, to be
exact, The Temporary Commission for the Organization of a Permanent
World League of Co-operating Sovereign Nations Dedicated to the Preservation of International Peace, Prosperity and Happiness—a title which in-
furiated [Winston] Churchill; there went his basic English. It is a chaos of
Quislings, an asylum of appeasers.

Mr. Bartlett is a journalist, an M.P., a liberal and an idealist. His European Preliminary Peace Conference, though more soberly treated, is hardly
less terrifying than the Baron's TCOPWLCSNDPIPPH. Again the appeasement element is strong and all the underlying antagonisms of the major powers are cruelly exploited.

Mrs. Hughes is a mystery novelist, a reviewer and it's a little hard to say
what else. The one factor that worries her is the renascence of German
militarism, on which she concentrates so thoroughly that the rest of her
political picture remains either nebulous or unbelievable.

The three books differ vastly in tone. They are in reverse order a spy
thriller, a scholar's diary and an outrageously bitter farce (the last accompanied by sketches from the invective pen of George Grosz which might
justly be called, after [the 19th-century artist Francisco] Goya, "The Disas-
ters of Peace"). But they agree on one thought: Peace must be earned.
Peace must be fought. It is not too early (we pray it is not too late) even
now to begin waging that peace. Admirers of the State Department and

Foreign Office may disagree strongly with the authors' concepts of what must be done and what avoided, but even they must concede:

In time of war prepare for peace. (White)

Edwin Honig, GARCIA LORCA (New Directions, $1.50).

Federico Garcia Lorca, murdered by Falangists in 1936, has become better known in this country than any other Spanish poet for generations but largely for false or at best irrelevant reasons. Mr. Honig sets out to correct this state of affairs by showing Lorca in his true place as part of the Spanish literary tradition, which enriches rather than diminishes his importance. The book contains a useful analysis of the poet's works, including synopses of unpublished material, and extensive quotations in the original and in unpretentiously good translations. (APW)

March 26, 1944

Helen MacInnes, WHILE STILL WE LIVE
(Little Brown, $2.75).

Sheila Matthews, English girl visiting Polish friends, is caught by the 1939 invasion and remains to fight on in the Polish underground and to find love with a handsome Polish cavalry captain.

In length, price and pretension, this is a serious novel of Poland, her sufferings and her struggles for freedom. It is also, as one expects from the author of ABOVE SUSPICION, a spy melodrama, with its English heroine posing as a Gestapo agent posing as herself, and many complications of counterplot which seem to underestimate the intelligence if not the evil of the Gestapo. It is also, particularly for the last 200 pages, a love story, in which the hero gallantly imperils the whole guerrilla movement which he leads in order to save the life of the heroine whom he has seen briefly three times but loved at first sight.

It is also, and subtly, a curious propaganda novel. Miss MacInnes' plea is for a future world in which we "will see many forms of political ideology living and working side by side." We have paid too much attention to political differences just as we used to pay too much attention to religious differences. The Polish feudal aristocrats, typified by our hero who tolerated pogroms, are extreme nationalists who refused to become Quislings; therefore they are not protofascists. Nationalism swallows all political differences, which are mainly based anyway on the fear of the haves and the envy of the have-nots. Some men, like our feudal hero, are naturally leaders and upon them depend their people's fates.

Miss MacInnes writes well and interestingly. Her minor characters are alive and absorbing. They are drawn of course from the Polish aristocracy, intelligentsia and peasantry, with no Jews or labor leaders to disturb the picture. (Boucher)

Norman Corwin, MORE BY CORWIN: 16 RADIO DRAMAS (with an
introduction by Clifton Fadiman
(Henry Holt, $3).

There's no need to say that Norman Corwin is the one authentic and ab-sorbing writing talent produced so far by American radio; you know that. But you may not know that most of his shows read nearly as well as they play, and that he adds to each in its printed form a set of "Studio Notes" which Mr. [Clifton] Fadiman [who wrote the introduction] compares justly to [playwright George Bernard] Shaw's prefaces.

These plays should delight and stimulate the most confirmed radio-hater and possibly even lead him to dial KQW on Tuesday evenings at 7, when *Columbia Presents Corwin*. (APW)

April 2, 1944

Vercors, THE SILENCE OF THE SEA (translated by Cyril Connolly)
(Macmillan, $1).

This is a skillful and sensitive short story by a pseudonymous French underground writer, depicting the unconquered silence with which France responds to her invaders' overtures. The circumstances of the book's production, detailed in a long and excellent preface by one M.D., are perhaps a finer tribute to the indomitable French spirit than the story itself. (AB)

Ernst Lothar, THE ANGEL WITH THE TRUMPET (translated by Eliza-beth Reynolds Hapgood) (Doubleday, $3).

Here is the history of Vienna from 1888 to date as reflected in the his-tory of one house and one family, which manages to be personally in-volved in everything from the tragedy at Mayerling through Hitler's failure at the Art Academy to the assassination of Dollfuss. As a novel this is somewhat heavy and contrived; as a sugarcoated summary of Austrian politics and problems it is absorbing. The translation, despite some incon-sistencies and errors, is readable. (AB)

Elizabeth Marion, THE KEYS TO THE HOUSE
(Crowell, $2.50).

Stolid Oregon farmer finds the body of his long-vanished father, with strong grounds for believing that his mother murdered him. His quest for the truth makes a good story of suspicion and suspense, so skillfully written as almost to fool you into accepting it as a valid novel of character. (AB)

April 9, 1944

Jane Beynon [Lange Lewis], CYPRESS MAN
(Bobbs-Merrill, $2.50).

Emotional pressures in a small group of career-minded young people build slowly to murder, the shadow of which you feel throughout the book without knowing until page 265 where it will strike. Jane Beynon is the pseudonym of a good Los Angeles mystery novelist; this, her first straight novel, is at times moving and perceptive, at other times as young as its characters, but never uninteresting. (AB)

Elmer Rice, A NEW LIFE: A PLAY IN NINE SCENES (Coward-McCann, $2).

The printed version of one of last fall's major failures retains the stock characterizations, stilted prose and endless ideological arguments of the stage original; the painstaking (and inaccurate) obstetrical details are somewhat more bearable in type than in the flesh. (APW)

Jack Barett, THE NATION'S CROSSWORD PUZZLE BOOK (Crown, $1).

These are British-type puzzles, in which each definition is an intellectual problem in itself; much harder than Albert Morehead's DOUBLETALK PUZZLES but not quite so terrifying as [the British crossword puzzle masters known as] Torquemada or Caliban. The true puzzle fan who wants something to chew on will find these rewarding and often brilliant, though he may doubt the author's claim to having "originated" the cryptic clue. (AB)

Ramon J. Sender, CHRONICLE OF DAWN (translated by Willard R. Trask) (Doubleday, $2.50).

The Spaniard Ramon Sender (now resident of Mexico) is possibly a great novelist and certainly an incredibly versatile one, whose work ranges from the high melodrama of DARK WEDDING to the moving realism of A MAN'S PLACE.
CHRONICLE OF DAWN is something else again—the story of a few months in the life of a 10-year-old boy in the northern Spain of some 20

years ago. Idyllic is the inevitable reviewer's epithet for this simple story of lessons and gang fights, of poetry and first love, of families and pigeons and the great adventure of exploring underground passages lost since the times of Alfonso the Wise, all of which adds up to something very like the puberty ritual whereby a boy attains manhood.

Only the prologue, in which we see the grown-up Pepe dying a self-willed death in a French concentration camp for Loyalists, ties directly into contemporary questions, but all of Pepe's middle-class childhood is an enlightening commentary on Spanish nature and culture. That's if you must have deeper significance; otherwise you can simply accept this as a sunny and delightful chronicle.

Mr. Trask's translation of the lucid prose is unusually alive; he is somewhat less fortunate in his renderings of Pepe's occasional verse. (APW)

April 23, 1944

C.S. Lewis, PERELANDRA (Macmillan), $2).

In Mr. Lewis' OUT OF THE SILENT PLANET the philologist Elwin Ransom accidentally visited Mars, or Malacandra. Now by the divine will he is transported to Venus (Perelandra), where a new race is coming into being and the drama of the temptation in the Garden must be re-enacted. And it is Ransom's duty to see that this time the drama has a happy ending; no easy task for a man whose principal weapons are a naked middle-aged body and a good command of Hressa-Hlab, the Old Solar language, and whose antagonist is Satan himself.

What Lewis, the brilliant Christian apologist, seems to be doing in his fantasy novels is inventing a new interplanetary mythology which accords perfectly with orthodox Christian theology. (Though the orthodox may boggle a bit at the literal psychophagy, if one may coin a word, of his soul-devouring devils.) It is a splendid intellectual game, with its allegorical implications concerning moral conduct here on this silent planet of Earth.

But where OUT OF THE SILENT PLANET was first-rate adventure-fantasy with incidental theology, PERELANDRA is fairly straight theology with only incidental fantasy trimmings. Mr. Lewis' clear, clean prose is always a joy and the insidious reasonings of his devil are fully worthy of His Excellency Screwtape, but the irreligious and skeptical may find this novel both dull and exasperating.

It is an odd thing to say as a warning in our theoretically Christian culture, but PERELANDRA is probably a novel for Christians only. They, however, will find in this novelistic guise one of the most suggestive and stimulating of devotional works. (AB)

Willard Wiener, FOUR BOYS AND A GUN
(Dial Press, $2.50).

Mr. Wiener goes behind a commonplace stickup episode to tell the life stories of the four boys involved and the factors that drove them to crime. An exceedingly hard-boiled novel, guaranteed to shock, somewhat mannered in its flashy and episodic telling, and apparently based on the thesis that juvenile delinquency results from depressions and unemployment—a thesis hardly supported by current evidence. (AB)

Michael Young, THE TRIAL OF ADOLF HITLER
(Dutton, $2.50).

Despite the sensational title and jacket, the body of this book is just another novel about Austrian Jews finding haven in America, undistinguished save by the intensely interesting (if sketchily developed) character of Jakob Schneidermann, modern "enlightened" skeptic who slowly returns to the mysticism of his religion and in an almost apocalyptic vision beholds the events of the future which give the novel its title.

As an indictment of Hitler and Hitlerism the vision is as indisputable as the sermon of [Calvin] Coolidge's minister who was against sin, and about as original; as a prophecy it is unconvincing in the extreme ease and rapidity with which all good things are accomplished and unsatisfactory in the supernatural ending which steals Hitler from human justice. Michael Young is indubitably on the side of the angels, but it is about as likely that man will attain world peace and unity in the next eight months as it is that a mob of thousands could (as it does in the vision) break out spontaneously into the Hallelujah Chorus. (AB)

Felix Riesenberg, Jr., THE PHANTOM FREIGHTER
(Dodd Mead, $2).

Submarines without and spies within imperil the freighter Princess on a mystery mission out of San Francisco. The son of Captain Felix Riesenberg is presumably authoritative in his maritime details (though one distrusts an author who can't tell a code from a cipher), but the older boys to whom the book is addressed may well feel insulted by the over-juvenile level of characterization and dialogue. (AB)

George S. Kaufman & Moss Hart, SIX PLAYS BY KAUFMAN AND
HART (with an introduction by Brooks Atkinson)
(Modern Library, 95 cents).

The 1942 Random House edition, now available as a Modern Library bargain, offers you a sound introduction by Brooks Atkinson, entertaining profiles of the two playwrights by each other, and a chance to study their collaborative progress from ONCE IN A LIFETIME (1930) to GEORGE WASHINGTON SLEPT HERE (1940)—if that's progress. (APW)

Margaret Mayorga (editor), THE BEST ONE-ACT PLAYS OF 1943 (Dodd Mead, $2.50).

Without the intensive knowledge of Miss Mayorga it would be impossible to say that these mediocre selections are not the best plays of last year; one must accept her judgment with wistful resignation. At least there are first-rate incisive episodes by Robert Ardrey and Doris Frankel, a possibly interesting experiment in dance drama by Arnold Sundgaard and a useful bibliography of one-act play publication in 1943. (APW)

May 7, 1944

Fremont Rider, MELVIL DEWEY (American Library Association, $2.75).

Melvil Dewey (1851-1931), who was almost single-handedly responsible for American libraries as we know them today and particularly for the system of classification still used by 96 per cent of our public libraries, is one of the most fantastic and fascinating eccentrics ever produced by the eccentric-breeding Anglo-Saxon race. This brief and meaty biography, though it touches on all his interests (spelling reform, the metric system, the rights of women, Lake Placid, anti-Semitism and what have you), is addressed almost exclusively to librarians. The layman may find much of it baffling, but one hopes it may fall into the hands of an American Hesketh Pearson [the first major biographer of Sir Arthur Conan Doyle] and stimulate him to what could easily be a masterpiece in the art of biography. (APW)

May 14, 1944

Virgil Partch, IT'S HOT IN HERE (edited by Gurney Williams) (McBride, $1).

There are many capable and sometimes convulsing cartoonists; then there are the satirists who take the life we know and heighten it to absurdity, like [Helen] Hokinson or [an unidentified cartoonist whose last name was] Barlow; then there are the magnificent zanies who create strange and terrifying worlds of their own, like [Charles] Addams or [George] Price. And then there is Virgil Partch. If you've ever looked at *Collier's* or *PM* you know VIP, of the great distorted heads and the greater and even more distorted thoughts—the one new and original master (with the possible exception of [Saul] Steinberg) to bless and addle our lives in the past several years. This collection of VIP's drawings (75 of them!) has a grand foreword by Kyle Crichton (in a style to remind you of the vanished Robert Forsythe) which warns against people who try to explain The Significance of Partch. It's enough to say: This is it. And if your soul is parched, try Partch! (APW)

William Steig, ABOUT PEOPLE
(Duell, Sloan & Pearce, $1.50).

You know from Steig's SMALL FRY and his Shell Oil billboards that he can be accurately funny. You know from last season's THE LONELY ONES that he can be accurately (and discomfortingly) analytical. But unless you were among the very few who rejoiced in the now reissued ABOUT PEOPLE when it appeared in 1939, you do not yet know the full humor and horror of his accuracy. These wonderful and unclassifiable drawings (part cartoon, part surrealism and part something that our language hasn't caught up with yet) are 105 exact pinnings down of the human psyche, so deftly accomplished that you can admire the perfection of the pin for minutes before realizing that it is thrust precisely through your own throat. Any intelligible description or review is impossible and must be reduced to the simple imperative: Go and buy. (APW)

May 21, 1944

Parker Tyler, THE HOLLYWOOD HALLUCINATION (Creative Age Press, $2.50).

Iris Barry of the Museum of Modern Art Film Library calls this "the first book in its field to deserve the name of creative criticism." It is that, and it is filled with shrewdly perceptive comments on films and such allied fields as Dostoevski, the detective novel, art in a democracy, and sex. It is also filled with careless syntax, errors of fact and pretentious jargon. Only those trained in jungle fighting amid luxuriant verbiage can hope to penetrate to Mr. Tyler's often rewarding ideas. (APW)

May 28, 1944

Willy Ley, ROCKETS: THE FUTURE OF TRAVEL BEYOND THE STRATOSPHERE (Viking, $2.50).

The history of rockets to date is the story of alternating emphasis on their values in war and in entertainment. The first recorded use of rockets (in China, A.D. 1232) was military. Their Occidental popularity has been chiefly for pyrotechnical display save for a brief period in the early nineteenth century when their military value was again exploited (and when Francis Scott Key saw "the rockets' red glare"). Now once more, with bazookas, Katyushas and Nebelwerfer, we think of rockets in terms of D-Day rather than the Fourth of July.

But the rocket in entertainment and the rocket in war (where it can supplement but never replace artillery) are only bypaths in what we shall someday consider the prehistory of the rocket. The rocket's greatest value lies in the fact that it is the one known means of propulsion which will function outside of the earth's atmosphere. Ever since man has conceived of the stars as something apart from earth, he has dreamed of reaching them. That dream is now on the threshold of fulfillment. It is not impossible that we will see the moon reached in our own lifetimes, and that our grandchildren will fulfill the invasion prediction of some Martian Orson Welles. And the dream will succeed through rockets.

The originally announced title of Mr. Ley's book, PRELUDE TO SPACEFLIGHT, was far more just than the opportunistic ROCKETS. Modern rocket weapons occupy little more than a footnote. Instead the book treats of the growth in the human mind of the concept of spaceflight (with fascinating excerpts from early romances), the technical development of the rocket, the activities in the past few decades of the semi-professional research groups (with a complete history of the German Rocket Society and its disruption by the Nazis), and a thorough scientific analysis of the problems (technological, physiological and economic) of the first steps to spaceflight.

Willy Ley, new weapons editor of *PM* and contributor to periodicals ranging from *Astounding Science Fiction* to the *United States Naval Institute Proceedings*, is the ideal man to produce such a book. He is a polyglot scholar of the history of science and has been actively engaged in rocket research (on the testing field as well as in the library) for almost 20 years. Other specialists may quarrel with him in details or regret that American rocket activities have not received more space, but even they must delight in his compendious and witty mind and hail him as the prophet of a new era. (White)

June 4, 1944

Elsa Valentine, NO MORTAL FIRE (Simon & Schuster, $2.50).

Augusta Fritzhoff is a ruthless, domineering, evil woman. Her crimes include murdering her stepmother, ruining the lives of her sisters and father, becoming a Nazi agent and straining the reader's credulity. She apparently symbolizes the German people, and the monotonous recital of her offenses is intended as a Vital and Significant Document. It emerges rather as a wooden and tasteless tract—the sort of blind, unbalanced propaganda which we shall be ashamed of after the war and which anyone with a fondness for the art of novel writing can start in being ashamed of right now. (Serialized as THERE IS SUCH STRENGTH.) (AB)

Arch Oboler & Stephen Longstreet (editors), FREE WORLD THEATER: NINETEEN NEW RADIO PLAYS (with an introduction by Thomas Mann and a preface by Arch Oboler) (Random House, $2.75)

A year ago the Hollywood Writers' Mobilization, the OWI [Office of War Information] and the Blue Network collaborated on a series of broadcasts to reach "the upper 10 percent intelligence quotient of the radio audience who were not listening to the ordinary bludgeoning war messages." Here is a collection of the plays, which should be as welcome in the library as they were on the air. A few to be sure are grandiose and diffused and suffocate rather than bludgeon, but many are alert, witty and stirring and all are resolutely on the side of the angels. The impressive roster of authors includes Arch Oboler, Pearl S. Buck, Arch Oboler, William Kozlenko, Samson Raphaelson and Arch Oboler. Aside to Mr. Oboler: The Loyalist slogan at Madrid was "No pasaran" [Spanish for "they shall not pass"]; your thrice-repeated "non passerons" is internationally-minded in that it is in no known language. (APW)

June 11, 1944

William Steig, ALL EMBARRASSED (with a foreword by Arthur Steig) (Duell, Sloan & Pearce, $2).

If you know [Steig's earlier books] THE LONELY ONES and ABOUT PEOPLE you need only be told that here is another Steig in the same vein. If you don't know those masterpieces of psychological satire, you might do better to start with them rather than with ALL EMBARRASSED; for here the Steig style frequently comes close to pure abstractionism, and you need the background of the earlier works to follow him.

The title of every drawing in this book is "Embarrassment," which the foreword calls "the normal sensation of the human being in our day"; and the best of the drawings belong to that perfection of visual satire which says clearly in its own medium what words can translate only by awkward fumbling. Words have nothing to do with what transcends words; the book should be wordlessly reviewed by a sketch conveying recognition, discomfort, gratification and a kind of ironic ecstasy—but it would take Steig himself to do that review. (APW)

Marcelle Michelin, LES RICHES HEURES: CONTES ET NOUVELLES
AU TEMPS DE JEANNE D'ARC ET DE LOUIS XI (with a foreword by
Gustave Cohen)
(Brentano's, $1.50).

Mlle. Michelin is a young Canadian medical student of French ancestry, Argentine birth and American education who has fallen in love with fifteenth century France. Impregnated with the lore and culture of the period, she has given birth to this her first book, a series of semi-fictional sketches of the times of Joan of Arc, Louis XI and Burgundy (whom to hell with). As stories they are slight; as archeological reconstructions they are precise, learned and evocative; as a political allegory they form a stirring and hopeful picture of the France which is "the fairest of all Frances, because she waxed great with the common sorrow of a people sorely tried—because she struggled with all the resolve of a people which knows not how to die." (APW)

June 18, 1944

Herbert A. Wise & Phyllis Fraser (editors), GREAT TALES OF TERROR
AND THE SUPERNATURAL
(Random House, $2.95);
Bennett Cerf (editor), FAMOUS GHOST STORIES (Modern Library, 95
cents); H.P. Lovecraft, THE WEIRD SHADOW OVER INNSMOUTH
AND OTHER STORIES OF THE SUPERNATURAL (Bartholomew
House, 25 cents).

There are two principal approaches to compiling an anthology. One is to present definitively the best work in the field, the other to discover unhackneyed, unanthologized excellence—for the reader of one anthology is sure to have read a half dozen others. And the ideal anthologist, like Ellery Queen [Frederic Dannay], manages to combine the two approaches.

It's hard to see which intent governed Wise and Fraser in their choice for the huge new Random House collection. If they aimed at a definitive survey of classics and the hell with repetition, it's difficult to justify the omission of Hugh Walpole, John Metcalfe, Stephen Vincent Benet, Max Beerbohm and a half dozen others. And they certainly were not aiming at the unhackneyed, despite the jacket blurb stating that they "combed old libraries and little-known collections." Of the 52 stories presented, at least 37 have been previously anthologized and at least 26 are available in collections currently on sale.

The editors' combs seem to have missed the pulp magazines completely. H.P. Lovecraft they know from the Arkham House volumes and represent by two of his best and most characteristic works, but they have not touched the rich fields to be found in back files of *Weird Tales* or *Unknown Worlds*, with the wacky supernatural comedy of L. Sprague de Camp or the modern metropolitan horror of Fritz Leiber, Jr.

With these reservations the Wise-Fraser collection can be recommended as offering a thousand pages of high-grade shuddering. There's hardly a poor story in it (though "The Boarded Window" is an odd choice for the only [Ambrose] Bierce), and most of them hold up excellently under re-reading—which is fortunate for the aficionado.

The Modern Library collection is of course smaller, less pretentious, cheaper, and quite satisfactory for what it is—a group of 16 topnotch chillers, mostly standard classics far more tastefully selected than in the older anthology which it replaces. The outstanding item that makes it a must for collectors is Mr. Cerf's "The Current Crop of Ghost Stories."

Both the Cerf and Wise-Fraser volumes deserve medals for including that strange magician Isak Dinesen—the first times, I believe, that she has been reprinted in fantasy anthologies.

If your palate is jaded and you want more unusual meat in the fantasy line, try Dashiell Hammett's CREEPS BY NIGHT, recently reissued in Forum Books; a collection which remains surprisingly fresh 13 years after its original publication. Or get the pocket-sized Bartholomew House edition of Lovecraft, the first popularly distributed book by the most influential pulp necromancer. Despite the unquestioned excellence of [Saki's] "The Open Window," [W.W. Jacobs'] "The Monkey's Paw" and [Oliver Onions'] "The Beckoning Fair One," there really are other ghost stories. (AB)

Laurence Dwight Smith, COUNTERFEITING: CRIME AGAINST THE PEOPLE (Norton, $3.50).

Counterfeiting is a crime that dates back as far as coinage itself. It is one of the most dangerous and anti-social of crimes; it victimizes not the billion-rich government but the small tradesman and the individual teller. It contributes to inflation and the debasement of legal currency and its profits go to finance other branches of organized crime. And it flourishes upon public ignorance. In the last decade the Secret Service of the Treasury Department has worked on a campaign to reduce that public ignorance.

This book, the latest step in the campaign, is, like Mr. Smith's CRYPTOGRAPHY, an admirable example of popular presentation without inaccuracy or condescension. It contains a brief history of coinage and counterfeiting, an explanation of the work of the Secret Service, and a detailed analysis of the nature and detection of counterfeits, particularly counterfeit bills. It has good illustrations (including specimens expressly designed by the Bureau of Engraving and Printing), a bibliography and a thorough index. Strongly recommended to collectors of numismatics and criminology and even more so to the average tradesman, who could take all the profit out of counterfeiting if he would look at a stranger's $20 bill with half the care he devotes to a customer's $5 check. (AB)

LORD HALIFAX'S GHOST BOOK: A COLLECTION OF STORIES OF HAUNTED HOUSES, APPARITIONS AND SUPERNATURAL OC-CURRENCES MADE BY CHARLES LINDLEY, VISCOUNT HALI-FAX (with a foreword by Viscount Halifax, Ambassador from Great Britain to the United States) (Didier, $2.75).

Mr. Noel Coward has forewarned us of the ghostly appurtenances of the stately homes of England, where the baby in the guest wing that crouches by the grate was walled up in the west wing in 1498; and those whose taste runs to such hauntings in aristocratic circles have long known in its English edition the admirable collection made by Viscount Halifax, father of the present British Ambassador. Lord Halifax's stories consist chiefly of documents from friends, many of them first-hand witnesses, though a few specimens of folklore or out and out fiction have crept in. Like most true ghost stories they are fragmentary and often pointless, but all are valuable to the student and a few are guaranteed to raise the back hackles of the amateur. Try for instance the story called "Here I Am Again!" or the malevolent episode of aviation entitled "I Will Pay You Tomorrow" and then give thanks to Didier for at last making this notable scrapbook available in America. (AB)

June 25, 1944

Dennis Wheatley, THE SWORD OF FATE
(Macmillan, $2.50).

It's hard to say just what this novel is. Much of it is the romance in Alexandria of two exceedingly star-crossed lovers. Some of it is spy stuff and revenge melodrama, a sequel to Mr. Wheatley's THE QUEST OF JULIAN DAY. And a great deal of it is straight military history of the African and Greek campaigns of 1940-41. The portions are not bad of their kind but they add up to a very long and somewhat uncertain book. (AB)

Alexandra Mazurova, REVELATION OF A RUSSIAN ACTOR
(introduction by Dr. Henry Lanz)
(privately printed, no price given).

This is the first of two proposed pamphlets on the life and theories of the great Russian actor Boris Glagolin. A blend of [John] Barrymore, [creator of "Method" acting Konstantin] Stanislavsky and a Christian revolutionist, he emerges as a splendid protagonist for a Russian novel. Proceeds from the book will go to establish a free studio of the Russian theater in the United States under the supervision of Mr. Glagolin, who two years ago, to give you a taste of his variety, was gardener for the James Gleasons in Beverly Hills. (APW)

F.C. Weiskopf, THE FIRING SQUAD
(translated by James A. Galston) (Knopf, $2.50).

"Before a battle, the old German Catti were chained one to another so that none of them could flee....The German soldiers are like the old Catti—they are all chained to one another, chained to the wrongs they have done or have failed to prevent."

These are the words of Hans Holler, German soldier, to the nurse in a Russian prison hospital where he lies dying after Stalingrad. THE FIRING SQUAD is Holler's story of the forging of that chain of wrongs.

It is a bitter story brilliantly told, the story of the destruction of men by the state which they have stupidly allowed to come into being and which they lack the energy to oppose.

Holler served chiefly with the army of occupation in Prague, an army which fought solely against civilians. He was not an evil or cruel man; in fact, of the five men in his barracks room only Dietz, the party fanatic, would be recognizable to a Hollywood casting director. But the simple Sudeten Holler, like Chabrun the Junker and Seelke the Berlin bourgeois, was lost in inertia and apathy, and the chain of evil bound him to Dietz and the SS.

It is unusual in wartime to find a novel with so understanding a treatment of the enemy. Not that this is appeasement propaganda; far from it. But it poses the unanswered question: "A great body of Germans once had the potentialities of good citizens; what is to be done with them now?" It is the reverse of the coin palmed off on us by the adherents of Vanstoutartism [Boucher's name for the view shared by Lord Vansittart and mystery writer Rex Stout that Germany and everyone and everything in it should be all but annihilated] and deserves our consideration, especially when presented in so distinguished and moving a novel.

Mr. Galston's translation is so satisfactory that you tend to think of the book as an excellent original in English. (White)

Admiral Sir W. Reginald Hall & Amos J. Peaslee,
THREE WARS WITH GERMANY
(edited and illustrated by Joseph P. Sims) (Putnam, $3).

The meat of this book is the correspondence between Admiral Hall, the fabulous director of British Naval Intelligence, and Mr. Peaslee, counsel for the American plaintiffs during the 17 years of international litigation in the Black Tom case—the attempt to secure German reparation for the most celebrated act of sabotage in the last war. The trimmings include anecdotes of the Silver Greyhounds, the dispatch-bearers whom Peaslee commanded in that war, and a long exchange of letters on military and philosophical aspects of this war. The whole, while often revealing the characters of two strong and interesting men, is so loosely organized and fragmentary as to be valuable only as source material. It is indexed and full of photographs. (AB)

July 2, 1944

Joseph Kessel, ARMY OF SHADOWS (translated by Haakon Chevalier) (Knopf, $2); Francoise Perrier & Claude Lebel, LA GARDE MONTANTE (with a foreword by Helen Mackay) (Brentano's, $1.50).

The novel of the Underground is already becoming a new literary genre and an admirable one, for at its best it fuses the tension and excitement of the spy story with the significance and compassion of the proletarian novel. Now that the invasion has made the French underground more than ever important to us, many readers will turn to these Underground novels for the true picture which for fear of reprisals can be revealed only as fiction.

ARMY OF SHADOWS was written by a novelist who himself worked with the Underground up to a year ago. The account is authentic and so is M. Kessel's novelistic talent. With the economy of a [Georges] Simenon and the humanity of a [John] Steinbeck he sketches a series of loosely connected episodes in the Underground career of one Philippe Gerbier—sometimes ironic, sometimes melodramatic and always real and moving. The translation is by Haakon Chevalier—which means that it is completely worthy of a book which should go down as a small classic of our times.

LA GARDE MONTANTE deals with a far less realistic and, in the French sense of the word, serious Underground than M. Kessel's—that of the very young who were university freshmen when the war began. The authors are as young as their characters and their hero, who is supposed to be poetically colorful, will strike most readers as simply tetched in the haid. But the dialogue, well larded with student slang, is vivid and spirited, and the young authors will bear watching. So will the French youths of whom they write with such confidence.

France fell, and many of the undefeated tend to look on her with scorn. But gold that has been through the crucible is purer than untried ore, and in the new-found strength and unity of the French lies (or can lie) much of the hope of Europe. These semi-fictional stories of the Underground are nec- essary footnotes to any post-war plans. (Boucher)

July 9, 1944

J.B.S. HARDMAN (editor), RENDEZVOUS WITH DESTINY: AD- DRESSES AND OPINIONS OF FRANKLIN DELANO ROOSEVELT (Dryden Press, $3).

No matter where you stand politically, you can hardly find more impor- tant source material for arguments in the coming campaign than the public papers and addresses of the President, which have hitherto been available only in the nine large volumes of the complete sets published by Random [House] and Macmillan. Mr. Hardman, president of the American Labor Press Association, has made an intelligent selection of Mr. Roosevelt's key utterances and supplemented them with notes on the aims and attainments of his administration. Twenty-five photographs of the President add to the book's usefulness; an index would have added even more. (APW)

July 23, 1944

Earl Browder, TEHERAN: OUR PATH IN WAR AND PEACE (Interna- tional Publishers, $1.50).

To Mr. Browder the eight paragraphs of the Declaration of Teheran are the essential key to the future of the world, and "every nation, every statesman, every individual who departs from the policy of Teheran will find himself walking off into a void." Step by step he takes up the implica- tions of the document as they affect the postwar world politically and eco- nomically, the internal affairs of the United States, and our 1944 elections, and argues for colonial emancipation, active support of anti-Fascism in liberated countries, the development of new world markets, the abolition of minority discriminations at home and a non-partisan 1944 campaign.

Red-baiters and extreme leftists will alike be disappointed in Mr. Browder's considered defense of "free enterprise" and in his persuasive argument to capital that support of [the Soviet-backed Yugoslav guerrilla leader] Tito and the Chinese "Communists" [i.e. the forces of Mao Tse- Tung] will pay better dividends than attempts to prop up [the right-wing Yugoslav guerrilla leader Draja] Mikhailovich and the Kuomintang [i.e. the forces of Chiang Kai-Shek].

One may quarrel with the author's statement that anti-Semitism is solely a Hitlerian import with no roots in the American past and with his pretense that there is no honest un-Fascistic anti-Communism. But even the most bitter of the honest anti-Communists must admit that this is a quietly cogent book of valuable arguments. Those who automatically disagree with the "party line" will find themselves in dubious company if they apply that principle here. (APW)

Lillian Hellman, THE SEARCHING WIND:
A PLAY IN TWO ACTS (Viking, $2).

The publisher's blurb says: "Few theatrical seasons bring to light a play which receives the unanimous critical acclaim accorded to" this one—a true if misleading statement since the critics were indeed unanimous, but in agreeing that Miss Hellman was not up to scratch this time. THE SEARCHING WIND is a confusing play—partly an impeachment of the appeasers of the past two decades, partly the story of a complex triangle in the life of one of those appeasers. The political intent of the play is certainly to be praised, and its statements may have seemed fresher on the stage than they do in the library. The emotional plot is unrelated to the thesis and solved by a disconcerting scene in which characters reverse themselves like least suspected persons in whodunits. Count this review in on the unanimity. (APW)

July 30, 1944

Julius Fast (editor), OUT OF THIS WORLD:
AN ANTHOLOGY (Penguin, 25 cents).

A few weeks ago I was complaining in these pages of the unimaginative sameness of fantasy anthologies which keep reprinting the same tried-and-terrible stories. If you also have been tempted to give up reading anthologies because you know their contents by heart in advance, here's the book to change your mind. Sergeant Fast has a fine lilting taste in pure fantasy, and he's read a few books and magazines besides other anthologies.

He has collected fourteen stories here, all highly indorsed by his army colleagues and by this reviewer, most of them never anthologized before and some of them even new to book form. They run from John Collier's grisly morsel about the invisible playmate to Jack London's picture of cave-humanity in the Bay Region after the scarlet plague of 2013, with Saki [H.H. Munro] and [Stephen Vincent] Benet of course, balanced by such less familiar names as Nelson Bond and Sergeant Fast himself. The time range is from 50,000 B.C. (Arch Oboler) to the last trump (H.G. Wells). All in all the blithest, most refreshing and least hackneyed supernatural anthology to come this way in a long time, and for only a quarter. (AB)

Mary Roberts Rinehart, ALIBI FOR ISABEL AND OTHER STORIES
(Farrar & Rinehart, $2.50).

Mrs. Rinehart's sixteenth book of short stories deals with murder, marital problems, Fifth Columnists and the reactions of the aristocratic rich to war. The stories on the last topic are by far the best (the criminous ones involve too many rabbits out of hats), but all have the slick Rinehart trademark. Odd coincidence: Mrs. Rinehart's "The Blackout" is almost identical in theme and situation with Sally Benson's "Men Really Rule the World"—a fine opportunity for comparison of tempers and techniques. (AB)

August 6, 1944

Sylvia G.L. Dannett & Edwin Bennett, DEFY THE TEMPEST (Messner, $2.50).

Meredith Hall is a nightmare of a girls' school, with sinister passages and a psychopathic faculty and a family crypt beneath it and a madhouse close by. The pretty young art teacher, who fatally resembles her dead predecessor, nearly loses life and sanity but comes through to win true love. The time is nominally around 1923; except for some grotesque allusions to psychoanalysis it seems more like 1823. This is a disarming book—haunted by ghosts of other novels from the Gothic to Daphne DuMaurier, dismally clanking their cliches, and yet for all its derivative amateurishness lots of fun, like a really good bad movie. (AB)

August 13, 1944

Robert M. Lindner, REBEL WITHOUT A CAUSE: THE HYPNOANALYSIS OF A CRIMINAL PSYCHOPATH
(with an introduction by Sheldon & Eleanor Glueck)
(Grune & Stratton, $4).

Essentially a record addressed to psychologists and criminologists, this 100,000-word transcript of the analysis of a psychopathic delinquent under hypnosis is of interest even to the layman for its short and meaty foreword on the nature and implications of psychopathic behavior and for its success in projecting character far more vividly and movingly than most "psychological" novels. (AB)

William J. Finn, THE CONDUCTOR RAISES HIS BATON (with a foreword by Leopold Stokowski) (Harper, $3.75).

The founder of the Paulist Choristers states and analyzes the principles which he has found valid for conducting in general and choral conducting in particular, with special emphasis on liturgical works of the Roman rite. Basically a stimulating text for young conductors, well indexed and fully illustrated with long quotations from musical scores, the book will also interest the more advanced layman with its ironic comments on modern conducting, its debunking of much pretentious patter about the Gregorian modes, and such evidences of Father Finn's vigorous common sense as "I have been unable to discover any valid reason for abandoning natural modes of expression when addressing religious subject matter." (APW)

August 20, 1944

Donald Wandrei, THE EYE AND THE FINGER
(Arkham House, $3).

Arkham House's latest boon to fantasy collectors is an assortment of horror stories and science fiction by Donald Wandrei, mostly reprinted from *Astounding*, *Weird Tales* and *Esquire*. Wandrei's work is always capable and often exciting if somewhat lacking in originality. Too often the aficionado can name the source of the plot idea and even of the style. Beside the earlier Arkham volumes of [Clark Ashton] Smith and [H.P.] Lovecraft, much of this book seems routine and derivative; but an occasional story, such as the vast and [Olaf] Stapledonian "Finality Unlimited" and the classic "The Red Brain," may help to show the reader who scorns pulps that he's been missing some magnificently imaginative story-telling. (AB)

September 3, 1944

Helen M. Morosco & Leonard Paul Dugger, THE ORACLE OF BROAD-WAY: LIFE OF OLIVER MOROSCO WRITTEN FROM HIS OWN NOTES AND COMMENTS (Caxton Printers, $4.25).

Here is a biography that has almost everything wrong with it: flat style, errors of facts and dates, careless proofreading, confused chronology, inadequate index, and an incredible device whereby Mrs. Morosco writes in her husband's first person as though it were an autobiography (the first person thinks well of Mrs. M). And yet, since Oliver Morosco was that rarest of biographical subjects, a man with a great theatrical career whose life had absorbing dramatic value even aside from the theater, the result is an intensely enjoyable book. Not since Ruth St. Denis' autobiography have I seen such a blending of theatrical record and human document. For all devotees of Californian or theater history and for all who relish a direct

narrative of emotional fireworks, this book with all its faults is a must—
even though it consistently calls our city (where Morosco grew up and began his career) Frisco. (APW)

September 10, 1944

Georges Simenon, ON THE DANGER LINE
(translated by Stuart Gilbert) (Harcourt Brace, $2).

Again the latest Simenon volume contains two short novels. HOME
TOWN (FAUBOURG) is the story of a minor crook returned to his home,
who feels himself drawn back from smart rackets to petit bourgeois respectability until the conflict resolves itself in murder. THE GREEN
THERMOS (LE SUSPECT) concerns the efforts of an idealistic anarchist
to prevent a bomb outrage plotted by his less idealistic comrades. Both are
restrained, skillful, moving, and marked by the artistic selection of realistic
detail, as we have come to expect of all Simenon's work. Both are also
inconclusive, the first ending too abruptly, the second reaching a false con-
clusion which solves and alters nothing. Those with a palate for Simenon
will welcome them gladly but class them as second grade—little more than
first installments of possible novels. (AB)

Vladimir Nabokov, NIKOLAI GOGOL
(New Directions, $1.50).

Vladimir Nabokov's GOGOL is an attempt by a brilliant and unclassifiable writer to depict for the American public a great Russian master even
more brilliant and unclassifiable. It analyzes his work, rescues him from
the doctrinaire theorists who have pigeonholed him as an early revolutionary, and leaves you with the impression that Gogol himself was a Gogol
character (and that Mr. Nabokov is not far from one). It's a remarkable job
of creative criticism, notable alike for its excellent prose, its understanding
sympathy with its subject, its irrational interludes, and above all its distinction as a vastly enjoyable book in its own right if you've never heard of
Gogol.

There is no question as to which biography will sell more this season.
Neither is there any doubt as to which will be still read and enjoyed ten
years from now. (APW)

September 17, 1944

Julien J. Proskauer, PUZZLES FOR EVERYONE
(illustrated by Robert A. Schoellhorn & Nancy P. Dryfoos) (Harper, $2).

Puzzles for Harper & Brothers: What persuaded you to publish this hap-hazard collection of simple, over-familiar and badly edited puzzles? And once persuaded, why didn't you at least bother to proofread it? (AB)

Robert Pick, THE TERHOVEN FILE
(Lippincott, $2.75).

The Terhoven file, in the possession of a Jewish Viennese lawyer, con-tained first-hand evidence concerning Hitler's private and incestuous mur-der of his niece. It had to be suppressed, and the search for the file and its owner affects remotely linked lives in Paris, London and Philadelphia. If this plot outline sounds like that of a rousing meller, you're in for a disap-pointment. Mr. Pick is a thoroughly earnest novelist who uses this frame-work only to enclose a world-wide picture of all nations and classes in their reactions to the problems of fascism, anti-Semitism and the refugee question. The result is an intelligent and very long novel, told in a spot-light-technique reminiscent of Jules Romains (but with all the action hap-pening between spots) and couched in a sort of Translator's English. (AB)

Denis de Rougemont, LE PART DU DIABLE: NOUVELLE VERSION
(Brentano's, $1.75).

M. de Rougemont's denunciation of the modern world and plea for spiri-tuality is as Gallic in style and content as [Philip Wylie's] GENERATION OF VIPERS is American or [C.S. Lewis'] THE SCREWTAPE LETTERS English; and yet the three works form a related trilogy, concerned in their several fashions with matters beyond the immediate what-shall-we do-with approach. This new edition is enriched by sixteen additional chapters, not padding, but rather so essential that it is hard to imagine the work without them. (APW)

September 24, 1944

Louis Verneuil, THEATRE COMPLET,
VOLUMES 3 AND 4 (Brentano's, $2.50 each).

These perfect specimens of the Parisian ability to write trifles so exceed-ingly deftly that they seem like masterpieces are rendered doubly delight-ful by M. Verneuil's prefaces of theatrical chitchat. A treasure for anyone who enjoys wit, craftsmanship or backstage gossip. (APW)

October 1, 1944

H.R. Hays, LIE DOWN IN DARKNESS
(Reynal & Hitchcock, $2.50).

Do you remember Mr. Hays' STRANGER ON THE HIGHWAY, one of the most distinguished murder novels of last year? Well, this second novel establishes H.R. Hays firmly in the front rank of—but that's a cliche, and this is of all books the last to deserve a cliche treatment. The publishers' blurb tells nothing of the plot and I'll follow its wise example; suspense melodrama doesn't summarize well.

But this is suspense melodrama with a difference; a build-up- to-murder that is as tense and horrifying as you could ask, but with an added quality of bitter (and not unjustified) hatred of humanity and its motives, expressed with such vicious vigor as to make Anne Parish and Sally Benson seem all sweetness and light. There is also (if I'm not reading things into it) a successful political allegory of the sort so wretchedly attempted a few months ago in [Elsa Valentine's] NO MORTAL FIRE, but that needn't bother you. As a thriller, as a psychological novel or as righteous invective, LIE DOWN IN DARKNESS is a grand job. (AB)

October 8, 1944

Lord Dunsany, GUERRILLA (Bobbs-Merrill, $2.50).

Lord Dunsany was lecturing at the University of Athens when the Axis invaded Greece. He knew the perilous hardships of the refugee at first hand. But there is none of the immediacy of his own suffering in GUERRILLA. Instead this story of the land (which might be Greece or might be any other small country of south Europe) has the beauty and remoteness of an ancient folk epic. Chastely and exquisitely written, the legend (for such it seems) of the heroic resistance of Hlaka and his guerrilla band is free of any such contemporary problems as internecine differences and quarrels with the government in exile. Despite airplanes and modern artillery it might deal with equally heroic resistance against Turks or Tartars. No poetic novel could better exemplify the definition of poetry as emotion recollected in tranquillity, and as a half-allegorical poem the book is a small masterpiece. (AB)

George Price, IS IT ANYONE WE KNOW?
(Murray Hill, $2.49).

This omnibus includes all of GOOD HUMOR MAN and IT'S SMART TO BE PEOPLE, plus some drawings new in book form and a redrawn version of the title cartoon. If you've ever seen a Price opus, you're on your way to the bookstore already. If not, lose no time in meeting the man whose blend of drab realism and mad concepts give the effect of Clifford Odets writing for the Marx brothers. (APW)

Miles Safranek, BOHUSLAV MARTINU:
THE MAN AND HIS MUSIC (Knopf, $3).

Bohuslav Martinu's music has been rarely performed in San Francisco and is almost entirely unrecorded. If he composes music as well as he thinks and writes about it, we've been missing something. Mr. Safranek's Boswellian tribute contains analyses of many compositions (including the composer's own unusually articulate program notes), a charmingly characterized biography and an exhaustive listing of the Martinu canon with full details of composition, publication and performance. Useful and pleasant in itself, the book makes you hungry for the orchestral and operatic works it describes. (APW)

October 15, 1944

Jerome Lawrence (editor), OFF MIKE: RADIO WRITING BY THE NA-
TION'S TOP RADIO WRITERS
(Essential Books, $2.50).

No book can tell you how to write but the intelligent shoptalk of success-ful writers can stimulate your ideas, give you some notion of the problems you're up against in professional writing, and often warn you at least how not to write. This symposium does all of that and in addition provides first-rate reading for the non-writing public that would like to understand radio better. Every kind of program from soap operas to news commentary is covered by a leading specialist, and there is even a provocative chapter on writing for television. (AB)

Erwin Lessner, PHANTOM VICTORY:
THE FOURTH REICH, 1945-1960 (Putnam, $2.50).

This fictional history of the future presents the events that follow upon our refusal to enforce a hard peace with Germany: the underground plots of the Wehrmacht, the sympathy for Germany fomented by a woman col-umnist, and the rise of the mystical shepherd Friedolin, who organizes Germany "for penance" and in 15 years takes over the world. Mr. Lessner is willing to grant intelligence only to his villains; the Allies (even the Russians) act throughout with a stupid disregard of their true interests that far surpasses 1938.

And it's hard to tell what the author does recommend (he dislikes and distrusts every political group from left through center to right, with the odd exception of the Hapsburgs) short of plowing salt into all Germany. But the book is a magnificent fantastic farce; the very exaggeration that weakens it as prophecy may also weaken your ribs with ironic laughter. Friedolin's penitence movement (In penitence lies salvation, or *In der Busse liegt das Heil*, shortened in speech of course to *Buss Heil*) is conceived from an exact and satiric knowledge of German culture; and Mr. Lessner, though a novice in writing English, can turn out a McCormick editorial, a Tass dispatch or a Churchill speech with every accuracy. But surely we can't be such complete idiots again—or can we? (AB)

Stefan Heym, OF SMILING PEACE (Little Brown, $2.50).

It was inevitable that the assassination of Admiral Darlan, the most melodramatic episode of the war, should inspire a novel; it was by no means inevitable that the novel should be as good as this one is. On one level OF SMILING PEACE is an action melodrama of the North African invasion, with plot and counterplot of American officers, Axis agents and cynically independent French operatives, culminating in the murder of "Colonel Monaitre." On a deeper level it is an admirably written study in human motives, rich and varied in its characterizations. While the excitement of the plot will take you through the book in no time, the people of that plot will long remain with you as individuals and as symbols and you'll end up with a better understanding of your enemies—and perhaps of yourself. (AB)

Lawrence Lariar (editor), BEST CARTOONS OF THE YEAR, 1944 (Crown, $2).

That's a brave title for a book that omits [Charles] Addams, [Peter] Arno, [George] Price, [Saul] Steinberg, [James] Thurber and all the other great individualists save Virgil Partch (who is represented not only in person but by that admirable ersatz-Partch, Leo Salkin). But if you look at it as BEST CONVENTIONAL CARTOONS OF 1944 it's a swell collection, full of quiet chuckles and an occasional helpless belly laugh. It is adorned with resolutely funny autobiographical notes by the artists. (APW)

Fremont Rider, THE SCHOLAR AND THE FUTURE OF THE RE-SEARCH LIBRARY: A PROBLEM AND ITS SOLUTION (Hadham Press, $4).

Under this awkward title the librarian of Wesleyan University advances a startling thesis: that entire books can be reproduced by microphotography on the backs of their catalogue cards, turning a card index into a complete library in itself. An admirably argued book—essential reading for any librarian or scholar. (APW)

October 22, 1944

Robert P. Tristram Coffin, MAINSTAYS OF MAINE (Macmillan, $2).

Mr. Coffin is a poet, a fact which he never lets you forget. He is also a careless author who tosses magazine essays into book form without checking their too frequent repetitions. But above all he is a man who loves eating and who loves Maine and who has fused his two loves into one of the most mouth-watering of books. Food, recipes (of a sort), sketches of the unnumbered Coffin family, food, descriptions of Maine scenery and character and more food, all recounted in vigorous Maine speech, make up a book that has settled my post-war planning: this reviewer is going to Maine for a year and eat. (APW)

Lawrence Lipton, IN SECRET BATTLE
(Appleton-Century, $2.75).

After Pearl Harbor we were apt to take for granted that American fascist activities could not survive our defensive entry into the war. We know better now, or should know better, and Mr. Lipton's novel is the latest effort to house our awareness of how fascist agents with or without Axis ties can turn the war effort itself to their advantage. A documented melodrama of the sabotage of what can still be the Century of the Common Man, IN SECRET BATTLE is an angry, humorless, crusading novel which would be even more valuable as propaganda if it were not inhabited by black and white stereotypes who make speeches. (APW)

Susanne Suba, SPOTS BY SUBA FROM THE NEW YORKER (Dutton, $1).

You know those graceful, perceptive little drawings of metropolitan life that appear occasionally in *The New Yorker*? You look a second time to see what the gag is and then you realize there isn't any gag—just a pleasing slice of truthful observation. Those "spots" are largely by Susanne Suba, and here she's gathered fifty of the best into a minute and charming book. Perfect for Christmas if you're thinking that far ahead. Perfect any time in fact. (APW)

October 29, 1944

William Gilmore Beymer, 12:20 P.M.
(Whittlesey House, $2.50).

At 12:20 P.M. myriads of people in each time-zone of the earth prayed for the death of Hitler; when the superstitious Fuhrer learned of this plan, the nervous shock slowly killed him. This notion, ingenious enough for a short story or a novelet, is here padded out to book length with such loose-knit irrelevancies as a Sioux uprising, espionage in Lisbon, and a long-drawn-out narrative of the German high command, all related in a prose which has been matched this season only by [Ruth Adams Knight and Jean Hersholt's] DR. CHRISTIAN'S OFFICE. You may like this opus if you too believe that the anguish of the earth was "all brought upon us by the bloody hands and black mind of one man" and if you relish a Sunday-supplement inside picture of Germany based on such new first-hand details as Goebbels limps, [Nazi labor czar Robert] Ley drinks and Von Ribben-trop was once a champagne salesman. Or you may find the book's over-simplification, which reduces a world revolution to the level of palace in-trigue and manages to waste 270 pages about Hitler without once mention-ing Fascism, not only silly but dangerous. (AB)

November 5, 1944

Allan Chase, THE FIVE ARROWS (Random House, $2.50).

Mr. Chase, author of FALANGE, has a great deal of significant material about Fascist infiltration in Latin America, and it's important that the North American audience should listen to him. But here he simply hasn't turned that material into a very good novel.

This story of how a free-lance newspaperman keeps the Falange from taking over the liberal republic of San Hermano is too heavy-handed for a spy story and often too melodramatic for a straight novel. It is written in a faithful pseudo-Hemingway style, fortunately without Hemingway's mock-Spanish but unfortunately without the complexities of his characters.

Mr. Chase writes about a nice simple world where all school teachers and union members are staunch democrats and all land owners and Catho-lics are Fascist dogs. Despite stirring scenes, the book is long and badly constructed; and the fictional setting leaves the reader uncertain as to how much of the author's documentation stems from research and how much from exigencies of plot. Mr. Chase's thesis is that Fascists are Fascists even when nominally neutral and blessed by our State Department. This cannot be said too often but it might be said better. (AB)

Clark Ashton Smith, LOST WORLDS (Arkham House, $3).

The second collected volume of a writer's stories is apt to consist of those tales advisedly omitted from the first volume, and LOST WORLDS is no match for Mr. Smith's previous OUT OF SPACE AND TIME. But there are a few first rate fantasies among these 23 stories, and even the more routine ones are enjoyably typical of the California pulp master whose legends deserve, perhaps even more than those of [Edgar Allan] Poe, the label of "Tales of the Grotesque and Arabesque." (AB)

Manya Gordon, HOW TO TELL PROGRESS FROM REACTION: ROADS TO INDUSTRIAL DEMOCRACY (Dutton, $3).

What is industrial democracy and how is it to be obtained and secured? To answer these questions the author takes Mr. Hopewell, an idealistic socialist, on a survey through time and space covering first the utopian commonwealths of past fiction and fact and then the leading democratic nations of today, studying in statistical detail the United States, Sweden, Great Britain and Russia and analyzing their achievements in such matters as wages, housing, education and trade union power. She argues in favor of public ownership (TVA or BBC) rather than government ownership and concludes, in the words of Lenin, that [since] "without political freedom all forms of workers' representation will continue to be a fraud," among the inherent rights of labor must be the right to strike even against the government employer. Despite the catchpenny title this is a serious exposition of views on the anti-Communist left, written with scholarship and admirable clarity. (APW)

William A. Lydgate, WHAT AMERICA THINKS
(Crowell, $2.50).

Editor of the American Institute of Public Opinion and assistant to [the pioneer pollster] Dr. [George] Gallup, Mr. Lydgate unconsciously demonstrates that polls prove what you want them to. A poll shows that Americans have some strange notions about diet; Americans must be educated. A poll shows that Americans have some strange notions about labor unions; the unions must mend their ways. In this survey of American thought you will look in vain for any references to religion, racial prejudice, the arts (even the liveliest), sports or the stock market; but in the limited fields covered you'll find many suggestive statistics—if you can disentangle them from the author's semantic slanting, his occasional misstatement of facts and his pose of impartiality so reminiscent of the *Reader's Digest*. (APW)

Frank J. Klingberg & Sigurd B. Hustvedt (editors), THE WARNING DRUM: THE BRITISH HOME FRONT FACES NAPOLEON: BROAD-SIDES OF 1803 (University of California Press, $4).

This choice collection of prose and verse from the days when every petty pamphleteer spoke with the tongue of a [Winston] Churchill and *Gallia delenda erat* [Latin for "France must be destroyed"] makes one mourn the passing of the broadside as a highly versatile and effective propaganda medium. As one has come to expect from the U.C. Press, the editing is intelligent, the scholarly apparatus complete and the typography a delight, providing a richly suggestive volume for connoisseurs of literary or historical oddments. (APW)

C.H.B. Wilkinson (editor), MORE DIVERSIONS (Oxford University Press, $1.75).

For a place of honor on the night table or in the coat pocket (which it conveniently fits) you can hardly do better than this collection of bits and pieces, prose and verse, satire, inspiration and the macabre—in all, like nothing so much as browsing in the well-stocked library of a scholar of catholic and curious tastes, where recognition and discovery are equal delights. (APW)

November 19, 1944

August Derleth (editor), SLEEP NO MORE: TWENTY MASTERPIECES OF HORROR FOR THE CONNOISSEUR (illustrated by Lee Brown Coye) (Farrar & Rinehart, $2.50); H.F. Heard, THE GREAT FOG AND OTHER WEIRD TALES (Vanguard Press, $2.50); Henry S. Whitehead, JUMBEE AND OTHER UNCANNY TALES (Arkham House, $3).

Here indeed is a fine feast for fanciers of fantastic figments. Of the 41 stories in these three volumes, only ten have appeared before in book form; here are new worlds for your perverse palates and terrorized tastes.

August Derleth, novelist, poet, pulp-writer and publisher, knows supernatural fiction as well as Ellery Queen [Frederic Dannay] knows detective stories. He knows too that anthologies are read by anthology readers and has wisely designed a post-graduate course of reading—taking for granted that you know the established classics and introducing you instead to such forgotten masterpieces as M.P. Shiel's magnificent "The House of Sounds," never before published in this country, or Alfred Noyes' haunting

"Midnight Express," plus a thorough representation of the great *Weird Tales* school founded by H.P. Lovecraft.

One may quarrel on such minor points as that Lee Brown Coye's sketches, gruesomely effective though they are, have a way of betraying too much of the stories, or that it is a pity to represent the vigorously original Robert Bloch by a mere imitation of Lovecraft; but for any reader sick of sameness, this is the most welcome collection of chills since Dashiell Hammett's CREEPS BY NIGHT.

The Derleth collection is deliberately limited to the grisly (two later volumes are to cover other fields of fantasy). If you want more varied matter, and if you want to get in on the ground floor ahead of the anthologists, try THE GREAT FOG. Mr. Heard, philosopher, metaphysician and mystery novelist, has here assembled a little of everything, from a straight detective story (and a clever one) to cataclysmic science fiction.

Yet the book has a unity in its clean good writing (save for once when Mr. Heard pitifully attempts to write in American) and its presentation of an unusual mind—an off-the-track creative talent that deserves to rank beside such purveyors of fine caviar as [M.P.] Shiel or John Collier (great sturgeons all). It's hard to pick favorites from such an entrancing book but I finished "Dromenon," the extraordinary story of an English Gothic cathedral and the rhythm of the universe, with the firm conviction that I had just read an all-time classic which future anthologists will try their best to make hackneyed.

Among the many authors anthologized for the first time in the Derleth volume is Henry S. Whitehead, an Episcopalian clergyman long stationed in the Virgin Islands who was one of the star writers for *Weird Tales* in the decade preceding his death in 1932. His work, now collected by Arkham House in the volume JUMBEE, seems far more impressive as a corpus than it ever did as individual stories. One by one, many of Whitehead's stories appear plotless and fragmentary, or grotesque almost to comedy. Taken together they form a fascinating and nightmarish record of the former Danish West Indies, with their formalized polyglot society existing artificially over a dark substratum of African survivals. Rev. Mr. Whitehead's prosaic, factual narration carries an eery conviction; he has created (or simply reported) a strange domain which you will not forget.

They tell me there was a rainy spell here recently. I wouldn't know; I was reviewing these three books. (Boucher)

Chris Massie, THE LOVE LETTERS
(Random House, $2.50).

When Maurice Quinton served in France in 1917, he dictated the love letters of a less articulate friend. When he returned to England, minus two fingers of his body and most of his soul, his thoughts kept reverting to this girl, now a widow, whom he had come to know so well through her letters. By chance he found her—an amnesiac, a convicted murderess and something of an idiot—or a saint. The attempt of these two shattered souls to bring each other to wholeness is a touching idyll of unreality—a fantasy of unearthly peace written with quiet convincing realism. You may never quite believe in the girl Singleton (a singular female version of the Fool of God), but you will not forget her and you would like a world in which you might believe. (AB)

Jules Romains, THE DEATH OF A NOBODY (translated by Desmond MacCarthy & Sidney Waterlow) (Knopf, $2).

This attractive reissue of the 1941 novelette has a new preface by the author (translated by Haakon Chevalier) clarifying its important position in his work and its relation to his doctrine of unanimism and to the cycle of MEN OF GOOD WILL. Readers of the cycle will welcome this early experiment and greet with mixed reactions the news that Romains expects to conclude in 1944 the twenty-seventh and final volume of his epic. (AB)

Oscar Ray, BORROWED NIGHT (Doubleday, $2.50).

Anton Conrad was an Alsatian, forced into the German army, who finally resolved in the siege of Leningrad to break loose and fight for freedom. He faked traumatic neurosis to escape the front, and a complex series of adventures, maneuvered by a friend in the underground, brought him at last to Africa. The adventures are familiar; we have read by now quite enough novels about crossing the border from Occupied and Unoccupied France. But the earlier episode of the fake neurosis which occupies two-thirds of the book is something new; here we have a long and detailed treatise on malingering, its methods and motivations, as exemplified by a dozen inmates of a base hospital. It's a unique subject, at once fascinating and repellent, here treated with a kind of mordant morbidity that should hold you spellbound—especially in the unusually readable translation of Joseph Szebenyei and Mary Finley. (AB)

November 26, 1944

Adeline Rumsey, CRYING AT THE LOCK
(Simon & Schuster, $2.50).

This reviewer did not read Miss Rumsey's first novel, WHEN THE BOUGH BREAKS, a Book League selection in 1940, but he is eager to do so at the first opportunity. And when a book reviewer is eager to read a novel non-professionally, that's news; it means that he's run up against an author who can, in the absolute, write.

Its plot might classify CRYING AT THE LOCK as a border-line murder novel. The outline is similar to that of [Daphne DuMaurier's] REBECCA: second wife probes into mystery behind suicide (or murder?) of first wife and gradually uncovers details of psychological tragedy. But the style and treatment have nothing in common with the slick romanticism of a Du-Maurier or even the ironic melodrama of a Francis Iles.

"Perceptive" is the word that most reviewers used for Miss Rumsey's first, and it can't be bettered for the second. Add wit, acerbity, understanding, an excellently undogmatic use of Freudian analysis and a talent for cruel dissection to be matched only in [Anne] Parrish and [John P.] Marquand at their best. For the seeking (and self-seeking) second wife here is no [Charlotte] Bronte derivative but as horrible a portrait of an efficient and capable homemaker as has been painted since [George Kelly's play] CRAIG'S WIFE.

This is a first rate job. Whether you want suspense, psychological characterization or simply good intelligent reading, don't miss it. (AB)

Elbert D. Thomas, THE FOUR FEARS (Ziff-Davis, $2).

Four great national phobias, stumbling blocks on our road to the future, are the fear of idealism, the fear of entangling alliances, the fear of England and Russia, and the fear of revolution. Senator Thomas examines the background of each fear and tries to dispel the ignorance and prejudice which have fostered it and goes on to a clear and scholarly discussion of the coming peace, which "must be based on a generous resolution to share America's social, political and economic security with the world." Only the most extreme sufferers from the first fear can fail to admire the senator from Utah as a model of the liberal statesman and to rejoice alike in his recent re-election and in this cogent presentation of the ends and means of good will. (APW)

Hoff, FEELING NO PAIN: AN ALBUM OF CARTOONS (Dial Press, $2.50).

Hoff is to cartooning what Arthur Kober is to prose humor—the bard of the Bronx, whose tender treatment of tenement turmoils is as realistic and funny as it often is unexpectedly touching. It was high time he had a book to himself, and despite the poor printing which speckles all black areas with tiny white dots, this collection of 180 Hoffs marks a high spot even in this golden age of cartoon humor. (APW)

December 3, 1944

Jennings Perry, DEMOCRACY BEGINS AT HOME:
THE TENNESSEE FIGHT ON THE POLL TAX
(with cartoons by Tom Little) (Lippincott, $3).

If you think the poll tax fight is basically a matter of white supremacy, if you think there's something to be said for a measure which keeps the riff-raff from the polls, if you believe the federal government has no business meddling in such private state affairs, above all if you feel that the whole battle is a Southern problem which doesn't affect you as a Californian, you will find this book an eye-opener.

Primarily Jennings Perry's book is the story of his crusade as editor of the Nashville *Tennesseean* to attain repeal of the state poll tax and thereby to crush the almost unbelievably omnipotent Crump machine. His victory in that crusade is one of the most stirring achievements of modern newspaper history, and there is no more bitter anticlimax than the novel and amazing decision of the state supreme court which frustrated that victory.

Indirectly the book is a general history of the poll tax, from which you will learn that it oppresses the white far more even than the Negro, that it facilitates the political activity of the riffraff, that there are excellent constitutional grounds (Article IV, Section 4) for federal intervention, and that you as a Californian are directly affected by the representatives whose endless minority-given tenure places them in the posts of seniority.

But even Mr. Perry, who marshals every other argument of constitutionality, logic and humanity, joins the conspiracy of silence concerning the second section of the Fourteenth Amendment. That section speaks for itself; read it and determine its relevancy to the question of the poll tax and federal intervention.

"....when the right to vote at any election for the choice of Electors for President and Vice President of the United States, Representatives in Congress, the executive or judicial officers of a State, or the members of the Legislature thereof, is denied to any of the male inhabitants of such State, being 21 years of age, and citizens of the United States, or in any way abridged, except for participation in rebellion, or other crime, the basis of representation therein shall be reduced in the proportion which the number of such male citizens shall bear to the whole number of male citizens 21 years of age in such State."

That's what it says. Read it over again. Notice especially "....or in any way abridged...." and "....shall be reduced...." Not may be. Shall. Think about it. Remember that one Illinois congressman receives more votes than fifty poll-tax congressmen. And wonder how loudmouths can fret over "constitutionality" when the Constitution itself remains unenforced.

Take it from there, Mr. Perry. It's another crusade—and you're just the guy to tackle it. (White)

December 10, 1944

Ronald A. Knox, THE NEW TESTAMENT OF OUR LORD AND SAV-
IOR JESUS CHRIST: NEWLY TRANSLATED FROM THE VULGATE
LATIN AT THE REQUEST OF THEIR LORDSHIPS, THE
ARCHBISHOPS OF ENGLAND AND WALES (Sheed & Ward, $3).

New translations of the Bible and particularly of the New Testament are healthy and necessary if the Book is to remain anything more than a grand antique poem. To read a new translation is to see as if for the first time the clear meaning of passages dulled by familiarity.

The recent New Testament authorized by the American Catholic bishops was only a revision, though an exceedingly helpful one, of Bishop Challoner's (1750), which in turn was based on the Rheims version of 1582. Father Knox's, like [Edgar S.] Goodspeed's, is a complete retranslation, founded for liturgical reasons upon the Vulgate of St. Jerome but making thorough use as well of the Greek manuscripts.

Monsignor Knox has hitherto been known in America chiefly for his excellent detective stories (for which he was once roundly denounced by that eccentric Jesuit, Montague Summers) and for his ESSAYS IN SATIRE, in which he laid the cornerstone of all later studies of Sherlock Holmes. He is a man of letters in the finest and broadest sense, uniquely able to render his classical scholarship into pellucid English prose.

In his hands the biblical episodes leap to new life. The familiar "I perceive that God is no respecter of persons" becomes "I see clearly enough that God makes no distinction between man and man"; and thereby the whole story of Cornelius (Acts, 10) takes on a living and timeless meaning.

Perhaps the virtues and the flaws of the new translation may be best illustrated by that great passage in Corinthians which reads in the King James version: "For now we see through a glass, darkly; but then face to face; now I know in part; but then shall I know even as also I am known."

The Knox version reads: "At present, we are looking at a confused reflection in a mirror; then we shall see face to face; now, I have only glimpses of knowledge; then, I shall recognize God as he has recognized me."

The conservative Bible reader will justly protest a loss of poetic quality but he must admit an equal gain in clarity and communication. It is so throughout: the "great lines," the poetic setpieces seem paler in Knox, but the intellectual portions—Christ debating with the Pharisees, Saint Paul discussing the problems of the early Church—are suddenly sharp and understandable. And it is possible, at that, that Father Knox's prose (which can hardly be matched in our time) seems poetically inferior only because it is of our own century. We are much more easily impressed by what is remote and not quite clear.

The Knox Testament is essential to all Catholics. It is recommended (particularly for its fine textual notes) to all Christians and students of Christianity. And it may in its simplicity appeal to many who have found the Bible hard to read. There is not one "amen, amen" nor a single "begat." (Boucher)

Thomas Kernan, NOW WITH THE MORNING STAR (Scribner, $2.50).

It was easy for the Nazis to evict the Cistercian monks from their valuable properties on framed immorality charges. It was not so easy for men accustomed to the strict Cistercian rule of silence, prayer and labor to adjust themselves to a Nazified Germany. This is the story of Andreas Hoffman, once Brother Nicholas, of his vain efforts to fit into the new world, of his service in the anti-Nazi Catholic Underground, and of how he found in a prison labor camp his place in the divine plan.

Mr. Kernan, author of FRANCE ON BERLIN TIME, wrote this, his first novel, while himself interned in a German concentration camp. He has a keen understanding of Germans and of Catholics and he can write. The result may seem a minor book among so many documents of horror but in its quiet simplicity, its gentle urge toward eternity, it holds, like Brother Nicholas in his labor camp, a fraction of truth safe against these times. (AB)

December 17, 1944

Fannie E. Ratchford (editor), LETTERS OF THOMAS J. WISE TO JOHN HENRY WRENN: A FURTHER INQUIRY INTO THE GUILT OF CERTAIN NINETEENTH-CENTURY FORGERIES (Knopf, $7.50).

Thomas J. Wise was a self-made scholar. From a poorly educated boy with a passion for rare books he built himself into one of England's foremost bibliographers and amassed the great Ashley Library, now owned by the British nation. He was an eminent Elder Bookman, dogmatic and respected, when in 1934 John Carter and Graham Pollard published their INQUIRY INTO THE NATURE OF CERTAIN NINETEENTH CENTURY PAMPHLETS.

One of the most exciting pieces of scholarly detection on record (a feat fully worthy of Elizabeth Daly's Henry Gamadge), the ENQUIRY proved conclusively, by the most detailed tests of text, paper and type, that some fifty fabulously rare "first editions" of Tennyson, Ruskin, the Brownings and others were forgeries—not even fakes of actual books but pure fabrications of editions that never existed.

Mr. Wise being still alive, the Enquirers restricted themselves to pointing out that almost all of these pamphlets came directly or indirectly through his hands and that the tales of their origins rested on his bibliographical authority. After Wise's death, Wilfred Partington was able, in FORGING AHEAD (1939), to detail the incredible Wise story—an epic of audacity unmatched in the combined histories of crime and scholarship.

One of Wise's chief clients was the wealthy John Henry Wrenn of Chicago, whose collection, almost equal to the Ashley, went to the University of Texas in 1918. With it went Wise's correspondence. The characteristic Wise sagacity forbade publication, but now at last Miss Ratchford, Rare Books Librarian of Texas, is able to present these fascinating documents.

The interest is two-fold: They contain much first-rate chat about book-collecting and many significant bibliographical observations, and they display admirably Wise's brilliant technique in luring the American into purchase of his fraudulent rarities.

Miss Ratchford's hundred-page introduction provides not only a good summary of the correspondence but some startling observations of her own on the forgeries. She presents evidence, some of it seemingly ineluctable, to prove that Wise was not alone in his fraud but consciously aided by several others including even the great Sir Edmund Gosse.

One may object that so large a conspiracy reduces Wise's profits too much and may ask what conceivable motive Gosse can have had to risk his reputation for a small cut. Miss Ratchford does not speculate about motives; she gives you the evidence and it, like the letters themselves, is indispensable to any further consideration of the past century's most absorbing book scandal.

The volume, a sumptuous specimen of Knopf bookmaking, contains twenty plates of photographs and photostats and a 16-page index. (Boucher)

James van der Veldt, O.F.M., THE CITY SET ON A HILL: THE STORY OF THE VATICAN (Dodd Mead, $2.50).

Through the eyes of the adolescent American son of an ambassador confined to Vatican City for the duration, Father van der Veldt paints a detailed picture of the arts, crafts, history and organization of the Vatican. Unfortunately it is through the eye only; there is not a word on music. The result is an authoritative and sumptuous picture, fascinating to Catholic and non-Catholic alike and marred only by the fact that the author never seems certain whether he is addressing a juvenile or an adult audience. (APW)

Mickey MacDougall, MacDOUGALL ON DICE AND CARDS (Coward-McCann, $1).

Hoyle was fine in 1744 but even the most modern editions of his classic are dated in their wording and slipshod in their odds. Here is the new definitive treatise on craps, poker, gin rummy and blackjack, written by an expert (remember his autobiography of a card-detective, DANGER ON THE CARDS?). From now on the phrase should read "according to Mac-Dougall." Note: That man in the service could use one of these books. (AB)

December 24, 1944

Archibald MacLeish, THE AMERICAN STORY: TEN BROADCASTS (Duell, Sloan & Pearce, $2).

This series of broadcasts, created by Mr. MacLeish and his associate Muna Lee for the NBC University of the Air, reveals not only poetic talent and creative radio technique, which one might expect, but a singular breadth and depth of understanding of America the hemisphere, the New Found Land. Based largely on the direct texts of the discoverers and explorers themselves, the broadcasts treat the history of North and South America as a unity and show the American story to be one not merely of a new land but of a new way of life. If American history can now be taught with such freshness, brevity and clarity, I envy my children. (APW)

December 31, 1944

Eric Linklater, THE WIND ON THE MOON (illustrated by Nicolas Bentley) (Macmillan, $2.75).

Dinah and Dorinda meant well but they knew that the better you mean the more apt the grownups are to think that you've been very naughty. So, since the wind on the moon meant that they were to be naughty for a year, they worked at becoming really and perfectly naughty and ended by rescuing their father, who was a Major, from a prison in Bombardy, because they had a good deal of experience in escaping acquired when they were kangaroos in Sir Lankaster Lemon's zoo. This is a summary of only the more reasonable aspects of Mr. Linklater's fantasy, obviously conceived during a severe case of moonstroke and related with the casual plausibility and realistic detail of a first-rate juvenile. Earnest readers are hereby warned off, but admirers of T.H. White and Eleanor Farjeon may revel in something that is not quite a satire, not quite a children's story and not quite anything in fact but pure absurd fun. Nicolas Bentley's pictures add a quarter to the price and are well worth it. (AB)

John Becker, THE NEGRO IN AMERICAN LIFE
(with a preface by Lillian Smith) (Messner, $1).

Not so much a book as a visual education exhibit, this large pamphlet sponsored by the Council Against Racial Intolerance in America vividly portrays the record of the Negro in our arts, sciences, sports and history. It's a fine job but I'd hate to prophesy its success. Christ opened the eyes of the blind but even he got nowhere with those who will not see. (APW)

January 7, 1945

J. B. Trend, THE CIVILIZATION OF SPAIN
(Oxford University Press, $1.25).

This latest volume in Oxford's Home University Library of Modern Knowledge is a succinct compendium of Spanish culture, history and politics. Mr. Trend's grace makes it enjoyable reading and his clarity and understanding make it an invaluable brief background for anyone who wants to comprehend the problematic Spain of today. (APW)

Helen Stevens Fisher (editor), RIDDLE-DE-QUIZ (Mill, $2).

Riddle: Why is this collection of pun-puzzles like a beautiful morning? Answer: Because the corn is as high as a elephant's eye. (APW)

January 14, 1945

Gerald Moore, THE UNASHAMED ACCOMPANIST (Macmillan, $2.50).

Mr. Moore's book is at once a defense of the often scorned art in which he is preeminent and a pamphlet urging young pianists to train themselves specifically for accompanying rather than falling back on it after failing as soloists. The volume is not only persuasive and instructive; it is also delightfully written, with a lucid charm that makes it a joy even to the layman, who will look forward hopefully to more detailed reminiscences from the long-suffering Mr. Moore. (APW)

January 21, 1945

Franz Werfel, BETWEEN HEAVEN AND EARTH (translated by Maxim
Newmark) (Philosophical Library, $3).

Many have wondered how a Jew who can write about Christianity with
the understanding and sympathy of Franz Werfel chooses to remain outside the church which he admires and even apparently agrees with. Mr.
Werfel gives his answer here in the essay "On Christ and Israel," and it is a
strange one indeed. "Even for a Jew who considers Jesus Christ to be...the
Son of God, baptism and conversion are inadequate....The Jew is not 'cur-
able' through baptism and faith alone....The Jew who goes to the baptismal
font deserts Christ himself, since he arbitrarily interrupts his historical suffering....Israel is...an order into which, according to the decree of God, one
enters by birth, never to be released until the last day but one."

There is poetic drama and a sort of stiffnecked nobility in this attitude.
But while theologians may dismiss it as eccentric nonsense, the Christian
layman cannot help hearing in Mr. Werfel's words a pernicious echo of
anti-Semitic screeds. If the Jews are still to be considered, even aside from
their historic role in the drama of revelation and redemption, a people set
apart, "as tragically barred by the profundity of the facts from being Christian as from being German or Russian," then the premises of a [Nazi
propagandist] Julius Streicher or a W.J. Cameron become irrefutable—
which, in the words of mathematics, is absurd.

This essay, though the most provocative section, is only 20 pages of Mr.
Werfel's new book. The rest consists of three lectures (1930-1937) and
assorted epigrams, meditations and short essays (1942-1944). These reveal
their author as a deeply religious man, bitterly shocked by "the cold banality of materialism," who possesses a fine gift for quasi-mystical gnomic
utterances and a somewhat irritating false logic in developing them. As a
purely devotional writer Mr. Werfel could be admirable; as an apologist he
is so vexatiously loose in the use of such terms as "the facts" and "indisputable proof" that he tempts the most devout to take up cudgels for materialism.

The unpublished original text probably had most of the faults of German
metaphysical prose, but one suspects the translator of adding a few of his
own. (White)

January 28, 1945

Marjorie Fischer & Rolfe Humphries (editors), PAUSE TO WONDER:
STORIES OF THE MARVELOUS AND STRANGE (Messner, $3).

If you feel with such authorities as Montague Summers and August Derleth that fantasy should be essentially grim and terrible, unsullied by humor or playfulness, this book is not for you. But if you liked Philip Van Doren Stern's blithe MIDNIGHT TRAVELER better than his ghastly MIDNIGHT READER, if among pulps you choose *Unknown Worlds* rather than *Weird Tales*, if in short you prefer fantasy to leave you aglow rather than aghast at the unforeseen possibilities of the universe, this is possibly the best anthology ever published for you.

A juvenile writer and a poet make a fine team for choosing fancies, and they have culled them from the least exhausted or even expected sources: the poems of Robert Frost, the newspaper writings of John Steinbeck and Finley Peter Dunne, the lives of the saints, and even such serious major figures as D.H. Lawrence and Virginia Woolf. Add to these unhackneyed specimens from such masters of fantasy as E.M. Forster, Max Beerbohm and Saki, sprinkle in a few freshly discovered masterpieces like Donald Cowle's "Lord Deliver Us," insert the entire text of David Garnett's short novel LADY INTO FOX, and you have six hundred pages of the freshest delight. (AB)

February 4, 1945

William Laurence Sullivan, UNDER ORDERS: THE AUTOBIOGRA-PHY OF WILLIAM LAURENCE SULLIVAN (Richard H. Smith, $2.50).

Dr. Sullivan was a Paulist who left the Catholic church and became one of the greatest of Unitarian preachers. The intellectual and spiritual reasons for this change are lucidly and movingly expounded in this autobiography, which is posthumous and incomplete but intelligently filled out by the anonymous editor. Dr. Sullivan's praise of the church which he left will confound the typical anti-Catholic, while his documented attacks on certain doctrines may perplex Catholic apologists; both however must admire him as a single-minded seeker after God. (APW)

Florence Ryerson & Colin Clements, SPRING GREEN: A COMEDY IN THREE ACTS (Samuel French, $1.50).

The authors of HARRIET add another to the endless current cycle of plays about adolescents, which differs markedly from the rest in that it is unimpeachably clean. It's light and lively, and the boy with a scientific passion for earthworms stands out as an ingratiatingly real character among a group of stock types—even down to the testy grandfather in the wheelchair. (APW)

Louis K. Anspacher, SHAKESPEARE AS POET AND LOVER AND
THE ENIGMA OF THE SONNETS
(Island Press, $1).

His careful researches have enabled Mr. Anspacher to announce that the
Dark Lady of the sonnets was Mary Fitton, that Mr. W.H. was William
Herbert, Earl of Pembroke, and that poetry differs markedly from prose.
Only an occasional deliberate misquotation could deter the sternest profes-
sor of freshman English from giving this paper an A plus. (APW)

Eugene Vale, THE TECHNIQUE OF SCREENPLAY WRITING: A
BOOK ABOUT THE DRAMATIC STRUCTURE OF MOTION PIC-
TURES (with a foreword by Marc Connelly) (Crown, $3.50).

Practiced European writer-director-producer here boils down the fruits
of his experience into a compote of truths and truisms. He is more concerned with the underlying theories (couched in a rather individual jargon)
of dramatic structure than with the routine mechanics. The book will
hardly enable you to produce a good script but it may help to show you
why a bad one is bad. (APW)

February 11, 1945

Judith Cape, THE SUN AND THE MOON
(Creative Age Press, $2.50).

Kristin was born during an eclipse of the moon and possessed a mystic
power to become one with inanimate objects. When she fell in love with a
painter, she knew that her power meant the danger of absorbing into herself her lover's personality and even his art. This study in psychic vampir-
ism has interesting possibilities but Miss Cape's prosaic writing lacks the
means to realize them. (AB)

February 18, 1945

Jack Karney, THERE GOES SHORTY HIGGINS
(Morrow, $2.50).

A reason sometimes advanced for reading mystery novels is that so little
other fiction is at once lightweight and literate. There's a gap between the
serious novel and pure trash, and that gap is what THERE GOES
SHORTY HIGGINS fits very neatly. It's a novel about the boxing game,
and there isn't a character or a situation that you haven't encountered before in [Clifford Odets' play] GOLDEN BOY or [Francis Wallace's novel]

KID GALAHAD or even (back in the days when the strip was about boxing) in *Joe Palooka*. But Jack Karney has the pure story-teller's gift; he writes hard and fast and you can't stop reading. The result is something like a first-rate detective story of the hard-boiled school without a detective, and for sheer readability it's hard to beat. (AB)

Marcelle Dorval (editor), LE COEUR SUR LA MAIN/THE HEART ON
THE SLEEVE: FRENCH AND AMERICAN IDIOMATIC SELEC-
TIONS (with illustrations by Jean Carlu and an introduction by Janet Flan-
ner)
(Brentano's, $2).

One of the joys of the 1943 season, this collection of the parallel picturesqueness of two languages is now reissued in a less expensive and hence even more welcome edition. As useful as it is delightful, it's a grand book. It is foot-breaking; *c'est un miel*. (APW)

February 25, 1945

Egon Hostovsky, THE HIDEOUT (translated by Fern Long) (Random
House, $1.75).

A nonpolitical Czech engineer, wanted by the Nazis for his invention of an anti-aircraft sight, is caught in France by the German invasion. He hides out in a cellar for months of darkness and animal inaction, from which he emerges to join the underground in an almost certainly fatal mission. Here's the plot of routine pursuit-melodrama or at most, you'd say, of the Graham Greene-Geoffrey Household kind of heightened drama, but the subtle and sensitive Hostovsky converts it into a novelette of curious spiritual conflicts which may remind you of Kafka or perhaps of Odon von Horvath. "The fourth age is coming," the engineer read in Dostoevsky; "something is going to happen which no one is expecting." And he dreamed of the indescribable thing whose name is Karutmon. You may dream too after this short book, so lucidly translated, and it will be a strange dream in which this war that absorbs us shrinks to a petty pang beside the agony of a world in labor with a new age. (AB)

Oscar Hammerstein II, CARMEN JONES (based on Meilhac and Halevy's
adaptation of Prosper Merimee's CARMEN) (Knopf, $2.50).

All the review this book needs is the mere announcement of its existence. If you're remotely interested in the theater or music, you already know that Mr. Hammerstein's adaptation of the CARMEN libretto is the most significant event to date in the erratic history of opera in English.

Here's the complete text, with photographs of the production and an important introductory essay on the problems involved. With this and the fine Decca album of the music you can keep yourself fairly content until CARMEN JONES hits the Coast—and incidentally you can realize that Mr. Hammerstein is an even better librettist than Meilhac and Halevy and wonder why he has never been commissioned for serious operatic work. (APW)

March 4, 1945

Louis Bachner, DYNAMIC SINGING: A NEW APPROACH TO FREE VOICE PRODUCTION (with an introduction by Marjorie Lawrence) (L.B. Fischer, $2.75).

The great German-American singing teacher whose pupils include [the then famous opera singers Sigurd] Onegin, [Heinrich] Schlusnus, [Frida] Leider, [Karin] Branzell and [Michael] Bohnen chops away a lot of the dead wood of vocalistic double-talk and insists primarily on a free voice production to be attained through correct posture and breathing. Unfortunately his highly sensible ideas, which would have made an excellent 10,000-word essay, are padded into a shapeless, repetitious book in which only the most ardent student will have the patience to grub. May we hope for a ghost-written second edition? (APW)

March 11, 1945

Elizabeth S. Kingsley, INVITATION TO DOUBLE-CROSTICS (Simon & Schuster, $1.50).

Mrs. Kingsley, puzzle-maker extraordinary to the intellectuals of America, here desists from skull-breakers to produce fifty simpler double-crostics for the novice. Like the composer who abandons his series of masses and fugues and opts to turn out a few divertimenti, she retains all her masterly skill and finesse. INVITATION should make unnumbered converts to this most literate of puzzles, and even old hands will not find it beneath their notice. (AB)

Alfred Einstein, MOZART: HIS CHARACTER, HIS WORK (translated by Arthur Mendel & Nathan Broder) (Oxford University Press, $5).

This is not an introduction to Mozart; Mr. Einstein presupposes a reasonable knowledge of the musical works and of a standard biography. But even for the Mozartian devotee he adds the difficulty of a curious formal structure. He first takes up each aspect of Mozart's character (lover, Free-mason, patriot, etc.) and examines it from the womb to the tomb, and then analyzes each separate musical sub-classification of his work again from the sperm to the worm, so that the reader has, before he finishes the book, traversed the years 1756 to 1791 over twenty times. A chronological chart to coordinate the several chapters might help in a future edition.

Despite these structural strictures the book is to be recommended for a great deal of stimulating and perceptive comment on the music, both in itself and in its relation to its times. A rich and rewarding causerie rather than an academic study, it is equipped with an index (of names only), a complete list of Koechel numbers, and the extant Mozart portraits. (APW)

March 18, 1945

William Carlos Williams, THE WEDGE
(Cummington Press, $3.50).

In this volume Dr. Williams addresses himself chiefly to such permanent themes of poetry as love and death and nature, and does so with the simplicity, directness and precision which he demands in "Writer's Prologue to a Play in Verse":

> "But believe that poetry will be
> in the terms you know, insist on that,
> and can and must break through everything,
> all the outward forms, to redress
> itself humbly in that which you
> yourself will say is the truth, the
> exceptional truth of ordinary people,
> the extraordinary truth."

A prose preface on the problems of the poet in wartime is clear and valuable.

The surprisingly high price of this small book is justified by its exceedingly attractive format and by the fact that the edition is limited to 380 copies—though one hopes that work of such quality will later reach a wider public. (APW)

W.J. Turner (editor), ROMANCE OF ENGLISH LITERATURE (with an introduction by Kate O'Brien) (Hastings House, $5).

If such a literary survey as this had appeared in either America or Germany, each department would have been entrusted to a recognized academic authority and each essay would have presented the latest definitive undebatable word on the subject. But the English often prefer the erratic amateur to the perfect professional, with the result that these essays are highly individualistic, highly debatable and highly enjoyable.

Graham Greene advances theories on "British Dramatists" which may exasperate or stimulate but will never bore you. Kate O'Brien opens her discussion of "English Diaries and Journals" with a simple avowal of distaste for [the famous English diarist Samuel] Pepys. F.L. Woodward treats cogently of "British Historians" without so much as mentioning the school of [Lytton] Strachey and [Philip] Guedalla. These and the other essays by Sir Herbert Grierson (the Bible), Lord David Cecil (poets), Elizabeth Bowen (novelists) and Kenneth Matthews (philosophers) are models of clear and graceful writing, intended to arouse rather than satiate, to prod rather than to inform. If you have seen these or any others of the "Britain in Pictures" series in their original form as separate pamphlets, you know the extraordinarily attractive reproductions with which they are embellished— possibly the best picture books issued cheaply in English. This collection of seven for $5 is an unrivaled treat for the eye and the mind. (APW)

Christine Price, CATALOGUE OF ROYAL BOOKPLATES FROM THE LOUISE E. WINTERBURN COLLECTION, SAN FRANCISCO COLLEGE FOR WOMEN (with a frontispiece by Dorothy Payne) (printed for the California Bookplate Society by the Saunders Press, $6.50).

For the devotee of bookplate collecting (surely there must be a fine Greek word for that ending in -ophily?) Miss Price's meticulous descriptions and genealogical notes will be invaluable. For the layman there's fun to be had in the curious glimpses of social history (such as the Frenchman whose plate reading "M. le Vicomte" is usually found with another pasted over it saying "Citoyen") and in the sumptuous reproductions of forty of the plates, from Henry VIII to the last Czar. The frontispiece is an original by the San Francisco artist Dorothy Payne, who was commissioned by Mrs. Winterburn for the job. It was completed after her death as a pleasing memorial. The edition is limited to 300 copies. (APW)

March 25, 1945

Jacques Soleymieu, DIMANCHE (Brentano's, $1.75).

A young couple drive up into the mountains one Sunday to see her parents and spend a quiet day with them. That's all the plot there is to the novel, but Soleymieu has managed to convey a completely memorable picture of an unmemorable day. Momentary characters are fine, such as the complex retired customs officer picked up in a cafe or the dull visitor who comes briefly alive in his shop talk; and the whole has the exact quality of a quiet family party—tenderness, warmth, and just a touch of boredom. Whether this lightweight work will be translated may be doubtful but the young Soleymieu, now living in America, is worth watching. (APW)

H.P. Lovecraft, MARGINALIA (collected by August Derleth & Donald Wandrei) (Arkham House, $3).

This is a volume of ana: juvenilia, fragments, photographs, poetical tributes, critical and biographical essays, by and about the great pulp writer who has already, in the eight years since his death, become the not unworthy focus of a cult. Of Lovecraft's own writing the only important item included here is "Imprisoned with the Pharaohs" which he ghosted for [magician Harry] Houdini in 1924—the first pulp horror story I remember vividly, and still effective. His own essays are, to me at least, unreadable; but the essays of others, particularly that of Winfield Townley Scott, are invaluable to the comprehension of the man whom Vincent Starrett has called "his own most fantastic creation." (AB)

April 1, 1945

Elissa Landi, THE PEAR TREE (Ziff-Davis, $2.50).

The sudden passing of a leading American poetess drives her disciple to probe through her relics and her friendships for the secret of her life, love and death. At times this novel is unbearably wordy, at others it is intelligent and moving, in a convincingly sketched setting of musical and theatrical circles. (AB)

Gregory d'Alessio, WELCOME HOME! (with an introduction by Fred Sparks) (McBride, $1).

If you agree with McBride's blurb writer that *Collier's* is "the outstanding purveyor of pictorial humor in this country," d'Alessio is undoubtedly your meat. And even if you like your humor a bit more individual and imaginative, you'll still find some pleasing chuckles in these warm depictions of the ludicrous problems of the returned soldier—even if some of the captions are as long as they used to be in *Punch*. (APW)

April 15, 1945

Nigel Balchin, THE SMALL BACK ROOM (Houghton Mifflin, $2.50).

This is the story of the men known as "Professor Mair's research group"—attached to a Ministry, with no official standing, to take the technical bugs out of scientifico-military problems. And especially it's the story of Sammy Rice, who had a good technician's mind, an artificial foot, and a biting sense of inferiority which lasted him even through his great achievement of dissecting a new trick booby-trap bomb.

Mr. Balchin is a playwright and a Lieutenant Colonel, general staff. The first fact is readily evident in his precisely right dialogue; the second is more surprising. For this is the sort of book that one expects ten years after a war, in its bitter exposal of the pettiness, the politics, the maneuvering that goes on in a setup where the war value of a weapon is secondary to the social connections of the man who proposes it.

A sardonic and terrible picture, it is also one hell of a good novel. The characters are vivid and accurate, the prose is as sound as it is readable, and the interplay of psychological themes and plot-threads is masterly, with the episode of the German bomb building to a point of naturalistic suspense which makes the most fantastic thriller look tame. This is a distinguished job—and not the least of its distinctions is the fact that it could be published in wartime. (Boucher)

William Sansom, FIREMAN FLOWER AND OTHER STORIES (Vanguard, $2.50);
Anne Goodwin Winslow, A WINTER IN GENEVA AND OTHER STORIES (Knopf, $2.50).

Even the nominally noncommercial short story is apt to be carefully slanted at *The New Yorker* or at *Story* or at some Little Review, but here are two practitioners of short fiction who aim at nothing but the careful examination of human character in skillful prose.

They resemble each other in little else. Mrs. Winslow, in a tradition deriving from [Henry] James through [Katharine Anne] Porter, studies the minute tragedies of human interaction—always a little remote in time and place, always a little faded and nostalgic, but subtly perceptive. Mr. Sansom employs the [Franz] Kafkan technique of fantastic allegory; and if the allegory is never precisely subtle, his scenes and symbols flame with a glowing reality that transcends realism.

Each book is a pleasure to the sensitive palate, and the reader will be a long time forgetting the maze and the lighthouse of Mr. Sansom's parables or the Army posts and Southern mansions of Mrs. Winslow's recollections. (AB)

W.A. Dwiggins, MILLENNIUM I (Knopf, $2).

The machines owned the world. They had a culture, a science, even a religion in which they ritually adored Man, Who had created them in His own image and Whom they never equated with the despised homogrubs, those soft pests which still infested the hills. Here in dramatic form is the story of how Man came again, and the homogrubs returned to human dignity. Mr. Dwiggins' exciting imagination is not limited to the creation of type faces; the play, though uneven and unstageable, is a fascinating one— and oddest in that the machines are so much more individually characterized than the human beings. (AB)

May 13, 1945

Donald Porter Geddes (editor), FRANKLIN DELANO ROOSEVELT: A MEMORIAL (Pocket Books, 25 cents).

This little volume in its black-edge [George] Salter-designed binding represents possibly the most astonishing feat in all publishing history; its first printing is dated April 18, 1945, six days after the tragic event which it commemorates.

But it has a value far beyond this freakish dazzle. It is no opportunistic hodgepodge but a moving, intelligent record of what [poet Archibald] MacLeish has called the "need to render greatness honor." Its opening section is a time-clocked chronicle of the coming of the news—the transcript of a universal impact possible only to our age of communications, recorded with a simple literalness that makes those hours live again in all their black incredibility.

There follows a selection of editorials and columns (who could find the words then?), a brief biography from the [New York] *Herald-Tribune*, an admirably edited collection of excerpts from the late president's speeches and writings, an able appraisal of the twelve years [of FDR's presidency] by [the distinguished historian] Henry Steele Commager, and a group of poems chosen as tributes by William Rose Benet. The book closes with the undelivered Jefferson Day address, ending: "The only limit to our realization of tomorrow will be our doubts of today. Let us move forward with strong and active faith."

One can only wish that Benet had included among the poems MacLeish's "Speech to the Detractors." We are still in the honeymoon of mourning, but in time "dying and wishing peace—the best are eaten by the envy round them." (Unsigned; carbon in Lilly Library)

John Van Druten, I REMEMBER MAMA: A PLAY IN TWO ACTS (adapted from Kathryn Forbes' MAMA'S BANK ACCOUNT) (Harcourt Brace, $2.50).

With even less pretense of formal drama thanLIFE WITH FATHER, John Van Druten has created a charming and memorable series of warm human incidents. The incidents themselves and the characters he owes to Mrs. Forbes' delightful recollections of 1910 San Francisco; the rich simplicity with which they come to life in this version, however, must be credited to Mr. Van Druten's exceedingly artful stagecraft. The deftness with which he sketches in his characters (and if some of them are fairly stock, others like Mama are fresh and wonderful), the ease with which he employs modern stage mechanisms to return the theater to the living flow it enjoyed in Elizabethan days—these are marvels of craftsmanship for which Mrs. Forbes and the public alike must be grateful. (APW)

May 20, 1945

Robert Lawson, MR. WILMER
(illustrated by the author) (Little Brown, $2);
Tom Powers, VIRGIN WITH BUTTERFLIES (illustrated by Roger Duvoisin) (Bobbs-Merrill, $2.50);
Richard Shattuck, THE HALF-HAUNTED SALOON
(Simon & Schuster, $2.50).

It is strange enough that there should appear practically simultaneously books about a Milquetoast who learns to talk Animal, a naive virgin who rescues India for the British Empire, and a respectable if insane family which inherits a saloon with a ghost. It is even stranger perhaps that these novels should be written by an illustrator, an actor and a murder-monger. But we are grateful for strange things when they set us off on such a happy merry-go-round as these three pieces of screwballiana succeed in spinning. The sternest connoisseurs of fantasy may be a little disappointed. Mr. Lawson's book has a splendid fantasy springboard but peters out into a routine Clarence Budington Kelland yarn with little plot and too many bothersome inconsistencies. Mr. Shattuck's story comes up with a last-chapter explanation which is only a notch above it-was-all-a-dream. But the Lawson offers wonderful pictures of animals, human and otherwise, and the Shattuck uses its fantastic framework to enclose some extraordinary funny dialogue and some acute comments on the dull degeneration of the human soul.

The Powers book, VIRGIN WITH BUTTERFLIES, is something special and indefinable. The unnamed Virgin is a sort of Parsifal or Johnny Johnson, a female version of the Perfect Fool who wanders with shrewd innocence through the wildest of melodrama from Chicago through India to Australia. Her precisely careless first-person style may bother you a little until you suddenly find yourself accepting it as perfect. The unusually inept jacket blurb makes the book sound like second-string Anita Loos, but it has honesty and integrity in its madness and even a curious understanding of very real evil—the subplot of Uncle Ulrich is as subtle and chilling a murder story as you're apt to come on this year.

Are the world and its problems too much for you? Then hole up this week-end with this set of books and a bottle of your choice. Who knows? Some day you too might learn Animal or inherit a ghost or even be a virgin. And it's just as well to know what happens then. (Boucher)

May 27, 1945

Moritz Jagendorf (editor), 20 NON-ROYALTY MYSTERY PLAYS (Greenberg, $2.50).

Well, what did you expect for no royalty? (AB)

June 10, 1945

Lillian de la Torre, ELIZABETH IS MISSING; OR, TRUTH TRIUMPHANT: AN EIGHTEENTH CENTURY MYSTERY (Knopf, $3.50).

One of the classic and inexhaustible mysteries, along with what song the sirens sang and who killed Sir Edmondbury Godfrey, is what became of Bet Canning.

Plain, proper, pleasant Miss Canning disappeared on New Year's Day of 1753. Four weeks later she returned ill and emaciated with a strange tale of imprisonment and starvation because she had refused a life of shame. She identified her captors, who produced so perfect an alibi that Elizabeth was herself convicted of perjury.

But simply to say that Elizabeth was lying leaves the whole story more mysterious than ever. Why? And where and how was the girl starved? For two centuries scholars and speculators (including Voltaire, [Andrew] Lang and [Arthur] Machen) have pondered over Miss Canning's lost four weeks.

Now Miss de la Torre, God bless her, has produced the definitive book on the subject. She has taken as her model John Dickson Carr's THE MURDER OF SIR EDMUND GODFREY, which treated an historical mystery with the technique of the mystery novel, presenting the reader with all the facts and out of them evolving the startling but inescapable new solution.

Miss de la Torre is ideally equipped to do this. Readers of *Ellery Queen's Mystery Magazine* know from her stories of Dr. Sam: Johnson,

Detector, that she is equally adept at mystery fiction technique and at eighteenth century reconstruction. Here in her story of Bet Canning she gives us the rich color and flavor of London in the 1750's, from coffee houses to bagnios, from Lord Mayors to hartshorn-scrapers; and she offers us a solution so unexpected, so well-founded and so convincing that I for one accept it without a murmur—or rather only with a murmur of pure delight. Knopf's ordinary trade books are beautiful enough. When the firm decides to spread itself as it did here, the result is something wonderful. From the magnificent pastiche title-page to the detailed index this is one of the year's most visually impressive books, and its contents are fully worthy of the superb format.

Here is a permanent classic of criminology and a unique treat for everyone from the historical sociologist to the ardent whodunit fan. (Boucher)

Philip Yordan, ANNA LUCASTA (Random House, $2).

Remember back in the '20s when Eugene O'Neill seemed to have created the American drama? Or again in the '30s when Clifford Odets appeared to revitalize it? Well, here's Philip Yordan, another great voice in the same tradition, who offers us a play—a true, bitter, tender and funny play—shining like a good deed in the naughty worldliness of machine-made Broadway products. This story of the tart who tries to make good (and whose sin is as snow beside the petty evil of her respectable family) is being played in New York by Negroes. It was written about Poles. And it is about neither and about both and about all of us—a cruel, moving study of the lowest middle class, couched in authentic dramatic language. (APW)

Ellen C. Philtine, THEY WALK IN DARKNESS
(Liveright, $2.50).

This is partly the story of Farland, a state insane asylum, and partly that of a young doctor and his wife who find their personal emotional tensions heightened by the ugliness and horror of the system in which they have to live. The book is overlong and undistinguished in its writing but the stories are highly effective. Mrs. Philtine, the wife of a psychiatrist, treats the shameful hospital conditions with a convincing bitterness and a Dickensian indignation, and she handles the problems of her protagonists with a fine sense of the petty evil inherent in the human tongue. A few well-sketched case histories of the inmates make the book even more interesting. (AB)

Ernst Lothar, THE PRISONER (translated by James A. Galston) (Doubleday, $2.75).

Toni was only ten at the time of Anschluss so he grew up unquestioningly as a good Hitler Youth, until the petty injustice which he himself suffered opened his eyes to the great injustices of Austria and the world. By that time he had been drafted; captured in France, he found himself in an American camp for prisoners of war where anti-Nazism is sternly frowned upon under the Geneva Convention. The situation is a bitterly meaningful one. Unfortunately the real story, the prison camp episode, forms only a sketchy prologue and epilogue to an over-detailed narrative of adolescence in post-Anschluss Vienna—told, to be sure, with the deft local color and sure portrayal of the Austrian mind at which Lothar excels, but disappointingly minor beside the terrible problems of re-education (of ourselves as well as our enemy) which the opening chapters pose and the book shirks. (AB)

June 17, 1945

Dorothy Caruso, ENRICO CARUSO: HIS LIFE AND DEATH (Simon & Schuster, $2.75).

A more accurate title would have been MY LIFE WITH CARUSO, for this is no definitive biography but a detailed record of the three wonderful years in Dorothy Park Benjamin's life when she was married to the immortal tenor. Its flaws are many. The young bride knew nothing of music (at least one of the stories she soberly relates is almost certainly a deadpan hoax of Caruso's); she resented and distrusted all of his other intimates; she has little sense of chronology and few details of his first 45 years. But the book is an invaluable source for its collection of Caruso photographs, for Jack L. Caidin's excellent discography, and above all for its many long selections from Caruso's letters, couched in a polyglot language approximating English and as fascinating to decipher as the richest passages of [James] Joyce. And with all her shortcomings Mrs. Caruso manages (sometimes even subconsciously) to give a magnificently rounded portrait of the best and wisest man she has ever known. (APW)

July 1, 1945

Emil Ludwig, THE MORAL CONQUEST OF GERMANY (Doubleday, $2).

"Music to me," [19th-century German chancellor Otto von] Bismarck once said, "calls forth two heterogeneous feelings: lust for war, and a desire for the idyllic." In this remark Ludwig finds the key to the much-debated German national character, which he analyzes through personal anecdote, sketched biographies of great Germans, and study of German self-revelation in art and politics. His what-to-do-about-it conclusions may be open at least to debate (his project of the ten-year quarantine of Germany is an astonishing one), but his preceding analysis deserves the most careful consideration from all the experts who propound their what-to-dos without the haziest notion of what makes the average German tick. A valuable background for any intelligent discussion of the German problem. (APW)

July 8, 1945

Frank Baker, MR. ALLENBY LOSES HIS WAY
(Coward-McCann, $2.75).

Mr. Baker is an intelligent, perceptive craftsman whose work is of interest even at its worst, and I'm afraid that his worst is just what this new novel is. Its opening promises a logical fantasy not unworthy of his classic MISS HARGREAVES but the fantasy is soon explained away as part of a semi-psychological, semi-mystical study in characters reminiscent of Philip Barry at his most groping, with a plot of lurid coincidences straight out of Mrs. E.D.E.N. Southworth. Recommended only to those who care to follow an important novelistic talent even when its possessor loses his way. (AB)

Robert Dean Frisbie, AMARU: A ROMANCE OF THE SOUTH SEAS
(Doubleday, $2.50).

If you want local color, a sketchy plot about buried treasure, a do-nothing hero, a heroine chiefly characterized by having breasts, more local color, a dose of adolescent philosophy, a sinister one-legged villain, a minimum of action and some local color, this is your dish, God help you. Mr. Frisbie showed a pretty appreciation of his coyly nauseous style when he entitled his first volume "The Book of Puka-Puka." (AB)

Margaret Mayorga (editor), THE BEST ONE-ACT PLAYS OF 1944
(Dodd Mead, $2.50).

Of the eleven plays in this eighth annual collection, seven are on war themes, two are by authors in the services and five are for radio rather than stage. Apparently 1944 was not a vintage year; only the contributions of Archibald MacLeish (already printed elsewhere) and Tennessee Williams are completely memorable. At least the collection offers only one thorough dud—a radio play by Ben Hecht which is possibly the most muddle-headed piece of propaganda to come out of this war yet. (APW)

July 15, 1945

Alan Hynd, THE GIANT KILLERS (McBride, $3).

The Intelligence Unit of the United States Treasury Department, the Davids who bring down the Goliaths of crime for tax evasion when all other law agencies are helpless, have certainly earned a book; and obscure Elmer Lincoln Irey, now Chief Coordinator of Treasury Enforcement Agencies, should become as popular a detective hero as J. Edgar Hoover. The importance of the material assembled in this book, from the fate of little-known con-men to the collapse of the [Al] Capone and [Tom] Pendergast empires, should make many readers tolerate the banality and carelessness of the writing. (AB)

July 22, 1945

Richard Brooks, THE BRICK FOXHOLE (Harper, $2.50); Robert Neumann, THE INQUEST (Dutton, $2.50).

Superficially these two novels are hardly comparable. Mr. Brooks' study of the spiritual corruption of the soldier stationed at a safe distance from combat is intensely American, direct in style and manner, angry and immediate. Mr. Neumann's probing into the interaction of politics and character in this uprooted century is cosmopolitan, experimental in technique (and masterly in its use of a borrowed language), detached and subtle.

But they are alike in demonstrating two points: that the post-war reaction literature of this war is being written during the war itself, and that the methods and techniques of the mystery novel are proving useful tools for the writer of serious fiction. Both of these are wartime books but no disillusioned writer of the twenties could more thoroughly have condemned war as a destroyer of men's inner values. Both are novels of importance and significance, yet Brooks uses a murder and its routine police investigation as the dramatic substance of his story of dry rot and Mr. Neumann shapes his entire novel on the detectival framework of tracking down a motive for a pointless suicide—even to a surprise solution.

As the pulpish Elizabethan revenge tragedy gave birth at last to HAMLET, so the final importance of the mystery may lie in providing a structural frame to hold together serious fictional commentary. And that such a frame can enclose startlingly valid subject matter is well attested by these two novels—both in their separate ways admirably capable of shaking the smug simplifications fostered by most of our reading. (AB)

August Derleth, SOMETHING NEAR (Arkham House, $3).

Mr. Derleth's umpteenth book offers twenty-one creepy stories, mostly reprinted from *Weird Tales*. Many of them are in the tradition of M.R. James and a few add interesting contributions to the mythology of H.P. Lovecraft. A varied and competent collection —especially impressive when you realize that Derleth's sizable pulp output is only a minute fraction of his annual wordage. (AB)

Alexander Granach, THERE GOES AN ACTOR
(translated by Willard Trask) (Doubleday, $2.75).

Theater devotees need no urging to read the memoirs of an actor, but tales of the theater are the least part of Mr. Granach's admirable book. A childhood as a Jewish villager in Galicia, an adolescence as a wandering baker, a young manhood as a reluctant conscript in the Austrian army, a fabulous escape from an Italian prison camp—all these form a story of a man's coming-of-age as rich and well-rounded as a good novel. And Granach can write—not simply pretty-good-for-an-actor but damned-good-for-a-professional. There is humor and tenderness and warmth and infinite skill in this narrative, all of which translator Trask has rendered ably. It adds up not merely to the best book I've ever read by a stage personality but to a sincere and moving document addressed to all men of good will, who will mourn Granach's death and pray that his publishers have another posthumous volume in store. (APW)

July 29, 1945

Ida Clyde Clark, MEN WHO WOULDN'T STAY DEAD (illustrated by Dorothea Braby) (Bernard Ackerman, $3).

These overfictionized and underdocumented ghost stories rely chiefly for their appeal on the value of names with a capital N; here you'll find the ghosts of Abraham Lincoln and Oscar Wilde and ghosts seen by David Belasco and Charles XII. You'll also find, twice repeated, a judgment on the late nineteenth century attributed to Dr. [Samuel] Johnson—which must be a psychic phenomenon too. The Braby woodcuts furnish agreeably grim decorations. (AB)

August 5, 1945

Sterling North & C.B. Boutell (editors), SPEAK OF THE DEVIL (Doubleday, $3).

There are enough good if not precisely unfamiliar diabolical accounts in this volume (by John Collier, F.O. Mann, Max Beerbohm and many others) almost to compensate for the sub-literate translations selected and for the incompetent excerpting, stupid prejudices and heavy-handed wit of the editors. The magnificent Salvador Dali jacket tips the scales completely in favor of purchase. (AB)

Zelda Popkin, THE JOURNEY HOME (Lippincott, $2.50).

Bombardier Don Corbett, home on leave after 35 missions and the DFC [Distinguished Flying Cross], takes the Palm Queen from Miami to New York, and on this semi-deluxe train confronts all the barriers which separate the serviceman from the smug citizens of this sheltered country. On one level this novel is a sort of GRAND HOTEL on wheels, with a typecast but well sketched set of characters heading toward a communal disaster, and as such it is highly readable, told with all the swift ease of Miss Popkin's mystery novels and presenting as vivid and recognizable a picture of train existence as I've read. On another level the book tries hard to say something significant about the readjustment to each other of the two segments of our split population—those who have and have not been through the ugliness of war. But the characters and events chosen effectively for melodramatic entertainment are none too satisfactory as symbols, and precisely what Miss Popkin is trying to say remains as confusing as her hero, who proudly bullies Negroes while resenting anti-Semitism. (AB)

August 29, 1945

Ernest Booth, WITH SIRENS SCREAMING
(Doubleday, $2.50).

The ex-convict author of STEALING THROUGH LIFE, LADIES OF THE BIG HOUSE, etc., has set himself a serious task in this new novel: the exposure of the over-complex and corrupt legalistic setup of the state of California, which turns innocent young people into branded delinquents and thence into hardened criminals. But he has most unwisely chosen to demonstrate his thesis by having every conceivable injustice, irony and cruelty happen in succession to one group of three characters, compared to whom Oedipus and Orestes were beloved of the fates. This black, blank piling up of horror, combined with the author's determination to see no possible good in anyone connected with politics or public welfare, produces the effect not so much of a novel of social injustice as of Little Orphan Annie's trial before Judge Fudge; and the characters' solution of their problems by extralegal individual force is about as socially sound as

Daddy Warbucks' intervention in that *cause celebre*. But despite these flaws and even despite his often stilted and "literary" dialogue, Mr. Booth is a born story-teller; and though your risibility may be excited as often as your indignation, you won't be bored by a page of this long, active and angry novel. (AB)

September 16, 1945

J. Bigelow Clark, THE DREAMERS (Doubleday, $2.50).

The small colony of expatriates on the Mediterranean island of Campagna led a quiet, civilized, South-Windish [referring to the novel of that name by Norman Douglas] existence even after the war had started—until the Germans took over Italy. Then their ex-patriotism was finally stirred, first by the indignities offered them as nationals of the countries they had foresworn, then by the arrival of an unobtrusive little British spy who might remind you of a second-string [Manning Coles' character] Tommy Hambledon.

This seems like the start of a routine suspense book—the small clever group of free men pitted against the vast impersonal Gestapo machine. But it develops with a difference. The small clever group does not succeed with Hitchcocked snoots in putting it all over the loutish fascists. The intellectual individuals instead get the bleeding bejeepers beaten out of them, and most of them are callously and inevitably killed.

The story is tense and well written. If the sympathetic characters are sketched in a bit lightly, the Nazis are as plausible models of studied psychological perversity as one could ask. The action is brutal, even shocking; and the author poses an interesting Freudian thesis on the essentially sexual elements of war-making. In all an unclassifiable book, and highly rewarding both as a piece of novel-writing and as a wry commentary on our time. (AB)

Gurney Williams (editor), STOP OR I'LL SCREAM! (McBride, $2).

This is the funniest yet of the collected *Collier's* volumes, with plenty of [cartoon characters] Alfred the Gob, Butch the Burglar, [cartoonists William] Steig, [Otto] Soglow, Gardner Rea and a host of masters topped of course by the incomparable Virgil Partch. It may be the Partch influence but there seems to be a higher percentage of pure outrageous macabre fantasy than *Collier's* ever indulged in before. (APW)

Ronald Hilton (editor), WHO'S WHO IN LATIN AMERICA, PART II: CENTRAL AMERICA AND PANAMA (Stanford University Press, $2.25 cloth, $1.50 paper).

The A.N. Marquis Company, publishers of WHO'S WHO IN AMER-ICA, join forces with the Stanford Press in presenting this third edition, revised and enlarged, of a standard and invaluable reference work. Volume II happens to be published first; the first volume, dealing with Mexico, should appear this summer, and five more will follow. (APW)

Eugene C. Davis, AMATEUR THEATER HANDBOOK: A COMPLETE
GUIDE TO SUCCESSFUL PLAY
PRODUCTION (Greenberg, $3).

The publisher's blurb calls this "a book destined to become the standard work of the Little Theater in America." It's hardly that. It deals rather with high school dramatics than with the Little Theater in general and it shies away from any such esthetic questions as the varying schools of acting, the development of the regional drama or the relation of the tributary to the commercial theater. It is at its best on the technical side of production and should be a useful guide to inexperienced high school teachers, and its detailed 60-page section on the design and construction of a unit set should be worth the price of the book to any amateur group. (APW)

September 23, 1945

Howard Phillips Lovecraft, SUPERNATURAL HORROR IN LITERA-TURE (with an introduction by August Derleth)
(Ben Abramson, $2.50);
T. Everett Harre (editor), BEWARE AFTER DARK: THE WORLD'S
MOST STUPENDOUS TALES OF MYSTERY, HORROR, THRILLS
AND TERROR
(Emerson Books, $2.50).

Here are two new reissues of out-of-print works indispensable to the serious collector of fantasy fiction. The Lovecraft essay is of little interest in itself (only his most devout admirers could take that limited and erratic scholar seriously as a critic) but highly valuable as showing the tastes and influences which guided his own creative work; and Messrs. Derleth and Abramson have provided it with an index and delightful format and typography. The Harre anthology still seems after 16 years one of the most satisfactory in its field, avoiding the hackneyed, hunting out unusual sources and presenting a first-rate selection of chillers by authors as varied as M.P. Shiel, Leonid Andreyeff and Gertrude Atherton. (AB)

Harley Granville-Barker, THE USE OF THE DRAMA (Princeton University Press, $1.50).

The 1944 Princeton lectures of the eminent British playwright-producer-critic touch on the fortunes of the arts in England, the place of the theater in the modern world and the proper academic approach to drama and end with a cogent plea for an established national theater. The author's flexible good prose well expresses his deep conviction that art "should leaven the daily life of a community." (APW)

Josephina Niggli, POINTERS ON PLAYWRITING
(The Writer, Inc., $2).

Miss Niggli, who knows, tells how to write non-royalty plays for the amateur theater. Even if that strikes you as a likely ambition, you've small business setting about it if you still need to be taught the commonplaces which the author proffers here. (APW)

September 30, 1945

Mary Anne Howard (editor), FIFTY SHORT SHORTS:
AN OMNIBUS OF SHORT STORIES (World, 49 cents).

These short shorts, all chosen from the files of the King Features Syndicate, average out at a trifle less than a cent apiece and may be worth just about exactly that. With very few exceptions these are magazine fiction at its most meretricious, with all integrity sacrificed to produce the cute slick twist. An anthology of the honest short short, however, would still seem a good idea. (AB)

Lajos Biro, GODS AND KINGS: SIX PLAYS
(Macmillan, $1.75).

These short plays range in time from Greek mythology to the next world-age, in place from the Tower of London to a Hungarian inn, and in style from realistic comedy to abstract allegory. They are unified by the wit and skill one has come to expect from Hungarian dramatists and by a querying philosophical irony which seems to be peculiarly Biro. Some are actable, some completely unstageable, but all are highly readable. And either Mr. Biro has learned to write admirable English or a distinguished translator is here left anonymous. (APW)

October 7, 1945

Donald A. Wollheim (editor), THE PORTABLE NOVELS OF SCIENCE (Viking, $2).

In the March 1944 issue of *Astounding Science Fiction* Cleve Cartmill published a short story called "Deadline." We scienti-fans who read it thought "Cartmill's slipping; this is just another routine yarn about a U-235 atomic bomb—hack stuff." But the F.B.I. was sufficiently interested to call on Cartmill and put him through the most serious of grillings as to where he'd got the idea for the story.

The concept of the atomic bomb, like the concepts of space ships, time travel and superior human mutants, has long been a commonplace to the readers of that branch of imaginative writing known to its devotees as sci-entifiction. The rest of the world is only now catching up with those devo-tees and beginning to realize, like the G-men in the affair Cartmill, that these fictional imaginings may dovetail remarkably with future fact.

Science-fiction, however, is still largely neglected by book publishers and restricted to the pulp magazines. Only one anthology of its short sto-ries has been compiled up to now, the excellent POCKET BOOK OF SCI-ENCE-FICTION [also edited by Wollheim, 1943]. A much larger collec-tion of shorts is being assembled by Random House, and now Viking of-fers us the first omnibus of imaginative science novels.

Mr. Wollheim's choices for this collection are impeccable. All have ap-peared before in American books but all are out of print and each is in its way a masterpiece.

Two of the novels are by American pulp writers. BEFORE THE DAWN by John Taine (pseudonym of Caltech mathematician Eric Temple Bell) combines the time-travel approach with a vivid scientific reconstruction of the world and life of the great dinosaurs. H.P. Lovecraft's THE SHADOW OUT OF TIME utilizes the patter of science to open up the same vistas of cosmic terror which the Providence master depicts in his purely supernatu-ral works.

The other two are by English men of letters, more reputable to the aver-age book reader. H.G. Wells' THE FIRST MEN IN THE MOON is one of the scarcest but most important imaginative novels of the one science-fiction writer whose work is widely accepted. I side with Willy Ley against Mr. Wollheim on the logical impossibility of the anti-gravity material ca-vorite, but the novel remains one of the first and best explorations of the problems of space-flight (problems which may soon be as real as those of the atomic bomb).

The last of the four novels is also the subtlest and most imaginative. Mr. Wollheim calls Olaf Stapledon "probably the greatest present-day writer of science-fictional fantasies," and I'd drop the "probably." His ODD JOHN, which he sagely subtitles A STORY BETWEEN JEST AND EARNEST, is the finest treatment ever accorded to the ironic and terrifying theme of Homo Superior—the mutant variation which may in time supplant Homo Sapiens. It is written with wit, skill and infinite plausibility—an off-trail and perfect book to delight any sensitive palate.

Mr. Wollheim has done us a fine service in making these four available and his notes add greatly to the book's interest. I wish his omnibus a success so resounding that publishers may at last realize that the reading public of the Atomic Age needs something a bit more imaginatively stimulating than internal-combustion-engine fiction. (Boucher)

October 21, 1945

R.A. Dick, THE GHOST AND MRS. MUIR (Ziff-Davis, $2); Evangeline Walton, WITCH HOUSE (Arkham House, $2.50).

These two contrasting novels are admirable illustrations of the two current approaches to the ghost story. Both are intelligent, modern and quite free of clanking-chain Gothic ghosting; both deal with a house possessed by an unliving being and with that being's effect on the living occupants; yet they could hardly be more unlike.

Mrs. Dick's story of how the bluff ghost of a sea captain roused a timid widow to vibrant life might be called whimsical if the word had not fallen into disrepute. It is light, logical and lovely in the best vein of blithe-hearted fantasy. Its humor is at once broad and deft, and the love between little Mrs. Muir and her domineering haunt is as touching as anything since [Oscar Wilde's] THE CANTERVILLE GHOST.

Miss Walton follows another path of fantasy: the grimly serious occultism of a William Hope Hodgson or a Jessie Douglas Kerruish. Her WITCH HOUSE, haunted by the lingering evil of three centuries of necromancers, is an abode of pure terror, and her sternly human Dr. Gaylord Carew is an earnest psychic detective worthy to rank beside, if not above, [William Hope Hodgson's] Carnacki and [Algernon Blackwood's] John Silence.

At a guess I'd say the Dick novel was for everybody and the Walton only for the more serious connoisseurs of chills (who should note that it's a limited edition and will probably, like all Arkham House books, become a collector's item). But both are valuable additions to the growing shelf of sound and literate fantasy novels. (AB)

Christopher La Farge, MESA VERDE
(New Directions, $2.50).

This poetic drama, guessing at the abandonment of the Colorado cliff dwellings, was originally intended as an opera libretto. No composer apparently having accepted it, it is now published (and most attractively) on its own. Mr. La Farge succeeds admirably, as he says of his brother Oliver [author of the Pulitzer Prize-winning 1929 novel LAUGHING BOY], "in writing of the Indian as a human being instead of an inaccurate symbol"; and if his play is a trifle operatic as a straight drama, it could be intensely dramatic as an opera. Let us hope that some composer will soon remedy the neglect of what is potentially one of the finest libretti in our language. (APW)

November 4, 1945

Robert Bloch, THE OPENER OF THE WAY
(Arkham House, $3).

Robert Bloch has one of the most original minds in modern pulp fiction. His specialty is a grisly gag-sense best exemplified by his answer to a reader who expressed surprise at his turning from horror to humor. "But I'm a very un-horrible person," Bloch protested. "I have the heart of a small boy—I keep it on my desk, in a jar." Those of us with a taste for the gruesome giggle—what the Germans call *Galgenhumor* [gallows humor]—have long found peculiar delight in Bloch; but unfortunately the editor of Arkham House believes that fantasy must be earnest, and this first collected volume of Bloch is chosen almost exclusively from his strictly deadpan efforts. They're not bad—largely resembling [H.P.] Lovecraft or even Lovecraft imitators; they're even very good when you consider that Bloch wrote many of them in his teens. But they could have been written by any of a dozen writers of the *Weird Tales* school, and I'm still waiting for a book of the mordant masterpieces which only Bloch can write. (AB)

November 11, 1945

Georges Simenon, THE SHADOW FALLS
(translated by Stuart Gilbert) Harcourt Brace, $2.50).

This chronicle of the collapse of a wealthy bourgeois family (published in France as LE TESTAMENT DONADIEU) is the first of Simenon's self-confessedly "serious" novels to be offered in English. There are occasional flashes of his old economical artistry, but the detailed listing of the murders, business frauds and rapes of the Donadieus adds up to Simenon's longest, most pretentious and least interesting book to date. (AB)

August Derleth, H.P.L.: A MEMOIR
(Ben Abramson, $2.50).

Mr. Derleth, who is almost single-handedly responsible for the current interest in H.P. Lovecraft, is a most suitable person to turn out a memoir of the Providence Master of supernatural horror. And if this book is more whetting than satisfying, it will do admirably until this most singular of eccentrics is finally treated by a biographer with psychoanalytic talents who will take his gloves off. The volume contains many hitherto unprinted excerpts from Lovecraft's letters and juvenilia, a thorough index and an excellent bibliography. (AB)

Alfred Neumann, SIX OF THEM (translated by Anatol Murad) (Macmillan, $2.75).

Mr. Neumann first attained success with such works as THE PATRIOT, in which he condensed the possible material of a vast historical novel into a brilliantly incisive novelette. In this story of the trial of a Munich professor and his students for disseminating anti-Nazi propaganda he reverses the process, straining every effort to expand a possible novelette to 327 wartime pages. Neumann here has interesting characters to present and a valuable contribution to the controversy about Good and Bad Germans, but the diffuse dullness of his form makes his ideas all but inaccessible. He is not helped by the translator, who achieves a painful prose that is neither German nor English. (AB)

C.E. Le Massena, GALLI-CURCI'S LIFE OF SONG
(Paebar, $3.75).

"The Catskills had ever proved hospitably pleasant for jaded bodies and tensioned nerves, so thither she cast about for a likely spot whereon to set up her Dolce far niente." This sample will show why Mr. Le Massena's book will be welcomed avidly by connoisseurs of great bad prose as a volume worthy to stand beside [an unidentified but no doubt atrociously written novel entitled] THE STRUGGLE; but devotees of Galli-Curci's art will find it a sadly unworthy and almost unintelligible tribute to their heroine. The book contains 45 pictures, a shoddy discography and no index. (APW)

December 9, 1945

Charles Henri Ford (editor), A NIGHT WITH JUPITER
AND OTHER FANTASTIC STORIES
(View Editions/Vanguard Press, $3).

The editor of *View: The Modern Magazine* has here assembled fifteen unclassifiable stories into a unique book as disconcertingly strange in its format as the stories are in their contents and techniques. Tales and fragments by Henry Miller, Leonora Carrington, Montague O'Reilly, Ramon Sender and Giorgio di Chirico are illuminated by sketches and designs by [Alexander] Calder, [Pavel] Tchelitchev and [Yves] Tanguy, mixed with anonymous commercial woodcuts of the nineteenth century. The result is a purely surrealist volume to delight the avant garde and perhaps even, through the occasional richness of its imagination and brilliance of its skill, to open the eyes of more conservative readers. (AB)

Mitchell Wilson, NONE SO BLIND
(Simon & Schuster, $2.50).

A lonely, battle-shocked man meets an enigmatically appealing woman and finds himself plunged into an affair with her despite the sinister presence of her blind husband—who may be feigning that blindness for dark ends of his own. Mr. Wilson's publishers are careful to stress that this "is NOT a mystery novel" but the author has not departed so far from his earlier successes as Simon & Schuster would like to think. There is a sudden surprise denouement based on well-planted clues, and the very nature of this surprise, whereby all the characters turn out to be very different from what you had thought, somewhat frustrates the effect of the book as a psychological novel. You never quite get at or believe in any of the people because the full revelation is being withheld to astonish you. But Mr. Wilson's skill in atmospheric suspense is in full evidence, and the novel, no matter how it may fall between two stools, will not fail to hold your interest and occasionally chill your blood. (AB)

Baynard Kendrick, LIGHTS OUT (Morrow, $2.50).

I don't know whether Baynard Kendrick's intense preoccupation with the problems of the blind is the cause or the result of his excellent series of mystery novels about blind detective Captain Duncan Maclain. At any rate there are few sighted individuals in America better equipped to handle the subject matter of Mr. Kendrick's first straight novel, the rehabilitation of a blinded veteran. Kendrick is a civilian instructor at Old Farms Convalescent Hospital, a founder of the Blinded Veterans' Association—and a sound professional novelist.

The story of LIGHTS OUT is a simple one. A Florida sergeant is blinded in France. The Army rehabilitation program teaches him that blindness is no handicap to a man of character and intelligence and his blindness teaches him something more: that the narrow prejudices of his Southern upbringing are meaningless in his new enlightened world of darkness.

The book is not a distinguished novel of character nor is it meant to be. Its people are sketched in casually. What is important—and infinitely exciting—is its detailed and authentic presentation of the intelligent adjustment of the blind. The fascinating minutiae which have been touched on in the Maclain books here become the main thing, and only the dullest reader can fail to be completely absorbed. Add a vigorous if totally materialistic argument for good will among men and you have an enthralling book—whose only flaw perhaps is that it makes the state of the blind seem almost one to be envied. (AB)

December 16, 1945

Laurence F. Hawkins, SPANISH HANDBOOK FOR MARINERS AND TRAVELERS IN LATIN AMERICA (Cornell Maritime Press, $2.50); Charles E. Kany, AMERICAN-SPANISH SYNTAX (University of Chicago Press, $6).

Mr. Hawkins' pocket-sized volume is an unusually useful book even for stay-at-homes—a combination of rapid instruction primer and what-do-I-say-now guidebook, well printed, accurately and ingeniously assembled, and even written with a certain style and good sense.

Professor Kany of Berkeley has composed a work which deserves the epithets "pioneer" and "monumental"—the first comprehensive volume treating the various American divergences from standard Castilian. This is not a Latin equivalent of [H.L.] Mencken's THE AMERICAN LANGUAGE; Kany interprets the word "syntax" in his title with an academic precision which somewhat limits the book. But it is still a sound and valuable work, indispensable to anyone interested in Latin American literature or people. (APW)

December 23, 1945

H.P. Lovecraft & August Derleth, THE LURKER AT THE THRESHOLD (Arkham House, $2.50); Donald M. Grant & Thomas P. Hadley (editors), RHODE ISLAND LOVECRAFT (illustrated by Betty Wells Halliday

(Grant-Hadley, no price given).

It begins to look as though the supernatural fiction of H.P. Lovecraft would in time spawn as large a body of derivative literature as has the canon of Sherlock Holmes. Of these latest items of Lovecraftiana, the pamphlet issued by Grant-Hadley (a new publishing house specializing like Arkham House in the book-resurrection of pulp fantasy) offers some interesting biographical source material and two critical articles with a refreshingly objective and iconoclastic approach. Mr. Derleth's novel, based on fragments by the Master, seems to be an attempt to systemize the vast mythos of cosmic terror which underlies all Lovecraft's writings, making everything perfectly clear. The result, beside the original more nebulous suggestions, is about as terrifying as a report from the Psychical Research Society. (AB)

December 30, 1945

J. Sheridan Le Fanu, GREEN TEA AND OTHER GHOST STORIES
(Arkham House, $3).

J. Sheridan Le Fanu is the father of the English ghost story as we know it. From M.R. James to Fritz Leiber the modern masters have all paid tribute to him. His work, notable for the meticulous naturalism with which he substantiates his supernatural terrors, is as interesting in itself as it is historically significant. And yet this is to my best knowledge the first collected volume of Le Fanu to appear in this country. August Derleth has chosen fourteen of his tales, once familiar from anthologies, many brand new even to addicts. One might wish for more bibliographical details and a less capricious arrangement but the book is certainly the most important publication of the year in the field of supernatural fiction. (AB)

Francis E. McMahon, A CATHOLIC LOOKS AT THE WORLD (Vanguard, $2.75).

The so-called liberal Catholic is a phenomenon which the editors of [secular liberal magazine] *The Nation* and of the Brooklyn *Tablet* [a right-wing Catholic periodical] find equally perplexing, though the author (and the reviewer) of this book sees in a progressive political attitude the inevitable consequence of orthodox Church doctrine. Professor McMahon expounds this position clearly and simply in a book well-equipped with index, bibliographies and extensive quotations from Doctors of the Church and papal encyclicals. (APW)

January 6, 1946

William Oliver Stevens, UNBIDDEN GUESTS: A BOOK OF REAL
GHOSTS (Dodd Mead, $3).

This is one of the better recent true-ghost collections, edited with as
much scholarship and responsibility as the regrettable anonymity of so
many ghost viewers will allow. There are a few strikingly good new stories, a sound retelling of many classics, and a laudable if not too successful
attempt to group and classify the stories. Your reaction will depend on
your feelings about orthodox psychic research (Mr. Stevens' interpretations lie entirely in that direction, even when his facts seem to demand the
consideration of modern time theories, [Charles] Fortean phenomena, psychoanalysis, or even conventional Christian religion); but he produces
enough reasonably valid data to make the reader echo C.E.M. Joad's remark at Borley Rectory: "Either the facts did not occur, or if they did, the
universe must in some respects be totally other than what one is accustomed to suppose." (AB)

Oliver St. John Gogarty, MR. PETUNIA
(Creative Age Press, $2.50).

Some philosophers, says Mr. Gogarty, "cannot imagine the chaotic,
ungermane and windy liberty of Creation." This novel, certainly one of the
most carelessly constructed of our time, might help them to understand it.
But the very chaos of this study of a paranoid watchmaker in the Virginia
of 1820 yields as many virtues as vices. If the melodramatic story is
strained and badly proportioned, the protagonist himself is (at least for
two-thirds of the book) an admirable portrait of a meticulous craftsman
with deep potentialities of evil. And if the other characters range from the
caricatured to the unlikely, they at least include many Irishmen who serve
as mouthpieces for the ever lively and delightful Gogarty wit. Read the
short anecdote on page 237 and see if you're apt to resist Gogarty with all
his faults. (AB)

H.R. Huse, READING AND SPEAKING FOREIGN LANGUAGES (University of North Carolina Press, $2.)

A professor of romance languages offers some highly sensible footnotes
to the discussion currently raging about the teaching of languages and ends
with a well-reasoned argument for a greater emphasis on reading ability.
An heretical book to modern theorists of linguistics, but a stimulating one.
(APW)

Max Graf, LEGEND OF A MUSICAL CITY
(Philosophical Library, $3).

The oldest of Austrian music critics sums up the history of Vienna as a musical center in a book nostalgic and charming when he writes of history, a trifle naive when politics intrude, and illuminatingly valuable when Graf sketches the composers from [Johannes] Brahms to [Arnold] Schoenberg whom he knew intimately. For all lovers of music, gossip or the flavor of Alt Wien. (APW)

February 10, 1946

L.M. McQuarrie, HALF ANGEL (Doubleday, $2).

"I leaped up from the table again, my eyes in line with his. 'If you mean by that, Bruce Billings, that I loved Lotus with all the respect and friendship and strength a man can give a woman in despair, you're right. I did love Lotus. If that's what you mean, I was one of Lotus' lovers.' "

The novel containing this seriously intended excerpt received honorable mention in the Doubleday $20,000 prize novel award. It also contains mysticism and many scenes set in a city whimsically called San Francisco, though any resemblance to the home of the *Chronicle* is as coincidental as the likeness of the characters to any members of the human race. (AB)

March 24, 1946

Groff Conklin (editor), THE BEST OF SCIENCE FICTION (with a preface by John W. Campbell, Jr.) (Crown, $3).
John Taine, THE TIME STREAM (Buffalo Book Co., $3).
Frank Belknap Long, THE HOUNDS OF TINDALOS (Arkham House, $3).
Paul Bailey, DELIVER ME FROM EVA
(Murray & Gee, $2).

THE BEST OF SCIENCE FICTION Groff Conklin (editor). This first comprehensive anthology of the prophetic literature of the pre-atomic age does not quite live up to its title, for reasons out of the editor's control. But within the limits imposed on him by the complication of reprint rights, Mr. Conklin has amassed an impressive collection. There's a scattering of Literary Names (not always at their best) but the backbone is the solid pulp masters—Lewis Padgett [a pseudonym of Henry Kuttner], Robert Heinlein, Don Stuart [a pseudonym of John W. Campbell, Jr.], A.E. Van Vogt—and their work is impressive enough to make clear to any intelligent reader that Buck Rogers represents science fiction, to quote the

Campbell introduction, "to precisely the extent that Dick Tracy is representative of detective fiction."

John Taine, THE TIME STREAM. First book appearance of one of the classics of time travel, written pseudonymously in 1931 by Professor E.T. Bell of Caltech. Set partly in San Francisco of 1906 and partly in the infinitely remote past (or future, for the author postulates an unending circular stream of time), it is equally effective as paradoxical speculation or as [H. Rider] Haggardesque romance—an excellent fantasy well deserving this resurrection.

Frank Belknap Long, THE HOUNDS OF TINDALOS. Short stories collected chiefly from *Weird Tales* and *Unknown Worlds* and ranging from straight science fiction to [M.R.] Jamesian ghost stories. Mr. Long has little creative individuality but marked assimilative skill; he has never developed a style of his own but proves a first-rate craftsman in any school of fantasy he turns to. Much imagination, some odd humor and a few authentic black chills.

Paul Bailey, DELIVER ME FROM EVA. Mad-scientist gibberish with sexual and mythical overtones. More lurid than the wildest pulps and couched in a pretentious "literary" style which results in some of the worst writing this reviewer has ever seen professionally published. (Boucher)

April 7, 1946

Dornford Yates, THE HOUSE THAT BERRY BUILT (Putnam, $2.50).

If you feel that the construction of a house in the Pyrenees by five idle aristocrats is meaty material for 120,000 words, this is your book—especially if you have a relish for British insularity, snobbery and coy humor. The transparent murder mystery which serves as subplot will hardly distract you from these pleasures. But if enough of the wrong people read this volume, the cause of the British loan is surely lost. (AB)

Phillips Rogers, STAG NIGHT (Prentice-Hall, $2.50).

The kaleidoscopic melodrama of the GRAND HOTEL technique is here revived to describe the 14th annual gentlemen's dinner of an important country club, from the green turtle soup to the feelthy pictures, from the white glitter of the toastmaster's table to the convenient darkness of the tennis pavilion, from the suave caddery of the club wolf to the suave humanity of the head waiter.

For a first novel (or for a 21st) it's a virtuoso's performance in its skilled handling of a multitude of characters and plot threads; Mr. Rogers manipulates the novel as adeptly as his incomparable head waiter manipulates the dinner. Though it avoids any direct "message," the book does contain by implication an indictment of a spiritual vacuum; but it is intended primarily as a novel of entertainment, on which level it should succeed resoundingly (save perhaps in Boston). (AB)

April 14, 1946

Philip Woodruff, CALL THE NEXT WITNESS
(Harcourt Brace, $2.50).

This is the story of a murder trial in India "where, by old tradition, an honest judge is one who takes presents from both sides and gives an impartial decision."

Pyari, Flame of the Forest, had dreamed of a husband handsome, brave and wise. By her one stroke of luck, Gopal Singh was at least handsome, but she was not long in discovering his lack of the other qualities. Then there were the money deceits and the other women and so finally the quarrel.

After Pyari's hushed-up death began the many-leveled official investigation (her father-in-law had underbribed the first investigator), and with the investigation came the witnesses. Truth had little to do with their evidence, but her own family happened to know the peculiar conduct of one Brahman, who thus testified for the prosecution, and her husband's family chanced on the cocaine-smuggling activities of one gypsy, who might otherwise have so testified. And behind all the witnesses was Pyari's old nurse, avenging her child.

Whether or not Pyari was murdered the reader is never told. Indeed much of the book's fascination is like that of a classic murder case, still proffering endless plausible arguments on either side. The impartial decision is difficult but the reader, like the honest judge, welcomes from both sides their presents, which here take the shape of a series of clear-cut vignettes filling in some part of the infinitely complex picture of Indian social life.

Mr. Woodruff is careful to take no sides on Indian political issues. He is even largely successful in avoiding the lofty viewpoint of the onlooking white man. He simply presents [an] alien and absorbing civilization as he has closely observed it, and presents it in the form of an unusually able and intelligent novel.

Kathleen Voute's delightful end-papers deserve special mention. (AB)

April 21, 1946

Algernon Blackwood, THE DOLL AND ONE OTHER (Arkham House, $1.50).
August Derleth (editor), WHO KNOCKS?:

TWENTY MASTERPIECES OF THE SPECTRAL FOR THE CON-
NOISSEUR (illustrated by Lee Brown Coye) (Rinehart, $2.50).

The first new Blackwood book to appear in America in many years is automatically a major event. Neither of the two long short stories here is first-water Blackwood; but "The Doll" deals extremely well not so much with the familiar subject of a vengeance-animated toy as with human reactions to it, and "The Trod," while full of Blackwood's verbose mysticism, displays also the eery plausibility with which he creates his own place-legends. I doubt if you'll forget either story easily.

August Derleth (editor), WHO KNOCKS?: TWENTY MASTER-PIECES OF THE SPECTRAL FOR THE CONNOISSEUR. After the admirable SLEEP NO MORE this second Derleth anthology is a bit disappointing. You'll find more familiar stories here and more dubious choices (the *Weird Tales* school especially is questionably represented). But perhaps half of the stories are both fine and unhackneyed fantasy. You wouldn't ask more of most anthologies—Mr. Derleth simply set himself too high a standard in his first. And any volume which offers the first book-appearance of Theodore Sturgeon's "It" (as imaginatively terrifying a pulp story as I know) is one to clasp to the collector's bosom.

BEST BUYS IN REPRINTS. Julius Fast (editor), OUT OF THIS WORLD (Penguin, 25 cents, uncut). (AB)

May 5, 1946

Albert Camus, THE STRANGER (translated by Stuart Gilbert) (Knopf, $2);
Georges Simenon, THE MAN WHO WATCHED THE TRAINS GO BY (translated by Stuart Gilbert) (Reynal & Hitchcock, $2.50).

Albert Camus is a young novelist of serious esthetic and philosophical stature who is one of the two key figures of the curious contemporary French movement of Existentialism.

Georges Simenon is an incredibly productive, popular crime fiction writer who represents the literature of sensation at its closest approach to "accepted" literature.

Two careers could hardly be more different, yet the recently published novels of both men treat in essence the same story: that of a man who cannot accept within himself the common conventions of society but who drifts along with them until a murder, committed almost by chance, sets him free of the social framework.

Simenon makes this story, in a Dutch and French setting, into a superlative underplayed melodrama of pursuit and capture—unquestionably the best of his non-Maigret stories yet to be translated, and the most effective murder study to come out of France since Jules Romains' Quinette episodes.

Camus devotes himself to the creation of an extraordinary character—a young bank clerk in Algiers whose reactions (or lack thereof) are simply not those which society demands. Commentators on Existentialism seem to give this character an extra-literary philosophical value; on the level of the novel itself he is an astonishingly well-realized portrayal of an absolute indifferentist.

The resemblance between the books may be a chance freak of publication or it may be an interesting example of a serious writer taking a theme from popular fiction to embody his ideas. Camus is a director of the publishing house of Gallimard, which printed THE STRANGER in 1942, four years after the same firm had published the Simenon novel.

In its own way each book is a notable and highly recommended work. As companion pieces they provide a fascinating study. And in each case Stuart Gilbert's translation is intelligent and unobtrusive. (AB)

May 12, 1946

George Orwell, DICKENS, DALI & OTHERS: STUDIES IN POPULAR CULTURE (Reynal & Hitchcock, $2.50).

"Though Fascism does not offer any real return to the past, those who yearn for the past will accept Fascism sooner than its probable alternatives." This observation, in connection with the politics of [the Irish poet] W[illiam] B[utler] Yeats, illustrates the directness and acuity of Mr. Orwell's socio-literary criticism. His esthetic sensibility and political intelligence casts new lights on such familiar subjects as [Salvador] Dali, [Rudyard] Kipling, [P.G.] Wodehouse and [Charles] Dickens (the analysis of Dickens as a "revolutionary" thinker is masterly) and open up to the American reader whole new fields fascinating to contemplate. Do you know anything of English boys' weeklies or comic postcards, or the peculiar art of James Hadley Chase, who so far out-Herods the American school of tough detection that American publishers have tended to leave him alone? You will learn from Mr. Orwell, and you could hardly desire a more witty or understanding instructor. (APW)

June 16, 1946

Anthony Quayle, EIGHT HOURS FROM ENGLAND (Doubleday, $2.50).

The author, a British actor, served during the war as liaison officer with the Albanian resistance movement—or movements rather, since the situation seems to have paralleled that in Yugoslavia. The problems of dealing with the Partisans and the Chetnik-like Balli, complicated by questions of personality and the overall question of grand strategy in hampering the German retreat from Greece, make absorbing material for what is not so much a novel (the personal plot is slight) as an impartial fictional account of military politics, written with style, intelligence and wit. (AB)

June 23, 1946

Tom Powers, SHEBA ON TRAMPLED GRASS
(Bobbs-Merrill, $2.50).

Tom Powers is an actor by profession and a prominent one, but his writing career is no press-agent's dream. As a novelist he's a solid craftsman in good standing, with qualities not quite like anyone else. A year ago he produced in VIRGIN WITH BUTTERFLIES one of the most entrancingly zany fantasies of the decade; if SHEBA is something less outstanding than that, it at least shows his admirable good sense in not trying to imitate his own hit.

Here he offers you a story of life in a traveling carnival, complete with the Human Rocket, the Tibetan Midget, the Wise Woman, the Girlie Show and the most wonderful merry-go-round you ever dreamed of. His carnival is a microcosm, and against its garish color he sets a pretty plot of good and evil and the infinite human gradations in between—almost the same sort of allegory that Philip Barry attempted in HERE COME THE CLOWNS but with less metaphysics and more straight story. It's a fresh, wise and likeable book, easily and vividly told; if you haven't caught up with Mr. Powers yet, you'd better start. (AB)

Ralph Morse Brown, THE SINGING VOICE
(Macmillan, $2.50).

Mr. Brown is unique among teachers of singing in that he has not devised a new and improved method. His contribution to this confused field of study is an orderly rearrangement of old principles. The result should be of interest to the teacher, who may argue with some of his statements; to the student interested in the larger plan behind his immediate problems; and to the bystander who wonders why teacher and student must talk so much gibberish. (APW)

September 22, 1946

Raymond J. Healy & J. Francis McComas (editors), ADVENTURES IN
TIME AND SPACE: AN ANTHOLOGY OF MODERN SCIENCE-
FICTION STORIES
(Random House, $2.95).
William Hope Hodgson, THE HOUSE ON THE BORDERLAND AND
OTHER NOVELS
(Arkham House, $5).
John Keir Cross, THE OTHER PASSENGER
(Lippincott, $2.75).
Robert E. Howard, SKULL-FACE AND OTHERS
(Arkham House, $5).
Will F. Jenkins, THE MURDER OF THE U.S.A.
(Crown, $2).
Barbara Hunt, SEA-CHANGE (Rinehart, $2.50).

Raymond J. Healy & J. Francis McComas (editors), ADVENTURES IN
TIME AND SPACE: AN ANTHOLOGY OF MODERN SCIENCE-
FICTION STORIES. By chronology this is the third anthology devoted
exclusively to science fiction. But chronology means little to us inveterate
time-rangers, and the Healy-McComas opus is hereby proclaimed the first
and foremost in its field—as definitive, say, as [Ellery] Queen's [Frederic
Dannay's] 101 YEARS' [ENTERTAINMENT] is among detective anthologies. The aficionado will need no luring, but this collection should
appeal beyond the circle of fans to any reader with curiosity and imagination, who will find here prophecy (sometimes already come true), fantasy,
satire, and (occasionally) fascinatingly off-beat psychological and literary
values.

William Hope Hodgson, THE HOUSE ON THE BORDERLAND AND
OTHER NOVELS. Until recently Hodgson has been almost unknown in
this country even among specialists. Now he is coming to be ranked
among the great masters of fantasy. His prose is often self-conscious and
even painful; his construction can be tortuous and difficult. But the fabulous imagination in his visions of the future of the world or of the horrors
of the sea demands comparison with such names as Olaf Stapledon or M.P.
Shiel. Arkham House is to be thanked even more warmly than usual for
this enormous omnibus volume.

John Keir Cross, THE OTHER PASSENGER. Eighteen wry imaginings
by a new young Scottish writer, dealing chiefly with the riddles of human
personalities and the odder aspects of death. Many of the plots are worthy
of John Collier; and if Keir Cross' style is a bit wordy and explicit for full
ironic impact, he can still be welcomed gladly to the macabre field in
which he has so lamentably few competitors.

Robert E. Howard, SKULL-FACE AND OTHERS. In a minority among fans I must confess that Robert Howard seems to me the least worthy of permanency of all the pulp writers that Arkham House has enshrined between covers (and a petulant little outburst against reviewers in the editor's preface doesn't improve my mood). If you care for subtlety or artistry in your terror, Howard is not apt to be your meat. But for rousing blood-and-thunder action he'll do very nicely, and the memoirs by H.P. Lovecraft and E. Hoffmann Price present the author as almost as curious a psychological study as Lovecraft himself.

Will F. Jenkins, THE MURDER OF THE U.S.A. Science-fiction fans will know Mr. Jenkins better as Murray Leinster and will recall his extraordinary ability to lend life to mechanical objects. He performs that trick here with atom bombs, which suddenly rain upon the entire United States from an unknown source. There are a hero and a girl and they finally frustrate the invasion (the author of which is tantalizingly never named), but what you'll remember are the magnificently animate descriptions of bombs and counter-bombs.

Barbara Hunt, SEA-CHANGE. New England woman (circa 1820) channels her frustrated sex impulses into witchcraft, to her final ironic self-destruction. Fascinating occult details (including a fine description of a Sabbath) embedded in careless scholarship. (Boucher)

October 20, 1946

Flora Armytage, SEBASTIAN (Doubleday, $2.50).

This book, described by the publishers as "a novel of fascination," begins: "I wonder how long it will be before that name pronounced soundlessly in the deep silence of my mind will fail to unleash in me such floods of nostalgia, rent through and through with fear and painful confusion, yet linked indissolubly with my memory of the strangest days I have ever known."

As a conscientious reviewer I read on for 246 pages beyond this impenetrable paragraph. I am happy to report that there is no reason for you to do so. (AB)

Sidney S. Lenz, CRIBBAGE: FUNDAMENTALS AND FINE POINTS (Greenberg, $1).

The rank beginner may find only confusion here but the experienced cribbage player will enjoy and profit by the fresh analysis of the subtleties of what Mr. Lenz calls with good reason "the finest two-handed card-game in the world." (AB)

November 24, 1946

Rhys Davies, THE TRIP TO LONDON
(Howell Soskin, $2.50);
James Reid Parker, THE PLEASURE WAS MINE (Current Books,
$2.50).

Two divergent masters of short fiction here offer the latest collection of their wares.

The title story of Mr. Davies' book is as subtle and plausible a portrait of a mass-murderer as I know—without one touch of gore or melodrama—and other stories range from a fine dissection of the silver-chord motif to the grotesque comedy of the undertaker who buried men only.

Mr. Parker's subjects range from an intolerably vigorous minister to the higher politics of dog breeding—and you will undoubtedly recall from *The New Yorker* such other figures as Mr. Hoon, the relentlessly glad taxi driver, and Mrs. Conley, who lived in her own interpretations of the news.

The two books share a gratifying perfection of technique. According to mood you may prefer Davies' psychological indirections or Parker's surface irony; each small volume offers enviable hours of reading and rereading. (AB)

Moritz Jagendorf (editor), TWENTY NON-ROYALTY ONE-ACT
GHOST PLAYS (Greenberg, $3).

A Pennsylvania Dutch play by Marion Wefer has a slight charm. As for the other nineteen—do you remember high school assemblies? (AB)

December 1, 1946

Stephen Leacock, THE LEACOCK ROUNDABOUT: A TREASURY OF
THE BEST WORKS OF STEPHEN LEACOCK (Dodd Mead, $3.50).

This omnibus opens with extremely sensible commentary on the comic subject of humor, closes with extremely comical commentary on the sensible subject of indexing. In other words this book is Leacock in his humor as he lived, alternately given to horse play and to horse sense and equally admirable in either. You'll find your favorites here, from the historical drama on Napoleon to the noble series of parodies on the mystery novel. The ideal book for the bedside table in the guest-room—where you'll bed yourself down till you've finished it. (AB)

Theodore Strauss, MOONRISE (Viking, $2.50).

Danny hadn't meant to kill a man. But the fact of killing shifted the balance of his life, changed him from a sullen half-ignorant hillbilly to a mature man, understanding his fellows and the compensation that he owed them for his involuntary crime. Mr. Strauss' style is self-consciously simple and his interpolated love story verges on the incredible but he has nonetheless achieved an effective short novel of crime and punishment. (AB)

Juliet Lowell, DEAR SIR OR MADAM (Duell,
Sloan & Pearce, $1).

Dear Miss Lowell:
As everybody who read DEAR SIR knows, you are wonderful. Rooting among endless files, you have the truffle-pig's unerring nose for the juiciest morsels. You convulse today's reader while documenting the future social history of this era of boards, forms and confusion. As long as it is human to write letters and to err magnificently in the writing, may you be with us to show us ourselves as others read us.
Sincerely yours,
APW

December 8, 1946

A.E. Van Vogt, SLAN (Arkham House, $2.50).
Jeanne de Lavigne, GHOST STORIES OF OLD NEW ORLEANS
(Rinehart, $3.50).
Joseph A. Margolies (editor), STRANGE AND FANTASTIC STORIES
(with an introduction by Christopher Morley) (Whittlesey House, $3.75).
THE AVON GHOST READER (Avon, 25 cents).
A.E. Coppard, FEARFUL PLEASURES
(Arkham House, $3).
Henry S. Whitehead, WEST INDIA LIGHTS
(Arkham House, $3).

A.E. Van Vogt, SLAN. One of the major themes of science fiction is the appearance of Homo Superior, the new mutation that will as far surpass the human race as Homo Sapiens does the anthropoid apes. And one of the finest treatments of this theme is Van Vogt's SLAN—an exciting melodrama, a fascinating study in scientific conjecture and a movingly human (or superhuman) story. In its magazine form this was the first pulp scientification novel I read; it converted me hopelessly and its concepts and vocabulary have become part of my thought patterns. Its book appearance is the signal for major jubilation among the devout and, unless I miss my guess badly, for the thronging in of new converts.

Jeanne de Lavigne, GHOST STORIES OF OLD NEW ORLEANS. Closer to fiction than to psychical research, these folk-tales make as grisly a collection of horrors as you'll find in a month of Sabbaths. You may think some of them revolting or even comical but never dull. Charles Richards' illustrations add to the ghastliness, and even some bad writing and worse proofreading can be overlooked in the proper self-terrifying mood.

Joseph A. Margolies (editor), STRANGE AND FANTASTIC STORIES (with an introduction by Christopher Morley). Mr. Margolies ranges from the terrible to the comic, from the supernatural to the sadistic, for 50 stories and 761 pages. The average of quality is high, but far too many of the stories are familiar revenants which haunt all standard anthologies.

THE AVON GHOST READER. This anonymously edited collection is a good quarter's worth, including several hitherto unanthologized stories and no bad ones. Stress is on the lighter, more ironic sides of fantasy, but you'll find a few solid chillers too.

A.E. Coppard, FEARFUL PLEASURES. Everyone from August Derleth to Clifton Fadiman proclaims Mr. Coppard as one of the greatest living masters so I'd better go easy except to say that here in one volume is a special collection, with a new preface by the author, of all the fantasy stories heretofore scattered among a dozen volumes.

Henry S. Whitehead, WEST INDIA LIGHTS. Despite its title this second Whitehead collection contains few of the reverend gentleman's first-hand fictions of West Indian magic. Most of it deals with stock fantasy themes in more prosaic settings and rarely rises above a publishable pulp level. Readable enough but a let-down after JUMBEE.

BEST BUYS IN REPRINTS. M.P. Shiel, THE PURPLE CLOUD (Forum, $1); William Sloane, TO WALK THE NIGHT (Tower, 49 cents). (Boucher)

Theodore F. Koop, WEAPON OF SILENCE
(University of Chicago Press, $3.50).

The jacket attempts to present this account of the Office of Censorship as an addition to the crop of postwar histories of espionage but you'll be disappointed if you're looking for a spy thriller. A small portion is devoted to a few dramatic cases, most of them told better elsewhere; the rest is a straightforward history related by the assistant director of the office. If the tone is somewhat partisan and uncritical (director Byron Price and his staff seem to have been unique among Washington agencies in possessing no weaknesses) and the style less than enthralling, the book is nonetheless valuable source material, well documented and indexed, on a highly successful operation. The sections on the voluntary censorship of press and radio are particularly interesting. (AB)

December 22, 1946

Agatha Christie Mallowan, COME, TELL ME HOW YOU LIVE (Dodd Mead, $3).

Probably no previous book-jacket ever advertised at once the travel books of H.V. Morton and the latest detectival exploit of Hercule Poirot. But as readers of, for instance, MURDER IN MESOPOTAMIA have long realized, Poirot's creator is not only Agatha Christie but also Mrs. Max Mallowan, wife of a noted archeologist, and fully equipped by first-hand experience to challenge Mr. Morton in his field of Near East travel. Not that you will learn profound things about Syria from what the author properly labels "this inconsequent chronicle" but you will emerge with a lively picture of the day-to-day life of an archeologist and particularly of an archeologist's wife, skillfully and delightfully presented. One of Christie's most agreeable books in any genre. (AB)

February 16, 1947

THE COMPLETE PROPHECIES OF NOSTRADAMUS (translated, edited and interpreted by Henry C. Roberts) (Crown, $3).

Although every war or crisis brings a rash of books on the sixteenth century French prophet, not since 1672 has a full translation of the Nostradamus oracles appeared in English. Since the start of the last war even the French text has been difficult to obtain, so the present bilingual edition should be welcome to the curious even with all its faults. It is not complete (it omits the sixains and presages), the proofreading of the French and the translation of the English are alike faulty, there is no introductory or explanatory material and the "interpretations" seem equally based on caprice and error. In the absence of an adequate edition, however, this may prove useful to those who have felt the lure of one of the few never-quite-discredited prophets. (AB)

March 9, 1947

H.F. Heard, DOPPELGANGERS (Vanguard, $2.75).
Mervyn Wall, THE UNFORTUNATE FURSEY (Crown, $2.75).
William Fryer Harvey, THE BEAST WITH FIVE FINGERS:

TWENTY TALES OF THE UNCANNY (edited by Maurice Richardson)
(Dutton, $2.50).
Alfred Hitchcock (editor), BAR THE DOORS: TERROR STORIES
(Dell, 25 cents).
Bennett Cerf (editor), FAMOUS GHOST STORIES
(Illustrated Modern Library, $2).
Anthony More, PUZZLE BOX (Trover Hall, $2.75).

H.F. Heard, DOPPELGANGERS. I shan't even attempt to summarize this strange tale of the benevolent dictatorship which followed the Fourth or Psychological Revolution and of the nameless man whose living clay was remodeled into the shape of the dictator himself. I'll only say that this is in style and imagination the most exciting and provocative piece of science fiction since the heyday of M.P. Shiel (even if the latter portion seems to stem more from philosopher Gerald Heard than from fantasist H.F.).

Mervyn Wall, THE UNFORTUNATE FURSEY. The magical perplexities and adventures of an innocent 10th-century Irish monk who all inadvertently becomes a sorcerer and a close personal friend of Lucifer, related by an author who knows his Irish, his period, his magic and his craft. A delightful book, witty, absurd and meaty, to be placed on your shelf not too far from T.H. White and Norman Douglas' THEY WENT.

William Fryer Harvey, THE BEAST WITH FIVE FINGERS: TWENTY TALES OF THE UNCANNY (edited by Maurice Richardson). One of the most notable English practitioners of understated terror, the late Dr. W.F. Harvey produced little, but that little of the highest quality. The present selection, chosen from three long out-of-print volumes, offers (in addition to the recently filmed title story and the classic "August Heat") a wide range of imagination, with chills that are as often psychological as supernatural. (Published in England as MIDNIGHT TALES.)

Alfred Hitchcock (editor), BAR THE DOORS: TERROR STORIES. From worn if never quite outworn classics Mr. Hitchcock ranges through less familiar eeriness (the Alfred Noyes and D.K. Broster stories deserve classic status) to such a little-known masterpiece as Margaret Irwin's "The Book." Most of the items have been previously anthologized, but all are good and the Irwin alone is worth your quarter.

Bennett Cerf (editor), FAMOUS GHOST STORIES. The same sound and varied text as the regular Modern Library edition, enhanced by chapter heads by Hugo Steiner-Prag and 10 color plates by William Sharp. As attractive a fantasy volume as you'll find.

Anthony More, PUZZLE BOX. The publishers are a newly founded S.F. firm which aims at specializing in fantasy and science fiction. Their first offering contains six short stories with provocative fantasy concepts; and if the treatment falls short of professional standards, both Mr. More and Trover Hall are worth keeping an aficionado's eye on.

BEST BUYS IN REPRINTS. David Garnett, LADY INTO FOX and A MAN IN THE ZOO (Penguin, one volume, 25 cents, uncut). (Boucher)

Jay Dratler, THE PITFALL (Crowell, $2).

Jon Forbes was a Hollywood rarity—a writer happily and faithfully married. That was before the cop Mac started putting ideas in his head—ideas that led to a strange kind of love and happiness and to a warped tragedy that demonstrated the infallibility of police methods.

The beginning of the plot is a little hard to accept; the ending is only neatly twisted melodrama. But the body of the book is a hard, tense, almost nerve-wracking study of the miseries of adultery, the torments of the man who wants both wife and mistress. The picture business background is unglamorously true and the fast easy tempo has a disquieting impact. (Unsigned; carbon in Lilly Library)

March 23, 1947

F.L. Green, ODD MAN OUT
(Reynal & Hitchcock, $2.75).

The leader of an Irish revolutionary group is wounded in a raid. His followers try unsuccessfully to rescue him but he wanders alone and dying through Belfast, his last moments impinging curiously on many lives.

This is almost two novels. The first, the story of the Organization's futile efforts to save its leader, is capably told but ineffective; the members of the Organization are mere names without identities and the whole is too reminiscent of too many stories of The Trouble three decades earlier.

The second, the odyssey of the dying Johnny, has striking moments of terror and suspense and much skilled evocation of the lower levels of Belfast. But this too suffers from irreality of character, from pretentious philosophizing, and from the author's obstinate insistence on writing a novel about a revolutionary organization without ever remotely discussing its revolutionary motives and intents.

This is Mr. Green's eighth novel but his first to be published in America. On its evidence he seems a writer who prefers to plunge ahead, trusting to his undeniable narrative competence, rather than to devote any time to exploring his people or his concepts. (AB)

April 6, 1947

Frank Baker, BEFORE I GO HENCE: FANTASIA ON A NOVEL (Cow-ard-McCann, $2.75).

In 1930 an old Anglican priest lay dying in a farmhouse. In 1943 a sensi-tive young novelist visits the deserted farmhouse and begins weaving a story about it. And gradually the two time levels intertwine until it is im-possible to say whether the events of 1930 imperceptibly influence those of 1943 or whether the novelist's creative powers are reaching back to alter the events of thirteen years before.

Mr. Baker has always been noted for his unusual and imaginative themes. BEFORE I GO HENCE lives fully up to his reputation. It is a delicate and highly skilled fantasy on a curious new twist of time theory. But it is more than that—it is a richly human novel, with much to say on the nature of the creative act and on the relation of man to his fellow man and to his God. In all this is probably Mr. Baker's most successful book since the classic MISS HARGREAVES—equally rewarding as a well-woven fantasy or as a novel, not of the currently popular psyche but of the soul. (AB)

April 20, 1947

Maria-Luisa Bombal, HOUSE OF MIST
(Farrar Straus, $2.75).

Love, death and a hint of the supernatural shape a somewhat dated and unreal romance set in the southernmost regions of South America. Latin critics praise the magic of Miss Bombal's style, which unfortunately does not survive her unwise decision to write directly in English. (AB)

April 27, 1947

Willy Ley, ROCKETS AND SPACE TRAVEL: THE FUTURE OF FLIGHT BEYOND THE STRATOSPHERE (Viking, $3.75).

Mr. Ley combines a preeminent knowledge of modern rocket research with a fine knack for entertaining exposition of scientific history for the intelligent layman—a combination which made his ROCKETS (1944) a memorable book. Now retitled and thoroughly rewritten, with the addition of much material on rockets in World War II and especially on the German researches at Peenemunde, it is more than ever indispensable, whether as a fascinating narrative of the past and present or as a signpost to man's pos-sible interplanetary future. (AB)

Caswell Adams (editor), GREAT AMERICAN SPORTS STORIES
(McKay, $3).

Caswell Adams, no mean sports writer himself, has compiled more than fifty top-flight accounts written under the King Features aegis in the past 38 years and has supplemented them with numerous action shots.

These stories, which date from Merkle's fabulous boner against the Chicago Cubs in 1908 to Assault's winning of the Dwyer Stakes last June, remain as fresh and spontaneous as the day they were pounded out on the scene by such proven reporters as Damon Runyon, John Kieran, Sid Mercer, Ed Frayne, Dan Parker and others.

A liberal amount of verse is included, such as Ernest Thayer's "Casey at the Bat" (conceived in San Francisco), Runyon's "A Handy Guy Like Sande" and "The Old Hop Horse."

Readers who wish to mull over the "Golden Era" of sports in the middle twenties will like this book. And those who can't tell a rain check from a trolley transfer will like it if they enjoy good writing. (AB)

May 4, 1947

Edward Wagenknecht (editor), THE FIRESIDE BOOK OF GHOST STO-
RIES (with decorations by Warren Chappell) (Bobbs-Merrill, $3.75).
Jules Verne, FROM THE EARTH TO THE MOON (including the sequel
ROUND THE MOON) (translated by Louis Mercier & Eleanor King, re-
vised by Carter Hull) (illustrated by John C. Wonsetler) (Didier, $3).
August Derleth (editor), DARK OF THE MOON: POEMS OF FANTASY
AND MACABRE (Arkham House, $3).
Cynthia Asquith, THIS MORTAL COIL
(Arkham House, $3).
R. DeWitt Miller, FORGOTTEN MYSTERIES
(Cloud, $2.50).

Edward Wagenknecht (editor), THE FIRESIDE BOOK OF GHOST STORIES. Mr. Wagenknecht has stuck closely and literally to his title of "ghost stories" and yet within that limitation he has found 40 specimens, all of high quality and mostly unfamiliar, to fill almost 600 pages of superlative reading. My own particular gratitude is for haunting narratives which I had not known from Joseph Shearing, Oliver Onions and Ann Bridge, but everyone will pick his own favorites in what is unquestionably one of the most tasteful and imaginative anthologies of supernatural fiction yet assembled.

Jules Verne, FROM THE EARTH TO THE MOON (including the sequel ROUND THE MOON). There can never (I warn you this is an ex cathedra utterance) be too many new editions of Jules Verne. The scientific qualities of his science fiction may date (though surprisingly little) but the fictional qualities—the elements of inventiveness, of character humor, of social satire—remain astonishingly fresh. Despite a mediocre translation and some shocking printing errors, this Didier revival (to be followed by more) is to be greeted with cheers.

August Derleth (editor), DARK OF THE MOON: POEMS OF FANTASY AND MACABRE. With all of the prose anthologies of the supernatural there's been only one previous volume of fantasy verse and that long out of print. Mr. Derleth's selection, which ranges from anonymous balladists to the newest young writers, is therefore far too welcome for any cavilling about inclusions or omissions. Whatever your taste, for long poems or short, satire or terror, fantastic narrative or evocative mood-magic, you'll be well rewarded here.

Cynthia Asquith, THIS MORTAL COIL. Lady Cynthia Asquith is well known as an admirable anthologist. This first collection of her own stories displays her creative fiction as literate but conventional and wordy.

R. DeWitt Miller, FORGOTTEN MYSTERIES. It's excellent that writers should emulate Charles Fort in collecting the data which science chooses to ignore, but must they emulate him in cryptic condensation and dim documentation? Critical commentary, argument and protest on this book would fill another volume of equal size, but the work may still prove of interest as bringing together, however crudely, a great group of provocative phenomena. Fantasy Note: Even book readers may have heard repercussions of The Great Shaver Controversy, which has split the ranks of magazine-fantasy enthusiasts. One Richard S. Shaver (whose prose style seems equally suited to founding a Southern California cult) has composed a series of narratives dealing with a terrible survivor-race which rules the world from subterranean caverns, and both Mr. Shaver and the editor of *Amazing Stories* choose to assert the factual truth of his revelations. If, like me, you came in late on all this and want to know just what it is that thousands of readers have come to accept as gospel, you should investigate the latest (June) issue of *Amazing*, which features a complete to-date resume of the Shaver Mystery—which stands there baldly revealed in all its pretentious sterility as one of the most peculiar phenomena in the history of fantasy fiction.

BEST BUYS IN REPRINTS. Dorothy Macardle, THE UNINVITED (Bantam, 25 cents, uncut). (Boucher)

May 25, 1947

Sylvia Townsend Warner, THE MUSEUM OF CHEATS (Viking, $2.50).

For delicacy and imagination, for the precise conception of an oddity of character or the loving re-creation of an oddity of culture, for clarity of style and wit of attitude, the fictions of Sylvia Townsend Warner are incomparable, and these 22 short stories will delight the same audience who have found few other novels so curiously satisfactory as LOLLY WILLOWES or MR. FORTUNE'S MAGGOT. (AB)

Ben Jones, SAM JONES: LAWYER (with drawings by Dick Underwood) (University of Oklahoma Press, $2.75).

Sam Jones was a shrewd, successful country lawyer in Kansas around the turn of the century; he was also, according to his filial Boswell, one part Clarence Day Sr., one part Ephraim Tutt and one part bumptious self-importance. His self-complacent cockiness may emerge somewhat less pleasantly than his son intended, but the book is rich in stories both of small-town life and of adroit legal maneuvers, including an admirable early episode in ballistics. (AB)

June 1, 1947

Mark Gayn & John Caldwell, AMERICAN AGENT (Henry Holt, $3).

John Caldwell, son of China missionaries, became an OWI [Office of War Information] agent in the southern coastal province of Fukien, fighting the Dark War—the unspectacular, quiet, deadly war of propaganda and morale. He worked skillfully among a people he knew well and he has a moving story to tell—a doubly valuable story now when our legislators mock the value of fighting with words and ideas. It's a pity that he was not allowed to tell it without the intervention of Mark Gayn, who has adopted an artificial, stilted and self-consciously "literary" technique which all but destroys the interest of Caldwell's invaluable report. (AB)

June 8, 1947

Georges Simenon, THE FIRST-BORN (translated by Geoffrey Sainsbury) (Reynal & Hitchcock, $2.75).

"At 33 he abandoned mystery novels and at last was able to devote himself to the writing of more personal works," runs the phrase that you find in most biographical notes on Georges Simenon. But these more personal works, as they emerge in this country, seem apt to prove not deeper or richer than the Simenon mysteries but simply much longer. The author has deliberately abandoned his incredibly virtuose technique of economy and offers nothing in its stead; he gets less under the skin of his characters in 100,000 long-pondered words than in a 40,000-word potboiler. This story of the decline of a French Congo exploiter and the rise (eventually over his literally dead body) of a slick and empty young arriviste might have been striking in the terse early Simenon manner; in its present meanderings it ranks only just above the dullness of THE SHADOW FALLS among his so far translated works. (AB)

Tris Coffin, MISSOURI COMPROMISE (Little Brown, $3).

Mr. Coffin, a Washington radio correspondent by profession and a Roosevelt liberal by conviction, has tried in this book "to tell the real story that I saw in these two fateful years when democracy was enduring one of its sternest trials."

The fateful years cover the period from the death of Franklin D. Roosevelt to the Republican victory of 1946, and Mr. Coffin has told the story as impartially as an honestly indignant man can. He gives detailed play-by-play accounts of such vital (and now half-forgotten) episodes as the railroad strike, the hearings on the Atomic Energy Commission, Mr. [Winston] Churchill's Fulton speech, the OPA crisis and the resignation of Henry Wallace. His reports, far more detailed than those we read at the time, make a fair substitute for careful perusal of the Congressional Record and state papers—and they will emphatically not be used for 1948 propaganda by either political party.

It's unfortunate that these reports are made in such a shapeless book, the first half of which is largely thumbnail sketches on the gossipy and even smartypants level. (Ex-Congressman John Tolan, the elder statesman of Alameda County, will be fascinated to find himself described as a "vigorous young liberal.") The absence not only of an index but even of chapter headings is infuriating in a volume so loosely organized. And I suggest a law that the next writer who refers to George Allen as "the court jester" be compelled to quote one mildly amusing remark.

But with all these faults, MISSOURI COMPROMISE is a document to be read and considered. The precise history of the year just past is more easily forgotten than that of ten years ago. The voter of 1948 needs the roll calls, the remarks in committee, the timetables of action of 1946. The most important are clearly and readably stated here, for future reference in checking against campaign leaflets. (White)

June 22, 1947

Ray Bradbury, DARK CARNIVAL (Arkham House, $3).
Christina Hole, WITCHCRAFT IN ENGLAND (illustrated by Mervyn Peake) (Scribner, $3).

Vance Randolph, OZARK SUPERSTITIONS
(Columbia University Press, $3.75).
August Derleth (editor), THE NIGHT SIDE: MASTERPIECES OF THE
STRANGE & TERRIBLE (illustrated by Lee Brown Coye) (Rinehart,
$2.50).
R.T.M. Scott, THE NAMELESS ONES
(Dutton, $2.50).

Ray Bradbury, DARK CARNIVAL. For years I have been prowling newsstands and buying any magazine with a Ray Bradbury story; to me he is the most fascinating and individual talent to appear in the fantasy field for a long time. He's not only a fantasy writer, he is also a writer, period, and there's no telling what may come of this still very young man. Meanwhile his best short stories form the most important book (and I'm remembering [H.P.] Lovecraft and [William Hope] Hodgson) that Arkham House has yet published; and you're strongly urged to latch onto it and discover the indefinable Mr. Bradbury's macabre perfections for yourself.

Christina Hole, WITCHCRAFT IN ENGLAND. Few writers have ever written so rationally about witchcraft as Miss Hole, who examines all of its bitter history in view of the concepts and premises of the period, avoiding both top-lofty modernity and the credulity of a Montague Summers. This sensible attitude, combined with a lucidity which compresses immense scholarship into readable briefness, makes WITCHCRAFT IN ENGLAND an indisputable classic in the field, to which Mervyn Peake's brilliantly grisly drawings add the final touch of grue.

Vance Randolph, OZARK SUPERSTITIONS. An invaluable supplement to Miss Hole's book, continuing its history with modern New World survivals. Mr. Randolph has produced a volume which is academically impeccable (including as admirable an annotated bibliography as I've ever seen) without the slightest hint of academic stiffness. His style is as agreeably easy-going as his research technique must have been, and the book ranges from occasional chills (I shan't soon forget the section on "dummy suppers") to absurdities which would supply splendid source material for [cartoonist and creator of Li'l Abner] Al Capp.

August Derleth (editor), THE NIGHT SIDE: MASTERPIECES OF THE STRANGE & TERRIBLE. It should be enough to say that Mr. Derleth is one of the few intelligent practicing anthologists and that this is probably his best collection. His extraordinary choices manage somehow to be slightly off-formula even within the essentially off-formula fantasy field. Almost none of the stories are elsewhere in print, and they include the first U.S. book-appearances of Arthur Machen's subtly perturbing "The Exalted Omega" and Henry Kuttner's (Lewis Padgett's) fine study in the nonhuman logic of childhood, "Mimsy Were the Borogoves." You can't do better.

R.T.M. Scott, THE NAMELESS ONES. Good and evil mahatmas and their disciples fight a spiritual battle for the mental control of America; Aurelius ("Secret Service") Smith, a detective not without psychic powers of his own, valiantly intervenes. A novel of the old school and as enjoyable as anything since [Thomas W.] Hanshew and [Sax] Rohmer, from its concepts of the reality of dream life to its agreement with Montague Summers' linkage between black magic and Communism. (Boucher)

Francis Rufus Bellamy, BLOOD MONEY: THE STORY OF U.S. TREASURY AGENTS (Dutton, $2.75).

Money not only pays for blood, it is itself the lifeblood of international espionage. And few civilian blows of the past struggle seem in retrospect more significant than President Roosevelt's creation of the Foreign Funds Control Division of the Treasury.

Mr. Bellamy relates with admirable clarity the story of how the Treasury persistently accomplished the financial frustration of Germany and Japan. He illustrates the story with vivid cases and tops it off with valuable profiles of two still flourishing financial enemies, Fritz Mandl and Juan March.

He makes an entry in a bank statement as exciting a clue as a blood-stained dagger and the possession of the Spanish tobacco monopoly more sinister than a battalion of Moorish mercenaries. Result: a book as thought-provoking as it is absorbingly melodramatic. (AB)

June 29, 1947

Gerald Kersh, PRELUDE TO A CERTAIN MIDNIGHT (Doubleday, $2.50).

With a variety rare among modern novelists, Gerald Kersh never writes the same novel twice. What he has produced this time has nothing to do with the Guards and little to do with the world of professional criminals; it is essentially a story of murder, perhaps even in a borderline way a mystery novel—but with a difference.

The Bar Bacchus in London was frequented by the flotsam cast up on the seacoasts of Bohemia. There was Mr. Pink, who rewrote the Bible in what he imagined to be the manner of Hemingway; there was The Tiger Fitzpatrick, who punchily longed for one chance at that so-called Braddock; there was Milton Catt, who devoted his life to physical perfection (outside of bed); there was Catchy, the soft-eyed symbol of round-heeled submissiveness; and above all there was Asta Thundersley, whose championship of lost causes was as deep and intense as her gaucherie in championing them.

And somewhere among these habitues (and, as the anecdote has it, sons thereof) there was the man who raped old Sabbatani's little girl and strangled her in the dank old house.

It was Asta who realized that the murderer must be one of this group and it was Detective Inspector Turpin who soberly, half-amusedly aided her bungling efforts at trapping him. It was not Asta who finally found the murderer and kept silent but it was Asta who learned what lay in Catchy's soft submission—that deeper evil than murder itself.

Much of Mr. Kersh's plotting derives from strict whodunit technique. He even amuses himself with a long sequence in which the reader may play armchair detective. But he is writing earnestly about the nature of the murderer and the nature of murder itself even while he is playing the game of withholding identity, and with results that place PRELUDE TO A CERTAIN MIDNIGHT, as a study in the sardonic macabre, beside the Quinette episodes of Jules Romains' MEN OF GOOD WILL.

And at the same time he is creating or re-creating a fantastic and self-consistent world—the crossroads where the upper criminal classes meet the fringes of the arts. It's a little like a miscegenation of [Evelyn] Waugh or early [Aldous] Huxley with Steinbeck and Hemingway. Which means that it's indescribable and simply exists, strongly, credibly and very satisfactorily.

I cannot leave this book without extending the writer of the jacket blurb a cordial "Drop dead!" Not only has he managed to give no indication of the theme of the novel; he has succeeded in misrepresenting most of the characters and flatly lying about two of the most important.

Perhaps his only true words are that Gerald Kersh "tells a remarkable story." It is all of that and may well become a minor classic of perverse psychology, dexterously and ironically related. (White)

Franz Werfel, VERDI: A NOVEL OF THE OPERA (translated by Helen Jessiman)
(Allen, Towne & Heath, $2.95).

Few novelists (and, it's a temptation to add, few opera composers) have understood and loved opera as did Franz Werfel. Out of that understanding and love (and his own great talent as a novelist) he shaped this early masterpiece, a study of Verdi's old age in that period of doubt and confusion out of which emerged his finest works. As a psychological novel or as a deeply perceptive commentary on the nature of opera, this reissue is most welcome. (AB)

Victor Alexander Fields, TRAINING THE SINGING VOICE: AN ANALYSIS OF THE WORKING CONCEPTS CONTAINED IN RE-CENT CONTRIBUTIONS TO VOCAL PEDAGOGY (King's Cross, $4).

"When I use a word," Humpty Dumpty said, "it means just what I choose it to mean—nothing more nor less." No doubt he was a singing master, and the royal gift of the ambiguous cravat-belt was a symbolic award for his services. Every voice expert has his own terminology. When he commits his method to print, his secrets are safe. Dr. Fields' study is a sifting and sorting of the published precepts now available "to provide basic orientations in this field for future investigators, as well as to provide a segment of organized information for the teaching profession." His annotated bibliography contains 702 items yielding nearly three thousand concepts used in voice training. These he has arranged in tables showing the complete disagreement among authorities on nearly all specific points. Dr. Fields gives the floor to each faction in turn, then gravely counts the votes and posts the results. Obviously no conclusions are reached, but the symposium is stimulating and the moderator unobtrusive. (APW)

July 13, 1947

Gilbert Neiman, THERE IS A TYRANT IN EVERY COUNTRY (Harcourt Brace, $3).

Freddie Connor had come to Mexico because he hated Mexicans and wanted to find the roots of his hate and cultivate them to even greater growth. And now the old woman whom he had thought to dominate was saying:

"This country will scorch you, boy, understand? You are strong, ambitious, but it will burn you like hay in a windstorm. You'll smolder like dung, smoke away. You'll sizzle in the sun. You'll be ashes before I am...."

And as he left he heard her mumbling "...if only his strength came from love..."

That was in World One, when he was only Mr. Unman's chauffeur. It was in World Two that he began to know Mexico and to understand what working for Mr. Unman meant. And in his third world, banished by Unman's clique to a small pueblo, he finally realized the depths of the Mexican character, threw his lot in with Mexico, and made the choice between life and renunciation of Unmanism. For Mr. Unman is the international tyrant who believes in progress for profit.

"My real birth," says Mr. Neiman on the jacket, "took place in Mexico, long before I was born," and it is obvious from the novel that he like his protagonist has cast his lot with the Mexican. One result and an extremely welcome one is a novel in which local color is used realistically rather than picturesquely, a novel which (almost uniquely in American publication) implies on every page an easy familiarity with the Mexican language.

It is a little more difficult to see what this sympathy is meant to imply. Mr. Neiman scatters his condemnations so broadside (upon politicians, upon unions, upon mestizos, upon literacy, upon foreigners, upon progress) that it's hard to gather what he wants done with Mexico by Mexicans.

And it's hard too to assess Mr. Neiman as a novelist. His style is not too unfairly represented by the speech quoted above; he has a certain conviction that saying a thing five ways is more impressive than saying it once and unforgettably. In characterization he is most successful with minor roles: Don Calixto the anachronistic Zapatista and Umberto the four-year-old tyrant-in-embryo are more memorable than the leading characters, most of whom seem contrived for their function in symbolism or plot-mechanics and far more fully realized than the inconsistent mouthpiece who serves as a first person.

Place against this a vigorous oppressive sense of actuality, a sharp (if sometimes almost fantastic) feeling of melodrama, a deep understanding of people in the mass—

And there you bump up against the difficulty. Mr. Neiman does have warmth and comprehension for people in the mass, for historical movements broadly viewed. Individuals, specific problems, he handles with chilling detachment. And the reader, admiring so much of Mr. Neiman's skill and knowledge, hoping for so much more from his later books, comes back to the words of the horrible old woman:

"...if only his strength came from love..." (Boucher)

H.W. Heinsheimer, MENAGERIE IN F SHARP
(Doubleday, $2.75).

Few conversationalists are so entertaining as the man who can talk his own shop-talk well; few conversationalists are so valuable as the outsider who can take the man-from-Mars attitude. Mr. Heinsheimer fulfills both requirements: he knows music thoroughly, as an art and even more as a business, and can write about it like a slightly (but only slightly) saner [Ludwig] Bemelmans; and he can, as a European, look upon the American musical scene with freshly stimulating wonder.

His main topics include the growth of local musical organizations in the United States, the nature and future of opera, the necessity of government subsidy of music, the incredible details of the technique of composition for the screen, and the history of music publishing in Vienna between wars.

But Mr. Heinsheimer is essentially a conversationalist, not an historian, and you will encounter digressions on such fascinating topics as the types of composers' wives, the plots of fiction about music, the relation between Fascism and Philistinism, and the function of blonde secretaries.

Oddly, it all adds up not only to a delightful book but to a coherent one, with one of the most sensible viewpoints yet presented on the place of music in our society—which does not detract in the least from its somewhat zany joy. It's a book as witty, as quotable and almost as malicious as Oscar Levant's A SMATTERING OF IGNORANCE—and if one-tenth of its wise ideas find fertile soil in one-twentieth of its (I hope) unnumbered readers, the future of American music will be a glowing one. (APW)

Michael Blankfort, THE BIG YANKEE: THE LIFE OF CARLSON OF
THE RAIDERS (Little Brown, $4).

The military hero in politics is traditionally reactionary, inept or dangerous—and possibly all three. Why then is Colonel Evans Carlson, hero of Makin, a devout and vigorous progressive, bent on revivifying democracy in our national life and even introducing it into our armed forces?

Mr. Blankfort examines Colonel Carlson's ministerial parentage, his experiences in the Army and Marine Corps, his contacts with the Chinese "Communists" and the creation of the legendary Raiders and produces a coherent picture of inevitable spiritual growth. If the author's attitude verges too often on the devotional and uncritical, the result is still a stirring American biography. (APW)

July 20, 1947

Leonard Engel & Emanuel S. Piller, WORLD AFLAME:
THE RUSSIAN-AMERICAN WAR OF 1950 (Dial Press, $2).

This is the first book review which the *Chronicle* has published in three years. The stringent newsprint shortage and the absolute official controls of public expression have all but abolished the publishing industry. And these same factors have made it impossible for the average man to reconstruct the detailed history of the war which absorbs all the energy of the 70,000,000 Americans who are left alive and able to work. For this reason the Secretary of War has authorized Ed Craig, whose broadcasts are familiar to all of us, to prepare this history. It is essential, before the President puts into force his new five-year plan for victory and recovery, that we understand our position.

Ed Craig has written a personal history which is the history of us all and Engel and Piller have edited it admirably, though one might have asked for more clarification of the domestic political picture (I refer particularly to the difficulties of the Communist question in 1950). We can only wish that some magic of time might have made this report available to the American and Russian peoples in 1947, when they found themselves drifting into the decisions whose results we know so bitterly. (AB)

Anthony Boucher

Adeline Rumsey, THE OTHER CHILDREN
(Simon & Schuster, $2.75).

The schoolhouse blew up at ten minutes before three on the 19th of December and in it perished every child over five in the town. Or almost every child; for there were the very few who had been ill or playing hookey, and upon them devolved the burden of being their whole generation in a community of sorrowing adults—a burden that brought about a forced growth, an unready maturity.

It's a fascinating novelistic problem that Miss Rumsey has set herself; and if the result is a little too tricksy, a little too methodically (and sometimes inconsistently) diagrammed, it is still written with the high technical skill, the odd combination of warmth and irony, the adroit characterization and the general satisfyingness of her earlier novels. (AB)

Barbara Hunt, A LITTLE NIGHT MUSIC (Rinehart, $2.75).

In a nightmare city called Chicago there was Gavin Macdowell, the gentle old second-hand bookdealer, who knew he was dying and leaving behind him an unfulfilled life, and there was Henry J. Stubbs, late Pfc, who had a touch of genius as a mathematician, an eery skill at extra-sensory perception and a conviction that the so lution of the mathematical problem of infinite series would solve the human problem of the nature of death. About the chance meeting of these two, and the largely loathsome minor characters who surround them, Miss Hunt weaves a free fantasia of plot and philosophy; and if it is somewhat less profound and significant than it pretends to be, it is at least extremely good reading on an odd level of sentiment, satire and supernatural. (AB)

Richard Curle, STAMP COLLECTING: A HANDBOOK (Knopf, $3).

The author, who describes himself as a philatelist but not a collector, outlines the past history, present trends and future possibilities of the making and collecting of postage stamps, addressing himself to the reasonably mature beginner and more to the British than to the American audience. It's a volume of sound scholarship, gentle charm and firm integrity, to arouse respect in the most scornful outsider and stir nostalgic yearnings in anyone who has ever licked a hinge. (AB)

July 27, 1947

American detective magazines, for years and even decades, concentrated pretty much on one type of story—the fast-action pulp yarn. Some of them concentrated to very good effect and produced [Dashiell] Hammett and [Raymond] Chandler, to say nothing of [Erle Stanley] Gardner and [Raoul] Whitfield and [Frank] Gruber and [George Harmon] Coxe and a few—like [Hugh] Pentecost and [Lawrence] Treat—who went on to develop other types of fiction in books.

Now, stimulated by the success of *Ellery Queen's Mystery Magazine*, many mags are developing more variety—trying to provide in short form the stories that appeal to readers of the various schools of crime novels.

Rex Stout's Mystery Monthly, which started, frankly, as a pretty hack job, has been improving recently under the new editorship of Herbert Williams. The latest issue contains (along with reprints) three original stories by Carlyn Coffin, Christopher La Farge and Luke Faust—the last particularly effective.

The same Herbert Williams is editing *Avon Detective Mysteries*, the latest of which includes several short reprints (including an uncharacteristic but excellent Carter Dickson [John Dickson Carr]) plus a long and highly satisfactory novelette, "Murder in Acapulco," by Los Gatos' Lange Lewis and her husband, Mal Bissell.

And *Shadow Mystery* continues its recent policy of mixing straight pulp with other kinds of stories, the current issue including another of the neatly ironic murder tales of Miriam Allen de Ford.

This is all a healthy sign of the revitalization of the mystery-short field—although I must confess, healthy and all, that it is nothing to worry Ellery Queen.

The same sort of phenomenon crops up in the fantasy field with *Avon Fantasy Reader*, edited by Donald A. Wollheim. So far this is using almost entirely reprints; in the current one the only original is a somewhat [Ray] Bradburian short by Stephen Grendon (whom the editor delicately describes as "a protege of August Derleth"). But Wollheim is choosing interesting reprints, including reasonably unhackneyed specimens of [H.P.] Lovecraft, [A.] Merritt, [C.L.] Moore and [H.G.] Wells, a chilling little item of his own, and—to crawl out on a limb—two of the finest fantasy stories ever written: John Collier's "Evening Primrose" and Ray Bradbury's "Homecoming."

The continuance of this sort of good reading, in either detective or fantasy fiction, at a quarter depends on only one thing—the still somewhat shaky state of the whole pocket-size market. (*Mystery Book Magazine* is shifting, I hear, to an old-style outsize which I haven't yet seen.) And that depends on you readers. Look around, sample, see what you like—and support it. (Boucher)

David Davidson, THE STEEPER CLIFF
(Random House, $3).

Lieutenant Andrew Cooper's problem started out simply. He was one of the men in charge of rehabilitating the press in Bavaria and he had to find a reliable anti-Nazi editor for the paper in Galensburg.

Not that anything would ever be quite simple for Cooper. He had been gnawed at all his life by the secret fear that he lacked courage, and a desk job in the States throughout the war had done nothing to remove it.

He kept hearing of a promising Galensburg writer who had been driven underground during the Third Reich. The other candidates were at best suspect and Cooper resolved, braving the disapproval of his major, to find this Adam Lorenz and place him in the job.

The search became an obsession. The more he heard of Lorenz, the more he came to identify himself with the German, even to the perilous extent of loving his lonely wife. More and more Cooper came to know that to learn all the truth about Lorenz would mean learning all the truth about himself—even to the ultimate test of his courage.

Mr. Davidson has produced a novel which exists on many levels at once and with complete satisfaction on all of them. In its basic plot of quest it is pure suspense-novel, as adroitly plotted, with twists as breath-taking as any [Alfred] Hitchcock or [Eric] Ambler opus. In its analysis (and resolution) of Cooper's courage-obsession it is a convincing and moving psychological novel, gratifyingly free of jargon. In the relationship between Cooper and Lorenz's wife Brigitte it offers one of the most tender and touching of love stories.

These factors, combined with Davidson's instinctive ability to write a novel, in structure, dialogue and characters, which no one could suspect of being a first, would be enough to make an outstanding book.

But beyond and above all this is his study, through the endless variety of Germans whom Cooper meets in his quest, of the reactions of a people (and of people) to fascistic tyranny. These varying characters, from authentic heroes to authentic heels, are so well drawn, so warmly understood, so adroitly paralleled by Americans, that they force upon the reader the same obsessing question that dominates the protagonist: What would you have done under those circumstances? (And possibly beyond that, the never stated question: What will you do, if ever....?)

I'm not sure of the reception of this book. It may be appearing too soon, before readers are willing to forget some of their extensive indoctrination on the difference between the noble Americans and the fiendish Germans. But—pause for long breath, and the reason why I waited a week instead of writing this review in my first enthusiasm.

In my five years of reviewing I have never flatly said, "This is a great novel." I'm saying it now: this is a great novel. Mr. Davidson is a new writer, it's true, but for once the word promising would be out of place; he's hit the first rank on his first book, which for ethical and political values, for probing of character or for sheer literary skill will be hard to match in any season. (Boucher)

Lillian Hellman, ANOTHER PART OF THE FOREST (Viking, $2).

Lillian Hellman has achieved what is a commonplace of the French theater but a rarity in our own—the ability to write tightly plotted melodrama with literary taste and skill. ANOTHER PART OF THE FOREST (probing back 20 years into the devious lives of the conniving Southern family known to us from THE LITTLE FOXES) is, if not her best, certainly her best-made play—an incomparably adroit blending of character and plot, with our knowledge of the characters' later life adding almost the ironic effect of Greek drama. (AB)

August 10, 1947

I.A. Richards, NATIONS AND PEACE (with pictures by Ramon Gordon) Simon & Schuster, $2).

Mr. Richards, noted advocate of Basic English, steps into Basic Politics with a primer designed to expose the fallacies of national sovereignty and to plead the case for a democratically constituted world government. His text is as brief, as sensible, as pointed and as well integrated with its adroit illustrations as one of Munro Leaf's books on behavior for children. One can only pray (if somewhat skeptically) that adults, laying aside their preconceptions, will be as willing to listen to Mr. Richards as children are to learn from Mr. Leaf. (APW)

C.S. Lewis, THE ABOLITION OF MAN
(Macmillan, $1.25).

In his Riddell memorial lectures at the University of Durham Mr. Lewis examines, with his expected clarity and wit, some deficiencies of modern materialistic education and argues for the necessity of accepting an a priori moral code—the "Tao," the Way of Life common to the teachings of Confucius, Plato and Jesus. Mr. Lewis writes as well as ever but his deliberate avoidance on this occasion of his usual spiritual and theological concerns tends to turn the Tao into something very like the Code of the Pukka Sahib. (AB)

Ronald Hilton (editor), WHO'S WHO IN LATIN AMERICA, PART IV: BOLIVIA, CHILE AND PERU (with a foreword by Ray Lyman Wilbur) (Stanford University Press, $2.50).

The latest supplement of Stanford's invaluable project proves equally rewarding as a sourcebook for facts or simply as entertainment-reading, in which you may encounter a character named Aurora Lira Lira. (APW)

Wesley McCune, THE NINE YOUNG MEN (Harper, $2.50).

A *Time* writer examines the character and records of the nine present Justices of the Supreme Court and sketches the trends and history of the Court in the past 10 years, including such causes celebres as the "court packing" episode and the Jackson-Black feud. A maddeningly repetitious book, written in a highly uncertain prose style, but nonetheless extremely valuable for any citizen desirous of understanding, for instance, [Justice Stanley] Reed's position as swing man between two court factions, [Justice Frank] Murphy's passionate devotion to civil liberties, or the curious phenomena by which [Hugo] Black has become one of the most liberal of Justices and [Felix] Frankfurter one of the most conservative. (APW)

Ruth Andreas-Friedrich, BERLIN UNDERGROUND, 1938-1945 (translated by Barrows Mussey) (with an introductory note by Joel Sayre) (Henry Holt, $3);
Allen Welsh Dulles, GERMANY'S UNDERGROUND (Macmillan, $3);
THEY ALMOST KILLED HITLER (based on the personal account of Fabian von Schlabrendorff) (prepared and edited by Gero von S. Gaevernitz) (Macmillan, $3.50).

Throughout the war we wondered and argued whether or not there was an underground German resistance movement. Now we know definitely that there was and now we know why it accomplished so little.

These three books in their several ways should help our understanding a little.

THEY ALMOST KILLED HITLER is the personal narrative of the all but sole survivor of the constantly frustrated conspiracy which exploded itself if not the Fuehrer in the abortive assassination attempt of July 1944—a limited and sketchy account with occasional highpoints of melodramatic suspense.

GERMANY'S UNDERGROUND is the thoroughly documented report of the OSS chief in Switzerland on his dealings with the conspirators and on the later revelations from the Nuernberg trials and the records of the Gestapo and the infamous "People's Court"—an invaluable source for all future research on the movement, if so dryly packed with data as to make difficult reading.

BERLIN UNDERGROUND is all but unrelated to the top-brass conspiracy. This is simply the story of a small cell of formerly nonpolitical professional people—a commercial writer, a symphony conductor, a physician, an actress—who rebelled against the inhumanity of the regime and worked in every small way to frustrate it, hiding Jews, forging papers, issuing fake medical certificates, playing on the cupidity of Party members.

And it is this book more than the others that helps to answer the question. The top-level conspiracy failed partly for lack of a clearly formulated program, largely from sheer ineptitude of leadership. But how about the people?

Ruth Andreas-Friedrich, using every skill of popular writing which she learned as an Ullstein professional, brings the question down to the level of the average middle-class citizen-of-good-will. She tells in a novelistically stirring narrative the little but vital things that she and her cell accomplished. And implicit in her whole story is the other side of the question: What more could you do if a tyrannical government takes over here?

Revolution in the days of the older monarchies was one thing. Revolution against once established totalitarianism is by definition all but impossible. The immediate value of the standard misquotation from Curran on "eternal vigilance" cannot be better demonstrated than by the study in these books of the tragically futile attempts to recapture a once lost liberty. (AB)

William Thomas Walsh, OUR LADY OF FATIMA (Macmillan, $2.75).

Not since the apparition at Lourdes has a miracle so affected the Catholic and even the non-Catholic world as the several appearances of the Virgin to three Portuguese shepherd children in 1917. It was a miracle with its theological side (the Virgin urged the spread of the devotion to her immaculate heart), its political side (she foretold the possible conversion of Russia) and—particularly moving to the lay reader—its dramatic side: the struggles of the privileged children with the skepticism of the clergy, the hostility of the civil authorities and the eager credulity of the devout, all culminating in that magnificent day on which the sun danced. Mr. Walsh's narrative is based upon first-hand observation of the scene and conversations with many of the people involved, including the only survivor of the three children, to which he adds his thorough knowledge of church history and doctrine and of Portuguese culture. (Unsigned; carbon in Lilly Library)

August 17, 1947

Edward Fenton, THE DOUBLE DARKNESS (Doubleday, $2.75).

A British soldier awakens in Athens lying beside a corpse and suffering from that currently epidemic affliction, amnesia literaria. For somewhat unclear reasons he assumes the corpse's identity, which consists of only a first name and a girl's photo, and embarks on a disjointed series of adventures which bring him love, political awareness and a passion for mankind without ever bestowing a recognizable human characterization upon him. This pretentious claptrap is all recounted in a precise blend of poetic prose and four-letter words. (AB)

September 7, 1947

Ronald Knox, THE PSALMS: A NEW TRANSLATION (Sheed & Ward, $2).

Readers of Father Knox's translation of the New Testament will know what to expect of his Psalms: scholarship, clarity and grace (in the literary as well as the theological sense). The translation is basically from the new Latin version, with reference to the Hebrew and notes on all important Greek and Vulgate variants. The volume also includes all canticles from other Biblical sources contained in the Roman breviary. Father Knox continues his ability to bring out fresh meaning in long-familiar passages and enjoys himself too with reproducing such devices as the Hebrew trick of beginning each verse with a successive letter of the alphabet. In all it is an admirable volume whether for study, meditation or pleasure. (AB)

September 21, 1947

Philip Van Doren Stern (editor), TRAVELERS IN TIME (Doubleday, $3.50).
Alexander M. Phillips, THE MISLAID CHARM (with illustrations by Herschel Levit) (Prime Press, $1.75).
Jack Williamson, THE LEGION OF SPACE (with illustrations by A.J. Donnell) (Fantasy Press, $3).
A.E. Van Vogt, THE WEAPON MAKERS
(Hadley Press, $3).
J.O. Bailey, PILGRIMS THROUGH SPACE AND TIME (Argus Books, $5).
Valentine Davies, MIRACLE ON 34TH STREET
(Harcourt Brace, $1.75).

Philip Van Doren Stern (editor), TRAVELERS IN TIME. Mr. Stern's anthologies have always ranked among the finest in the fantasy field for sheer good taste and literary quality, and if anything he's outdone himself in this collection of tales of time-travel. It's regrettable that he has resolutely neglected the pulps, whose standards are often higher than his curt introductory note assumes, but even without them he has assembled some two dozen time-twists, some familiar, some novel and all excellent.

Alexander M. Phillips, THE MISLAID CHARM. How a dull young man achieved a memorably expansive evening by encountering, at once and all for the first time, intoxication, an Amazon, and the pilfered talisman of the Pennsylvania Dutch Little Men. A sort of Thorne Smith with fig leaves—lightweight but delightfully refreshing. And I hope if Prime Press continues this admirable policy of publishing novelettes from the palmy days of *Unknown,* they'll do a more professional job of printing and format.

Jack Williamson, THE LEGION OF SPACE. Eons hence, the fate of all mankind is threatened when a would-be dictator invokes the aid of mysterious allies from another system, and four heroes (including the virile John Star and the Falstaffian Giles Habibula) battle alone against unspeakable forces. Not so much true science-fiction as pure swashbuckling adventure set in the future—something below Williamson's best, but grand fun.

A.E. Van Vogt, THE WEAPON MAKERS. Far in the distant future, the solar system is dually governed by the tyrannical pomp of the Isher Empire and the underground intellects of the Weapon Makers, with one immortal man holding the balance between them—a balance perilously upset when interstellar travel is at last achieved. A vast fantastic melodrama, sometimes stirring in its wild concepts, sometimes shockingly flat in its writing—and probably only for the postgraduate fan who has worked gradually up to its wonders.

J.O. Bailey, PILGRIMS THROUGH SPACE AND TIME. For years enthusiasts have patiently awaited this long-promised book, which could have been to science fiction what [Howard] Haycraft's MURDER FOR PLEASURE is to the detective story. I regret to report that it is dully written, repetitiously constructed, critically insecure, and based on insufficient and capriciously selected material. The only usefulness I can see in it is as a source of many detailed plot synopses—in which good books sound just as silly as bad ones.

Valentine Davies, MIRACLE ON 34TH STREET. By now you've seen or at least heard of the film about how the Christmas spirit was brought to Macy and Gimbel by an old man who might really be Santa Claus. It's a completely joyous story idea with nice satiric slants; unfortunately this novelette version is written with all the literary grace and skill of a fairly promising rough synopsis. (Boucher)

Rex Stout, HOW LIKE A GOD (Vanguard, $2.50).

It's almost twenty years since Rex Stout wrote this first novel, the study of a man recapitulating the events of his tortured petty life as he tries to steel himself to murder. If the empty protagonist never quite seems worth 300 pages, the trick of suspense, the Krafft-Ebingesque details and the already evident narrative skill make the early novel well worth reissuing and rereading. (AB)

Edward J. Flynn, YOU'RE THE BOSS (Viking, $3);
William M. Reddig, TOM'S TOWN: KANSAS CITY AND THE
PENDERGAST LEGEND (Lippincott, $4).

The *Chronicle*'s political editor and the wire services have covered extensively the gossip angles of Mr. Flynn's autobiography, from his story of how [President Harry S.] Truman came to be nominated to his resolute insistence that it was he who dreamed up the use of "Happy Days Are Here Again" as the Roosevelt theme song in '32.

But for once a politician's memoirs are not important for their gossip value. Inevitably Mr. Flynn tries to show himself in the best possible light in controversial episodes and to lash back at those who would scandalize his name; inevitably he reveals a few "now-it-can-be-told" items, none of them markedly world-shaking.

But the body of the book is devoted to something very different: an explanation, a rationale, even an apologia on bossism, curiously combined with a precise description of how bossism can be reformed or even destroyed.

Mr. Flynn knows how many of our idealistic liberals shrink from politics and exalt a nebulous and impotent figure labelled "The Independent Voter." Mr. Flynn also knows that a general election is meaningless once the primary is lost and that the primary can be won only by those voters working politically within a party.

The story of his rise from Assembly candidate to quarter-century Boss of the Bronx and ultimately to Democratic National Chairman (without being Postmaster General yet!) he tells with such candor and clarity as to make it the perfect illustration of his thesis: "The one and only way that political organizations can be cleaned up is at primary time, not at election time....The voter who says in effect 'Let George do it' need not be too surprised to wake up to find that he has."

The publishers state that the book was not ghosted—in which case Mr. Flynn is further to be congratulated on a highly readable style and sense of organization as effective with words and thoughts as with voters. He has produced a small classic of politics—most urgently recommended to the general reader, who may therein discover his own political potential.

A less rationalized and exalted picture of bossism in action may be found in Mr. Reddig's TOM'S TOWN. Those who wish to use the Pendergast scandals chiefly as national political ammunition will be disappointed by the scant space which the author devotes to Harry Truman, but anyone basically interested in the growth and function of one of America's most powerful machines will find no details omitted.

In fact that's just the trouble. Mr. Reddig has long been feature and book editor of the Kansas City *Star*, Pendergast's great antagonist. He knows every angle of every slightest event that has ever befallen the Democrats of Kansas City and he tells all, for almost 200,000 words. The result at times is sheer numbness as details pile on details. But the book is nonetheless invaluable documentation—and a sound corrective if Mr. Flynn oversells you on bossism. (White)

October 12, 1947

Michael F. Reilly (as told to William J. Slocum), REILLY OF THE WHITE HOUSE (Simon & Schuster, $3).

Mike Reilly is as tough, as Irish, as sentimental, as shrewd and as wise-cracking as any private cop in the lists of hardboiled fiction; but his memoirs, admirably and vividly transcribed by Mr. Slocum, are not criminous entertainment but flashing sidelights on history. Reilly headed the White House detail of the Secret Service from Pearl Harbor till that day of death at Warm Springs which proved that April is indeed the cruelest month. He tells us here the absorbing details of the strategies and tactics involved in guarding a president's life and he illuminates his story with wonderful anecdotes, ranging from his awe at the drinking capacity of the Prime Minister [Winston Churchill] and his helplessness before the treasonable activities of Fala [FDR's dog] to the occasion when General [Charles] de Gaulle drove him, for the only time in his service, to draw his pistol from its holster to guard the Boss. Above all else this book is the heartwarming account of Reilly's devotion to that Boss. Perhaps only a tough Irishman could feel so deep a love and only an FDR could inspire it; it makes good reassuring reading in these tepid days when full-blooded devotion to Roosevelt is slipping out of style. (AB)

October 19, 1947

C.S. Lewis, MIRACLES: A PRELIMINARY STUDY (Macmillan, $2.50).

In this, perhaps his finest book since THE SCREWTAPE LETTERS, Mr. Lewis pursues his heterodox approach to Christian orthodoxy in an investigation of the relation of God to nature and the possibilities of divine intervention in the natural order.

It is, I confess, extremely difficult to review a book by Lewis. His easy command of logic, his quietly perfect prose style, his humor and his sudden glints of fancy (there are in this book seeds which could equally well produce a dozen great metaphysical poems or a dozen great fantasy novels) should commend him to every reader.

But materialism is so dominant in our popular culture—as irrationally dominant perhaps as was ever the rankest superstition —that one wonders how many readers will be willing to follow this flawless exposition of non-material doctrine.

It is doubtful whether even Mr. Lewis will win over the slavishly devout materialist. But it is hard to imagine the Christian (and particularly the Catholic, Anglican or Roman) who will not find his spiritual perception immeasurably deepened—at the same time that he is enjoying an entrancing literary performance. (AB)

October 26, 1947

Hinko Gottlieb, THE KEY TO THE GREAT GATE (translated by Fred Belman & Ruth Morris) (with illustrations by Sam Fischer) (Simon & Schuster, $2.75).
A.G. Spectorsky (editor), MAN INTO BEAST: STRANGE TALES OF TRANSFORMATION (Doubleday, $3.75).
George O. Smith, VENUS EQUILATERAL (with illustrations by Sol Levin) (Prime Press, $3).
Tiffany Thayer, THE GREEK (with decorations by Edward Staloff) (Old Wine Press, $1.98).

Hinko Gottlieb, THE KEY TO THE GREAT GATE. When the Nazis tossed Warsaw Jew Dov Tarnopolski into their Vienna prison, the life of the Master Race went slightly askew; for Tarnopolski had mastered the post-Einsteinian principles of a varying and autonomic space, and used his knowledge first to produce food in the prison cell, then a radio (which became a piano), and finally—But the "finally" is Mr. Gottlieb's story, and a wonderful story it is—equally rich in its glib scientific patter, in its study of prison psychology, in its odd and human humor and in its affirmative philosophy of man's nature and fate. A small classic of science fantasy, delightfully translated and illustrated and worthy to rank beside the unclassifiable imaginings of such other Central European writers as Leo Perutz and Karel Capek.

A.G. Spectorsky (editor), MAN INTO BEAST: STRANGE TALES OF TRANSFORMATION. Five short stories and five brief novels of metamorphosis carry that curious entity the mind of man into every form of life from ant to orchid, from fish to "some monstrous kind of vermin." The shorts are all pretty well-worn but the brief novels form an admirably selected treasury, with special credit going to the inclusion of [Theodore] Pratt's pleasantly absurd "Mr. Limpet" and [Franz] Kafka's wonderful "Metamorphosis," which has long deserved to be rescued from the metaphysicians and cultists and restored to the fantasy fans who can honestly enjoy it.

George O. Smith, VENUS EQUILATERAL. A fan once said that [the science-fiction magazine] *Astounding* developed around 1943 a new story-formula: "the technical problems of a technician in a technological technocracy." Prime examples of this trend are these ten interrelated stories of the complex uses of electronics in interplanetary communication, written by a professional technician with brilliantly plausible scientific gimmickry—and a pretty thorough lack of style and characterization. Interesting and sensible preface by [*Astounding* editor] John W. Campbell, Jr.

Tiffany Thayer, THE GREEK. Reissue of the most curious novel of America's most curious novelist—the story of how Mr. Thayer himself became dictator of America and instituted his own form of aristocratic totalitarianism. To denounce the book as vicious or fascistic would be to take it too seriously, but it's not without interest for its heavy satire, its erotic passages or its occasional M.P. Shiel wildness. (Boucher)

Leslie M. Lecron & Jean Bordeaux, HYPNOTISM TODAY (Grune & Stratton, $4).

Two consulting psychologists have produced a useful and well-written revaluation of hypnotism including a brief sketch of its history, a suggestive study of its (still somewhat unsolved) nature, and an examination of its role in psychoanalysis. Readers of Dr. [Robert] Lindner's memorable REBEL WITHOUT A CAUSE will find particular interest in this further discussion of hypnanalysis. Local note: Dr. Bordeaux is a former San Franciscan—a fact less important than that he and his collaborator have written a stimulating book well within the grasp of the intelligent layman. (AB)

Ivan Martynov, SHOSTAKOVICH: THE MAN AND HIS WORK (translated by T. Guaralsky)
(Philosophical Library, $3.75).

There is no questioning the popularity or the importance of [Dmitri] Shostakovich's music. But Mr. Martynov approaches his subject with a wholehearted partisan enthusiasm which might seem extravagant in a critical study of Mozart. He does, however, offer interesting politico-musical analyses of all the symphonies and the major chamber works, some fascinating details on the composer's operas, and a useful complete set of opus numbers. There is no bibliography or discography and (despite the high price) almost no illustrations, musical or otherwise. It's uncertain whether the author or the translator is responsible for the unfortunate dialectical jargon which makes the prose almost unreadable. (APW)

November 9, 1947

Cortez A.M. Ewing, CONGRESSIONAL ELECTIONS 1896-1944 (University of Oklahoma Press, $2).

In clear charts and graphs, accompanied by a readable and perceptive commentary, Dr. Ewing has assembled every conceivable type of statistic dealing with the congressional elections of the past fifty years—invaluable data for anyone concerned with such questions as the nature of sectional representation, the function of the Solid South or the role of third parties. (APW)

November 16, 1947

G.H. Estabrooks, Ph.D., SPIRITISM (Dutton, $3).

Dr. Estabrooks, professor of psychology at Colgate University, approaches psychic research with the advantage over the average spiritualist of a training in scientific method and the advantage over the average psychologist of a freedom from overstrict materialism. He draws interesting analogies between spiritism and his own special field of hypnotism, finds no evidence for survival in physical mediumship but a possible unexplained residue in mental phenomena, and concludes that "Humanity cannot afford to throw away the religious heritage of the past...in order to base its hopes on the meager results of psychical research, or to sink those hopes entirely by accepting the teachings of mechanism." An unorthodox and stimulating book, well written and well organized and crammed with absorbing case histories. (AB)

November 23, 1947

Philip Woodruff, THE WILD SWEET WITCH
(Harcourt Brace, $3).

Mr. Woodruff's CALL THE NEXT WITNESS was a memorable study of Indian life and customs which also managed to provide a universal commentary on murder and justice. The same adroit blend of local color and wider impact distinguishes his new novel, in which the setting is still India but the subject changed from murder to politics.

Kalyanu was an obscure hillsman whose qualities of leadership and initiative uprooted him from his tribal background. These same qualities, backed by a modern education, made his grandson Jodh Singh a potentially great political leader in the movement for independence; but perverse circumstances (including even the circumstantial suspicion that he was a were-panther!), the machinations of rivals, and above all the flaws of impetuosity and insecurity within Jodh Singh himself finally combined to destroy him.

In certain respects the novel is unsatisfactory; too much of its hero's career is synopsized and the final catastrophe is disproportionate to the problem. But the sensitive style and the well-sketched minor characters make for excellent reading, and Jodh Singh is a magnificently conceived and projected portrait not merely of a Hindu nationalist but of every idealistic young politician who falls precisely and pitifully short of greatness. (AB)

November 30, 1947

Emro Joseph Gergely, HUNGARIAN DRAMA IN NEW YORK: ADAP-
TATIONS 1908-1940
(University of Pennsylvania Press, $3).

For much of this century, particularly in the '20s, adaptations from the Hungarian have been prominent in the Broadway theater—partly because of their consummate craftsmanship, partly because of their erotic titillation. Mr. Gergely examines in detail every Hungarian play produced in New York, with special emphasis on those of the masterly [Ferenc] Molnar; and if his conclusions as to their influence on the American theater are sketchy (he nowhere mentions for instance Samson Raphaelson, Molnar's most direct heir), he offers an illuminating study. (Unsigned; carbon in Lilly Library)

December 21, 1947

Edward J. Dent, MOZART'S OPERAS: A CRITICAL STUDY (Oxford
University Press, $5.50).

When Mr. Dent first published this valuable study in 1913, he had to argue vigorously for the popular acceptance of the Mozart operas and for opera in English. Since then public taste, especially in England, has matured so rapidly (largely because of Dent's own efforts as critic and translator) that this welcome new edition no longer needs to devote itself to missionary effort but can settle down comfortably to discuss the scores and their libretti, the way in which they fit into Mozart's life and development, and their relation to other operatic music of the time—this last point illustrated by many quotations from all but inaccessible contemporary scores. The result is an absorbing study, gratifyingly clear and tasteful both in judgment and in expression. (APW)

August Heckscher, A PATTERN OF POLITICS
(Reynal & Hitchcock, $3).

Mr. Heckscher, scholar and newspaper editor, talks so articulately, so readably, so learnedly upon the contradictory problems of democracy and constitutionalism, expounds so ably the influence of Transcendentalism on American political thought or the neglected theories of Francis Lieber, that one closes the book with reluctant amazement, realizing that he has said precisely nothing. (APW)

January 4, 1948

Benjamin Appel, BUT NOT YET SLAIN (A.A. Wyn, $2.50).

The disillusionment of a liberal in contemporary Washington bureaucracy, where adherence to New Deal thinking may mean a "loyalty" investigation and loss of a job, is worthwhile novelistic material, but platitudinous dialogue and cardboard characters produce a wooden book, far below Mr. Appel's standard. (AB)

January 25, 1948

Dorothy L. Sayers, UNPOPULAR OPINIONS
(Harcourt Brace, $3).

What is your particular taste in the subject-matter of essays? No matter what it is, if you have an inquiring mind and a subtle palate, you will find something to delight you in Miss Sayers' *omnium gatherum.* Her theological essays follow the lines suggested in her unforgettable THE MIND OF THE MAKER, and her witty orthodoxy on such topics as the historicity of the Gospels or the dramatic interpretation of the role of the Savior demands comparison with [the Anglican religious writer] C.S. Lewis.

Another group of essays treats, wisely and amusingly, of the English—their origins, their language, their press and their politics; and if Miss Sayers' political views resemble somewhat those of Winston Churchill, so (God be praised) does her sense of English prose. All initiates of the Baker Street myths will eagerly welcome four essays on the life and letters of Holmes and Watson (and an ingenious plea in the Foreword for the serious value of such scholarly games). And the closing essay, "Aristotle on Detective Fiction," is a landmark in the history of detective critique. Even the most devout devotees of the [Lord Peter] Wimsey saga should forgive its creator for abandoning it when she sets before them such a feast as this. (AB)

INDEX

RAMBLE HOUSE's

HARRY STEPHEN KEELER WEBWORK MYSTERIES

(RH) indicates the title is available ONLY in the **RAMBLE HOUSE** edition

The Ace of Spades Murder
The Affair of the Bottled Deuce (RH)
The Amazing Web
The Barking Clock
Behind That Mask
The Book with the Orange Leaves
The Bottle with the Green Wax Seal
The Box from Japan
The Case of the Canny Killer
The Case of the Crazy Corpse (RH)
The Case of the Flying Hands (RH)
The Case of the Ivory Arrow
The Case of the Jeweled Ragpicker
The Case of the Lavender Gripsack
The Case of the Mysterious Moll
The Case of the 16 Beans
The Case of the Transparent Nude (RH)
The Case of the Transposed Legs
The Case of the Two-Headed Idiot (RH)
The Case of the Two Strange Ladies
The Circus Stealers (RH)
Cleopatra's Tears
A Copy of Beowulf (RH)
The Crimson Cube (RH)
The Face of the Man From Saturn
Find the Clock
The Five Silver Buddhas
The 4th King
The Gallows Waits, My Lord! (RH)
The Green Jade Hand
Finger! Finger!
Hangman's Nights (RH)
I, Chameleon (RH)
I Killed Lincoln at 10:13! (RH)
The Iron Ring
The Man Who Changed His Skin (RH)
The Man with the Crimson Box
The Man with the Magic Eardrums
The Man with the Wooden Spectacles
The Marceau Case
The Matilda Hunter Murder
The Monocled Monster

The Murder of London Lew
The Murdered Mathematician
The Mysterious Card (RH)
The Mysterious Ivory Ball of Wong Shing Li (RH)
The Mystery of the Fiddling Cracksman
The Peacock Fan
The Photo of Lady X (RH)
The Portrait of Jirjohn Cobb
Report on Vanessa Hewstone (RH)
Riddle of the Travelling Skull
Riddle of the Wooden Parrakeet (RH)
The Scarlet Mummy (RH)
The Search for X-Y-Z
The Sharkskin Book
Sing Sing Nights
The Six From Nowhere (RH)
The Skull of the Waltzing Clown
The Spectacles of Mr. Cagliostro
Stand By—London Calling!
The Steeltown Strangler
The Stolen Gravestone (RH)
Strange Journey (RH)
The Strange Will
The Straw Hat Murders (RH)
The Street of 1000 Eyes (RH)
Thieves' Nights
Three Novellos (RH)
The Tiger Snake
The Trap (RH)
Vagabond Nights (Defrauded Yeggman)
Vagabond Nights 2 (10 Hours)
The Vanishing Gold Truck
The Voice of the Seven Sparrows
The Washington Square Enigma
When Thief Meets Thief
The White Circle (RH)
The Wonderful Scheme of Mr. Christopher Thorne
X. Jones—of Scotland Yard
Y. Cheung, Business Detective

Keeler Related Works

A To Izzard: A Harry Stephen Keeler Companion by Fender Tucker — Articles and stories about Harry, by Harry, and in his style. Included is a compleat bibliography.

Wild About Harry: Reviews of Keeler Novels — Edited by Richard Polt & Fender Tucker — 22 reviews of works by Harry Stephen Keeler from *Keeler News.* A perfect introduction to the author.

The Keeler Keyhole Collection: Annotated newsletter rants from Harry Stephen Keeler, edited by Francis M. Nevins. Over 400 pages of incredibly personal Keeleriana.

Fakealoo — Pastiches of the style of Harry Stephen Keeler by selected demented members of the HSK Society. Updated every year with the new winner.

RAMBLE HOUSE's OTHER LOONS

Strands of the Web: Short Stories of Harry Stephen Keeler — Edited and Introduced by Fred Cleaver

The Sam McCain Novels — Ed Gorman's terrific series includes *The Day the Music Died*, *Wake Up Little Susie* and *Will You Still Love Me Tomorrow?*

A Shot Rang Out — Three decades of reviews from Jon Breen

Blood Moon — The first of the Robert Payne series by Ed Gorman

The Time Armada — Fox B. Holden's 1953 SF gem.

Black River Falls — Suspense from the master, Ed Gorman

Sideslip — 1968 SF masterpiece by Ted White and Dave Van Arnam

The Triune Man — Mindscrambling science fiction from Richard A. Lupoff

Detective Duff Unravels It — Episodic mysteries by Harvey O'Higgins

Mysterious Martin, the Master of Murder — Two versions of a strange 1912 novel by Tod Robbins about a man who writes books that can kill.

The Master of Mysteries — 1912 novel of supernatural sleuthing by Gelett Burgess

Dago Red — 22 tales of dark suspense by Bill Pronzini

The Night Remembers — A 1991 Jack Walsh mystery from Ed Gorman

Rough Cut & New, Improved Murder — Ed Gorman's first two novels

Hollywood Dreams — A novel of the Depression by Richard O'Brien

Six Gelett Burgess Novels — *The Master of Mysteries, The White Cat, Two O'Clock Courage, Ladies in Boxes, Find the Woman, The Heart Line*

The Organ Reader — A huge compilation of just about everything published in the 1971-1972 radical bay-area newspaper, *THE ORGAN*.

A Clear Path to Cross — Sharon Knowles short mystery stories by Ed Lynskey

Old Times' Sake — Short stories by James Reasoner from Mike Shayne Magazine

Freaks and Fantasies — Eerie tales by Tod Robbins, collaborator of Tod Browning on the film FREAKS.

Five Jim Harmon Sleaze Double Novels — *Vixen Hollow/Celluloid Scandal, The Man Who Made Maniacs/Silent Siren, Ape Rape/Wanton Witch, Sex Burns Like Fire/Twist Session*, and *Sudden Lust/Passion Strip*. More doubles to come!

Marblehead: A Novel of H.P. Lovecraft — A long-lost masterpiece from Richard A. Lupoff. Published for the first time!

The Compleat Ova Hamlet — Parodies of SF authors by Richard A. Lupoff – New edition!

The Secret Adventures of Sherlock Holmes — Three Sherlockian pastiches by the Brooklyn author/publisher, Gary Lovisi.

The Universal Holmes — Richard A. Lupoff's 2007 collection of five Holmesian pastiches and a recipe for giant rat stew.

Four Joel Townsley Rogers Novels — By the author of *The Red Right Hand: Once In a Red Moon, Lady With the Dice, The Stopped Clock, Never Leave My Bed*

Two Joel Townsley Rogers Story Collections — Night of Horror and Killing Time

Twenty Norman Berrow Novels — *The Bishop's Sword, Ghost House, Don't Go Out After Dark, Claws of the Cougar, The Smokers of Hashish, The Secret Dancer, Don't Jump Mr. Boland!, The Footprints of Satan, Fingers for Ransom, The Three Tiers of Fantasy, The Spaniard's Thumb, The Eleventh Plague, Words Have Wings, One Thrilling Night, The Lady's in Danger, It Howls at Night, The Terror in the Fog, Oil Under the Window, Murder in the Melody, The Singing Room*

The N. R. De Mexico Novels — Robert Bragg presents *Marijuana Girl, Madman on a Drum, Private Chauffeur* in one volume.

Four Chelsea Quinn Yarbro Novels featuring Charlie Moon — *Ogilvie, Tallant and Moon, Music When the Sweet Voice Dies, Poisonous Fruit* and *Dead Mice*

Four Walter S. Masterman Mysteries — *The Green Toad, The Flying Beast, The Yellow Mistletoe* and *The Wrong Verdict*, fantastic impossible plots. More to come.

Two Hake Talbot Novels — *Rim of the Pit, The Hangman's Handyman*. Classic locked room mysteries.

Two Alexander Laing Novels — *The Motives of Nicholas Holtz* and *Dr. Scarlett*, stories of medical mayhem and intrigue from the 30s.

Four David Hume Novels — *Corpses Never Argue, Cemetery First Stop, Make Way for the Mourners, Eternity Here I Come*, and more to come.

Three Wade Wright Novels — *Echo of Fear, Death At Nostalgia Street* and *It Leads to Murder*, with more to come!

Five Rupert Penny Novels — *Policeman's Holiday, Policeman's Evidence, Lucky Policeman, Sealed Room Murder* and *Sweet Poison*, classic impossible mysteries.

Five Jack Mann Novels — Strange murder in the English countryside. *Gees' First Case, Nightmare Farm, Grey Shapes, The Ninth Life, The Glass Too Many.*

Seven Max Afford Novels — *Owl of Darkness, Death's Mannikins, Blood on His Hands, The Dead Are Blind, The Sheep and the Wolves, Sinners in Paradise* and *Two Locked Room Mysteries and a Ripping Yarn* by one of Australia's finest novelists.

Five Joseph Shallit Novels — *The Case of the Billion Dollar Body, Lady Don't Die on My Doorstep, Kiss the Killer, Yell Bloody Murder, Take Your Last Look.* One of America's best 50's authors.

Two Crimson Clown Novels — By Johnston McCulley, author of the Zorro novels, *The Crimson Clown* and *The Crimson Clown Again.*

The Best of 10-Story Book — edited by Chris Mikul, over 35 stories from the literary magazine Harry Stephen Keeler edited.

A Young Man's Heart — A forgotten early classic by Cornell Woolrich

The Anthony Boucher Chronicles — edited by Francis M. Nevins
Book reviews by Anthony Boucher written for the *San Francisco Chronicle,* 1942 – 1947. Essential and fascinating reading.

Muddled Mind: Complete Works of Ed Wood, Jr. — David Hayes and Hayden Davis deconstruct the life and works of a mad genius.

Gadsby — A lipogram (a novel without the letter E). Ernest Vincent Wright's last work, published in 1939 right before his death.

My First Time: The One Experience You Never Forget — Michael Birchwood — 64 true first-person narratives of how they lost it.

Automaton — Brilliant treatise on robotics: 1928-style! By H. Stafford Hatfield

The Incredible Adventures of Rowland Hern — Rousing 1928 impossible crimes by Nicholas Olde.

Slammer Days — Two full-length prison memoirs: *Men into Beasts* (1952) by George Sylvester Viereck and *Home Away From Home* (1962) by Jack Woodford

Murder in Black and White — 1931 classic tennis whodunit by Evelyn Elder

Killer's Caress — Cary Moran's 1936 hardboiled thriller

The Golden Dagger — 1951 Scotland Yard yarn by E. R. Punshon

Beat Books #1 — Two beatnik classics, *A Sea of Thighs* by Ray Kainen and *Village Hipster* by J.X. Williams

A Smell of Smoke — 1951 English countryside thriller by Miles Burton

Ruled By Radio — 1925 futuristic novel by Robert L. Hadfield & Frank E. Farncombe

Murder in Silk — A 1937 Yellow Peril novel of the silk trade by Ralph Trevor

The Case of the Withered Hand — 1936 potboiler by John G. Brandon

Finger-prints Never Lie — A 1939 classic detective novel by John G. Brandon

Inclination to Murder — 1966 thriller by New Zealand's Harriet Hunter

Invaders from the Dark — Classic werewolf tale from Greye La Spina

Fatal Accident — Murder by automobile, a 1936 mystery by Cecil M. Wills

The Devil Drives — A prison and lost treasure novel by Virgil Markham

Dr. Odin — Douglas Newton's 1933 potboiler comes back to life.

The Chinese Jar Mystery — Murder in the manor by John Stephen Strange, 1934

The Julius Caesar Murder Case — A classic 1935 re-telling of the assassination by Wallace Irwin that's much more fun than the Shakespeare version

West Texas War and Other Western Stories — by Gary Lovisi

The Contested Earth and Other SF Stories — A never-before published space opera and seven short stories by Jim Harmon.

Tales of the Macabre and Ordinary — Modern twisted horror by Chris Mikul, author of the *Bizarrism* series.

The Gold Star Line — Seaboard adventure from L.T. Reade and Robert Eustace.

The Werewolf vs the Vampire Woman — Hard to believe ultraviolence by either Arthur M. Scarm or Arthur M. Scram.

Black Hogan Strikes Again — Australia's Peter Renwick pens a tale of the outback.

Don Diablo: Book of a Lost Film — Two-volume treatment of a western by Paul Landres, with diagrams. Intro by Francis M. Nevins.

The Charlie Chaplin Murder Mystery — Movie hijinks by Wes D. Gehring

The Koky Comics — A collection of all of the 1978-1981 Sunday and daily comic strips by Richard O'Brien and Mort Gerberg, in two volumes.

Suzy — Another collection of comic strips from Richard O'Brien and Bob Vojtko

Dime Novels: Ramble House's 10-Cent Books — *Knife in the Dark* by Robert Leslie Bellem, *Hot Lead* and *Song of Death* by Ed Earl Repp, *A Hashish House in New York* by H.H. Kane, and five more.

Blood in a Snap — The *Finnegan's Wake* of the 21st century, by Jim Weiler and Al Gorithm

Stakeout on Millennium Drive — Award-winning Indianapolis Noir — Ian Woollen.

Dope Tales #1 — Two dope-riddled classics; *Dope Runners* by Gerald Grantham and *Death Takes the Joystick* by Phillip Condé.

Dope Tales #2 — Two more narco-classics; *The Invisible Hand* by Rex Dark and *The Smokers of Hashish* by Norman Berrow.

Dope Tales #3 — Two enchanting novels of opium by the master, Sax Rohmer. *Dope* and *The Yellow Claw.*

Tenebrae — Ernest G. Henham's 1898 horror tale brought back.

The Singular Problem of the Stygian House-Boat — Two classic tales by John Kendrick Bangs about the denizens of Hades.

Tiresias — Psychotic modern horror novel by Jonathan M. Sweet.

The One After Snelling — Kickass modern noir from Richard O'Brien.

The Sign of the Scorpion — 1935 Edmund Snell tale of oriental evil.

The House of the Vampire — 1907 poetic thriller by George S. Viereck.

An Angel in the Street — Modern hardboiled noir by Peter Genovese.

The Devil's Mistress — Scottish gothic tale by J. W. Brodie-Innes.

The Lord of Terror — 1925 mystery with master-criminal, Fantômas.

The Lady of the Terraces — 1925 adventure by E. Charles Vivian.

My Deadly Angel — 1955 Cold War drama by John Chelton

Prose Bowl — Futuristic satire — Bill Pronzini & Barry N. Malzberg .

Satan's Den Exposed — True crime in Truth or Consequences New Mexico — Award-winning journalism by the *Desert Journal.*

The Amorous Intrigues & Adventures of Aaron Burr — by Anonymous — Hot historical action.

I Stole $16,000,000 — A true story by cracksman Herbert E. Wilson.

The Black Dark Murders — Vintage 50s college murder yarn by Milt Ozaki, writing as Robert O. Saber.

Sex Slave — Potboiler of lust in the days of Cleopatra — Dion Leclerq.

You'll Die Laughing — Bruce Elliott's 1945 novel of murder at a practical joker's English countryside manor.

The Private Journal & Diary of John H. Surratt — The memoirs of the man who conspired to assassinate President Lincoln.

Dead Man Talks Too Much — Hollywood boozer by Weed Dickenson

Red Light — History of legal prostitution in Shreveport Louisiana by Eric Brock. Includes wonderful photos of the houses and the ladies.

A Snark Selection — Lewis Carroll's *The Hunting of the Snark* with two Snarkian chapters by Harry Stephen Keeler — Illustrated by Gavin L. O'Keefe.

Ripped from the Headlines! — The Jack the Ripper story as told in the newspaper articles in the *New York* and *London Times.*

Geronimo — S. M. Barrett's 1905 autobiography of a noble American.

The White Peril in the Far East — Sidney Lewis Gulick's 1905 indictment of the West and assurance that Japan would never attack the U.S.

The Compleat Calhoon — All of Fender Tucker's works: Includes *The Totah Trilogy, Weed, Women and Song* and *Tales from the Tower,* plus a CD of all of his songs.

RAMBLE HOUSE
Fender Tucker, Prop.
www.ramblehouse.com   fender@ramblehouse.com
228-826-1783   10329 Sheephead Drive, Vancleave MS 39565

www.ingramcontent.com/pod-product-compliance
Lightning Source LLC
Chambersburg PA
CBHW020921020726
47495CB00002B/289